BETWEEN BURNING WORLDS

ALSO BY JESSICA BRODY
& JOANNE RENDELL
Sky Without Stars

BETWEEN BURNING WORLDS

SYSTEM DIVINE: BOOK II

JESSICA BRODY & JOANNE RENDELL

SIMON PULSE
NEW YORK   LONDON   TORONTO   SYDNEY   NEW DELHI

SIMON PULSE

An imprint of Simon & Schuster Children's Publishing Division
1230 Avenue of the Americas, New York, New York 10020
First Simon Pulse hardcover edition March 2020
Text copyright © 2020 by Jessica Brody Entertainment, LLC and Joanne Rendell
Jacket illustration copyright © 2020 by Billelis
Map illustration copyright © 2020 by Francesca Baerald
All rights reserved, including the right of reproduction in whole or in part in any form.
SIMON PULSE and colophon are registered trademarks of Simon & Schuster, Inc.
For information about special discounts for bulk purchases, please contact Simon & Schuster
Special Sales at 1-866-506-1949 or business@simonandschuster.com.
The Simon & Schuster Speakers Bureau can bring authors to your live event.
For more information or to book an event contact the Simon & Schuster Speakers Bureau
at 1-866-248-3049 or visit our website at www.simonspeakers.com.
Jacket designed by Heather Palisi
Interior designed by Mike Rosamilia
The text of this book was set in Adobe Caslon Pro.
Manufactured in the United States of America
2 4 6 8 10 9 7 5 3 1
Library of Congress Cataloging-in-Publication Data
Names: Brody, Jessica, author. | Rendell, Joanne, author.
Title: Between burning worlds / by Jessica Brody & Joanne Rendell.
Description: First edition. | New York : Simon Pulse, 2020. | Series: System Divine ; book 2 |
Audience: Ages 12 up. | Audience: Grades 10-12. | Summary: As Laterre stands on the brink of
war, Marcellus, Chatine, and Alouette must rush to stop The General from gaining access to a
weapon that would mean complete control of the planet.
Identifiers: LCCN 2019035422 | ISBN 9781534410664 (hardcover) | ISBN 9781534410688 (eBook)
Subjects: CYAC: Space colonies—Fiction. | Soldiers—Fiction. |
Revolutions—Fiction. | Science fiction.
Classification: LCC PZ7.B786157 Bg 2019 | DDC [Fic]—dc23
LC record available at https://lccn.loc.gov/2019035422

To Jessica Khoury,
our guiding star in the Darkest Night

L'etat, c'est moi.
(I am the state.)
—Louis XIV

OVERVIEW OF BOOK 1,
Sky Without Stars

Marcellus Bonnefaçon:

Second Estate. Officer of the Ministère. Grandson of General Bonnefaçon and son of Julien Bonnefaçon (an infamous traitor and member of a rebel group known as the Vangarde). As the general's protégé, Marcellus was a loyal member of the Regime until recently, when he discovered that seventeen years ago his grandfather framed his father for the crime that sent Julien Bonnefaçon to prison. Marcellus now suspects the general is responsible for murdering Marie Paresse, the Premier Enfant, and plotting to take control of the Regime by force.

Chatine Renard:

Third Estate. A skilled thief and the daughter of con artists. Grew up in the Frets (slums) of Vallonay after moving from the mining city of Montfer with her family when she was a child. For the past ten years, she posed as a boy named Théo to avoid the blood bordels, which prey on young women. She was hired by General Bonnefaçon to spy on his grandson, Marcellus, and was later sent to the prison moon of Bastille for refusing to give up the location of the Vangarde's rebel base.

Alouette "Little Lark" Taureau (aka Madeline):
Third Estate. Daughter of wanted fugitive, Hugo Taureau, recently revealed not to be her biological father. When she was a young child, her mother left her in the care of the Renards who badly mistreated her. She was later rescued by Hugo and brought to live in the Refuge of the Sisterhood, an off-grid, underground bunker. For the past twelve years, she's served as a guardian of the First World knowledge and the Forgotten Word before recently discovering that the sisterhood is actually the Vangarde and the Refuge their secret rebel base.

Hugo Taureau (aka Jean LeGrand):
Third Estate. Alouette's adoptive father and wanted Bastille fugitive, Prisoner 2.4.6.0.1. Intimately acquainted with Alouette's mother. Hugo recently escaped to the planet of Reichenstat after being discovered by his longtime pursuer and nemesis, Inspecteur Limier.

Inspecteur Limier:
Second Estate. Cyborg and head of the Vallonay Policier. For years, he's been hunting down runaway convict, Hugo Taureau, and recently tracked him to the Forest Verdure where he managed to capture Taureau. He was soon after incapacitated by Alouette, allowing Hugo to escape again.

General Bonnefaçon:
Second Estate. Marcellus's grandfather and Julien Bonnefaçon's father. As head of the Ministère and chief advisor to the Patriarche, he is one of the most powerful men on Laterre. When Marcellus confronted the general about hiring a spy to follow him, the general responded by brutally beating Marcellus. A ruthless strategist, the general is determined to take control of the Regime by any means necessary.

Julien Bonnefaçon:
Second Estate. Son of General Bonnefaçon and father to Marcellus. As a member of the Vangarde, he was framed by the general for a copper

exploit bombing that killed 600 workers and brought an end to the Rebellion of 488. Julien was sent to Bastille when Marcellus was a baby and recently died in prison. He left behind a message sewn into his uniform, directing Marcellus to find Mabelle Dubois.

Mabelle Dubois:
Third Estate. Marcellus's childhood governess, who secretly taught Marcellus to read and write the Forgotten Word. When Marcellus was eleven years old, Mabelle was discovered to be a Vangarde spy—and sent to Bastille. A recent message left by his father led Marcellus to Montfer where he tracked down Mabelle who tried, and failed, to recruit him to join the Vangarde.

Patriarche Lyon Paresse:
First Estate. Leader of Laterre and direct descendant of the founding Paresse family. Lyon lives in the Grand Palais in the center of Ledôme and has always been more interested in hunting than running the Regime—until his young daughter, Marie, was poisoned. The Patriarche suspects that Citizen Rousseau, the imprisoned leader of the Vangarde, was somehow behind the murder.

Matrone Veronik Paresse:
First Estate. Wife of Patriarche Paresse and mother to the Premier Enfant, Marie Paresse. Before the shocking death of her daughter, she spent most of her time dressing in the latest Laterrian fashions and drinking champagne.

Premier Enfant Marie Paresse:
First Estate. Daughter of the Patriarche and Matrone and only heir to the Regime. Just before her third birthday, Marie was poisoned and her murder (and the subsequent cancellation of the Ascension lottery) ignited riots on Laterre.

Nadette Epernay:
Third Estate. Governess to the Premier Enfant. She was recently accused of working with the Vangarde to murder her charge, Marie

Paresse, and was soon after put to death by exécuteur (aka "the Blade") in the Marsh, the central marketplace of the Frets.

Citizen Rousseau:
Third Estate. Former leader of the Vangarde. In 488, Citizen Rousseau led a rebellion that sought to end the Regime's inequality and injustice, but was eventually arrested and sent to Bastille where she has been kept in solitary confinement for the past seventeen years.

Monsieur and Madame Renard:
Third Estate. Con artists and parents of Chatine, Azelle, and Henri Renard. Former owners of the Jondrette Inn in Montfer, they moved to Vallonay ten years ago where Monsieur Renard became the leader of the formidable Délabré gang. After Hugo Taureau, the escaped convict, was spotted in the Frets, the Renards pursued and kidnapped him, in an attempt to secure his bounty, but were soon after arrested by Inspecteur Limier.

Azelle Renard:
Third Estate. Oldest daughter of the Renards and sister to Chatine and Henri. A law-abiding employee of the TéléSkin fabrique, she dreamed of winning the Ascension lottery and ascending to the Second Estate. But in the recent spate of unrest, the TéléSkin fabrique was bombed by an unknown attacker, killing Azelle and eleven other workers.

Henri Renard:
Third Estate. Youngest child of the Renards and baby brother to Chatine and Azelle. Chatine believed him to be dead until recently when it was discovered that her parents sold him off to pay their debts.

Sergent Chacal:
Second Estate. A bullheaded Vallonay Policier sergent who reports to Inspecteur Limier. Chacal is ruthless, cruel, and doles out violent punishments with a metal baton.

Commandeur Vernay:

Second Estate. The general's closest friend and former commandeur of the Ministère. She was killed on a failed mission to assassinate Queen Mathilda, the "Mad Queen" of Albion (Laterre's longtime enemy) during Usonia's recent war of independence. Since her death, General Bonnefaçon has been grooming Marcellus to take Vernay's place as commandeur.

Roche:

Third Estate. An orphan—or "Oublie"—who grew up in the Frets of Vallonay. He was recently arrested for delivering messages for the Vangarde. In an attempt to prove he's innocent, Marcellus recruited Chatine to interrogate Roche which inadvertently resulted in Roche's imprisonment on Bastille.

The Sisters of the Refuge:

A secret society of ten women who protect the Forgotten Word and an extensive library of books rescued from the First World. Led by Principale Francine, all ten sisters live in a bunker hidden beneath the Frets and wear a string of "devotion beads" around their necks. For the past twelve years, Alouette Taureau has lived and studied with the sisters, unaware until recently that they are also the leaders of a rebel group known as the Vangarde.

The Vangarde:

A rebel group believed to be dead after their leader, Citizen Rousseau, was arrested and sent to Bastille during the Rebellion of 488. They've spent the past seventeen years in hiding, building their numbers in preparation for a resurgence. The Refuge of the Sisterhood is their central base of operations. Two of their operatives—Sister Jacqui and Sister Denise—were recently captured during a mission to break into the office of the Warden of Bastille in an attempt to free their imprisoned leader.

PART 1

CITIZEN ROUSSEAU

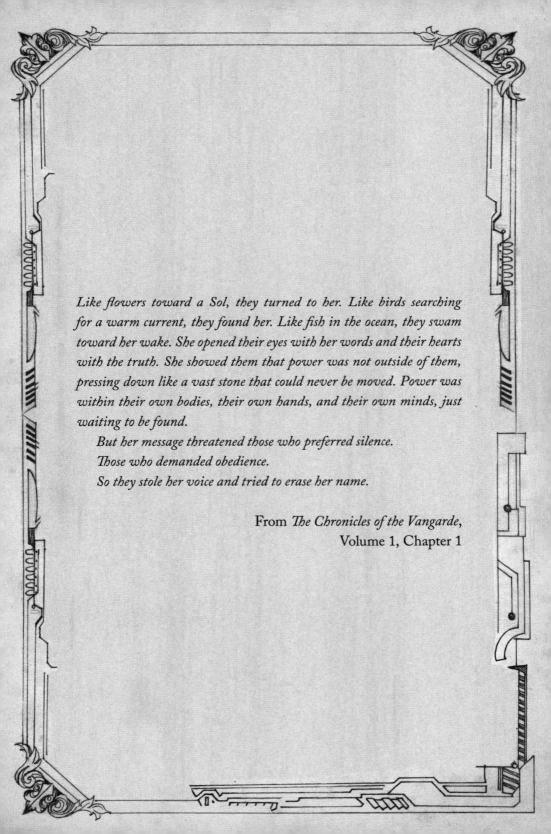

Like flowers toward a Sol, they turned to her. Like birds searching for a warm current, they found her. Like fish in the ocean, they swam toward her wake. She opened their eyes with her words and their hearts with the truth. She showed them that power was not outside of them, pressing down like a vast stone that could never be moved. Power was within their own bodies, their own hands, and their own minds, just waiting to be found.

But her message threatened those who preferred silence.

Those who demanded obedience.

So they stole her voice and tried to erase her name.

From *The Chronicles of the Vangarde,*
Volume 1, Chapter 1

- CHAPTER 1 -
MARCELLUS

MARCELLUS BONNEFAÇON MOVED LIKE A SHADOW among shadows, ducking under cables and darting around rusty cages that sat empty and gaping like sinister, hungry mouths. With every step he took through the abandoned exploit, his heart pounded harder, making him feel more and more like the traitor he had become.

The traitor his grandfather always knew he *would* become.

You were right, Grand-père. I am just like my father.

Rain splattered up from the puddles as Marcellus wound his way past a collapsed hoist tower that lay twisted and decaying on the uneven ground. The old copper exploit hadn't been operational in seventeen years, but it felt as if it had been deserted for centuries. It was an eerie, ominous place, with rows of abandoned shaft entrances, dark and empty like black holes in a galaxy. Two weeks ago, Marcellus might have turned around, his fear sending him scurrying back to his plush, well-lit rooms in the Grand Palais. But not now. Not with the memory of the Premier Enfant's tiny red coffin still vivid in his mind. Not with this bruise on his rib cage still tender and throbbing.

Everything was different now. His senses were sharper. Sights and sounds and smells were stronger. His eyes were wide open.

And the world had turned red.

A dark, crimson red.

The color of death. The color of rage. The color of fire.

But you were also wrong, Grand-père. I can fight back.

As Marcellus shimmied along the wall of one of the old processing plants, he caught a glimpse of his own reflection in the warped metal siding and nearly jumped at the sight. He barely recognized himself. The young man looking back at him was too unkempt. Too rebellious. Not the buttoned-up, obedient officer his grandfather had raised him to be over the past eighteen years.

Before leaving the Grand Palais earlier this evening, he'd washed the gel from his thick, dark hair, letting it dry tousled and wavy. He'd donned this stolen exploit coat and streaked mud across his cheeks and neck. It was an effective disguise. A good way to disappear. A Fret rat had once taught him that. Someone he used to know.

But he tried not to think about Chatine Renard now.

Much.

Marcellus peered up at the sky, hoping to catch a rare glimpse of the prison moon of Bastille. But of course, he saw nothing. Nothing but a dark, unfathomable abyss. The constant cloud coverage of Laterre's atmosphere made it impossible to see anything else.

There were no Sols. No moon. No light. It was a sky entirely without stars.

But Marcellus didn't need the stars or the moon to guide him tonight. He had the fire to do that. A red-hot blaze that had been lit deep inside of him. A flame that he was certain would never die.

And of course, he had his instructions. Mysterious words written on a piece of paper by an unseen hand. Words that had lured him out to an abandoned exploit in the dark hours of morning.

I will meet you at the beginning of the end.

Marcellus followed a narrow path through a cluster of buildings, passing piles and piles of debris: discarded boots, cracked helmets, decomposing jackets, and a canvas gurney streaked with blood.

Some people believed that the old copper exploit was haunted. That the ghosts of the six hundred workers who had perished in the bombing seventeen years ago still lingered here. Trapped underground forever.

Marcellus didn't want to believe that. But walking through this forsaken place, he could understand why no one ever came out here.

This was a picture stained with death and grief and time.

A picture no one should have to see.

But that Marcellus *needed* to see.

This was the reason his father, Julien Bonnefaçon, had spent the last seventeen years of his life in prison.

And this was where the mysterious instructions had been leading Marcellus. He was certain of it.

The beginning of the end. For his father. For the Vangarde. For the Rebellion of 488.

The sinister silence was suddenly shattered by the sound of footsteps. Panicked, Marcellus flipped up the hood of his stolen coat and tucked himself into one of the rusty metal cages. The suspension cable above creaked and whined, and Marcellus felt his stomach drop as he glanced down into the two-hundred-mètre deep chasm below. He sucked in a breath and kept perfectly still, praying those footsteps didn't belong to a droid.

All it would take was one scan. One encounter, and his disguise would be rendered useless. His biometrics would be detected. His identity known. And then it would all be over. This perilous task that loomed before him would no longer matter. Nothing would matter. Because he'd be rotting away on the moon with the rest of the traitors.

The footsteps grew closer. Marcellus listened in the darkness, his heart hammering in his chest. Peering out from under his hood, he tried to pinpoint where they were coming from, but the exploit had fallen silent again.

Had he imagined them? He wouldn't be surprised. After the events of the past few weeks, he'd been imagining all manner of ghastly things. His visions kept him awake at night. He'd hardly slept since the funeral.

A damp breeze kicked up and started to batter at his coat. Hearing a soft creaking noise up ahead, he stepped out from the rickety cage and squinted into the darkness where he was just able to make out a small, rundown hut with a lopsided door swinging on the hinges. Marcellus plunged his cold, shaky fingers into his pocket and pulled out a small container of matches. The first one struggled to catch light in the wet air, but the second sparked and bloomed into a brilliant orange flame. Protecting the glow with his cupped hand, he held the light up to the hut until he could see the distinct marking slashed across the door in mud.

Two diagonal lines descending toward each other.

The letter V, he remembered with a jolt of anticipation. He was in the right place.

The roof of the structure sagged at a strange angle, and the hut's rusting walls seemed to billow as the angry wind picked up speed. Marcellus pushed open the corroded door and stepped inside.

Shadows swallowed him. It took a moment for his eyes to adjust to the low light. And then he saw her.

She was sitting on a wooden bench, her hands tucked into her lap, her head turned so that Marcellus could see her profile. A face pulled straight from both his darkest and brightest memories. When she turned toward him, her lips curled into a warm, familiar smile. "Marcellou. I hoped you'd come."

Marcellus's legs gave out from under him. He sank to his knees in front of his former governess, feeling every emotion that he'd blocked out for the past seven years suddenly wash over him at once. Anger, frustration, betrayal, regret, guilt, longing.

It was the longing more than anything. Mabelle had been marked as a traitor to the Regime. An enemy spy. He was forbidden from missing her. From thinking of her in any way but resentment. But, Sols, how he'd missed her.

There was so much to say. And yet all he could utter as he knelt by her feet was, "I'm sorry. I'm so sorry."

What was he apologizing for? For treating her like a criminal when he'd come face-to-face with her three weeks ago in Montfer? For believing his grandfather's lies about her? Even when they scratched against his heart in the most uncomfortable of ways? For not saving her that day seven years ago when the droids dragged her away?

But he knew the answer.

All of it.

He was sorry for all of it.

Suddenly, he felt Mabelle's gentle yet reassuring hand on his head. "It's okay, Marcellou. It's okay." And for the briefest of moments, every last drop of his anger melted right off him. He felt safe. He felt protected. The decrepit and wind-beaten hut he'd entered had turned into a warm place, a familiar place, a place of love and light. Suddenly, he was a little boy again, playing with his little plastique transporteurs at Mabelle's feet while she read aloud from one of the books she'd smuggled into the Palais.

"Does anyone know you're here?" Mabelle asked, her voice suddenly taking on a grave tone. "Were you followed?"

Marcellus momentarily thought of the footsteps he'd heard earlier. The ones he was now certain he'd imagined. "No."

"Are you sure?" Mabelle asked. "The general has spies working for him all over the planet."

And just like that, the bubble burst. Marcellus was thrust back into the present moment. Everything flooded into focus: the leaking, rundown hut; the cold, uneven floor under his knees; Mabelle's drawn, weather-beaten skin; and the splintered bench where she sat. The anger came flooding back too, seeping into his bones, returning his vision to red.

"I know all about his spies," he muttered, thinking once again of Chatine. "I took precautions." He pushed himself back to his feet. "I left my TéléCom back at the Palais. I exited the grounds through the gaps in the perimeter you showed me when I was little. I parked my moto far away from the exploit."

Mabelle exhaled audibly. "Good. Good boy."

Marcellus's lips quirked involuntarily at the praise. She might have aged a lifetime on Bastille, but she was still the same woman who had raised him for eleven years.

She patted the bench next to her, and Marcellus sat down.

"I must say," Mabelle said as the cruel wind beat at the walls and the rain oozed through the cracks in the roof, "I wasn't entirely sure you'd come."

"I almost didn't," he said, and when Mabelle cocked an eyebrow, he smiled bashfully and explained. "It took me a while to read the message."

When he'd first discovered the piece of paper that had been slipped into his pocket during one of his patrols in the Frets, the letters felt impossible to decipher. It had been over seven years since he'd practiced reading and writing them. He'd spent hours tracing the curves and loops with his fingertips, until slowly, the memories of learning those letters came back to him, like lost lyrics. Once you start humming the first verse, the entire song suddenly reappears in your mind.

Perhaps the Forgotten Word was not so easily forgotten to him.

"Well, you're here. That's what matters," Mabelle said, taking his hand in hers. Her hand, which once swallowed his own, now felt impossibly small. But it was warm. The only warm thing in this whole miserable place.

Marcellus nodded, trying to pull comfort from Mabelle's words. The truth was, he wished he'd gotten that message sooner, decoded it faster. They'd already lost so much time. General Bonnefaçon had already caused so much unrest and upheaval and . . . *death*. The Premier Enfant—little Marie Paresse—on a one-way trip to Sol 2. Nadette Epernay, who was framed—and *executed*—for Marie's murder. Who was next? How many more lives would the general sacrifice in his quest for power?

"I watched the footage," Marcellus said, feeling the now-familiar rage well up inside of him. "The proof that my father was innocent in the bombing of this exploit seventeen years ago. I found the microcam in the painting in your old room at the Grand Palais, just where you said it would be. I know Julien Bonnefaçon was framed and that my grandfather and the former Patriarche were the ones behind the attack."

Mabelle nodded. "I'm glad you've finally seen the truth."

"We have to stop him," Marcellus said urgently. "Not just stop him.

Destroy him. He betrayed me. He betrayed my father. He betrayed everyone on this planet. He must be brought down."

He took a deep breath and then finally said the words that had been running through his mind for the past two weeks. Maybe even for his entire life. Maybe they'd always been there. Buried deep inside his DNA. Calling out to him from his very veins. Just waiting for him to wake up and hear them. "I want to join the Vangarde."

A flicker of pride passed over Mabelle's face, but it was quickly replaced by a grave, warning look. "Marcellus, this is a very important decision that you should not take lightly. Joining us is a dangerous choice. It will put everything you know and love in danger. Your home. Your job. Your family."

"I don't have a family," Marcellus snapped. "My father died trying to fight for the right side. And my mother died mourning him. *You* are my only family. And as for my home and my job? I don't care about any of it anymore. The Regime, the Ministère, my promotion to commandeur, that cursed officer uniform. I'm done with all of it. I'm done being the general's dutiful, doting protégé. I'm done following in *his* footsteps. It's time I follow in the right footsteps. The ones I should have followed all along."

Mabelle looked at him with deep, pitying eyes. "Marcellus, joining the Vangarde won't bring your father back."

Marcellus stood up, his hands clenched by his sides. "I'm not doing this to bring my father back. I'm doing this to honor his memory." He nodded toward the rickety door that led to what was left of the copper exploit. "To honor *all* of their memories. I'm doing this to defeat the general. I want to pick up where my father left off. I'm ready now. I'll fight. I'll run messages. I'll recruit. I'll travel across the System Divine. Usonia, Kaishi, Reichenstat, wherever the Vangarde wants to send me. I'll leave the Palais tomorrow. I'll—"

"Marcellou." Mabelle held up a hand to stop him, looking slightly pained. "You don't understand. We don't want you to do any of that."

Marcellus squinted, confused. And just a little bit panicked. It had never even occurred to him that the Vangarde might turn him down. "But you said in Montfer . . . You said when I've seen the truth that I should come to you. That I could join you."

"Yes, that's true. We do need you, Marcellus. But not on the *outside*."

His confusion quickly gave way to dread. He suddenly felt nauseous. Sick. Cold. He shook his head. "No. I can't. I—"

"You're the only one who can get close to him."

Marcellus clawed his fingers through his hair, letting Mabelle's words sink in. "You want me to go back there? You want me to be in the same room as him and pretend that nothing happened? That he's innocent? I can't just go back to being blind."

"Not blind," Mabelle corrected. "The *opposite* of blind. Your eyes are wide open now. And we need those eyes inside the Palais. We haven't been able to get anyone inside since my arrest seven years ago. And now it's more important than ever that we do."

Marcellus swallowed, feeling like he might throw up.

"Why do you think I sent you that message in your father's prison shirt?" Mabelle went on. She was suddenly on her feet too, forcing him to look at her. "You have to understand; we didn't expect any of this. We thought we were fighting against the Regime, the Patriarche, a five-hundred-year-old corrupt institution. The Vangarde didn't know until a few months ago that the general was *also* fighting against the Regime. We are up against not one enemy, but two. And that uniform you wear is not a curse. It's a gift. It's a key. To go where no one else can go. To see and hear things that no one else can. If we're going to defeat General Bonnefaçon and stop him from taking over the Regime, we need your eyes and your ears. We need you to continue to be the general's dutiful, doting protégé."

Mabelle's gaze was so intense and piercing, Marcellus had to look away. He tried to rein in his wild, tempestuous breath, but it was like trying to rein in the storm outside.

"Did you know?" he whispered sharply. "That he was planning to murder the Premier Enfant?"

"No," Mabelle said emphatically. "Not until it was too late."

"But you have proof, right? That he killed her? We can use that. We can show the Patriarche and get my grandfather arrested and—"

"We don't have proof. Like you, we only have our suspicions. Our instincts."

"So that's what you want me to do? Get proof that he's guilty?"

Mabelle shook her head. "You won't find it. The general is a clever, careful man. He would have covered his tracks too well. Distanced himself from the crime to ensure it could never be traced back to him."

Marcellus shut his eyes as the memories bombarded him once more.

The head of Nadette Epernay thumping into a metal can.

The tiny coffin of Marie Paresse shooting into space.

"May she rest with the Sols."

"How did you know?" Marcellus blurted out.

The weathered skin on Mabelle's forehead crinkled in confusion.

"You said, 'The Vangarde didn't know until a few months ago that the general was also fighting against the Regime.' How did you know that?"

Mabelle sighed, looking forlorn. "We have intel that the general is working on something. Something horrible and destructive that will threaten the lives of everyone on this planet."

An icy chill trickled down Marcellus's spine. "What?"

For a moment, Mabelle's gaze drifted out the window, as though she were trying to summon strength from something—*anything*—out there. "He's building a weapon."

Marcellus felt the planet tilt beneath his feet. Was this what it felt like when that explosif went off seventeen years ago? Like the ground was giving way beneath them? Like the sky was crashing down around them? Like they might never breath again? It was several seconds before he could speak. Yet the words came out minced and mutilated. "What *kind* of weapon?"

"We don't know," Mabelle admitted. "But we believe it to be the general's endgame. The way he plans to take control of the Regime. Our intel comes from a source who is working directly with the general.

Unfortunately, the operative who has been in communication with that source was captured by the Ministère two weeks ago."

"The two women," Marcellus said with sudden realization, remembering the Vangarde operatives that he'd questioned at the Policier Precinct. The tall, rangy one who called herself Jacqui, and the shorter, dark-haired one who barely spoke. "They were caught trying to break into the Bastille warden's office."

"Yes," Mabelle confirmed. "One of them goes by the name of Denise."

"The one with the scars on her face?"

Mabelle nodded. "She used to be a cyborg. Before she joined the Vangarde."

Used to be?

Suddenly, everything about that woman's face started to make more sense. The pattern and placement of her scars, the lines running down her left cheek. He had no idea that a cyborg could have their circuitries removed. He'd always assumed that cyborgs were cyborgs for life.

"She was the only person who knew how to contact the source," Mabelle went on. "She was our only lead for finding out what the general was working on and how to stop it."

Marcellus felt his throat go dry. Those two operatives had vanished from the Policier Precinct only hours after Marcellus had questioned them.

"I don't know where they are," Marcellus said desperately. "The general has a secret facility somewhere. He's never told me much about it. I just know that every so often prisoners—high-profile ones—will disappear from the Precinct and come back days or weeks later, completely broken. Or they don't come back at all." He swallowed. "I'm sorry."

"It's okay," said Mabelle. "This is helpful information. We will try to root out their location, but in the meantime, we need someone to track down this weapon." Mabelle caught Marcellus's gaze with a meaningful look.

The realization sank into the pit of his stomach. "That's what you want me to do. You want me to find out what he's working on."

"What he's working on. Where he's working on it. Who he's working with. When it will be ready. Whatever you can find. We have exhausted countless resources on this, and we have still uncovered nothing."

Marcellus felt the weight of impossibility bearing down on him. He pressed his fingertips into his temples. "If the Vangarde can't find anything, what makes you think *I* can?"

A knowing smile tweaked at Mabelle's lips. "Because I raised you, ma chéri. I *know* you. I believe in you."

Marcellus began to pace the length of the tiny hut. "But the general already suspects me of working with you. He even hired a girl from the Frets to spy on me. He's *already* distrustful."

"Then you'll have to work extra hard to convince him of your loyalty."

Marcellus let out a growl of frustration. "He's the greatest military strategist this planet has ever seen! If he finds out I'm spying on him, he . . . he . . ." A shudder worked its way down his spine. "All of you would be in danger." For the first time since he'd left the Palais that night, Marcellus felt hopelessness settle over him. An entire ocean of it.

"This is the only way to stop him," Mabelle said, and Marcellus caught the air of finality in her voice. It reminded him of when he was little, and he would try to negotiate for five more minutes before bed.

But this was so different. They weren't negotiating for extra hours of playtime. They were negotiating for his life.

"What about the captured operative?" he asked desperately. "The one who knows how to contact the source working with the general. If I can dig around and find out where my grandfather is holding her—"

"Then, yes, of course, we will organize an extraction team," Mabelle said, "but that will take time, and we're running out of it. We need to find that weapon now."

Marcellus's eyes narrowed. "An extraction team? You mean to break them out?"

"Yes."

"Like you're planning to break out Citizen Rousseau?"

Mabelle fell quiet, her expression as placid as a lake.

It was no secret around the Ministère what those two operatives had been trying to do when they were captured in the warden's office. They had been attempting to infiltrate Bastille's security system so they could rescue their infamous incarcerated leader, Citizen Rousseau, the woman who had rallied thousands of people to her cause in the Rebellion of 488. The operatives had failed, but the general was certain that the Vangarde would try again.

But if Mabelle knew anything about another attempt to break into Bastille, she was not letting on.

"Isn't that what you're ultimately planning?" Marcellus pressed. "To bring back Rousseau so you can launch a full-scale revolution?"

"I'm afraid I cannot divulge that."

Marcellus felt a small flicker of indignation. "Why not?"

"You have to understand, Marcellus," Mabelle said gently. "You are still new to our cause. You are not yet trained to keep our secrets."

That silenced him. He knew exactly what she was saying. If he was caught, if he was tortured, he couldn't be trusted not to talk. He dug his fingernails into his palms. "Will you just tell me one thing?"

Mabelle's lips quirked into a ghost of a smile. "Depends on what it is."

Marcellus clenched his eyes shut, taking himself back to that night, two weeks ago, in the hallway of Fret 7. The last time he'd ever seen the girl named Alouette Taureau. He could still picture her vanishing form as she darted away from him. He could still picture her dark eyes, wide with shock and disbelief, as he'd told her the truth.

That she'd been unknowingly living with the Vangarde.

"There was a girl," he whispered before remembering the code name that was written on a metal tag that hung around her neck on a string of beads. "Little Lark." Marcellus opened his eyes. "What is her role in all of this? Please tell me she's not going to be involved in . . . in anything dangerous."

Mabelle's reaction made Marcellus's stomach clench. "Little Lark is . . ." She paused, lowering her gaze. "Little Lark is no longer with the Vangarde."

Marcellus felt all the blood drain from his head. "What? What do you mean? I thought she—"

"She left."

"Left?" Marcellus repeated. "Left where?"

"This is not something you need to concern yourself with," Mabelle said calmly, assuredly. "She will be fine. We will make sure of it."

Marcellus was breathing heavily now, the gravity of everything seeming to crash down on him at once. "But—" he began to say.

"We all have our role to play in the story of this planet, Marcellus. And right now, if you join us, your role is to find that weapon." Mabelle slowly extended her foot and dragged it across the floor of the hut, cutting an angled line through the dirt. "By accepting this assignment, you are swearing to pledge your life to our purpose. You are swearing your commitment to a better Laterre and your loyalty to that future planet."

Marcellus stared numbly down at the line that Mabelle had drawn on the floor, eventually recognizing what it represented.

It was one half of the same symbol that had been marked on the door of this hut.

One half of a letter.

Just waiting for him to make it complete.

Marcellus began to sweat inside his exploit coat. When he finally spoke again, his voice was quiet, resigned. "The general is always three moves ahead of everyone."

"Which is why you must do this. So *we* can stay ahead of *him*. So he can't hurt anyone else."

Marcellus placed a hand to the side of his rib cage, feeling the fading bruise where his grandfather's boot had driven into him over and over and over. He winced at the memory of lying on that cold marble floor of his grandfather's study. Beaten. Humiliated. Defeated.

"Look at you! You are pathetic. You can't even fight back."

Suddenly, the embers inside of him caught light again. The flames roared. The thought of returning to the Palais, donning that scratchy white uniform, and seeing his grandfather's face was enough to make

Marcellus's heart race, but he knew he couldn't just stand idly by and watch his grandfather tear this planet apart.

After all, he was no longer that scared, helpless boy lying on the floor. That Marcellus Bonnefaçon was gone. Incinerated instantly in the smoldering remains of his grandfather's lies.

Marcellus had been reborn that day. When he rose up from that cold hard floor to discover the truth about his father, his past, and his grandfather's deceptive games, he became someone else. Someone stronger. Someone angrier.

Someone who fought back.

Outside the cracked windows of the hut, light began to push its way through the dark, dark night. The three Sols were rising, turning Laterre's vast blanket of clouds into a glowing patchwork of gold, orange, and gray.

Mabelle stepped closer to Marcellus, her brown eyes sparkling in the dawn light. "Do you swear?"

Marcellus stood up straighter and—with one swift, decisive motion—swiped his foot across the dirty floor at a sharp angle. "I swear."

They both looked down at the now-complete letter *V* that blazed between them. Like it was on fire. Like it had been branded right into the ground. It was a letter that had lost its meaning on Laterre hundreds of years ago. But now, it suddenly had the power to tilt the planet on its axis. Realign the stars around the entire System Divine.

Mabelle smiled a mysterious little smile. "Welcome to the Vangarde."

Marcellus exhaled a breath that he swore he'd been holding for eighteen years. Joining the Vangarde might not bring his father back, but, in that moment, Marcellus had never felt closer to Julien Bonnefaçon.

- CHAPTER 2 -
MARCELLUS

IN THE CENTER OF LEDÔME, THE GRAND BOULEVARD
bustled with Second Estaters, promenading and shopping, gossiping
with friends and flaunting their latest fashions. Cruiseurs and motos
flitted up and down the street, delivering passengers to the hundreds of
shops and restaurants lining the sidewalk.

Marcellus steered his moto past the Opéra and the Musée of the First
World before pulling to a stop near a large roundabout where the Grand
Boulevard ended and other smaller avenues jutted out like spokes on an
old-fashioned wheel. He tugged at the collar of his stiff officer uniform,
feeling like it was already cutting off the circulation to his brain.

Before returning to Ledôme, he'd washed the dirt from his face and
changed back into the crisp white trousers and lapelled jacket that he
loathed so much. He was, once again, Officer Bonnefaçon, the grandson
of General César Bonnefaçon, and the son of the notorious dead traitor,
Julien Bonnefaçon. He was, once again, Laterre's commandeur-in-training,
a dutiful servant of the Ministère.

And today, he would have to look his grandfather in the eye and pretend that he didn't just pledge his life to bringing the general down.

He felt sick with dread and impossibility. He couldn't help but think that the Vangarde had made a huge mistake in entrusting this task to him. It still felt like a fool's errand. The general was too clever, too secretive, too strategic. How was Marcellus ever going to find this weapon? Where would he even begin?

Releasing a sigh, he tipped his head back and glanced up at the Paresse Tower that stood tall and regal at the center of the roundabout, watching over every street and park, every manoir and garden. Erected twenty years ago by the former Patriarche, Claude Paresse, to celebrate the Laterrian Regime, the tower used to be one of Marcellus's favorite sights in Ledôme. The view of the magnificent structure, motionless and vast, shooting up into the TéléSky, used to inspire him.

But today, like everything else around him, the Paresse Tower felt gaudy and grandiose and so very wrong. Now Marcellus could see it for what it really was: a tower erected to mark centuries of oppression and inequality. A landmark built to celebrate the elite few who were fortunate enough to live in luxury in this climate-controlled biodome while the rest of the planet starved and froze.

Today, the tower only served to make him angrier.

He kicked off from the ground and sped the rest of the way back to the Grand Palais. After docking his moto outside the gates, Marcellus walked the length of the perimeter, scanning the little fleur-de-lis ornaments that topped each post of the titan fence, until he located the one that was bent at a slight angle. He climbed the fence and slipped through the invisible breach in the security shields, silently thanking Mabelle for her ingenuity.

He remembered the first time she had shown him the bent ornaments, when he was just a little boy. She'd made a game out of locating them. *"Which ones are not like the others?"* It wasn't until years later, after Mabelle had been arrested as a Vangarde spy, that Marcellus realized Mabelle had bent them on purpose. To mark the loopholes where she had compromised the shields surrounding the Palais grounds, allowing her to come and go without being noticed or tracked.

Marcellus let himself in through the servants' entrance and climbed one of the back staircases to the south wing, where he and his grandfather lived. As the head of the Ministère and the Patriarche's primary advisor, General Bonnefaçon was awarded dedicated residences in the Palais. It was an honor that used to make Marcellus feel lucky, privileged, prestigious. Now these walls felt like prison bars. And the spacious, well-appointed rooms that he passed along the way only served to remind him that this morning's visit to the copper exploit had *not* gone as he'd planned.

When he'd crept through the dark, sleeping Palais only a few hours ago, he thought he was leaving it for good. He thought he'd never have to return. He was fueled by the idea that he would never have to be in the same room as his grandfather again. He'd thought that joining the Vangarde would take him *away* from all of this. Just as it had for his father.

And yet, here he was. Back within these suffocating walls. With his grandfather's loathsome lies clinging to every fiber of every tapestry.

"Access granted." The door to his rooms opened and Marcellus lifted his palm from the panel on the biometric lock and barged inside. He stalked over to the bed, collapsed down onto it, and screamed into one of the silk pillows. Loud and hard until his throat burned and the sound silenced the voices of doubt and helplessness in his head.

"Are you finished?"

Marcellus sprang up from the bed and glanced around, his heart leaping into his throat when he saw his grandfather standing near the door to the balcony. The general's tall, muscular frame was half silhouetted by the artificial Sol-light streaming in through the gap in the curtains.

"G-G-Grand-père," Marcellus said, stammering slightly. How long had he been standing there? "What are you doing here?"

"I've been waiting for you," his grandfather said coolly.

Marcellus's pulse spiked as a hundred thousand crimes filtered through his mind at once.

Does he know where I've been?

Marcellus glanced back down at the ruffled comforter of his bed, where he'd just thrown his little tantrum. His grandfather had *seen* that.

"You weren't answering your AirLinks." The general nodded to the TéléCom that was folded up and sitting idly on Marcellus's bedside table. Even though the tracking capabilities on the device were deactivated, he'd still left it behind as a precaution.

"Yes . . . um . . . ," Marcellus began, wishing that, just this once, he could talk to the general without stammering like an imbecile. "I just stepped out to get some air and I . . . forgot it."

His grandfather lifted an eyebrow. "And Chacal says he stopped by the TéléSkin fabrique yesterday—where you were supposed to be investigating the recent attack—but you weren't there."

Marcellus felt a storm brewing in his chest. His grandfather had appointed him lead officer on the investigation of the recent TéléSkin fabrique attack. It had killed twelve workers, including Chatine's sister, and they still had no idea who was responsible. But Marcellus had been so busy deciphering the message that the Vangarde had slipped to him in the Frets and mentally preparing himself for his meeting with Mabelle, he'd let some of his officer duties slide. But he never thought that clochard Chacal would rat him out for it.

Marcellus fought to keep his face neutral as he tried to come up with a believable excuse. "I'm sorry, Grand-père. I haven't been myself since the funeral."

The general's cool hazel eyes bored into Marcellus. "Must I remind you that Laterre is in a precarious state right now?"

Thanks to you, Marcellus thought bitterly but he shook his head and muttered, "No, sir."

"Tensions are mounting. The Third Estate are getting out of control, rioting almost daily. And with Inspecteur Limier still missing, we need everyone around here to pull their weight."

The fearsome head of the Vallonay Policier had vanished two weeks ago. He'd ventured out to the Forest Verdure to arrest two wanted criminals and never came back.

"*This* is not the time to be lazy and distracted, Marcellus."

Marcellus felt his blood start to boil. His fists clenched at his sides, desperate to strike, to pound, to pummel. But he forced himself to remember Mabelle's words.

"*. . . you'll have to work extra hard to convince him of your loyalty.*"

Marcellus swallowed down the rage. "Of course, Grand-père. I apologize for my actions. It will not happen again."

The general scrutinized him, the edge of his jaw pulsing. It's what his grandfather did when he was holding something back. Then, silently, he stepped forward and reached a hand toward Marcellus's face. Marcellus flinched as his grandfather dragged a single finger across his cheek. When his hand retracted, Marcellus could see the smear of mud on the general's fingertip. Remnants of his disguise.

For a long, tense moment, both of them just stared down at it.

Finally, his grandfather spoke. "You need to come with me."

The room tilted. Marcellus wished he could grab on to something for balance. For a moment, he considered running. He eyed the balcony, trying to gauge how far down it was to the forecourt below. Would he survive the jump?

"Why?" he whispered.

The general released a heavy sigh. "The Patriarche has summoned us to go hunting."

Hunting?

For a full three seconds, Marcellus was certain he had misunderstood.

"Prepare your status report on the investigation and make yourself presentable." The general nodded dismissively toward Marcellus's face and then strode toward the hallway. "And meet me in the foyer in thirty minutes."

The moment the door slid shut behind the general, Marcellus let out a shuddering breath. The beautiful air flooded back into his lungs. He darted to the bathroom and splashed ice-cold water on his face, trying to bring the sensation back to his skin. Tilting his chin at various angles, he searched for any more traces of mud before drying his face with a towel and turning back toward the door. But something out of the corner of his eye caught his attention and pulled him up short.

He spun around and stared down into the corner of the bathroom. Beside the toilette, a single floor tile glinted in the light. He'd accidentally wrenched it loose when he was a little boy, and it had been his secret hiding place ever since. When he was younger and Mabelle was teaching him the Forgotten Word, he used to hide folded-up pieces of paper in there, lines and lines of practiced letters and shaky misspelled words. Now the small nook under the tile held the microcam he'd found two weeks ago, hidden in the painting in Mabelle's old room. Proof that his grandfather was guilty in the bombing of that copper exploit seventeen years ago.

His heart started to pound again in his chest as he glared at the tile.

What had his grandfather *really* been doing in his rooms? Looking for Marcellus, as he'd said? Or looking for something else?

Slowly, tentatively, Marcellus walked over to the toilette, crouched down, and used his fingernails to peel up the loose floor tile. He almost didn't have to look. He almost knew what he would find before he saw it.

Nothing.

He found nothing.

Because the microcam was gone.

- CHAPTER 3 -
CHATINE

CHATINE RENARD HAD KNOWN DARKNESS ALL HER
life. From the moment she was born eighteen years ago, it had surrounded
her, clinging to her like a cloak. But nothing compared to the darkness
that lurked two hundred mètres below the surface of Bastille. This was a
darkness like Chatine had never known. It was a living, breathing thing.
A murkiness that seeped into her bones and coated her lungs.

This was the kind of darkness that brought the dead back to life.

The droid closed the metal cage with a bang that reverberated down
Chatine's spine. The lift started to descend, slow and painful and creaking, into the ground. With every centimètre they lowered, Chatine's
teeth chattered harder. Not because of the temperature. It was mercifully
warmer down here than on the surface of the moon. But if Chatine had
learned anything since arriving on Bastille, it was that the cold wasn't the
only thing here that could make you shiver.

The lift wrenched to a stop and the door of the cage creaked open,
revealing a warren of gloomy passageways that extended out from the
main shaft. Two more bashers stood watch, their bright orange eyes
cutting through the darkness. No human guards dared set foot on this

wretched moon. The prison was manned entirely by droids while some overpaid warden supervised from his plush, cushy office back in Ledôme.

"Single-file line," one of them droned. "Look down. No talking. No running."

Chatine almost snorted aloud at the warning. *Running? Seriously? Where would they even run to?* The craggy walls and looming ceilings of the exploit tunnels snaked and dipped, burrowed and crisscrossed through the Bastille rock, going nowhere. Always ending in cold, dark nothingness.

And even if it weren't for the dead-end tunnels, Chatine was barely capable of crawling out of her bunk each morning, let alone *running*. Her body had never felt so useless and heavy and beaten. Her head was almost always pounding, her mouth was constantly dirt dry, every centimètre of her ached, and no matter how tired she was at the end of her twelve-hour shift down here in the darkness, she could never *ever* seem to get enough sleep.

The inmates called the condition the "grippe." Chatine could certainly understand why. It felt like every organ in her body—including her mind—had been placed in a merciless vise. It was the result of the thinner air on Bastille. Chatine had heard that it could take up to six months for your body to adapt to the climate.

She had been here two weeks.

The inmates formed a line and began to shuffle into the tunnel. Beside them, the droids paced, their heavy metal footsteps clanking, the rayonettes embedded in their arms glowing menacingly in the dim light. After grabbing a headlamp and a pick, Chatine followed the procession into the tunnel. With each collective step they took, the walls and ceilings rumbled ominously around them.

Chatine hated the crackles and pops that came from above, rippling through the ground and threatening to bring two hundred mètres of hard rock crashing down on top of her. She'd heard stories of prisoners dying in the zyttrium exploits. They were some of the first stories told to newcomers on Bastille.

She paused, glanced up, and cringed as a scattering of loose dust and debris rained down on her face.

"Prisoner 51562," one of the droids boomed, "look down and keep walking."

Chatine lowered her gaze and scuffled forward. They seemed to be walking forever today. Much farther than Chatine had ever ventured into the tunnels. The light from the headlamp clipped onto her helmet was a poor contender for the murky depths of the exploit. And the farther away they got from the main shaft, the darker the tunnel became.

Chatine pushed back the sleeve of her prison uniform and touched the darkened screen just above her wrist. It blinked to life, providing a dim halo of light. The Skins had limited functionality on Bastille. There were no broadcasts, no AirLink messages, no Universal Alerts, no Ascension points or tokens. Up here on the moon, the Skins were only used to track time and people. Including, now, Chatine. All her former Skin hacks had been removed by the droids when she'd first arrived. But Chatine liked to look at her Skin from time to time, if for no other reason than to remind her of why she was really here. Why all of them were here. This small rectangular device that had been implanted in her flesh since childhood was the reason the Regime spent millions of tokens a year running this Sol-forsaken prison.

The Skins were needed to keep the Third Estate in line.

Zyttrium was needed to make the Skins.

And the dusty craters of Bastille held the last known deposits of zyttrium in the entire System Divine.

Chatine spotted the glint of metal up ahead, and the procession finally slowed to a stop. In front of them, the giant machines that dug the tunnels and secured the supports stood motionless, idling like sleeping silver beasts.

"Every inmate is required to excavate one hundred grammes of zyttrium," the nearest droid announced, causing a stirring among the prisoners.

"One hundred grammes?!" shouted one of the inmates. "That's double what we had to dig yesterday."

"No talking!" the droid boomed, its eerie monotone voice ricocheting off the low-ceilinged tunnels, making it sound even *less* human than it already did. "Look down, start digging."

Silently, Chatine positioned herself in front of the tunnel wall and got to work, jamming her pick into the hard rock. With each strike, she paused and waited, listening, expecting, holding her breath. Would today finally be the day the voice in her head didn't come? The day that Chatine's mind finally got ahold of itself and came back to its senses?

Chatine couldn't decide what was worse: a mental breakdown, or losing that voice all over again.

And then, finally, after the tenth strike of her pick against the wall, Chatine heard it. From deep in the dark corners of her mind.

"Brrr! It is so chilly here. Way colder than on Laterre."

Chatine's shoulders slumped in relief. Azelle was here. For at least one more day, Chatine would not be alone on this moon.

"How are you not *freezing*, Chatine?" the voice asked.

Chatine didn't reply. She never replied to the voice of her dead sister. But just like in life, it didn't stop Azelle from talking.

"Did you hear those new quotas? You're going to be here forever. How do they expect you to mine one hundred grammes in a day?"

Chatine shone her headlamp into the heap of rock that had gathered by her feet. There wasn't a single hint of glowing blue zyttrium. She'd heard prisoners whispering about the shortage on Bastille. How each week, the tunnels stretched farther and farther, and the exploit carts came back less and less full.

"I remember this being a problem back at the Skin fabrique," Dead Azelle said knowledgably. "Not enough zyttrium to make the new Skins. The superviseurs tried to hide it from us but we weren't stupide. We saw the supply transporteurs coming in. How many of these prisoners do you think are here because of an actual crime they committed? And how many are here because the Ministère just needed more people to dig?"

Chatine momentarily glanced up at the inmates lining the tunnel, wondering if Azelle was right. Was Chatine's existence here—as well as the existence of every other prisoner on this moon—no more complicated than a dwindling supply of zyttrium? Chatine had never known her older sister to be very wise or observant in life. But often, as Chatine lay in the cold, damp prison bunks, she wondered if she'd underestimated her sister. If maybe there had been more to Azelle Renard than Chatine ever knew.

Of course, she'd never have a chance to find out now. An explosif in the Skin fabrique two weeks ago had made sure of that.

"It also kind of stinks down here," Azelle added. "Much worse than the Frets."

Chatine *almost* smiled at that one. She knew that the Azelle who spoke to her down here in the dark exploits wasn't real. Obviously, she knew that. She just assumed it was another symptom of the grippe. A symptom that—unlike the bone-splitting headaches and waves of dizziness—was not entirely unwelcome. It gave her something to listen to besides the monotonous banging of the picks hitting rocks and the ominous rattles and tremors that followed.

And also, it kept her mind off Henri.

Because Dead Azelle knew better than to talk about *him*.

One ghost to distract you from another.

"Is this how it's going to be every day?"

Chatine reared back her pick and slammed it into the wall, bringing down a fresh cascade of rock to add to her pile.

"How long do we have to be down here? It's really dark. I didn't think it would be this dark. Cold, yes. You always hear about the cold. But no one ever tells you about the darkness."

Chatine sighed and pitched her pick back again, letting Azelle's quiet prattling voice continue to envelop her like a blanket.

"Excuse me. Can you hear me? Or are you just ignoring me? People often do ignore me."

The pick paused over Chatine's head. She looked to her right, where a slender girl in an exploit coat too big for her small frame was waving her hand back and forth, trying to get Chatine's attention.

How long had *this* girl been talking? She sounded just like Azelle.

"I know we're not supposed to talk," the girl went on in a low voice.

"You're right," Chatine snapped with a cautious look over her shoulder for nearby droids. "We're not."

"But I'm going a little bit insane," she said, shaking her head. Her helmet—like her exploit coat—was too big, and it rattled haphazardly, causing the light from her headlamp to flash and bob. "No one here talks to anyone. It's my first day, and I haven't been able to get anyone to say a single word to me."

Chatine sighed. Of all the people she could get stuck next to, she'd ended up with a babbler.

"And why is everyone so mean here?" the girl continued.

"They're not mean," Chatine whispered harshly. "They're tired and cranky. And don't want to get tazed for talking."

"I'm Anaïs," the girl went on, clearly interpreting Chatine's dismissal as an invitation to introduce herself. "What's your name?"

Chatine didn't reply. Maybe if she just ignored her, the girl would give up and stop talking.

"Did you come from Vallonay?"

Chatine kept digging.

"I came from Delaine in the Northern Région. Do you know it? Probably not. It's a very boring town. Mostly just sheep. You're probably wondering why I'm on Bastille."

Actually, Chatine thought bitterly. *I wasn't.*

"I got rounded up for being out after curfew. They're being really strict now. Anyone out after hours gets sent straight to Bastille. It's not fair. I wasn't even doing anything wrong! I swear. I was just—" The girl's voice was cut off by her own scream as her body convulsed violently and her pick fell to the ground. Chatine glanced over to see the nearest droid retracting its tazeur.

As she watched Anaïs's eyes roll back into place, Chatine couldn't help but feel the slightest bit sorry for the girl. But also the slightest bit relieved. Maybe now she would finally understand the consequences and shut up.

"Look down, keep digging," the droid admonished.

Whimpering slightly, Anaïs picked up her fallen pick, and the basher moved on. Chatine watched as the girl wiped tears from her face and tried to shake off the lingering effects of the tazeur. Then she hoisted back her pick, nearly collapsing under its weight, and brought it crashing clumsily and noisily down into the rock, mere centimètres from the nearest anchor bolt.

"What are you doing!?" Chatine hissed. "Are you trying to kill us?"

Anaïs sniffled. "No."

"You have to dig *around* the rock bolts. If you knock one out of place, you could bring the whole tunnel down on top of us."

Anaïs glanced in confusion between her pick and the tunnel wall.

Chatine huffed. "Watch me." She demonstrated, carefully aiming her pick at the space between the two nearest anchor bolts. "See?"

The girl nodded but didn't go back to work. Instead, she leaned on her pick and let out a melancholy sigh. "Do you think he'll wait for me?"

Chatine's grip around her pick handle tightened as she buried it into the wall with more force than she'd ever used before. Rock skittered around her feet, and there was a flash of blue under the light from her headlamp. It was a thread of zyttrium laced through a shard of rubble. That would barely make up five percent of her quota today.

Anaïs turned her head upward and stared at the ceiling of the tunnel, as though she could see right through it, all the way back to Laterre. "We were going to get married. I didn't even get a chance to say good-bye to him before they took me away. But he'll wait for me, right? They only gave me eighteen months. He'll be true to me, right?"

"He's probably already forgotten you," Chatine murmured to herself, and then, with a clench of her stomach, silently added in her head, *Just like he's forgotten me.*

She had no doubt that whatever Marcellus Bonnefaçon was doing back on Laterre, he wasn't thinking about her.

"What did you say?" Anaïs asked, her eyes twinkling in the low light of Chatine's headlamp.

"Nothing," Chatine said, feeling a flicker of guilt. She softened her voice. "You need to be quiet, or that droid is going to come back. Just keep your head down. Don't look up. There's nothing to look up for."

Thankfully, this time Anaïs listened to her. With another sigh, she grabbed her pick and, struggling to even lift it over her head, brought it smashing recklessly down against the side of the tunnel. Right on top of the anchor bolt.

"No!" Chatine cried, lunging toward her. But it was too late. A terrible cracking sound rang out above them as a plume of dust billowed down from the low ceiling, followed by a cascade of small rocks that rained and smacked onto their helmets.

"Watch out!" Chatine jumped back from the falling debris. Anaïs looked up just long enough for Chatine to peer into her wide, terrified eyes before a giant slab of rock shook loose from the ceiling and collapsed, in another thundering wave of dust, right on top of the girl's head.

For several heart-pounding seconds, Chatine could only stare. Stare at the girl's frail, unmoving body peeking out from beneath the stone. Stare at her frail shoulders and slender arms and scuffed boot . . . which suddenly twitched. Chatine stumbled backward, tripping over her pile of excavated rock and slamming into the wall.

"Sols!" she cried, glancing up the tunnel. The other inmates had stopped working and were gathered around Anaïs's body, staring incredulously at her foot, which now jerked and trembled.

"She's alive!" Chatine called, lunging toward the massive boulder and trying to shove it out of the way. But it was so heavy, and she was so weak, it barely moved. "Someone help! She's alive and she's trapped!"

The sound of whirring metal clanked down the hallway as a droid fought to make its way through the debris. The gigantic metal monster paused in front of the girl, the glow of its orange eyes roving up and down her quivering body.

"Don't just stand there!" Chatine screamed. She'd never raised her voice at a basher before. "Do something! Help her!"

The droid continued its scan, its robotic face emotionless and calculating. Finally, it took a step forward, extending its arm toward the girl. Chatine let out the breath she'd been holding. Anaïs would be okay. She would be taken to the Bastille Med Center. Her wounds would be treated. She would be fine. She would live. She would—

Whoosh.

The girl's twitching limbs fell still. Very still. The droid lowered its arm, which Chatine now saw was glowing, the deadly rayonette still armed. A deep, soul-splitting shiver traveled through her body.

"You . . ." Chatine stared up at the droid, her voice frail and thin and hollow. "What did you do? Why did you do that?"

The droid's orange eyes tracked over her entire face, as though searching for signs of life left in Chatine, too. She honestly wondered if it would find any. The day she was shipped off to this abominable moon was the day she'd stopped living. Stopped caring. Stopped climbing. Stopped conning. Stopped looking up to the skies, hoping for something better.

Stopped being Chatine Renard.

Now she had become someone else. A cursed soul who brought about nothing but chaos and destruction and *death* wherever she went. A shell of a person reduced to nothing more than a number.

"Look down, keep digging, Prisoner 51562," the droid said before turning and disappearing into the darkness of the tunnels.

- CHAPTER 4 -
MARCELLUS

PATRIARCHE LYON PARESSE SNAPPED HIS RIFLE CLOSED
with a resounding crack and snatched it up to his shoulder. He closed
one eye and aimed upward at the bright TéléSky, just as a swarm of
unsuspecting doves fluttered by.

Bang. Bang. Bang. Bang.

The gunshots rang sharp and fierce in Marcellus's ears. But the
sound was soon replaced by a cacophony of barks from the Patriarche's
hunting dogs. The dappled and straggly eared animals yipped and
bounded in circles, anxiously awaiting the prey to fall from the fake
blue sky.

But no birds fell.

Because the Patriarche had missed again.

"Damn the Sols," he roared, yanking the antique hunting gun from
his shoulder and snapping it open again. With chubby, agitated fingers,
he jammed more cartridges into the chamber.

Marcellus felt General Bonnefaçon wince and stiffen beside him. It
was one thing Marcellus had in common with his grandfather: They both
hated meeting with the Patriarche while he was hunting. Marcellus hated

the echoing gunshots, the terrible flutter of the dying birds' wings, the frantic yapping of the bloodthirsty dogs.

And his grandfather simply hated the distraction.

"Monsieur Patriarche," the general called out before the Patriarche could raise his gun again. "As I was saying, you put in an order for a fivefold increase in droid production at the fabrique." He pointed at the TéléCom unfurled and glowing in his hand. "I don't remember us discussing this incr—"

"This is no time for *discussions*," the Patriarche barked. "I'm done with *discussions*, General. This planet is falling apart at the seams and we need a stronger military presence in the cities. The other planets in the System Alliance are starting to get worried. Our ambassador just returned from Kaishi this week and said there was 'talk' of instability on Laterre. *Talk*, General! We simply can't have this. In case you've forgotten, my precious daughter—the only heir to the Laterrian Regime—has been killed. The Matrone is sick with grief. She barely gets out of bed. And now the Vangarde have attacked one of my fabriques!"

His hands shook furiously as he tried to close his gun. Pascal Chaumont, the Patriarche's most-trusted advisor, stepped wordlessly forward to assist him, snapping the weapon closed with an efficient click and handing it back to the Patriarche, before returning to stand with the rest of the green-robed advisors.

"I agree this is the moment for action—" the general began to say, but the Patriarche didn't allow him to finish.

"What is the status of the investigation?" he asked, turning toward Marcellus.

Marcellus stood up straighter, shifting his rifle to his other hand. "I have been interviewing workers and foremen at the TéléSkin fabrique for the past two weeks, but so far no one seems to know who set off the explosif. I have more interviews scheduled for tomorrow, but based on the evidence we've collected, we believe someone broke into the fabrique—"

"I know exactly who set off that explosif!" the Patriarche roared, as though Marcellus's update was a massive waste of his time. "It was that Citizen Rousseau woman! She's responsible for all of this. I just know it."

Marcellus opened his mouth to reply, but the general stepped in. "I assure you, Monsieur Patriarche, Citizen Rousseau is not a danger to us. She remains in maximum security lockdown on Bastille, where she's been for the past seventeen years."

"Until those Vangarde monsters tried to break her out!" the Patriarche reminded him.

"*Tried*," the general emphasized. "And failed."

The Patriarche harrumphed. He had become unbearably paranoid in the past few weeks, convinced that Citizen Rousseau had somehow orchestrated everything that had happened on Laterre—the murder of his only child, the riots in the Frets, the bombing of the TéléSkin fabrique—all from solitary confinement. Which, of course, was ludicrous. Solitary confinement meant no contact with the outside world. But it didn't stop the Patriarche from spending his days watching security footage of Citizen Rousseau's cell.

Even if Marcellus hadn't been the lead officer on the investigation, he would still be willing to bet his life that the Vangarde had not orchestrated that attack. The problem was, he still didn't know who had.

"Regardless," the Patriarche snapped, "this planet needs to be brought to order. And *clearly*, I have to do that myself." He tossed a furious glance at the general before raising the weapon to his shoulder again and peering up at the sky.

Marcellus braved a look at his grandfather and immediately noticed the general's jaw tensing. This had become the new way of things around the Palais. Since the Premier Enfant's funeral, the Patriarche had started taking matters of state into his own hands, making important decisions on a whim and changing protocols whenever it struck his fancy, all without the general knowing about it.

And Marcellus knew this would only make the general more desperate. More eager to push his plans forward.

"He's building a weapon."

Bang. Bang. Bang. Bang.

The gunshots shook Marcellus from his thoughts. They were followed by the maniacal yapping of the hunting dogs who, once again, had no prey to chase for. The Patriarche's bullets had hit nothing but the artificial Ledôme breeze.

"Monsieur Patriarche," the general began calmly, "please be assured that I am *well* in control of the situation on Laterre. New security procedures are being carried out in the Frets and the fabrique district, suspects are being interrogated daily, curfews are being strongly enforced. . . ."

Marcellus startled as a small ping reverberated through his audio patch, notifying him of an incoming alert. As the general continued to list all the new protocols he'd initiated since the Premier Enfant's funeral, Marcellus furtively pulled his TéléCom out of his pocket, unfolded it, and tapped on the screen.

"Tunnel collapse on Bastille in Exploit 5," the TéléCom's smooth, pleasant voice announced. "One fatality."

Marcellus's heart stopped. *Exploit 5.* That was Chatine's exploit.

Normally officers weren't alerted of every single death or accident on Bastille. The prison moon was a dangerous place, and there were simply too many. Instead, the warden received a summary report at the end of each day and only passed it along to the other members of the Ministère if there was something noteworthy to share. But as soon as Marcellus had learned that Chatine had been sent to the moon, he had instantly memorized her prisoner number, cell block tower, and exploit assignment and set up a series of alerts to notify him of any accidents or fatalities on Bastille. And every time that TéléCom dinged softly in his ear, he felt like he couldn't breathe.

He clicked on the alert flashing on the screen and gripped the edges of the TéléCom, as though this flimsy device could possibly hold him up if his legs gave out.

"Today at 11.02 Laterrian time, Bastille Central Command logged a tunnel collapse in Exploit 5 caused by a compromised anchor bolt. One fatality was reported by the supervising droid. Female. Eighteen years old . . ."

No. Marcellus felt the ground beneath him give way.

"Prisoner number 515. . . ."

He was suddenly plummeting into Laterre's red hot core. He was burning alive. His skin was on fire. His lungs burned.

". . . 98."

Marcellus blinked, certain he had misheard. He hastily tapped to replay the alert.

"...Female. Eighteen years old. Prisoner 51598."

5.1.5.9.8.? It wasn't her. He was sure of it. Chatine's prison number was 5.1.5.6.2. His breath returned like a gust of warm air. She was still alive.

"Officer Bonnefaçon?"

Marcellus's head popped up at the sound of his grandfather's voice. The entire hunting party was now staring at him like he was a smoking cruiseur wreck. "Yes? Sorry. I was just . . ." But he gave up trying to make an excuse and pocketed his TéléCom. He could feel the general's eyes on him.

"I was telling the Patriarche," his grandfather said tightly, "that the couchette searches in the Frets are proving effective in rooting out poten-tial rebel activity."

Marcellus nodded. "Yes, very much so. Three arrests have been made this week."

"So, you see, Monsieur Patriarche," the general went on, "I'm confi-dent that these new initiatives are—"

The Patriarche snorted as he angrily uncocked his gun. "I want wages docked too."

The general raised one of his neatly groomed silver eyebrows. "With all due respect, Monsieur Patriarche, I'm not sure docking wages will—"

"If the people cannot behave, they must be punished. Cancelling their Ascension was clearly not enough. Maybe they need to go hungry for a while. See what *that* feels like."

Hungry?

Anger immediately bloomed in Marcellus's chest. The Third Estate were *already* hungry. Already starving and wet and cold, not to mention completely overworked for the meager wages they did receive.

The Patriarche glanced up from his gun, where he was stuffing a fresh round of cartridges into the chamber. "And if you're so 'in control' of the situation, General, then why, may I ask, have you not yet found the Vangarde base and eliminated those terrorist rats once and for all?"

Bang. Bang. Bang. Bang.

This time the Patriarche managed to clip the edge of a dove's wing, causing a lone white feather to puff away on the breeze. But the bird didn't fall. It spiraled and veered awkwardly for a moment, but then righted itself and flew off in a dancing and mocking loop into the dazzling blue TéléSky.

The Patriarche growled furiously and shoved his antique rifle back at Chaumont, snapping for the advisor to hand him a different one.

"We are still actively working on rooting out the Vangarde's base," the general replied vaguely.

Marcellus braved another sidelong glance at him. He'd been unable to look his grandfather in the eye since they'd left the Palais. Neither of them had uttered a word about the microcam that had vanished from beneath the loose floor tile in Marcellus's bathroom. Marcellus assumed the general hadn't had a chance to watch the footage yet. But it would only be a matter of time. And then, his grandfather would know.

That Marcellus had learned the truth about the copper exploit bombing.

That Marcellus had been in contact with a convicted Vangarde spy.

That Marcellus knew his father—the man he'd been taught to despise, to distrust, to banish from his thoughts—was innocent.

Which meant that the time Marcellus had to find this weapon his grandfather was building just got a whole lot shorter.

"What about those operatives you arrested?" Marcellus barely recognized his own voice as the words charged out of him. He cleared his throat and continued. "The ones who tried to break into the warden's office and infiltrate Bastille's security system? Surely, they should be able to tell us where the base is."

The general shot Marcellus a scathing look as the Patriarche pounced on his suggestion. "Exactly! Why haven't you extracted information from them, General?"

"They are still our best leads, yes," the general said tensely as he ripped his gaze from Marcellus. "But unfortunately, despite vigorous interrogation, they are proving difficult to crack."

Marcellus's stomach rolled.

Vigorous interrogation.

He didn't have to be a trained officer of the Ministère to infer what that meant.

"Obviously not vigorous *enough*," the Patriarche blustered.

"I assure you," the general replied, the slightest hint of annoyance cracking through his façade, "they will break eventually."

"Perhaps I might have a try," Marcellus offered, attempting to sound nonchalant. If he could be allowed to interrogate the operatives, if his grandfather told him where they were being kept, Marcellus could find out what Denise knew about the weapon. "If I'm going to be commandeur one day, I need to be well versed in these . . . interrogation tactics."

The general scrutinized his grandson, his eyes narrowing ever so slightly. "I appreciate your newfound initiative, but that won't be necessary. As these operatives are our most important leads on the Vangarde, *I* am handling the situation personally."

Disappointment stabbed Marcellus. He had been right. This was an impossible task. If his grandfather was keeping a secret, there was no way Marcellus was going to be able to uncover it. He'd need a miracle.

"In the meantime," the general continued as the Patriarche once again took aim at the TéléSky, "we are analyzing the devices found on the Vangarde operatives when they were captured."

Lyon Paresse lowered his gun. "What devices?"

"Necklaces, sir. Made of what appeared to be some sort of metal beads. But we believe they are more than just decorative. Possibly communication devices of some kind. Directeur Chevalier's team at the Ministère's

Cyborg and Technology Labs is working on them now. We hope that they might provide a legitimate lead to the base."

Metal beads.

With a shiver, Marcellus's thoughts raced back to that night two weeks ago, in the hallways of Fret 7, when a similar necklace hanging from Alouette's neck had triggered a mysterious message to appear on his TéléCom. A message he still didn't know the contents of, but that he was *certain* had been sent by Denise.

"Very good," the Patriarche said. "But if those operatives won't talk, we do have other means of dealing with them." He aimed his gun at a flock of birds that had just fluttered up from the ground.

Bang, bang, bang, bang, bang.

"Blast." He lowered his weapon and glared at the general. "What is the progress on the exécuteur, General?"

"My techniciens in the munitions fabrique are working on the reconstruction. I have been told it will be completed in the next week."

Marcellus shuddered at the thought of seeing that monstrous contraption again. The Third Estate were already calling it by a much more appropriate name—the Blade. After witnessing the sick swiftness with which it had sliced Nadette Epernay's head from her body, Marcellus had been glad to hear that the rioters in the Marsh had ripped it to pieces.

"But they've already been working on it for *two* weeks!" the Patriarche boomed. "Why is it taking so long?"

"We've had to rebuild the device from scratch. The last one was completely destroyed in the recent riot. We were not able to salvage any parts."

The Patriarche huffed and then, under his breath, muttered, "I'm sure the scientists on Albion wouldn't need this long."

Marcellus could almost feel his grandfather's muscles tense. It was a well-known fact that Albion had the most superior tech-development program in the system. Far more advanced than any other planet. But no one on Laterre—Albion's long-standing enemy—liked to admit that, especially not the general.

"I want that thing finished as soon as possible," the Patriarche went on. "And I want the entire Third Estate to know when it is. Those ungrateful wretches need to understand that there are consequences for rising up against *me*."

"Yes, Monsieur Patriarche," the general said with a swift nod. Then he cut his eyes to Marcellus, and in a cool monotone voice that sent chills down Marcellus's spine, he added, "Treason against the Regime should *never* be taken lightly. I think you would agree, Officer Bonnefaçon."

Marcellus's throat went dry.

Treason against the Regime.

Was that what his grandfather would accuse Marcellus of once he watched that microcam footage? Would Marcellus be the first to find himself in the path of the newly built Blade?

Marcellus tried to picture his grandfather's expression when he would eventually connect the tiny device to his TéléCom. When he would press play. When he would discover that the Vangarde had been watching him that day he'd agreed to bomb the copper exploit and pin the blame on his own son.

Watching.

Marcellus felt a shiver travel through him as he remembered the day *he'd* first found the microcam and viewed its contents. He'd been shocked to learn that the footage had been captured right inside General Bonnefaçon's study. Where all of his most private and *secret* conversations took place.

Marcellus's heart started to pound as he suddenly realized what he had to do.

The idea made him feel physically sick, but it was the only way. His only chance of finding out what his grandfather was working on.

It was the very miracle he needed.

If Mabelle had managed to plant a microcam inside his grandfather's office, then Marcellus could do it too.

"Now, enough business," the Patriarche commanded. "General, put that TéléCom away. It's time for you to shoot."

The general tossed another glance at Marcellus before folding up his TéléCom and slipping it into the pocket of his pristine white jacket. He stepped forward, took a gun from one of the Patriarche's advisors, and with ease and an austere calm, loaded the chamber.

Marcellus felt another chill run down his spine as he watched his grandfather carefully pull the weapon to his shoulder and squint up, with unrelenting focus and determination, at the TéléSky above. Even the dogs seemed to quiet as the general watched and waited.

Finally, a flock of doves whisked into view and looped above the heads of the hunting party.

Bang.

Marcellus winced as a mess of feathers scattered into the wind, followed by the awful flutter and flap of dying wings. A great arc of bird blood sprayed like a rainbow of red through the sky. The dogs took off after the fallen prey, yapping excitedly.

"Sols!" came a thundering roar from the other side of the general. When Marcellus glanced over at Laterre's leader, his stomach clenched at the sight of the bright red streak of blood that had splattered across the Patriarche's cheek and forehead and was now dripping down into the folds of his wide, plump neck.

Silently, Chaumont handed the Patriarche a handkerchief, which Lyon Paresse snatched violently from his advisor's hand.

"Nice shot, General," the Patriarche muttered as he wiped the blood from his face and neck. "Nice shot."

The general lowered the gun with a contented expression and immediately reached for his TéléCom again. "Apologies, Monsieur Patriarche, but I've just received an urgent AirLink from Directeur Chevalier."

The Patriarche waved one permissive hand toward the general as he used the other to continue mopping bird blood from his neck.

Marcellus noticed the general's expression shift drastically as he watched the AirLink message play out on his screen. He almost looked, dare Marcellus think it, *elated*.

"I'm sorry," the general said, handing his gun to the nearest advisor.

"But I must cut this visit short. Officer Bonnefaçon and I are needed at the Ministère headquarters."

"What is it?" the Patriarche asked gruffly.

The general shot Marcellus a cryptic look before turning back to the Patriarche. "It appears Inspecteur Limier has been found."

CHAPTER 5

MARCELLUS

THE HALLWAYS OF THE MINISTÈRE HEADQUARTERS were buzzing with activity. Officers and cyborgs crisscrossed the pristine, chrome-tiled hallways, their heads bent over the broadcasts playing out on their TéléComs. Marcellus followed behind his grandfather and watched as people saluted and then scattered at the sight of the almighty general, the Regime's most dedicated and loyal servant.

If only they knew, Marcellus thought bitterly.

The door to the Ministère's Cyborg and Technology labs whooshed open, and Marcellus and the general stepped through into another hallway, this one brilliant white and immaculately sterile. Marcellus squinted under the bright, harsh lights as their boots clicked rhythmically and purposefully across the polished floors.

Marcellus knew exactly where they were heading. He'd walked this route many times in his years of training as an officer and now a commandeur. Past the labs where new state-of-the-art tech was developed, the hallway that housed the cyborg initiation and training facilities, and the myriad of server rooms where Laterre's intricate communication networks and power grids were controlled. The difference was, today,

Marcellus's mind was filled with thoughts of deception and treason.

Somehow, he had to plant a surveillance device in his grandfather's study. He knew he'd never be able to gain access to the office alone. No one was allowed in there without the general. Even the maids had to clean the room while he was present. Which meant that Marcellus would have to do it right under his grandfather's nose.

And then there was the problem of acquiring the device itself. These hallways were packed full of every kind of surveillance equipment imaginable. But all Ministère-issued devices were trackable. He couldn't risk it being found.

He had to find another way.

"Access granted."

The biometric lock on the infirmerie door disengaged and the general didn't hesitate. He pushed the door open and blustered inside. Marcellus followed after him, decidedly less enthusiastic. The thought of seeing the cyborg inspecteur again was making him break out in a cold sweat. He had never liked Inspecteur Limier. The man was suspicious of everything and dogged to a fault. In short, the very last person you wanted to have around when you had a secret to hide. And right now, Marcellus didn't need another pair of eyes watching him.

But as he stepped inside the infirmerie a moment later, he felt his tensed muscles instantly relax. This was not the Inspecteur Limier of Marcellus's memories. The once fearsome cyborg now looked helpless and vulnerable. He lay unmoving and silent on a gurney under a crisp green sheet, while a collection of monitors blinked and hummed around him. A bandage had been wrapped in a complicated crisscrossing pattern over the top of his head, and a breathing tube snaked between his colorless lips like a grim, glowing serpent.

"What's his status?" the general asked.

"It's hard to tell at this point," replied a voice, and Marcellus turned to find Gustave Chevalier—Directeur of the Ministère's Cyborg and Technology Labs—standing behind them. The directeur's cropped hair and narrow moustache were, per usual, as spotless and gleaming as his white coat. "His vitals seem stable for now, but we won't know anything for certain until we run some tests."

"Where was he found?" asked the general.

At this question, an officer in a white uniform stepped forward. Marcellus recognized him as Officer Meudon. "A ferme superviseur found him unconscious in the wheat-fleur fields this afternoon and called it in. We believe he must have collapsed there. He was still breathing, but unresponsive."

Marcellus braved another glance at Vallonay's most-prized and celebrated inspecteur. Limier's taut skin appeared to be made of wax. His once-flickering circuitry, which was threaded across his forehead and cheek, was lifeless and gray, like a forlorn and abandoned spiderweb. Marcellus was grateful the cyborg's eyes were closed, so he couldn't see his enhanced left eye. The same eye that used to unnerve Marcellus every time it glowed bright orange and roved over him, assessing and inspecting and searching for signs of weakness. Signs of treachery and deceit.

"Who did this to him?" The question emerged like a growl from the back of the general's throat.

"We don't know," Officer Meudon replied.

"Access his memory chip," General Bonnefaçon ordered. "Whatever he saw last will have been captured by his cybernetic eye."

Directeur Chevalier winced slightly. "Unfortunately, his entire cybernetic system has been compromised. We believe he was shot in the face by a rayonette pulse, and it scorched his circuitry. It's likely that his memory chip was severely damaged in the attack. But I will see what I can find."

The general nodded, and Directeur Chevalier walked over to a small control panel near the inspecteur's bed. He tapped on the interface and the light from the screen illuminated his smooth, unblemished features, most likely the result of youth injections. Marcellus often thought it peculiar that the man who was personally in charge of recruiting and vetting candidates for the Cyborg Initiation Program was not a cyborg himself.

"Accessing the files now," he announced. "It will take a few minutes to process them."

The general sighed and lowered himself into a chair in the corner, all the while never taking his steady gaze off Limier. For a brief moment, Marcellus caught a glimpse of something on his grandfather's face that he had only ever seen once before in his life. It was when the general had lost his previous commandeur, Michele Vernay. Vernay had been captured and killed while trying to assassinate Queen Matilda, the "Mad Queen" of Albion, during the Usonian War of Independence. Marcellus had been there when the general had received the alert. He'd seen the pain flash in his grandfather's eyes. And then he'd seen that pain turn to anger.

All of that had transpired in less than a minute. A fleeting moment of vulnerability. Once it was over, his grandfather had returned to his stoic, impervious self again.

But now Marcellus could see the same torment flash in his grandfather's eyes as he watched Limier's chest precariously rise and fall in an uneven rhythm. The general cared about this man. Marcellus knew that. And in that moment—and that moment *only*—Marcellus felt the tiniest drop of sympathy for his grandfather. He was a man who had known loss. And Limier had been his grandfather's most loyal inspecteur for years. He entrusted the cyborg with things he didn't share with anyone else. Even his own grandson.

The thought pulled Marcellus up short, and his gaze darted back to Limier and Directeur Chevalier, who was still trying to connect to the inspecteur's memory chip.

If memory files could be accessed from the moments before Limier was attacked, could *other* files be accessed as well? Memories from further back?

Marcellus's fingers twitched as an idea began to form in his mind. The inspecteur was the general's most prized interrogator. No one could pull the truth out of a criminal like Limier. Which meant he *had* to know the location of his grandfather's secret facility. The very facility where Marcellus was certain the Vangarde operatives Jacqui and Denise were being held. His gaze zeroed in on Directeur Chevalier's control panel, where files were slowly appearing on the screen. If he could search those files and find out where the operatives were being held, Denise could tell him what she knows about the general's weapon and perhaps direct him to the source she's been—

"Papa! There you are!" A shrill voice punctured Marcellus's thoughts, and he turned to see a tall, slender girl sweep through the door and hurry toward Directeur Chevalier. She wore a bright purple velvet dress, cinched at the waist with an oversized belt, and her shiny obsidian-black hair was fashioned atop her head in a ridiculous construction that Marcellus thought resembled a willow tree in the Palais gardens.

"I've sent you nearly a thousand AirLinks," the girl went on, her chipper voice a startling contrast to the somber tension in the room. "Are you ignoring me again, silly Papa? Oh, hi, General. Hi, Marcellus. Didn't see you there. Marcellus, you're looking . . . *dapper* as always."

"Hi, Cerise," Marcellus said as politely as he could muster. It wasn't that he disliked the daughter of Gustave Chevalier. He honestly didn't think about her much. She was like every other Second Estate teenage girl who lived in Ledôme. Sparkle-headed and spoiled and obsessed with mundane things like clothes and hair fashions. And now, after everything that had happened in the past few weeks, he had even less patience than ever for girls like Cerise Chevalier.

"I'm very busy here," Chevalier snapped at his daughter. "I will respond to your AirLinks as soon as I'm done."

"I know, I know," Cerise said with a wave of her hand. "You're always busy. But if you had watched *any* of my messages, you would know that this is very important. I really *really* need your TéléCom to track a shipment of dresses arriving from Samsara today. There's only one in my size in the entire shipment. And I *have* to have it for Petale's birthday fête this weekend. If I don't get to the shops the moment the dresses are put on the rack, I won't get one."

Marcellus fought back a roll of his eyes. Could this girl not see that they were dealing with a very morbid situation right now? Inspecteur Limier was lying unconscious on a gurney only centimètres away, and she was babbling about dresses?

The directeur looked mortified by the interruption. He muttered an apology to the general before quickly ushering his daughter back toward the door. "Cerise," he hissed under his breath, as they disappeared into the hallway. Marcellus could only hear bits and pieces of their conversation.

". . . this is not a good time . . ."

". . . but Papa . . ."

". . . tired of this behavior. It won't change my mind about anything. . . ."

". . . I'm totally serious about the dress. . . ."

". . . fine. Take the TéléCom. We will discuss this later. . . ."

When Chevalier reappeared, he looked flustered and agitated. "Apologies again, General and officers." He smoothed down his short hair, walked back to the console, and frowned at the screen. "It appears we do have some viable footage from the hour before Limier was attacked, but it looks to be corrupted."

The general rose from his chair and walked over to the wall monitor. "Play it."

"Yes, sir," the directeur said as he tapped on the screen.

The monitor glowed to life, and for the longest time, Marcellus could not make sense of what he was looking at. He moved closer and stood next to his grandfather, squinting at the screen.

At first, there was nothing but shadowy blurs of green and an intermittent flashing light, accompanied by faint scraping and crackling noises. If all the files on the memory chip looked like this, finding the general's facility was not going to be easy. A few seconds later, the distorted footage cleared somewhat, and Marcellus could make out what looked to be a thicket of trees.

"The Forest Verdure," Officer Meudon declared, stepping up beside Marcellus. "That's where he went to make the arrests."

"Who was he arresting?" the general asked.

"Two criminals by the name of Renard. They both had about a hundred outstanding warrants logged in the Communiqué."

Marcellus's gaze snapped toward Officer Meudon. He had to be talking about Chatine's parents. "Were they sent to Bastille?"

The officer shook his head. "They escaped shortly after the droids led them out of the forest."

Wisps of movement drew Marcellus's attention back to the screen where he could just make out a collection of small stones on the forest floor. They appeared to be arranged in some type of pattern. It took Marcellus a moment to connect the image to his memory and then, in a flash of certainty, he knew exactly where this footage had been captured. It was the old Défecteur camp that he sometimes liked to escape to when he needed to be alone. A place once inhabited by people who had tried to live outside the rules of the Regime. Until his grandfather rounded them all up in a spate of brutal raids. Now, all that was left of the Défecteurs were abandoned camps like this one.

The footage began to bounce violently again, as though Inspecteur Limier was running. Jumping, maybe? Shaky blurs of movement kept whisking through the frame, and the soundtrack continued to squeak, making Marcellus feel dizzy and disoriented.

Then the image juddered and cut out, and the screen went black.

"Is that it?" the general said in a gruff, dissatisfied whisper.

But just as Directeur Chevalier was about to utter a clearly confused reply, the monitor flickered, and a new image blurred in and out of focus. Marcellus tilted his head, trying to make out the strange black object that filled the entire screen.

"What is that?" he asked.

Officer Meudon squinted. "It looks like a . . ."

"A boot," the general replied flatly.

Suddenly, the shaky image made sense. It was a heavy, black, Ministère-issued boot. Limier's, presumably. And it was pushing down on something. The footage cut out again and returned a second later. And Marcellus could now see the boot was standing on a hand. A hand desperately clutching hold of a rayonette.

The three men leaned in closer. There was a violent crash of movement and Marcellus nearly leapt back. The image blurred and shuddered, flickering rapidly in and out. The squeaks and crackles seemed to reach a fever-pitch. Suddenly, the rayonette was clutched in Limier's own hand and pointed down at the ground. At someone crouching below him. A girl?

And then, in a confusion of light and motion and trees, Marcellus saw them.

Deep dark eyes, like two vast pools of night sky.

Alouette?

Marcellus bit down on his lip to keep the shock from barreling out of him.

For a long time, the image was frozen on her terrified face. Marcellus glanced uneasily over at his grandfather, who was gritting his teeth, as though he wished he could reach through the screen and grab her. Marcellus's heart hammered in his chest as he thought about Mabelle's words to him earlier this morning.

"Little Lark is no longer with the Vangarde. . . . She left."

Marcellus tore his gaze away from the monitor and glanced uneasily at the unconscious inspecteur lying only a mètre away, the bandages on his head concealing a wealth of untold secrets.

"When was this footage captured?" The question fired out of Marcellus like an explosif.

The directeur tapped on his console and reported back. "Month 7, Day 15, 28.12."

Marcellus's mind whirled as he thought back to the last time he'd seen Alouette. In the hallway of Fret 7 in the very early morning of Month 7, Day 16. This footage was captured *before* that. Which meant . . .

But he never finished the thought, because suddenly, Alouette was on her feet. She was descending upon the inspecteur with a speed that astonished Marcellus. Fists punching and arms swinging and elbows arcing. He had never seen anything like it. Her movements were fast yet fluid. Powerful yet graceful. All the while her eyes flashed and sparked with fury and determination.

"What on Laterre?" Officer Meudon spat. "Who is that?"

The general said nothing in response, just continued to glare at the screen.

The footage shook again as Limier was thrust backward. Then everyone in the room drew in a collective breath as Alouette filled the entire frame once more, and her huge black eyes stared straight back at them.

But no one was looking at her eyes. Because clutched in her slim fingers . . . was the rayonette.

And it was pointed straight at Limier.

CRASH!

Marcellus spun around to see a smashed monitor lying on the floor and the serpentlike breathing tube dangling from the handrail of the gurney. The cyborg inspecteur was no longer unconscious. He was now thrashing violently. His whole body bucking. His hands scratching at his face as though he could claw the memory right out of his mind.

"I need a médecin in here now!" the directeur shouted.

Seconds later, two cyborgs in green scrubs strode briskly into the room, their faces the epitome of serene despite the chaos around them. The inspecteur continued to spasm as the cyborgs attempted to examine him. Foam pooled at the corners of his mouth and his circuitry, which was inert and dull only moments ago, now sparked frenetically like broken stars.

"Subdural hematoma," one of the médecins said in an even monotone. "We need to get him into surgery immediately and remove the blood clot from his brain."

The directeur nodded once and the cyborgs were instantly on the move, guiding the gurney toward the door of the infirmerie. Marcellus jumped back, out of the way, and watched helplessly as Inspecteur Limier disappeared down the hallway, taking all his secrets with him.

Stunned, Marcellus turned his gaze back to the monitor on the wall, which he now saw was frozen on the image of Alouette's determined glare and the glint of the rayonette in her hands. He didn't have to watch the rest of the footage to know what came next. The proof had just vanished out the door.

Marcellus stole another glance at his grandfather. The general was also staring at the frozen footage. But this time, Marcellus swore he saw something else reflected in those cryptic hazel eyes. Something that went beyond hatred and rage. It almost looked like fear.

With a snarl, the general turned away from the monitor and stalked toward the door, pausing just long enough to point at Officer Meudon and then at the screen. "I want that girl found."

- CHAPTER 6 -
CHATINE

"LEAVE THEM ALONE! THEY'RE INNOCENT!"

Chatine's legs burned and her heart raced as she ran through the Frets, chasing after the vanishing forms of the droids. They were faster. Nimbler. They were gigantic. As tall as the Frets themselves. And she was running through mud.

Then she was swimming. The Frets had flooded, sucking all the dirt and waste and muck into a giant sea of filth. But Chatine kept sinking, something gripping at her feet.

Finally, she managed to pull herself to dry land. Her body heaving. A lifetime of grime and poverty spewing from her lungs. She coughed up impossible things: an entire loaf of chou bread; a plastique doll arm; a gold medallion she'd once stolen from a Second Estate foreman, chain and all; a disconnected Skin. And then one of her own lungs, blackened and corroded from a lifetime of breathing in grime.

She wiped at her mouth and stood up to find she was in the Marsh. It was crammed full of people. A platform had been erected. On it stood a humming, glowing, monstrous contraption that Chatine recognized at once. The Blade.

That horrible machine that had been used to execute the Premier Enfant's governess.

Except this time, it wasn't a lovely, auburn-haired woman that the droids were leading to the block. It was Chatine's sister, Azelle. And cradled in her arms was their little baby brother, Henri. His precious plump cheeks, tiny chin, and clear gray eyes were exactly as Chatine had last seen them.

The droids tried to grab Henri from Azelle. She screamed and attempted to fight them off, but her efforts were futile. The blanket slipped from around Henri's tiny body, revealing the small, raindrop-shaped birthmark on the back of his right shoulder. The very birthmark Chatine used to kiss when he cried.

"Leave them alone! They're innocent!" Chatine screamed again, but no one heard.

The droids wrenched baby Henri free and began to lead Azelle toward the Blade. She thrashed and kicked and cried as they forced her face down onto the platform, binding her wrists and ankles with metal clamps.

Henri wailed in the fists of a droid. Chatine fought to get to him, but the crowd was too thick. Her legs were useless. Paralyzed.

And his cries continued to pierce the sky.

The Blade turned on, drowning out all the noise with its high-pitched, screeching buzz. The droids held Azelle's head down on the block. The thin beam of blue light, which stretched between the two columns of the contraption, began to descend. Crawling its way toward her slender, exposed neck.

"Stop it!" Chatine shouted. "Someone has to stop it! Someone please save her!"

But no one stopped it. And no one saved her.

A silent, choked sob escaped Chatine as the Blade continued to descend, crackling through the air. She heard a faint sizzle, the sound of fire on flesh. Then she smelled it. Burning. Decaying. Putrefying.

Azelle's mouth opened, letting out a scream to end all screams.

Chatine jolted awake, gasping. She blinked and stared through the gloom at the sagging bunk above her, the dream coming back to her in grim fragments. Of course, it was about Henri and Azelle. All her dreams these days were about her lost siblings.

Ever since Chatine had learned that Henri hadn't died as a baby—as she'd believed for the past twelve years—and that her parents had, instead, sold him off like a sac of turnips to pay a debt, Chatine had been plagued by nightmares of him.

In the glow of the small orange lights that shone down all night around the perimeter of the cell block, she could see the other bunks, stacked four beds high and crammed in a circle around the eleventh floor of the Trésor tower. She was still here. Still locked away on Bastille. Stuck in this stinking overcrowded cell.

Chatine turned onto her side, trying to get comfortable on the thin, drooping mattress, but it was near impossible. Chatine had quickly learned that everything about this prison—from the serving sizes of the food, to the conditions of the bunks, to the lengths of shifts in the exploits—was designed to keep the inmates just alive *enough*. Strong, healthy prisoners meant riots and escape attempts. But dead prisoners meant less zyttrium sent to Laterre. It was a delicate balance.

The nearest orange light shone straight into her face, searing her vision even when her lids were closed. She'd heard some of the inmates call them "the eyes" because, while they glowed, they also watched. Blinding and brutal, they were always observing, always scanning—an extension of the droids that patrolled Bastille.

Chatine shuddered and pulled the threadbare blanket over her head, shutting her eyes tight. But the dream immediately started to suck her back in, like a cruel and grasping joke. The faces of Azelle and Henri cycled in her mind, blurring into one distorted mess of eyes and mouths and wispy hair. Finally, she gave up and flipped onto her back, her eyes wide open.

"Can't sleep?" a voice asked, and Chatine breathed out a sigh of relief. She never quite knew when Dead Azelle would speak to her, but she was always grateful when she did.

"That's the third dream you've had about me this week. I would say I'm flattered, but I'm not exactly sure I like how I'm being portrayed. Why am I always so helpless?"

Chatine stared up at the bunk above her and listened to her own breathing. It was coarse and ragged. She hadn't been able to take a deep breath since the droids had hauled Anaïs's body to the morgue yesterday.

Chatine had warned herself not to look when the hulking creature pushed aside the rubble from the girl's fragile, young face. She'd done everything in her power to turn away. But, in the end, she knew she owed it to the girl to look. To remember her crushed skull and blood-stained scalp. To capture it in her mind, no matter how much she knew it would haunt her.

Because if Chatine didn't remember, who would?

"It wasn't your fault," Azelle said, her voice taking on a careful tone, like she was skirting around the edge of a cliff. "There was nothing you could do. About either of us."

Of course, Chatine knew that.

Didn't she?

Azelle sighed. "Do you ever wonder what happened to Maman and Papa?"

Chatine flipped onto her stomach. She did wonder that. Almost daily. Even though her parents had been arrested only a few hours before Chatine, they'd mysteriously never showed up on Bastille, once again somehow managing to dodge their fate.

"Do you think they escaped?" Azelle asked. "Or maybe they're dead?"

For the sake of the entire System Divine, Chatine hoped it was the latter. She closed her eyes and tried to fall back asleep, but it was quickly becoming obvious that it wasn't going to happen.

"I think it might be one of *those* nights," Azelle said, and Chatine knew she was right.

Careful to keep her hands out of view of the "eyes," Chatine reached into the small tear in her mattress and felt around for the tiny object she kept hidden inside. Every night, she was terrified she'd come back to her bunk to find it stolen. But she knew better than to keep it on her, where the droids could find it. She nudged around with her fingertip until her skin touched metal.

Then she closed her eyes, for just a moment, and pictured the silver ring. *His* ring. She hadn't actually seen it since she'd arrived on Bastille and stashed it in the first hiding place she could find. But every night, as she lay here on this bunk, she could feel it. With every turn of her body, she could sense it pulsing. As though it were its own moon with its own gravitational pull.

The feel of the cool metal against her skin brought back a wave of memories. The kind of memories she only allowed herself to indulge in on the worst of nights here.

Marcellus.

Sitting across from her in a cruiseur, his hazel eyes twinkling, his lips quirked into a small smile.

Marcellus.

Kissing her on the rooftop of the garment fabrique. Deeply. Intensely. Endlessly.

And then finally, *Marcellus.*

Turning away from her. Calling her a traitor and a déchet. Walking out of her life forever.

Chatine's heart wrenched. Would he ever forgive her for betraying him? For spying on him for the general? For stealing his mother's ring? Somehow, she doubted it.

Yet, somehow, it still mattered to her that he did.

Eventually. Maybe. Someday.

"All prisoners rise." A robotic voice blared through Chatine's audio chip like a monster in her head. Chatine yanked her hand out from the tear in the mattress as the dingy overhead lights illuminated. All around her, she heard the groans of people waking up and stumbling out of their beds.

Chatine kicked off the scratchy sheet, climbed down from her bunk, pulled on her boots, and followed the slow procession of prisoners making their way toward the stairs. The languid, mechanical movements of her fellow inmates made them look almost dead. And on some level, Chatine supposed they were. Being alive was only half the battle on

Bastille. You had to have something to live *for*. And most of the prisoners here did not.

The Trésor tower cell block was a shadowy, circular chamber made up of twelve floors, each linked to a winding central staircase by a series of metal gangways.

Stepping onto the nearest bridge, Chatine glanced precariously over the railing. Normally, heights didn't bother her. She was used to being up high, looking down at the world. But this dizzying, eleven-floor drop always made her stomach roll. She swept her gaze down to the ground floor, trying to imagine the place that was rumored to be buried beneath it. A place shrouded in even more darkness than the exploits.

The inmates called it the Black Hole, where the most dangerous prisoners of Bastille were kept. Chatine had heard that the walls down there were made of thick, solid PermaSteel and that there was one cell in particular that was guarded thirty hours a day by droids. This was where the most famous criminal on Laterre was kept.

Citizen Rousseau.

The woman who had led the only known rebellion against the Regime . . . and failed.

Of course, no one on Bastille had ever seen her in person. Being confined to the Black Hole meant no contact with the outside world. No contact at all. Chatine had been told that even the droids didn't set foot inside that cell.

It was thirty hours a day of absolute nothingness.

Shivering, Chatine pulled her gaze back up to the line of ripped uniforms and grime-covered bodies descending the steps in front of her. As she wound around the staircase, she caught sight of one inmate who stood far shorter than the rest. A boy. Only thirteen years old. Chatine recognized him at once. Despite his grimy blue uniform and shaved head, there was no mistaking his scrawny shoulders, the determined dimple in his cheek, and the slight limp that still lingered from his last encounter with the Policier.

Chatine let out a breath. *He's still alive.*

The sight of him each morning always gave her a reason to keep walking. Keep digging. Keep living. He was a small ray of Sol-light in this dark, dark place. The *only* Sol-light.

The prisoners shuffled lethargically down the twisting staircase until they reached the ground floor. Chatine checked for nearby droids before pushing her way through the line and positioning herself right behind the boy whose life she'd single-handedly destroyed.

"Roche," she whispered.

His body visibly stiffened at the sound of her voice, but he said nothing.

"Please," she said softly. "Talk to me."

He didn't respond, and Chatine felt a punch of disappointment. Although, she honestly wasn't sure why she thought today would be different from any other day. Roche hadn't spoken to her since he'd been arrested. And she couldn't exactly blame him for the silence. *She* was the reason he'd been sent to Bastille in the first place.

She sighed. "Fine. You don't have to talk. But just listen to what I have to say. I'm sorry about what happened at the Policier Precinct. I—"

Just then, a massive body maneuvered in front of her. She could tell by the long hair and half-chewed ear that it was Clovis, an older member of Roche's exploit crew who had taken on the unofficial role of his bodyguard.

"Roche kindly requests that you stop trying to make contact with him," Clovis snapped over his shoulder, his voice low and gruff.

Chatine gritted her teeth and attempted to maneuver herself around him.

"Roche," she hissed. "Please. I need to explain—"

"Get in line, Prisoner 51562," boomed a nearby droid.

Chatine did as she was told, veering back into place behind Clovis. She stared intently at his dark shoulder-length hair before her gaze shifted to his left shirtsleeve, which had been rolled with precision.

A Vétéran.

That's what Chatine secretly called his kind because of how long they'd clearly been on Bastille. She could always tell how much time someone had served based on the length of their hair. Every prisoner's head was shaved before they left Laterre. And no sharp objects on Bastille meant no haircuts. After two weeks, Chatine's own head was already covered with a soft fuzz of growth, and every time she touched it, she flinched at the strange bumpiness of her scalp.

The Vétérans were mostly older prisoners. Many of them too old to even work in the exploits. Instead, they held jobs all over the prison—kitchen staff, janitors, morgue workers. Every one of them had long hair and every one of them wore their left shirtsleeve rolled up, like a badge of honor for how long they'd lasted.

But what intrigued Chatine the most about Vétérans like Clovis was that they never spoke to one another. Never looked at one another. Never sat together in the cantine. Never even seemed to acknowledge one another.

The line of inmates progressed sluggishly forward, nearing the cantine. Chatine knew it would be only a matter of minutes before she and Roche were separated.

"Roche," she whispered, stepping around Clovis again. "You have to believe me. I never meant to betray you. I was just trying to—"

Clovis sidestepped, blocking her with his back once again. "Roche kindly requests that you follow protocol and refrain from speaking to your fellow inmates."

"Why don't you let him tell me that," Chatine snapped. She was getting very tired of always being thwarted by this clochard every time she tried to get close to Roche.

Clovis's heavy footsteps slowed, and for a moment, his large frame looked to be coiling up, preparing to spin around and spring toward Chatine. But he didn't. He kept walking, his neck muscles visibly straining under the collar of his prison shirt. And when he did speak again, his tone reverberated with pure malice. "Roche kindly reminds you that he doesn't speak to *mouchards.*"

Chatine felt the stab in her gut at the word. It was exactly what Roche had called her when he'd found out she'd betrayed him, the day he'd been arrested and his fate on Bastille was cast in PermaSteel.

Now, every day, as she watched Roche board the rickety lift and descend into the depths of the zyttrium exploits, the guilt consumed her a little more, until she felt like nothing more than a skeleton. A corpse eaten away by the rot. He was just a scrawny kid. A thirteen-year-old Oublie, forgotten and abandoned and parentless. He'd just been trying to make his way in the harsh world of the Frets. And Chatine had ruined his life.

Chatine nodded, swallowing the sourness that was rising up in her throat. "Fine," she said stiffly. "But you can tell Roche that I'm not giving up. He can ignore me, he can turn his stupid one-eared guard dogs on me, I don't care. I'm not going to stop trying to talk to him until he forgives me. I won't—"

She felt the shock of the tazeur against her skin before she even saw the droid. Her body convulsed for a second, lightning bolts of pain shooting through her bones and veins. Her vision blurred, her muscles cramped, and something began to clang relentlessly in her ears.

Her legs wobbled beneath her. Suddenly, all she wanted to do was lie down and never move again. But then she felt a shove at her back as the line moved forward and inmates pushed to get into the cantine and consume their meager rations of food. She stumbled, struggling to put one useless foot in front of the other, as a voice broke through the ringing in her ears. It was Clovis. And he was laughing. A sharp, derisive sound. "Forgive you?" he spat. "Don't hold your breath, Renard."

- CHAPTER 7 -
MARCELLUS

MARCELLUS HAD NEVER LIKED THE FRETS. THE SIGHTS and sounds and smells were too sharp. Too immediate. Too disturbing. But today, as he darted through the alleyways, it seemed like everything here had been amplified overnight. The garbage and debris seemed to be piled up even higher than usual. The rusted edges of the walls and broken pipes seemed to jut out at sharper, more severe angles. The massive crumbling freightships seemed even more unstable, threatening to collapse and kill everyone at any moment.

And then there were the droids.

The Ministère's ground troops. Three-mètre-high PermaSteel monsters that stalked the alleyways, scanning, observing, punishing. Thanks to the Patriarche's increased production, there were now more on patrol today than Marcellus had ever seen.

The rickety stairwell was empty. Everyone was out in the Marsh, protesting the wage cuts the Patriarche had ordered yesterday. By the time Marcellus reached the tenth floor he was slightly winded and stopped to pause at the end of a long hallway dotted with small porthole windows.

From way up here, the city below looked peaceful. The dense layer of clouds seemed to swaddle the tops of the buildings like a soft, downy blanket. The bustle from the crowded marketplace could no longer be heard. And the rain—the constant, ever-present rain that pinged gently on the corroded walls and dingy streets—almost sounded like a soothing lullaby. And Marcellus could almost bring himself to believe that everyone down there was safe.

But of course, he knew the truth.

No one down there was safe.

Laterre was on the brink of war. The Third Estate were protesting daily in the streets. The Patriarche's grief had turned him from an apathetic leader to a brutal, irrational one. And General Bonnefaçon was developing a weapon that threatened the lives of everyone on this planet.

Unless Marcellus could figure out a way to stop him.

He turned and pounded on the PermaSteel door at the end of the hall, gripping his rayonette tightly in his hand.

"Ministère! Open up!"

The heavy door squeaked open and a voice boomed from the murkiness inside. "What do you want?"

Marcellus looked up to see a huge guard with a mouthful of missing teeth glaring back at him, and he nearly lost his nerve. Until he remembered that he was dressed in his officer uniform. And he was armed. *He* had all the power here.

He waved the rayonette in the man's face. "I am conducting an authorized search of this facility in the name of the Ministère."

The guard began to shut the door, but Marcellus blocked it with his boot. "I need to speak to whoever is in charge here. Things will go a lot easier for you if you comply."

The guard looked more annoyed than afraid. As though he had much better things to do than entertain Ministère officers in the middle of the day. Without a word, he opened the door wider and gestured for Marcellus to enter.

Marcellus followed the guard down a dark corridor strewn with puddles. Just like all the other Frets in Vallonay, Fret 17 used to be a freightship that once soared majestically across the galaxies, bringing survivors from the First World to Laterre hundreds of years ago. Now the old structure sat lopsided and decomposing in the mud, housing thousands upon thousands of people in the cramped couchettes that filled the floors below.

This floor, however, held no rooms except for the one that stood at the end of the hallway.

Marcellus had never been up here before. Up until a few hours ago, he hadn't known this place and its one solitary resident even existed.

"It's all yours," the guard mumbled unceremoniously as they reached the door. Then, before Marcellus could blink, he took off down the hallway, scurrying away faster than a cockroach from the light.

Marcellus rolled his eyes and pushed on the rusting handle. The door eased open with a whine and he stepped inside, jerking to an abrupt halt at the sight in front of him. It was one of the most incredible views Marcellus had ever seen.

Huge windows made of clear sheets of plastique looked out over the whole of Vallonay. Under the cloudy gray sky, Laterre's capital stretched out for kilomètres. Marcellus could make out the shimmering curve of Ledôme high up on its hill and in the flatlands below, he could see the outlines of hothouses and fermes. To his left, the docklands hugged the edge of the Secana Sea, which stretched out dark blue and endless into the distance.

"It's quite the view isn't it?"

The voice startled Marcellus and his gaze snapped around, landing on a huge chair stationed in the center of the room, in front of a vast, decrepit flight console. In the chair sat the man Marcellus had come to see. He just never imagined he would look like this.

The man's face was a collage of scars, craters, and pockmarks, and his left eye drooped like it was being pulled down by an invisible weight. It was a face unlike anything Marcellus had seen before. A face wrecked and transfigured by . . . he couldn't even imagine what.

"I haven't gotten fully used to the sight myself," the man in the chair said. "It still startles me from time to time."

Marcellus now wasn't sure whether the man was talking about the view out the window or his face.

"Welcome to the Bridge, Officer," the man said, eyeing Marcellus's crisp white uniform with a twinkle of approval.

"The *Bridge*?"

The man gestured around the vast room. "That's what all of this used to be. Back when these hunks of metal could fly. They call me the Capitaine." He winked his good eye. "It's a little play on words. Now, to what do I owe the honor?"

Marcellus holstered his rayonette and forced himself to meet the man's eye. "I was told you could help me."

The Capitaine cocked his head. "You were, were you? And who told you that?"

Marcellus thought of the convict at the Policier Precinct that he'd bribed for information leading him here. And the promise of silence Marcellus had made in return. "I can't say."

"Of course, you can't." The Capitaine croaked out a laugh, and Marcellus couldn't shake the feeling that the man was mocking him. "Help you with what, mon ami? I must warn you, though. If you're looking for a mouchard, I don't do deals with the Ministère."

Marcellus shook his head. He was not looking for a snitch. "I need a microcam. Something untraceable and discreet."

"I see." The Capitaine leaned back in his seat. "And what would you want with an untraceable, *discreet* microcam?"

"I—" Marcellus started to say, but the Capitaine cut him off with another cackle.

"Let me guess, you can't say, right?"

The man was *definitely* mocking him.

"I suppose you want to eavesdrop on someone," the Capitaine went on, rising from his chair and walking over to a bank of metal cabinets. He pulled one open and riffled through a small bin. "A suspect, perhaps?"

Marcellus swallowed the lump in his throat. "Yes. A suspect," and then, he quickly added, "believed to be working with the Vangarde."

The Capitaine turned to flash him a thin smile. "Right."

As the Capitaine continued to sift through his cabinet, Marcellus caught brief glimpses of a grand assortment of contraband: TéléComs, a pair of Policier cuffs, even a glinting rayonette. All the things the Ministère didn't want the Third Estate to have. And every single one of them stolen, Marcellus had no doubt. If he were really here on a Ministère-sanctioned search, as he'd claimed to be, this place would be the mother lode.

"Here we are." The Capitaine closed the cabinet, walked back to his chair, sat down, and held out his hand. In his leathered palm sat a tiny wafer-thin device, no bigger than a pea. A web of glimmering filaments threaded across its smooth surface.

Marcellus frowned down at it. "That doesn't look like a microcam."

"That's because I don't have a microcam."

"What?"

"Fresh out, I'm afraid. This is the next best thing. An auditeur."

An auditeur? Marcellus felt his hopes sink once again. He didn't want a listening device. He wanted a cam. He wanted visual. He wanted no mistakes. Nothing left unseen.

"It's a very advanced device," the Capitaine said encouragingly. "Invisible to scans. It will connect directly to your TéléCom via regular communication channels. The signal will be encrypted to look like an AirLink. No one will ever discover it. Including your . . . *suspect.*" He flashed Marcellus another wry grin.

"But I want a microcam," Marcellus said.

"Well, we don't always get what we want, do we?"

Marcellus let out a huff and dropped his gaze back down to the Capitaine's open palm.

"You're welcome to take your business elsewhere," the Capitaine said. "But anyone will tell you—as I'm sure the person who sent you here already did—that I'm the most trustworthy shop in town. As well as the most"—he winked again at Marcellus—"*discreet.*"

Marcellus pondered his options. He could leave and try to find someone else who could sell him an illegal microcam, or he could attempt to plant this auditeur instead. It was, as the Capitaine said, the next best thing. If his grandfather conducted *any* business in his office, either in person or by AirLink, Marcellus would be able to hear it.

Plus, he was running out of time.

It had been a full day since his grandfather had stolen Mabelle's microcam from Marcellus's rooms. He'd, undoubtably, watched the footage by now.

And tonight was their weekly game of Regiments in the general's study. It was the perfect moment for Marcellus to find a place to hide the device. Possibly the *only* moment. Because who knew when Marcellus would be invited back into his grandfather's office . . . if ever?

"Fine," Marcellus said as he reached into his pocket and pulled out the ten titan buttons he'd removed from one of his officer uniforms earlier. He spread them out on the console. But for the longest time, the Capitaine simply stared at them, his one sagging eye twitching as though he were computing something.

"I was told that would be enough," Marcellus said nervously, remembering the convict's instructions.

The Capitaine leaned back in his chair with a sigh. "Seems you get told a lot of things, mon ami." His gaze roved over Marcellus from head to toe. "Anyone ever *tell* you not to believe everything you're told?"

"How much?" Marcellus asked briskly.

The Capitaine scanned the ten titan buttons. "Triple."

Marcellus's stomach lurched. "I don't have triple."

The Capitaine's hand that was holding the device shifted out of reach. "Then it seems you don't have an auditeur."

Marcellus felt that familiar rush of anger. This criminal was trying to take advantage of him. Take advantage of the fact that he knew Marcellus not only needed this device, but needed it to be kept a secret.

But Marcellus was done being taken advantage of.

He stood up straighter. "How about I resist the urge to shut down this whole establishment right here and now, and we call it even?"

"Oh, I don't think you'll do that."

"You're right," Marcellus said hotly. "I won't. Because you're going to take the *ten* titan buttons and you're going to keep your Sol-damn mouth shut. Because you're not a mouchard who does deals with the Ministère, remember?"

Marcellus stepped forward and grabbed the auditeur, swiftly and decisively, from the Capitaine's hand. Then, without another word, he turned and headed for the door, stomping noisily down the corridor and the stairs to the ground floor.

By the time Marcellus exited out of Fret 17, the Marsh was more crowded than ever. People shoved and jostled amongst the market stalls, and the walkways thrummed with energy and noise. The protest over the Patriarche's wage cuts seemed to be reaching a pinnacle, and Marcellus couldn't shake the feeling that he was walking through the center of an unstable Sol on the brink of imploding.

At the center of the marketplace, a group of Third Estaters was congregated around the resurrected statue of Thibault Paresse, the founding Patriarche of Laterre, shouting and punching their fists into the air. Their synchronized, echoing chant reverberated through the Frets.

"Honest work for an honest wage! Honest work for an honest wage!"

Policier sergents tried desperately to keep the crowd contained, but Marcellus knew it was only a matter of minutes before another riot broke out. Today, however, he was grateful for the commotion. It would conceal what he had to do and keep the local authorities distracted.

After checking to make sure he wasn't being followed, Marcellus ducked through the entrance of Fret 7. Once inside, memories began to swarm him. He suddenly saw her everywhere. Tending to his bleeding head in the hallway. Reading the message sewn into his father's prison shirt. Vanishing around the corner the last night he'd seen her.

It wasn't the first time he'd been back here since that night he'd watched Alouette run away from him. But now, with Mabelle's words ringing in his ears, the hallway of Fret 7 felt different. Emptier somehow.

"Little Lark is no longer with the Vangarde."

He'd stayed awake almost the entire night searching for her on his TéléCom. Scouring countless hours of security footage from the droids patrolling the Frets. Scanning a hundred thousand faces, looking for her face. But it was like trying to find a single drop of water in all of the Secana sea.

Alouette Taureau, it would seem, had turned back into a ghost.

With a sigh, he attempted to push her from his thoughts as he scurried toward the old collapsed stairwell at the end of the hall. Reaching into his pocket, he retrieved the balled-up piece of paper he'd scrawled a message on earlier this morning, informing the Vangarde that he was going to attempt to bug his grandfather's office.

He squeezed the message in his palm before surreptitiously stuffing it between two broken slats in the staircase. Then, as he headed back down the long, dank corridor, he bent over and dragged his fingertip through the mud on the ground. When he reached the Fret's entrance, he stopped and drew a large letter *V* on the wall.

The signal to the Vangarde that a new drop had been made.

Marcellus didn't know who picked up or delivered the messages—perhaps more Fret rats like that boy he'd interrogated two weeks ago, who had been sent to Bastille for being a Vangarde courier. All Marcellus knew was that, by the time he returned tomorrow, a response would be waiting for him in the stairwell. At least, that's what Mabelle had told him before he'd left the copper exploit yesterday morning, when she'd given him the instructions on how to make contact.

Exiting the Fret, he could hear the commotion building in the Marsh. Becoming more volatile. More violent. Soon, the droids would start firing into the crowd. Bodies would fall limp. More arrests would be made. More prisoners sent to Bastille to mine the zyttrium required to make more Skins. More chains for the Third Estate. It was a vicious cycle that Marcellus knew had to change.

But his grandfather was *not* the one to do it. He was not the better solution. If there was anything Marcellus was certain of, it was that.

"Is this really where you're supposed to be?"

Marcellus froze at the sound of the voice. The icy, cold, inflectionless tone. He closed his eyes, praying that the voice was talking to someone else—a rioter escaped from the marketplace, perhaps. But then the footsteps approached from behind him. Their stiff, rhythmic cadence snapped through the damp air. A tingle shot down Marcellus's spine. He spun around and his gaze landed on a pair of shiny black boots as they emerged from the Fret hallway and came toe to toe with Marcellus's own.

His pulse spiked. Had he been followed?

Marcellus took a deep breath and looked unwaveringly into the eyes of the man who stood now a mere whisper away from him.

If you could even still call him a *man*.

The newly implanted circuitry in the left side of the cyborg's face blinked furiously as a look of satisfaction passed over his harsh features.

Marcellus kept his gaze steady and tried to infuse nonchalance into his words. "Inspecteur Chacal. How good to see you."

The inspecteur glared back at him. "Officer Bonnefaçon. What are you doing here? My TéléCom says you're supposed to be at the TéléSkin fabrique right now, interrogating the déchets."

Marcellus tried not to cringe at the inspecteur's use of that vulgar word for the Third Estates. Déchets. Garbage. Scum.

"I'm on a special assignment," Marcellus replied, fighting to keep his voice steady. Chacal had already snitched on him to his grandfather once. He had to assume he would do it again. "Confidential. It's not logged."

The inspecteur's gaze raked up and down Marcellus, his circuitry flashing with suspicion. The auditeur in Marcellus's pocket suddenly felt like a boulder.

The inspecteur couldn't search him, could he? He didn't have the authority.

Marcellus heard the crisp *smack, smack, smack* of Chacal's infamous metal baton slapping against his palm as he considered the validity of Marcellus's claim. The weapon glinted ominously in the afternoon light.

"And I'm running behind," Marcellus continued, anxious to get as far away from Chacal as possible, "so I better get back to it."

He began to push his way past the inspecteur, but Chacal flicked his baton in front of him, blocking his path. Chacal's one orange eye bore into him.

Marcellus knew the inspecteur could use that eye to seek the truth, to pick up on Marcellus's heart rate and body heat. A human lie detector. But he was certain Chacal was also using it as a method of intimidation. Chacal had always been predatory, with a taste for terrorization. But after his recent promotion from sergent to inspecteur—and subsequent cyborg operation—the power had immediately gone to his cybernetically enhanced brain.

"What *kind* of special assignment?" Chacal asked.

Marcellus allowed a small smile to cross his lips. "I would share more details with you, Inspecteur, but I'm afraid it's above your clearance level."

The insult registered on the man's face, and Marcellus could see the fury flash in his one human eye.

"Shall I AirLink in a quick confirmation to the general that you *are* indeed supposed to be here? And not in the Fabrique District as my TéléCom says?" Chacal asked.

Marcellus could hear his heart thudding in his ears, but somehow, he managed to keep his panic concealed. "If you must," he replied casually. "And while you're at it, perhaps you could also explain to him why the newly appointed inspecteur of the Vallonay Policier Precinct has abandoned his sergents in the midst of a potential riot."

The embedded circuits in Chacal's face flashed once more, but this time, Marcellus could read the difference in their frenetic flickering. This time, it wasn't anger or suspicion that played out on the cyborg's face. It was fear. Followed by subtle resignation.

Chacal slowly raised his baton, allowing Marcellus to pass. "Good luck on your assignment," he muttered, refusing to meet Marcellus's eye.

"Merci," Marcellus replied jovially, giving the inspecteur an undeserved salute. "And Vive Laterre."

"Vive Laterre," Chacal repeated, barely audible through his clenched teeth.

- CHAPTER 8 -
CHATINE

THE HEAVY PERMASTEEL COLLAR CLAMPED AROUND
Chatine's neck, and she felt herself being tugged forward. She shuffled
her feet, following the inmate in front of her as they walked slowly and
arduously out of the exploit complex.

Another day over.

Only ten thousand, one hundred and eighty-five to go.

She stumbled across the moon's dusty amber-colored surface while
the collar dragged at her throat, causing her to cough and wheeze.

Chatine wasn't sure why they even needed these collars and the heavy
PermaSteel chain hitching each prisoner together in a long miserable
line. What was the point when there were droids stationed all along their
route back to the prison building, ready to send ruthless volts of electricity through your body if you dared try to run?

The walk to and from the exploit complex was long and laborious.
Chatine and the other prisoners moved like a single, lumbering snake, the
great chain between them clanking and jangling in the cold Bastille air.

Chatine shivered as a gust of wind whistled through her exploit coat
and spread across her skin. She glanced up and squinted against the light

of the stars. They were mere pinpricks in the sky, but after twelve hours of darkness in the exploits, it took her eyes a moment to adjust.

The three Sols of the System Divine were still invisible to her on Bastille. The prison complex was positioned so far north on the moon's surface, it was almost always night here. But the stars, they were everywhere. Like an infinite blanket of shimmering and dancing light across the sky. More stars than she could ever hope to count. More than she even thought existed.

"Look down, keep walking," said a nearby droid.

Chatine trudged forward, relieved when she could finally make out the glittering lights of Bastille's spaceport to her right. They were almost there.

Up ahead, the prison building loomed. Flanked by an impenetrable curtain wall, its six towers glowed like unwavering sentinels. Chatine's gaze tracked across to the Trésor tower, where her own cell block was located. Up on its roof, she could just make out a long silver chute glinting in the starlight. Chatine shivered, thinking about the terrible machine that was attached to that chimney. The disintegrateur. And even though she warned herself not to, she couldn't help but think about Anaïs, the girl from the exploit. Somewhere up there, in the dingy, cold morgue on the top floor of the tower, her body was waiting to be loaded into that machine, which blasted, froze, and turned everything to nothing. Chatine was grateful that at least today wasn't a disintegration day. Even though the ice dust of the dead wasn't supposed to have an odor, Chatine swore she could smell the stench as the frozen fragments billowed up the gleaming chimney into the dark skies above.

Chatine pulled her gaze from the roof as the heavy airlock of the dispatch bunker yawned open and the line of chained prisoners filed inside. The doors sealed shut, and one by one, they stepped into a narrow chamber where, amid a deafening cranking and squealing noise, the chains from their necks were removed. As soon as the metal collar was unfastened, Chatine felt like she could breathe again.

The dispatch bunker was a desolate room with nothing but a few benches, floors covered in Bastille dust, and rows of hooks for exploit coats. Chatine shrugged out of her own and was just about to hang it up when a loud clatter rang out, causing her to jump. She turned to see a man sprawled out on the floor. His head was smooth and shiny from the razor. Fresh off the voyageur.

"Watch your step, Nov," a harsh voice spat, using the nickname new arrivals were given on Bastille.

Chatine turned around to see another man standing just behind her, glaring down at the prisoner on the floor. He'd evidently been the one to put him there. The standing man's hair was long, falling to the middle of his back. Chatine's gaze zeroed in on his left shirt sleeve, rolled with precision.

Another Vétéran. Like Roche's bodyguard, Clovis.

"Sorry," the newcomer muttered through clenched teeth. "Calm the fric down, all right?"

There was something eerily familiar about him. But as hard as she tried, Chatine couldn't manage to place him in her memories.

"Everyone has to learn their place here," the Vétéran growled, taking a few steps forward until he stood directly over the fallen inmate. "And right now, you are exactly where you belong. On the floor like the Nov scum that you are."

A ripple of trepidation passed through Chatine. She'd never seen a Vétéran instigate a fight before. Most of them were too old. And while inmates like Clovis were intimidating, they mostly stayed out of trouble.

So what was this man doing?

The newcomer tried to stand, but the Vétéran immediately kicked him back down to the floor.

Chatine's muscles coiled. This would not end well. Fights between inmates broke out often, and she'd learned quickly to be as far away from the scene as possible when they did. She tossed her coat onto the hook and backed away from the two men just as the newcomer let out a roar, launched to his feet, and barreled into the Vétéran.

The older man staggered backward, taking the hit, and soon the two prisoners were on the floor together, wrestling for position, punches being thrown and ducked. Out of the corner of her eye, Chatine saw the nearest droid register the fight and start to make its way over. She turned, preparing to remove herself from the crime of proximity, when just then, something caught her eye. The two scrabbling prisoners were still on the ground. The Vétéran had grabbed a stray boot from nearby and was holding it high above his head, preparing to slam it down on the other man's face.

But it was the newcomer—lying on his back—who Chatine was watching, transfixed. One of his hands was raised to protect his face from the blow, while the other was reaching toward the pocket of the Vétéran's prison uniform. Chatine caught a glimpse of something small and white—like a tiny vial—before it was gone. Deposited into the pocket. The heavy boot came down. The newcomer rolled left and was instantly back on his feet. He landed a kick right in the Vétéran's stomach. The Vétéran collapsed. The newcomer went for a second blow, but it never connected because he was suddenly flung back as the droid grabbed him by the scruff of the neck like a dog. Dangling from its metal fist, the Nov wriggled and whipped his body, but it was no use. Hardly anyone broke free from the grasp of a droid. A split second later, the droid's tazeur made contact with the newcomer's neck. His whole body juddered and seized before the droid dropped him to the floor in a quivering, convulsing heap.

And that's when Chatine saw it.

The cuff of the newcomer's left shirt sleeve.

It, too, had been rolled up.

Just like Clovis's. Just like the old man who had started the fight.

Chatine's body stiffened.

He couldn't be one of *them*. He'd only just arrived. It didn't make any sense. The Vétérans were all ancient prisoners, with hair that fell at least to their chins. This man didn't fit in.

"Prisoner 51616," announced the droid, which still loomed over the newcomer. "This is your first warning. Any future altercations or breaches in protocol will earn you two days in solitary confinement."

As Chatine watched the man hobble away, she was struck, once again, by that same twinge of recognition. His prominent brow and hooked nose seemed so familiar to her. But still, she couldn't figure out how she knew him. The haze of the grippe was holding her brain and her memories hostage. Trying to recall this man's face was like trying to swim through thick sludge.

Chatine followed the newcomer with her eyes, watching as he pulled off his exploit coat and hung it up. Her good sense told her to let it go. Stop obsessing over this. It was none of her business, and she was better off not getting involved anyway.

But another part of her—the part that had been tamped down, drowned out by the grippe, forgotten back on Laterre—wouldn't allow her to let it go. It was the very part of Chatine that had helped her survive the streets of Vallonay.

It was the Fret rat in her.

She'd thought it was dead and incinerated. She'd thought it had been killed the moment that prisoner number had been tattooed into her arm. But now she could feel it rising back up, screaming through the thick fog, telling her there was something going on here. Something she had to figure out.

Chatine studied the new inmate as he joined the line of prisoners exiting the dispatch bunker and heading for the cantine. His long muscular limbs, broad shoulders, and square jaw tugged at the corners of her memory.

Where had she seen him before?

He turned his head to rub at the back of his neck, giving Chatine a perfect view of his face. And that's when a flimsy memory pushed its way into her mind. She could suddenly see wisps of fog in the air. His large, menacing frame emerging from a wall of mist.

Montfer.

The Tourbay.

Mabelle.

He was one of Mabelle's bodyguards. Chatine had seen the man when she'd accompanied Marcellus to Montfer to meet with his former governess, an escaped Vangarde prisoner. That was back when Chatine was still working as a spy for General Bonnefaçon. The decision that had eventually landed her on Bastille.

Chatine cursed the thick haze that was constantly swirling around her brain, keeping her thoughts blurry, keeping her stupide. She shut her eyes tight, trying to push her way through the fog—both the one in her memory and the one that was holding her mind hostage. Until the jagged, fragmented pieces of that day in Montfer finally started to take shape and fuse together.

Mabelle was Vangarde.

This man was one of her operatives. And he had just staged a fight to slip something into the pocket of another prisoner. Something he'd obviously brought from Laterre and smuggled onto Bastille.

Chatine had gotten it all wrong. She'd misread the signs from the start. The rolled-up sleeves, the long hair, the lack of eye contact and acknowledgement.

The Vétérans weren't just some random group of old prisoners. They were the *Vangarde*. They'd infiltrated Bastille, getting jobs in the kitchen, and the Med Center, and the morgue. They'd been here for years, maybe even as far back as the Rebellion of 488.

And now, they were planning something.

CHAPTER 9

MARCELLUS

THE THREE ARTIFICIAL SOLS WERE SETTING IN THE
TéléSky outside, and the last of their golden light cast shimmering,
glowing shafts across General Bonnefaçon's office. Marcellus couldn't
help but think they looked like gleaming prison bars, slashing their way
through the room.

Flicking his eyes across the vast, wood-paneled study, Marcellus scrutinized every light fixture, every nook and dark corner, every First World
relic lining the shelves. He zeroed in on a promising-looking lamp on the
general's desk, but then ruled it out a second later.

Too close to his eyeline.

"Your move, Marcellus." His grandfather's deep voice pulled Marcellus's
attention back to the center of the room until he was staring directly at his
grandfather, sitting in the leather chair across from him, hands steepled
under his chin. The general's dark brows were furrowed in concentration
and his eyes looked flat and hard, like two shards of unbreakable rock, as
he studied the three-tiered game board between them.

Looking down, Marcellus noticed that the general had pushed one
of his infanterie pieces toward Marcellus's troop of unarmed peasants.

Without a moment's hesitation, Marcellus moved one of his own infanterie pieces in to protect the peasants. Then, once he was certain his grandfather's attention was still locked on the game, Marcellus let his gaze return to the room, discerningly rejecting one potential hiding place after another.

Too big.

Too small.

Too risky.

For a moment, he really liked the look of the great twisting, forked horns on the head of the First World beast that hung on the wall. But then—after gauging their distance from his grandfather's desk, where the general conducted most of his business—Marcellus quickly decided it was too far away. To have any hope of finding out what kind of weapon his grandfather was developing, the listening device had to be closer to the action.

"Marcellus!" his grandfather snapped, and Marcellus quickly turned to see that the general had made his next move and was now glaring at Marcellus with a dissatisfied expression.

"Sorry, Grand-père," Marcellus muttered, avoiding his grandfather's stern eyes, and returning his gaze to the game.

"You've been awfully distracted this evening," his grandfather noted. "Is there somewhere else you'd rather be?"

Marcellus swallowed through the growing lump in his throat. "No, sir." He tucked his hands under his chin as he studied the board. His grandfather had moved one of his cavalerie pieces up to the second level, where Marcellus's artillerie were lined up.

Sweat pooled beneath the stiff collar of his uniform. Being inside this room was making him uneasy. Not just because of the seemingly impossible task in front of him. But because he'd been in here for nearly half an hour and so far, his grandfather had made no indication that he'd watched the footage on Mabelle's microcam. He hadn't even so much as hinted that he knew Marcellus had been harboring evidence from a Vangarde spy. Even though Marcellus was fairly certain that he *had* watched that footage. That he *did* know.

Which meant General Bonnefaçon was currently playing *two* differ-ent games in this office tonight. The one that was playing out on the board between them, and the one that Marcellus couldn't see. That was the scarier game. Because that was the game that toyed not with little stone pieces representing great battalions of the First World, but with Marcellus's mind.

Marcellus picked up one of his artillerie pieces and rubbed his thumb over the ornately carved stone. He'd never liked the game of Regiments. The rules were complicated, and the strategy took years to master. Marcellus had, indeed, been playing for years, but it seemed no matter how many times he played, how many lessons his grandfather doled out, he couldn't seem to get a handle on the game. He'd stopped caring years ago whether he won or lost. Not that he *ever* won.

He eyed his grandfather's brigadier piece, gradually making its way across the top level of the board, toward Marcellus's Monarch. Swiftly and decisively, Marcellus placed his artillerie piece on the same tier.

The general made a clucking sound with his tongue, and Marcellus glanced up to see he was shaking his head disapprovingly. "Always so hasty to act, aren't you, Marcellus? Always rushing into things. You must learn to be more strategic. Plan your attack. Analyze your opponent. Play with your head, not your emotions."

You mean be more like you? Marcellus thought scornfully. That was something he would *never* do.

"Sooner or later, Marcellus," his grandfather went on, "you're going to have to start playing the game like someone who actually wants to *win*."

Marcellus sighed and allowed his gaze to dart back to the walls of the office, trying to block out the sound of his grandfather's voice. He didn't give a damn about winning the *game*.

His eyes flitted over the contents of the shelf closest to the general's desk. The small statue of the First World military officer? Perhaps he could hide the auditeur in the man's billowing cape or under his rearing, wild-eyed horse? No. The marble was too smooth. Too white. The device would surely stand out.

A knock on the door pulled Marcellus's attention away from the shelf. A Palais servant entered carrying a large rectangular package wrapped in a white sheet. "General Bonnefaçon," said the man anxiously. "I have the painting you requested."

The general barely glanced at the servant as he waved his hand toward the desk. "Just set it down over there."

The servant hurriedly crossed the office and propped the artwork up against the desk. "Would you like me to unwrap it?"

The general kept his gaze locked on the game board as he replied, "Yes, that's fine. Merci." Then, presumably to Marcellus, he explained, "It's quite a painting. I found it in the servants' quarters, of all places. I have no idea how such a valuable piece ended up *there*. So I asked for it to be transferred here. For safekeeping."

There was a rustling sound as the sheet was removed, and Marcellus only had to glimpse a tiny speck of the corner—swirls of blue and pale yellow—before his heart plummeted straight down to his feet.

It wasn't just *a* painting.

It was *the* painting.

The one that used to be in Nadette Epernay's room and, before that, in his own governess Mabelle's room.

It was buried inside this very painting that Marcellus had first found Mabelle's microcam, setting off a chain of events that had led him right here.

"Check."

Marcellus cut his eyes back to the game board to see his that grandfather had snuck one of his cavalerie pieces up to the third tier and placed it in striking distance of Marcellus's Monarch. But Marcellus was far more interested in his grandfather's *other* move. The painting had certainly not been delivered here at this very moment by accident. His grandfather wanted him to see it.

"Your move," the general prompted as the servant darted back out the door.

Marcellus squinted at the complicated game board, trying to focus his thoughts. But his vision kept blurring. He was having a hard time concentrating on the pieces. Not just because now, with his Monarch in check, he was quickly running out of time to find a place to plant the auditeur, but because now he knew for *sure* that his grandfather had watched that footage.

He knew that Marcellus had learned the truth. About his father. About the general. About the real reason the Rebellion of 488 had failed.

But now the question was, what would the general do about it?

Sucking in a deep breath, Marcellus reached for his légionnaire and quickly moved it between the general's cavalerie piece and his own exposed Monarch. The general immediately responded by pushing his brigadier piece directly in striking distance of Marcellus's légionnaire.

Marcellus blinked down at the board for a long moment, unable to believe his grandfather had made such a stupide move. Even Marcellus knew not to put your brigadier—one of the most valuable pieces in the game—in the path of another player's powerful légionnaire.

Had his grandfather made a mistake?

Was it possible he too was distracted this evening?

Swiftly, Marcellus knocked the brigadier piece over and swiped it off from the board.

"Check mate," his grandfather announced.

What? Marcellus's eyes struggled to make sense of what he was seeing as the general moved his own légionnaire up to the top level and, with a swift and purposeful flick of his wrist, tipped Marcellus's Monarch onto its side. The heavy stone piece fell against the marble game board with an unsettling *clink*.

"Sometimes," the general leaned back his chair, "we must sacrifice important pieces for the sake of the larger goal."

And suddenly, Marcellus knew his grandfather was no longer talking about the game. He was talking about his own son. Julien Bonnefaçon. The one who went to prison in the general's place. And now the only proof was in the general's possession.

Marcellus stared numbly down at his fallen Monarch. That was it.

Game over. And worse yet, he still hadn't found a place to hide the auditeur. A defeat on all fronts.

Outside the general's study, the golden Sol-light had disappeared entirely from the TéléSky, and through the windows now, there was nothing but darkness.

"Reset the game, won't you?" His grandfather rose to his feet and immediately reached for the TéléCom on his desk, already getting pulled into a barrage of AirLinks and broadcasts.

Marcellus got to work arranging the Regiments pieces back into their starting formations. He saved his Monarch for last. With its crowned head resting against the marble surface of the game board, the stone piece looked so helpless and deserted, like Marcellus imagined so many of the monarchs had looked after those bloody battles for power and wealth that had been fought on the First World.

He supposed not much had changed since then, however. Laterre and Albion had been fighting since the first days of the System Divine. Battles for land and titan and influence had kept their leaders at odds for more than five centuries. The general, himself, had lost his own commandeur and friend, Michele Vernay, because of that grudge.

Marcellus sighed and picked up his defeated Monarch, turning it over in his hands. Over the years, he'd seen this piece fall time and time again at the hands of his grandfather. The general was just too clever, too strategic, too manipulative. And Marcellus felt like one of those lonely peasant pieces on the bottom tier of the board. Always unarmed and unprepared. Always outsmarted in the end.

But this time, as he studied the intricate carvings and bell-like shape of the Monarch, he noticed something he'd never noticed before. The piece was not made of solid stone, as it appeared. But rather, it was hollow in the middle. As he subtly lifted it up to eye level, Marcellus could see a narrow indentation carved into the base of the stone.

Deep and cavernous and . . .

Perfect.

"General Bonnefaçon!"

Marcellus and his grandfather both looked toward the door of the study to find one of the Palais maids, dressed in her usual black-and-blue uniform, panting breathlessly, as though she'd just been running laps around Ledôme.

"Yes?" The general looked more confused than angry by the intrusion.

"The Patriarche . . ."—her words were punctuated by short, ragged breaths—". . . has insisted . . . you come . . . now."

The general checked the time on his TéléCom. "Right now?"

The maid clutched her heaving chest. "He says . . . it's urgent. . . . He's in the . . . imperial appartements."

A flash of irritation crossed over the general's face. He evidently believed this to be just another pointless summoning from a man suffering from severe paranoia. "We'll be right there," he muttered to the servant, who bowed her head and slipped back out the door.

Marcellus gripped the Monarch piece tightly in his shaking hands. This could be his only chance. Carefully reaching into his pocket, he pinched the auditeur between his fingers. Tiny and round with a row of protruding filaments, it felt like an insect. And weighed nothing more than one too.

His grandfather had been right. Marcellus *had* been distracted tonight. So distracted, he didn't even see what was right in front of him. The Regiments board was positioned on a small round table directly in the center of the study. It was equal distance from the general's desk, the sitting area, and the large windows in front of which his grandfather often paced when he was on long AirLink conversations.

"Marcellus," his grandfather said sharply as he stalked toward the door. "Let's go."

"Coming, Grand-Père," Marcellus replied. And then, with his back turned to the general, he hastily shoved the auditeur into the hollow groove at the base of the Monarch and, with a soft clink, repositioned the stone piece on the top tier of the board. It stood stoic and regal. Ready for action.

Ready for the next game to begin.

- CHAPTER 10 -
MARCELLUS

"THANK THE SOLS YOU'RE HERE!" THE PATRIARCHE said urgently before grabbing the general and Marcellus by the sleeves and pulling them through the door.

It was the first time Marcellus had ever been inside the imperial appartements. The walls were lined with velvet, and beautiful handwoven rugs covered the floors underfoot. Hundreds of tiny crystals on an intricate chandelier glimmered above, and in the center of the room, in a gigantic canopied bed, lay Veronik Paresse, fast asleep.

"This is a catastrophe!" the Patriarche ranted in a hushed voice as he paced in front of the bed. He was dressed in crumpled silk pajamas the color of apricots and a pair of fluffy wool slippers. At the crown of his head, a few strands of his thin hair tented upward like antennae on the top of the Paresse Tower. "An absolute disaster."

"Perhaps we should take this meeting elsewhere?" the general nodded discreetly toward the sleeping Matrone. Her dark hair, usually so immaculate, resembled a nest of twisted, anxious snakes on the satin pillow. Her cheeks were sunken, her jaw taut, and two large gray shadows hung like rainclouds under her sleeping eyes.

The Patriarche scoffed and waved a dismissive hand toward his wife. "She's so knocked out on sleeping médicaments, a droid army couldn't wake her."

"Madame Matrone has been through a lot," the general said to the Patriarche in a calm, measured voice.

"Of course, she's been through a lot," the Patriarche snapped. "She lost her child—our *only* heir—to a bunch of Vangarde terrorists. And now they're at it *again*."

Marcellus started. "Again, sir?"

The Patriarche glanced anxiously around the room, as though checking for spies, and then lowered his voice to a conspiratorial whisper. "Citizen Rousseau has *escaped*."

Marcellus peered sideways at his grandfather to gauge his reaction, but the general looked more inconvenienced than concerned.

"As we've discussed many times," the general began, "Citizen Rousseau remains in solitary confinement on permanent watch. You have no reason to worry about—"

But the Patriarche didn't allow him to finish. "No, you're wrong. I saw it with my own eyes. I couldn't sleep, so I logged into the security feeds and saw that her cell was empty. The Vangarde have broken her out!"

"You must be mistaken," the general replied diplomatically. "If there was a break-in attempt on Bastille, I would have been alerted immediately. The prison is as secure and impenetrable as always."

The Patriarche snatched a TéléCom off a nearby settee and thrust it under the general's nose. "I'm telling you, General, she's *gone*. Look." He pointed at the TéléCom, but the screen was dark. His cheeks flamed with fury as he jabbed violently at the screen. The flimsy device slipped in his hand, and he had to fumble to catch it.

"Damn the Sols!" he spat.

Until recently, the Patriarche had never owned a TéléCom because he, his wife, and the rest of the First Estate thought such technology to be crass and inferior. But after the death of his only daughter, he'd insisted on having his own TéléCom with the same security clearance as the general's so he could be alerted instantly of any updates and, of course, keep a vigilant watch on Citizen Rousseau's cell.

The problem was, he still hadn't quite mastered how to operate the device.

"It was just here!" he thundered. "Where is it now? Where did it go? This stupide contraption!"

Marcellus noticed the general's shoulders rise and fall in what was obviously an attempt at a deep breath. It was for this very reason that the general had secretly installed guardian controls on the TéléCom before he'd delivered it to the Patriarche. They weren't too dissimilar from the controls Second Estate parents installed on their children's devices. They allowed the general to keep tabs on what the Patriarche was doing with his TéléCom and prohibit him from accidentally—or *intentionally*—starting a war with the Mad Queen of Albion.

"If I may," the general said, easing the TéléCom from the Patriarche's grip. He tapped proficiently on the screen a few times, eventually pulling up what Marcellus recognized as the portal for Bastille's Central Command before tapping on the security feed of Citizen Rousseau's cell.

Marcellus glanced away, knowing exactly what he would see next. It would be the same thing he always saw: a frail skeleton of a woman curled up on the grimy floor. He would not see the strong, charismatic woman who had led a rebellion seventeen years ago and had almost won. The woman who was feared by every Ministère officer on the planet. He would see a shell. A useless heap of flesh and bones.

He'd witnessed the ghastly sight so many times, he'd almost become desensitized to it.

Almost.

"What on Laterre—"

Marcellus heard his grandfather's words but could not make sense of the bewilderment in his voice until a moment later, when Marcellus glanced at the Patriarche's TéléCom, still clutched in the general's hands. The screen displayed the usual view of a dreary, cement cell with no windows and only one PermaSteel door. But instead of revealing a withered, gaunt-faced woman huddled in a corner, Marcellus could see that the cell was, indeed, empty.

"I told you!" the Patriarche said, pointing his finger in the general's face. "I told you she escaped!"

The general ignored him and continued to prod and poke desperately at the screen, looking not too dissimilar from the Patriarche only a few moments ago.

"It's not possible," the general whispered, his brow crumpled, his eyes narrowed. The sight of the general's face made Marcellus's stomach flip. He'd never seen his grandfather look quite so . . . so . . .

But Marcellus couldn't even think of the right word. It didn't exist. Not for the almighty General Bonnefaçon.

"Well, don't just stand there like an imbecile, General," the Patriarche roared. "FIND HER!"

The general shoved the Patriarche's TéléCom into Marcellus's chest before reaching into his pocket for his own. He hastily unfurled it and began punching at the screen.

"Chéri?" cried a small, fragile voice. Marcellus turned to see the Matrone now sitting bolt upright in bed, her eyes wide open. "What's happening? Why are you shouting?"

The Patriarche turned toward his wife, looking like he was about to say something to try to appease her, but was interrupted by the general bellowing into his TéléCom.

"Warden Gallant. This is General Bonnefaçon. I am reporting a code orange. I repeat, a code orange. Prisoner 40102 has disappeared from her—"

The general halted abruptly and listened, his eyes blinking in response to the incoming information. Marcellus peered at the TéléCom to see the warden's face staring back at the general, his thin lips moving rapidly. Marcellus could not hear what the warden was saying, but he noticed his grandfather swallow and stand up straighter, pushing his shoulders back and reasserting his usual rigid stance. It was as though he was physically preparing himself for everything that came next. For the repercussions of what he was about to hear.

For *war*.

"I understand," the general said stiffly. "Yes, I am with Monsieur Patriarche right now. I will relay the information. Merci, Warden Gallant."

The general disconnected the AirLink and turned toward the Patriarche, who met his stare with dark, furious eyes. "What is going on? Where is the wretched woman? Tell me what's going on right this instant, or I swear to the Sols, General, I will—"

The general held up a hand, halting the Patriarche midsentence. "Monsieur Patriarche. I am delighted to be the one to deliver you this news."

Delighted?

The Patriarche and Marcellus exchanged confused glances before turning back to the general.

"The warden has just received word from the droid stationed outside of Citizen Rousseau's cell. Earlier tonight, scanners picked up a significant change in her vitals. By the time the droid entered her cell to perform a scan, her heart had stopped beating. Her body is presently being transferred to the Bastille morgue for disintegration."

The Patriarche stared vacantly at the general, as though he were a droid with a faulty processing chip, unable to compute the words he was hearing.

From somewhere behind them, the Matrone let out a small sob. "Oh, thank the Sols," she whispered into her hands. "Thank the Sols."

But the Patriarche still didn't seem to register the news. The general reached out and patted him congenially on the back. "Congratulations, Monsieur Patriarche. Citizen Rousseau is dead."

- PART 2 -

BASTILLE

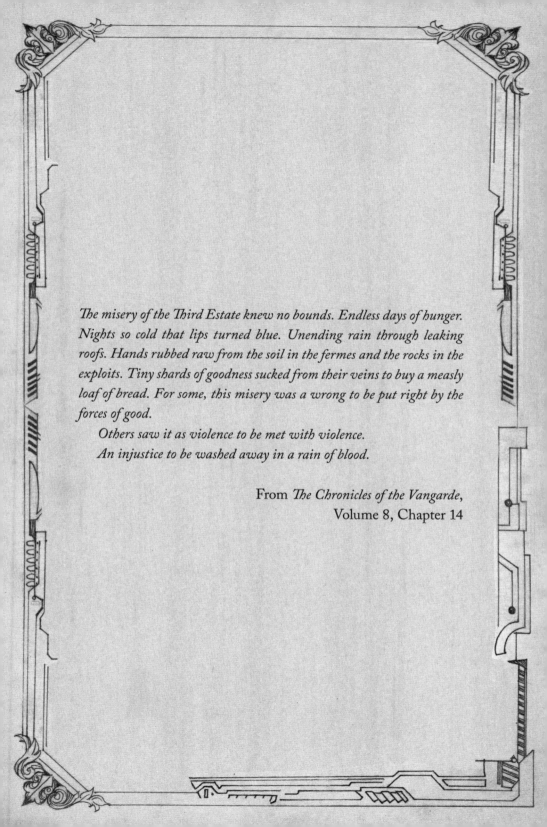

The misery of the Third Estate knew no bounds. Endless days of hunger. Nights so cold that lips turned blue. Unending rain through leaking roofs. Hands rubbed raw from the soil in the fermes and the rocks in the exploits. Tiny shards of goodness sucked from their veins to buy a measly loaf of bread. For some, this misery was a wrong to be put right by the forces of good.

Others saw it as violence to be met with violence.

An injustice to be washed away in a rain of blood.

From *The Chronicles of the Vangarde*,
Volume 8, Chapter 14

- CHAPTER 11 -
ALOUETTE

ALOUETTE TAUREAU HAD LIVED THE LAST TWELVE
years of her life in the dark.

Not because she'd lived in a Refuge hidden ten mètres below the surface of Laterre. Nor because she'd grown up protecting a secret library of
First World books that hadn't seen the light of day for centuries.

The darkness that had surrounded Alouette for all those years consisted of lies.

Deep, dark, all-encompassing lies.

She'd been told the Refuge was a sanctuary. A place for quiet contem-
plation and study.

Lie.

She'd been told the sisters were peaceful people who'd taken a vow
of secrecy and solitude so they could protect the First World knowledge
from destruction.

Lie.

She'd been told that their purpose for living ten mètres underground,
in a bunker hidden away from the rest of the planet, was to guard the

Chronicles—the heavy, clothbound, handwritten books that lined the back shelf of the Refuge library.

More lies.

As the giant door of the disembarkation bay creaked open and the bateau's great loading ramp began to unfurl, Alouette could feel those lies lurking behind her in the shadows, ready to follow her off the bateau and into this faraway city that filled the sea air with the smell of burnt metal. The light from the dock streamed into the belly of the ship, and the crowd jostled in anticipation. Alouette held tight to the sac strapped around her chest, clutching the only possessions she had left in the world.

As she waited to disembark, the memories of the events that had brought her here, to the other side of the Secana Sea, cycled through her mind on an endless loop. She could still see it all so clearly. She could see herself flying down the low hallways of the Refuge, the place she and her father had called home for so many years. She could see herself storming into the sisters' Assemblée room—a room she'd always been told was for private meditation and prayer. She could see her own face twisted in shock and disbelief as she tried to make sense of her surroundings.

It was *not* a room for private meditation and prayer.

It was a control center.

The heart of an underground movement.

It was a deep, dark secret that Alouette had been shielded from her entire life.

"Sit down. We need to talk."

Principale Francine's words came back to her now like sharp daggers in her side. The words that had turned Alouette's world from a familiar place of safety and surety to an unknown place of danger and uncertainty.

"We, the sisters, are the leaders of an underground movement, working to bring about an end to poverty, sickness, and suffering on Laterre," Principale Francine said. "We call ourselves the Vangarde."

Alouette stood frozen in shock, unable to move. Her eyes glazed over as she took in the wires and cables and circuit boards. The books and papers and screens.

So many screens. She simply couldn't stop staring at this strange new world that had somehow been part of her world the whole time. But she'd never seen it. Never known. How could the sisters have kept this from her for twelve years?

Her eyes drifted to the seven other women in the room—Sister Laurel, Sister Muriel, Sister Marguerite, Sister Nicolette, Sister Léonie, Sister Clare, Sister Noëlle—all of them stationed at various monitors and control panels. These were the sisters Alouette had grown up with, eaten meals in grateful silence with, practiced Tranquil Forme with. These were the women who had raised her and fed her and cared for her when she was sick. And they were all in on this?

"You, Little Lark, are part of a very important legacy," Principale Francine continued. "A legacy that is destined to heal our broken planet. We, the Vangarde, are Laterre's last hope. The people's last hope."

Alouette felt like every organ inside her body was shutting down, one by one. Her liver, her spleen, her brain, her lungs, her heart. When she finally found her voice again, it was cracked and shaky. "I don't understand."

Principale Francine sighed. "The Regime is extremely corrupt. The very origins of Laterre were unjust and divisive, designed to keep the poor downtrodden and defeated and ignorant. Seventeen years ago, we tried to do something about it. Our rebellion began peacefully. Our former leader, Citizen Rousseau, rallied the people behind our cause with words and emotion and a shift in perspective. But eventually, the movement got away from us. It escalated. It became violent. Instead of peacefully demanding change from the Regime—the way we envisioned it—the people started fighting the Regime. And the Regime fought back. Not just with their droids, but also with their lies. They framed us for violent acts that we were innocent of. They turned the people against us. Citizen Rousseau was captured and incarcerated on Bastille. The spirit of what she represented—what we all represented—died. And our rebellion died right along with it."

Alouette pressed her fingertips into her temples. She was vaguely aware that Principale Francine was speaking, but the words came to Alouette in floating fragments. Space debris that seemed to drift by before Alouette could make sense of it. The sisters had another leader who was in prison?

Her gaze found its way to the black pedestal that stood in the dead center of the Assemblée room. Just above it, a hologram hovered and glowed, like it was burned right into the air.

She'd recognized the image the moment she'd first walked into this room.

It was a map of Bastille. The prison moon of Laterre.

But now, as she peered closer to the hologram, Alouette spotted details she hadn't noticed before. The crisscrossing lines, precise angles, and tiny annotations led her to believe it was more than just a map.

It was a blueprint.

"Citizen Rousseau." Alouette repeated the unfamiliar name Francine had just uttered, feeling a chill tingle down her spine. "You're going to break her out."

Francine clasped her hands in her lap and jutted out her chin. "The situation on Laterre has escalated. Exponentially. If we don't act quickly, the planet will fall into the wrong hands, and we shall all be doomed. Rousseau is our best chance at launching a successful revolution. The people will rally around her again, just as they did before. She understands their suffering, she articulates their pain, and when she is free again, she will be their glowing lamp in a dark forest. With her eloquence, her fearlessness, and her compassion, she will light the path of change. The peaceful path. Which is why we must rescue her from Bastille."

Something snapped together in Alouette's mind. Marcellus had just told her, only moments ago, that two Vangarde operatives had been captured trying to break into the office of the warden of Bastille.

"Sister Jacqui and Sister Denise!" she cried. "They were . . . That's what they were doing. That's why they were arrested."

Francine nodded, a solemn shadow passing over her face. "Their capture was an unfortunate setback."

"Unfortunate setback?" Alouette repeated, disgusted at Francine's blatant coldness. "The Ministère has them. They could be tortured or killed or worse! We have to help them. We have to break them out. If you can break out Citizen Rousseau, you can break them out too, right?"

Francine sighed again. "Jacqui and Denise understood the risks when they agreed to the mission."

Numbness started spreading through Alouette's toes. She had to remind herself to keep breathing. "But you can't . . . You can't just leave them. . . ."

"We don't even know where the Ministère is holding them. Trust me, we are trying to find them, but until then, Citizen Rousseau is our top priority. And the sisters know that."

"No!" Alouette said forcefully. The numbness was already spreading through her legs. Tears were already blurring her vision.

"We need time. And more resources. Freeing Rousseau is a vital step, but it is only the first step. We have a very long road ahead of us before we see true change on Laterre." Principale Francine's eyes settled intensely on Alouette. "Which is why we need your help, Little Lark."

Rage suddenly flared up inside Alouette. "My help? Why would you ever need my help? I know nothing about any of this! You've kept me in the dark for twelve years! What use could I ever be to your . . . your . . . movement?"

"You are more useful than you realize, Alouette," Francine said with a rare twinkle in her eye. "And you have not spent those twelve years in the dark. You have spent them in training. In learning. In becoming the sister—the woman—we always knew you could be. And now I am offering you a choice to join us. To help us."

Alouette hastily shook her head and gritted her teeth. "No, you're not. You stole that choice! You didn't offer it to me, you thrust it upon me, without asking. The moment I stepped foot inside this Refuge, the moment you put that first Chronicles volume in my hand, that choice was robbed from me. My life was robbed from me. You can't give it back." She wiped her cheeks where tears were beginning to fall. "And I don't want it back. I don't want any of it."

"All passengers disembark!"

The thundering voice yanked Alouette out of her reverie, and she felt the crowd around her start to move. As she followed the stream of people shuffling toward the bateau's disembarkation ramp, she tried to push away the memory of Principale Francine's face as Alouette had shouted those words.

She could not allow herself to be distracted by painful memories of things she couldn't change. She had come here, to this city, with a purpose. A burning question to answer. She'd escaped from the Refuge—from that hidden-away bunker with its low ceilings; heavy, suffocating doors; and secret rooms. She'd gathered up what few possessions she had and left the only home she'd ever known. She'd boarded a bateau and sailed around the great single landmass of Laterre, journeying as far away as she possibly could from that darkness and those lies.

Until she'd arrived right here. In the city of Montfer. Which had twinkled on the horizon like a city of jewels. A city of hope.

And now she was finally, *finally* heading toward the light.

Toward the stories that had been hidden from her for far too long.

Toward the truth of who she was.

But the moment she stepped off the bateau and into the icy night air, something shifted inside of her. All her resolve seemed to shrivel up at once.

The dock of Montfer was a bustling cesspool of noise and activity, even though the Sols had set hours ago. Rain drizzled softly from the dark sky, and the wind from the Secana Sea behind her was both biting and refreshing, offering a momentary reprieve from the foul smell that seemed to hang over the darkened city like a layer of fog. Disembarking passengers mixed chaotically with passengers trying to board the bateau that would soon head out into the night, making its return trip to Vallonay. Alouette quickly became lost and dizzy in the confusion. She wedged herself into an empty space on the dock and struggled to catch her breath.

It seemed like ever since she'd left the safety of the Refuge, it had been one overwhelming situation after the next: navigating the Marsh; negotiating with stall owners for new clothes and passage to Montfer; endless days at sea enduring violent storms, towering waves, and grueling seasickness. And now this. A strange world that felt galaxies away from the world she grew up in. The sisters may have taught her to read and write, but what good did that do now? Alouette had never felt less certain and more ill prepared than she did at this moment.

"First time on the east coast, chéri?"

The voice seemed to float out of nowhere. Alouette turned to see a frail older woman standing nearby, her wispy white hair matted with rain and clinging to her face. She looked like she hadn't eaten in weeks.

Alouette pressed her lips together, wondering whether or not she should reply. She'd learned from her time aboard the bateau that people couldn't always be trusted. But there was something in the woman's hungry, hooded eyes that found Alouette murmuring, "First time in a long time."

The woman chuckled. "I suspected as much. You look terrified."

Admonishing herself, Alouette tried to loosen her face. She wasn't going to get anywhere if everyone could see the fear written all over her.

"Let me help you out," the woman said with a smile, revealing yellowed, rotting teeth. "I know this city backward and forward. What are you looking for?"

Alouette hesitated, wondering how much she should reveal to this woman. But the thought of venturing out there, into that chaos, alone, made her want to turn right back around and reboard the bateau. "I'm looking for . . ."—she lowered her voice—"the blood bordel?" She pronounced the words like a question. Like she wasn't sure they actually existed.

Something flickered in the woman's eyes. It looked like comprehension and sympathy and pity all wrapped up in one blink. "Of course. I see girls like you arriving every day. Desperate. Hungry. Craving something just out of reach."

"No, I—" Alouette started to correct the woman. She had her all wrong. But she stopped herself when she realized that perhaps that was the perfect description of Alouette right now. Desperate and craving something that was just out of reach.

The truth was, she had a sinking feeling that she was chasing dust, hunting down infinitesimal particles of matter that were thrown on the wind long ago.

But that dust was all Alouette had.

"I can take you there," the woman said before curling her lips into a sneer. "For a price."

Alouette nodded. She was starting to learn that this was how things worked in places like this. Nothing was free. Everything was for sale. Alouette rummaged through her sac, pulled out her last slice of chou bread, and offered it to the woman. She clearly deemed it worthy, because she devoured the bread and then, in a gruff voice, muttered, "Follow me," before wading into the crowd.

Clutching her elbow tight against her bag, Alouette followed behind. They wove through the docks and up a winding street lined with dilapidated and shuttered stalls. In the morning, the vendors would probably sell fish heads and sea snails that, according to the Chronicles, were food staples in Montfer.

The farther away from the docks they got, the more Alouette felt she could breathe again. Soon the stalls gave way to much larger buildings. Fabriques, Alouette guessed, because of the discarded crates littering the muddy streets. They made their way through an alley between two of these industrial buildings whose corrugated walls loomed over them like rusting battlements. The nearby streetlamps did little to chase away the all-consuming blackness of Laterre's Darkest Night or the terrors that seemed to lurk around every corner of this town.

"I'm Dahlia." The woman introduced herself without turning around.

"Nice to meet you," Alouette muttered, caught between her inclination to be nice and the guardedness she was quickly developing.

Dahlia snorted. "And do you have a name?"

Alouette swallowed. "My name is Alou—" But she stopped herself, realizing she probably shouldn't be using that name anymore, especially to someone like Dahlia. *Alouette* was the daughter of an escaped convict named Jean Legrand. And now, through no fault of her own, *Alouette* was also associated with the Vangarde. Despite having left the Refuge, she was still in hiding. And she feared she would be for the rest of her life. Whether she liked it or not.

"I mean," Alouette said, "My name is . . . Madeline."

The name still sounded foreign on her lips. She'd only just found out about it two weeks ago. It was the name her mother had given her. Before her father had changed it to Alouette when they'd come to the Refuge.

The woman chuckled again. "Are you sure about that, chéri?"

Despite her trepidation, Alouette found herself smiling at the question. "No," she admitted. She wasn't sure about anything anymore.

"Well, you better make up your mind. And fast. You're not going to get very far on this planet if you don't know who you are." She picked up her pace as they passed by another long alleyway. Alouette made the mistake of peering down it, into the darkness, and immediately wished she hadn't. Through the gloom, a dozen pairs of eyes flashed and stared back at her, and on the ground, there was a series of strange, misshapen shadows. Almost like a row of bony carcasses—

"That's the Taudis," Dahlia whispered. "Gang territory. I wouldn't linger."

Alouette scurried away, a chill seeping into her skin that had nothing to do with the damp, cold air. Somehow, this place, this city, seemed even worse than Vallonay. Worse than the Frets. She didn't know how that was possible. She didn't know such worseness could exist.

"This your first time at a blood bordel?" Dahlia asked, casting a doubtful, sidelong look at Alouette.

"Yes," Alouette said quietly, debating whether or not she should elaborate. She quickly decided not.

"I remember my first time."

The shock on Alouette's face made Dahlia laugh. "Don't look so surprised, chéri. Every girl around here has done it at least once. When the babies are screaming from hunger or freezing from the cold, you'll do just about anything to make it stop."

Alouette cleared her throat, unsure what to say to that. So she simply asked, "Does it . . . Did it hurt?"

Dahlia shook her head. "Maybe for a second. But it's over pretty quick. It's the next few days you have to worry about. That's when the regret sinks in. When your body is too tired to do anything, and the bruises start to appear, and no amount of food seems to quench the hunger. Not that there *is* any food."

Alouette's mouth went dry. There was still so much of this world she didn't yet know. So much the sisters hadn't prepared her for, despite how many volumes of the Chronicles she'd read.

She clutched her arm tighter around her sac as they passed by another darkened alleyway. At the end of this one, however, Alouette could see a warm, golden glow. Almost like a Sol rising in the distance. Which of course, she knew was impossible. Night had fallen hours ago. And even if it were dawn, she would never actually be able to *see* a Sol rise on Laterre. The cloud coverage was too thick.

"Second Estate quartier," Dahlia said, as though she could read the question right on Alouette's face. "Where the superviseurs and foremen have their manoirs. They couldn't be bothered to live over here with the rest of us dirty déchets, so they built a wall."

"How long have you lived here?" Alouette asked uneasily.

"All my life," Dahlia replied, and Alouette remarked on something unusual in her voice. It wasn't pride exactly. It was more like dignity. "Don't worry. You get used to it after a while. Home is home."

Home.

The word was like an angry punch in the gut for Alouette. Four simple letters that had sent her chasing dust across the Secana Sea.

Sols, how she longed to be as certain as Dahlia about that word.

She remembered the message Sister Denise had sent Alouette through Marcellus's TéléCom two weeks ago. The message that had launched this slow decline of her certainty and sanity.

When the Lark flies home, the Regime will fall.

Alouette still wasn't entirely sure what it meant. What was Sister Denise trying to tell her? To go home to the Refuge and join the sisters? Help them bring down this faulty Regime with all its cracks and injustices? That was definitely the most convincing answer.

But Alouette wasn't convinced.

Because the Refuge would never be her home again. Not in the way she remembered it, anyway. Never again would she eat her meals in Grateful Silence, lulled by the gentle clink of soup spoons. Never again would she dust the precious volumes of the Chronicles in the library. Or sit on the bed in the room that Sister Jacqui and Sister Denise shared, chattering on about what she'd read that day while Jacqui paced and asked insightful questions, and Denise prodded at some disassembled Ministère device that lay open on her desk.

That Refuge had been a lie. A delusion that had crumbled before her very eyes the moment Principale Francine had revealed the truth.

Alouette felt her fists clench in frustration. The sisters might have wanted her to fly home. To be their "Little Lark." A member of the Vangarde. But Alouette's feathers were wilted now. Her wings ached from flying so far.

She was a lost lark with no home.

"Here we are," Dahlia said.

Alouette blinked and glanced up at the building that loomed above them.

"This is it?" Alouette asked, suddenly wondering if Dahlia had led her to the wrong place. She wasn't expecting the Grand Palais, but she certainly wasn't expecting this. The crooked structure sat slumped in the Montfer mud, its low, rusted roof dangling at an awkward angle and its small, grated windows like a row of lopsided mouths. An old wooden door, whose slats had been gnawed and pummeled by the damp air, was the only perpendicular part of the building. "Is this the only bordel in the city?"

"Yes, but don't be nervous," Dahlia said, her gruff voice softening ever so slightly. "Madame Blanchard has been here for years. She'll take good care of you."

That's what I'm counting on, Alouette thought with a shudder. She glanced back up at the ominous building, trying to work up the courage to go inside. She was thousands of kilomètres from where she'd started, and yet, still so far from where she wanted to be. But that door was a step in the right direction, right? Or, at least, a step in *a* direction. She had to take it.

"Merci," she murmured, without pulling her gaze away from the door. She wanted to say more to the woman who had guided her here. She felt like she *should* say more. But everything on the tip of her tongue felt trite and pointless. *I'm sorry you have to live like this. I'm sorry I can't help. I'm sorry the planet is so broken.* But it didn't seem to matter. Because when Alouette turned back around and gazed into the mist, Dahlia was gone.

And the answers to the questions Alouette had been asking her whole life were waiting behind that weather-beaten door.

CHAPTER 12

MARCELLUS

"WHAT'S TAKING SO LONG?" THE PATRIARCHE GRUMBLED. "Why can't we see her yet?"

Marcellus stood tucked in the corner of Warden Gallant's office, watching the Patriarche pace the room in his fluttering silk dressing gown. Meanwhile, Chaumont, the Patriarche's favorite advisor, stood like a statue, with his hands clasped behind his back. Shimmering on the front pocket of his dark green robe were the two lions of the Paresse family crest.

The moment the words had left General Bonnefaçon's lips—"Citizen Rousseau is dead"—the Patriarche had demanded he see the body for himself. But after more than thirty seconds of the general trying to connect his TéléCom to the morgue security cams, the Patriarche stormed out of the imperial appartements and marched straight to the Ministère headquarters, with the general and Marcellus in tow.

"We're pulling up the feed now, Monsieur Patriarche." Warden Gallant ran a hand through his usually immaculate silver hair. "This is not a sector of the prison that we access regularly." He turned to a technicien currently standing in front of a vast control panel, deftly maneuvering her hands across the screens. "Rolland, what is the status?"

"I'm connecting to the microcam network for the Med Center now," she replied in that affectless tone that all cyborgs seemed to have. "Just a few more moments."

The Patriarche began to pace again. Marcellus stood back, behind his grandfather, afraid to even breathe.

Citizen Rousseau is dead.

He was still numb with shock. As if metal was dripping through his veins. And that word—"dead"—it felt so heavy. So final. So hopeless.

The Patriarche stopped pacing to yell at the technicien. "I want that feed up right this second—"

"The feed is up," Rolland announced. She didn't even blink in the face of the Patriarche's wrath.

Frantically, the Patriarche spun around to face one of the dozens of screens that lined the walls of the warden's office. His gaze flicked to each one, unsure where to look. A moment later, the center screen blinked to life, and Marcellus felt his heart skitter at the sight before him.

On the screen was a dark and dingy room crammed full of gurneys. Each one held an emaciated body, pummeled, beaten, and eroded from life on Bastille. The microcam scanned the room, panning over every body, every face. Their features were all different, and yet they were the same in their wretchedness. They had all died the same bleak, arduous, and miserable death in captivity. And in every single one of their faces, Marcellus saw his own father. Eyes glassy, hands spotted, fingertips blackened.

Thank the Sols Chatine was still alive up there. He couldn't even begin to imagine what his heart would do if he had to see her in a place like this. Unable to stomach the sight of any more bodies, Marcellus turned away and searched the warden's office for a safe place to look. His gaze finally landed on the glowing sculpture sitting on the small table next to him. He knew this elaborate model of the System Divine well. Marcellus had spent so many hours staring at it during the countless security briefings his grandfather had dragged him to over the years, he had the whole thing memorized. Every moon of Albion, every crater of Usonia, every floating rock in the Asteroid Channel. Each item was so carefully rendered with tiny lights, shimmering filaments, and delicate plastique molding. There was even a cluster of miniscule laser beams depicting the rings of Samsara.

"Move left," the warden directed Rolland. "More. More. There!"

Marcellus reluctantly returned his gaze to the monitor. To the face that was now emblazoned on the screen. The face that everyone in this room had come here to see.

Citizen Rousseau.

Her cheeks had sunken into dark craters; her lips had shriveled to a thin, puckered line; and her skin was so dried out and wrinkled, it seemed to fold in on itself a thousand times. Gray hair fanned out in brittle waves, and her eyes—the same eyes that Marcellus had seen blaze with such fire and passion in old footage from the last rebellion—now stared blank and vacant, like two lifeless pebbles on the shores of the Secana Sea.

A stunned silence descended over the room. Over the planet. Marcellus took a step forward, out of his corner, just to make sure he was seeing the image clearly.

Seconds passed that felt like hours. There was no movement. No breath. No life.

"We have confirmation," the warden announced. "Citizen Rousseau is dead."

There was a hesitant stillness in the room, as though everyone was afraid to move. Afraid to even release a single breath that might cause this fragile hope to vanish into the air.

Then, celebration.

The room erupted in applause. Chaumont cheered. The warden pumped his fist in the air. The Patriarche's face transformed into an exuberant smile as he gave the warden a congratulatory pat on the back. Even the implanted circuitry in Rolland's face seemed to flicker a little faster.

Laterre's most dangerous enemy was finally gone.

And everyone was rejoicing.

Everyone except Marcellus.

Marcellus turned away from the monitor, trying to collect his chaotic thoughts.

She's really dead. What did this mean? For his grandfather? For the Vangarde? For the planet?

He knew the Vangarde had recently tried to break Citizen Rousseau out of Bastille. They had been unsuccessful, but his grandfather had been certain they would try again. Citizen Rousseau was the Vangarde's most powerful weapon. Their best hope at a resurgence. They knew it. He knew it. Even the Patriarche knew it.

And now she was gone.

Marcellus itched to get out of this room, ride to the Frets, and drop another message to the Vangarde. If they *were* planning a second escape attempt, they had to call it off immediately. They had to know she was dead.

Marcellus scanned the office, watching the exalted faces and triumphant smiles, wondering if he could possibly slip out unseen. It wasn't until he'd circled back to the monitor—to the image of Citizen Rousseau on the screen—that he noticed there was someone else in the room not celebrating.

General Bonnefaçon stood centimètres away from the screen, staring at Citizen Rousseau's unmoving body dressed in her flimsy blue prisoner uniform. His gaze was intense, focused, his expression completely unreadable.

Marcellus felt the burning urge to jump inside his grandfather's head and watch all his thoughts on repeat like a looped broadcast.

What are you thinking?

What are you plotting?

How does this affect your plan?

The general's gaze suddenly snapped toward Marcellus, as though he knew Marcellus had been staring at him. "Contact Bastille Central Command. Tell the droids to power up the disintegrateur and start preparing the body."

"Me?" Marcellus asked warily, glancing around the office for the warden. But Warden Gallant had disappeared behind his desk, busying himself with something on his TéléCom.

"Now, Marcellus," his grandfather boomed.

Marcellus fumbled for his TéléCom, trying to keep the room from spinning at the thought of that word. "Disintegration." Soon, Citizen Rousseau would be reduced to nothing more than fragments of ice to be shot off into space. Her name would fizzle out. Her memory would slowly be erased from the people's minds. She would become like a distant dream, fading with each passing day.

"Officer Bonnefaçon to Bastille Central Command," Marcellus spoke shakily into his TéléCom.

"Stop."

Marcellus glanced up to see the Patriarche stalking toward him, his eyes fierce and determined. "No disintegration."

Marcellus's brow furrowed. "I-I'm not sure I understand."

"I want her body brought back here," the Patriarche said in a low growl. "I want her head on display in the center of the Marsh. I want the entire planet to see it. The threat she poses to the Regime isn't over until the people see her dead."

Marcellus swallowed. "Of course, Monsieur Patriarche. I will make arrangements for a voyageur to be dispatched and—"

"I would strongly advise against that," the general warned.

The Patriarche glanced anxiously around the room, his nostrils flaring. He did not like being contradicted. Especially in front of people. "What was that, General?"

"I would strongly advise against bringing Rousseau's body back to Laterre," the general repeated, his voice unwavering. "In fact, I would advise against anyone outside this room being made aware of her death."

The Patriarche let out a hoarse chuckle. "Oh, really? So you just want everyone on Laterre to go on thinking she's still alive?"

"Yes."

The Patriarche huffed indignantly. "That's the most stupid idea I've ever heard!"

"It might behoove us to listen to what the general has to say," Chaumont calmly advised his boss.

But the Patriarche was adamant. "The people have to know she's dead! Every planet in the System Alliance must be alerted. And the Vangarde have to know their precious Rousseau is gone."

"The Vangarde will use her death to rally the people around their cause," the general said. "This is a highly volatile time on our planet, and martyrs make for much better motivators than prisoners. It's the reason we made the decision not to kill her when she was first captured."

"*You* made that decision," the Patriarche said, jabbing a finger in the general's direction.

Marcellus kneaded his hands together. The energy in the room was making him antsy. He was desperate to get this whole catastrophe over with so he could get out of here and contact the Vangarde.

"The final decision to incarcerate Rousseau was your father's," the general replied tightly to the Patriarche. "I simply provided council."

"Well, my father was an imbecile," the Patriarche raged. "He was the one who let the planet break out in rebellion in the first place. I'm sorry, General. I cannot let my people go on thinking she is still alive and well. I want her dead face broadcast on every TéléSkin on Laterre." He turned back to Marcellus. "Contact the droids. Tell them to start preparations for the body to be retrieved."

Marcellus glanced momentarily at his grandfather before reaching a shaking hand toward his screen.

"Arrête," the general commanded. "Put the TéléCom down, Marcellus."

The Patriarche snarled at the general's blatant disobedience. Marcellus paused, his chest tightening as his gaze bounced between his superior and his superior's superior. But General Bonnefaçon was no longer even looking at Marcellus *or* the Patriarche. He was back to looking at the monitor. Something on it had caught his attention.

"Proceed," the Patriarche commanded Marcellus.

"No." The general stepped even closer to the monitor, his eyes dark and intense, his jaw hardened.

"General Bonnefaçon," the Patriarche spat, the rage rolling off him in thick waves. "How dare you—"

"Shut up!" the general said, holding up a hand to the Patriarche's face.

Marcellus was certain the Patriarche was going to have a heart attack right then and there. Eyes blazing, Lyon Paresse took a furious step toward the general, but was suddenly held back by Chaumont who whispered something in his ear.

The Patriarche's fists clenched, but he reluctantly stayed put.

Marcellus studied the general, trying to figure out what had caught his attention. He approached carefully and stood beside the general. He stared up at the monitor, which still displayed Citizen Rousseau's lifeless body sprawled out on the gurney.

"What is it?" the warden asked, walking over from his desk.

For a long moment, the general didn't respond. He just continued to stare at the monitor, his eyes flicking furiously over the screen. Then, out of nowhere, he roared out a command. "Rolland, zoom in on her left hand!"

The technicien jabbed furiously at her control panel until the microcam pushed forward and to the left, focusing entirely on the prisoner's hand.

"More," the general said.

Rolland did as she was told until Rousseau's long, skeletal fingers were the only thing in the frame.

The Patriarche hurried over and stood on the other side of the general. "What's wrong?"

"Wait," the general said, his eyes narrowing.

Everyone in the room was as still and silent as that corpse. All eyes were trained on the monitor.

And then, it happened.

It was so small, so fast, it was almost imperceptible. In fact, it *was* imperceptible until just a few moments ago. But now, it was all Marcellus could see.

The smallest finger on Citizen Rousseau's left hand twitched ever so slightly, before falling still again.

"There!" the general called out.

The Patriarche gasped and stumbled back, away from the screen, as though Citizen Rousseau might come crawling through the monitor to strangle him. Marcellus took a step forward, leaning in to get a better look.

"She's alive?" he whispered.

But before anyone could answer, it happened again. The smallest finger. The smallest movement. But there was something very strange about it. Something almost familiar. As though it were the exact *same* movement. The same twitch, followed by the same stillness.

The general must have come to an identical conclusion, because a second later, he reached into his pocket, unfolded his TéléCom, and bellowed into the screen. "This is General Bonnefaçon to Bastille Central Command. We need an immediate status update for prisoner 40102. Please send the nearest droid to the morgue for visual confirmation."

The general waited. Everyone waited. Finally, the Patriarche stomped forward, and before the general could stop him, he jabbed his finger against the screen of the general's TéléCom, routing the audio to the device's external speakers just in time to hear the response. The robotic voice was coming from thousands of kilomètres away, but Marcellus still felt it as though it were being whispered directly into his ear.

"There is currently one droid stationed in the Med Center. Visual status cannot be confirmed. Prisoner 40102 is no longer in the Bastille morgue."

"Sols!" General Bonnefaçon shouted.

"What's going on?" the Patriarche demanded. "I don't understand. How can she not be in the morgue?" He swatted at the screen. "I can see her right there with my own eyes."

"The feed has been looped," the general explained hastily. "She's not there. She's gone. We're watching an archive."

Gone.

The impossible word tumbled around Marcellus's brain as he stared at the image on the screen. At that tiny finger and that tiny intermittent twitch.

"Looped?" the Patriarche repeated, as though it were far too advanced a term for him and he was still having trouble keeping up.

But the general didn't have time for any more explanations. He was already back on his TéléCom. Even though his face was twisted with rage, his voice was eerily calm. "This is General Bonnefaçon to flight dispatch. I want every combatteur we have on the Masséna Spacecraft carrier en route to Bastille immediately." There was a short pause before General Bonnefaçon spoke again, and this time, the words sent a thrill of anticipation ricocheting down Marcellus's spine. A thrill of, dare he think it, *hope*. "The Vangarde have just declared war on the Regime."

- CHAPTER 13 -
ALOUETTE

THE RECEPTION ROOM OF THE BLOOD BORDEL WAS small, dotted with rickety tables, threadbare rugs, and low-hanging lamps. Through the dim glow, Alouette could make out chairs covered with worn-out velvet, and on a long, sagging couch that had seen better days, a few girls huddled together. The moment Alouette stepped into the room, they looked up at her, their eyes big and round and glassy. More girls emerged from the corners and shadows, like small creatures poking tentatively out from a cave.

Alouette hesitated for a moment, unsure where to go or what to say. The haunted, round eyes just stared at her, and no one said a word.

Until Alouette felt something touch her elbow, light and gentle like a butterfly.

"What lovely hair," a voice whispered.

Alouette looked down to see a tiny girl in a silky azure dress, stained at its collar and shabby at its hems. The girl's eyes were wider and more haunted than all the others in the room. But she was gazing up at Alouette with a shy smile. "Is this your first time?"

"Actually, I—" Alouette tried to say, but another girl in an ill-fitting yellow dress sidled up to them.

"If you relax, it doesn't hurt at all," she said. Her voice was rough and harsh, but her expression was kind.

Alouette's gaze moved quickly over the girls. She tried to picture her mother sitting there, on that couch, in this room, huddled and staring. But she simply couldn't grip the image in her mind. It was too loose, too slippery. And she didn't have enough to hold on to. She had no real memories of her mother. No kind eyes. No gentle, reassuring arms embracing her. No scents. Nothing.

All she had was a small titan box stashed away in her bag.

And those words flitting around her like nasty, biting insects.

"... *the daughter of a worthless blood whore.*"

That horrible cyborg inspecteur, Limier, had said this about Alouette back in the Forest Verdure. The words were spiteful and malicious, and at first, Alouette hadn't dared believe them. Until she remembered that cyborgs were incapable of lying. It was part of their programming. And that's when Alouette realized the words—as painful as they were to hear— were a clue.

Her mother had once been one of these girls. She'd sold her blood in a bordel. *This* bordel. It had to be. Montfer was the last known location Alouette had for her mother, and Dahlia had said this was the only bordel in the city.

"Just remember, don't accept the first offer they give you," said the girl in yellow, nudging Alouette with her pointy elbow. "You can always negotiate a higher price."

"She's right," the tiny girl in blue whispered, still smiling. "I learned that lesson too late."

"But I'm not here to—"Alouette began, but she was cut off again as an authoritative voice rang across the room.

"Heloise! What are you doing, standing there chattering?"

An older woman emerged from the darkness wearing green medical scrubs as threadbare and stained as the rugs on the floor. Her hair was pulled back into a severe bun and her small, shrewish eyes glimmered in the room's low light.

"I called you five minutes ago," she went on. "It's time for your treatment."

The small girl in the blue dress—Heloise—gave Alouette one last smile, before wordlessly slinking away and disappearing behind an unmarked door at the other end of the reception area.

"And Zéphine," continued the woman. "You can go in now too."

As Alouette watched the girl in the yellow dress follow Heloise through the door, she suddenly couldn't help but notice how young she was. So frail and thin, she looked almost sickly. All of them did, in fact. There was a drabness about their complexions, a hint of bruises and rashes on their bare shoulders, and their eyes were sunken and tired.

Alouette had read about the illegal blood trade in the Chronicles. Young girls being lured to the bordels to have the nutrients stripped from their blood and shipped off to some fabrique to turn them into rejuvenating face creams and injections for the upper estates. Girls could make ten times what they made in a Ministère-assigned job. But many girls went too far. Sold too much. They grew thin and sick and wasted. And many of them ended up in the morgue.

All for the sake of a larg.

Was that how her mother had died? Had she sold too much? Alouette had always been told her mother had gotten very sick, but no one had divulged more than that. Was this place responsible for her death?

"Welcome, chérie." Alouette turned toward the woman in the green scrubs who was now speaking directly to her. "It's always nice to see a new face here. And such a pretty one too. I'm Médecin Clodie."

Alouette studied the woman's clean, unmarked features. There was no way she was a true médecin. She would have had cyborg circuitry implanted. Alouette guessed it was a made-up title. Something they told girls to make them feel more comfortable. To make the establishment feel more professional.

A blatant lie.

There was nothing professional about murder.

Despite her disdain, Alouette forced herself to smile back, trying to match the woman's kind, open expression. If she was going to get any answers here, she couldn't let her disgust show.

"We're glad you came to visit us tonight," said Clodie, still smiling. "Would you please come with me?"

The woman led Alouette into an adjacent room as dimly lit and shabby as the reception area. But there were no sagging couches or faded rugs here. Instead, the bare floor was grimy and stained—with what, Alouette shuddered to imagine—and in the middle of the room sat a long row of reclining chairs with tattered leather seats and rusting armrests. Next to each chair was a sinister gray machine covered in wheezing pumps, clanking pistons, and small spinning filters. Half of the recliners held young girls, some seemingly no older than twelve, whose spindly arms were connected to the whirring contraptions by long tubes filled with dark crimson liquid.

The other recliners were empty.

Waiting for their next victims.

Alouette watched in horror as Heloise climbed onto one of the empty chairs, pushed back the ragged sleeve of her blue dress, and extended her left arm. Next to her, another woman in dirty scrubs prepared a long needle. Alouette's stomach flipped at the sight, and she had to look away.

"Right in here," said Clodie, ushering Alouette through another door. This room was small and held nothing but an old desk and two scuffed chairs. Clodie closed the door and took the seat behind the desk before gesturing for Alouette to sit. "I'm just going to ask you some preliminary questions." She flashed Alouette another fake smile.

"Actually . . . ," Alouette said, glancing nervously at the closed door. She turned back to Clodie, who had pulled a TéléCom from the desk drawer and was now tapping into it. "You see . . . I was just hoping I might speak with whoever is in charge."

"The madame is very busy," said Clodie dismissively. "What is your age?"

"I really need to speak to her."

Clodie's smile grew tighter. "I will check if she's available as soon as we're done here. Your age?"

"Sixteen."

The woman tapped something into the TéléCom and looked up again. "And where do you live?"

"Can you check if she's available now?" Alouette asked, growing restless. "It's very important."

The woman pursed her lips and spoke into the TéléCom. "Client prefers not to divulge location." She turned back to Alouette. "Have you recently been exposed to any metals or disease like the rot?"

"Please," Alouette said. "I only need a few minutes of her time."

The woman sighed and stood up. "Apparently, we have to do this the *other* way." She reached into the drawer of her desk, pulled out a small spherical object, and handed it to Alouette. "Hold this please."

Alouette took the object and studied it curiously. It looked like one of the marbles Jacqui used to let Alouette play with back in the Refuge when she was little, except this was twice the size and had strange rectangular indentations covering the surface. "What is—OUCH!" She dropped it on the desk and stared at her index finger, which now had a small pin prick of blood on the tip.

Clodie picked up the sphere and turned it around, examining a row of tiny colored lights that had appeared on the surface. "Oh my," she said delightedly, a genuine smile swiftly replacing the artificial one. "You are a prime candidate for extraction. Your blood nutrient level is off the charts."

Alouette tensed, frustration coursing through her nutrient-dense veins. The woman had tricked her.

"I'm happy to report we can offer you fifty largs in exchange for an extraction. The procedure is quite simple. And painless. We don't actually *take* your blood—that's a popular misconception. We simply draw it out, a little at a time, extract the nutrients we need and return the blood back to your—"

"No," Alouette said, narrowing her eyes.

"If you need something to help you relax, we can offer you that too."

"I'm not selling you my blood. I want to talk to the madame."

Clodie flinched but quickly recomposed herself. "It's a very competitive offer. More than you can expect from any other establishment."

Alouette jumped out of her seat. This place was making her too anxious. Maybe she should just forget the whole thing. The madame probably didn't even remember her mother. It had been more than fifteen years ago. "I'm sorry," she murmured. "This was a mistake. I'm—"

"Wait," Clodie stood up and smoothed out the front of her scrubs. "We don't normally do this, so please don't tell the other girls. But"—she paused, lowering her voice and taking in a breath—"a hundred largs."

Alouette stared at the woman, dumbfounded. She was really going to offer her a hundred largs for the nutrients in her blood? That was ludicrous. That was appalling. That was . . .

Desperate.

Alouette scanned the woman's angular features, which were taut in what could only be described as desperation. Alouette remembered what the girl in yellow had told her back in the reception area—"*don't accept the first offer*"—and an idea came to her. She arranged her face in what she hoped was a tenacious expression and stood up straight. "I'm not agreeing to anything until I talk to the madame."

"I assure you the madame has given me full authority to negotiate on the establishment's behalf."

"Good," said Alouette defiantly. "Then, if you want the nutrients in my"—she fought back a gag—"*blood*, I'm sure you'll have no problem getting me a meeting with her."

The woman's jaw tightened. She stared long and hard at Alouette. Despite her churning stomach, Alouette forced herself to stare long and hard back. "Fine," the woman finally relented. "Wait here. I'll see if she's available."

As soon as Clodie was gone, Alouette collapsed back into the chair, like she'd just swum the Secana Sea. But she also felt a swell of pride. Two weeks away from the Refuge, and Alouette was already becoming a different person.

"You asked to see me?" came a woman's voice a few minutes later. Alouette pivoted in her chair as her gaze landed first on a shiny, heeled shoe, then a sleek gold dress and even sleeker shoulder-length golden hair, before finally resting on the most disturbing face Alouette had ever seen. The woman's eyebrows were arched unnaturally high, as though a string were pulling them straight toward the ceiling. The skin of her forehead looked as though it had been peeled off, stretched to the limit, and then pasted back on. And her cheekbones appeared to be in the entirely wrong place. Was this what those poor girls' blood was being used for? To make someone look like *that*? Alouette fought hard to not react to the sight.

The woman, however, clearly was not fighting as hard. Because as soon as her gaze landed on Alouette, a gasp escaped her lips, and her eyes widened with a look of pure disbelief.

Alouette self-consciously touched her hair, her face, the front of her sweater.

The madame blinked, as though trying to disengage herself from a bad dream, and let out a tinkling laugh. "Oh my. That was rude. So sorry about that. You'll have to excuse me. I thought—you just look like someone I used to—" The madame squinted at Alouette again before shaking her head. "It's uncanny, really."

With a squeeze of her chest, Alouette suddenly understood.

I look like her. I look like my mother.

Straightaway, hope fluttered inside Alouette. Perhaps this hadn't been a mistake after all.

Alouette remained silent as the woman composed herself and then continued into the small room and took a seat in Clodie's chair. She folded her hands regally across her lap. "I'm Madame Blanchard. I am in charge of this facility. My médecin informed me that you are an ideal candidate for extraction but are having some reservations about the process. And while that is to be understood for someone who is experiencing it for the first time, I can assure you that it's quite safe."

The lie slid so easily out of the woman's red-stained lips, it made

Alouette's teeth clench. "That's not why I'm here, actually. I'm looking for information about—"

"Lisole," the madame said with a knowing smile.

Alouette felt a tingle race through her body. Was that her name? Her *mother's* name?

How many years had she been waiting for this? Lying awake at night dreaming about it. Just one name—two syllables—and suddenly she felt more complete than she had in years.

Lisole.

"You *must* be related to her," Madame Blanchard went on. "I feel like I'm looking at a ghost. You're almost an exact replica. Your face, your hair, even your blood. Hers was quite rich in nutrients as well." The madame's gaze went wistful for a moment, as though her thoughts had snagged on some distant memory. "She was an ideal client. While she was around." She blinked out of her brief trance and refocused on Alouette. "Are you a niece? A cousin?"

"No," Alouette said, slightly confused by the question. "I'm her daughter."

The madame flinched as though someone had slapped her. "Her daughter? Surely you can't be—"

"I'm Madeline."

Madame Blanchard's eyes narrowed, almost distrustfully. She shifted in her chair.

"I was hoping you could tell me a little about her," Alouette forged on. "Where she was from. Who her family was. Even her last name would help. Anything. Please. All I know was that she used to come here and then . . ." Alouette dropped her gaze to the floor, trying to conceal the malice she felt toward this place, this woman, this whole operation. "And then she died."

"Yes," Madame Blanchard said, although there was something suddenly cold about her tone. Distant. "I was very sorry to hear about her passing. Like I said, she was a good client. And had become somewhat of a friend. She used to rent a room from me upstairs."

Alouette's small seed of hope suddenly blossomed until it filled her entire body, chasing all the resentment away. "Really? What was she like? Did you know my father? Did you ever meet me?"

Madame Blanchard laughed at Alouette's eagerness. "She was lovely. Bright and beautiful and very full of life. She loved you quite dearly. She used to bring you in here when she would come for her extractions. You were just a little baby then. The other girls would play with you while Lisole was in the extraction room. But I'm sorry I don't know who your father is. She never spoke of him. And most people in here don't use any last names. So, I'm afraid I'm not much help there either."

Alouette scooted to the edge of her chair, desperate to keep this woman talking. She'd had a taste of truth—her truth—and like the girls plugged into those dreadful machines in the next room, she was hooked. She wanted more. She craved it. "Do you remember anything else?"

The madame closed her eyes, thinking. "Lisole was a sweet girl. I had grown quite fond of her."

Alouette reached into her sac and cradled the little titan box that had belonged to her mother, squeezing it hopefully between her fingers. She desperately wished she knew what was inside. That she could see what was hiding underneath the two majestic creatures carved onto its lid. But no matter how hard she'd tried to pry the box open, it had stayed sealed shut.

The madame opened her eyes and smiled at Alouette, but it was a crooked smile that never seemed to reach her eyes.

"I was very sorry when she left town," Madame Blanchard went on.

"Left?" Alouette withdrew her hand from the bag. "What do you mean? When did she leave? Where did she go?"

Alouette knew her mother had left her with the Renards because she couldn't afford to take care of her, but she'd always assumed her mother had stayed in Montfer. After all, Sister Jacqui had told her that her mother had died in Montfer.

"I don't know where she went. She just left. Skipped out on the rent. Four months of rent, actually." There was a sudden edge to the madame's voice.

"When was this?" Alouette asked.

The madame sighed. "Let's see. It was about two years after the end of the rebellion. Probably around Month 7 or 8 of 490."

Alouette quickly did the calculations in her head. Month 7 or 8 of 490, she would have been not quite two years old. Which means her mother had left Montfer right after she'd dropped Alouette at the Renards.

"Do you know *why* she left?"

The madame shifted in her seat, suddenly looking uncomfortable with the question.

"Do you?" Alouette pressed.

"I always assumed she left because she was in mourning and wanted to escape her grief." The madame stared down at her hands, trying to avoid eye contact with Alouette. "But now I'm not so sure."

"In mourning? Over who?"

The madame tittered uneasily. "See, that's where my confusion starts. Up until five minutes ago, I thought—and with good reason—that she was mourning *you*."

Alouette's stomach dropped. "Me?" she whispered, hardly able to form the word. "B-b-but why would she be mourning me?"

"Good question." The madame clucked her tongue. "One I've been trying to answer since you *claimed* to be Madeline."

Alouette's heart raced at the madame's accusatory tone. She *was* Madeline, wasn't she? She was the daughter of Lisole, the woman they'd been talking about.

The madame went on. "And if you *are* who you claim to be—which, let's face it, how could you not be, looking like that—then the next obvious question is, whose funeral did I attend in 490?"

The small room began to spin.

Dead.

She was supposed to be dead. There had been a funeral. For her?

Alouette barely had time to register the madame's words before she heard a soft click of the door opening behind her. She turned around but Clodie was already there. Already upon her. By the time Alouette felt the pinch at her neck, it was too late. Dizziness instantly overtook her, and she fell straight into clouds.

**SYED... ,
AIM...**

Date shelved:
12/20/2021

Patron number: 1272945
Item barcode: 39078095432960

Exp Date:
12/28/2021

E. D. Locke Public Library

5920 Milwaukee St.

McFarland, WI 53716

608-838-9030

mcfarlandlibrary.org

Date: 12/21/2021

Time: 7:34:47 PM

Fines/Fees Owed: $0.00

Total Checked Out This Session: 2

Checked Out

Title: The righteous /
Barcode: 39078105102066
Due Date: 2022-01-19

Title: Between burning worlds /
Barcode: 39078095432960
Due Date: 2022-01-19

Thank you for visiting the library!

- CHAPTER 14 -
MARCELLUS

"ARRIVAL ON BASTILLE IN SEVENTEEN MINUTES." THE voice of Capitaine Apolline Moreau blasted into Marcellus's audio patch, making him feel as though the combatteurs were soaring through the next room, as opposed to thousands of kilomètres away en route to Bastille.

Marcellus tried to inhale, but it felt like he was drowning on dry land. He hadn't been able to take a proper breath since it was announced that Citizen Rousseau was dead. And then, *not* dead. He felt helpless. Out of control. He didn't know what the Vangarde were up to on Bastille, but he knew, that in seventeen minutes, they would be in for a very big surprise. And Marcellus had no way to warn them.

"Seventeen minutes?" the Patriarche barked. "Can't those blasted things move any faster?"

Marcellus saw his grandfather flinch. "These are state-of-the-art crafts," the general explained defensively. "Bastille is more than a hundred thousand kilomètres from the spacecraft carrier. It takes time to get there."

The Patriarche harrumphed. "Well, meanwhile, the Vangarde are getting away with Citizen Rousseau!"

Marcellus retreated back to his corner, tucking himself next to the table that held the giant lit-up model of the System Divine. It was the only place in the room that felt relatively safe right now.

The general turned to Rolland. "Have you located the source of the hack yet?"

The technicien was currently sitting in the midst of what looked like the wreckage of a tornado. Monitors had been stripped from the walls, plastique panels had been yanked from consoles, and wires and motherboards hung in twisted loops. Rolland had torn apart the entire left side of the warden's office, trying to figure out what was corrupting the morgue security feeds. Meanwhile, the archived footage of "dead" Citizen Rousseau was still playing on a loop on the center monitor, and all around it were views from other parts of the prison compound: the spaceport, the cantine, the cell blocks, the dispatch bunker, even the washrooms.

They all *looked* normal. But it was now impossible to tell if any of them had been looped as well.

"Negative," Rolland replied, the circuitry in her cheek and forehead humming calmly. "I can't isolate the breach. There is no evidence of any tampering."

"We already checked the integrity of the security systems after the two Vangarde operatives were arrested," the warden reminded the general. "Nothing had been compromised."

"Well, they're managing to hack that morgue feed somehow!" the general thundered to Rolland. "And Sols know how many others. Find out how!"

Rolland nodded and disappeared back into her tangle of wires.

"What are the droids reporting?" the general asked Warden Gallant.

The small, stocky man wiped sweat from his brow. "No unusual activity reported. And there are currently droids stationed all over the spaceport. If the Vangarde try to land a ship on Bastille—"

"Who says they'll use the spaceport?" the general snapped. "Our own ships can land on almost any flat surface. They could be on the far side of the moon for all we know."

The warden's lips puckered like a fish. He clearly hadn't thought of that.

"Continue to search everywhere," the general commanded. "I want droids covering every square centimètre of that moon. Tell them to fire on anyone and any ships on sight. *Lethal* mode only."

The warden nodded and returned to his desk to relay the orders into his TéléCom.

"Arrival on Bastille in fourteen minutes," Capitaine Moreau reported.

"Tell them to speed up!" The Patriarche stepped forward but soon retreated after a sharp but mollifying look from his advisor.

"Rolland," the general said suddenly, as though an idea had just occurred to him. "Don't the satellite feeds for Bastille run through a different network? Which means it's likely they wouldn't be compromised by the same hack?"

Rolland nodded and the general was immediately in motion, his fingers flying across the screen of his TéléCom. A moment later, one of the monitors on the wall filled with a grainy, distorted view of the prison compound from space. As the general zoomed in, the image got closer but only slightly less blurry.

"How are you going to find them?" the Patriarche asked incredulously, echoing Marcellus's own thoughts. "They could be anywhere!"

The general ignored him and continued dragging his fingertip across the screen of his TéléCom. The satellite imagery shifted around, showing what looked like nothing more than a quiet, sleeping prison.

Are the Vangarde even there? Marcellus wondered. Whatever was happening on that moon, the Vangarde were doing a stellar job of making it look like just another night on Bastille. But he supposed he should expect nothing less from a rebel group that had spent the past seventeen years in hiding.

"Arrival on Bastille in eleven minutes," Moreau reported to the room.

Marcellus returned his attention to the large replica of the System Divine sitting on the table next to him, trying to imagine that fleet of combatteurs racing through the skies, getting closer and closer to Bastille with each passing second.

"The droids are currently searching the exterior of the main prison building, and multiple teams are en route to the zyttrium exploits," the warden reported from his desk.

Marcellus was about to pull his gaze away from the model when something strange caught his eye. There was something *off* about it. He couldn't quite put his finger on what it was, but the model looked different somehow. If he hadn't spent countless hours over the years staring at that thing, wishing he were on any other planet but this one, he probably wouldn't have noticed. But now he couldn't *un*-notice.

Inconspicuously, he hunched down, trying to get a better look at the model. It wasn't the alignment of the planets that was off. They all looked intact, all twelve of them hovering in perfect orbit around Sol 1 at the center, with Sols 2 and 3 dancing alone in the farthest reaches of the system. Laterre hung perfectly positioned between the ice-white planet of their ally Reichenstat and the marbled blue-and-green globe of their enemy, Albion. But it was the luminous, amber-colored moon suspended next to Laterre that seemed altered somehow.

Bastille.

"Still no progress on locating the source of the breach," Rolland reported from her position in front of the open control panel. "I've tried rebooting the system and reconfiguring all connections, but nothing has worked. The Vangarde must somehow be overriding the signals from the outside."

"How on Laterre are they doing that?" the warden asked.

"I do not know, sir," replied Rolland. "But I'm working on it."

Marcellus squinted at the glowing miniscule replica of Laterre's moon. There was definitely something different about it. The color was off. It was just a tad too orange. And the size was just a touch too large. He reached out a finger and curiously pushed the tiny sphere around its orbit.

"What was that?" the Patriarche shouted, and Marcellus glanced up to see him staring at the center monitor, where Citizen Rousseau's body still filled the screen.

"What was what?" the general asked impatiently.

"The footage from the morgue. It just . . . flickered."

The general turned to Rolland. "Did you do that?"

Rolland's circuitry flashed in concentration as her gaze darted between the monitor and the control panel. "I don't believe so, sir."

Marcellus glanced down at his hand which was still lingering near the replica of Bastille. A shiver ricocheted down his spine.

Could it be . . . ?

Careful to make sure everyone's back was still turned to him, he reached out and touched the model again, this time, wrapping his entire hand around the tiny illuminated sphere of Bastille.

The center monitor filled with static. Everyone reacted at once. Marcellus released the replica as though it were hot to the touch and the screen instantly returned to normal.

"Damn the Sols!" the general swore. "Rolland, what is going on? We need those feeds fixed. We are completely blind here!"

Marcellus's gaze darted suspiciously back to the model. He thought of those two women who had been caught breaking into this very office two weeks ago. Jacqui and Denise.

"We already checked the integrity of the security systems after the two Vangarde operatives were arrested. Nothing had been compromised."

That's what the warden had just said. And the general had told Marcellus something similar two weeks ago. Everyone was so certain the two operatives had failed in their mission.

But what if they hadn't?

"Arrival on Bastille in nine minutes."

The general stood up straighter. "Moreau, connect me to your cockpit cam."

"Copy. Connecting."

A second later, one of the monitors on the wall switched to the view from Capitaine Moreau's combatteur.

And there it was. Embedded in a vast mantle of blackness and surrounded by a thousand shimmering stars, Bastille glowed a goldish-yellow. Its amber rocks like the burning embers of a fire. Marcellus felt like his heart might thud right out of his chest.

"General!" the warden shouted, jumping up from his desk. "There's an update from the droids. The power has just gone out in the Trésor tower."

"WHAT?" the Patriarche boomed. "What does that mean?"

"What caused the outage?" the general asked with impressive composure.

The warden paused to listen to the rest of the update. "Source of the outage is unclear. There was a disturbance in the nearest power cell. The droids are currently running diagnostics on the grid, but this can't be a coincidence, right?"

Marcellus watched as his grandfather calmly and thoughtfully approached the center monitor, which was still displaying the looped footage from the morgue. He stood before it, hands clasped behind his back, and stared deeply into the screen, as though he were trying to look *through* the Vangarde's hack and see what was really happening on that moon. The light from the monitor's screen lit up the harsh lines and crevices of the general's face, making him suddenly look ten years older than he was, and ten years more hardened.

"Where is the morgue?" the general finally asked, turning toward the warden.

Gallant's eyes went wide as everything seemed to clatter into place in his mind. "It's on the top floor of the Trésor tower, sir."

The general was back on his TéléCom in a flash, whisking his fingertip across the screen. The satellite imagery on the monitor blurred and fuzzed in response. Then, a moment later, the view came to a juddering stop and the general zoomed in as far as the distant cam would allow.

A loud gasp erupted around the room. Marcellus stared speechlessly at the roof of the Trésor tower. In the center of a neat grid of cooling vents, crisscrossing pipes, and water towers, stood three figures huddled close together. As though trying to stay warm or hidden or both.

"Are those prisoners?" Chaumont asked, squinting at the slightly blurry image on the screen.

Marcellus leaned in for a closer look. Through the darkness, he could see that the three figures were dressed in Bastille blue uniforms, just like the one his father had worn. And they all had hair that fell to the middles of their backs.

"What is that?" Warden Gallant cried out, suddenly pointing at something behind one of the vents.

The general maneuvered the satellite cam to the right, and as the image processed and began to clear, Marcellus felt the last sips of air get sucked right out of the room.

"It's her!" the Patriarche called out, as though he were the only one in the room to recognize her. But of course, he wasn't. Of course, they *all* recognized her instantly.

It was Citizen Rousseau. Lying on a makeshift stretcher. Looking one shudder away from death.

"Gallant!" the general shouted, startling Marcellus away from the frail, white-haired woman on the screen. "Send droids to the roof of the Trésor tower immediately."

The warden glanced up from his TéléCom with panic scrawled all over his face. "Sir, the blackout cut the power to the exterior elevator. It's the only access to the roof."

Fragile hope began to flutter in Marcellus's stomach like a flock of beautiful songbirds. They were doing it. The Vangarde were outsmarting the Ministère.

"That's ridiculous. It can't be!" the Patriarche blustered. "Tell them to climb up the side of the Sol-damn building if they have to."

The warden shared a knowing look with the general and Marcellus instantly recognized the defeat in both of their eyes. But it was Warden Gallant who relayed the bad news, looking like he might actually start crying. "Droids can't climb, sir. Until the power is restored, there is no way they can get onto that roof."

The general slammed his TéléCom down on the warden's desk, causing everyone in the room to jump. "Can't you see what's going on here? The Vangarde are using our own tech against us."

Marcellus had never seen his grandfather look so wild and unhinged. He had the eyes of a mad man.

"I-I don't understand how this could happen!" the warden stammered, glancing anxiously between the looped footage of Citizen Rousseau in the morgue and the satellite image of her on the roof, weak and fragile but very much alive. As though he couldn't quite believe they were the same person. "She's the most-guarded prisoner on Bastille."

The general turned his vengeful eyes back to the monitors. "My guess is somehow they were able to make it look like Rousseau was dead," he stated, his composure slowly returning. "Or, at least dead enough to fool the droids. Probably something slipped into her food by a kitchen worker. That got her out of solitary confinement, the most secure area of the prison. Then, these prisoners—Med Center workers I imagine—got her out of the morgue while we watched looped footage of her dead body. And now . . ." his voice trailed off as something flickered on the satellite imagery. A slender beam of light cut across the rooftop, momentarily illuminating the faces of the prisoners.

The general snatched up his TéléCom again and zoomed out on the image, until they could see almost the entire prison complex.

"The combatteurs?" the warden asked him hopefully. "Have they arrived?"

The general shook his head as a shadow passed over his face. "Negative."

And that's when Marcellus saw it. The lone ship descending from the sky. Heading straight toward the Trésor tower.

"What on Laterre?" The Patriarche stared wide-eyed at the monitor.

"That's certainly not one of ours," Chaumont said, echoing the disbelief in everyone's eyes.

"How on Laterre did they get past our shields?" the warden bellowed, his face twisting with sudden rage.

Marcellus's mouth fell open. It was the strangest ship he had ever seen. With a hull made up of a series of mismatched panels, it looked as if it had been cobbled together with parts of decommissioned cruiseurs and perhaps a transporteur or two. The wings jutted out in odd directions and a large window bubbled up over the top of the cockpit like a single protruding eye.

"Gallant!" the general seethed, his gaze locked on the descending craft. "We need power restored to the tower. Now."

The warden nodded and murmured a series of hushed, angry commands into his TéléCom.

"So, we're just supposed to sit here and watch them take her?" the Patriarche asked, looking from Marcellus to the warden to the general. But no one dared reply. The entire room was in shock at the sight playing out before them. A tense silence filled the air, as the obvious and irrefutable answer to the Patriarche's question seemed to descend over the room as slowly and surely as that strange craft descending over the surface of Bastille.

Yes.

"Arrival on Bastille in six minutes." Capitaine Moreau's voice crashed through the silence.

The general snapped to attention, grabbed for his TéléCom, and in an assertive and unwavering voice said, "Capitaine Moreau. This is General Bonnefaçon. We are running out of time. The enemy is descending toward the roof of the Trésor tower. As soon as the target is in sight, I want all explosifs deployed. Spare nothing. Blow up the whole tower if you have to, but no one is getting off that moon alive."

Marcellus froze as the general's directives reverberated in his mind like a clap of thunder.

The Trésor tower?

"But, sir," Moreau replied, sounding slightly unsettled by the command. "There will be prisoners inside. At least a thousand human lives at risk."

"This is Citizen Rousseau we're talking about!" the general roared. "She gets out and there will be even *more* lives at risk."

"Copy," Moreau said, uncertainty still lingering in her voice. "Pilotes, prime your weapons."

Marcellus's gaze darted from the satellite image of the roof to the view from Moreau's cockpit cam. The great burning globe of Bastille was growing larger by the second. He had to do *something*. Fueled by a new wave of urgency, he moved silently toward the door and slipped, unseen, into the hallway. The second he was alone, he unfolded his TéléCom and clicked on the screen. "Access Bastille Central Command," he whispered into the device. "Locate Prisoner 51562."

"Locating," the TéléCom reported. Then, a moment later, Marcellus's pulse ratcheted up three notches as a little blinking dot appeared on the screen and the device confirmed his worst nightmare. "Prisoner 51562. Location found. Trésor tower."

CHAPTER 15

CHATINE

ZAP.

The noise was unlike anything Chatine had ever heard. Like a fly buzzing its last buzz. A loose wire shorting out in the rain. Chatine snapped awake and opened her eyes. But all she saw in the cramped eleventh-floor cell block of the Trésor tower was darkness.

No orange glow, no unblinking eyes staring back at her, only a shroud of black. Was she dreaming? Chatine groggily pushed herself up onto her elbow and peered around. It was as dark as the exploits.

Then, a series of lights flickered on in the bunks around her. Not the small orange eyes that blanketed this entire building. Instead, it was the familiar, bluish glow of Skins.

Chatine tapped on her own embedded screen and leaned over the side of her bunk to whisper to the woman who slept below. "What's happening?"

The woman shook her head, fear glazing her eyes.

Tentatively, Chatine climbed out of her bunk and pulled on her boots. She could hear a commotion coming from the center of the tower, the unmistakable sound of feet pounding on the metal steps of the stairwell.

Someone pushed past her and she grabbed him by the shirt sleeve. "What the fric is going on?"

"The cell block door is open!" he whispered giddily before wriggling from her grasp and darting toward the nearest bridge.

Chatine shook her head, trying to clear the last cobwebs of sleep from her mind.

The cell block door is open?

"Power must be out," someone murmured to another inmate as they pushed past Chatine. "Let's go!"

Chatine blinked, still unable to process what was happening. Had these people lost their minds? Had the thin atmosphere of Bastille fritzed their brains? Even if the door of the tower was open, where were they planning to go? They were on the Sol-damn moon! What were they going to do? Stand out on the craggy surface and flag down a passing voyageur? And that's if they even *got* out the door. More droids were appearing by the second. This whole stupid lot was going to get themselves tazed or paralyzed before they'd even reached the central stairwell.

"Idiots," Chatine muttered under her breath as she shoved her way through the crowd, back toward her bunk. Let the stupid sots do whatever they wanted. There was no way *she* was going to run the fool's errand of trying to escape an inescapable prison.

"Prisoner 51562."

A metal claw clamped down on her shoulder, stopping her in her tracks. Chatine shuddered and turned around to see a pair of piercing orange droid eyes boring down on her from behind its PermaSteel exoskeleton.

Fear thundered through her. "I-I was just trying to get back to my bunk," she stammered. "I had nothing to do with any of this, I swear. I'm not trying to escape."

Muscles clenching, she braced herself for another painful jolt of the tazeur. Or even a paralyzing rayonette pulse. But the basher didn't move; instead its eyes flickered coolly. "Urgent message for prisoner 51562," it said in a clicking, rhythmic monotone, as though it were reciting some new, unfamiliar programming.

"Message?" she croaked.

"Your life is in danger. You must leave the Trésor tower immediately," the droid continued in the same robotic tone. "It is not safe for you to stay here."

Chatine stared up at the droid, dumbfounded, certain she had misunderstood, or it had malfunctioned. "What?"

"Your life is in danger," the droid repeated. "You must leave the Trésor tower immediately. It is not safe for you to stay here."

It almost sounded like a trap. Were droids even capable of setting traps? She didn't think so. She racked her fog-filled brain, trying to figure out what to do. Was it possible the droid was really trying to warn her about something?

She nearly laughed aloud at the thought. Bashers don't warn prisoners. *Then again, they don't send messages either.*

"Who is the message from?" she blurted out.

The droid's eyes flickered for just a moment, processing her question . . . and its answer.

"Message sent by PompFlic," the droid stated before turning around and clanking back into the fray.

Every molecule and nerve ending in Chatine's body seemed to implode in on itself. Now she was *certain* she had misunderstood. Or permanently lost her mind to the grippe. Because there was no way that droid had just said what she thought it said.

"No, I'm pretty sure it said PompFlic," said another voice. This one was high-pitched and familiar.

Dead Azelle was back.

Maybe Chatine really *was* going insane.

"PompFlic," Azelle repeated curiously. "Isn't that what you called Marcellus Bonnefaçon?"

Chatine's mind was reeling. She glanced out into the commotion of the dark cell block. Inmates were still shoving their way toward the bridges, trying to reach the tower's central staircase.

"Oh, no, I remember now," Azelle went on inside her head. "It's what

Marcellus called *himself.*" She giggled. "That boy is cute, but he really couldn't get the hang of Third Estate slang, could he?"

Chatine shut her eyes, trying to block out the shouts and the thundering sounds of footsteps. She needed to think.

"What's to think about?" Azelle asked. "Marcellus Bonnefaçon sent you that message. Something is happening. Something bad. And he's trying to warn you. You need to find . . ."

Roche.

Chatine's eyes flew open. And suddenly, she was on the move. She sprinted back to her bunk and threw herself up the rungs of the rickety ladder. Reaching into the small tear in her mattress, she searched for the silver ring.

Marcellus's ring.

As her hand clasped around it, she felt a surge of hope. A surge of energy. And more important, a surge of courage.

Azelle was right. He *was* warning her of something. Warning her all the way from Laterre. Which meant . . .

He *hadn't* forgotten about her.

She slipped the ring into the pocket of her uniform and jumped back down to the floor. She was suddenly wide awake. More awake than she'd felt in over two weeks. She jabbed at her Skin, using its dull glow to navigate her way around the neighboring bunks. The commotion had now consumed the whole cell floor. Inmates were charging toward the bridges. Rayonette blasts whooshed past her, burying themselves into unsuspecting flesh.

Chatine dropped to her hands and knees, remembering an old trick her parents had taught her for maneuvering around during a riot. *If the bashers are shooting high, you stay low.*

Crawling through the pandemonium, Chatine headed for Roche's bunk, which was on the other side of the cell block. But even on her hands and knees, it was arduous to move. She was forced to dodge crumpled bodies, trampling footsteps, and the glimmering, terrifying legs of the droids trying to keep order.

"Roche!" she called out as she reached his bunk. She climbed up to the second-level mattress and cringed when she saw the bed was empty. Had he already left? Was he out there in that anarchy?

Chatine pushed toward the cell's inner railing and looked out over the gaping eleven-floor drop. In the low light of the Skins, she could see the winding stairwell in the center of the tower, linked by gangways to the prison cells on each floor. Every single one was crammed full of people shoving and stumbling toward the staircase, causing the PermaSteel grating under their feet to rattle in the gloom. Droids stood behind the railings of each floor, firing their rayonettes toward the stairs. Prisoners stumbled and fell as pulses buried into their flesh, but it only seemed to cause more chaos as the other inmates tried to maneuver around them.

Chatine felt a surge of frustration. How was she even supposed to get down there? What good was Marcellus's warning if she couldn't escape the tower?

A scream broke into her thoughts, and she looked out just in time to see a body being shoved over the edge of one of the gangways. Chatine gripped the railing as the inmate accelerated down, down, down, toward the bottom of the tower far below.

The thud echoed through the entire building, reaching her, even eleven floors up.

Chatine turned away, her heart galloping in her chest. She knew better than to peer over the railing and look. Her nightmares were already bad enough.

Trying to catch her breath, Chatine struggled to come up with a plan. This whole scene reminded her of that horrible riot in the Marsh after Nadette Epernay's execution. The bedlam of bodies and droids and rayonette pulses whooshing past her ears. That had been the day she'd first met Roche. She'd been crawling around on the Marsh floor, and she'd ducked under a stall to find him hiding—

Her thoughts screeched to a halt.

She raced back to the bunk and dropped to her knees again, peering under the lowest mattress. She almost smiled from the relief that rushed through her.

There he was. Tucked into a tiny, shaking ball, with his head buried between his knees. The light from her Skin illuminated his soft, recently shaved head. It reminded her of the baby chicks that were sold in the Marsh.

"Roche" she whispered.

He looked up briefly but stiffened and snapped his gaze away the moment he recognized her in the darkness.

Chatine climbed into the cramped space and crouched in front of him. "Roche. Look at me. We need to get out of here."

Roche's jaw pulsed, but still he would not meet her eye.

"Roche, please." Chatine pulled at his elbow. "You have to come with me. We have to get out of here. It's not safe."

He yanked his arm away from her. "I'm not going anywhere with you! You're the one who got me sent here in the first place, *Chatine*," he spat the pronunciation of her real name.

She felt the familiar hollowness of shame spread through her. "I know. I know. I'm sorry. But you need to trust me right now."

"Why?" he asked spitefully. "Why would I ever trust *you* again?"

"Because I got a message!" she shouted, her frustration boiling over. "That said our lives are in danger and that we have to leave the tower immediately."

Roche stared at her, unblinking. "A message? From who?"

"Someone I trust," she said, but Roche only narrowed his eyes in suspicion. "Look," Chatine tried another tack, lowering her voice into what she hoped was a grave, firm tone. "Something is happening on Bastille. Something to do with the power going out."

Roche's gaze softened from suspicion to curiosity. "What do you mean?"

"I don't know," Chatine said helplessly. "And I don't want to wait around to find out. So, come with me right now. We need to get as far away from this tower as possible."

She pulled again on Roche's arm. He didn't move, but he didn't fight back either. His body was as limp as a wet rag. "Roche!"

"Shh!" he said. "I'm thinking."

"There's no time to think!" Chatine cried. "We have to go now."

"Go. Now." Roche repeated slowly, pensively. He peered up at the sagging mattress above their heads as though he were trying to look *through* it, straight out of the tower and all the way to the stars. "'. . . the only way off this moon.'" He sounded like he was in a trance. "It's happening *now*."

Then, suddenly, he was unfurling himself and scrabbling out from under the bunk. Relieved, Chatine darted after him. But to her surprise and then, dread, she saw he was *not* moving toward the nearest stairwell bridge. He was heading toward the railing. He was—she gasped aloud— climbing *onto* the railing!

"Roche!" she screamed, charging forward.

"Watch where you're going, Nov," a giant man barked at her as she screamed past, accidentally stomping on his foot.

Reaching the railing, Chatine glanced up to see Roche hoisting himself up onto the next floor, his legs dangling just above her eyeline. "What the fric are you doing?" she yelled up at him. "Are you out of your Sol-damn mind?"

"The roof!" he called back. "We have to get to the roof."

"What?" Chatine asked, certain now that he *was* out of his Sol-damn mind. But he also was not stopping.

Roche's small boots disappeared above her head, and Chatine felt a rush of annoyance and then determination as she grabbed for the railing and launched herself upward. Her muscles must have weakened during her short time on Bastille, because her climbing skills weren't what they used to be. By the time she pulled herself up to the next floor, her arms ached and she was panting from the effort.

The twelfth-floor cell block was mostly deserted. Everyone had already made their way to the stairwell and the droids had inevitably followed. Chatine and Roche were the only sots trying to get *up* instead of down. And she still had no idea why.

She heard a small grunting sound and stumbled in the darkness until she found Roche kneeling down on the ground, struggling to open an air vent in the wall. The vents were normally secured to keep prisoners from trying to escape, but the power outage must have disabled the locking mechanism, because a moment later, the rusty metal grate swung open and Roche dove inside.

With a groan, Chatine followed after him. The duct was narrow. She could barely wedge her shoulders through, and she had to slither on her belly to keep from knocking her head. "Roche," she said in a harsh whisper. "Are you insane? What the fric are you—"

"Don't you see what's happening?" Roche called back to her, maneuvering deftly on his elbows like he'd climbed through a thousand air ducts before. And he probably had. He *was* a Fret rat, after all. Just like her. "Don't you think it's strange that the power just happened to go out on the very same night that the Vangarde started that fight in the dispatch bunker?"

The Vangarde.

Chatine's crawling slowed. She had nearly forgotten about the man she'd recognized as one of Mabelle's operatives, slipping that that strange vial into the pocket of the long-haired inmate.

"Wait, you *knew* they were Vangarde? How did you—" But the answer came to Chatine a second later. "Clovis," she murmured, remembering the same precisely rolled shirt sleeve on Roche's unofficial bodyguard.

"Did you forget I also used to run messages for them in the Frets?"

Chatine felt a simmer of guilt. Of course she hadn't forgotten that. She could *never* forget that. Those messages were one of the two reasons Roche was here on Bastille. Chatine was the other.

Roche reached a right angle where the air duct bent straight up, and he crept forward until he could stand. Then, using his hands and feet for leverage, he began to shimmy up the narrow shaft.

Chatine followed behind him, her sore muscles aching from the effort, until Roche popped open another vent and they crawled out into a dingy room engulfed in shadows. But it wasn't the darkness that made Chatine falter. It was the smell. A smell worse than anything she had ever experienced in the Frets. This wasn't the unpleasant stink of old vegetables, or unwashed bodies, or rusting PermaSteel. This was death and rot and decay all mixed up into one stomach-curdling stench.

They were *inside* the Bastille morgue.

"Roche," she barked out, coughing from the stink. "What are we doing in here?"

There was no reply. Through the darkness, Chatine could hear the thump of footsteps and the creak and scrape of something being shoved across the floor. Burying her nose in the crook of her elbow, she shone her Skin around the pitch-black room. Then immediately wished she hadn't. The slim beam of light revealed a row of gurneys stacked with wrecked, beaten bodies. Arms dangled by tendons from shoulders. Feet bent downward at odd, terrible angles. Great gashes gnawed their way across dust-splattered skin. And from the faces that were still intact, dead eyes stared up into the darkness and mouths gaped open like they were still gasping for a last drop of clean air.

At the far end of the room, she could see some kind of huge metallic box glinting in the glow from her Skin. But before she could fully make it out, she heard another scraping noise and redirected her light toward Roche, who was pushing through a pile-up of gurneys, clearly looking for something.

"What are you doing?" she whispered, darting over to him.

"I kept overhearing Clovis talk about the morgue," Roche explained hurriedly as he ran his hand along the surface of one of the walls. "'The morgue is the only way off this moon,' he kept saying. The whole time, I just thought he was being morbid. You know, death is the only escape? But now I realize"—he paused and peered curiously up at the ceiling—"he wasn't."

"Wait a minute," Chatine said, trying to follow his whacked line of reasoning. "What exactly are you saying?"

"I'm saying they're breaking her out. Right now. They somehow got her up to the roof from this very room, and we need to figure out how."

Something inside of Chatine started to stir. A memory shoved its way through the fog. Unlike every other memory held captive in her brain, this one was somehow crisp and vivid and sharp.

"This will certainly not be the Vangarde's last attempt to free Citizen Rousseau. They will try again."

Chatine shut her eyes and could suddenly see it all again. As though she were living it now. As though she were right there, sitting in the general's combatteur, soaring over the dark Laterrian landscape on the way back to Vallonay. The general had been talking to Marcellus on his TéléCom, telling him about the Vangarde's attempt to break Citizen Rousseau out of Bastille.

"They will try again."

Chatine felt her heart start to pound. This was ridiculous. This was insane. Citizen Rousseau was locked in solitary confinement deep underground. How on Laterre would the Vangarde even get her into the morgue, let alone up to the roof?

"Roche! Are you saying the Vangarde are—"

"Halt!"

A set of metallic footsteps clanged from behind. Chatine spun to find a lone droid coming toward them, clobbering through the crowded morgue. Its glowing orange eyes sliced through the darkness, and its weaponized arm was aimed straight at Roche's chest.

"Get down!" she screamed.

They dropped to their knees, scrabbling under the gurneys. Rayonette pulses whizzed above their heads. The basher barreled after them, shoving aside gurneys as it went. Dead bodies rolled off and dropped to the floor with the most sickening of sounds.

They kept crawling. But the farther they went, the clearer it became that the droid was chasing them straight toward a dead end. Eventually they would reach the far end of the morgue, and then there was nothing over there but that strange metallic box. . . .

Chatine slowed as the realization began to seep into her bones. Her mind flashed to every single long, labored walk back from the exploits with the chain around her neck and the prison complex looming in the distance. She thought of that glimmering silver chimney shooting up into the sky from the roof of the Trésor tower.

The roof.

"This way!" she bellowed to Roche, scrambling ahead of him.

"Halt!" More rayonette pulses exploded into the dead bodies around them as the droid charged through the morgue.

"The disintegrateur?" Roche cried out as they drew closer to the large hulking machine. "Are you—" But he must have suddenly come to the same conclusion as Chatine, because he started crawling faster. "Yes," he whispered eagerly.

Roche was ahead of her now, and he immediately clambered up on a conveyor belt that led into the big, metallic chamber. He had to shuffle on his elbows to pass through the small opening and into the belly of the machine. Chatine had seen a disintegrateur back on Vallonay. It had given her the creeps there, and it certainly wasn't any more comforting here.

But now it was their only way out.

Chatine scrabbled up on the conveyor belt and was about to climb inside after Roche when the bouncing glow of her Skin suddenly snagged on something. Some*body*. And a tiny cry crawled out from the back of her throat.

A few mètres away, on a rickety, rusting gurney, with a skull half caved in like a mutilated monster, was Anaïs.

The dark room spun. Chatine swore she was going to pass out. She felt the air around her head twist and bend.

"Chatine!"

A voice shot out from the opening of the disintegrateur and yanked her out of her stupor. She felt the air around her twist again as another pulse from the droid's rayonette missed her face by a centimètre. Glancing back, she saw the basher was right behind her, reaching for her. She shrieked and clambered up the conveyer belt just as its metal claws grasped at her ankle. She gave a forceful kick and broke free before launching herself through the small opening of the machine.

Inside, the chamber was dark and cramped, and Chatine could barely lift her head.

"Roche?" she called out, trying to maneuver the light of her Skin.

She could see him just up ahead, furiously patting, slamming, and kicking at the walls around him. "Where's the fric-ing chimney?"

Just then, the whole chamber began to shudder around them with the force of a mighty storm. Chatine peered over her shoulder and her stomach heaved at the sight of a single beam of orange light slicing through the darkness.

"The basher!" she cried. "It's trying to get in."

"There's no way it can fit," Roche said.

But it soon became apparent that it wouldn't have to. Because a second later, the deafening sound of ripping metal exploded in Chatine's ears. The floor rumbled beneath them like the whole moon was breaking apart.

"We have to get out of here!" Chatine patted desperately at the walls and ceiling of the chamber.

"I know! But I can't find the opening for the chimney. It must be sealed off."

Chatine's stomach heaved again. This time in defeat. Had she been wrong? Had the Vangarde gotten to the roof another way? They were trapped. The droid would tear this metal tomb apart to get to them. There was nothing else to do.

Chatine reached into the pocket of her uniform, drawing out Marcellus's ring, remembering the first time she'd ever seen it. It was in a place much like this. And much like now, it seemed to serve as the only ray of light in the darkness.

The chamber continued to shriek and judder as the droid ripped through the metal.

Please, she whispered to the Sols, sliding the ring onto her finger. *Please help us.*

Back on Laterre, Chatine had never been the praying type. But then again, she'd never tried to escape a prison on the moon before.

People change.

"Look!"

Chatine opened her eyes to see Roche staring upward, shining the light of his Skin at a narrow panel above their heads. With a loud scrape, he pushed it aside, and that's when Chatine saw it.

A single rope dangling down from the chimney.

Amazed, she peered at the ring on her finger, and then back up at the rope.

At salvation.

With one final, earsplitting screech, the disintegrateur split apart. Orange light flooded the chamber. Roche grabbed onto the rope and began to climb, quickly disappearing into the darkness of the chute. The droid heaved away a giant piece of the machine and aimed its rayonette inside. Chatine shimmied forward, latched onto the end of the rope, and heaved herself up. Three pulses were fired off, each one grazing the fabric of her prison uniform.

She continued to climb until she could just make out the first few pinpricks of stars in the sky above her head. *Almost there.* With each hasty pull of the rope, she felt Marcellus's ring digging into her finger. Once again, the touch of the cool metal seemed to bring her strength. Courage. Luck. And, as she continued to scrabble upward toward the roof of the Trésor tower, she also couldn't help but feel hope. That maybe, just maybe, Marcellus's stolen ring might actually find its way back to him.

- CHAPTER 16 -
CHATINE

IT WAS THE STRANGEST SHIP CHATINE HAD EVER SEEN.
With its stubby wings, discolored paneling, and glowing bulbous cockpit, it looked like a giant fly perched hungrily over a plate of food.

This was no sleek Ministère ship shimmering in the starlight.

This was something else.

And it was about to take off.

Lights along the underbelly glowed, and Chatine squinted through
the darkness to see several figures darting around an open hatch on the
side of the ship. Three of them looked like prisoners—dressed in Bastille
blue with long hair—while the others wore all black, their faces concealed
beneath dark hats. They were carrying what appeared to be a stretcher up
the loading ramp toward the open hatch.

"Come on!" Roche cried, already on the run. "We have to get on
that ship!"

Chatine raced after him. Her heart was pounding. But not from
the running. Chatine couldn't shake the sensation that something was
very wrong. Apart from the hovering ship, this rooftop was empty. *Too*
empty. She thought back to Marcellus's message, sent to her through

the droid. He had told her to *leave* the Trésor tower. He had said her life was in danger.

But why?

They were halfway across the roof when the air started to shift. The wind picked up and shimmering moon dust swirled violently around them, like a sudden storm come to life. The breath caught in Chatine's throat. She remembered that storm. She remembered that wind. The way it whipped and battered her like an invisible assailant.

She looked up at Roche just in time to see him disappear into a cloud of amber-colored dust.

"Ro—" she tried to cry out to him, but the word was swallowed up by a sound that Chatine swore she would remember for the rest of her life.

BOOOOOMMM!

The ground shook. Her vision exploded in a tempest of blazing light. All around her, the world was on fire. She glanced up into the dark Bastille sky just in time to see them soaring amid the stars. Ships she knew all too well. Wielding a destructive power that would forever haunt her memories.

Combatteurs.

And suddenly, everything about Marcellus's warning message made sense. The Ministère was here. They knew about the breakout. And they were retaliating.

"ROCHE!" she screamed again, barreling forward, tripping over her own desperate feet. The ringing in her ears was so loud, she could barely hear her own voice shouting, "FASTER!"

But a second explosion drowned out the word.

BOOOOOMMM!

The explosif hit the far side of the tower, and up ahead, Chatine saw the lights from the strange ship shudder and flicker.

Oh Sols, no. Please don't let it be hit.

The third explosif came not a second later. The ground shook and Chatine was thrown forward. She heard a long guttural scream, and every molecule of air in her body felt like it was being sucked out of her.

Roche?!

She searched the surrounding area, but she couldn't see him anywhere. The smoke and dust were too thick. Her eyes burned. She tried to push herself back to her feet, but that's when she heard the scream again. It was coming from *her.* A pain so fierce and hot was ripping through her leg with the force of a thousand paralyzeur pulses.

"Chatine!" Roche's voice broke through the smoke and the ringing in her ears. Suddenly he was there, next to her, helping her back to her feet. The shirt of his uniform was ripped almost clean off. His face was covered in ash. But he was alive.

The ground, however, was crumbling beneath them.

Roche grabbed Chatine by the hand and they surged forward. Chatine's left leg screamed in agony, but she didn't dare look down for fear of what she might find there. With every thundering step of their feet, the rooftop seemed to dissolve further into nothing.

Coughing and fighting to see through the nearly impenetrable wall of smoke and debris, Chatine could just make out the black-clad figures loading the stretcher into the open door of the ship.

"Cargo aboard!" a voice called out. "Close the hatch. Prepare for liftoff."

"Watch out!" someone else shouted.

BOOOOOMMM!

Another explosif hit the roof. The ship juddered. Debris erupted like upside down rain. A huge object came flying toward Chatine. She ducked as it disappeared into the thick smoke.

Then, to her horror, the ship's loading ramp began to retract.

"It's leaving!" Roche screamed, and they sprinted faster toward the ship. But a few seconds later, Chatine's foot caught on something and she went down again, landing painfully on her injured knee. She bit back a horrendous scream that bubbled up in her throat. But then, as she looked down to see what she had tripped over, she suddenly understood what she had ducked only moments ago. And the scream finally broke free.

It was a body.

A very *dead* body.

And there was something familiar about her face. . . .

Another streak of fire tore across the sky, and the world around her exploded in a dizzying blaze of light.

"Chatine!" Roche cried again from somewhere in the chaos. Chatine scrambled back to her feet. Her outstretched hand found Roche's, and they raced toward the hatch of the ship, which was now just a shrinking patch of light in the smoke.

And it was slowly rising.

The door was closing, and the ship was taking off.

They charged forward and pulled to a halt directly below the rising craft. Thinking fast, Chatine positioned herself behind Roche and locked her grip into a makeshift step. "I'm going to hoist you up!" she shouted over the noise, the whipping wind and blazing fires. "Once you're on, you can reach down and pull me in."

He nodded and tucked one foot into her hands. Chatine peered up at the ascending ship. Bracing against the pain in her leg, she prepared to thrust Roche upward.

"Ready? One, two . . ."

But she never got to three. Because the moment her gaze traveled back down to Roche and her eyes landed on his bare left shoulder, her whole body—legs, arms, heart, lungs, everything—froze.

For a full second, the world became silent.

And still.

And infinite.

A vacuum of time and space.

Until all that was left was Chatine and a small raindrop-shaped birthmark on the back of Roche's shoulder.

His birthmark.

His shoulder.

Her mind emptied, apart from one endlessly looping thought:

It's impossible.

It's impossible.

It's—

"Chatine!" Roche was screaming at her. She blinked and focused back on his face.

His face?

It's impossible.

"The ship!"

Chatine shook herself out of her trance and looked up. The small patch of light had picked up speed. The ship was now a few mètres above their heads. It was rising too fast. They weren't going to make it.

No, Chatine thought with a ferocious determination that stemmed from the deepest parts of her subconscious.

I'm *not going to make it.*

"Go!" she shouted. Then, with all the strength she could muster, she launched Roche into the air.

BOOOOOMMM!

Another explosif fell from the sky and imploded in a fiery cloud that sent Chatine flying backward. It seemed to take forever for her to land, but once she did, the pain in her left leg reverberated even louder than the blast. She swallowed down a scream as her gaze shot upward, back toward the Vangarde ship. Her chest squeezed when she saw that Roche had gripped onto the frame of the rapidly closing door and was now dangling there as the ship continued its ascent into the sky.

Panic hurtled through Chatine as she helplessly watched Roche's spindly legs swing back and forth, his hands struggling to gain purchase.

Please. She said one more final prayer to the Sols. The Sols that had always been invisible to her. That had always seemed too far away to do any good. But now, she felt they were closer than ever. They had heard her prayers. They had brought her little brother back to her. Even if just for a moment.

And evidently, they were *still* listening, because just then, a pair of hands reached out from the door of the ship and grabbed Roche by the shoulders. Chatine collapsed in relief as she watched his body disappear through the narrowing sliver of light, just before the door closed completely.

Only then did she dare look down at what was left of her leg.

Only then did she see how bad the wound really was.

And only then did she allow herself to pass out.

- CHAPTER 17 -
MARCELLUS

"ONE SHIP STILL DETECTED," CAPITAINE MOREAU'S voice cut through the tense silence in the warden's office. The view from the cockpit cam, as Moreau's combatteur slowly circled above the wreckage of the Trésor tower, showed nothing but smoke.

Marcellus's gaze was latched onto the monitor, his heart in his throat as he searched for a sign of her. Any sign. His emotions were as rippling and disorienting as that smoke. A heady mix of fear and dread and anger.

He'd told Chatine to *leave* the tower. Not climb up to the roof! But apparently that was exactly what she'd done, because not a few moments ago, he'd watched her run headlong toward the departing ship. He'd watched an explosif detonate just mètres away from her. He'd watched her tiny, frail body get thrown backward. And then he'd watched the smoke conceal everything, until there was nothing but gray.

Swirling, shimmering, and billowing gray.

"Take it down already!" the general shouted.

"Do not let that ship leave!" Moreau called out to her pilotes.

The smoke on the screen started to clear as the combatteurs repositioned themselves. Marcellus desperately scanned what was left of the roof. But still, he could not find her.

Where are you? he wanted to scream straight into the monitor.

Through the undulating patches of gray, Marcellus could see the Ministère's fighters swarming the Vangarde ship, firing relentlessly at the helpless little craft. It buffeted and jerked, trying in vain to dodge the blasts. But it was hopeless. They were one ship against an entire fleet. The Ministère had them surrounded. And they weren't even firing back. Marcellus knew there was no way they would get off Bastille alive.

"One ship still detected," Moreau repeated, her voice weary and laced with frustration.

The view from the cockpit cam juddered as Moreau steered her combatteur down closer to the tower. The small Vangarde craft below her seemed to flash in and out of view as the fire blazed and the smoke swished.

Then, three more combatteurs streaked past her, their sleek bodies nothing more than blurs of shimmering silver. Explosifs began to fall on the tower like a rainstorm in the Frets.

Except this was no rainstorm.

Marcellus balled his fists until he felt blood seep from his palms.

The Vangarde ship continued to shudder and sway until finally, in a blinding flash of fiery light, it was gone.

Winked out of existence like a dying star.

Leaving nothing but smoke and ash in its wake.

The entire room was silent. Marcellus stared at the screen as a strange buzzing noise started to ring in his ears. Everyone waited. The Patriarche grabbed Chaumont's hand and squeezed it. General Bonnefaçon folded his arms across his chest. Marcellus sucked in what felt like the last drop of air in the room.

"No ships detected," Moreau reported.

A collective breath was released. Shudders of relief echoed through the warden's office. And, for the second time that night, the room broke into applause.

Marcellus continued to stare at the screen filled with billowing gray ash. He clamped his teeth down hard on his bottom lip. Stopping himself from yelling out. Stopping himself from running forward and placing his hand on the screen. Like he could reverse the footage, replay it with a different outcome. A different end.

But no. He could not do that. This was the only end. And, as the storm of gray began to eddy, glow, and then puff away, Marcellus was certain it *was* the end.

For the Vangarde. For Citizen Rousseau. And most likely for Chatine Renard, too.

Because, as the ash and debris continued to clear, and Marcellus could finally see what was left of the tower—a fiery, smoking mess with twisted beams of PermaSteel and a mountain of charred mortar—he knew no one could possibly have survived that.

And yet, it didn't stop him from searching. As Moreau continued to circle the wreckage, Marcellus's gaze flitted desperately over the monitor. A moment later, a gust of wind appeared to sweep across the moon, chasing away a large plume of smoke from the roof of the tower, and that's when he saw her.

Her body had been ripped apart by the explosifs. But her face was just as he remembered it. Just as he would *always* remember it.

Except it wasn't Chatine.

It was Mabelle.

Marcellus stepped up closer to the screen, placing his palm flat across the surface. At the sight of her body—dressed all in black—lying on that demolished rooftop, something thick and hot and bitter filled his throat. A scream rising up. A scream that he could not let break free.

She was there. On Bastille. She'd refused to tell Marcellus anything about this mission when he'd asked, and she was a *part* of it. Even after escaping that horrible place, she had chosen to go back. And now he had lost her all over again. His beloved governess was gone.

Gone.

Gone.

Her word clanged through Marcellus's mind as every last molecule of air in his constricted lungs finally just left. Puffed away like the great storm of smoke on the Trésor tower of Bastille.

Taking her ashes with it.

Pop!

Marcellus jumped and turned from the screen to see Chaumont trying to catch a stream of gold, bubbling liquid overflowing from a champagne bottle in crystal flutes. "Congratulations, Monsieur Patriarche. Congratulations, General. Warden. That was nothing short of brilliant." He handed a glass to everyone in the room except the general who stiffly refused.

The Patriarche beamed as he took a long swig, looking happier than Marcellus had ever seen him. The nonexistent contents of Marcellus's stomach threatened to rise up at the sight of that smile.

"Central Command is reporting a few prisoner casualties," Warden Gallant reported, peering down at his TéléCom. "But because of the escape attempt from the tower, most of them were far enough away from the attack."

"Well done, pilotes," the general praised the squad of combatteurs who were still circling the remains of the roof. "Good work, Capitaine Moreau. Your swift actions and bravery here tonight have saved the Regime from a dangerous enemy. Never again will Citizen Rousseau threaten the peace and prosperity of our planet."

Marcellus clutched his glass, not daring to take a sip. His eyes kept drifting back to the monitor. To the wreckage that had been left behind on Bastille. And in every fiber of his being. Nothing but wreckage.

"Officer Bonnefaçon!" the Patriarche's gruff voice rang out. "Don't look so glum! This is a cause for celebration." He clinked his glass against Marcellus's and took another long gulp before immediately passing his flute to Chaumont for a refill.

Marcellus took a sip, trying to keep the liquid from bubbling right back up.

"Excellent work, General." The Patriarche slapped Marcellus's grandfather heartily on the back. "I had no doubt you could do it. The Regime is lucky to have you on our side."

The general nodded curtly, accepting the commendation. "Just doing my job, Monsieur Patriarche."

"If I could promote you any higher than you already are, General, I would." The Patriarche snorted at his own joke, the champagne clearly already going to his head.

"We'll need to get the tower rebuilt," the warden said to the general as he continued to monitor the reports coming in from Bastille.

"Just have the prisoners do it!" the Patriarche replied jovially as he finished off his second glass of champagne. "They're already up there and they have nothing better to do."

"I think perhaps it's time for you to return to your bed chambers." Chaumont gripped the Patriarche's elbow hard as he swayed. "It's been a very long and exciting night, hasn't it, Monsieur Patriarche?"

"Citizen Rousseau is dead!" the Patriarche cheered, raising his champagne flute in the air. It slipped from between his thick fingers and smashed to the floor, shattering.

Marcellus watched the spectacle with numb, deadened eyes. He could barely even feel his limbs anymore. The shock of what he had just witnessed was spreading through him like deadly gas through a windowless chamber.

As the fires continued to burn and smolder on Bastille, a different fire was burning inside his chest, growing stronger by the second. He glared over at his grandfather. The general was hiding his reaction well, but Marcellus knew that inside he must be celebrating. Now that the Vangarde had failed and Citizen Rousseau was dead, what else could possibly stand in his way?

The warden called for a servant to clean up the shattered glass while Chaumont led the drunk Patriarche out of the office. Marcellus's gaze was still focused in on the surface of Bastille. On the debris and rubble and destruction on the screen.

Is that what will become of our planet?

Is this the kind of carnage the general's new weapon will unleash?

Marcellus could feel the pressure building inside of him. He had to get out of this room. He could not stay here, surrounded by these screens—that wreckage, her face—any longer.

"General." Capitaine Moreau's voice cut through Marcellus's thoughts. "Our detection scans are showing a second ship."

General Bonnefaçon and Warden Gallant both turned back toward the monitors. "What?" the general asked. "Where?"

"We're trying to triangulate the location. The signal seems to be inconsistent. Possibly the result of the smoke and debris. It's probably a back-up team."

"Find them!" the general commanded.

Marcellus tore his gaze away from the monitors. He couldn't watch another slaughter. Because it would surely be another slaughter. Just like the last one. And Marcellus didn't have the head, the heart, or the stomach for it.

With his grandfather's attention diverted, Marcellus slinked toward the door of the warden's office, slipped into the hallway, and finally let his body be overtaken by sobs.

- CHAPTER 18 -
CHATINE

WARMTH. THAT WAS THE ONLY WAY CHATINE COULD describe the sensation pulsing through her left leg. Like a warm, velvety glow. But she knew she shouldn't be feeling warm, velvety glows. She should be feeling pain. Anguishing, heart-racing pain.

She'd seen the mess the explosif had made of her leg. It hadn't been pretty. There had been blood and muscle and possibly even bone, she couldn't be sure. She'd passed out before she'd been able to take a thorough look.

And then what?

She couldn't remember. Her mind felt mushy. Cloudy. Like it was soaked with rain. Beautiful, warm, soothing rain. As delicious and blissful as the energy radiating through her leg.

Delicious? Blissful?

What on Laterre was she thinking? Since when did she *ever* use the word "beautiful" to describe the rain? Who was she right now?

"Come on, baby. Work for Papa."

Chatine startled at the sound of the foreign voice. It was male and it was close. Too close. Like it was hovering right above her.

"You know you want to. You know I love you. You *know* you love *me*. So let's make gorgeous love together and get the fric out of here."

Chatine was lying on her back. The ground beneath her was hard and cold. She dragged her eyes open, struggling to take in what she was seeing. What exactly *was* she seeing?

The sky. Dark and sinister.

The stars. Endless and profound.

Was she still on Bastille?

She glanced to the left, and her gaze landed on some kind of console scattered with dials, switches, and glowing screens of varying sizes and colors. She turned her head to the right and saw a bank of metal cabinets built into a curving, riveted wall.

Then, Chatine heard another voice. "Stealth mode deactivated." This one seemed to come from all around her. Like the sky was speaking. It was a decidedly more pleasant voice. Female.

"No!" the male voice boomed. "That is *not* how we demonstrate our love for each other."

Chatine tipped her head back, pointing her chin to the ceiling and casting her gaze behind her.

A man sat in a large capitaine's chair, his hands moving furiously over a vast control panel. His hair sprang out of his head in short coiled braids, and his forearms were taut with muscles.

And he was upside down.

No, *she* was upside down. Or her head was, at least. Something rumbled beneath her and Chatine soon realized she was lying on the floor of some type of compartment.

The cockpit of a ship?

But how did she even get here? Wherever *here* was.

She shut her eyes and tried to draw out the memories. They felt hazy but fresh. As though they'd just happened a few minutes ago. She remembered the power going off in the tower. She remembered climbing through the vents, the morgue, clambering onto the Trésor tower roof. She remembered Ministère combatteurs soaring overhead, raining down fire. Then finally, she remembered hoisting Roche onto the mysterious ship and seeing the tiny raindrop-shaped birthmark on his left shoulder. The same birthmark she used to kiss. The same birthmark she'd dreamed about for years.

Roche.

His name pulsed through her mind like a heartbeat—*Roche. Roche. Roche.*—before suddenly morphing into something else. Another name. Another beat. Same heart.

Henri. Henri. Henri.

Roche *was* Henri?

Roche was her lost little brother? The one she'd thought was dead for years, only to learn he'd been sold off by her parents for extra largs?

She still couldn't wrap her mind around that. All this time she'd been trying to save her baby brother in her dreams and trying to save Roche in real life, and they were the exact same person?

"Stealth mode activated," the ethereal female voice announced.

"Stay with me, baby," the man said, his hands flying over the controls. "Stay. With. Me."

"Stealth mode deactivated," the other voice replied a moment later.

The man's body sagged in his chair. "You do realize that is the opposite of staying with me?"

Chatine blinked hard, trying to dispel the fog from her brain. Was he talking to her?

"How about we try this again? Can you try it again for Papa? Can you?" There was a pause, and then he said, "Oh good, you're awake."

Chatine glanced up to see the man was now leaning over the edge of his chair, staring straight down at her, his huge head filling up her entire field of vision. In the glow from the control panel, his dark eyes sparkled. He was definitely speaking to *her* now. She squinted, trying to bring his face into focus. It was a nice face. From what she could tell. A little too chiseled and perfect to look real, but nice.

"I don't suppose you have any advanced knowledge in stealth management systems, do you?"

Chatine tried to formulate a reply, but the only sound she seemed capable of making was, "Huh?"

The man twisted his mouth to the side and sat back up in his chair. "Didn't think so."

Chatine tried to speak again but was promptly cut off.

"Look, I'd love to chat, but I've got to figure out how to fix this or we're both going to get turned into moon dust. There are Ministère combatteurs swarming this place. Their scans have detected us, but up until now, they haven't been able to locate us. That won't last long, though, if I can't get this generator to work." He rose from his chair and leapt right over Chatine's head in a blur of color and movement. She tried to track him with her eyes, but he moved too fast for her to keep up. He reached the control panel to her left and began fiddling with knobs and jabbing at screens.

"Stealth mode activat— Stealth mode deactivated."

"Not good, baby!" the man said, shaking his head. "Not good at all."

Chatine ground her teeth. This man was making no sense whatsoever. Nothing about this whole situation was making any sense. And he was still upside down.

She slowly pushed herself to a sitting position, seeing her surroundings clearly for the first time. There were glowing screens. More rows of dials. More riveted walls and small metal cabinets. Chatine glanced up and took in the stars again. Except she now realized she was looking at them through a plate of curved plastique. The vast, scuffed window above her stretched all the way down in front of the young man at the control panel, and through it, she spotted the burning wreckage of the Trésor tower roof. Her heart immediately sank. She *was* still on Bastille. Tucked away behind a water tank, from the looks of it, yet definitely *still* on this Sol-forsaken moon.

And this ship didn't look like any ship Chatine had ever been in before. Not that riding in one combatteur and one prisoner transport voyageur made her an expert on the subject, but there was something about the controls. They felt old somehow. Like the entire ship was made up of parts she could find at Monsieur Ferraille's junk stall in the Marsh. Relics of a lost world.

"Okay, I'm going to try something a little extreme," the man said, staring intently at the controls in front of him, "so bear with me, baby." He gripped a metallic toggle with pinched fingers, flicked it down and then back up.

Chatine felt the floor beneath her rattle, and then the entire ship shook violently. She braced her hands on either side of her for balance. And that's when her gaze fell upon her left leg. Her prison uniform was ripped open, and there was a gash just below her knee cap. Bloodied and deep and oozing. The sight of it nearly made her faint again. She took deep breaths to push away the curtaining blackness and then gently prodded at the skin around the open wound.

Still, no pain.

How strange.

"Did you paralyze me?" she asked, finally finding her voice. But as soon as the question was out of her mouth, she knew it was wrong. She'd been paralyzed by enough rayonettes to know what it felt like, and this wasn't it. Her leg wasn't numb and cold. It was tingly and . . . *warm.*

There was that word again. It was so foreign to her. Chatine had spent her entire life freezing in the Frets and then on Bastille. This was the first time she could ever remember feeling so Sol-damn warm.

Without warning, the man—presumably the pilot of this ship—leapt back over Chatine and collapsed down in the capitaine's seat again. "Paralyzeurs? No way. We don't get near that toxic stuff. Too much of that and it starts to do permanent damage. Messes with your brain."

Chatine wondered if that's exactly what was happening to her. Too much paralyzeur in her system from years of being shot at by bashers and cyborg inspecteurs, and now her brain was hallucinating being inside some ancient-looking ship with a wild-eyed, chisel-jawed man flipping switches and saying things like, "This is for the whole baguette, baby. Come on. Make Papa proud."

A red light on the panel flickered on. "Stealth mode activated," said the breathy voice.

The man flung his hands into the air. "And we have engagement. That's right. Who is the best pilote in all of Laterre?" But then, a second later, the light flickered off and his entire body seemed to deflate. "Okay, not me, apparently."

"Stealth mode deactivated."

"Yeah, I get it," the man snapped in the general direction of the ship's ceiling. "You don't need to rub it in!" Then, a moment later, he hung his head and, looking ashamed, added in a soft voice, "I'm sorry. I didn't mean to raise my voice. I don't want to fight. Let's try this again."

Chatine, once again, glanced around the empty compartment. "*Who* are you talking to?" she asked.

The man pulled his gaze away from the controls long enough to flash her a strange look. "The ship," he said as if it were the only rational answer to *any* question.

Chatine stared at him, trying to gauge whether or not he was pranking her. "Are you serious?"

"Dead serious."

"You talk to a ship?"

"I don't talk to *a* ship. I talk to *my* ship. We're inseparable. We do everything together. She's my baby. Isn't that right, baby?"

The ship remained silent.

The man snorted and pointed at a red light on the console that was blinking erratically. "She got injured when I pulsed the power on Bastille, and now I can't get stealth mode to stay activated." He reached out and caressed the console. "Poor baby."

Chatine stared incredulously. "Okay."

The man was suddenly out of his chair again, darting to the back of the cockpit. He flipped open a panel on the wall and shone a small flashlight at the tangle of wires inside. His lips tugged into a frown. "Hmm. So it's not the reactor. It's definitely not the power cell. It could be . . ." He switched his flashlight to the other hand before pulling a wire from a port and studying the ends. "Nope. Not the thermal matrix."

Chatine felt another warm rush of tingles shoot up her leg. She glanced down and curiously prodded at the skin around the giant gash again, marveling at how she felt nothing but that soothing glow. "So, why doesn't it hurt?"

"Oh, it will," the man replied distractedly as he continued to poke at wires inside the panel. "Just not for a while. You got a nasty shrapnel wound there. I pumped you full of goldenroot. The strong kind. A lot of it. You'll be feeling pretty good for a few hours."

"Goldenroot? What on Laterre is goldenroot?"

"Just a little remedy we use. Made with Maman's finest herbs. Works wonders on menstrual cramps." He paused and turned to add, "So I've been told."

"How did I get in here?" Chatine asked.

The man closed the panel and returned to his chair in the center of the cockpit. "I saw you go down. On the roof. We don't normally get involved, but I was hovering nearby and we have a kind of code back at the camp: If you can help without getting yourself killed, do it. So I did."

Herbs?

Camp?

Something familiar was tickling the fuzzy edges of Chatine's memory. She could only think of one kind of people who lived in a camp.

She let out a gasp. "Are you a Défecteur?"

The man's arms fell limply to his sides, and he spun his chair away from the console to glare at her. "First of all, that name is offensive. Secondly, we didn't *defect* from society. We simply chose not to partake in it. There's a difference. One that the Regime clearly doesn't understand."

Chatine's thoughts were whirling.

The Défecteurs have ships? With stealth mode?

"And thirdly—"

"Incoming explosif detected," the ship interrupted. "Impact in five seconds."

The pilote spun his chair back to the console. "Discussion to be continued." He maneuvered a series of dials and then took control of the ship's throttle and yanked it hard to the left. The ship, which was hovering a few mètres above what was left of the roof, sliced through the air.

Out the front window, Chatine watched a beam of light whiz by, just narrowly missing the ship. The air around them still seemed to sizzle, as though the explosif had gone right through the cockpit.

"Sols!" Chatine cried out, grabbing onto the first thing she saw. Unfortunately, it was the pilote's leg. She quickly moved her grip to the base of his chair. "They're firing at us!"

"Yeah, that tends to happen when you try to break someone out of prison."

"Incoming explosif detect—" the ship began to say, but there wasn't even time for her to finish. The pilote wrenched the contrôleur, and Chatine was knocked back as the ship leapt into the air to avoid another hit.

"Might be best to strap in," he advised. He punched another button on his console, and a moment later, a narrow jump seat unfolded from the wall next to Chatine. Favoring her good leg, she quickly maneuvered into it and fastened the harnesses around her, just as another streak of light crackled across the sky. The ship pitched to the left.

"Can't you do something!?" Chatine had to shout to be heard over the thunder of relentless explosions outside the window.

"I told you," he replied breathlessly with another fierce yank on the throttle. "The stealth mode is on the fritz. Otherwise we would be hidden from these clochards."

"Well, you need to fix it!" Chatine yelled.

"I'm only one person!" the man yelled back. "Do you want to dodge Ministère explosifs while I continue trying to fix the ship?"

"I—" Chatine started to say.

"That was a rhetorical question. Like I'd *ever* let you fly my ship." The pilote swerved hard to the right and Chatine slammed against her harness.

"Then, why don't you fly us out of here already? Why are we just hovering here like sitting ducks?"

The pilote sighed. "Because I can't get past Bastille's outer shields without stealth mode. We'll be destroyed. Wait! I have an idea! Can you reach the emergency access panel?"

"The what?"

His jaw tightened as he spun the ship in a half circle. Fiery sparks exploded outside the window. "The little red door!"

Chatine glanced next to her and noticed a small red panel cut into the side of the hull. "Why don't you just call it the little red door?"

"Because it's—" the pilote huffed. "Never mind. Can you reach it?"

"Yes." Chatine strained against her harness until she could reach the panel. She dug her fingernails into the groove and yanked it open. "Got it."

"Good." The pilote kept his gaze out the front window at the combatteurs that whooshed and buzzed around them like insects. "Do you see a large lever?"

Chatine grabbed the lever with her extended hand, ready to yank it down. "Yes!"

"Whatever you do, *don't* pull that lever!"

Chatine pulled her hand away as though she'd been burned. The pilote chuckled. "Just kidding. Pull that lever."

"I'm going to kill you when this is over. You do realize that, right?"

The pilote shrugged as he successfully dodged another incoming explosif. "Risk I take for picking up a runaway Bastille convict, I guess. Are you going to pull the lever or not?"

"What does it do?" Chatine asked, now suddenly distrustful.

"It's a system override."

"That doesn't sound good."

"Well, you know what they say. When all else fails, reboot."

"What does that even mean?" Chatine asked impatiently.

"We have to shut down the whole system and restart it. It's risky but it might be the only way to reset the stealth management system. The only problem is, I won't be able to steer the ship when it's down."

Chatine drew her hand away from the lever again. "WHAT? Are you crazy? They'll shoot us for sure."

"The system will only be down for a few seconds. As soon as it's back up, stealth mode will reengage automatically, and we'll disappear from their monitors and detection scans."

"Okay," Chatine said, steeling herself and reaching for the lever again. The ship shuddered as another explosif whizzed by.

"That is, *if* it works."

She pulled back. *"If?"*

"Just do it!"

Chatine took a breath, grabbed for the lever, and thrust it down hard. She felt a low rumbling beneath her as the ship powered down and sunk back onto what was left of the roof. Every light on every panel extinguished, and they were plunged into darkness. Only the stars cast their measly light inside the small cockpit.

Then, three blinding streaks cracked through the sky like lightning, heading straight toward them.

Chatine held her breath and shut her eyes. After all of this, after everything she'd done today, she couldn't believe she was *still* going to die on Bastille.

She opened her eyes to see the explosifs coming straight toward them. They were going to crash right through the cockpit window. They were going to slice her in half. She opened her mouth to scream.

"Stealth mode activated."

The lights of the cockpit flickered on, one by one, and Chatine felt a jolt as the pilote took command of the contrôleur again and tore the ship up into the air, banking hard to the left. The explosifs detonated on the roof of the prison in a ball of blazing light.

Chatine coughed, expelling all the air from her lungs. She stared back at the roof, where a barrage of more explosifs was detonating, combusting nothing but air.

The pilote let out a whoop of self-congratulation. "Aha! Let's see how good your aim is now, you stupide Ministère monkeys."

"Is it over?" Chatine asked breathlessly.

"It's over, baby."

Chatine wasn't sure if he was talking to her or the ship, but at this point she didn't care.

The pilote jabbed at his controls and flipped two switches on a panel by his feet.

"Thrusters initiated," the ship announced. "Ready for launch."

"Better put this on." The pilote tossed Chatine a large metal clamp and nodded toward her left wrist.

"What is it?" Chatine asked, turning it around in her hands.

"It blocks the signal from your Skin. So they can't track us."

Chatine pushed back her sleeve and fastened the heavy, clunky object around her wrist. Despite its weight, she felt instantly comforted.

The young man turned to check that her Skin was fully concealed before flashing Chatine a sparkling, roguish grin. "Okay, then. Let's blow this joint. I, for one, am getting very tired of this view."

CHAPTER 19

MARCELLUS

IT WAS ALMOST THE MIDDLE OF THE NIGHT WHEN
Marcellus finally made it back to the Grand Palais. He'd been wandering the streets of Ledôme for over an hour. Like a lost planet without an orbit, he didn't know where to go. What to do. How to escape those gruesome images: Chatine being blasted into the air by an explosive, and Mabelle's mangled body lying on that tower roof.

He staggered between the sculpted hedges and immaculate flowerbeds of the Palais gardens, before entering the Palais through the back terrace. He had just reached the base of the imperial staircase when his TéléCom dinged in his ear and he heard the familiar chime of a Universal Alert starting.

Confused, Marcellus unfolded his TéléCom and startled when he saw not his grandfather's face on the screen, but Pascal Chaumont.

"Good evening, fellow Laterrians. I apologize for the late-night interruption, but this good news could not wait. Patriarche Lyon Paresse is pleased to announce that, as of this evening, Citizen Rousseau, prisoner of Bastille and former Vangarde leader, is dead."

Marcellus angrily flicked the alert from his screen and returned his

TéléCom to his pocket. Apparently, the Patriarche couldn't even wait until morning to do the *very* thing the general advised him not to do.

He pounded up the steps of the imperial staircase and stalked down the corridors to the south wing. He just wanted to be alone. He wanted to lock the door. Shut the drapes. Shroud himself in darkness.

He rounded the corner and approached his rooms at the end of the hallway. But it wasn't until he lifted his hand to the biometric lock that he noticed the door was already ajar.

Marcellus froze.

Had he forgotten to shut his door when he'd left?

Then Marcellus heard something inside. A scraping. A rustling. The squeak of furniture across polished floors, followed by a series of thuds and bangs. It sounded like a wild animal was scrounging around his rooms for scraps of food. He crept toward the open door and peered through the crack. His heart leapt into his throat when he saw the ragged, dust-covered coat he'd worn to meet with Mabelle at the copper exploit. The disguise was no longer tucked into the back of his closet, where he'd hidden it. It now lay exposed in the middle of the floor.

Like it had been dug up.

Uncovered.

Found.

And then came the voice.

"Keep looking. I know it's in here somewhere."

Every nerve inside Marcellus felt as if it were unraveling. That voice—harsh and gruff and, now thanks to his recent enhancements, disturbingly robotic—was the last voice Marcellus wanted to hear inside his rooms.

Standing up straighter, he shoved the door open and barged inside. "What do you think you're doing?"

The state of the room brought Marcellus up short. Every drawer had been opened and emptied. His dressing room was completely torn apart. His bedsheets lay tangled on the ground. Even the paintings had been removed from the walls.

And just as he suspected, Inspecteur Chacal stood in the middle of the carnage, slapping his metal baton rhythmically against his palm, surveying the debris.

"Officer Bonnefaçon," he said with a slight sneer, his circuitry flashing once. "Welcome back. Don't worry. Just a routine search."

"An *unauthorized* search," Marcellus growled. "I order you to cease immediately or I will have you arrested for trespassing and disobeying orders from an officer of the Ministère."

Marcellus heard a crash and looked over to see that one of Chacal's deputies had overturned his bedside table and was now rifling through the contents of its small drawer. Furiously, he rushed toward the man. "What on Laterre—"

But he stopped when something hard was thrust into his stomach. He glanced down to see Chacal had extended his baton, blocking Marcellus's path.

"I am not disobeying orders," the inspecteur said in a chillingly calm tone. "I am following them."

Marcellus seethed. "Well, whoever gave you those orders, as Commandeur-in-training, I outrank them."

"You see, that's where you're wrong, Officer Bonnefaçon." Chacal's voice hissed ominously on the last syllable of Marcellus's name. "I have every right to search this room. I would share more details with you, but I'm afraid it's above *your* clearance level."

Marcellus recognized his own words echoed back at him. The same words he'd said to Chacal earlier today, when the inspecteur had cornered him outside of Fret 7.

"We found something," a voice announced, causing both Chacal and Marcellus to dart into the bathroom, where a uniformed deputy was kneeling over a small gap in the floor. Marcellus's childhood hiding spot. The loose tile had been pulled up and tossed aside. And lying at the base of the shallow nook, where only days ago there was nothing, there was now, indeed, *something*.

A microcam.

Marcellus could tell from its crude design and shape that it was the same one his grandfather had stolen from that very spot. *Mabelle's* microcam.

A chill worked its way down Marcellus's spine as Inspecteur Chacal reached into the floor and pinched the tiny object between two gloved fingers. He held it up to the light, examining it. "And what is this, Officer?"

"I have no idea how that got there," Marcellus said and, even though it was the truth, his voice still wavered.

The inspecteur raised an eyebrow, clearly not believing Marcellus. He stalked into the bedroom and tapped on the wall monitor. "Well, let's find out, shall we?"

Marcellus stood back, dread coating his stomach. Something was going on here. Something that made the back of Marcellus's neck prickle with sweat.

The screen blinked to life as it connected to the small device, and a moment later, an image appeared. An image Marcellus was certain he'd never seen before. It appeared to be captured from within the warden's office, the room Marcellus had just left. Except now it was dark and empty. As though this footage had been taken at night. The image panned around the room, closing in on various objects: the warden's desk, the monitors on the wall, the control panel. Then, the image shifted, replaced by what looked to be three-dimensional blueprints of some kind. The complicated schematics rotated and zoomed out, until Marcellus started to recognize the shapes and patterns of the design.

And the blood froze to ice in his veins.

Bastille.

These were blueprints for the prison. Marcellus could see the whole compound now. The towers, the spaceport, the zyttrium exploits—all of it cracked open and displayed in great detail.

Inspecteur Chacal tapped on the screen to pause the playback. "Marcellus Bonnefaçon, you are under arrest for collusion with the Vangarde in the attempted break-out of Citizen Rousseau."

"What?" Marcellus barely had time to sputter out the word before one of the deputies was on him, grabbing his wrists and pinning them behind his back. Marcellus struggled, but the second deputy was there in an instant, restraining him and swiping Marcellus's rayonette from its holster. "Chacal! I had nothing to do with that!"

But the inspecteur ignored Marcellus's protests, jabbing a finger at the frozen blueprint on the screen. "This evidence suggests otherwise. And I, personally, am witness to the fact that you disobeyed direct orders and met secretly with two Vangarde operatives in the Policier Precinct, shortly after they were arrested for attempting to break into the office of the Warden of Bastille. The very office documented on this microcam." He shoved the device under Marcellus's nose.

"Chacal!" Marcellus wrestled uselessly against his captors. "This is a mistake. I. . ."

Then, like lightning hitting a conductor, realization struck, and the words died on Marcellus's tongue.

Of course. How could he have been so blind. So stupid?

This was no mistake. This was intentional. *Very* intentional. His grandfather had put that microcam there. Exactly where he'd found it the other day. Except obviously, it didn't still have the incriminating footage that Mabelle had captured seventeen years ago. The general couldn't risk *that* getting out. Which is why he'd replaced it with something that incriminated Marcellus instead.

Because, as always, the general had been three moves ahead of Marcellus the whole time.

He knew. He knew from the moment he'd watched that footage that Marcellus had been in contact with the Vangarde and was probably now working with them. He just couldn't prove it. So, the general had to do what he did best.

Frame.

Marcellus glared at Inspecteur Chacal, who was clearly in on this. "So, this is how you got your promotion?" Marcellus asked in amazement. "You became his new lackey? Willing to go along with anything in order to get ahead?"

The newly implanted circuitry across Chacal's face flickered, confirming everything Marcellus needed to know.

"Take him in," the inspecteur growled.

The two deputies shoved hard at Marcellus's back, compelling him forward. Moving him closer to the fate that was awaiting him at the Policier Precinct. At the prisoner transport center. And finally, on the moon.

"Just like your father . . ."

In his mind, like a flash of lightning, Marcellus suddenly saw his father's body, wracked and frozen and decimated. Julien Bonnefaçon had been framed for the murder of six hundred exploit workers. He'd been sent to Bastille and had died there, many grueling and freezing years later.

And now, so would Marcellus.

From the day he was born, he had been destined to walk this path.

Destined to follow in the footsteps of a traitor.

As the deputies led him down the hallway of the south wing, down the imperial staircase, and through the Grand Foyer, Marcellus's whole body was numb. All he could feel was the failure. The defeat.

General Bonnefaçon had won. Again. Just like he always did. In every game. Every maneuver. Every challenge. Every battle. He was the planet's greatest military strategist. And Marcellus was nothing.

Now his grandfather was going to get away with all of it. He was going to develop this deadly weapon and take control of the Regime, and there was no one left to stop him. Citizen Rousseau was dead. Mabelle was dead. His grandfather had killed them both.

They stepped outside, into the warm night air of Ledôme, where Marcellus could see a Policier patroleur waiting in the forecourt. As the deputies led him toward the vehicle, Marcellus felt a shiver in his bones. It was as though he could feel someone watching him. He pulled to a stop and glanced back, into the night. No one was there, but Marcellus's gaze was instantly drawn upward. To a large window with a single light illuminated inside. Standing in the center of the frame, like a First World portrait, was General Bonnefaçon. He glared down at Marcellus, his expression made of pure PermaSteel, his eyes made of fire.

Marcellus's gaze locked into his grandfather's, and in one brief, burning moment, everything was exchanged. Every horrible insult the general had ever thrown at him. And every heated reply Marcellus had never had the courage to throw back. Every doubt and every tense silence.

An eighteen-year-old schism opened up in the short distance that now stood between them.

The deputies shoved at his back, urging him to keep walking, but just then something detonated inside of Marcellus. Something deep and dark and determined.

A roar ripped out of him, shocking everyone, including himself. He threw off the two deputies holding on to his arms with such force that both of them were flung to the ground.

"Get up you imbeciles!" Chacal shouted from somewhere behind him. "Stop him!"

But Marcellus was already on the move. He sprinted across the forecourt, heading for the docking station just behind the patroleur. A second later, he heard something sizzle past his left ear. His gaze whipped to the side and he saw it.

The warping, the twisting, the blurring of the air around him.

Rayonette pulses.

Marcellus gasped and ran faster. He was now halfway across the forecourt, the docking station in sight.

"Don't let him get away!" Chacal shouted.

Whoosh. Whoosh.

Two more pulses tore through the air, one after the other. Marcellus took cover behind a sculpture of a partially dressed woman that stood guard in the center of the forecourt. The first pulse ricocheted off her chest, causing the marble to crack and splinter, before shooting upward toward the TéléSky.

The second pulse glanced Marcellus's right shoulder. He bit back a scream that bubbled up in his throat and kept running, even though it felt as if his whole arm and shoulder had been ripped through by a jagged knife.

"You filthy déchet lover," the inspecteur growled at him. "You will pay for this."

Footsteps echoed across the flagstones. Three more pulses surged through the air. Marcellus dove behind the idling patroleur and scrambled toward the docking station where his moto gleamed and hovered, like it was eagerly awaiting his arrival. As he mounted the bike and disengaged the lock, he could feel numbness spreading to his fingers. The paralyzeur was working its way through his nerves, shutting down all feeling, all sensation. He shook out his right hand, trying to bring some of the sensation back. But it was a lost cause. The paralyzeur would take hours to wear off. He was going to have to somehow drive this moto one-handed.

Revving the engine, Marcellus took one final glance up at the window. General Bonnefaçon still stood there, watching him with an almost amused expression. And, for a moment, Marcellus swore he could hear his grandfather's thoughts as clearly as if the general were whispering them right into his ear.

"Always so hasty to act, aren't you, Marcellus?"

The moto roared beneath him, anxious to take him far away from this place. From that steely gaze. From those words that Marcellus feared were all too true.

Just as Chacal and his deputies came barreling around the patroleur with their rayonettes raised, Marcellus lifted his feet and sped out of the gates, out of Ledôme, and into the night. He refused to turn around. Refused to glance behind him. Even though he was certain he was never coming back.

CHAPTER 20

ALOUETTE

"WHY DIDN'T YOU JUST TELL ME?"
  "We were always going to tell you, Little Lark. We've just been waiting."
  "Waiting for what?"
  "Waiting for you to be ready. And now you are."

Everything around Alouette was blurry and hazy, covered in clouds. The memory of her last night in the Refuge seeped in and out of her consciousness like wisps of smoke. Too thick to ignore. Too thin to grasp on to.

  "You lied! You should have told me! You should have trusted me!"
  "I'm sorry. But please know, we only lied to protect you. Little Lark—"
  "Don't call me that! I am not your Little Lark. Not anymore."

Colors flashed in and out of her view—green, silver, a dirty, muted brown. She tried to blink, but she wasn't sure if her eyelids were actually moving or not. Her muscles were millions of kilomètres away from her mind. Out of reach. Out of contact.

She felt something hard and plastique beneath her. A chair? But she couldn't sit up. Her body was weighed down. And her arms—why couldn't she move her arms?

The clouds finally started to clear from her vision, but she was still seeing two of everything. Two hulking silver machines. Two sets of spindly tubes snaking out of the top, filled with a dark red liquid. She attempted to follow them with her eyes, until they disappeared into the flesh of two arms.

Her arm.

Her blood.

Whisking out of her, into that giant, whirring contraption.

And that's when the clouds started to clear from her brain, too. She was lying in a chair in the extraction room of the blood bordel. Metal clamps encircled her wrists, holding them in place. She managed to cast a single glance around the room, but it was strangely vacant now. All the other chairs were empty.

"Wha ahr yoo doin . . . ?" Alouette's words were mangled and deformed.

Madame Blanchard's face appeared over her, her harsh features blurring in and out of focus as she leaned in close. "I'm sorry to do this, Madeline, but your blood is just too valuable to let you walk out the door."

Alouette's brain registered the fear, but for some reason she couldn't feel it. Whatever médicament they had injected her with was too strong. "Buh my mama . . . ," she garbled. She wanted to remind the madame that her mother had been a friend. The woman had said so herself.

Somehow the madame's tightly drawn face restricted even further as something passionate and vengeful flashed in her eyes. "Your *maman* was a croc. Obviously, she conned us both. She lied about you being dead, and, like a sot, I believed her. She's a good liar, that Lisole. She put on quite a show. Tears, shaking, the whole bit. She had me wrapped around her scrawny little finger. But now, seeing you here—quite alive, I might add—I realize what a fool I was. Clearly, it was all just a hoax—the death, the funeral, the grieving. A stunt so she could sneak out of town without paying her debts." The madame let out a bitter laugh. "And it worked! I felt sorry for her. Which is exactly why I didn't chase after her to collect the four months of rent she owed me . . . *and* the fifteen-hundred-larg advance I gave her on her next extractions."

A woman in green scrubs appeared beside the madame. Alouette vaguely remembered her introducing herself earlier as Clodie. She examined the tube twisting out of Alouette's arm before cranking a dial on a nearby control panel. The big silver machine let out a vicious roar as its pumps began to whir faster. The blood from Alouette's veins continued to snake and coil its way up the clear plastique tube.

"But now," Madame Blanchard continued with a heavy sigh, as though this whole ordeal were fatiguing her, "fortunately, I know exactly how to get back what she owes me."

A shiver passed over Alouette as she suddenly understood why the other stations in the room were empty. This wasn't just an extraction. This was a violation. They were *stealing* the nutrients right out of her veins.

Alouette tried to fight. She tried to sit up. She tried to *move*. But her muscles were held hostage.

"No," was all she could mutter in her weak, groggy voice as she watched the blood flow out of her body, into the ravenous, whirring machine.

"You see?" Clodie said with another one of her artificial smiles. "It's really not that bad, is it?"

Alouette wasn't sure if it was the medicament flowing through her, or the blood flowing out of her, but she felt herself start to drift away again, the clouds pulling her back in.

"That's a good girl," she heard Clodie whisper in her ear. "Just a few more—"

"Arrête!"

A voice rang out across the extraction room, crashing through the clouds in Alouette's mind and causing a flurry of panicked footsteps around her. Clodie yelped and jumped back from the machine that was still spinning and churning with Alouette's blood trapped inside.

Through her hazy vision, Alouette saw two male figures approach, both dressed head-to-toe in glistening white.

Pristine white.

Ministère white.

"You are commanded to abort all extractions," One of the men announced. "I am Officer Leclair and this is Officer Sauvage. We are shutting down this facility."

In that moment, it felt as though every molecule of Alouette's blood shot out of her vein and into the monstrous machine.

Officers? Of the Ministère?

Clodie scuttled to the corner of the room like an insect. But the madame looked unfazed by the disruption. She strode toward the uniformed men, her sleek gold dress fluttering around her slim calves. "Officers, how nice of you to stop by." Her voice was coy, playful. Nothing like the vengeful tone Alouette had heard only moments ago. "How can I help you today?"

"Your establishment is being shut down," said Officer Leclair. "With immediate effect."

Madame Blanchard's face remained unwrinkled, unlined, and unmoving. "I see. How much will it be this time, Officer?"

Officer Leclair ignored the question. "You and everyone inside this facility are under arrest. We have already detained the girls in the reception area."

"Your price has gone up, I take it," Madame Blanchard said with a tight smile.

Officer Leclair stepped forward. "You don't seem to be hearing me, madame. This is not a joke. Laterre is currently in a precarious state of instability, and it is a known fact that illegal establishments like this one are breeding grounds for rebel activity."

Rebel activity. The words slammed into Alouette. The officers *knew*. They knew who she'd been living with for the past twelve years. They were looking for *her*.

"Rebel activity?" the madame scoffed. "Here? Are you serious?"

"I am very serious," said Officer Leclair. "If everyone complies quietly and promptly, I will not be forced to call in the droids."

He snapped his fingers at his colleague, and Officer Sauvage leapt into action, coaxing Clodie out of her hiding place with a wave of his rayonette.

The smile instantly vanished from the madame's face, and where there was once a flawless brow, lines started to appear. "I'm sure we can figure this out, Officers," Madame Blanchard pleaded. "I'm sure we can come to some kind of arrangement. If you just speak to Sergent Langlais at the Montfer Policier Precinct, he can tell you that—"

"This is not a Policier matter," Leclair snapped. "This is a Ministère matter. We've been sent here by General Bonnefaçon himself."

The madame closed her mouth, looking chastised and defeated.

Alouette's brain fought to break through her drug-induced haze. *General Bonnefaçon? Marcellus's grandfather.* Had Marcellus turned her in? No, he would never do that. The general had found her some other way. She'd made a wrong step somewhere. Or the general had spies in Montfer who had tracked her down.

Leclair's beady gray eyes scanned the extraction room, landing promptly on Alouette. For a moment, the officer just stared, his tongue jabbing the inside of his cheek, as though he were trying to make sense of something.

Alouette tensed, afraid to even breathe.

The man's eyes raked up and down Alouette before cutting back to Clodie who stood huddled and shaking in the custody of the other officer. Then, in a quick decision, Leclair snapped his fingers again and nodded to Clodie. "You. Disconnect this girl. Now."

- CHAPTER 21 -
MARCELLUS

MARCELLUS'S FOOT SLAMMED INTO THE RUSTY DOOR of the couchette for the third time, and the faulty lock finally gave way. The door burst open and he barreled inside, his eyes immediately landing on a small rickety table piled high with titan spoons, clearly stolen. He grabbed hold of the table and, with a yank that sent the spoons scattering to the floor, dragged it across the room and shoved it against the busted door until it felt somewhat secure.

Not that Marcellus really cared if someone were to break in. Let them come. Let them rob him and beat him and take everything he had left. It certainly wasn't much.

He glanced around the abandoned couchette in shock and horror. He'd seen glimpses of Third Estate dwellings during his door-to-door interrogations, but he'd never actually been inside one before. It was worse than he'd imagined.

Dust and grease clung to every nook, corner, and surface. In a tiny kitchen, which took up the back part of the room, cockroaches skittered over a pile of rotting turnips. A leak from the low ceiling dripped into a foul-colored puddle on the floor, and between two sagging chairs in the living space, rats nosed and sniffed at a stack of empty weed wine bottles.

So this is how she lived.

Marcellus felt a pang of remorse and longing rip through him. He'd been so blind for so long. Too long. Maybe if he'd opened his eyes sooner, realized the truth sooner, taken action sooner, things would be different.

Chatine Renard might still be here.

He scanned every centimètre of the decaying couchette, trying to imagine her here. Living inside these walls. Walking across these floors. Eating at that table. Dodging cockroaches, and rats, and puddles.

He knew the Renards' old couchette would be abandoned. Chatine's parents wouldn't dare return here after they'd escaped arrest. And her sister, Azelle, was dead. Perished in the bombing of the TéléSkin fabrique.

Now all that was left of any of them was this dirty, dilapidated furniture, a few rotten turnips, and a handful of stolen spoons. No wonder Chatine had spied on him for the general. No wonder she had done *everything* and anything she could to try to escape this. Marcellus was now certain he would have done the same.

Fatigue and grief overtook him, turning his mind to fog and his muscles to mud. He staggered into one of the bedrooms and sat down on the unmade bed. Then, he took out his TéléCom and, after confirming that the tracking feature was still deactivated, spoke the words he'd been dreading to speak for the entire moto ride to the Frets. Terrified of what the response might be. And even more terrified that he already knew.

"Locate Prisoner 51562."

The search seemed to take forever. Like the TéléCom was purposefully trying to torture him. Marcellus held his breath.

"Prisoner 51562. Location unknown."

Marcellus's heart skipped.

Unknown?

That had to be a mistake. He'd seen her on that roof. He'd watched her get flung into the air from that explosif. He'd seen her . . .

His thoughts juddered to a halt. He *hadn't* seen her die. He'd never found her body. He'd found Mabelle's instead.

Is it possible?

He didn't want to allow himself to hope. It felt too dangerous. Like wading into deep water with stones tied to your feet.

"Locate Prisoner 51562," he said again, careful to keep his voice steady and clear. No misunderstandings. No mistakes.

"Prisoner 51562. Location unknown."

Marcellus let out a hesitant breath. Unknown was good. Unknown was alive. If she was dead, if her life had been snuffed out by that explosif, her Skin would have registered it. She'd be marked dead in the Communiqué, and the search results would have reported that. Which meant . . . she was still out there. Alive. Somewhere.

Just like Alouette.

The two were both now painfully lost to him. Vanished. Locations unknown.

Marcellus glanced around the empty room, his gaze eventually snagging on a small tin box on a table next to the bed. Curious, he opened it and rifled through the assortment of stray wires, metal fasteners, and clips. He suddenly remembered the ripped pants and hooded coat Chatine had worn. The fabric had been held together with random pieces of metal like these.

This must be *her* room.

Guilt started to splinter its way through his mind. The same guilt that had plagued him ever since he'd first watched her arrest report. *"Treason,"* the TéléCom had said. Marcellus didn't understand exactly what that meant, but regardless, he knew she was sent to that moon because of him. His grandfather's suspicion of *him* is what had gotten her embroiled with the general in the first place. And her yearning to escape all of this—this squalor and misery—had turned her into just another piece in the general's deadly game.

Marcellus was just about to close the lid of the box when he noticed something else lying at the bottom. Something that stood out amongst the rusted scraps of metal.

Digging his fingers inside, he pulled out the strangest looking object. It was hard and smooth and clearly made of plastique. It almost looked like . . .

An arm?

Yes, Marcellus was now certain it was. A little plastique arm complete with a hand and five tiny fingers, most likely once belonging to a doll.

What was Chatine doing with a detached doll arm?

Marcellus had no idea. He started to return it to the tin box, but something compelled him to stop. He wasn't sure what that something was. A feeling of some sort. An intuition that this was important to her. Why else would she keep such a strange item locked in a box near her bed?

He tucked the tiny arm into the pocket of his uniform and lay back on the bed, his gaze fanning around the room. It was stuffy and dingy and, like the rest of the couchette, covered in a layer of grime. But there was something about it—something about her lingering presence here—that eased the clutch in his chest the slightest bit. Enough for his eyes to close and the darkness of the past few hours to consume him.

Marcellus wasn't sure how long he'd been asleep when he heard the soft click of a door being opened and footsteps entering the room.

He sat bolt upright and lunged for his bedside lamp, only to remember that he wasn't in his own bed. He was in Chatine Renard's dirty, abandoned couchette.

He squinted groggily into the darkness. "Who's there?"

There was no response. Just a faint squeak. Like someone sitting down in a nearby chair.

Marcellus reached for his rayonette, but it had been confiscated during his arrest. His heart pounded beneath his rib cage. Had Inspecteur Chacal found him so quickly?

The soft squeak came again, followed by what sounded like the tapping of fingers on a hard surface.

Marcellus pulled his TéléCom out of his pocket and unfolded it, using the light from the screen to illuminate the small bedroom.

It was empty. Apart from the vermin, of course.

"Good evening," came a rich, smooth voice in Marcellus's ear.

His *grandfather's* voice.

Marcellus jumped out of bed and spun around, casting the light from his TéléCom every which way.

"I'm sorry I could not speak sooner. Another pressing matter detained me."

And that's when Marcellus realized that the voice wasn't coming from *this* room. It was coming from his audio patch.

The auditeur. He'd planted it in his grandfather's office just before they'd been summoned to the imperial appartements earlier tonight. After the horrific events of the evening, Marcellus had completely forgotten about the tiny listening device hidden in the Monarch piece of the Regiments game, streaming his grandfather's most private conversations straight to Marcellus's TéléCom.

For a moment, Marcellus's grief and aching sense of defeat gave way to a flicker of pride. The general had no idea Marcellus was listening.

"That's good to hear," his grandfather was now saying. "The timing of your update couldn't be better. A great enemy of Laterre has just been defeated. The Patriarche is thrilled and, more important, *appeased*. He believes the biggest threat to the Regime is dealt with. Which makes it the perfect moment for us to move forward with our plans. How long until the project is ready to initiate?"

Marcellus's skin prickled with apprehension.

Project?

This was it. This *had* to be the weapon Mabelle had told him about.

There was a torturously long pause, during which Marcellus desperately wished he could hear the other side of the conversation. But his grandfather must have been on an AirLink, because Marcellus could only hear silence.

The general let out a grunt of approval. "Excellent. I'm am so grateful for your generous support and hard work. It will not be forgotten."

Who was the general talking to? Could it be the source Denise had been in contact with? Mabelle had said that it was someone on the inside. Someone working *with* the general to build the weapon.

"I am certain that this marks the beginning of a new age," the general continued, his voice ringing with a pride that Marcellus had never heard before. This was not the artificial patriotism with which the general delivered his Universal Alerts, nor the unwavering loyalty he exuded when speaking to the Patriarche. This was something else. Pure, untarnished conviction. "The scum of Laterre will soon be eliminated. The fat will be trimmed. The Regime will finally rid itself of the déchets and be brought to order." The general let out a satisfied puff of air. "Our dark nights will be over and a new Laterre will be born. Streamlined and functioning, lean and clean, just as it should be."

Marcellus struggled to recapture his breath, but it was as though all the air in the room had been sucked out.

Eliminated. Streamlined. Rid itself of the déchets?

His grandfather was planning to eliminate the Third Estate? *All* of the Third Estate? But that didn't make any sense. General Bonnefaçon, of all people, knew how necessary the Third Estate was. Without them, the planet would surely crumble.

"Our two planets have been enemies for far too long," the general went on. "It is time we become allies. When Laterre is under my control, I will make sure that the new and improved Regime benefits us both. Her majesty will not regret her investment in this joint venture."

Thoughts swirled in Marcellus's head like a hurricane forming over the Secana Sea, threatening to move inland and wipe out entire cities and towns.

Her majesty?

No. It couldn't be. The general would never . . .

Would he?

"Keep me apprised as things progress on your end, and I will do the same."

There was a soft tap, and then silence filled Marcellus's audio patch. Deep, dark silence that spread across the couchette like a poisonous gas.

It slithered out of the general's office, traveled the corridors of the Grand Palais, slinked across the vast landscape of Vallonay, all the way to the Frets. It permeated Marcellus's skin and sank straight down into his bones. Until that deadly silence was all he could see, hear, and feel.

CHAPTER 22

ALOUETTE

THIS HAD NOT BEEN A PART OF ALOUETTE'S PLAN. She'd left Vallonay and the Refuge and come to Montfer to escape the darkness, to finally shed light on her past, and to find her truth.

And now, this was where she'd ended up.

Arrested and cuffed.

Shoved into a cramped, windowless cell in the Montfer Policier Precinct.

Back in the darkness.

With even more questions than she'd started with.

Even though she was huddled together with the other girls who had been arrested at the bordel, Alouette still shivered from the cold. The cell's somber black ceiling and walls seemed to loom menacingly all around, and the air hung damp and thick.

The effects of the extraction were starting to gnaw at her. Her head felt woozy, and she could see bruises blooming on her arms. Purplish-blue memories of the nutrients that had been taken from her.

Even though it caused the cuffs to cut into her wrists, she clutched her sac tightly to her chest. For some reason, the officers hadn't searched any of them when they'd detained them in the bordel. But Alouette still feared that her sac might eventually be taken from her. All of her precious items confiscated.

"When are you planning to let us go?" Madame Blanchard called out. She stood at the cell's heavy door, still in her slinky gold dress. "Come on," she snapped when she received no answer from the officers outside. "We've been in here for hours."

Only silence met her from the other side of the door.

The madame banged again with her cuffed fists, getting more desperate. "Someone at the Ministère obviously got their AirLinks crossed because this lot are about as likely to be rebels as I am to be First Estate!" Defeated, the madame finally collapsed down onto one of the benches. Beside her, Clodie sat shivering in her threadbare green scrubs, her eyes closed, her lips moving silently as though she were praying.

Alouette glanced over at the other girls crammed onto the bench next to her. They had thankfully stopped crying an hour ago, but their faces were still haunted. Guilt coursed through Alouette, mixing with the fear knotting up her stomach. If the officers *had* tracked Alouette to Montfer because they knew she'd been living with the Vangarde, then this was all her fault.

"I'm scared," a small voice said, breaking through Alouette's thoughts. She turned to see Heloise looking up at her with wide, desperate eyes. She was so petite, so skinny, and the cold had turned her lips so blue they almost matched the azure of her flimsy dress.

Alouette didn't know what to say or how to chase away the terror in Heloise's gaze. Because, in truth, she felt the same. She knew her own eyes were probably brimming with the same fear.

Alouette scooted along the bench, pressing herself closer to Heloise's shivering body. "It's okay. Fear is like a wave. It comes and then it goes away. Just try to breathe."

As soon as the words whispered out of her, she knew instantly where they'd come from. They were the same words Sister Jacqui used to say to her when Alouette was a child and had woken from a nightmare.

With a sigh, Heloise laid her head on Alouette's shoulder and—as the girl's shudders subsided, turning into the long, whispery breaths of sleep—Alouette's mind returned to her mother. Lisole. She had once been thin and sickly just like this girl. She had once sold her blood to make ends meet. But that still didn't answer the larger, burning questions that were searing holes in Alouette's mind.

Why had her mother really left Montfer? Where did she go? And why had she told Madame Blanchard that her baby was dead before giving Alouette to the Renards?

Alouette exhaled a long breath and, with her cuffed hands, reached into the sac strapped around her body. She'd kept it close to her the entire voyage here, never once letting it out of her sight. Each item inside had been chosen with care and purpose. When she'd left the Refuge, she knew she could only take a few things with her. And now, just like she'd done countless times during her journey, she brushed her fingertips lightly over the items, trying to draw strength from each one.

A flashlight, to light her way.

Her metal devotion beads, because despite her anger at the lies and the darkness, she still couldn't bring herself to leave them behind.

One of the titan blocs Hugo Taureau had given her before he'd left for Reichenstat. She'd traded the other in the Marsh for passage on the bateau and new clothes.

The locked titan box with the delicate engraving of two First World beasts on its lid that had once belonged to her mother.

And of course, her trusty screwdriver. Sister Denise had given it to her for her eighth birthday, and that same day, she'd showed Alouette how to disassemble a Ministère device. It was an old biometric lock that Denise had said she'd bought from a stall in the Marsh. Alouette could still feel Denise's hands on hers, guiding the screwdriver, pointing out the various wires and mechanisms and circuitry. And Sister Jacqui—dear Sister Jacqui—smiling over from her desk, watching the two of them work.

Suddenly, in the shadow of everything that had happened, that memory began to change shape, take on new meaning. Alouette had always believed Sister Denise's obsession with dismantling Ministère devices was just a hobby. Now she realized it had been a necessity.

Was that how she and Jacqui had broken into the Ministère head-quarters? Because Denise knew the innerworkings of a biometric lock?

As Alouette's fingertips brushed against the screwdriver's plastique handle now, she had to blink back the tears that threatened to blur her vision as, once again, Principale Francine's painful words sliced through her memory.

"We don't even know where the Ministère is holding them."

Alouette didn't have to be a member of the Vangarde to know what was happening to Jacqui and Denise now. She knew how brutal the Ministère could be. And the thought of her beloved sisters being tortured made Alouette's stomach clench with agony and uselessness and guilt.

She could have stayed. She could have joined the Vangarde and tried to help find Jacqui and Denise. But instead she'd chosen to leave. To travel the Secana Sea in search of answers. Answers that now seemed farther away than ever.

What if she'd left the Refuge for nothing? What if she'd come all this way for nothing?

Alouette shoved the thought away and dug her cuffed hands farther into the bag, until finally her fingertips brushed against the very last item. The one thing that didn't really belong to her. The one thing she'd *stolen* from the Refuge that night.

The cell door opened with a clank, and Alouette ripped her bound hands out of the sac.

"Let's go," came the gruff voice of Officer Leclair. "Everyone out."

"What's happening?" Heloise asked, startling awake.

"By order of General Bonnefaçon, you're being transferred to Vallonay."

"What?" Heloise squeaked, tears welling up in her eyes again. "Why?"

"Shhh. It's okay," Alouette whispered. She reached out with her cuffed hands and linked her little finger around Heloise's. "Just stay close to me."

Heloise cried quietly against Alouette's shoulder as they were all marched out of the cell and down a long corridor. Just as they neared the Precinct's entrance, another door opened and out stepped Officer

Sauvage, leading a cuffed young man from the cell. The prisoner was tall with shaggy dark hair and a stubbly beard. Sauvage gave him a rough push and he stumbled into the moving line, right in front of Alouette.

"Well, well, do my eyes deceive me?" Officer Leclair said when his gaze fell upon the prisoner. "I never thought I'd live to see the day. The infamous Gabriel Courfey. Captured at last."

"We caught him trying to tunnel under the wall to the Second Estate quartier," Sauvage said.

"Good," replied Leclair. "It's about time you were shipped off to Bastille where you belong."

The young man—Gabriel—flashed a roguish grin. "C'mon, mec. You don't want to do this. If I go to Bastille, what will you people around here do all day? Your lives will be so incredibly boring without me here to run you around in circles."

"Shut up and keep walking." Officer Leclair menacingly waved his rayonette.

Gabriel snapped his spine straight. "Yes, sir. By the way, how is *Madame* Leclair?" He winked at the officer. "Will you tell her Gabriel says bonjour?"

Officer Leclair gave the young man a swift kick in the back of the leg, and he went down, landing hard on his knees. When he made no attempt to stand again, Leclair snapped his fingers again at Sauvage. "Get him up."

"All right, all right, mec," Gabriel said as the officer lifted him to his feet. "No need to get handsy. If you want to cop a feel, all you have to do is ask." At that moment, he finally seemed to notice the line of girls shuffling down the hallway with him, and he spun around, his gaze flickering inquisitively over each of their faces.

"What is all this? You mecs bust a female crime ring or something?" Then his eyes swiveled from Madame Blanchard to Clodie before landing on the bandaged puncture wound still throbbing on Alouette's arm, and his mouth fell open. "They're busting the blood bordels now? Sols, is no one safe around here anymore?"

"Keep walking, Courfey!" Officer Leclair boomed.

Gabriel started to turn back around but his gaze suddenly latched onto Alouette and his expression shifted. He stared curiously at her, a shadow of recognition passing over his eyes. "Hey," he said slowly, raising his bound wrists to point at her. "Don't I know you from somewhere?"

Alouette shook her head, growing uncomfortable from the man's inquisitive gaze. "I don't think so."

"Walk, déchet!" Leclair shouted.

Gabriel shuffled his feet backward as he continued to gape at Alouette. "No, I definitely know you. *How* do I know you?"

Alouette kept walking and tried to ignore the niggling sensation that the young man *did* look vaguely familiar. Although she didn't have the slightest idea why he would. In the past twelve years, she'd had virtually no contact with anyone but Hugo Taureau and the sisters.

As the line moved forward, out the front doors of the Policier Precinct and toward an idling transporteur, Gabriel sidled up next to Alouette and whispered, "Did we knock off a manoir together a few years back?"

Alouette blinked in shock. "What? No. I—"

"The Tremblay job, then." He pointed another finger at her. "That was it. You drove the getaway moto."

"I-I'm sorry," she stammered, "but you must have me confused with someone else."

"So, what? You're not a croc?"

"A what?"

"A criminal."

Alouette shook her head but then immediately thought about the stolen object that lurked at the bottom of her bag.

"Shut your mouth, Courfey," Sauvage warned. "Or you'll spend the entire ride to Vallonay with a numb face."

"Will it look like yours?" Gabriel shot back, stifling a laugh at his own joke.

Sauvage raised his weapon, taking aim at Gabriel's forehead, when suddenly, a voice from nearby snatched his attention.

"Well, would you look at that. A bunch of blood whores got themselves arrested."

Alouette looked over to see two men leering at the girls from the street. They were dressed in tailored velvet jackets and shiny leather boots, and their perfectly coiffed hair blew in the damp breeze.

"Good riddance," the taller of the two men guffawed. He waved a nonchalant hand at Officer Leclair. "Just shoot them, Officer. Don't even bother with Bastille. It's a waste of time to get them there. Set your rayonettes to kill and do us all a favor. We could do with a few less déchets in Montfer."

Beside her, Gabriel's whole body stiffened, and Alouette saw his wrists strain against his cuffs.

"Oh fric off!" the madame shouted at the men. "You're going to miss these girls, and their blood, when you have to go home to your wrinkled old wives who can't get their hands on any more rejuvenation creams."

Anger flashed over the taller man's face. And then, in an instant, he was stalking toward them, rage in his dark eyes. But he didn't go for the madame, as Alouette expected. Instead, he scooped up a handful of wet, sticky mud, and lunged for the girl closest to him. Zéphine.

Alouette felt every one of her muscles tense as she watched the man shove the handful of mud down the back of Zéphine's dress, staining her skin and the dull yellow fabric.

Zéphine let out a piercing howl that filled the damp morning air. "How dare you, you rotten clochard!" she growled before leaping like a wild animal toward the man and sinking her fingernails into his smooth, clean-shaven cheek.

Everyone froze in their tracks. Alouette felt Heloise's little finger clutch even tighter to her own. And then, suddenly, a strange sensation began to trickle through Alouette. It started in her chest. A clenching and tightening. Her palms tingled, like tiny needles were puncturing her skin. She felt oddly alert and numb at the same time.

It was the same sensation she'd felt in the Forest Verdure, right before she'd fought off Inspecteur Limier.

She could feel her limbs aching to move. Her hands yearning to arch, loop, strike. But the cuffs were holding her back, limiting her movement.

"You filthy blood whore!" the man yelled, his hand flying up to his scratched face. He turned to Officer Sauvage. "Keep this girl in line, will you?"

But Sauvage was already on the move. He grabbed Zéphine by the hair, spun her around, and slapped her hard across her face.

At the sound of his palm hitting Zéphine's sickly and hollowed cheek, something unleashed inside Alouette. A million stars suddenly colliding and exploding. She felt it everywhere, from the roots of her hair to the soles of her feet.

Sparking.

Burning.

A searing hot lightning strike through every part of her being.

And Alouette knew, cuffs or no, she would not, *could* not, hold it in.

Shoving Heloise behind her, Alouette lunged forward. Her bound fists struck. Her elbows jabbed. Her feet wheeled and sliced through the air. Every movement her body knew. Every kick and stab was written directly into her nerves and into her muscles. These were the moves of the Tranquil Forme, the meditation sequences taught to her by the sisters in the Refuge.

Except now they were sped up a thousand times.

Now they were fast and furious and powerful. Even with her hands bound.

Within seconds, Officer Leclair was on the ground. Officer Sauvage rushed forward, coming to his colleague's aid, but another swift sweeping kick flung him backward, into the mud. His rayonette looped off in a soaring arc toward the transporteur. The two well-dressed men, who moments ago were all swagger and smirk, scurried off down the street, vanishing like terrified rats into the gray drizzle.

"Holy Fric!" Gabriel shouted from somewhere behind her. "Are you sure you're not a croc?"

But Alouette wasn't listening. Officer Sauvage had scrabbled up from the ground and was diving toward her. She whipped around and faced him dead on, her mind and body still alight with fire.

"And now we move into the third sequence," she could hear Sister Laurel's soft voice in her head. *"Orbit of the Divine."*

Alouette's elbow arched up, and with a crack, it met the officer's jaw, throwing him off-balance and into the mud once again.

"RUN!" Alouette shouted to Madame Blanchard. "Get them out of here!"

After a stunned beat, the girls, Clodie, and the madame scattered like a flock of panicked birds. Alouette turned back, immediately noticing the empty space in the mud where Leclair had fallen. Her gaze snapped up, searching for the officer. But a second later, her stomach curdled when she heard three consecutive rayonette pulses searing through the air, followed by a body crumpling to the ground.

Alouette spun back toward the girls, fully expecting to see one of them lying in the street. But it was Officer Leclair who was on the ground. And holding his rayonette was Gabriel.

Somehow, he'd gotten out of his cuffs and was now staring down, utterly dumbfounded, at the weapon in his hands, like he wasn't quite sure how he'd managed to wrangle it from the officer.

But a second later, Sauvage leapt up from the mud and swiped the rayonette from Gabriel's grasp. He took aim at Alouette.

"Watch out!" Gabriel cried. Alouette attempted another kick, but Sauvage was ready this time, dodging the blow. He fired the rayonette. The pulse tore past her, missing her face by a centimètre. But the force knocked her off balance and she went down, landing in a patch of mud. Alouette struggled to get back to her feet, but her cuffed hands and the slick ground were making it difficult.

Officer Sauvage stepped closer, his rayonette outstretched. "You'll pay for that, blood whore."

There was a flash of movement. The rayonette fired again. Alouette shuddered. She heard the sickening sound of the pulse burying itself into flesh but was surprised to feel no pain anywhere.

"Holy fric, that hurts!"

Confused, Alouette glanced around to see Gabriel on his knees next to her, clutching his shoulder.

But before Alouette could fully grasp what had happened, Gabriel had crawled toward her. She felt a tug on her wrists, and a split second later, the two PermaSteel loops clattered to the ground.

Officer Sauvage took aim again, but Alouette didn't hesitate. She was a bird let out of its cage. A prisoner broken from chains. Her whole body coursed with newfound energy. With freedom. She sprang to her feet, landing in a deep squat. Then, using the force of her legs, she launched forward. Her liberated hands arched up and around and across, with a flow, strength, and precision she'd never felt before.

The fourth sequence: *The Darkest Night.*

There was a grunt, followed by the sound of bones breaking, and by the time Alouette was released from her trance, Sauvage was on the ground, moaning in pain and holding his bloody, shattered nose.

Alouette stared down at the fallen officer, her mind whirring with questions and adrenaline. But then the sound of sirens crashed into her. She looked up at the building of the Montfer Policier Precinct, where orange lights were flashing from the roof.

"Come on," Gabriel said, grabbing her by the arm and pulling her away. "We have to get out of here."

- CHAPTER 23 -
MARCELLUS

THE BITTER COLD OF THE TERRAIN PERDU SLICED through Marcellus's flimsy coat and stabbed at his skin. As the rough, frozen tundra skimmed beneath his moto and the frigid air bit at his fingers, one word crashed endlessly through his mind like a recurrent clap of thunder.

Albion.

Laterre's longest standing enemy.

Albion.

Home of the Mad Queen.

Albion.

General Bonnefaçon's new ally.

Marcellus banked his moto into a shallow turn. It felt like he'd been riding for days. For weeks. For lifetimes. Even though it had only been a few hours. Finally, the twinkling lights of the exploit city of Montfer came into view on the horizon. Right now, that city was his only hope. His *last* hope. He had to tell the Vangarde what he'd discovered. But when he'd gone back to his dead drop location before leaving the Frets, he'd found his last message was still there.

Untouched.

Unreceived.

Unanswered.

And he just couldn't shake the feeling that, after the devastation on Bastille, the Vangarde might never answer him again. That it was the end. That the general had already won.

The thought sent a ripple of determination through him, and he leaned into the throttle, pushing his moto faster.

No. It couldn't be the end. There had to be more Vangarde operatives out there. Mabelle had told him there were cells rising up everywhere. Like in Montfer, where he'd first made contact with Mabelle three weeks ago.

The landscape whizzed by in a blur, made even hazier by the cold pricking at his eyes, causing them to water. All the while, he kept his grandfather's voice firmly in his mind, letting it stoke that fire that was burning inside of him. Right now, that fire was the only thing keeping him going. And the only thing keeping him warm.

"*. . . the perfect moment for us to move forward . . .*

"*. . . the Regime will finally rid itself of the déchets and be brought to order . . .*

"*. . . our dark nights will be over.*"

"Or they're just beginning," Marcellus muttered into his helmet.

On some level, an alliance between the general and the Mad Queen made sense. What better place to develop a game-changing weapon than on the planet that had been the leader in weapons development for centuries? And Queen Matilda would certainly love nothing more than to see the Patriarche overthrown. In a disturbing way, it *was* the perfect alliance.

But, in so many other ways, it was completely senseless.

What about Commandeur Vernay? Queen Matilda had executed the general's closest confidante and friend—and perhaps the only woman he'd ever loved. Was the general so willing to simply forget that? Was that how desperate he was for control?

And Marcellus also couldn't shake another unanswered question. One that chilled him to the bone:

What was Albion getting out of this alliance?

On the horizon, the city grew larger, and Marcellus's teeth were beginning to chatter from the cold. There was a reason no one crossed the Terrain Perdu on a moto. But Marcellus had no other choice. He couldn't hire a cruiseur. Inspecteur Chacal would surely be tracking for that. He was a fugitive now. A wanted traitor.

Something flickered across the rear view on the moto's console. It looked unnervingly like a headlight. Marcellus jerked his head back over his shoulder, causing the moto to swerve and dip. He fought to regain control as his eyes desperately scanned the vast horizon. But he saw only the cold, bleak landscape of the Terrain Perdu. Swathes of frozen grass, rocks jutting violently out of the ground, forlorn and tangled shrubs, and vast sheets of slick, unforgiving ice.

Was his sleep-deprived brain still imagining things?

He leaned farther into the throttle, pushing the moto up to top speed. The bitter wind tore through him and battered noisily against his helmet. By the time he careened into the city limits of Montfer and through the Bidon slums, he could no longer feel half of his body.

The muddied, trash-strewn streets were quiet, the city still asleep. He passed by rows of rusting makeshift dwellings before finally coming to a halt in front of the two-story ramshackle building at the end of a deserted alleyway.

After parking his moto where it wouldn't be spotted, he approached the Jondrette Inn with caution, checking to make sure his disguise was well in place. He remembered all too well how the people in this city treated unwanted members of the Second Estate. The bruises of that beating were still fading from his skin and his memories. Which was why, before leaving the couchette, Marcellus had stolen some of Monsieur Renard's clothes and, not wanting to leave any evidence behind, had stashed his officer uniform in a sac which was now strapped around his chest.

Steeling himself with a breath, Marcellus slowly climbed the steps of the inn and slipped through the rickety front door. But the moment he was inside, he came to a crashing halt.

This was *not* the inn he remembered from three weeks ago. The walls and ceiling and floors were the same, but there were no longer any tables or chairs in the room. The entire first floor of the building had been emptied of all furniture and replaced with people. So many people. Apart from the Marsh on Ascension Day, Marcellus had never seen so many bodies crammed into one place before. The inn was *swarming* with Third Estaters. Far too many for Marcellus to even take in at once. And there was a buzzing energy about them that unnerved him. It was electric, energized, bubbling like a pot just about to boil.

Marcellus's stomach tightened like a vise. He pulled up the hood of Monsieur Renard's coat and stood on his tiptoes, searching through the ocean of faces for the man he'd come to see. Would Marcellus even recognize him if he saw him? He dug into the back corners of his mind, grasping at the memory of the last time he was here. He couldn't remember exactly what the man looked like, but he remembered him standing behind the bar when Chatine had asked him about Mabelle.

Marcellus was only a few paces from the bar now, but with the crowd this thick, he may as well have been planets away. He began to push his way through, scanning every face. There were so many of them.

What are all these people even doing—

Marcellus's thought was cut off by a commotion. Shouts and cheers erupted all around him as everyone's attention was suddenly directed toward the back of the room.

"Welcome, camarades," a commanding voice called out, immediately bringing a hush over the crowd.

Marcellus glanced up, following the countless gazes to a woman who was now standing on top of the bar, addressing the crowd. She was dressed in a dark red coat, the hood thrown back to reveal a shaven head and fierce gray eyes.

"You know why you're here," she went on, her voice grave and authoritative. "You recognize the pang in your chest that guided you out of your beds and brought you to this place. That is the pang of injustice. That is the pang of knowing you want more than this pitiful existence you've been given. That you *deserve* more."

Marcellus watched in awe as every person in the room stared at the mysterious woman with reverent, glassy eyes. As though just the sound of her voice had lulled them into a trance.

"But they don't want you to know that," the woman went on. "They don't want you to feel that pang, and they definitely don't want you to listen to it. The Regime wants us to live in fear. Numb, mindless fear. They want us to stay hungry and weak. They want us to stare at our Skins all day long. They want us to collect our Ascension points and dream of living out the rest of our days high up on a hill in their precious Ledôme."

Murmurs broke out across the room. Some people raised their fists in the air and shouted their agreement. Marcellus noticed that, beside the speaker on the bar, a tall man with glimmering pale eyes, a high brow, and flowing, curly hair stood with his arms crossed defiantly. And, on the floor below, eight soldier-like men and women were standing rigid with their legs spread apart and their hands clasped behind their back.

They all wore the same hooded coats as the speaker.

Red.

Laterre's official color of death and mourning.

But this was certainly no funeral.

"They want us to work. Work and work and work. Even when they unjustly cut our wages, they still want us to make the silk dresses *they* wear, the satin sheets *they* sleep in, the cruiseurs *they* ride in, and the sugared treats *they* eat all day while we starve." The speaker paused, letting her audience jeer and nod and shout obscenities about the Regime. More fists shot into the air in a show of solidarity.

For a moment, Marcellus forgot why he was even here. He was too mesmerized by the woman standing on top of the bar. But try as he might, he just couldn't manage to grasp what was so captivating about her. She had a way of pulling you in with her impassioned words and intense stares. In spite of her fierce tone and ferocious eyes, there was something delicate about her. The arch of her top lip, her high cheekbones, the curve of her hips and waist. And something vaguely familiar, even though Marcellus was certain he'd never met her before.

"But most of all," she continued once the shouts had died down, "they want us to stay quiet. They want us to stay docile and passive. But now is not the time to be quiet. Now is not the time to be docile or passive, is it?"

"NO!" yelled the audience in unison.

The woman jabbed her own fist in the air and shouted, "Now is the time to RISE UP."

At these words, the crowd seemed to congeal around Marcellus, as if it were one living, breathing being. He wondered if this is what it was like back in 488, before the rebellion was stamped out. He'd heard rumors that Citizen Rousseau had led rallies like this in secret, spreading her message, moving people to her cause.

The speaker lowered her gaze and shook her head. The crowd quieted, sensing a shift. "Unlike us, however, too many of our fellow Laterrians are asleep. Too many Third Estaters are passive and docile, just as the Regime wants them to be. They do not feel the pang like you do. Like *I* do. They listen obediently to their Universal Alerts. They are content with their Skins, their Ascension points, their ridiculous hopes for winning a better life in Ledôme. Their apathy makes them hungry and cold, miserable and wretched." The speaker paused and straightened her spine, her eyes suddenly glittering. "But we must show them. We must awaken our sleeping camarades. We must call them from their deadly slumber." She raised her own fist in the air. "This is a war! And we are the first soldiers in that war."

Just then, Marcellus's gaze suddenly snagged on the curly haired man who stood protectively beside the speaker. His gleaming pale eyes weren't staring out at the crowd like his fellow guards on the ground below. Instead, they were staring straight at Marcellus.

For a moment, their gazes locked, and Marcellus immediately recognized the look that flashed across the man's face. He'd seen that same look a thousand times in his life. It was the price he paid, the burden he bore, for being an officer of the Ministère. And not just any officer. The grandson of the general and the son of a renowned traitor.

It was the look of recognition.

Despite the Third Estate disguise, this man knew who he was. Which meant it wouldn't be long until others did as well. Marcellus dropped his gaze and faded farther back into the crowd. He had to find the person he had come here to see. He had to get word to the Vangarde about the general's weapon.

Marcellus pushed his way through the throng, trying to reach the far end of the bar.

"The planet is wounded," the speaker was now saying, "and we are the new growth that has risen up around that wound. We are the scar of a corrupt regime. We are doing the work that the Vangarde failed to do."

A stunned hush fell over the crowd. Marcellus's feet froze, his attention snapping back up to the speaker.

"Yes, that's right," she said. "The Vangarde failed you. You heard the alert tonight. Their precious leader, Citizen Rousseau, is dead. The Vangarde are no more. They are not the hope they once were. They are not the saviors we once turned to. They are *nothing*. *We* are that hope now. We are those saviors." She gestured to the red-hooded men and women standing guard below her. "We are the Red Scar of this crooked Regime, and we are the ones who will finally bring it to its knees."

The crowd started to chant, "Red Scar! Red Scar! Red Scar!"

The speaker raised a hand to quiet them. "This a Regime of thieves. Not only do they steal our hard-earned largs and food and shelter. They steal our loved ones. Like my little sister—poor, innocent Nadette Epernay—who was executed for a crime she did not commit."

Sister?

Marcellus gaped in wonder at the speaker, suddenly realizing why she felt so familiar. It was because she looked like *her*. Like Nadette.

"They stole her from me. Just like they stole so many of your loved ones from you. And now we will steal something back from them. I, Maximilienne Pierre Epernay, am here to tell you that we can do this. We can awaken the people and overthrow this corrupt Regime. And we will do it by any means possible. We will take back what is rightfully ours. Our freedom. Our power. *And* our planet. It is time, camarades. It is time to take up whatever arms we can find and FIGHT BACK!"

At these last words, the whole inn boiled over with a cacophony of applause and stamping feet. Soon, everyone in the room was shouting, "Fight back! Fight back!"

Marcellus glanced uneasily around at the sea of dirty yet eager faces and then back up at the speaker and her legion of guards. A shiver of fear and trepidation shot through him. Now that Citizen Rousseau was dead, now that there was a big empty hole left in her place, was this what would fill it? This thirst for violence and war?

The crowd continued to chatter, working their way into a frenzy. Marcellus was being shoved from all sides. He no longer felt like he had control of his own feet. He looked helplessly around him, searching for something to grab on to. An anchor in this stormy sea. And that's when his gaze landed on a man standing at the edge of the bar. Up until now, his face had been shielded by Maximilienne and her red-hooded soldiers.

But the moment Marcellus's eyes landed on him—his tall, lanky frame and thick beard—Marcellus knew it was him. The man he had come here to find. The man who had once provided instructions on how to find Mabelle. This man was Marcellus's last hope at locating the Vangarde.

Pushing his way through the chanting crowd, Marcellus stumbled up to the side of the bar. The man shot him a wary look and Marcellus wondered if he remembered him too.

"Back for another beating?" the man said with a twinge of amusement.

Yes, he definitely remembered him.

"I need your help," Marcellus whispered. Although he wasn't sure why he bothered. The crowd's excitement had reached an earsplitting peak. "My name is Marcellus. But you might remember me as *Marcellou*."

The man said nothing in response, just nodded that he was listening.

Marcellus drew in a breath. "I'm looking for some people. People I think you might know how to find." He gave the man a pointed look that he hoped was meaningful.

But the man still did not speak.

Marcellus glanced over both shoulders before leaning in closer and carefully dragging his fingertip across the surface bar. Once. Twice.

The man glanced down at the perfectly formed V that Marcellus had etched into the layer of grime. He flinched before hurriedly collecting his features back into a stern, impassive façade. Marcellus waited, his heart squeezing in his chest.

Then, the man gave an infinitesimal, nearly imperceptible shake of his head. "Sorry, mec. That channel's gone dead."

"Dead?" Marcellus repeated in confusion. "What do you mean dead?"

"I mean no traffic. No communication. No nothing."

"Do you know—" Marcellus started to ask, but just then, the crowd around him fell to a hush. The chanting had stopped, and suddenly, every pair of eyes was trained on the front of the inn where two more Red Scar guards were making their way from the door to the bar. And they were carrying something.

No, not something. Some*one*.

A girl.

At least, Marcellus assumed it was a girl from the sound of her cries. Her head was covered by a burlap sac, but he could see she was willowy and tall, and dressed entirely in black.

Silent and rapt, the crowd parted for the two burly guards. The girl bucked and writhed and tried to kick the tallest one in the face. "Get your hands off me! Let me go!"

But it was all in vain. The men were too strong. They effortlessly pinned her flailing arms and legs in place. As they approached the bar, the speaker's guard knelt down to address the approaching men. An exchange took place, before the guard on the bar nodded, stood up, and whispered something into Maximilienne's ear.

A smile slowly tweaked at her mouth.

"Well, well," she said, turning back to the crowd. "You are all in for a treat tonight. My brother, Jolras, informs me that we have caught ourselves a little fish."

Brother.

Marcellus stared at the pale-eyed guard on the bar, his thoughts racing. Nadette's sister and brother were behind this group. Exacting revenge for their sister's unjust murder.

The speaker smiled again. "Who would like to witness a demonstration?"

The crowd erupted once more, and Marcellus felt his stomach turn.

"By the sheer luck of the Sols, this girl was born into the Second Estate." The speaker gestured to the figure under the burlap sac, who was now being hauled up onto the bar by Jolras. "She was raised with a titan spoon in her mouth and a beautiful TéléSky over her head. She has eaten more fruit and gâteau and cheeses imported from distant planets than you and I could ever begin to imagine. She has gone to sleep every night of her life certain that the Sols would rise tomorrow. She has been given every assurance of health, prosperity, and happiness that we have never had."

A series of boos permeated the crowd. Once again, the girl tried to shout something, but Jolras nudged an elbow into her rib cage, promptly shutting her up.

"Would you like to see the face of your enemy?" Maximilienne asked.

The boos quickly turned to raucous cheers as fists jabbed into the air again. Maximilienne stepped up to the girl and ceremoniously yanked the sac from her head.

Marcellus froze, every centimètre of his body suddenly paralyzed.

He took in the girl's long, usually sleek, black hair, now tousled from the sac; her slender face, stained with tears; and her small, heart-shaped mouth. He blinked rapidly, struggling to make sense of what he was seeing. *Who* he was seeing.

Cerise Chevalier?

But it couldn't be. What was she doing here? In the middle of a Third Estate protest in Montfer? Only the other day, Marcellus had seen her in the Ministère Cyborg and Technology Labs, jabbering on about borrowing her father's TéléCom so she could secure a new dress for some fête. How on Laterre had the directeur's daughter ended up embroiled in this mess?

"No, listen, you have me all wrong," Cerise insisted in that famil-iar petulant voice that always made it sound like she was negotiating. "I swear. I'm not like them. I want to help you. I want to change things—" A dirty cloth was stuffed into her mouth, muffling her voice.

Maximilienne continued. "Our ancestors—the ancestors of the *Third Estate*—built this planet. They arrived here from a broken world and made Laterre a habitable place to live. *They* labored and suffered so that this girl could live out her days in blissful extravagance."

The crowd roared and hurled angry assaults at Cerise. She shook her head, shouting incomprehensibly into her gag.

The speaker quieted the noise with a single raised hand. "It's time, camarades, for the First and Second Estates to feel our pain. It's time for them to feel the anguish of backbreaking work, unceasing hunger, need-less sickness and death."

The audience let out a low, ominous hiss.

"And so," Maximilienne went on, her gray eyes glimmering with something that made Marcellus's throat go dry—something dark and vengeful, "we will brand this girl the way they have branded us for cen-turies. We will give her the scar that we, the Third Estate, all wear. The Red Scar of oppression and subjugation and, most of all, humiliation."

Suddenly, the speaker's face glowed blue as a small laser hummed in her hand. Marcellus recognized it as a scalpel that the médecins used for operations in the med centers of Ledôme. How had the Red Scar gotten ahold of one?

Jolras grabbed Cerise's slender, bound wrists and pushed them toward Maximilienne.

"We already hindered their ability to enslave us when we attacked their Skin fabrique," she yelled, pushing the laser closer. "But it is not enough."

Comprehension smashed into Marcellus. These people were responsible for the explosif in the TéléSkin fabrique. These "first soldiers" dressed in red had stolen the lives of twelve innocent workers, including Chatine's sister.

"Now *we* are the chainmakers," Maximilienne announced. "We are the builders of the manacles." The blue light of the laser glowed on the inside of Cerise's wrist. Cerise thrashed harder, screaming into her gag, until one of her captors slapped her hard across the face and she finally stopped fighting. Tears of resignation filled her eyes as she watched the speaker push the humming laser closer to her flesh.

The breath hitched in Marcellus's chest as he realized that this was not a charade. That this woman—with her fierce, familiar gray eyes and shaven head—was actually going to brand Cerise.

Marcellus knew he had to do something. He could not let this happen. But he was a lone, unarmed man in an inn full of angry Third Estaters. What could he possibly—

Suddenly, he caught sight of something near one of the front windows. A towering stack of furniture was pushed up against the wall, obviously having been piled away to make room for all the people.

Tables and chairs and barstools. All made entirely of *wood*.

Adrenaline spiked through Marcellus as he reached into the bag strapped across his chest and rooted around in the pocket of his Ministère uniform.

Sols, please tell me I still have it.

His fist closed around the small, unmarked container, and his hopes soared.

Pushing his way through the crowd, Marcellus moved toward the front corner. Behind him, he heard the crowd start to chant something new. It was low and garbled at first, getting clearer with each iteration: "Skin her! Skin her! Skin her!"

Marcellus reached the stack of furniture, and with desperate, trembling hands, he yanked at the hem of Monsieur Renard's tattered coat. The garment was so old and threadbare that a big chunk of the fabric ripped off easily. He placed the scrap at the base of the tower, positioning it carefully between two wooden legs of an old chair.

"You will feel the burn of our burden," Maximilienne shouted from the bar. "You will feel the scar of our enslavement!"

Marcellus's fingers fumbled to open the container in his hand. The slim piece of wood felt splintery and dangerous between his fingertips. The smallest weapon he'd ever held.

The crowd fell silent, the sizzle of the blue laser the only sound for kilomètres.

Marcellus struck the match. The small flame ignited instantly. Cerise shouted through her gag again. He held the match to the piece of fabric. Just as he intended, the threadbare material caught light straightaway. But then, a second later, Marcellus watched in shock and confusion as the entire tower of wood exploded into flames. Bigger and wilder than Marcellus had ever seen before.

What on Laterre . . . ?

He'd barely had time to form the question in his mind before the blow sent him flying backward and crashing into a support beam. His head hit the wood with a *crack* that sent the room spinning and his vision spiraling into darkness.

- CHAPTER 24 -
ALOUETTE

RAIN DRIZZLED SOFTLY FROM THE DARK SKIES OVER Montfer as Alouette and Gabriel hurried through a maze of crumbling shacks and makeshift shelters that looked like they were sinking into the mud below. Alouette had seen poverty in the Frets, but nothing could have prepared her for this. Hungry eyes looked out at her from shadowy doorways, and a few shoeless children ran up, yanked on her coat, and pleaded for chou bread. But she'd traded her last piece to Dahlia hours ago.

"What is this place?" she whispered to Gabriel, her voice cold and horror-struck.

"The Bidon," Gabriel replied. "Housing for the exploit workers."

Housing? Alouette thought as she glanced around again, shuddering at the rusting shacks, with their pockmarked roofs and off-kilter doors. *That's a generous term.*

"This is where the Third Estate live in Montfer?"

"Most of them," Gabriel said. "Some are lucky and get jobs as live-in servants in the Second Estate quartier on the other side of the wall. But most everyone in Montfer is somehow connected to the exploits. If they're not digging the iron from the ground, they're processing it into PermaSteel in the fabriques. Or catching fish in the harbor to feed the workers."

Alouette peered into one of the crooked shacks and saw a young woman trying to rock a crying baby to sleep. She locked eyes with Alouette, and the desperation in the woman's gaze made Alouette's stomach clench.

She looked away. "Someone should . . . *do* something about this," she whispered to Gabriel. "The Ministère should—"

"The Ministère doesn't care."

The reply came like a slap in the face. She suddenly heard Principale Francine's words echoed back at her:

"The Regime is extremely corrupt. The very origins of Laterre were unjust and divisive, designed to keep the poor downtrodden and defeated and ignorant."

Then, with a flinch, Alouette realized that someone *was* trying to do something about this. The Vangarde. The sisters she'd left behind.

Gabriel massaged his left shoulder. "Sols, that paralyzeur works fast."

Alouette cringed as she watched him shake out his dead arm. "Merci for that, by the way. No one has ever taken a rayonette pulse for me before."

"Honored to be the first."

Alouette still couldn't seem to process what had happened back there, outside the Precinct. She'd taken down two Ministère officers. With her Tranquil Forme. The same way she'd been able to defeat Inspecteur Limier in the Forest Verdure.

She'd somehow convinced herself that the incident in the forest had just been an accident. A fluke. The sisters' Tranquil Forme wasn't a weapon. It was a practice of mindful meditation. But clearly *that* had been a lie too. Just like all the rest of the things she'd been told about the Refuge over the past twelve years.

"Oh, and before I forget," Gabriel added, "here's this back."

He reached into his pocket and withdrew a long metal object. It was familiar, but it still took Alouette a second to make sense of it in Gabriel's hand.

"My screwdriver?" she asked, immediately looking down at her sac to check for holes in the fabric. "Where did you— How did you—?"

"I swiped it outside the Precinct," Gabriel said nonchalantly.

"Swiped it?" she repeated curiously, still trying to keep up. "But why?"

He waved the screwdriver at her. "To get out of the cuffs."

Alouette grabbed the tool and turned it around in her hands, like it had suddenly turned into a *magic* screwdriver.

"Ministère cuffs have a weak point at one of the seams. I found it years ago." He chuckled like this was highly amusing. "They still haven't figured out how I keep escaping."

Alouette returned the screwdriver to her sac. "Where are we going?" She glanced uneasily at her surroundings. It wasn't just the poverty that unsettled Alouette about the Bidon. There was something else, too. The stench of smelting iron in the air. The suck and pull of the heavy mud under her feet. The damp, stinging breeze swirling from the ocean to the east.

Alouette soon realized that it felt . . . *familiar.*

Not in her mind, exactly, but in her body. Her bones suddenly felt cold. Her stomach seemed to ache and clench with hunger. And her skin could distinctly remember the touch of a rough hand, slapping quick and fierce across her cheek.

"There's an inn right up here. The Jondrette. They're sympathetic to our kind." He turned to wink at her. "You know, us crocs. We can hide out there until the commotion dies down."

An inn?

And just as the thought entered her mind, she saw it. Straight ahead. A ramshackle two-story building that sat sagging and crooked in the mud.

Every droplet of blood in Alouette's body seemed to pool down to her toes. She knew this place. She knew it in every part of her. She knew its tall rusting walls and how it towered above the shacks and hovels below. She remembered the overhang from the roof where a swing had once hung. A lone wooden broom was propped against the wall outside the entrance, and suddenly Alouette felt the sting of old blisters in her palms.

It was all coming back to her now. The memories, like shards of glass, slipping and sliding back together into something almost whole. Working for measly scraps of bread and small helpings of stew. Sleeping under a small table where the feet of strangers would kick against her and the drip of sticky weed wine would trickle through the slats. Scrubbing and sweeping and hauling reeds from the misty boglands for their foul-smelling homemade wine.

Her life with the Renards.

"Are you okay?" Gabriel asked, and it was only then that she realized she'd stopped walking. Her eyes fluttered open. Gabriel was a few paces ahead of her, his face perfectly framed between the posts of the inn's front porch. The low light danced across his cheeks, and suddenly, Alouette was struck with another sense of familiarity. For a moment, she swore she'd seen his face before.

She followed behind Gabriel as he scurried up to the inn and yanked hard on the door. The moment it opened, Alouette felt like she'd been punched.

Tables and chairs had been swept aside, and every square-mètre of the inn was jammed with people. Their pulsating, pent-up energy was palpable in the air.

"Is it always like this?" Alouette asked.

She could read the answer on Gabriel's stunned face. "I have no idea what's going on."

At the back of the room, a fierce-eyed woman dressed entirely in red stood on top of the bar, wielding a glowing blue laser. Beside her, a young girl squirmed and kicked as the flickering device moved closer to the inside of her wrist.

"Sols!" Alouette cried out. "What is she—"

But the words caught in her throat as she spotted a man pushing his way through the crowd, heading for the front corner of the inn. His hair was dark and wavy. His stature tall and achingly familiar. Her heart skipped.

Marcellus?

She instantly shook the thought away. It was ridiculous. And impossible. It couldn't be him. What would he be doing *here* at this hour? In this middle of this commotion?

But for some reason, she couldn't tear her eyes off him.

There was something about the way he walked. With both purpose and hesitation. She took a step closer, tracking the young man as he approached a towering stack of furniture in the corner of the inn. He ripped a piece of fabric from his threadbare coat and inserted it between two legs of a chair. But it wasn't until he struck the match that she knew, for sure, it was him.

Suddenly, she wasn't inside the Jondrette. She was back in the Forest Verdure, sitting beside a warm fire. With his eyes dancing across from her. Those eyes that now danced in the flame of the tiny match.

Alouette gasped with realization as her gaze darted back to the bar where the woman with the laser was mere centimètres away from searing that girl's skin.

He's causing a diversion.

Marcellus held the fire to the cloth, and before Alouette could blink, the world exploded into flames. They shot out the windows of the inn, breaking effortlessly through the thick plastique. They rippled across the Jondrette floor like lava from a First World volcano.

Alouette staggered backward, smashing into Gabriel.

"What the fric?" he cried, staring wide-eyed at the blaze. "Is that . . ."

"Fire!" Alouette bellowed, expelling every gramme of oxygen in her already-burning lungs.

Screams broke out around the inn. Flames licked up the walls like giant, glowing tongues, and smoke billowed everywhere in choking waves. Alouette searched frantically for Marcellus, but she couldn't see him anywhere. The smoke was already too thick. She charged headlong toward the flames only to be pulled back a split second later by Gabriel. "I don't know much about fire, but I don't think you're supposed to run *toward* it!"

With a frustrated yelp, she yanked her arm free and kept running. But with everyone else rushing toward the door, she felt like a fish swimming upstream. Heat from the flames blazed her skin as she scanned the room, searching for his face, until she finally spotted a body slumped against a wooden support beam only mètres away from the voracious flames. He was unconscious, his chin lolling against his chest.

"Marcellus!" Alouette cried out, shock and fear rippling through her.

At the sound of her voice, Marcellus's eyelids dragged open. He smiled wistfully up at her, like he wasn't seconds away from being burned alive.

"Alouette?" he said in a misty, far-off tone. "Am I dreaming?"

Alouette wrapped her arms around him and tried to lift him to his feet. "No, you're not dreaming. But you need to get up."

"Dead, then?"

She grunted from the effort of trying to hoist him up. "Not dead, either. Marcellus, please. Help me. I can't lift you."

Then, all at once, he seemed to register the flames, the burning building, the danger. His eyes snapped open and he looked urgently from Alouette to the fire. "What happened?"

"I don't know." She gestured desperately to the encroaching flames. "But you need to move."

Leaning on Alouette for strength, Marcellus rose unsteadily to his feet, and they hobbled quickly out of reach of the fire. Marcellus held his hand to his head as though he were trying to steady the room. "You're real," he whispered, finally focusing on her with clear eyes. He shook his head. "What are you doing—?" But his question was stopped short by a soft, muffled cry coming from somewhere behind them.

"Sols! Cerise," Marcellus exclaimed.

Alouette spun around to find the dark-haired girl from the bar writhing on the ground with a dirty rag stuffed into her mouth. Her hands and ankles were bound. Marcellus charged toward her, dropped to his knees, and began fumbling with the ropes bound around her ankles. Alouette went to work on her wrists. A second later, a loud cracking noise rang out above and, as they turned toward the sound, a ceiling beam engulfed in hungry, blinding flames came crashing down to the floor behind them.

"Hurry!" Alouette cried as her trembling fingers fought to untie the rope.

Just then, the kitchen door swung open and Gabriel emerged with a knife clutched in one hand. "Move aside," he commanded as he knelt down beside the girl and began to saw through the rope.

"Cerise," Marcellus spoke directly to the girl. He obviously knew her somehow. "Can you walk?"

The girl nodded, her dark eyes brimming with gratitude.

"C'mon." Marcellus yanked Cerise to her feet and they charged toward the front door. But it was a dead end. The fallen beam from the ceiling had completely blocked the entrance. The old door and half the wall around it were now consumed in flames. Panic clawed at Alouette's chest, and now, in the consuming heat and smothering smoke, she fully understood why starting fires had been banned on Laterre. They were volatile and ravenous and out of control.

"I don't understand," Marcellus called out, stumbling away from the flames. "I've never seen a fire catch so fast. It was just supposed to be a small flame. To scare everyone away."

"The weed wine," Alouette said with sudden realization. She remembered the stickiness of the tables and floors from when she was little. The noxious alcohol that clung to everything. "It must be flammable."

Marcellus glanced anxiously around the burning inn. "How do we get out?"

"Over here!" Gabriel darted behind the bar and they all followed after him, through a rickety door, and into the grimy kitchen. Alouette held her breath, trying to stave off the bitter memories of this place that swarmed around her like flies, biting at her skin.

"Fric," Gabriel said, pulling to a sudden halt in the middle of the room. Alouette followed his gaze until they were both staring out the same window, at the flashing orange lights of Policier patroleurs, transporteurs, and . . .

Her heart clattered to a halt behind her ribs.

Droids.

She'd prayed she'd never have to see another one of those metal monsters for as long as she lived.

"They must have followed us here," Gabriel said to Alouette.

"Followed *you*?" Marcellus asked with wide eyes.

"We're trapped." Gabriel collapsed against the counter.

"Hold on." The girl named Cerise pulled a TéléCom from her pocket and bent over it, her long dark hair curtaining her face. "I have an idea. Follow me."

Before anyone could respond, she spun around and headed out of the kitchen, right back toward the flames.

"Cerise!" Marcellus called after her. "Where are you going?"

"Does no one understand what fire is?" Gabriel shouted in exasperation. "You're not supposed to run toward it!"

"Trust me!" Cerise yelled over her shoulder.

Reluctantly, they all followed Cerise out of the kitchen to find the fire had overtaken the entire room. Ravenous flames were eating through the old bar, floorboards glowed like exploding Sols, and the walls could barely be seen behind the curtain of smoke.

"You can't go up there!" Gabriel bellowed to Cerise, who was now making her way through the flames toward a decrepit staircase that looked one second away from collapsing. "There's no exit up there!"

Cerise paused long enough to shout back, "If you want to stay down there and take your chances with the fire and the droids, be my guest!"

Gabriel gestured helplessly at Alouette, his face stained with soot and ash. "That girl is whacked. I'm not going—" But he was cut off by a loud crash as the front door of the inn gave way and three enormous droids barreled inside.

Gabriel let out a small shriek. "Upstairs it is!"

He bounded up the steps after Cerise, followed closely by Alouette and Marcellus. One of the droids gave chase, ascending the staircase behind them, its hulking silver frame shaking the foundation with every step.

"Faster!" Marcellus urged.

The droid reached the first landing and made a swipe at Marcellus, just managing to grip the sleeve of his coat in its metal fist. Marcellus cried out and staggered back.

"Marcellus!" Alouette grabbed his hand and pulled him out of the droid's grip. The droid took another step, but the staircase was already weakened by the flames, and its massive metal foot crashed right through the wood.

"Go!" Marcellus shouted.

They charged up the rest of the steps. A terrible creaking noise followed, and Alouette spun around just in time to see every step they'd just climbed disintegrating right before their eyes, pulling the droid down into a storm cloud of fire and smoke.

"In here!" Cerise called, beckoning them from an open doorway. They stumbled inside and Marcellus slammed the door shut. Smoke immediately began to slither underneath the door frame.

Terrified and out of breath, Alouette quickly took in her surroundings. She remembered these low, sloping ceilings, sagging, unmade bed, and old wardrobe. This used to be the Renards' bedroom. Not much had changed, and just as Gabriel had warned them, there was no exit up here. Only a single dirty plastique window.

"Fric!" Gabriel swore, punching his hand into the mattress of the bed.

But Cerise wasn't even listening. She stalked purposefully toward the window and shoved it open. The cool night air instantly rushed inside like a lost traveler, desperate for the warmth of the fire. Then, they all watched in horror as the girl climbed up onto the windowsill and stepped straight off the edge.

"No!" Alouette sprinted toward the window, cringing in anticipation of the sight she was certain was waiting for her: a mangled body crushed against the ground. But a second later, a sleek silver cruiseur rose up into the air, causing Alouette to jump back. Cerise was perched in the open doorway, a look of urgency on her face. "What are you all staring at? Get in already!"

Alouette, Marcellus, and Gabriel dove inside the hovering vehicle. The door slid shut and Cerise called out, "Go!"

Alouette was wrenched backward onto the leather seat as the cruiseur launched away from the burning building. The flames were destroying everything in their path. Not just wood and mortar, but the memories they held too: the terrifying sound of pounding footsteps, the suffocating stench of hot, angry breath in her face. Blisters and splinters and aching feet. The piercing wail of a baby crying in the distance.

The fire consumed it all, until the old inn finally collapsed in on itself in a fountain of sparks, flying debris, and pluming, choking smoke. And as it all disappeared—every wall, every chair, every table, every child-hood memory—Alouette felt something deep inside of her break free.

CHAPTER 25

MARCELLUS

THE JONDRETTE WAS GONE. DISINTEGRATED. NOTH-
ing left but rubble and ash. Marcellus stared numbly out the window as
the cruiseur soared high above the darkened streets of Montfer, putting
welcome distance between them and the line of Policier patroleurs and
transporteurs stationed outside the wreckage.

What happened back there?

It had all transpired so fast, Marcellus barely had a second to wrap his
mind around it. First the Red Scar were claiming responsibility for the
TéléSkin bombing, and then there was a laser, something about Nadette
Epernay's sister, and before he knew it, the whole inn was ablaze.

"That fire wasn't exactly discreet, mec. But it worked."

Marcellus tore his eyes away from the window and stared at the
shaggy-haired man with soot on his face who was sitting across from
him. "I'm sorry, who are you?"

"This is Gabriel," Alouette explained. "He and I—"

"We met back at the Policier Precinct," Gabriel cut in, beaming like
this was something to be proud of.

"Why were you at the Policier Precinct?"

Alouette shook her head. "It's a long story."

"Well, *that* was the most excitement I've had all year!" a voice squealed, pulling Marcellus's attention toward Cerise, who was breathing heavily and fanning herself with both hands. "What a rush!"

Gabriel, who was sitting next to her, surreptitiously scooted away.

"Excitement?" Marcellus repeated in disbelief. If he didn't know any better, he would have thought Cerise had *enjoyed* that. "We nearly died, Cerise."

"But we didn't!" Cerise pointed out.

"Those people were about to *brand* you," Gabriel said condescendingly. "With a laser."

Cerise scoffed as though everyone was being overdramatic. "They weren't really going to brand me. It was just for show. They were trying to make a point."

"No, I'm pretty sure they were going to brand you," said Gabriel.

Cerise waved that away as she unlatched a nearby storage compartment, pulled out a sparkly black hat, and placed it on her head with a flourish. "I would have talked my way out of it eventually."

"Don't be naïve, Cerise," Marcellus warned, already losing patience with her. "This isn't Ledôme."

"I know this isn't Ledôme," Cerise snapped back.

Alouette glanced between Cerise and Marcellus, looking uneasy. "How do you two know each other?"

Cerise refreshed her chipper tone. "Well, we don't exactly run in the same circles, but my father works with his grandfather and I see him around from time to time. All my friends are *in love* with him. But seriously, can you blame them? Look at those eyelashes!"

Alouette cracked a smile and Marcellus felt his entire face grow hot. He exhaled loudly. "Cerise, I don't know what you were doing at that inn, but you put yourself in grave danger."

Cerise rolled her eyes. "Don't worry about me, Officer. I can take care of myself."

Gabriel snorted. "Yeah, right. This is *Montfer*," he pronounced the name like he was teaching a toddler how to speak. "They don't like the Second Estate here. Trust me, you wouldn't last a day—"

"Wait, how did you know I'm Second Estate?"

Gabriel coughed. "Are you serious?"

"Yes!"

Gabriel looked her up and down, taking in her rhinestone-studded hat and belted, black jumpsuit. "You don't exactly blend in, Sparkles."

"What?" she asked, defensively touching her hat. "This is my spy look. I made it myself. And I happen to believe that the care of one's personal appearance represents the care of one's mind." She gave Gabriel's shabby coat and thick stubble a disdainful once-over.

Marcellus sighed. He didn't have the time nor the energy to argue with the likes of Cerise Chevalier. "Are you going to tell me what you were doing in Montfer at a Third Estate protest?"

"Are you going to tell me how you learned to start fires?" Cerise shot back.

"Um," Marcellus stammered before remembering that *he* was in charge here. He was the one who had rescued *her*. He got to ask the questions. "Answer me first."

She huffed. "Fine. I was following you."

"What?" Marcellus sputtered. He was certainly not expecting *that*. "Why?"

"Because you're Vangarde," she replied as though this were the most obvious answer in the world.

"You are?" Alouette and Gabriel asked in unison.

"Well, I . . . ," Marcellus began haltingly, feeling caught out. He narrowed his eyes at Cerise. "What makes you think I'm Vangarde?"

She spat out a laugh. "Who's being naïve now?"

Marcellus furrowed his brow. "What?"

Cerise sighed and tapped hastily on the TéléCom on her lap. Then, with a flick of her finger, she sent the contents of her screen to the cruiseur's internal hologram unit. Suddenly, the familiar footage of an arrest warrant appeared. The Ministère emblem—a pair of crossed rayonettes protecting the planet of Laterre—glowed in the air, and just below it, hovering in the center of the cruiseur like a disembodied head on a spike, was Marcellus's face.

"Arrest warrant for Marcellus Bonnefaçon issued on Month 7, Day 32, Year 505," a voice announced through the cruiser's speaker system. "Marcellus Bonnefaçon is wanted for collusion with a terrorist group known as the Vangarde. Suspect is dangerous and potentially armed. Anyone with information on his whereabouts is to contact the Ministère or their local Policier Precinct."

Marcellus felt his whole body melt right into the seat.

Of course, his grandfather and Chacal would have issued a warrant. The entire *planet* knew he was Vangarde now.

"I mean, I had my suspicions earlier," Cerise went on breezily. "You *are* the son of Julien Bonnefaçon, the famous Vangarde traitor, after all."

Again, Alouette's expression was incredulous. "Is that true?"

Marcellus nodded, a familiar flicker of pain clutching at his chest. "Yeah. It's true."

"And then, when you went to the copper exploit—"

"Wait." Marcellus gaped at Cerise. "You followed me there too? Those were *your* footsteps I heard?"

"But I wasn't entirely convinced until the arrest warrant was issued earlier," Cerise went on, relishing in Marcellus's disbelief. "That's when I decided to follow you here."

"B-b-but *why*?" Marcellus asked, feeling like his brain might explode.

"Oh," Cerise said, "Right. Because I'm a sympathizeur and I—"

"A what?" asked Gabriel in a deadpan voice.

"A sympathizeur. I'm sympathetic. To the Third Estate cause."

"That's not a thing," Gabriel protested.

"Of course it is. What I said back there at the inn wasn't just a lie to convince them to let me go." She turned and flashed Gabriel a winning smile. "I'm on *your* side. I want change on Laterre. I want justice for the Third Estate. There are tons of us. We're starting a movement."

Gabriel scoffed. "A movement of what? Wearing ridiculous hats?"

Cerise's nostrils flared. "It's not a hat. It's a *beret.*"

"Whatever it is," Gabriel snapped, "we don't need your 'sympathy.'"

Cerise glared at him. "What exactly are you doing in my cruiseur?"

"I've been asking myself the same question," he grumbled.

Cerise turned back to Alouette and Marcellus. "Shall I eject him?" She looked hopeful at the proposition.

"No!" Alouette said. She cast a glance at Gabriel. "He's . . . He helped me. I trust him."

Marcellus still wasn't sure what to make of that. Since when did Alouette hang out with Third Estate criminals? And why had she been in the Policier Precinct? But he decided to file all those questions away until a time when he had more brain space to devote to them.

"Fine," Cerise said, looking slightly disappointed that she didn't get to eject anyone. "Then, at least give me back my hairbrush." She narrowed her eyes at Gabriel.

"What?" Gabriel asked, confused. "What are you talking about?"

Cerise said nothing, just extended her hand, palm up, across the cruiseur.

Gabriel flashed her an exaggerated sad face before reaching into his pocket and retrieving a small titan-backed brush studded with twinkling gemstones. He handed it to Cerise, who returned it to one of the many pockets of her jumpsuit.

Marcellus watched the whole spectacle with fascination.

Gabriel shot Alouette a sheepish look. "It's not like she needed it. I'm sure she has a hundred just like it."

Cerise let out an exasperated huff before turning back to Marcellus. "*Anyway,*" she said emphatically, "I followed you to Montfer because I have recently come into possession of some very important intel that the Vangarde will definitely want to know about."

Marcellus eyed her dubiously. "What do you mean you've 'come into possession'?"

She leaned back in her seat with a self-satisfied smile. "I have a lot of skills that you don't know about, Marcellus Bonnefaçon." She motioned to the TéléCom in her lap. "For instance, I happen to be an expert hacker."

Gabriel rolled his eyes. "Yeah, and I'm the Matrone's little white dog, Fluffy."

"Well, *Fluffy*," Cerise shot back, her tone heavy with sarcasm. "You're certainly in need of a groom."

"Look, Sparkles—" Gabriel began.

"My name is Cerise," she snapped.

"Sparkles," Gabriel continued unfazed. "You may think you're on our side, but until you've gone to bed hungry and slept in the mud and worked until your fingers bled, you cannot claim to be *sympathetic* to the Third Estate 'cause.' Which, by the way, is not a cause. It's not something for you to discuss over champagne and gateaux while you glue rhinestones to hats. It is our *life*. Not an idle hobby for bored Second Estaters."

"At least what I'm doing is honest!" Cerise fired back. "Do you really expect to improve your lot in life by stealing?"

"Hey, I don't need some sparkle-headed bimbo telling me how to improve my life. I'm doing just fine on my own."

Cerise's eyes flashed with fury and Marcellus quickly intervened. "Cerise, why don't you just tell us what you found?"

Cerise took a moment to calm herself down. Then, once she'd gathered her face back into a smile, she exhaled and said, "Well, two days ago, I was out in Céleste, on the Southern Peninsula, scanning signals from the satellites—"

"Wait, you were *what*?" spat Marcellus.

"Scanning signals from the satellites," Cerise repeated, slowly enunciating each word.

"In the Southern Peninsula?"

"Céleste is gorgeous this time of year. Have you been? Brilliant pure white skies. And it's where the Laterrian cloud coverage is thinnest, so you get the best signal strength from the satellites."

"Really?" Alouette asked, sounding genuinely interested. "I never read about—" she caught herself and cleared her throat. "I mean, I've never heard that before."

"Why were you scanning satellite signals?" Marcellus asked.

"Because I was looking for the kill switch," Cerise replied matter-of-factly.

Marcellus fought back a groan. "Seriously, Cerise?"

"What's the kill switch?" Alouette asked.

"It's a master switch that can deactivate all the Skins," Cerise explained at the exact same moment as Marcellus said, "It's a hoax that only extremely gullible people believe."

Alouette swung her gaze from Cerise to Marcellus and then finally to Gabriel.

"I'm going to side with fire boy here," Gabriel said. "It's totally a hoax."

"No, it's not," Cerise insisted. "It's real."

Marcellus rolled his eyes. "No. It's an urban legend that's been around for years. A fantasy. It's just fodder for conspiracy theorists."

"Yeah. You've got to be pretty stupid to believe that all the Skins on the planet can be shut down with one button." Gabriel snorted and then muttered under his breath. "Expert hacker, my foot."

Cerise's jaw visibly clenched. "I'm not stupid. A lot of people believe the kill switch is real. And as an *expert* hacker"—she shot Gabriel a steely look—"I know from personal experience that you should never build any system without some kind of emergency shut-off mechanism, in case anything goes wrong."

Marcellus clenched his fists against the seat. This conversation was going nowhere. He was this close to ordering the cruiseur to stop so he could jump out. "Trust me, Cerise," he said with a sigh, "if such a thing existed, I would know about it. I'm second-in-command of the Ministère after General Bonnefaçon." He glanced at the arrest warrant still displayed on the hologram unit and cleared his throat. "Or, *was* anyway."

"But what if the general doesn't even know about it?" she countered. "I mean, it makes sense to hide it, right? So, no one can ever use it? But I figured, if there *is* a switch somewhere, it has to be connected to a network, so it can reach all the Skins at once. That's why I was scanning the satellites. I thought that if I could locate the right signal, I could track it back to the switch."

Gabriel crossed his arms over his chest. "And? Did you find it?"

Cerise deflated. "Well, no."

"Okay, that was a charming story," Gabriel said. "How about you just drop me off somewhere and I'll walk home."

"I'm not finished," Cerise said through gritted teeth. Then, she refreshed her breezy smile again and continued. "I may not have located the kill switch"—she flashed another scathing look at Gabriel—"*yet*. But I did end up stumbling upon something else. Something very, *very* interesting."

"And that would be?" Marcellus prompted. He was getting a little fatigued by Cerise's flair for the dramatics. And he still wasn't entirely convinced he should believe anything she had to say. Cerise Chevalier? A sympathizeur? A hacker? And now a conspiracy theorist, too? Just the other day she was whining about dresses for a fête like it was the end of the world.

"I found an encrypted message being sent through one of the old Human Conservation Commission probes."

"Those probes still exist?" Alouette cut in, staring wide-eyed at Cerise. "I thought they were all destroyed once the planets of the System Divine were inhabited."

"Me too," Cerise said, sounding thrilled to have someone in this cruiseur who seemed as excited about this development as she was.

"What's this about probes?" Gabriel asked.

Cerise let out a huff, but Alouette turned patiently to Gabriel and explained, "Before the Last Days, the Human Conservation Commission sent probes from the First World into space to locate a new place for human beings to live. That's how they found the twelve planets of the System Divine. But after the planets were terraformed and inhabited, the probes weren't needed anymore, and they just sort of disappeared."

"But not *all* of them," Cerise said. "One, I've discovered, is apparently still floating around in the Asteroid Channel, and someone is using it to send messages through an abandoned First World communication network." Cerise leaned forward and swiveled her gaze purposefully between

Alouette and Marcellus. She paused for a second, making sure her next words carried the weight she wanted. "Someone on *Albion*."

Marcellus felt as though the cruiseur had suddenly lost altitude and they were falling. Plummeting straight to the ground.

"And you found one of these messages?" Marcellus asked.

Cerise crossed her arms over her chest. "Mmm-hmm."

"What did it say?" Alouette and Marcellus blurted out at the same moment.

Cerise's eager expression slid right off her face. She uncrossed her arms. "Well, see, that's the problem. I can't interpret it."

"Why not?" Gabriel chided. "I thought you were an *expert* hacker."

"I am," she snapped. "But this isn't about hacking. The message was transmitted in some kind of code that I can't decipher. I even tried running it through my father's TéléCom because he has access to more advanced decryption software, but it didn't work."

Comprehension flashed in Marcellus's mind. "*That's* why you needed his TéléCom the other day? It wasn't about a dress for a fête?"

Cerise rolled her eyes. "Keep up, Marcellus. I don't give a fric about a fête. I was trying to figure out who had transmitted a message from Albion through an old space probe. But every time I listen to it, it just sounds like a bunch of beeps. I thought maybe the Vangarde could help."

Marcellus pressed his fingertips into his temples. None of this was making any sense. "But . . . you always seemed so . . . so . . ."

"Spoiled and sparkle-headed?" Cerise suggested.

Marcellus balked, uncomfortable. "Well, yes."

"Yeah, that's just an act. To keep Papa from getting too suspicious. He's the last person I want knowing what I can do."

"So you *pretend* to be . . . superficial?"

Cerise rolled her eyes. "Trust me, when your father is the head of the Cyborg and Technology Labs, superficial is the safest thing *to* be."

"What does that mean?" Marcellus asked.

"Never mind," Cerise muttered, looking almost uncomfortable.

"What kind of beeps?" Alouette suddenly asked, and Marcellus turned to see her eyes were locked on Cerise.

"Huh?" said Cerise.

"You said the message was encoded, and it sounded like a bunch of beeps."

"Oh." Cerise shrugged. "I don't know. Just beeps."

"Were they different lengths?"

Marcellus glanced curiously between Alouette and Cerise as Cerise considered the question.

"Yeah," she said slowly. "Actually, they were."

"Can you play it?"

"Why?" Cerise's gaze roved over Alouette as though she were seeing her for the first time.

"Just play it."

Hesitantly, Cerise pulled her attention from Alouette and focused back on her TéléCom. Marcellus sensed something in the air. A buzzing anticipation. It made his heart beat faster. Cerise tapped proficiently on the screen until, finally, a soft crackle emanated from the speakers, like an AirLink being sent over a faulty connection. Then, a moment later, the cruiseur was filled with the most peculiar series of sounds Marcellus had ever heard.

Dah . . . Dit . . . Dit . . . Dit . . . Dit . . . Dit . . . Dit . . . . . . Dit . . . Dah . . . Dah . . . Dit . . .

It seemed to go on forever. How was anyone supposed to make sense of this? But when he glanced over at Alouette, he saw she was staring, with slightly glazed eyes, at some invisible space in front of her. Her lips were moving ever so slightly with each beep, as though she were mouthing along to a song she'd memorized.

The beeps came to an abrupt end, and the cruiseur filled with heavy silence.

"Alouette," Marcellus began hesitantly. "Do you know what that—"

"Play it again!" she commanded.

Cerise obliged, tapping on the screen. The same series of beeps replayed on the speakers, and once again, Alouette seemed to fall into some kind of trance. Marcellus listened carefully, trying to hear what she was hearing, but it just sounded like nonsensical noise to him.

When the message finally concluded, Alouette sat very still for a long moment, her eyes closed, her lips moving silently.

Then, without warning, her eyelids fluttered open, and in a steady, almost droid-like voice, she said, "Weapon nearly complete. Delivery in two weeks. I can stop it. Come now."

An instant chill corkscrewed through Marcellus's body, slicing at his legs and neck and ribcage.

Everyone stared at Alouette in silence. Gabriel was the first to break it.

"WHAT. THE. FRIC?" he exploded.

"That's what the message says," Alouette clarified, as though *this* was the part Gabriel was questioning.

Marcellus numbly shook his head, trying to make sense of everything. He turned to Alouette. "How—how did you do that? How did you know what it said?"

Alouette swallowed, clearly trying to absorb all of this shocking news as well. "It's an old First World code. Sister—" but she stopped herself. "I mean, one of the people I lived with taught it to me."

"Wait a minute." Cerise reeled on Alouette, her mind clearly calculating something. "Who are you exactly?"

Alouette hesitated. "I'm . . . It's complicated."

"A weapon?" Gabriel repeated in disbelief. "Being delivered from Albion? What weapon? Who is it being delivered *to*?"

"My grandfather." The words were barely audible through Marcellus's taut lips. Yet they were clearly loud enough, because everyone in the cruiseur turned toward him at once, question marks blazing in their eyes. "He's been developing a weapon with Albion."

There was no point keeping it a secret anymore. The planet would know soon enough. And by then it would be too late.

"What?" Alouette asked in a shaky voice.

Marcellus nodded. "The Vangarde recruited me to try to track it

down. I don't know what it is or what it does. All I know is that he's
going to somehow use it in his grand plan to take control of the planet.
Or as he put it, 'rid' the Regime of the déchets and eliminate the 'scum
of Laterre.'"

More silence followed. But this time it was different. It was the kind of
silence that keeps you awake at night. The kind that's filled with menacing
shadows and lurking horrors. Once again, Gabriel was the first to speak.

"Stop the cruiseur!"

"What do you mean, 'stop the cruiseur'?" Cerise shot back.

"I mean, STOP THE CRUISEUR! I have to get out."

Cerise directed the vehicle to a halt and opened the door. Mist immediately seeped inside, and Marcellus realized they were in the middle of
the Tourbay, Montfer's infamous boglands where he'd met Mabelle only
three weeks ago. The memory was like a splinter twisting in his heart.
Three weeks ago, she had been alive. And now she wasn't.

Gabriel tumbled out through the door and bent over, hands on his
knees, sucking in air with great, full-body spasms like he was drowning
in the mist. Alouette immediately hurried after him and placed a tender
hand on his back.

Marcellus fought to keep his own breathing steady. Suddenly everything was lining up in his mind. Pieces that had once seemed like random
floating debris circling his thoughts clattered into place. The AirLink
conversation overheard in his grandfather's study. His mission from
Mabelle.

*"She was the only person who knew how to contact the source. She was our
only lead for finding out what the general was working on and how to stop it."*

Marcellus leapt to his feet and jumped out of the cruiseur. He strode
purposefully toward Alouette, feeling his heart thud faster with every
step he took. "This person who taught you that First World code. Is her
name Denise?"

The shock that registered in Alouette's eyes was all Marcellus needed
to see to know he was right. "Y-yes," she stammered. "How did you know
that?"

Marcellus felt the misty air around him catch fire again. The blaze and heat were all too familiar now. Like an intimate friend, whispering in his ear. And strangely enough, it was that very fire—smoke and flames and all—that allowed him to see the world clearly. That allowed him to see his path clearly.

Citizen Rousseau might be dead. Mabelle might be dead. The Vangarde might have lost that battle. But this war against his grandfather was not over.

General Bonnefaçon still had to be stopped.

"Because that message was meant for her," he said. "Denise has been working with a source on Albion. Someone involved in the development of the weapon. The same person who, I imagine, sent that message. Whoever this person is, Denise is supposed to go to Albion to meet with them so she can stop the general from using the weapon to take control of the Regime."

"But," Alouette struggled, looking pained, "isn't she still being held captive? Didn't the general arrest her?"

"Yes," Marcellus said, drawing in a long, burdened breath, "which is why I have to go in her place."

- PART 3 -
ALBION

The twelve planets in the System Divine orbited together like a string of jewels, precious and dazzling and rare. But one jewel stood out amid the others. A memory made real and a dream brought to life. An echo of the First World, with reminiscent whispers of the old world's breezes blowing across its lands. One family secured this wondrous place for their people and their home.

But not without bitterness from those who lost out.

And not without deep resentments held across the skies.

From *The Chronicles of the Vangarde*,
Volume 3, Chapter 10

- CHAPTER 26 -
CHATINE

THE LAST TIME CHATINE HAD SEEN LATERRE FROM space, she was leaving it behind. Heading toward Bastille to serve a twenty-five-year sentence. Now, as the strange Défecteur man's even stranger ship surged through space, and she saw the giant white-and-gray planet looming in front of them, Chatine felt a curious sense of peace. She was going back. She was going home.

And she was going to find her brother.

The pilote eased his hand off the contrôleur and flipped a switch on the console.

"Autopilote engaged," the breathy voice of the ship announced.

"Okay," he said, swiveling his capitaine's chair around to face Chatine, who was still strapped into the jump seat, her injured leg extended out in front of her. "Lives saved. Autopilote engaged. Now for pleasantries." He held out his fist like he was going to punch Chatine in the face. She ducked out of striking distance.

The young man laughed. "Oh. Right, sorry. I keep forgetting you don't do this." He nodded toward his fist. "We tap to say hello. Well, Maman likes to kiss on the lips, but I won't do that to you."

Chatine instantly felt her cheeks flush with heat and berated herself for it. She'd learned her lesson about blushing for pretty-faced boys. And although this boy was decidedly rougher-looking than Marcellus—with shabbier clothes, short braided hair, and a scoundrel's smile—his face was definitely still pretty.

He extended his closed fist forward. "I'm Etienne."

Chatine remained silent.

"And you are?" he prompted slowly.

"Oh. Um, my name is . . ." A rush of exhilaration shot through her at the endless possibilities. This was her chance. Her chance to reinvent herself again. To become someone completely new. Without a past. Without a criminal record. Without a heart that had been shattered by a pair of dark hazel eyes. But, as countless new names and identities filtered through her mind, she found herself feeling not inspired, but exhausted. She'd been someone else for so long—Théo, the Fret rat; prisoner 5.1.5.6.2.—she found herself actually wondering what it would be like to simply say . . .

"Chatine," she whispered. And once it was out, she was grateful that she couldn't take it back. Couldn't change her mind. This is who she had to be now.

Chatine, the sister of Henri and Azelle.

Etienne tilted his head, as though he were listening for something. "Chatine," he repeated and Chatine felt like she was hearing her name for the first time. "Hmm." He tapped his fingers on the armrest of his chair before finally deciding. "I like it."

She scoffed. "Well, thanks. I'm so glad you approve."

"Okay. Let me show you how it's done." Etienne proffered his fist again. "Make a fist like this."

She did as she was told, but she kept it close to her body and Etienne had to lean forward—nearly falling out of his chair—to tap his fist against hers. He pushed himself back with a dramatic grunt. "Okay, we'll work on the extension part later. In the meantime"—he spread his arms wide—"welcome aboard Marilyn!"

Chatine rolled her eyes. "I just told you my name is Chatine."

He shook his head. "No, not 'welcome aboard, Marilyn.'" He pointed to Chatine and then gestured grandly again to the interior of the ship. "Welcome aboard *Marilyn*."

Chatine stared blankly back at him.

His arms collapsed. "The ship is *named* Marilyn."

"You named your ship?"

"Of course I named my ship."

"Who names their ship?"

"Everyone names their ship."

"I don't think everyone names their ship."

Etienne crossed his arms over his chest in a challenge. "Oh really? You know a lot of people with ships?"

"Well, I definitely didn't know *Défecteurs* had ships." Chatine was still trying to wrap her mind around that part.

The man quirked his lips into a knowing smile. "What did you think? We just hold hands, sing songs, and eat wood chips all day?"

Chatine bowed her head, feeling heat warm her cheeks. "No."

"Sure, sure," the man said. "I know what you gridders think of us."

Chatine's head whipped up. "Excuse me? What did you just call me?"

"A gridder. Someone who lives on the Regime's grid. Watches all the Ministère broadcasts and Universal Alerts with wide, hopeful eyes. Buys into the whole three-Estates-divided-by-nature thing. Prays to win the Ascension. Plays by the rules—"

"Whoa. Whoa. I do *not* play by their rules."

He looked her up and down, taking in her blue prison uniform. "Fine. But you're still a slave to that." He pointed to her Skin, which was still covered by the giant metal cuff he'd insisted she put on to block the tracker.

Embarrassed, Chatine hid her hand behind her back as she stole a glance at Etienne's left arm. There was nothing there but smooth, untarnished flesh. Not even a scar. A Défecteur born outside the Regime. Outside the cruel laws of the Ministère.

"That's not fair," she said. "They implanted this thing in me when I was a child. I didn't have a choice. Besides, you don't even know me."

"I know you're gullible enough to believe what the Regime wants you to believe about us." Chatine opened her mouth to argue, but the man interrupted her once more. "What was it you called me again? A Défecteur? Now, let me see, who came up with that word?"

She crossed her arms. "Fine. What do *you* call yourselves?"

The man smiled, clearly enjoying the question. "Well, we don't really like labels. We're more of a you-be-you type of people."

Chatine snorted. "Why am I not surprised?"

"But," he went on, ignoring her snide remark, "if I had to pick, I would say you could call us"—he began to count on his fingers—"renegades, bon vivants, zealous nonconformists."

Chatine fought hard not to roll her eyes. "Or . . . how about . . . I don't know . . . Défecteurs?"

Annoyance flashed across the young man's chiseled features before he quickly composed himself.

"It's as good of a name as *Marilyn*," Chatine jabbed.

"What wrong with Marilyn?" The pilote was clearly insulted.

"It's . . ." Chatine searched for the right word. "I don't know, kind of stupide."

Etienne made a choking sound and pounded his fist against his chest as though trying to dispel something caught there. "Marilyn happens to be a very beloved name on the First World."

Chatine unfastened her harness and, with effort, pushed herself to standing and limped over to the console. She gazed out at the view of her home planet growing closer. "Oh, right, I forgot you people have an obsession with the First World."

Etienne twisted his mouth to the side. "I wouldn't call it an obsession. I'd say it's more of an appreciation. There were a lot of things they did well on the First World."

"The First World died," Chatine reminded him. "In a fiery explosion. Of their own making."

"Okay," Etienne allowed. "So, they didn't do *everything* well. But there were *some* beliefs and traditions held by different people on the First World that we happen to like upholding."

Chatine glanced back over her shoulder. "Like eating wood chips?"

He snickered. "Hey, don't knock it until you try it. With a little salt, they're pretty tasty."

Chatine allowed herself a chuckle. "Well, I have to say Marilyn is . . ."

Etienne leaned forward, his eyes narrowing. "Yes?"

"Interesting," she finished with a smirk.

Etienne considered. "Interesting good or interesting bad?"

"I've never seen anything like it, that's for sure."

"That's because she's one of a kind."

"Hmm." Chatine reached out and ran her fingertips lightly across the console.

Etienne hastily shooed her away. "Whoa, whoa. Time to set some ground rules. Rule number one: Only *I* touch the controls, okay?"

Chatine theatrically tucked her hands into her armpits. "And rule number two?"

"There is no rule number two. There doesn't have to be. Because rule number one is everything. Marilyn is my ship. I am the only one allowed to fly her. And you don't touch anything unless I tell you to. Understood?"

Chatine intentionally ignored the question. "What class of ship is this, anyway?"

Etienne folded his hands contentedly on his lap. "There is no *class*. Like I said, she's one of a kind. The only one. My own invention."

"Wait a minute, you *built* this ship yourself?"

Etienne opened his mouth to reply but then seemed to think better of it. "You know what? I've told you too much already. And you don't exactly strike me as a super trustworthy type of person."

Chatine gasped in mock offense. "Me? I'm completely trustworthy."

Etienne spun around and faced out the front window, adjusting a few dials.

"So, you built this ship yourself, huh?" Chatine sidled casually up to the console. "And it actually flies?"

Etienne flashed her another warning look. "It has excellent ejection capabilities as well, in case you want to test out that feature."

She smirked. "That's okay. I *trust* you."

He sneered at her obvious jab. "Good. Because Maman says trust is the building block of all good relationships."

Chatine instinctively backed away from his chair. "Okay, I'm going to stop you right there. We don't have a *relationship*. Good or otherwise."

Etienne exploded in laughter. "Wow. Your buttons are, like, displayed right across your face."

Confused, Chatine glared. "What buttons?"

He gestured to the series of colored dials and switches on his console. "You know, your push buttons. Your hot spots. You press them and *bam!*" He slammed his palm down. "Instant outrage." He looked up at Chatine's face, squinting as though he were searching for something. "Hmm. Let's see here. I bet you have an auto-engage disgust lever somewhere on there too."

Chatine felt every ounce of fluid in her body start to boil. And she did *not* like the feeling of this guy scrutinizing her face. She turned away with a grunt. "Shut up."

"Wow. That one was even easier to find than I thought."

She bristled. This Défecteur was really starting to grate her nerves. "So, how did you get involved in a mission to break out Citizen Rousseau? Do you work for the Vangarde or something?"

"We don't work for anyone," Etienne said sharply. "And I'm not telling you anything else."

"So, they blackmailed you?"

The pilot turned back around, clearly attempting to ignore her. Chatine flicked her gaze over the controls, selecting one at random. "Hmm. What does this one do?"

Etienne dove toward her hand and smacked it away. "Fine. The Vangarde hired us for the mission. Sometimes we offer our services for a price. Happy?"

Chatine thought about Roche, who was also Henri, who was also on that other ship with Citizen Rousseau.

"How many ships were there on the mission?"

Etienne pressed his lips together. Chatine reached for another switch on the console.

"Okay!" he shouted in surrender. "There were two. Two ships. The primary-extraction ship and the bounty ship." He jabbed his thumbs at his chest. "That would be me. Now stop trying to touch things."

"Bounty? What bounty?"

With a relenting sigh, Etienne punched a button on the console, and one of the monitors flickered to life, displaying a view of a small, darkened cargo hold full of metal shelves and steel lockers. Strapped into one of the shelves, Chatine could make out a row of clear boxes, stacked to their lids with blocs of a glowing blue metal she knew all too well.

Her mouth fell open. "You stole zyttrium from Bastille?"

"Like I said. We offer our services for a price."

Chatine's mind churned. What did the Défecteurs want with zyttrium? They obviously weren't in the business of making Skins.

"So, the other ship." Chatine refocused her thoughts. "You know the person flying it?"

"Yes. Faustine. She's a friend of mine. A fine pilote, too."

"Then, you know where the ship is going?"

"Nope," Etienne said, and when Chatine extended her hand toward a large blue dial, he swiped it away and cried, "I swear! I don't know. The Vangarde didn't give us the location up front. We were just ordered to fly their operatives to Bastille, pick up their precious cargo, and fly back to Laterre. We were told they would direct the extraction ship to a destination once the cargo was aboard."

"By cargo, you mean Citizen Rousseau, right?" Chatine asked.

"Yeah, sure, whoever. Don't know. Don't care. We try not to get involved with matters of the Regime."

"But isn't that exactly what you just did? Get involved? I mean, breaking out Citizen Rousseau is an act of war against the Regime."

"Maybe for them. But for us, it was a simple business deal." He tapped on the view of the cargo hold.

"So you're mercenaries?"

Etienne cocked his head, looking unsettled. "No. We try to keep to ourselves most of the time. Until we need something that we can't make or grow ourselves—like zyttrium—and then we sell our services."

"That's a mercenary."

"And here we go again with the labels. What's up with that?"

"You're the one who called me a gridder."

"That's . . ."—he hesitated, quirking his lips—". . . different."

"Uh-huh. So you have no idea where the other ship is going?"

"Not a clue."

"Can't you AirLink them or something?"

"We don't do AirLinks. And the Vangarde specifically requested no communication. As an extra precaution."

Chatine felt frustration swell in her chest. "But I need to know. My brother is on that ship."

A chill splintered through her at the sound of that word. It was the first time she'd said it aloud in years.

My brother.

My brother.

Etienne shrugged. "Sorry. I can't help you."

With a huff, Chatine turned her gaze out the window, checking to see how far away from Laterre they were. Once they landed, she would just have to go looking for Henri herself. She knew where the Vangarde base was. She'd found it just before she was sent to Bastille. She would start there. And she would not stop until she found him again.

"When are we landing?" she asked.

Etienne swiveled his chair back toward the control console and glanced at one of the monitors. "One minute until atmosphere break."

"Great," Chatine said tightly.

Etienne jabbed at a switch on the console.

"Autopilote disabled," the ship said.

Etienne took hold of the throttle and yanked it back. The engines made a hiccupping noise and then roared to life. Grabbing the contrôleur, he began to steer the ship down toward the great blanket of clouds that encompassed Laterre. As they descended, the ship's dials and switches wobbled in their plates and the small metal cabinets built into the cockpit's hull rattled like a mouthful of loose teeth.

Hobbling as fast as she could back to her seat, Chatine quickly buckled her restraints and stared out at the approaching planet. The clouds came closer and closer until, with a slam and judder, the ship was diving into them. Through them. White and gray consumed every window while the engines whinnied and revved under their seats.

And then, in a burst of light and rain, she was back. Back beneath the canopy of clouds and soaring above a vast, dark ocean.

The Secana Sea, Chatine thought, a bubble of nostalgia rising up inside of her.

She'd only been gone from Laterre for two weeks. She couldn't believe she'd actually missed it, but she had.

Chatine stared out the cockpit window as Etienne guided the ship over swells of choppy water that seemed to go on forever. Morning had just started to push its way through the night, and the ocean was beginning to glimmer and brighten. Before long, Chatine could see land coming into view. She spotted the vast green mass of the Forest Verdure first. A seemingly endless expanse of trees, hugging every hill and mountain, with the lumber town of Bûcheron almost hidden at its center. To the left, she saw the Frets, huddled around each other like a group of rusting beasts at a watering hole. And, off in the distance, Chatine could see Ledôme up on its hill, twinkling and glowing amid the heavy dawn mist.

Vallonay, she thought to herself.

She'd made it.

She grabbed hold of her seat restraints, bracing herself for another sharp turn. But then, a second later, she realized that the ship was not banking. It was not even slowing. Etienne continued to fly over the trees, past the Frets, Ledôme, and the low-lying ferme-lands.

"Where are we going?" Chatine asked warily.

Etienne shook his head. "Sorry. Can't tell you. Top secret." He leaned over, opened one of the metal cabinets next to Chatine, and pulled out a long strip of fabric. "Which reminds me, you'll have to put this blindfold on."

"What? No."

"Those are the rules."

"I thought there was only one rule."

"Which you've already broken, like, three times."

Chatine let out an exasperated sigh. "Just drop me off in Vallonay, please."

This made Etienne cackle. "Sure, right, right. Me, a member of a community that the Ministère doesn't even know exists, I'll just land my ship, which the Ministère doesn't know I have, in the middle of Laterre's capital. Yeah, I'll get right on that."

Chatine threw up her hands. "I thought this ship had stealth mode."

"Yeah, *stealth* mode. Not stupidity override mode."

"Well, then just drop me off at the edge of the city. In the Forest Verdure or something. I'll find my way back."

"Brilliant plan," Etienne commended, steering the ship into a sharp left turn. "Now, tell me, will you be *walking* on that wounded leg of yours? Or crawling? Just wondering."

Chatine balled her fists, trying to keep her temper under control. "I have to find him!"

"Look," Etienne said, his voice softening with what sounded like sympathy. "We're nearly there. As soon as the other ship gets back, you can ask Faustine about your brother, okay?"

Chatine froze, a debilitating shiver running down her spine. "Nearly *where?*"

"Just put on the blindfold please so I can land."

"Still don't trust me, huh?"

"Trust is a two-way street, Gridder."

With a grunt, Chatine snatched the fabric from Etienne and tied it around the back of her head. She could feel Etienne's hand waving in front of her face. "I can't see anything," she muttered.

A moment later, Chatine felt a familiar tug in her stomach. The pressure building behind her ears, threatening to pop. They were descending.

"Where are you taking me?" Chatine asked.

"To the camp."

"A *Défecteur* camp?" she screeched.

The pilote huffed at the word but ignored her.

With the blindfold on, Chatine felt vulnerable and disoriented. She had a hard time tracking the ship's sharp turns and deceleration. Then, finally, the engine settled into a low hum and Etienne removed the fabric from her eyes.

Desperately, Chatine searched the horizon for any sign of civilization, but there was nothing in front of them, behind them, or to either side of them except vast stretches of ice and frozen grass, punctuated by craggy outcrops of rock.

"Um," she said anxiously, glancing around at the unforgiving landscape, "This is the *Terrain Perdu.*"

Etienne shrugged, as though this were an insignificant detail. As though it weren't a well-known fact that no one had ever survived a single night out here in this frozen tundra.

"You call it the Terrain Perdu," he said nonchalantly. "We just call it home."

- CHAPTER 27 -
MARCELLUS

OVER THE SPAN OF HIS NINETEEN YEARS OF LIFE, Marcellus had seen many things and visited many places. He'd circled this planet countless times. He'd flown billions of kilomètres amongst the stars. He'd traveled to every planet in the System Divine.

Except Albion.

Because no one from Laterre *ever* visited Albion.

Marcellus had heard plenty of stories about its picturesque blue skies and flawless weather. Being the most similar in landscape and climate to the First World, the families of the Human Conservation Commission had squabbled ruthlessly over the planet when the System Divine had first been discovered. But no two families had fought harder than the Paresse family and the Bellingham family. It had been the start of a five-century-long feud that still waged to this day, marking Albion the number-one enemy of Laterre.

And now, Marcellus had just volunteered to go there.

"Are you insane?" Gabriel shouted. "You can't go to *Albion*."

"Didn't you hear him?" Cerise fired back. "The general is building a weapon that will be delivered in two weeks. He must be stopped!"

They were standing in the middle of the Tourbay, with Cerise's crui-seur idling nearby. Even though the Sols were rising and the skies were slowly brightening, the abundant mist of the boglands provided an effec-tive cover. Just as it once had for Mabelle and her Montfer cell of the Vangarde. Before her life was snuffed out in an instant.

Marcellus hastily pushed the thought from his mind. He had to com-partmentalize. He could not find the courage to do what he'd just sworn to do *and* grieve at the same time.

"But you can't just *go* to Albion!" Gabriel said, exasperated. "It's an enemy planet. You'll get shot right out of space before you even get close! It's a suicide mission."

Marcellus kneaded his hands together, his heart pounding in his chest.

Was he insane?

Was this a suicide mission?

"Maybe so," Marcellus admitted. "But I have no other choice. This has to be done."

Gabriel scoffed. "Oh, so you're just going to waltz right onto Albion and be like, 'Hey! I hear you're making a weapon for General Bonnefaçon. Any idea who's working on that, because I'd like to talk to them.'"

"No, genius," Cerise snapped. "I can send a message back to the source through the probe. Alouette can code it, right?" She looked at Alouette who nodded. "We'll pretend to be this Denise person, because clearly the source trusts her, and we'll ask the source where to meet."

Marcellus gaped at Cerise, thoroughly impressed.

"Are you *all* insane?" Gabriel screeched. "Even if you do somehow miraculously manage to get into Albion airspace, have you not heard the rumors about the Albion Royal Guard? Plucked out of their houses as infants and trained to be killers?"

"No one is asking you to come with us," Cerise snapped.

Marcellus blinked and reeled on Cerise. "Wait a minute, *us*?"

"I'm coming with you," Cerise said, as though this had already been decided and the detail had simply slipped Marcellus's mind.

"You absolutely are *not* coming with me."

"Yes, I am," she declared. "You're going to need my help."

"No, I won't. Just go back to Ledôme and—"

"I can't go back to Ledôme!" she shouted, startling Marcellus.

"Why not?"

"Because . . ." She took a breath, steadying herself. "Because I just can't, okay? I'm going with you, Marcellus, and that's the end of it. You're going to need a good hacker. *And* you're going to need someone who can get you a voyageur. Have you already forgotten about this?"

Cerise tapped on her TéléCom and turned it around so everyone could see Marcellus's arrest warrant glowing on the screen.

Marcellus felt like he was being sucked right into the marshy ground beneath his feet. He *had* almost forgotten about that. The entire planet would be out looking for him. He couldn't just walk into the Vallonay spaceport and order a voyageur.

"And you're not the only one who's wanted," Cerise shot a pointed look at Alouette and Gabriel.

"What?" Alouette asked.

Cerise sighed, like she was growing impatient with being the smartest person in the group. She flicked her finger across the screen of the TéléCom again. The image of Marcellus's face grew smaller, and then, beside it, two more faces appeared: Alouette and Gabriel.

"Arrest warrant for Gabriel Courfey and Unknown Female, last seen escaping from the Montfer Policier Precinct. Female is considered a high-priority fugitive. Any information leading to her whereabouts should be AirLinked directly to the Ministère headquarters."

Alouette sucked in a sharp breath.

"Don't worry," Gabriel whispered to her. "I've got, like, a hundred of those. And they haven't caught me yet." He stopped, a thought just occurring to him. "'Unknown Female'? Wait, how are you not in the Communiqué?"

"In fact," Cerise said, ignoring Gabriel. "I seem to be the only person here who's *not* wanted by the Policier." She narrowed her eyes at Marcellus. "Which, right now, makes me your greatest asset."

Surrendering a sigh, Marcellus looked from the TéléCom to Cerise. "Okay, how do you propose we do this?"

Cerise beamed triumphantly as she flipped her TéléCom back around. "I'm glad you asked. Once we're out of Laterrian airspace, I can place a cloaking code on the ship and override the navigation system to reroute us to Albion."

"You can do that?" Marcellus asked.

"Like I said before," Cerise flashed him a pointed look. "I'm an expert hacker. One could even say I'm *soop*."

"Don't say 'soop,'" Gabriel said warningly.

"Why not? It's Third Estate slang meaning 'the best.'"

"I know what it means," Gabriel said. "But you can't wear that hat and say 'soop.'"

Cerise huffed and straightened her rhinestone-studded beret. "I told you, it's not a hat—"

"Just order the voyageur," Marcellus cut her off before another argument could break out between them.

"On it!" Cerise chirped. She bounded back toward the cruiseur and disappeared inside.

"It's confirmed. You *are* all insane." Gabriel threw up his hands and, with a sigh, followed after Cerise.

Marcellus turned to reboard the cruiseur but was stopped by a gentle hand on his arm. "Wait." Alouette's kind, compassionate face almost seemed to glow in the mist. "I think Gabriel might be right. I think you should take a breath and really think this through."

"I don't have time to take a breath," Marcellus said. "You heard the message. This source knows how to stop the weapon. Someone has to go to Albion. Now. Or the general wins."

"Yes, but have you considered your other options?" Alouette asked reasonably.

"What other options?"

"Don't you think you should try to . . ."—Alouette paused, looking like the next words were difficult for her to say—"contact the Vangarde?

They might be able to help. Or, at the very least, shouldn't you tell them about the message? If Albion is delivering a weapon to the general in two weeks, they should know about it."

Marcellus felt a stab of guilt as he looked into Alouette's large, dark eyes, and the realization hit him. "You don't know."

Of course she didn't know. She'd left the Vangarde. And she didn't have a Skin, so she couldn't have seen the Universal Alert from earlier tonight.

"Don't know what?" she asked.

Marcellus rubbed at the stubble that was forming on his jaw. He'd barely slept a full hour in the Renards' couchette and the fatigue was starting to creep in. How could he possibly break this news to her? He glanced anxiously around the Tourbay, as though searching for help.

"Last night," he began hesitantly, "the Vangarde tried to break Citizen Rousseau out of Bastille."

Something flickered in Alouette's eyes that Marcellus couldn't identify. For a moment, he wondered if she even knew who Citizen Rousseau was. Last time he'd seen her, she didn't even seem to know who the *Vangarde* was.

But then, in a tentative voice, she asked, "Did they— Did they succeed? Did they get her out?"

Marcellus let out a heavy sigh as the memory of that ship vanishing in a deadly flash of light replayed in his mind. "No. My grandfather discovered the Vangarde's plan. He sent in a fleet of combatteurs, and they shot down her ship as it was taking off." He lowered his head. "I'm so sorry."

Alouette stood motionless next to him, her face gaunt, her breathing shallow. Then, as though remembering something, she reached into the bag strapped around her chest and pulled out a long string of metallic beads. Marcellus recognized them as the same ones she'd been wearing that day in the Forest Verdure, when they'd sat around the fire and she'd helped him remember how to read the Forgotten Word. The ones with the metal tag that said: LITTLE LARK.

"Who else was on the ship?" she asked vacantly as she ran the beads through her fingers in a slow, methodical rhythm. "How many others are . . ." her voice broke off. She couldn't bring herself to say the word.

"I don't know," Marcellus said hastily, once again trying to push that dreadful memory of Mabelle's face from his mind. "I'm sorry. All I know is that"—he dragged the toe of his boot anxiously through the mud—"I haven't been able to make contact with the Vangarde since."

A small sound escaped Alouette's lips, almost like a hiccup. And for a long time, she just stood there, unblinking and unseeing, her eyes locked on the mist, her mind somewhere far, far away from here.

"What does that mean?" she managed to say at last, her voice a cracked whisper.

Marcellus shook his head. He didn't want to say it. Up until now, he hadn't said it. He'd barely managed to think it. But he had a feeling he *needed* to say it. For Alouette. For himself. For Laterre.

He shuddered out a breath. "I think it means that I'm on my own."

He closed his eyes, letting the truth sink in like heavy fog in his bones. He felt something slip into his hand, and he was certain it was the mist. But when he opened his eyes, he saw Alouette's fingers interlaced with his own.

"No, you're not." Her eyes blazed with a familiar, fierce determination. Familiar because he'd seen it on his own face. Every time he looked in the mirror. It was a sensation he knew all too well. A determination he was confident would either save Laterre from certain death or plunge them all straight into it. "I'm coming with you."

- CHAPTER 28 -
CHATINE

"NO." CHATINE STARED IN HORROR AT THE DESOLATE, frozen landscape that stretched out for kilomètres around Etienne's ship. "No way. Take me back to Vallonay. Or Montfer. Or the Southern Peninsula. Anywhere. I am *not* going to a Défecteur camp."

"Uh, I don't think you have a choice. And besides, that leg of yours needs immediate attention. It's not going to stay warm and tingly like that forever. The shrapnel dug itself in there pretty bad. If you don't get it taken care of, you're looking at a one-legged future."

"Oh, so not only do you *live* in the Terrain Perdu, you have a med center out here too?" Chatine asked skeptically.

Etienne scoffed at this. "Med centers are useless. We have something better."

"I'm afraid to ask."

"Healers."

Chatine scowled. "What is a healer?"

"A healer treats the body as a whole, instead of relying solely on médicaments and invasive procedures to fix the individual parts. And my maman happens to the best healer in our community."

"You're kidding, right?" Chatine glanced at Etienne's sober expression. "You're not kidding."

Etienne eased on the contrôleur until the ship glided to a halt just above the ground. Lakes of ice, blankets of rigid grass, spindly bushes, and jagged, misshapen rocks stretched out in front of them for kilomètres. The same monotonous and unchanging pattern as far as Chatine could see.

"Here we are!" he said, making a sweeping gesture toward the front window. "Home sweet home."

Chatine glanced out again. All she saw was deserted, frozen wilderness. "I don't see anything."

Etienne turned to her with panicked eyes. "You don't?! Are you sure?! It's right there!"

Anxiety trickled through Chatine's stomach. She turned back and stared out the cockpit window. She blinked a few times, but still saw nothing.

"No!" she said. "I don't see anything! Did that stupid goldenroot you gave me do something to my vision? I knew I shouldn't have trusted a dropout Defect—"

Etienne laughed. "Relax, I'm kidding. Do you honestly think we'd be able to survive out here for this long by living in plain sight? But on the bright side, looks like I found your panic button."

Chatine jabbed a fist out to punch him in the side, but he was too quick, ducking just out of her reach.

Etienne dipped the ship's contrôleur, and Chatine was thrust forward in her harness as they careened down a sharp incline. Suddenly, a cluster of metallic structures seemed to emerge from the frozen nothingness. The small, flat-roofed buildings were connected by crisscrossing walkways, each shielded by a similar flat roof that was held up by narrow stilts.

They reached the bottom of the slope, and Chatine gazed in astonishment at the scattering of buildings. Invisible one second and there the next.

"Stealth technology isn't just for ships," Etienne said, reading her expression.

He steered them into a wide open-mouthed hangar that was cut into the side of the slope and flipped a single switch on the console. Slowly the engines grew still and quiet. Then he jabbed a button over his head, and a door appeared in one of the walls, which then folded over itself to form a short set of stairs.

"Primary hatch deployed," Marilyn announced.

Chatine instantly shivered as the cold air of the hangar rushed inside the ship, slapping against her arms and face. Etienne began to make his way toward the stairs but stopped when he noticed that Chatine hadn't moved.

"Are you coming? Do you need help? I can carry you. I'd rather not, but I will."

Chatine gripped on to her harness. "No way. I am *not* stepping foot inside a camp full of Défecteurs. I've never trusted you people, and now I know why. You're insane. You can't *live* in the Terrain Perdu. No one can live in the Terrain Perdu. That's why people call it Dead Man's Land! Everyone dies there!"

Etienne shrugged. "Fine. Suit yourself." He continued toward the stairs but stopped again a moment later, as though remembering something. He opened up a small compartment next to the hatch; pulled out a strange, palm-sized device; and tossed it to Chatine, who just barely managed to catch it. She studied it with curiosity. On one end was a crooked antenna, while the other end sported a scuffed dial next to a clunky red button.

"Radio me when you change your mind and want me to come get you."

"I'm not going to change my mind."

He smiled. "Okay, I'll rephrase. Radio me when the goldenroot wears off."

Then, with a knowing raise of his brow, Etienne hopped down the steps of the hatch door and disappeared into the hangar.

The moment he was out of view, Chatine leapt into action. She tossed the device to the side, unbuckled her harness, and hobbled over to the capitaine's chair, sweeping her gaze over the giant console.

"Okay," she whispered to herself. "You can do this. It's just a stupid Défecteur ship. It can't be that complicated." She just had to find the right control, engage the engines, and fly the fric out of there.

She pinched one of the levers between her fingers and flicked it upward. Nothing happened. She toggled it back and forth, but the engine remained quiet. She eyed a second, nearly identical switch, three centimètres to the left, and gave it a swift flick.

A loud blaring siren rang out across the ship. Chatine startled and scrambled away from the console, stumbling over her injured leg and falling backward.

"Owww!" she cried as lights along the baseboards began to flash fierce and red.

Then, came a voice.

"Intruder aboard. Intruder aboard."

Her mouth fell open. The wretched ship was ratting her out. That mouchard!

"You know," she muttered aloud. "Where I come from, you can lose a few toes for being a snitch."

Suddenly, everything halted. The flashing lights flickered off. The alarm fell silent.

"Will you stop trying to steal my ship and just come out of there already?"

Chatine jumped and spun around, ready to face off with the pilote again, but there was no one there.

"Marilyn is never going to let you fly her. Only I know how to start that ship."

The voice was coming from somewhere behind her. And it was only now she noticed that there was a scratchiness to it. A crackle. Her gaze landed on the strange, antennaed device lying in the center of the cockpit. She crept forward and cautiously poked at it.

"Have you had enough of your antics?"

With a squeak, she retracted her finger.

"How are you doing that?" she asked the box.

The box let out a sigh. "Press the red button."

She glanced around the cockpit. "The red button?"

"On the radio," Etienne said, sounding impatient and just the tiniest bit amused. It made Chatine's hackles rise. "It shouldn't be hard for you. You're familiar with buttons, right?"

There was a snicker and Chatine wanted to snatch up the device and throw it out the hatch. But instead, she picked it up and pressed down tentatively on the button. "Hello?"

"So, now that you've figured out that Marilyn's anti-theft system is impenetrable, are you ready to come out?"

"No," she said stubbornly.

"So you're just going to sit out there all day and night? Even when the temperature drops?"

She lowered back down into the capitaine's chair. "Yes."

Etienne didn't reply. And Chatine commended herself for winning the argument. But then, not a full minute later, she felt something sharp and stabbing in her left leg, right where the shrapnel had hit her. It was like nothing she'd ever experienced before. A searing pain that seemed to ricochet through her body, faster than a paralyzeur pulse from a rayonette. The warm, tingling sensation in her leg waned, and all that was left in its place was pure, unbearable anguish.

Chatine let out a scream that echoed around the small cockpit, out the open hatch, and deep into the silent hangar. The pain was all-consuming. It blurred her vision and screeched in her ears. It seemed to go on so long, Chatine could swear an entire season had passed on Laterre. They were no longer in the Darkest Night. They had entered the Blue Dawn. And yet, the pain was still there.

Finally, the radio crackled again, and she felt boundless relief when Etienne said, "That's it. I'm coming to get you."

- CHAPTER 29 -
ALOUETTE

"ARRIVAL AT MONTFER SPACEPORT IN FIVE MINUTES," the cruiseur announced before banking sharply and descending through the drizzly air. Alouette pressed her nose to the window as the last remaining traces of the boglands rushed past. The morning Sols shone behind the clouds above, turning them into a vast glowing blanket of gray, and up ahead, Alouette could see the city of Montfer waking up.

Tears stung her eyes, blurring her reflection in the cruiseur's plastique windows. She couldn't stop thinking about what Marcellus had told her in the Tourbay.

The sisters' plan had failed.

Citizen Rousseau was dead.

Along with who else?

No. Don't think like that. She hastily wiped her eyes and forced the morbid thoughts from her mind. She couldn't afford to think like that. They were heading to an enemy planet to track down Denise's source and stop the general from unleashing some disastrous weapon. She had to stay focused. Stay sharp. Stay *positive*.

"So, you're really going through with this?" The voice belonged to Gabriel. It ripped Alouette from her thoughts and the window.

"Yes," said Cerise, peering over the top of her TéléCom. "I've already made all the arrangements."

Gabriel darted a look at Alouette. "Fine. I guess that means I'll have to come too."

Cerise lowered her TéléCom, looking suspicious. "Why? You just said you thought we were all insane."

"Yes. And that's exactly why I *have* to go. You pampered idiots have no idea what you're getting into. You're going to get yourselves killed. I'm your best chance at survival."

"So, *you* are going to help us stop the general?" Cerise confirmed. She didn't sound convinced. And to be honest, Alouette wasn't convinced either.

"Yes," Gabriel said, folding his arms over his chest.

"*You* are going to help save the planet."

"Is that so hard for you to believe?" Gabriel challenged.

"Yes."

"Gabriel," Alouette said gently. She had a feeling he was hiding something from them, she just wasn't sure what it was. "You don't have to do this."

Gabriel uncrossed his arms and began to fidget with the edge of the seat. "I know. I *want* to do it." He shot Alouette a look that she interpreted as, *just let it go.*

"Okay," she said. "Well, I'm glad you're coming."

"Me too," he said hastily before turning toward the window, clearly avoiding her gaze.

The cruiseur banked again, and the spaceport loomed into view. In the early morning, it was a collage of shadows, tiny blinking lights, and dark shapes extending far into the distance. But Alouette could easily make out the terminal, a massive egg-shaped hangar at the center of the complex. Even under the gloomy skies, the great dome seemed to shimmer and shine. A moment later, there was a sudden burst of light from the rear side of the port, and in a cascade of rumbles and smoke, a voyageur shot up toward the sky. As it tore through Laterre's layer of constant clouds, Alouette imagined she could see a glimpse of the stars above.

Stars that, in just a few hours, she would see up close.

Stars that would soon surround her in infinite space.

"Okay," Cerise said, setting down her TéléCom. "The voyageur is all ready to go. As soon as we're onboard, we'll send a message to the source on Albion to request the coordinates for a meeting."

Marcellus nodded pensively, his eyes never leaving the window. Alouette felt a rush of anticipation. They were really doing this. They were really going to Albion. Alouette never thought she'd ever get to travel to another planet, let alone Laterre's longest-standing enemy.

"All right! This is it. Here we go." Gabriel rubbed his hands together as though trying to warm them. "Now, I don't want anyone to be nervous. People fly to other planets every single day. Just a normal occurrence. Voyageurs *very* rarely explode into fiery balls of light when leaving the atmosphere. There's absolutely no reason to be scared."

"No one is scared but you," Cerise deadpanned.

Gabriel scoffed, which quickly turned into a cough. "Scared? Me? No way. I've been waiting my whole life to fly on one of those fancy voyageurs. Do you think they'll serve gâteau? I've never had gâteau before. Or maybe duck paté? What does paté even taste like? I can't say it sounds particularly appealing. Did you know that duck paté comes from Usonia? Why is that? Do they have a duck infestation problem there? Do ducks just roam about freely in those giant plastique bubbles? Like the chickens in the Marsh?"

Cerise let out a groan. "Are you going to blab all the way to Albion? Because I'm not sure I can take five days of that."

Gabriel winked at Cerise. "Don't worry, Sparkles. I'm an acquired taste. I imagine much like duck paté."

"If you don't shut up, I'm not bringing you."

"Hold on," Marcellus said, ripping his gaze from the window as though a thought had just occurred to him. "She's right."

Gabriel scoffed again. "No, she's not. Wait. About what?"

"About bringing you. About bringing all of us. How do you expect to get us on that voyageur?" He gestured at Alouette, Gabriel, and himself. "We're all wanted criminals now. It's not like the three of us can just walk into the spaceport and board a ship."

Cerise flashed a crafty smile that, for some reason, made Alouette's stomach flip. "Don't worry. I've already thought of that."

Gabriel snorted. "What, are you going to smuggle us on in your luggage? Along with your collection of ridiculous hats?"

Cerise's eyes twinkled with mischief. "Actually . . ."

Gabriel flinched. "I was joking." He turned to Alouette. "She knows I was joking, right?"

Cerise pulled her TéléCom out of her pocket and tapped on the screen. "Bonjour, ma chéri," she crooned in a sickeningly sweet voice. "How is the son of Montfer's esteemed inspecteur doing this morning?"

"Who are you talking to?" Gabriel demanded before turning to Alouette. "Who is she talking to?"

Cerise winked at Gabriel and whispered, "I have friends in very high places."

Gabriel rolled his eyes. "Of course she does."

Cerise focused back on her AirLink. "So, remember that favor you owe me?" She let out a playful chuckle at whatever was just said in response. "Right, so, here's the deal. I'm going to be flying out with a *very* large shipment of cargo this morning, and I need some help getting it past security."

CHAPTER 30

MARCELLUS

"LIFTOFF IN THIRTY SECONDS." THE COMPUTERIZED voice of the autopilote system drifted through the cargo hold of the Galactique-class voyageur.

Marcellus shivered. He had never been so cold in his life. The ice packs wedged tightly against his body were starting to make his skin burn. He could feel Alouette's hand beside his, cold as the ground of the Terrain Perdu. And on his other side, Gabriel shivered so hard, it rattled the walls of the crate that surrounded them like a tomb.

"Twenty-two, twenty-one, twenty . . ."

"I can't believe I let that sparkle-headed lunatic talk us into this," Gabriel whispered.

"Shh," said Marcellus.

"They barely even checked the cargo," Gabriel went on, undeterred. "She just did this to torture me."

When they'd arrived at the spaceport thirty minutes ago, Cerise had directed the cruiseur to the cargo-loading center, where they'd been met by a gregarious young man named Grantaire, the son of Montfer's Policier inspecteur. According to Cerise, he was a fellow "sympathizeur," but given Marcellus's previous encounters with Policier inspecteurs, he had been hesitant to trust him. They hadn't disclosed any details about what they were doing or why, but it hadn't really mattered in the end. Marcellus had seen the look of recognition on Grantaire's face the moment he'd first laid eyes on Marcellus. It was the same look Marcellus had seen on the face of that Red Scar guard in the Jondrette. He knew *exactly* who Marcellus was.

Now Marcellus just had to hope that Cerise had been right to trust him.

It had been Grantaire's idea to pack Marcellus, Alouette, and Gabriel—the three fugitives—into a large shipping crate full of ice, in order to fool the body-heat scanners at the security checkpoint.

And Marcellus was about as happy about the solution as Gabriel.

"Body-heat scanners?" Gabriel snorted. "Yeah, right. They probably don't even *have* body-heat scanners at that port."

"Shh!" came Alouette's voice from Marcellus's other side.

"And that's another thing," Gabriel ranted. "Why are we still in here? There's no one else on this ship!"

Marcellus shivered again. The ice packs were creating condensation, and it was soaking through his coat.

"Fifteen . . . fourteen . . . thirteen . . ."

"She's probably up there right now, sitting pretty on a sateen chaise and sipping champagne, while we're down here freezing to death. Sols, I can't stand that little—"

"Ten . . . nine . . . eight . . ."

Gabriel let out a small yelp but mercifully fell quiet.

Through the thick walls of the crate, Marcellus could feel the spacecraft's giant engines beginning to rumble beneath them. Alouette's hand brushed up against his in the darkness, searching for him. He grabbed it and squeezed. "Don't be scared," he whispered. "Once we break atmosphere, it'll be smooth."

"For the last time, I'm *not* scared," Gabriel snapped.

"Shh!" Marcellus and Alouette said at once.

"Five . . . four . . . three . . . two . . . one . . ."

The engines roared and pulsed, until it felt like the whole ship might be on the brink of exploding.

"Okay, I lied," Gabriel said. "I'm scared!"

Marcellus reached out in the darkness and grabbed his hand too. This seemed to calm him down. Marcellus had never experienced a voyageur takeoff from the cargo hold, without the proper safety restraints and counter stabilization. It was an entirely different experience. The force of the liftoff was so strong, Marcellus wondered if they would be pushed clean out of the crate, through the thick PermaSteel hull of the voyageur, and into the nothingness of the air outside.

He shut his eyes and felt both Alouette and Gabriel squeeze his hands tighter.

But then, like a wave finally hitting the shore, all the power and fury of the last few minutes suddenly seemed to fade away. The voyageur broke through Laterre's atmosphere, and the world went calm and still and quiet.

Beside him, Gabriel exhaled as though he'd been holding his breath. "Was that it? Did the ship explode? Are we dead?"

Alouette chuckled. "No. We're not dead."

"Well, we're going to be soon if Sparkles doesn't put down her paté and open this crate right now."

"Surprise, surprise," came a familiar voice from the cargo hold. "Gabriel is complaining. I never would have guessed."

"You know," Gabriel yelled, "I've had about enough of your sarcasm. Just get us—"

But his words were cut off by a banging sound, followed by a loud creak, and then blinding light flooded into the crate as the lid was yanked open. Cerise beamed down at them. "Awww . . . don't you three look cozy?"

Gabriel immediately released Marcellus's hand and climbed hastily and clumsily out of the crate. He shook out his fingers. "Not funny. Next time *you* can ride in the ice box."

"Too bad it didn't freeze off your tongue," Cerise said as she grabbed

Alouette's hand and helped her out of the crate. Marcellus clambered out after her, wobbling slightly on his still-frozen legs.

They followed Cerise out of the dim, windowless cargo hold; through a maze of low-ceilinged gangways; and up a series of grated PermaSteel staircases. Finally, they reached the voyageur's flight bridge, a semicircular room with a bank of blinking consoles, plush flight seats, and glowing monitors on every free surface.

Marcellus nearly crashed into Alouette, who had stopped suddenly in her tracks.

"Oh my Sols," she whispered as she stared, speechless and gaping.

Marcellus followed her gaze toward the vast window that wrapped around the front half of the flight bridge, and it was only then that he understood her reaction.

She had never left Laterre before.

Which meant, she had never seen stars before.

And as he stood beside her, staring out the window, he suddenly felt like he, too, was seeing the stars for the first time. Through her eyes. There were thousands—no *millions*—of them. Twinkling and glowing. As though someone had thrown a shaker of salt crystals across a vast, beautiful blanket. A blanket so endless and infinite and black.

And there, nestled amongst the stars, hanging in the voyageur's window like a priceless piece of First World art, was Laterre. A marble of swirling white and gray.

"Whoa," Gabriel said, stepping up to the window. "Titanique."

"Titanique?" Marcellus repeated.

"Yeah, you know. Soop, stellar, awesome."

"Yes," said Alouette, turning to share a smile with Gabriel. "It really is titanique, isn't it?"

Gabriel chuckled. "The planet almost looks *nice* from here."

Marcellus squinted into the sky, where he could just make out the faint shadow of Bastille, peeking up over the horizon of Laterre. For a fleeting moment, he let his thoughts drift back to Mabelle. And then to Chatine. He'd checked her location twice since leaving her couchette and both times he'd gotten the same frustrating response.

"Location unknown."

Where was she?

"I've installed the cloaking code," Cerise announced, and Marcellus turned to see she was seated in front of the main flight console with her TéléCom open in front of her. He left the window and walked over to look at her screen. "The ship's flight log will display Reichenstat as the destination, but the coordinates in the nav system are set to Albion."

In the center of the flight bridge, a hologram map glowed above a small pedestal, illustrating their flight path from Laterre, across the Asteroid Channel, to the pristine blue-and-green planet of Laterre's long-time enemy. And suspended above the two planets, like the countdown of an explosif, was a giant clock, ticking down the time until their arrival.

05.02.32

5 days. 2 hours. 32 minutes.

"I'm going to explore the ship!" Gabriel said, his eyes lighting up at the idea. "Anyone want to join me?" He glanced from Cerise to Alouette to Marcellus who all stared blankly back at him. "No takers? Okay then."

Once Gabriel had scurried off toward the stairs to the lower decks, Cerise rolled her eyes and continued, "I also managed to hijack an inactive Albion call signal to mask the Laterrian one on this ship. So that should allow us to cross into Albion airspace without any problems. But we can't just land a Laterrian voyageur in an Albion spaceport. So we're going to have to figure out another place to land. Maybe a private port outside of Queenstead, somewhere in the countryside. Hopefully our source can help us with that. Alouette, are you ready to transmit the message?"

Alouette nodded and Cerise tilted the TéléCom toward her. The screen was empty apart from a single green circle in the center. "I built this while you were in the ice box. It's a bit rudimentary, but it should do the trick."

Alouette tested it out, tapping her fingertip rhythmically against the circle in a sequence of long and short beeps. She looked up at Cerise with a smile. "That works."

"Okay, once you record the message, I'll transmit it through the same network in the probe. Remember, you are sending this message as Denise. Tell the source you will be there in five days, and request coordinates for a meeting."

Alouette nodded and closed her eyes. On her thigh, her fingers bounced tentatively up and down, like she was pulling the secret rhythmic code out of her memories. Finally, she opened her eyes, took a deep breath, and reached for the TéléCom.

As the sound of soft beeps filled the flight bridge, Marcellus's gaze drifted back to the window. To the millions of kilomètres of space that stood between them and Albion. He couldn't stop the last coded message from circling through his mind on a constant loop.

"Weapon nearly complete. Delivery in two weeks. I can stop it. Come now."

That message had been meant for Denise. What would the source do when four strangers showed up in her place?

Once Alouette had completed the recording, Cerise took over, her hands flying over the TéléCom, accessing screens and portals that Marcellus had never seen before. It reminded him of when he'd first met Denise at the Vallonay Policier Precinct and she'd hacked his TéléCom right before his very eyes.

"Okay. The transmission is sent," Cerise announced. "Now I guess we just have to wait for a response."

Marcellus clenched his fists tightly at his sides. He didn't like the fact that their entire plan depended on some mysterious source on Albion responding to a bunch of beeps sent through a space probe that hadn't been operational in five hundred years.

But he supposed it was the only plan they had.

"Did you know this ship has seven bathrooms *and* a full kitchen?" Gabriel suddenly came barreling back into the flight bridge, looking winded.

"It's called a *galley*," Cerise said with a roll of her eyes.

Gabriel ignored her. "And *six* bedrooms."

"Couchettes," Cerise corrected.

"And three escape pods!" Gabriel's enthusiasm suddenly clouded over with fear. "Wait a minute, why does the ship need escape pods?"

Just then, the voyageur began to rumble beneath their feet, and Marcellus instinctively grabbed on to the edge of the flight console, bracing himself.

"What was that!?" Gabriel asked, his eyes wide. "Did we hit an asteroid?"

"Don't be such an idiot," Cerise said, securing the harness of her flight seat. "It's just the engines preparing to boost into supervoyage. You better strap in."

Gabriel practically dove into the seat next to her and fumbled to fasten the restraints.

"Acceleration stabilizeurs activated." The voice of the ship's autopilote slipped into the air. "Accelerating to supervoyage in ten . . . nine . . . eight . . ."

Marcellus and Alouette took two of the other seats and secured their restraints. This was the part of space travel that Marcellus disliked the most. Even with the stablizeurs, the acceleration into supervoyage was still intense and almost painful. But he loved the idea of how fast they were traveling once it was over. Not as fast as hypervoyage, of course, but still fast enough to cross half a system in less than two weeks.

Marcellus had never actually experienced hypervoyage before. It was reserved for long journeys across galaxies. But he'd heard that it was fast enough to bend space and blur the stars.

"Five . . . four . . . three . . . two . . . one."

The hum of the supervoyage engines shook the floors, the consoles, and the flight seats, making it feel like the ship might break apart around them. Then, a few seconds later, Marcellus felt it. The tug on his muscles, the clench of his bones, every follicle of hair on his head tingling. Finally, the pressure became too much, and Marcellus had to close his eyes.

He wasn't sure how long they'd remained closed. Maybe he'd passed out as people often do, or maybe he'd simply fallen asleep. But when he opened his eyes again, the tugging sensation in his chest was gone. Outside the window, the stars still shone bright and infinite. Laterre was now little more than a muted gray speck lost in the darkness. And somewhere out there, millions of kilomètres away, in the deep shadows of space, an enemy planet awaited their arrival.

- CHAPTER 31 -
CHATINE

THEY WEREN'T NORMAL DREAMS. THAT MUCH CHATINE
could be sure of. Because in normal dreams, Chatine was always running. Running toward something she could never catch, or running
away from something she could never escape.

In this dream, however, Chatine was floating. In water? No, in
clouds. Chatine didn't even know you could float in clouds. The clouds
on Laterre always looked too menacing. Too dark and dangerous, as
though they would pull you in and drown you in an instant. But these
were not Laterrian clouds. They were not gray and soaked in rain. These
clouds were white. Buoyant. Soft. They drifted through her fingers.
They danced across the nape of her neck. They brushed up against her
flesh, tickling the spot just above her left wrist, where her Skin was. She
giggled at the sensation. When was the last time she'd actually *giggled*?
She couldn't even remember.

The thought made her giggle harder.

"She's coming around." A deep, male voice broke through the clouds.
It was a nice voice. A soothing voice. It made Chatine giggle again.
"What is that noise she's making? It sounds like she's being strangled."

A bright light shone into Chatine's left eye. It was white and warm and beautiful. Was it a Sol? She tried to close her eye and bask in its warmth, but someone was holding her eyelid open.

She vaguely registered that this should annoy her, but she couldn't seem to pinpoint why. She normally didn't like people touching her. But right now, she simply couldn't bring herself to care. She felt so peaceful. So . . . *fluffy*. Yes, that was the word, she quickly decided. She felt as fluffy and buoyant as those beautiful white clouds.

"Her pupils are dilating normally. That's good. Still, I don't like the look of that leg. We've got to keep her off it for at least another few days." This, Chatine immediately recognized, was a different voice. Higher and tinklier. A woman's voice.

The man snorted. "Yeah, good luck with that. She's been a total pest since I picked her up. I should have left her back on Bastille."

"But you didn't," said the woman. "Because you're not heartless. You're my sweet, kindhearted, heroic boy."

The other voice let out a whine. "Maman, stop. No. No more kisses. Please."

Chatine's eyes fluttered open, and she tried to blink her vision into focus. Was that a ceiling above her? Yes, it was. A ceiling with soft white lights. Beautiful lights. Then a face popped into view, hovering directly above her. She recognized the man's slender, chiseled features and deep-set, dark eyes.

"Hey. I know you," she garbled. "You're that nice pilote man."

Etienne nodded. "Yup. That's me. Monsieur Nice. How are you doing, Gridder?"

Chatine smiled a loopy, crooked smile. "I feel good. I feel really good."

He snickered. "That would be the goldenroot talking. I told you, Maman makes the best."

Just then, another face popped into view. A woman. The sight of her made Chatine flinch. She seemed to have the same dark eyes as Etienne, but dripping down the left side of her face was a river of twisted, angry red scars. When the woman smiled, though, it immediately put Chatine back at ease. It was a kind smile. A smile that seemed to chase the scars away. Or, at the very least, soothe their anger.

"Bonjour, Chatine."

"Bonjour, pretty lady," Chatine replied.

The woman chuckled. "You can call me Brigitte. It's nice to see you awake."

Chatine grinned. "It's nice to be awake."

"What do you think about trying to sit up and drink some water?" the woman asked.

Chatine was instantly filled with delight. "I think it's the best idea in the world."

Etienne laughed again. "Maman, how much did you give her?"

Brigitte waved the question away. "She's post-op."

Etienne scooped one hand under each of Chatine's shoulders and gave her a push.

"Okay, up you go. Jeez, you weigh nothing. We need to put some meat on your bones."

Chatine giggled again. "Meat on bones. That's funny." She turned and cupped one of Etienne's cheeks with her hand and gazed deeply into his intense, dark eyes, feeling like she could easily get lost in them. "You're funny. And very handsome."

He cleared his throat. "Yup. Definitely the goldenroot talking."

Brigitte brought a small cup of water to Chatine's lips. Chatine sipped it slowly. It was cold and refreshing and so much cleaner than the water she drank back in the Frets or on Bastille. It tasted like it came straight from the sky.

"Not too much," Brigitte warned, pulling the cup away.

Chatine licked her lips with a smacking sound as she glanced around the room. It wasn't much bigger than her family's old couchette back in the Frets. Except here, there were no rusting walls, no empty weed wine bottles strewn on the table, no cockroaches skittering across the floor. Instead, this room was neat and clean and cozily lit by tiny lights cupped into the ceiling. The whole space was bordered by shelves filled with what appeared to be various medical supplies, and, in the center of the room, a handful of neatly made cots sat side by side in a row. Cots just like the one Chatine was currently sitting on.

She tried to remember coming in here, but her mind was blank. The last thing she could remember was being on the ship. What was its name again? Margaret? Martha?

"Where am I?" she asked groggily as Etienne laid her back down.

Brigitte pressed two fingers to the inside of Chatine's right wrist and tilted her head, as though listening for something. "You're inside my treatment center."

"How long have I been in here?"

Brigitte released Chatine's hand and placed it back on the bed. "Almost a full day."

Chatine startled, the fluffy, peaceful feeling running through her veins ebbing for just a second. "What!?"

"Shhh," Brigitte said, gently rubbing Chatine's shoulder. "Relax. Try not to let yourself get too worked up. My son here says you have a tendency to overreact."

Chatine shot a look at Etienne who grinned back at her. She felt another strange inkling that this, too, should annoy her but it was as though the feeling was a slippery fish that she couldn't keep grasped in her hand.

"Normally, procedures don't require that much healing time, but in conjunction with the shrapnel in your leg—which I was thankfully able to remove—we had to increase your recovery period."

Chatine could hear the woman speaking. She could pluck out words she understood as they floated by her. But she couldn't seem to make sense of them.

The woman nodded to Chatine's left arm. "I'll continue to monitor you until you're healthy enough to leave; in the meantime, we'll just have to keep the incisions clean."

Slowly, Chatine turned her head and let her gaze fall to the side. She knew the sight in front of her should have elicited some kind of strong reaction, but all she could feel in that moment was curiosity.

Running up and down the inside of her left wrist was a rectangle of red seams. Four neat lines, where her flesh had been pinched and sewn together with what looked like thread.

Had that been there before?

Chatine was almost certain it hadn't. But her mind struggled to remember what *used* to be there. *Something* used to be there.

"You'll have a scar, but it should heal nicely," Brigitte said. "Skin removals are one of my specialties. In fact, I did two just this month."

Skin removal?

And then suddenly, Chatine could see it. The faint shadow of a small, rectangular screen. The ghost of what used to be and was no more.

The fluffy fog around her mind vanished, and all she was left with was disbelief. And joy. Pure, unclouded joy that she knew had nothing to do with any strange Défecteur herbs and everything to do with the sight of her Skin-less arm.

How many largs had she spent hacking that Sol-damn device, every time the Ministère sent out another mandatory update? How many years had she spent trying to escape their watch? And now it was over. It was all over. Never again would they remind her to check in for her job assignment, or go to the Med Center for her vitamin D injection, or return to her couchette for curfew. Never again would they be able to track her, contact her, control her.

"Sorry, not to consult you," Brigitte said in an apologetic tone, "but it's a community rule. No one who stays with us can be linked to the Ministère in any way. We don't trust any of their devices. Especially not the Skins."

Chatine pulled her gaze away from her arm to stare at the woman in confusion. Did she think she was *angry* at her? She could have kissed her right now!

"I—" Chatine tried to speak, but she couldn't seem to form her thoughts into words. Everything that filtered through her mind felt insufficient. So, she opted for just a blurry yet heartfelt "Merci."

Brigitte smiled. The expression warped her jagged scars, but it still lit up her face and warmed her eyes. "You're welcome." She straightened the sheets around Chatine's legs. "Once you're recovered, we can walk you through your options. Where to live, how to survive off the grid, all those things. Obviously, you can't go back to your old life. Not that you'd want to, I presume."

Chatine's heart lifted at the thought of living outside the Regime. Where would she go? The Southern Peninsula, maybe? Or even a whole other planet. Perhaps Chatine could finally make it to Usonia. And her little brother could come too!

Suddenly, thoughts of Henri flooded back into her mind. She pushed herself back up to sitting with a burst of determination. "The pilote! Of the other ship! Where is she? Is she back yet? I need to talk to her. I need to ask her where she took—"

The look that passed between Etienne and his mother stopped her words in their tracks and set Chatine's chest on fire.

Brigitte tried to ease Chatine back down onto the bed. "You should probably rest."

But the moment Chatine's head hit the pillow, she was up again. "No. I need to talk to that pilote. My little brother was on her ship. I need to know where she took him."

"There's nothing you can do about it right now, ma chérie," Brigitte said gently. "Right now, all you can do is heal and gather your strength."

Chatine glanced uneasily from Brigitte to Etienne. But Etienne seemed to be going to great efforts *not* to look back at her. A bitter hollowness began to bloom in Chatine's stomach, chasing away any remnants of the blissful warmth that was there.

She glared at Etienne. "What's going on?"

Etienne opened his mouth to speak but was stopped by his mother's hand on his shoulder.

"Not. Now." Her words were quiet yet sharp, almost threatening.

There was something in the air. Something Chatine did not like the smell of. It was dark and hovering, turning her fluffy, white clouds into rain.

She hastily pushed back the thick blanket but paused when she noticed that her prison uniform was gone. Instead, she'd been dressed in a strange pair of white pants flecked with gray and stitched with a myriad of pockets and zips.

Who had dressed her in this?

She pulled up the left cuff of the pants to see that her wound was now clean and impeccably bandaged. She tried to rise to her feet, but Brigitte pushed her back down. "Stop. You are not well enough to get up."

"Then tell me what's going on," Chatine demanded.

"It's not important right now," Brigitte said.

"Maman!" Etienne cried.

"It's not important *right now*," she repeated, directing her heavy words at her son. "She needs to rest. Skin removals are very taxing on the system and—"

"I'm not resting until someone tells me what the fric is happening," Chatine said, her gaze still swiveling between Etienne and his mother.

Etienne glared at Brigitte for a long, tense moment before muttering, "She deserves to know." Then he stormed out the door, and Chatine was left alone with the woman and her long, rigid scars, which now looked redder and more furious than ever.

Chatine waited. The room seemed to drop a hundred degrees in an instant, and she thought she could see puffs of her own breath hanging in the air.

Like clouds.

Dark, heavy, sinister clouds.

"Where is the pilote?" Chatine asked again.

"Do you want to try to eat something?" Brigitte's voice was masked with a thin layer of cheerfulness that Chatine could see right through.

"No."

"I really think you should have some food. You haven't eaten in—"

"TELL ME NOW!" The fire and ferocity in her voice caused the stitched seams on her left arm to burn.

Brigitte turned away from her. Her shoulders sagged. Her body shuddered. When she turned back, the cheerful façade was gone, replaced with a somber expression that made Chatine feel like she was being suffocated slowly. It was as though she knew what was coming before Brigitte even spoke. It was as though her body was already preparing for the blow, and her mind was already scolding her for hoping. For thinking, for even a moment, that the Sols might have given her a second chance.

For thinking that he was ever hers to keep.

"The other ship never came back," Brigitte said quietly.

The room spun.

"We lost contact with the pilote."

The floor dropped out.

"We sent out a search party, but so far, they've found no sign of them."

The chasm opened up beneath her.

"We believe they never made it off Bastille."

And the planet of Laterre swallowed Chatine whole.

CHAPTER 32

MARCELLUS

THERE WAS SOMETHING ABOUT SPACE TRAVEL THAT made it feel like time was moving in slow motion. Or maybe it was just *this* space travel. Marcellus stood in the middle of the bridge, watching the flight clock tick down.

4 days. 13 hours. 9 minutes.

It seemed for every minute that passed on the hologram, a thousand hours would pass in his mind.

At this rate, he'd be an old man by the time they reached Albion. And his grandfather would rule Laterre. And they would be too late.

"I just can't get over how endless it is."

Marcellus startled at the sound of the voice and peered up to see Alouette standing in the doorway.

"The flight?" Marcellus asked, certain she, too, was experiencing this strange sense of time paralysis.

She shook her head. "The view."

"Ah. Right." Marcellus turned toward the massive domed windows and sighed. "Yes. It's almost unfathomable."

Alouette moved through the flight bridge and came to stand next to him. The glow from the console seemed to turn her curls a beautiful indigo blue, and her dark brown eyes twinkled like jewels in one of the Matrone's ceremonial tiaras. Marcellus stole a quick glance at her from the corner of his eye. He still couldn't believe she was actually here. With him. On a voyageur destined for Albion. So much had happened since he'd first seen her in the Jondrette. And now that he was finally able to breathe and think, all the questions that had been queuing up in his mind came flooding back.

"So," he said, trying to keep his voice light, conversational. "You've been busy."

She turned and flashed him a confused look. "Busy?"

He counted on his fingers. "Running away from the Vangarde, getting arrested, escaping the Policier, incapacitating Inspecteur Limier—"

"Is he dead?" The question darted out of her, fast and desperate, as though it had been plaguing her for weeks.

"Limier? No. I mean, I don't think so." Marcellus's mind flashed back to the inspecteur convulsing violently on that gurney in the infirmerie. "Last I heard, the médecins were still working on him, but they didn't know whether or not he'd fully recover."

Alouette dropped her gaze to the ground, looking pained. "It was an accident. I was just defending myself."

"I know. It's okay." Marcellus felt the sudden urge to reach out and comfort her, but he didn't know how. It had only been a few weeks since they'd sat at that fireside together in the Forest Verdure, but somehow it felt like years ago. Like they'd been different people back then, leading different lives. And now they had to start all over again.

"He came after my father," Alouette said, her gaze still trained on the floor, as though it were the only safe place to look.

"Jean LeGrand?"

She nodded. "Yes. But he goes by Hugo Taureau now, and as it turns out, he wasn't my real father. That's why I was in Montfer. I was trying to learn the truth about my past. Mostly about my mother."

"Your mother?" Marcellus had never heard Alouette talk about her mother.

"Her name was Lisole. She died a long time ago." Alouette's voice fell to a cracked whisper. "I don't even remember her."

Marcellus glanced away as something sharp jabbed him from the inside. An old wound he'd thought he'd healed from. He couldn't remember his mother either.

"I just wanted answers," Alouette went on, sounding like she was being stabbed by that same sharp object. "I just wanted to know where I came from."

"And?" Marcellus asked. "Did you find out?"

She shook her head. "Not really. I followed a clue to a bordel in Montfer, where my mother used to sell her blood when I was a baby. To try to make ends meet. I thought the madame would be helpful. But she just made everything more confusing. She seemed to be under the impression that I was . . ." Her voice trailed off, as though whatever was supposed to come next was too difficult to say aloud.

"That you were what?"

She let out a deep shudder. "Dead."

Marcellus flinched. That was certainly not what he'd expected her to say. "Dead?"

"That's what my mother told her."

"Why would she do that?"

Alouette shook her head. "I don't know. Then the madame turned on me, and the Policier came, and it was sort of a mess." She reached down and rubbed at her wrist where Marcellus could see hints of dark purple bruises. "Anyway, the whole thing was just one big dead end. And now . . ." Alouette bit her lip as though her next words terrified her. "Now I'm starting to wonder if I ever should have left."

"Why *did* you leave?" Marcellus asked. "My contact at the Vangarde said you were no longer with them."

"I was never with them," Alouette said, somewhat forcefully. Then she took a breath that seemed to calm her. "I mean, not that I knew about. They told me *nothing*."

"And you never even suspected?"

"No," she said. "Never. They were always just sisters to me. Teachers and scholars. They were never . . ."—she paused, hesitating—"*revolutionaries*. I guess that makes me the fool, doesn't it?"

"That's not what I meant," Marcellus rushed to say.

Alouette's face softened. "I know. I'm sorry. I'm still just trying to process it all. Twelve years of lies is a lot to sort through. I didn't find out who they really were until that night I saw you in the Frets. After you showed me those images of Sister Jacqui and Sister Denise."

Marcellus knew the moment she was referring to. He could still see the look in her eyes when they'd stood in that hallway of Fret 7 and he'd told her about the Vangarde operatives who had been captured breaking into the warden's office. She'd looked at him like he was speaking in another language.

"Do you know where they are?" Alouette blurted out, the possibility clearly just occurring to her.

Marcellus shook his head, hating to disappoint her. "I'm sorry. I don't. My grandfather has a detention facility hidden somewhere. It's where he takes prisoners to . . ."

He didn't dare finish that sentence. But the darkness that passed over her eyes told him without a doubt that she knew. She understood *exactly* what happened at a facility like that.

"And you have no idea where this"—Alouette swallowed—"*facility* might be?"

"No. My grandfather never told me. I'm pretty sure there are only two people on the planet who know where it is: the general and Limier. At least Limier *did* know, at one point. His circuitry was pretty fried from the rayonette pulse. And it damaged his memory chip."

Alouette nodded, her fingers fidgeting absentmindedly with something inside her sac. Marcellus glanced down to see a glint of silver from her string of metal beads. He stared at them, remembering the night he'd stood in that same dark and dingy hallway of Fret 7 and that necklace had somehow triggered a strange message to appear on the screen of his TéléCom.

"You never told me what it said." Marcellus's voice was quiet and hesitant. Alouette looked at him, confused.

"The message that Denise sent you through my TéléCom."

At first, Alouette didn't respond. She just continued to thread her fingers pensively through the beads. And Marcellus worried that she still wouldn't tell him. Even after everything that had just happened. But then, in a distant, trance-like voice, she whispered, "*When the Lark flies home, the Regime will fall.*"

Marcellus stood stunned and silent for a long moment, trying to make sense of these peculiar words.

When the Lark flies home, the Regime will fall?

"What does that mean?"

Alouette shrugged. "I don't know. Honestly, I don't know what to think about anything anymore. Fly home? I don't even know where that is. I'm not entirely sure I *have* a home. I just . . ." She dropped her gaze back to the floor. "I just feel so . . . lost."

Marcellus's brain squeezed as he tried to make sense of all this. But it was like trying to look at a picture through broken plastique. The edges were blurry, the image was warped, and nothing seemed to fit together.

The pounding of footsteps jolted Marcellus out of his thoughts, and he turned toward the flight bridge door just as Cerise barreled through it, clutching a TéléCom in her hand.

Panic instantly spiraled through him. Had their mission failed already?

"Marcellus!" she said, winded. "You need to hear this."

"Hear what?"

"I was just working on your TéléCom, to check that the tracking capabilities were still deactivated, and I found"—she paused and put a hand to her heaving chest, trying to catch her breath—"a signal."

"What kind of signal?" he asked.

"An open AirLink signal. It's encrypted but it's coming straight from the south wing of the Grand Palais."

Comprehension flooded Marcellus, and he exhaled a sigh of relief. "That's an auditeur. I planted it in the general's office before I left."

Cerise scoffed. "I *know*. I figured that part out on my own. Merci for telling me, by the way. It nearly gave me a heart attack. I thought the general was tracking us."

Marcellus cringed. "Sorry. There's been a lot going on. And I honestly didn't think the signal would reach out here."

"The *signal* does. But I had to amplify it to be able to hear what was being said." Cerise hastily tapped on the TéléCom. "I think you should hear this. It's about the Vangarde."

Alouette flinched and looked to Marcellus with wide, fearful eyes. He nodded to Cerise. "Play it through the speakers."

Cerise tapped on the screen and Marcellus felt Alouette's hand slip shakily into his. He gave it a reassuring squeeze.

"When I recognized my father's voice," Cerise explained, "I immediately started logging the transmission."

"Your father?" Marcellus had rarely known Directeur Chevalier to come to the general's private study in the Palais. They normally met in the Ministère's Cyborg and Technology Labs.

Cerise nodded gravely and Marcellus recognized the regret that flashed in her dark eyes. As though she really despised being the one to convey whatever they were about to hear.

"What's all the commotion?" Gabriel appeared in the doorway, rubbing at his eyes. "I was trying to sleep."

"Shh," Cerise urged him and pressed play on the TéléCom.

At first there was nothing but a low hum through the speakers. Then, with a sharp click, Directeur Chevalier's voice began speaking, midsentence. ". . . the results of the analysis you requested for the devices found on the captured Vangarde operatives."

Devices?

It took Marcellus a moment to connect the dots in his mind. He remembered something his grandfather had said during their last hunting trip with the Patriarche. He'd told the Patriarche that Directeur Chevalier's team was analyzing the necklaces that had been found on Jacqui and Denise when they were arrested.

Necklaces just like the one still peeking out from Alouette's sac.

"As we suspected," the directeur went on, "they are not just decorative. The two devices we analyzed are part of a larger communication network that the Vangarde have been using."

Alouette turned to Marcellus with desperate, searching eyes. "What is he talking about?"

Marcellus drew in a heavy breath and nodded toward Alouette's bag. "He's talking about the beads."

Alouette's whole body went rigid. "The sisters' beads?"

"What can you tell me about this network?" the general's voice boomed out from the TéléCom, causing Marcellus to flinch.

"The devices were still active when we apprehended the operatives," the directeur said, "so we were able to trace the signal back to a server. Unfortunately, we've been unable to discern the location yet. But what we did discover is that there are eleven devices total, all connecting through the same network."

"Eleven?" the general repeated gruffly. "What is the significance of that?"

"There's no way to know for sure," the directeur replied. "But our working hypothesis is that the eleven necklaces belong to current leaders of the Vangarde. The highest-ranking members of their organization."

Dazedly, slowly, Alouette reached into her sac and withdrew her string of metallic beads. Cerise jabbed the TéléCom to pause the playback and stared openmouthed at the necklace now dangling from Alouette's fingertip, the little metal tag glinting in the console lights.

"Wait a minute. *You're* Vangarde too?" Gabriel, who up until this moment had been lingering in the back of the flight bridge, suddenly pushed his way into the middle of the group. "Am I the only one on this ship who is *not* Vangarde?"

Alouette ignored him as her eyes swiveled back and forth, following the metal tag that was swinging like a pendulum. When she finally spoke, her voice was so quiet, it was as though the words were only meant to be heard by her. Disjointed thoughts whispered aloud in search of meaning. "Ten sisters. Ten strings of devotion beads. Plus mine equals eleven. Connected to the same network." She gasped with a sudden epiphany. "Principale Francine! She gave me my devotion beads the night before I snuck out of the Refuge for the second time. She told me it was because they were going to make me a sister. But they knew. Of course they did. They knew I was sneaking out. They gave these to me so they could keep me safe." Her head snapped up, her gaze finding Marcellus's. "They're tracking me."

"Were," Cerise replied in a low, somber tone that sent a ripple of dread through Marcellus.

Alouette's brow furrowed. "What do you mean?"

Tears were already glistening in Cerise's eyes as she let out a burdened breath and resumed the playback on the TéléCom.

It was the general who spoke next. And even though his voice was coming from all the way back on Laterre, it still felt like he was standing right there in the flight bridge with them. His imposing presence translating across millions of miles of space. "So, if we have two of them in custody, that means there are nine Vangarde leaders still out there?"

There was a long pause, during which Marcellus felt sweat start to pool on the back of his neck. When the directeur finally replied, there was something different about his voice. A levity that made Marcellus queasy. "That's the good news, sir."

"Good news?" the general repeated.

"We were able to run a trace through the server and pull status updates on all eleven devices. One is offline. Two are still active—those are the ones we analyzed, belonging to the operatives in custody. But the remaining eight are all dead."

Dead.

The word felt like a stone sinking to the pit of Marcellus's stomach. He glanced over at Alouette. She looked frozen. Paralyzed. A statue of disbelief.

"What do you mean 'dead'?" The general's gravelly voice held a hint of hope.

"The last time the remaining eight devices connected to the server was on Month 7, Day 32. The night of Rousseau's attempted escape."

Silence filled the general's office. A silence so thick and so laced with insinuation, it seeped out of the TéléCom like a poisonous gas, spreading through the flight bridge, leaving charred streaks in the atmosphere.

Then the general asked the final question that stood between him and his long-fought victory over a rebel group called the Vangarde. "Where did the last connection come from?"

Marcellus felt the stars shift even before the answer came. Even before the directeur said those two words that confirmed everything Marcellus had been fearing for days.

"From Bastille."

They really were on their own.

- CHAPTER 33 -
ALOUETTE

IN THE DARK COUCHETTE OF THE VOYAGEUR, ALOUETTE felt like she was drowning. Drowning in space. Drowning in memories and regrets and shadows.

Drowning in sobs.

The tears drenched her face, her sweater, the sheets of the bed. The shudders shook her entire body. Until she forgot what it felt like to be still. Until she feared she might never be still again.

How could she ever be okay? How could she ever not blame herself for leaving them? If she hadn't, maybe all the sisters would still be alive.

Or maybe, Alouette would be dead too. But at least then, she wouldn't feel this ocean of regret crashing down on her over and over again. At least then, she wouldn't have to endure the image of their ship exploding in a devastating ball of light with eight of her beloved sisters—her family—locked inside.

Did they scream?

Did they feel any pain?

Or was it over before they even realized what had happened?

The pain was almost too much to bear. It crushed down on Alouette.

It suffocated her. It gnawed at her from the inside until she was just an empty shell. A doll made of whisper-thin paper.

She clutched her devotion beads in her hands and brought the little metal tag up to her trembling lips, whispering silent prayers to the Sols against its cool surface. For Principale Francine, Sister Laurel, Sister Muriel, Léonie, Marguerite, Nicolette, Clare, and Noëlle, who had perished on that moon, she prayed they had felt no pain. And for brave Sister Jacqui and stoic Sister Denise, now the only family she had left, she prayed—no, *vowed*—that she would one day see them again. That she would track them down. She would find this ghastly detention facility where the general was holding them captive, and she would set them free.

Alouette curled up on the couchette's narrow bed and tried to sleep. Everyone else was sleeping, and she knew she should be as well. In less than three days they would be arriving on the enemy planet of Albion. She would need her strength, her wits, her courage. But every time she closed her eyes, gruesome images of an exploding ship came flooding back. Her mind was so far from the calm, peaceful garden the sisters had taught her to cultivate. It was a messy, knotted tangle of grief.

She pushed herself up and stared out the window of her couchette. But the view did nothing to soothe her. They were almost through the infamous Asteroid Channel which divided Laterre from its longtime enemy neighbor of Albion, and the giant space rocks floating all around the voyageur made Alouette feel anxious and vulnerable.

Pulling her gaze from the window, she immediately spotted her sac lying on the floor, where she'd dropped it the moment she'd run from the flight bridge and locked herself inside this couchette. Alouette hastily scooped up the bag and emptied all the contents out onto the bed until everything that she had left in the world was scattered around her. As jumbled and disorderly as her thoughts.

The screwdriver that Sister Denise had given her. Her father's titan bloc. Her trusty flashlight. Her mother's small titan box. Alouette's eyes roved over each one before finally coming to rest on the thing that she stole.

With a quiet sniffle, she traced her fingertips over the rugged, time-weathered spine of the old leather-bound book with its handstitched seams and crinkled paper. And then, just as it always did, the memory of that night began to shove its way back into her mind, like an unwanted visitor barging through the door. That fateful, regretful night that she'd learned the truth about the sisters and the Vangarde.

She was suddenly back in the middle of that Assemblée room, surrounded by twisting wires and cables, a collage of monitors and circuit boards, and the faces of the sisters she'd left behind. The sisters who were now all gone.

"We knew right away that you were destined to be one of us," Principale Francine told her. "From the moment you walked through that door with Hugo twelve years ago, you had a curiosity for knowledge. You drank in the world and questioned everything."

Tears pricked at Alouette's eyes, as the years of secrets and darkness spread over her skin, puncturing her like a thousand tiny knives. "Does my father— Does Hugo know? About . . . you?"

"No," Francine replied with a shake of her head. "When Hugo brought you to the Refuge, we decided not to tell him. While he is a good, honest man, he never showed a propensity for learning. Or a desire for change. He was just too hardened. Too jaded by the Regime. But you, Little Lark . . ." She released a nostalgic sigh. "Your heart was so pure. And so good. You read about the injustices on the planet, and you wanted to change them. So we started to train you. Sister Jacqui became responsible for your philosophical education. Sister Denise ensured you had technical skills for the field. And I took charge of teaching you the history of our world and the world that came before it."

"Yes!" Alouette blurted out breathlessly. "The books! I've read every book in that library. Because you told me we were protecting them. You told me that's what the Sisterhood was for."

"We are still here to protect the books. The books are a symbol, can't you see? The books represent the kind of life we want for the people of Laterre. A life of knowledge and freedom and ideas. Do you remember why the written word

was forgotten? It was deemed too powerful a tool. Too potentially destructive to the new way of life. So it was gradually phased out by the people who feared it. When we rescued those books from the First World, we were rescuing a philosophy. We were rescuing hope. And now we need to find that hope again. That's why we continue to write and update the Chronicles. That's why we continue to protect the written word."

"B-b-but," Alouette stammered, shaking her head. "But I've read the Chronicles. Every volume. They don't say anything about any of this. About Citizen Rousseau or the rebellion or the Vangarde."

Francine lowered her gaze to the floor, looking almost ashamed. "Actually, they do."

Alouette was about to speak again when suddenly Principale Francine stood up and walked over to the far wall where Alouette could see a large, metal cabinet. Then, slowly, Francine cranked on a heavy, round handle and the glimmering doors on the cabinet winched back to reveal shelves and shelves, filled top to bottom with clothbound books. Alouette let out a tiny gasp as Francine continued to wind the handle and the first set of shelves moved away, revealing even more shelves behind them. And even more books. Books upon books. Packed tightly onto the revolving shelves, with spines of all different colors.

"Chronicles," she murmured under her breath.

But these weren't the Chronicles Alouette had grown up reading and dusting and protecting in the Refuge's library. These were something different. Something Alouette had never seen before. These were the chronicles of the sisters' deepest, darkest secrets.

The Chronicles of the Vangarde.

"Remember, Little Lark. Knowledge is always available for those who seek it." Francine ran her fingertips over the books before plucking a single red-spined volume from the shelf. She handed it to Alouette. "Start with this one."

Alouette had felt the weight of the book as Principale Francine had placed it in her hands that night. The weight of all those unread words, unknown histories. Truths that Alouette had been denied access to for all these years.

When she'd left the Refuge that very next morning, she'd taken this book with her as a reminder. A promise. That never again would she allow herself to live in the dark. She hadn't read it yet. She hadn't been able to. Twice on the bateau to Montfer, she had tried. But both times, she'd barely been able to lift the cover. The pain of the sisters' lies and betrayal had still been too fresh. Too pulsing.

But now, she knew it was time.

She pulled the volume toward her and, with a steady breath, flipped open the cover.

Her gaze scanned over the long title on the first page.

Full Compendium of Operative Reports from 488 to 489

Alouette frowned at the words. Operative reports? She certainly hadn't expected that. She'd assumed this was another volume of the Chronicles, like the ones kept in the library: beautiful, poetic histories and accounts of their world and the world that existed before them. But as her eyes roved over the table of contents, listing operative names and corresponding page numbers, she realized this book, with its bright red spine, was something different.

Had this really been what Principale Francine had meant to give her? Of all the books in that vast vault, why had she chosen this one?

A gentle knock came at the couchette door, startling Alouette. She closed the book and pushed it aside. "Yes?" she called.

A second later, Gabriel tentatively poked his head into the room. "Were you sleeping?"

She shook her head. "No. Come in."

He stepped inside but halted when he saw Alouette's face. "Are you okay?"

It was only then Alouette realized what she must look like. Tear-stained cheeks, red-rimmed eyes, and disheveled hair. She wiped her face with the heel of her hand. "Not really."

Gabriel walked over and sat down on the edge of the bed, looking slightly uncomfortable. "Do you . . . want to talk about it?"

"Not really," Alouette said again, even though she was certain Sister Jacqui would tell her that she *should* talk about it. But she knew if she talked about the sisters, she would only start crying again. And she was so sick of crying.

"Are you hungry?"

As soon as Gabriel asked the question, Alouette's stomach rumbled. "Yes, actually. Famished."

"I thought so." He dug into his pocket and pulled out a small loaf of bread, which he broke in half and offered to Alouette.

For a long moment, all she could do was stare down at the jagged half loaf. A chill passed through her as a hazy memory tickled the corners of her mind. Something about this situation felt achingly familiar.

"It's okay," Gabriel said, nudging it closer. "I washed my hands."

She looked up into his dark eyes and then back down at the loaf. And that's when it hit her. The memory slammed its way back into her mind. She saw those same eyes, that same hand unfurling to revealing a tiny piece of chou bread.

"I remember," she whispered. "I remember *you*. From the Renards's inn. You used to sneak me food under the table where I slept."

"Well, it's about *time*."

Her brow furrowed. "Wait, you already knew this?"

"I knew you looked familiar when I saw you at the Precinct. But I didn't figure it out until we were walking to the inn and the place clearly creeped you out. Understandably so. I was hoping you'd eventually remember me, too." He paused and lowered his voice. "They used to call you Madeline, right?"

Another chill ran through her. "So, you were *there*?"

"I started working there when I was six."

"Six?!" Alouette exclaimed, although she wasn't sure why she was so surprised. The Renards had put her to work when she was barely four years old.

"My papa used to work in the kitchens," Gabriel explained. "He would bring me with him every day, and I would help out. Until he got sick and couldn't work anymore. That's when I learned how to steal. It was mostly just médicaments and food at first. Then I moved onto the hard stuff."

"Hard stuff?"

"Manoir jobs mostly. The amount of wealth the Second Estate has just lying around their gardens would blow your mind." He cleared his throat. "Anyway, yes, I was there. At the Jondrette. With the Renards." He shuddered. "Horrible people. And total criminals, too."

Alouette cocked a teasing eyebrow at him.

"Hey! I only steal from the Second Estate. They have plenty. The Renards cheat their own kind. They used to make us fill the sausages with frog limbs and mice guts." He lowered his head, his tone suddenly turning somber. "They were awful to you. I remember Madame Renard yelling at you. All the time. You were so small, and she would tower over you. They used to . . ." but his voice trailed off, as though he couldn't even bring himself to say it aloud.

Alouette cast her gaze to the floor. Because she knew. They both knew.

Gabriel cleared his throat. "So, yeah, I used to steal food for you sometimes." He gestured down to the half loaf in his hand again. "I stole this from the kitchen too." He winked. "Don't tell Sparkles."

Alouette flashed a weak smile. "I don't think she would mind if you took a loaf of bread."

"I mean don't tell her that I called it the *kitchen*. She'll freak out. 'It's a *galley*, you uneducated, unwashed Third Estate clochard.'" His impersonation of Cerise was over the top but it still made Alouette smile. It felt good to smile. Even if just for a moment.

She grabbed the bread from Gabriel's hand and took a small bite. "Cerise is not that bad."

Gabriel scoffed. "She is *worse* than that bad. Of all the things wrong with our planet, calling things by their proper names is top of her priority list."

"If it's any consolation, I think she really is just genuinely trying to help. Her heart seems to be in the right place."

Gabriel bit off a piece of bread. "She doesn't get it. This is all a game to her. I mean, think about it. She spends her days searching for magical switches that can shut off the Skins."

"The kill switch," Alouette said, remembering the strange term.

"Exactly. She thinks this planet can be fixed with the touch of a button. She's delusional."

"You don't think it exists?"

"Of course it doesn't exist. It's a fantasy! And unlike her, I can't afford to believe in fantasies. I have real problems to deal with." He sighed and took another bite of bread.

Alouette had to admit she was doubtful too. She'd read about the Skins in the Chronicles. Countless pages about their origins, their functionality, the neuroelectricity they ran on. But there had never been any mention of an off switch. She had a hard time believing the Regime would allow such a thing to exist.

"The point is," Gabriel continued after a large swallow, "whether you all succeed in stopping the general or not, it doesn't affect Cerise in any real way. When this is all over, she'll go back to her manoir, and her life will be more or less the same."

"Whether *we* succeed?"

Gabriel fell quiet and Alouette instantly knew her suspicions back in the cruiseur had been right. He was hiding something.

"Why did you really agree to come with us?" she asked. "I have a feeling it has nothing to do with the general's weapon."

He quirked an eyebrow. "Am I that predictable?"

Alouette just smiled.

Gabriel popped the last piece of bread into his mouth and leaned back on his hands. "Oh, I don't know. I heard the words 'weapon' and 'rid the Regime of the déchets' and I freaked. I figured bad things were about to go down, and anywhere had to be better than Laterre." He snorted. "Even Albion."

"So, what? When we land, you're going to get off the ship and enlist in the Albion Royal Guard?"

He shrugged. "I'll figure something out."

"Well, just be sure to thank Cerise for the ride."

He cringed. "Are you mad?"

"Mad?"

"That I'm not along to save the world?"

Alouette glanced down at the closed book beside her. The Vangarde's mysterious compendium of reports. "I'm starting to think that saving the world is a pretty foolish ambition."

"And yet, here you are."

She let out a heavy sigh. "Here I am."

"What is this?" Gabriel shifted uncomfortably. He leaned forward and picked up her mother's titan box from the bed before turning it around in his hands and studying the ornate design on the top. "Is this—"

Alouette hastily snatched the box back from him. She didn't like the sensation that came over her from watching someone else hold it. "Sorry, it's . . . It belonged to my mother." She squeezed the box in her hand. It felt like years ago that she'd found it in Hugo's room. She had come so far since then. And yet, right now, Alouette felt just as lost and hopeless and naïve as that girl snooping around the Refuge, looking for answers. "It's the only thing I have left of her."

"What's in it?" Gabriel asked.

Alouette ran her fingertips over the seam. "I don't know. It's locked."

Gabriel guffawed.

"What?" She glanced up at him.

"That would *never* stop me."

"What do you . . . ?" But her voice trailed off as her gaze fell back down to the bed and landed on her screwdriver. The same one Gabriel had used to break them out of their Ministère cuffs. She stared intently at the sharp-tipped tool, her jumbled thoughts focusing into one single, resolute goal. Then, before she could second-guess herself, she snatched up the screwdriver and, with more desperation than precision, jammed the flat end under the lid of the box and wrenched up. With a crack and a hiss, the top flew open. Alouette was so shocked that her forceful tactic had worked, she nearly dropped the box.

In a split second, all her former anger and grief simply melted away, replaced by a thrumming, burning curiosity.

Slowly, warily, Alouette leaned forward and peered inside.

She had never known what to expect when she finally got a glimpse at her mother's long-lost treasure. Anything probably would have surprised her at this point. But she still let out a tiny gasp.

Nestled in a bed of soft purple velvet was a small plait of braided hair. Two distinct strands woven together: one dark and curly, so much like her own, and the other thick and reddish-brown.

Her father's?

Was she looking at a piece of her real father?

She reached out and gently touched the strands, feeling a tingle travel through her.

"What is it?" Gabriel asked, peering over her shoulder into the box.

But before she could answer, the door to her couchette whooshed open again and Cerise barged in, looking eager and flushed. She opened her mouth to say something, but then her gaze fell upon Gabriel and Alouette, sitting side by side on the bed, and she seemed to lose her train of thought.

"Did you want something?" Gabriel prompted, leaning back on his hands again as though he were making a grand show of looking comfortable.

"Not from you," she snapped.

Gabriel flashed Alouette an I-told-you-so look and stood up from the bed. "Fine. If anyone needs me, I'll be raiding the *galley*." He pushed past Cerise and sauntered out of the room. Once he was gone, Cerise turned to Alouette, and Alouette's stomach instantly clenched at the anticipation of more bad news. She didn't think she could take any more.

But then Cerise's eyes flashed with unmistakable excitement. "We got it."

Alouette frowned. "Got what?"

"A response. From the source on Albion."

- CHAPTER 34 -
MARCELLUS

"THOSE WRETCHES! ALL OF THEM. THE WHOLE BLASTED Third Estate!"

Marcellus woke with a start to the sound of Patriarche Lyon Paresse ranting in his ear. He sat up and grappled around in the darkness of his couchette for the light panel, fighting through the bleariness of sleep.

"Have you seen it, General?!" the Patriarche roared. "Have you seen what they've done?"

It took Marcellus a moment to realize the sound was coming from the auditeur back on Laterre. He was listening to another conversation from his grandfather's study.

"Yes, Monsieur Patriarche," the general replied calmly. "I just watched the footage. It is dreadful news."

"Three superviseurs dead!" the Patriarche said. "And an entire hothouse obliterated!"

Marcellus's stomach clenched. Another attack on Laterre?

"These victims are members of the *Second Estate*!" the Patriarche went on. "And they've been murdered! Murdered right in their own hothouse. Who will be next? Will it be us? Will they come after the *First* Estate?

Are we all going to be murdered in our beds *right here in Ledôme*!?" The Patriarche's voice was trembling now.

"No," came the general's reassuring reply a moment later. "Of course not. That will never happen. Ledôme is impenetrable. Its perimeter is guarded by droids, and officers are on patrol throughout the interior at all times. If anyone wanted to get inside Ledôme, they'd have to go through me first."

Marcellus shivered at the words. They almost sounded like a threat.

"I assure you, Monsieur Patriarche," the general went on, "this assault on the Regime will not be taken lightly."

The Patriarche sniffed a skeptical sniff. "And who are these people anyway? I've never even heard of this *Red Scar*."

The entire couchette seemed to tilt underneath Marcellus. He gripped the side of the bed for balance as images from the Jondrette came flooding back to him. Those stoic guards in their red hoods. That fanatical woman with her steely gaze and provoking rhetoric.

First the TéléSkin fabrique and now a hothouse?

"I don't know," the general admitted. "I'd never heard of this organization until today."

"So they're *not* associated with the Vangarde?" the Patriarche confirmed.

"It would appear not."

"Well, they're making a mockery of the Regime," the Patriarche thundered, "sending that horrible footage to the entire Ministère. How did they even do that?"

Marcellus moved like lightning, snatching up his TéléCom from the table. The Red Scar had sent a message to the entire Ministère? Why hadn't he received it?

"Access Ministère portal," he commanded the TéléCom.

"Access denied," came the chilling response not a second later. "All clearance levels have been revoked."

Right, he thought miserably, letting the TéléCom fall back onto the table with a clank. *Wanted criminals don't have security clearances.*

"My officers are working on tracking down the perpetrators of this heinous act," the general was now saying, and Marcellus could hear the frustration in his voice. This was clearly not a twist his grandfather had foreseen. "Once found, their punishment will be swift."

"Exactly," said the Patriarche. "They must be dealt with. Is the exécuteur ready?"

"My techniciens in the munitions fabrique have just completed the final product today," said the general.

"Good. Once these murderers are found, I want their heads to be the first ones under that blade."

"Yes, Monsieur Patriarche."

Heavy footsteps filled Marcellus's audio patch, and he imagined the Patriarche pacing back and forth in front of the Regiments board that hid the auditeur. "Ungrateful sots! My ancestors built this planet from nothing. They rescued these people from the Last Days. From a horrible fiery death on a collapsing planet. They gave them a place to live. Food. Shelter. Jobs. And five hundred years later, this is the thanks we get?! Murdering my superviseurs, destroying my fabriques, and rioting in my streets? You would think the news of Citizen Rousseau's death would have scared them off, but instead it has only seemed to rile them up more!"

"Perhaps," the general said, still maintaining his trademark impassiveness, "the Third Estate simply need a reminder of your . . . generosity."

The heavy footsteps paused, and Marcellus's brow lifted.

"What do you mean?" the Patriarche asked.

The general cleared his throat. "It's quite possible that, with all of these disturbances, the people have simply lost sight of what's important and what a just and fair ruler you are."

"Obviously."

"Might I suggest, then, that you reschedule the Ascension?"

"WHAT?" the Patriarche roared. "You mean to *reward* them for this treachery?"

"I mean to pacify them in the *midst* of it."

The Patriarche grunted in response.

"The people need to remember who is in control here," General Bonnefaçon continued. "And most of all, they need something else to *think* about outside of these attacks. Something to hope for."

"Uh-huh." The Patriarche did not sound convinced. "So you're suggesting we reschedule the Ascension as a distraction?"

The general faltered for a moment. "I'm simply saying it might help. It's kept the Third Estate in line thus far, it might do it again."

Marcellus narrowed his eyes, immediately suspicious. Why was his grandfather pressing for this so hard?

"And you think this will quell any future disturbances?" the Patriarche confirmed.

"I think it's worth a try."

"Because I will not have this Regime fall under my watch. My father successfully stamped out a rebellion seventeen years ago. We cannot allow another one to break out. We must get this planet under control once and for all."

"We will," the general assured him. "Just . . . think about it."

Marcellus heard a grunt, then the sound of footsteps retreating, followed by the door of the study opening and closing as the Patriarche made another one of his dramatic exits.

As soon as the general's office had fallen quiet again, Marcellus was on his feet. He barreled out of the couchette, down the hallway, and up the stairs to the bridge, where he found Alouette and Cerise gathered around the flight console, talking in hushed voices.

"Bonjour, sleepy head," Cerise said brightly.

He ignored her and focused on Alouette. He'd been worried sick about her for the past day. After listening to the general's conversation with Directeur Chevalier, she'd disappeared into her couchette and hadn't come out since. He'd tried talking to her, but she'd said she wanted to be alone.

Are you okay? He mouthed to her now.

She shrugged in response and refused to meet his eye.

He turned his attention to Cerise and the glowing console. "What's going on?"

Cerise beamed at him. "We got the coordinates for the meeting with the source. Alouette just decoded the message, and I've already entered the new destination into the nav system. It looks like it's a small town on the outskirts of Queenstead."

Marcellus nodded numbly, barely able to follow her words. "I guess that's good."

"What's wrong?" Cerise asked, clearly noticing the haunted expression on his face.

"I—" he tried to figure out where to begin, but then was struck by an idea. "Wait. Cerise, do you still have access to the Ministère portal on your TéléCom?"

"Yes, why?"

Marcellus let out a shaky breath. "Pull it up. Now."

A minute later, Alouette, Cerise, and Marcellus were all gathered around Cerise's TéléCom as the mysterious footage began to play on the screen.

It was juddering and slightly grainy, as though whoever had captured it was on the move. But Marcellus could make out a nearby hothouse glowing under an inky sky and a field of crops stretching out into the distance. The image suddenly jerked to the left, revealing three men kneeling on the muddy ground. They wore regulation green jackets and matching felt hats, marking them as hothouse superviseurs.

Two of them had their eyes shut, but the third had his wide open.

And they shone with terror.

The footage tilted upward. Five figures stood behind the kneeling men. All of them were in matching coats with hoods pulled down to obscure most of their faces.

They were dressed head to toe in the color of blood.

The color of death.

"The Red Scar," Alouette whispered.

One of the figures stepped forward. Marcellus couldn't see much beyond the hood of the jacket. But when she spoke, he knew it was *her*.

Maximilienne.

"These men are guilty of enslavement and oppression." She gestured to the kneeling superviseurs. "They are yet another cog in the great broken machine that is this planet. And they will pay for their complicity with chains of their own."

"Oh my Sols!" Alouette cried. "What is she going to—"

But her words were swallowed up by a flash of blue light across the screen. Marcellus's eyes blurred for a second before he saw the laser clutched in Maximilienne's hand.

Dread squeezed his lungs as two of the hooded figures grabbed one of the kneeling men and yanked back the sleeve of his jacket. Maximilienne stepped toward him, the tip of her laser glowing a vivid blue.

The humming, sparking sound filled Marcellus's ears, followed by the screams and pleas of the superviseur.

The laser bore down, scorching and carving and burning the man's skin into a smoking and sickening rectangle. With one final yelp, he fainted from the pain.

Marcellus glanced over at Cerise, whose face was twisted in disbelief and horror. He could almost see the realization play out on her face. What happened at the Jondrette wasn't just for show. That could have been her.

On the screen, Maximilienne moved on, and in a cacophony of whirs and sparks and screams, the two other Second Estate men underwent the same torture, their arms branded with the same terrible scar.

As the Red Scar guards grabbed each of the kneeling men and yanked them to their feet, Marcellus could swear he recognized one of the hooded figures. His gaze zeroed in on the guard on the far left, and the single long curl that sprang out from under his hood.

Jolras, he remembered, picturing the guard who had stood so defiantly and protectively next to Maximilienne on the bar at the Jondrette, and who had clearly recognized Marcellus. The one who Maximilienne had called her brother.

Two siblings of Nadette Epernay, driven to these horrible acts of revenge.

The branded men were spun roughly around and shoved toward the nearest hothouse.

Then Maximilienne spoke again.

"No longer will the First and Second Estates enjoy the fruits of *our* labor," she shouted in an impassioned cry. "Soon every member of the upper estates will come to fear the name Red Scar."

Suddenly, the screen of the TéléCom flashed a blinding white as a deafening, thunderous boom exploded out of the speakers. Startled, Marcellus blinked to clear his vision, and when he was finally able to focus on the screen again, he saw that the hothouse was gone.

Its plastique roof had been blown completely off, and all of its large paneled windows had disintegrated into nothing. Plumes of dust and rocks engulfed the screen, and where the three superviseurs had been standing moments ago, only a lone boot in the mud remained.

- CHAPTER 35 -
CHATINE

WHEN CHATINE WAS SEVEN YEARS OLD, SHE FOUND an injured mouse in the Tourbay. Back then, she often wandered around the boglands to pass the time. It was the only place she could go to escape Henri's ghost. It had been haunting their inn for a year now, and the misty fields near Montfer seemed to keep it at bay. As though it were afraid of getting lost in the dense fog.

She came upon the mouse near a muddy stream. Chatine could tell right away that there was something wrong with it. She cornered it between her feet and picked it up by its tail. It dangled in front of her, squirming in an attempt to break free. And that's when Chatine noticed that its back left foot had been cut clean off, leaving behind a bleeding stump.

Chatine deposited the wriggling creature into the pocket of her coat and returned to the inn. She knew her mother would slap her dizzy if she found out Chatine had brought a mouse into the inn. The only rodents allowed through the doors were the ones being cooked into her father's "famous Jondrette sausages."

But Chatine wanted to cure the little animal. She thought that with enough time and patience, she could not only make him better, but maybe she could make him love her too.

She placed the mouse in an old bread box that she'd found in a trash heap in the Bidon and hid the box under her bed. Every day, she cleaned the mouse's wound and fed him scraps from the kitchen. And every day, he seemed to get a little better. Each time she opened the lid to check on him or bring him water, he would scurry around the bottom of the box, back and forth, like he was excited to see her.

Until one day, when she opened the lid and he was dead.

She couldn't understand why. She'd given him everything he needed. Food, water, attention, care. What could have happened? She showed the dead mouse to her older sister, Azelle, who studied the creature for a long moment before taking the box from Chatine's small hands and turning it around and around like she was inspecting it for defects.

Finally, she gave her very official-sounding diagnosis.

"You suffocated it, Chatine."

"Suffo-what?" Chatine had never heard this word before.

"This box has no holes for air. It couldn't breathe."

Chatine felt frustration well up inside her. And suddenly *she* was the one who couldn't breathe. "But I only put it in the box so it wouldn't run away and get killed out there. By Papa or a cat or the cold."

Azelle shrugged and handed the mouse coffin back to Chatine. "Looks like it was dead either way, then."

Chatine stared at the fresh bandages on her left leg. In the past two days, they were the only things that had changed in this room. Everything else had remained exactly the same. The yellow lights cupped in the ceiling, the shelves of neatly stacked medical supplies, the untouched tray full of food sitting on a table next to her cot. And the numbness. The heavy, mind-crushing numbness that hung in the air like the stink of the Frets. It clung to everything. It slowed everything. Until it felt like the space between breaths lasted an entire day, and the lull between heartbeats, a lifetime.

It was better this way, though. She preferred the numbness. A mind full of fog was easier than a mind razor-sharp with thoughts. With memories. With regrets.

And Chatine had so many of those.

"Azelle?" she whispered into the empty room. "Are you there?"

But as predicted, she got no response. Azelle hadn't spoken to her since she'd left Bastille, confirming that Chatine was alone again.

She wanted to hope. Truly, she did. She wanted to believe that Henri wasn't dead. That the Sols weren't cruel enough to bring him back to her only to take him away again. But she knew hope was a dangerous game to play. To Chatine, hope was like that wounded mouse in a box. Whether you tried to hold onto it—to protect it from all the dangers of the world— or you let it go, it didn't matter.

It died either way.

"Will you try to eat something for me today?" The door to the treatment center creaked open and Brigitte appeared, carrying a fresh tray of food. Through Chatine's fog-filled vision, she could make out dried fruit and a boiled egg. She expected her stomach to rumble, to remind her that she'd barely eaten anything since her last meager ration on Bastille. But even her stomach seemed to have given up.

Brigitte sighed and placed the tray down next to the other one. "Okay. How about a trip then?"

Mildly interested, Chatine swiveled her gaze to the woman. "What kind of trip?"

Brigitte smiled. "Just a chance to see more than the walls of this chalet."

Chatine lazily looked back at the wall. "I'm fine here," she muttered, even though it was a lie. She wasn't fine here. She wasn't fine anywhere.

Absentmindedly, she rubbed her forefinger over her thumb, searching for Marcellus's ring, only to remember that it had disappeared when she'd first arrived at the camp. Chatine had convinced herself that the Défecteurs had stolen it, even though Brigitte had sworn she hadn't seen it when she'd operated on Chatine. Now the absence of that ring—the notion that she might have lost it after keeping it safe for all those days and nights on Bastille—carved a hole inside of her as big as a Sol.

"I want to show you something," Brigitte said.

"What is it?"

"Ah, you see, that's the catch. You won't know until you agree to come with me."

"I can't walk," Chatine reminded her. "You're the médecin. I shouldn't have to tell you that."

Brigitte smiled, seemingly unfazed by Chatine's sourness. "I'm not a médecin."

"Sorry," Chatine muttered. "*Healer.* Whatever."

"I haven't been a médecin for"—she sighed—"wow . . . years. But I never got to work with people, like I always wanted. The Ministère assigned me to the medical research field."

Chatine cut her eyes back to Brigitte. Silently, in response, Brigitte pointed to the deep grooves carved into the side of her face. They weren't angry today. They were just there.

Realization slammed into Chatine, momentarily stealing the breath from her lungs. "Wait, you were a—"

"Cyborg? Yes."

For a blissful second, Chatine's mind emptied of everything else except those strange, miraculous scars. She didn't know a cyborg could have their circuitry removed. And then what? They were just normal people again? The only cyborgs she'd ever known were cruel and cold and heartless. As though the circuitry had been implanted as a blocker to their emotions. Because, as Chatine well knew, emotions only impeded your ability to do your job well.

A thousand questions flooded her mind, and they all seemed to be forcing their way out of her mouth at once. "What . . . How . . . Do . . ." She took a deep breath and plucked the simplest one from the stack. "*Why?*"

Brigitte chuckled. "Have you ever *met* a cyborg?"

The faintest ghost of a smile passed over Chatine's face, only to vanish a second later.

"I was recruited into the Cyborg Initiation Program when I turned eighteen. I quickly climbed the ranks and eventually became a very prominent and well-respected research médecin."

"And then you just left?" she asked, gesturing around the chalet. "For this?"

Brigitte's eyes twinkled. "I'll tell you what. I will answer all of your questions. . . *if* you agree to leave this chalet with me."

Chatine considered. Her curiosity was strong, and she soon realized her desire to get out of this room was equally strong. She glanced down at her bandaged leg and was about to remind Brigitte once again that she was in no condition to walk when Brigitte made her way to a cabinet on the far side of the room, opened the door, and removed a pair of metal crutches. "These will help you get around the camp."

Chatine eyed them with skepticism. She'd seen maimed Third Estaters hobbling around the Frets on crutches before, but she'd never actually used any herself. For their simplistic construction, they looked oddly complicated.

"Don't worry," Brigitte assured her, clearly interpreting her hesitation. "You'll get the hang of them quickly. I'm sure you're looking forward to being mobile again."

Mobile.

It was the magic word. Chatine had never felt so trapped in her life. And she had been to prison. She continued to eye the crutches still in Brigitte's hands, her Fret-rat determination returning like a punch of cold air. If she could scale walls and dangle from rafters, she could certainly manage a pair of Défecteur crutches.

With Brigitte's help, she pushed herself up to sitting and swung her legs off the bed. Her bandaged leg pulsed in response, but the pain was minimal.

"Put this on." Brigitte pulled an odd piece of clothing from the closet where she'd retrieved the crutches. "It will keep you warm outside."

Chatine stared warily at the strange garment. It looked like a coat, but it was unlike any coat she'd ever seen before. It was patched together, like the pants she used to wear back in the Frets. But these patches were thick and tough and so shiny they seemed to reflect everything in the room like a jumble of undulating mirrors. And unlike her old threadbare clothes, the moment this jacket was on and the hood was pulled up, Chatine felt nothing but rich, glowing warmth.

"These, too," Brigitte said, holding out a pair of mittens made of the same material.

"Does all this really keep you warm out there?" Chatine asked, still skeptical but slipping on the mittens anyway. She'd known cold in Vallonay and on Bastille. But she knew it was nothing compared to the cruel, biting winds that swept through the Terrain Perdu.

Brigitte extended the pair of crutches toward Chatine with a smile. "I guess there's only one way to find out."

The jacket was magic. Ridiculously puffy but impossibly warm. As Chatine hobbled on her crutches through the intricate grid of box-shaped structures and roofed walkways that made up the Défecteur camp, she felt none of the chill of being outside. Brigitte walked slowly beside her, pointing out the various buildings—which the Défecteurs called "chalets."

"Every roof in our camp is built with stealth technology," Brigitte explained as they continued down the walkway. "Just like our ships. This allows us to stay hidden from any passing crafts."

Chatine stared in awe at the structure above her head. If she hadn't seen it with her very own eyes, she wouldn't have believed that the roof of the passageway was invisible from above.

"How did you figure out how to do that?" she asked.

"The technology is actually not complicated. The Ministère has had the resources to develop it for more than five hundred years."

Chatine's brow furrowed as she continued to maneuver down the walkway on her crutches. They were nearing a cluster of chalets that was much larger than the others in the camp. "The Ministère has stealth tech?"

"No." Brigitte shook her head. "That's the thing. They've been so focused on using those resources for another purpose, they failed to recognize what they had."

"What resources?"

Brigitte nodded ahead of them, and when Chatine looked up, her crutches nearly slipped out from under her. She froze, staring in awe at the large structure. Along the chalet's frontside, there was a long row of slitted windows through which glowed a shimmering, iridescent blue.

"Zyttrium," Chatine murmured numbly.

She suddenly remembered the transparent boxes in the cargo hold of Etienne's ship. Processed zyttrium stolen from Bastille. Evidently, it hadn't been the first batch.

"As you probably already know, the Regime uses the metal to manufacture the Skins. We found another purpose for it."

Chatine gaped. "So you *steal* it from them?"

Brigitte let out a tinkling laugh. "One could argue that *they* steal it from Bastille. And that they steal the thousands of lives lost in mining it."

"Oh, I'm not judging you," Chatine was quick to say. She was the last person on the planet to condemn a thief. "I'm just . . . impressed."

"Well, merci." Brigitte continued down the walkway. Chatine hobbled beside her, unable to take her eyes off the blue light radiating from the windows. "Stealth technology is crucial to our way of life. As you probably know, we have a long history of . . . well, I guess you could call it 'conflict' with the Regime."

Chatine did know. For years, General Bonnefaçon and his minions at the Ministère had been rounding up Défecteurs all over the planet. Those who resisted the raids were either killed or sent to Bastille, while those who cooperated were Skinned and assimilated into society.

And others, it would seem, had somehow managed to escape. To live here.

"We are the last of the communities," Brigitte continued. "After the most recent roundups, there were so few of us left, we decided to join together and create this camp. It was a challenging adjustment. Not all the communities operated the same way. We've had to make many compromises, but all in all it seems to work."

Brigitte paused to point to a chalet to their left. "This is the lodge. When you feel well enough, you can join us there for meals, if you'd like."

Chatine peered through the window at a room filled with large, round tables and a kitchen at the far end. It was evidently mealtime right now, because each table was crammed full of people. Everyone talked and laughed as they ate from plates bursting with food. And at one of the tables, she spotted Etienne. He was seated between two younger girls. Both looked no older than seven. He was pretending not to notice while they each snuck pieces of meat from his plate. Then he glanced down and acted astonished to find the food gone. The girls giggled in delight at the charade.

Chatine felt something harden inside of her, and she tore her gaze away.

"Is this the trip?" she asked sharply. "Did you trick me into going on a tour of your camp so you could give me a Défecteur history lesson?" Chatine immediately felt guilty for the edge in her voice. Brigitte had been nothing but kind to her since she'd arrived. And she was, admittedly, somewhat interested in what Brigitte was saying. Chatine had always considered the Défecteurs to be backward and ignorant. But walking around this camp, she could see they were just the opposite.

Despite Chatine's venom, Brigitte still offered her a smile. "Maybe," she admitted. "But what I really wanted to show you is up here."

Balancing on her crutches, Chatine followed after her, surprised when the woman reached the end of the covered walkway and kept going, straight out from under the protective shields of the roofs and into the wild, frozen tundra of the Terrain Perdu. Chatine could see nothing in front of her for kilomètres except the ice, the frozen grass, a few scraggly bushes, and rocks that made up this endless landscape. With no roofs or chalets out here, the wind was brutal and relentless. It stung Chatine's cheeks and eyes, but the giant padded coat Brigitte had given her miraculously still kept out most of the cold.

"This is what you wanted to show me?" Chatine asked, confused. "The Terrain Perdu?"

"It's beautiful isn't it?"

Chatine shot Brigitte a strange look. Was the woman on goldenroot? "Sure, yeah. It's also very cold. So . . ." She dug her crutches into the ground and started to turn back toward the camp, but her foot snagged over something, drawing her attention to the pile of rocks she'd nearly tripped over.

She silently cursed the stones and prepared to maneuver around them when she noticed the rocks weren't arranged in a pile, as they'd first appeared. They were arranged in a shape.

Chatine tilted her head to the side to get a better look.

Is that a . . .

"It's a star," Brigitte said, evidently reading her mind. She did that far too often for Chatine's liking. "It represents hope." Brigitte pointed to another cluster of stones a few mètres away. "And that one is a circle, which to us represents the interconnectedness of all things."

Chatine glanced around her, suddenly seeing the landscape with new eyes and new wonderment. There were hundreds of them. Tiny clusters of stones arranged in so many different shapes. Squares, triangles, crosses, parallel lines, and several more that Chatine couldn't even begin to identify.

"What are they?" she asked, jutting her chin toward the mètres and mètres of stone patterns that surrounded them.

"They're memories."

"Memories?" Chatine was certain she'd misheard.

"Of those we've lost."

"I don't understand."

Brigitte walked over to one of the clusters. It was a simple design. Just eight tiny pebbles in the shape of an arrow. She knelt down reverently in front of it. "We bury our dead."

Horrified, Chatine tried to leap back, but the crutches made it impossible. Instead she found herself hobbling away from the stone cluster by her feet. But another cluster was only a few paces behind her. She yelped and tried to escape that one as well. But it was no use. The patterns were everywhere. She was surrounded.

"So . . . ," she stammered. "So these are all . . . There are *cavs* under the ground?"

Brigitte looked somewhat amused by Chatine's reaction. "Are you afraid of the dead?"

"No," Chatine asserted. But they both knew it was a lie. She was terrified of the dead. She'd spent far too much time sneaking around Third Estate morgues. She'd seen enough cavs to last a lifetime.

"The dead can't hurt you."

"I'm not sure that's true," Chatine muttered under her breath. The dead most definitely could hurt you. They could hurt you a *lot*.

Brigitte stared at her for so long, Chatine began to squirm.

"These stones don't mark actual graves," the woman went on. "At least not all of them. During the roundups, we were forced to leave many of our graveyards behind. We placed these stones as a reminder of those we lost." Brigitte ran her fingertip across a stone by her feet, and for a moment Chatine could swear she saw something that looked like longing cross Brigitte's face.

The wind swept over the great, barren landscape and bit at Chatine's ears and the tip of her nose. She shivered and stared down at the pattern next to Brigitte. "Whose memory is that?" she asked, although her voice was so small, she was surprised that Brigitte even heard her over all that wind.

"Etienne's father." She didn't look up as she spoke. "He died in the last roundup."

Chatine's stomach turned. "I'm . . . ," she started to speak, but she quickly realized she didn't know what to say. The polite way to finish that sentence was to say "I'm sorry." But sorry wasn't enough. If anyone understood that, it was her.

Sorry wasn't enough for Azelle.

It wasn't enough for Henri, the first time he left her.

And now—if, Sols forbid, he was gone again—she knew, with the certainty of the clouds in the Laterrian sky, that it would never, *ever* be enough.

Chatine swallowed, finding her voice again. It was no longer small and uncertain. It was strong and tempestuous. "I don't get it. Why aren't you angrier? Why didn't you fight back against the Ministère? They took your people. They *killed* your people. Why do you act like it's all some magical gift from the Sols?"

"I *was* angry," Brigitte admitted. "Very angry. At first. But I—like the rest of our community—chose to confront the anger instead of the Ministère."

Chatine scowled at her. "What?"

"Life is full of monsters, Chatine. We can't fight them all. We have to choose. Some monsters are not worth confronting. Some we are better off stepping away from. We *choose* to step away from the Ministère. From the Regime. By not engaging in their battles and their politics and their wars, by not participating, we are making a silent stand against them. Our lives out here," she gestured to the wild, rugged terrain around her, "away from their power cells and technology and food source and rules, is an opposition in and of itself. So you see, sometimes not fighting is fighting. Do you understand?"

Chatine balanced precariously on her crutches, trying to wrap her mind around what this woman was saying. But her rage was blinding her and turning her vision red. "Are you telling me to run away?"

"Well," Brigitte replied with a mysterious smile, "that all depends on what you're running away *from*."

Chatine shook her head. "I don't know what you're talking about."

"Some monsters are not worth confronting," Brigitte repeated. "But some—" she placed a hand to her chest— "like the ones that live in here, *must* be confronted. Because those are the ones that can truly destroy us, by turning us into our own worst villains. The challenge is knowing which is which." Brigitte reached out again and touched one of the tiny pebbles on the ground in front of her. "It's harder for some."

Chatine snorted. "You mean, you? I find that hard to believe."

Brigitte shook her head, momentarily lost in her thoughts. "Not me."

She stood up but kept her gaze locked on the ground. On the stones. On the memory of who those stones represented. "The dead can only hurt you when you try to forget them."

At these words, Chatine felt something pulse inside of her. A deep, bitter wound that she thought she'd closed long ago. But that had recently been ripped open again, and was now bleeding from the inside.

"So that's why you brought me out here?" Chatine's voice was venomous and cold. "Because you think my brother is dead?"

"I never said that," Brigitte said sternly.

"But that's what you think, right? That the ship is gone? And the search party will never find them?"

"I couldn't possibly know that. The outcome is not up to me. Or you. Only your reaction is."

"So you want me to gather up a bunch of stones and put them in some stupid raindrop-shaped pattern to honor his memory? Because he may as well be dead?" The words were firing out of Chatine now like explosifs dropped from a combatteur. "Well, I'm not going to do that. In my world, we don't bury our dead. We disintegrate them. We turn them to ice dust. And they become *nothing*."

"Chatine—" Brigitte tried to say, but Chatine cut her off.

"Save it. I've heard enough. You know, for people who pride themselves on not conforming to the Regime, you certainly seem to have a lot of ideas on who I should be and how I should live."

Then, before Brigitte could spew out any more Défecteur nonsense, Chatine turned awkwardly on her crutches and hobbled back to the camp.

CHAPTER 36

ALOUETTE

"THIS IS THE MONARCH PIECE. YOU HAVE TO PROTECT it throughout the entire game. If you can capture the other player's Monarch, you win. That's the end goal."

Alouette was barely listening as Cerise attempted to explain the rules of Regiments to Gabriel from across a glowing, holographic game board. Alouette was sitting in a chaise on the other side of the viewing lounge, facing out the window, with Marcellus's TéléCom open on her lap.

"Every other piece can move," Cerise continued, pointing to the three-tiered board. "But the Monarch always has to stay in the same place."

"Why?" Gabriel asked. "Why can't he just cross the board and destroy all the other pieces? He's the Monarch."

"First of all," Cerise snapped, "the Monarch has no gender. It's not a he or a she. It's just *the* Monarch."

"And that matters because?"

"And secondly," Cerise continued, ignoring the question, "the Monarch can't move because it has to stay here, in the palace, where it can be protected." She'd been explaining this game to Gabriel for the past hour, and she'd lost her patience about two minutes into the explanation.

But Alouette knew they were only playing to keep their minds off everything else. Like the fact that amid the infinite stars in front of them loomed a great enemy, while in the abyss of space behind them was a planet on the brink of war.

It had been two days since they'd watched that disturbing footage from the Red Scar. And none of them had even so much as uttered a single word about it. It was almost as though they were all pretending it had never happened. Alouette supposed it was easier that way. She'd been doing everything in her power to keep all thoughts of the sisters at bay too. After all, how many potential disasters could they deal with at once? Right now, their first priority had to be the general's weapon. The rest—the grief, the sorrow, the turmoil back home—had to come later.

"Well, that's just stupid," Gabriel said.

"No, *you're* stupid," Cerise countered.

"I'm not stupid. The whole game is stupid!"

Alouette glanced over at the flight map on the wall of the viewing lounge.

Eighteen more hours until they arrived on Albion. Eighteen more hours until they came face-to-face with Sister Denise's mysterious source and discovered what the general was planning.

"I have to agree with Gabriel." Marcellus appeared in the doorway of the galley holding two full plates of food. "The game is pretty stupid."

"Wait, you know how to play too?" Gabriel asked.

Marcellus set down a plate of cheese and fruit on the table under the glowing game board. "Unfortunately, yes. My grandfather taught me when I was little. For the past ten years we've played every single week. But I've always been dreadful at it. According to my grandfather, it's an effective way to learn and practice strategy and military maneuvering. He said it would make me a great leader one day." Marcellus's tone went from bitter to morose in an instant. "Like him."

Everyone in the ship fell silent, as though afraid to go near Marcellus's words. Everyone except Gabriel, that is, who seemed oblivious to the tension in the air. "So, is this what you pomps all do for fun? Sit up there in your fancy manoirs and play stupide, pointless games all day, while the rest of us are working ourselves to death?"

"Working?" Cerise said with a snort. "Really? You work?"

"Yes," Gabriel said. "Unlike *some* people, I earn what I eat."

"I wouldn't call what *you* do earning."

"I'll have you know it takes a lot of skill to do what I do."

Cerise snorted. "Yes, I'm sure pickpocketing handkerchiefs from little old ladies is very challenging."

"First of all, I don't rob little old ladies. And secondly, I'm not just a pickpocket. I happen to be a criminal mastermind."

"Mastermind? Really? You steal stuff."

"The Second Estate steals. The Third Estate only steals *back*."

Cerise rolled her eyes. "Oh please. You steal for yourself. Not because you're trying to make some kind of grand political statement."

"My whole life is a grand political statement! While yours is a joke."

"How many times do I have to tell you?" Cerise shouted. "I'm on your side. I'm a sympathizeur."

Gabriel launched out of his chair. "That's. Not. A. Thing!"

"Yes. It. Is!"

"No," Gabriel said, his voice turning dark and determined, "it's not. Until you have one of these"—he roughly pulled up the sleeve of his shirt to reveal the darkened screen just above his left wrist—"implanted in your flesh against your will, you cannot sympathize with us. We're told these are here for our own safety. But they're nothing but chains. These are here to enslave us."

"Just because you're Third Estate, doesn't mean you have a monopoly on pain," Cerise muttered.

"What the fric does that mean?"

"You're not the only one with problems."

"Yeah, right," Gabriel snorted. "Your biggest problem is what dress to wear to what fête. My biggest problem is where my next meal is coming from."

"I think you already solved that when you raided the galley. I'm surprised there's any food left."

"Sucks to be hungry, doesn't it?"

"I'm just saying"—Cerise tried for a deep breath—"not all chains are visible."

"Whatever," Gabriel mumbled collapsing back into his seat. "Let's just play."

Cerise nodded, restoring herself, and sat back down. "Actually, there's a few more rules to explain first."

"Of course there are."

Alouette let out an uneasy sigh. The tension in this voyageur had been suffocating for days. They may have all been doing an effective job at pretending the world wasn't falling apart, but clearly the anxiety was showing itself in other ways.

Returning her attention to the TéléCom in her lap, Alouette turned up the volume on the audio patch Cerise had lent her and continued to scroll through the search results on the screen.

"With those two onboard, who needs in-flight entertainment, right?"

Alouette glanced up to see Marcellus standing next to her with a wry smile. She knew he was trying for a joke, an attempt to diffuse the friction in the air. And she was grateful for the distraction. He set a second plate of food down on a nearby table before lowering himself onto the edge of the chaise and nodding toward the TéléCom. "Any luck?"

Alouette shook her head. "Not much. At least not anything new."

Cerise had set up Marcellus's TéléCom with her Ministère portal access, and Alouette had spent nearly the entire day watching broadcasts and reports and archived footage, searching for more information about her mother, but she was still at a dead end. With each file she watched and discarded, she could feel another one of her fragile hopes popping like a soap bubble.

She tipped her head back against the chaise. "I did find a profile for a Madeline Villette, daughter of Lisole Villette, who died in Montfer in Month 8, 490. That date matches up to what the madame at the bordel told me. So that must be me. Madeline Villette." The name felt so foreign. Like borrowed clothes. Ill-fitting in all the wrong places.

"Villette," Marcellus repeated pensively, tilting his head. "Where have I heard that name before?"

Alouette shrugged. "I can't imagine where. There's not much in here about Madeline or Lisole. After the death of her daughter, Lisole Villette just disappeared. The madame said she left town. She probably changed her name. And there's absolutely nothing about Madeline Villette's father."

Marcellus proffered the plate of food toward her. "Here. Eat something. You need sustenance."

Alouette took a piece of cheese and popped it into her mouth. It did make her feel a little better. She immediately grabbed for another.

"Anything more from the auditeur?" she asked.

Marcellus sighed. "A little. Fortunately, the general still has no idea where we are. He doesn't even seem to know we left Laterre, but it won't be long until he sniffs something out. He's got his new hunting dog, Inspecteur Chacal, out scouring the planet looking for us."

"So, the best way to win the game," Cerise's voice rang out from across the lounge, "is to maneuver your most powerful pieces—like your brigadier or legionnaires—up the levels of the board to eventually capture the other player's Monarch."

"That's it?" Gabriel asked. "That's the only way to win?"

"Yes. That's how you win. By capturing the Monarch."

"And the brigadier and legionnaires are the only ones who can do that?"

"Not necessarily," Marcellus cut in, causing everyone in the lounge to turn to him. "You can always try for the Peasant's Revolt."

"The what?" Gabriel asked, looking between Marcellus and Cerise.

"You don't want to try for the Peasant's Revolt," Cerise said decisively. "It's a fool's move."

"I *am* a fool," Gabriel replied.

"Well, at least we agree on that."

"So tell me what it is already."

"Fine," said Cerise. "The Peasant's Revolt is when you use your peasant pieces to surround and capture the other player's Monarch."

"What's so foolish about that?" asked Gabriel.

"It's just incredibly risky," Marcellus replied. "Because in order to get enough peasants up to the top tier of the board to trap the Monarch, it usually requires you to sacrifice several of your more valuable pieces, leaving your own Monarch vulnerable."

Cerise scoffed. "Which is foolish, because the peasants are the weakest pieces on the board."

"*Individually*, they're weak," Alouette corrected.

Marcellus peered at her in surprise. "You know how to play?"

Alouette nodded.

Gabriel stood up from the table. "That's it. I'm done. This game is stupid and confusing and—"

"Oh, sit down," Cerise said impatiently. "You just have to start playing. You'll pick it up eventually."

Gabriel succumbed and plopped back down into his chair.

"Where did you learn to play Regiments?" Marcellus asked Alouette.

She flashed him a sad smile. "Sister Jacqui taught me."

Marcellus fell silent for a long time as he stared down at his hands. Alouette knew he was thinking about Jacqui and Denise, the last remaining leaders of the Vangarde, locked up in some facility somewhere, being tortured by the general. A small part of her—the saddest part of her—almost wished they were dead too.

"I met her, you know?" Marcellus said softly. "Both of them. Jacqui and Denise. I met them right before the general relocated them. She was . . ." He paused, seemingly searching for the right word. "Intriguing."

Alouette nodded. It was the perfect word for Sister Jacqui. She felt tears sting her eyes and quickly blinked them away. "Is that how you got recruited to join the Vangarde?"

He shook his head. "Actually, no. It was Mabelle Dubois who recruited me."

Alouette's breath unexpectedly hitched in her chest at the name. There was something achingly familiar about it. She swore she'd heard it before. Or read it before? "Why do I know that name?"

"It was sewn into my father's prisoner shirt. Remember? You read it to me in the Frets? The day we met?"

"Oh, yes. Right." But something was still niggling at her. "She was your . . . governess?"

Marcellus nodded, and Alouette recognized fresh pain on his face. "She had been an undercover spy in the Palais for more than ten years before they found out she was a Vangarde operative. She started working there during the Rebellion of 488."

Alouette's mind was churning now, dates and names spinning across her vision.

Mabelle Dubois. Operative. 488.

"Oh my Sols!" she said, launching out of the chaise.

Marcellus stood up too. "What? What's wrong?"

But Alouette didn't answer. She couldn't answer until she was sure. Until this gnawing feeling in her chest was either confirmed or denied. Darting through the viewing lounge, she brushed past Cerise and Gabriel, tore down the stairs, and barged into her couchette with Marcellus close behind her.

The thick red-spined book that Principale Francine had given her was lying on the bedside table. *Full Compendium of Operative Reports from 488 to 489.* She scooped it up and flipped to the table of contents, running her fingertip down the list of headings scrawled in neat cursive handwriting.

And there it was.

Her finger froze halfway down the page, on the line that read:

Surveillance Reports from Operative Mabelle Dubois

The connection to the name must have slipped her mind when she'd read this yesterday. It was too out of context. Too far buried in the haze of the past few weeks. But now the connection seemed far too strong to be a coincidence.

"What is that?" Marcellus asked. He'd stepped up beside her and was staring down at the words half-hidden by her fingertip.

"I think . . ." Alouette felt a shiver run through her. "I think they're reports from when Mabelle was working as your governess. Principale Francine gave me this book before I left the Refuge."

Marcellus stared incredulously between Alouette and the open page. "Why?"

Alouette shook her head. "I don't know."

"Well, read it!"

With shaky hands, Alouette turned to the correct section and read aloud from the first report. It was about an upcoming interplanetary visit from Novayan delegates. She flipped to the next report, and together, she and Marcellus skimmed over a diagram illustrating Mabelle's suggested placements for a new batch of surveillance microcams and another diagram that laid out the locations of four loopholes that Mabelle had engineered in the security shields around the Palais, so she could sneak on and off the grounds without being seen.

"Yes!" Marcellus said eagerly, pointing at the page. "She told me about those. I was using them to come and go from the Palais before I was arrested."

In the next report, Alouette read aloud from a full hour-by-hour account of Patriarche Claude's daily activities, including what he ate for breakfast, lunch, and dinner. And then there was a review of the former Matrone's comings and goings. But after skimming through more than ten subsequent reports, Alouette was still no closer to answering that nagging question: *Why* had Principale Francine given this to her?

She blew out a breath and turned to the next report, convinced that this one would be just as unhelpful as the last. But something near the top of the page instantly caught her eye. A word. A *name*.

The only name that seemed to matter to Alouette anymore.

Her heart started to pound. She warned herself not to get her hopes up. There were probably countless women on the planet of Laterre that had that same name. It didn't necessarily mean anything.

But she just couldn't help the adrenaline coursing through her as she bent her head toward the worn, yellowed page of Mabelle's report and read aloud.

Date: Month 6, Day 1, 488
Operative: Mabelle Dubois
Location: Grand Palais

Today I came back to my room in the servants' wing and heard the sound of muffled sobs. I knew instantly that it was Lisole in the room next to mine. Today was the "big day," as she'd been calling it for weeks. But clearly it had not gone as planned.

I called to her through the crack in the wall, the one we always use to whisper to each other late into the night. But she didn't answer. Nor did she come to dinner with the other maids.

I fear it is the worst news. I fear she has gotten herself in too deep. She has waded into the water with sharks, and she can't swim.

I worry about her. Lisole has become my one true friend here in the Palais. I remember how she used to be such a happy girl. Before she got herself embroiled in this mess. She used to sing while she scrubbed the floors. She smiled at the flowers in the garden. And her big, dark eyes drank in the stars in the vast TéléSky.

But tonight, I fall asleep to the sound of her cries.

"Lisole," Marcellus echoed once Alouette had reached the end of the report. He turned to her, the shock on his face matching her own. "Your mother?"

Alouette's breaths were coming fast and furious now. She could barely move her head enough to nod. "I think . . . maybe?"

"Keep reading!" Marcellus urged.

She turned the page.

Date: Month 6, Day 2, 488
Operative: Mabelle Dubois
Location: Grand Palais

This morning, I awoke to the sound of a commotion outside my door. I rushed into the hallway to find Lisole fighting with a handsome auburn-haired

Palais guard. Her eyes were puffy and red. Her hair was a mess, and across her cheek, I saw an angry red mark. I knew, immediately, that she'd been struck.

I asked the guard what was happening.

"Mademoiselle Villette has been relieved of her duties at the Palais," he said in a cold, detached tone. He wouldn't even look at her as he spoke.

"Is there a reason?" I asked, even though I was certain I already knew. Lisole's tears last night had told me everything.

"For theft," the guard announced.

Lisole bowed her head in shame, and my worst fears were confirmed.

"She was caught stealing directly from the Patriarche himself," the guard went on. "She is fortunate Patriarche Claude is only dismissing her, and not sending her straight to Bastille."

I nodded but said nothing. For there was nothing I could say.

As the guard escorted her away, Lisole caught my eye, and in a single desperate glance, we both knew that this was the beginning of the end for her.

Alouette's heart pounded faster as she turned eagerly to the next report.

Date: Month 6, Day 3, 488
Operative: Mabelle Dubois
Location: Grand Palais

The Patriarche and the general have been locking themselves in the general's private study for hours on end. This change of protocol is clearly indicative of . . .

Alouette glanced up from the book and stared incredulously at Marcellus. "That's it?" She hastily flipped to the next page and scanned the lines of handwritten words for another mention of her mother's name. But there was nothing. The next page contained a reconnaissance report from the delegation meetings, followed by five separate reports on a new TéléSkin update that the Ministère was working on.

Alouette kept flipping, desperation filling her with every turn of the page, until she was quite certain she would rip the paper clean out of the spine.

"Hey." Marcellus's gentle tone broke into her thoughts, and his warm fingers stopped her hand. "It's okay."

"It's not okay!" she cried, feeling the crushing blow of disappointment. "I'm so tired of all these dead ends! All of this, just to discover that my mother was a Palais servant and a *criminal*? Just like Hugo?"

"Maybe there's more to it than that?" Marcellus suggested.

"What more would there be? She wasn't special. She wasn't this long-lost secret that I've been destined to find. She was just a common thief."

Suddenly, Alouette remembered the words Madame Blanchard had said to her back at the bordel.

Your maman was a croc. Obviously, she conned us both. . . . She's a good liar, that Lisole.

Furiously, Alouette closed the book with a snap and tossed it onto the bed. A deep and guttural scream was building up inside of her, threatening to shake the walls of the couchette and echo out into the deepest depths of space.

But it never released. Because someone else beat her to it. "Nooooooo!" A piercing wail echoed from the upper deck. Alouette and Marcellus shared a panicked look before barreling out of the couchette and back up the stairs to the viewing lounge.

The Regiments game had been abandoned. Cerise was standing in the middle of the room, gripping her TéléCom, a look of sheer dread on her face.

"What's wrong?" Marcellus asked, slightly winded.

"Our cloaking code," Cerise replied in a shaky voice without lifting her eyes from the TéléCom. "It's been . . . overridden."

"Overridden?" Marcellus echoed. "What does that mean?"

But before Cerise could respond, the ship began to rumble, the floors beneath their feet juddering so forcefully, Alouette had to grab on to a nearby chaise to steady herself.

Gabriel yelped. "Oh Sols! What's happening? Are we dying? Is the ship exploding?"

"No," said Marcellus, sounding confused. "It's just the stabilizeurs. We're decelerating."

"Why?" Alouette asked, glancing at the hologram map. "We still have over seventeen hours of flight time left."

"I know," said Marcellus. His tone did little to comfort Alouette.

Then, suddenly, Cerise was on the move, crossing the viewing lounge and marching into the flight bridge with quick, purposeful strides. Alouette darted after her with Marcellus and Gabriel close behind.

"Why is it slowing down now?" Gabriel asked breathlessly.

They all looked to Cerise, but her eyes were trained out the window of the bridge, her face gaunt. "Because of *that*."

Alouette turned, and all the blood in her veins drained instantly to her feet. Outside the window loomed something so vast, so colossal, it blocked out every star and every centimètre of space, overshadowing their tiny voyageur like a behemoth to a gnat. Wider than the Terrain Perdu, sleeker and steelier than the exoskeleton of a droid, it moved like a great block of ice in a waveless ocean.

Silent and slow and deadly.

"What *is* that?" Gabriel asked, his voice strained.

It took Alouette a moment to match the gargantuan ship to the sketches she'd studied in the Chronicles, but once the connection was made, she knew their journey was over. "It's a Trafalgar 4000," she whispered.

"A what?" Gabriel asked.

But it was Marcellus who answered, his voice as brittle as aged paper. "Albion's most powerful warship."

CHAPTER 37

MARCELLUS

MARCELLUS COULDN'T BREATHE. THE TRAFALGAR 4000 hung above the voyageur, vast and menacing and hungry, looking like it might swallow them whole. In one gulping second, they would be gone. Consumed, chewed, and digested inside the gigantic warship. Marcellus had learned about these types of Albion spacecraft during his training at the Ministère. He knew of their might and their power. And now, as he stared up at the beast of a warship, it felt as though every molecule of oxygen in the flight bridge was being sucked out into space.

"Oh my Sols! We're going to die!" someone screamed behind him. He was fairly certain it was Gabriel. But it sounded like it was coming from galaxies away, drowned out by the sound of the warship's colossal engines humming just outside the window.

Whomp.

Whomp.

Whomp.

But Marcellus knew he had to be imagining it. There was no sound in space. No engines whirring. No weapons firing.

No screams.

"We're not going to die!" Cerise shouted back at Gabriel. "Stop panicking."

"Stop panicking?! Have you *looked* outside the window?"

"How did they even find us?" Alouette asked. Marcellus could feel her presence behind him. Serene and composed, even in the face of this catastrophe.

Meanwhile, Marcellus felt as though his entire body was shutting down. One essential organ at a time. He still hadn't brought himself to move, speak, breathe. He stood motionless at the window, trying desperately to come up with a plan. A strategy. Something! But his mind was as empty as the endless void of space outside.

"I don't know!" Cerise cried. "But now they've taken control of the navigation system."

Just then, the voyageur lurched beneath their feet, knocking them all off balance. Marcellus reached out to steady himself before whipping his gaze back to the window. His chest squeezed.

The Trafalgar.

It was getting closer.

"They're pulling us in." Cerise voiced his fear.

Gabriel let out another yelp. "They're *what*?"

"Will you stop whining!" Cerise shouted. "You are the most unsmooth criminal I've ever met. How have you ever managed to steal anything?!"

"What do we do?" Alouette asked.

Marcellus was still too numb to speak, but he knew the answer.
Nothing.

There was nothing to do now. They were flying in Albion airspace on a Laterrian ship. They were being reeled in by a Trafalgar 4000, like a tiny fish on a line, and soon they would be captured. They would stand trial. They would be convicted as spies, and they would spend the rest of their lives in "The Tower," Albion's infamous prison, rotting in one of its dank and pitch-black cells.

And his grandfather would win.

Just as he always did.

Cerise prodded frantically at the controls on the console. Alouette stood beside her, her steady gaze trying to follow Cerise's rapidly moving hands. Marcellus turned toward the hologram map in the center of the bridge, which now showed their ship, caught between the Asteroid Channel and the planet of Albion.

"I can't do anything," Cerise said. "They've completely locked us out. Even the backup nav systems have been overridden."

"This is it!" Gabriel cried, frantically pacing the length of the bridge like a mad man. "It's all over. We're all going to die. I knew this was a mistake. I knew I should never have stepped foot on this death trap. It wasn't even that nice of a ship. Sure, it has seven bathrooms, but what good are seven bathrooms when you're dead? And the kitchen didn't even *have* paté. Or gateaux! And now I will never know what either of them taste like. I'm going to die without ever tasting gateaux and—"

POW!

Cerise's fist slammed into Gabriel's face with such force, he stumbled back, crashing into the holographic map, causing the planets to fritz and fuzz.

"Hey!" Gabriel shouted, holding his nose with both hands. "You punched me! You punched me in the face! You don't punch people in the face."

"I had to shut you up," Cerise said, pivoting back to the flight console.

Gabriel turned to Marcellus. "Did you see that? She punched me. In the *face.*"

But Marcellus was barely listening. Because the voyageur had started to rumble again, this time with far more intensity. Everyone's gazes jumped back to the window. They were heading toward a large latticed grid on the side of the Trafalgar, dotted with thousands of blinking lights. Beneath the grid, a vast fleet of tiny crafts clung to the surface of the ship like bats on the branches of a tree. Their sleek black shells shimmered ominously.

Albion Micro-fighters.

Marcellus had heard about their deadly capabilities. One small swarm could take out entire cities, entire fleets.

Alouette turned to him. "What's happening?"

Marcellus squeezed his fists at his sides. "They're docking us."

The docking port grew larger in front of them, and soon its lights dazzled so brightly in the voyageur's window that Marcellus was momentarily blinded.

But he could still feel the vibrations underfoot.

The whirring of vast machinery.

And the deafening clanking sound, which Marcellus knew meant only one thing.

"We're docked," said Cerise.

A squealing noise echoed from the voyageur's speaker system, followed by an unfamiliar, chilling voice. "This is Admiral Wellington of the Albion Royal Space Fleet. We are commandeering this ship."

The long vowels and clipped consonants of the admiral's accent made Marcellus's whole spine shudder.

"Do not try to run or escape, or you will be shot."

With these words, the speakers clicked off. But on the screens of the flight console, Marcellus could see them. The primary hatch of the voyageur had been opened, and a squad of Albion guards were already trooping onboard.

Terrified, Marcellus searched for something reassuring to grasp on to, his fingers finally entangling with Alouette's. He grabbed on to her hand, vowing not to let go, no matter what happened in the next few minutes. She looked over at him, and he saw something in those large, dark eyes of hers. Something he hoped to never see again.

Fear.

He squeezed her hand, hoping it would comfort her, although he had no idea why it would. What was his feeble hand compared to the Albion Royal Guard? They were known across the System Divine for being monsters. Murderers. Killing machines. And the scariest part was, they were 100 percent human. These men and women were no droids. They weren't even cyborgs. They were flesh and bone, rumored to be recruited from birth, raised in captivity, brainwashed from infancy, trained to hunt and invade and leave no survivors.

And an entire fleet of them had just boarded this ship.

Marcellus's hands had never felt more useless.

"They're coming," Cerise squeaked, her voice strangled and panicked.

Gabriel looked like he might be sick.

Then all they could hear were footsteps. Heavy, clomping footsteps, which were getting louder and louder . . .

Until finally, the door to the bridge whooshed open.

Marcellus sucked in a breath at the sight of them. At least twelve guards stood in the doorway dressed in pristine red uniforms and fur-trimmed black helmets that almost covered their eyes. From the way the fabric stretched across their bodies, Marcellus could see these soldiers were built to fight. Solid muscles. Supple tendons. A power and force barely kept in check by their stiff wool uniforms. And strapped to their sides were gleaming assault lancers. Marcellus had heard about these Albion weapons with their lethal cluster bullets that could unleash a spray of tiny shrapnel inside a victim's body. They made Laterrian paralyzeurs seem almost kind.

From amid the group of guards, a man in a metallic-gray, floor-length coat pushed his way to the front. He wore no hat, and over one of his hard, dark eyes was a round disk that winked and glowed in the bluish lights of the flight bridge.

A monoglass, Marcellus realized. Albion tech that could scan the world like a cyborg eye. It tracked across the flight bridge, monitoring and analyzing each of them in turn.

"I expected something rather more . . ." The man trailed off and sniffed the air with his hawkish nose, clearly searching for the right word. ". . . daunting. But all we seem to have found here is a little gaggle of peculiarly dressed *children.* How very disappointing."

Marcellus flinched at the man's haughty Albion accent and scornful eyes. It was the same voice he'd heard over the ship's speakers only moments ago. Admiral Wellington.

"Nevertheless, you are still flying a Laterrian ship and trespassing in

Albion airspace, which, according to royal decree, warrants immediate arrest and imprisonment."

He took one last chilling look at each of them before flicking his fingers dismissively and turning back toward the door. "Seize them."

The guards stalked menacingly forward, their weapons raised and ready to fire at a moment's provocation.

Searing heat charged through Marcellus. His muscles coiled, preparing to fight. But then he felt Alouette squeeze his hand in a gentle warning. Calmly reminding him that taking on this troop of Albion guards by force would not only be rash and foolish; it would be deadly.

But what else were they supposed to do? They *had* to fight. The general *had* to be stopped. Marcellus dropped Alouette's hand and formed his fingers into a tight fist.

"We are accompanying Officer Marcellus Bonnefaçon, grandson of César Bonnefaçon, the General of the Laterrian Ministère."

Marcellus blinked, uncertain who had just spoken. Then Alouette stepped forward, addressing the admiral with a smooth, diplomatic voice. "Her majesty, Queen Matilda Bellingham, is expecting us. We are here to check on the progress of a top-secret project that General Bonnefaçon is developing with your planet."

Admiral Wellington paused and slowly turned back around, something between a grimace and a sneer playing out on his otherwise austere face. "I have no knowledge of this so-called project. Nor do I have any reason to believe that Her Majesty would be expecting an officer of the *Laterrian* Regime." He pronounced the word Laterrian as though it were diseased.

"What are you doing?" Marcellus hissed to Alouette, blood pumping wildly through his veins.

But she ignored him, taking another step forward. One of the guards advanced and pushed the barrel of his assault lancer into Alouette's chest. Marcellus felt the fire inside him flare, but Alouette looked perfectly composed. As though she wasn't one finger twitch away from dying a gruesome, painful death.

"I'm not surprised you have no knowledge of it," she said, standing rigid and unyielding in front of Admiral Wellington. Her expression was as unreadable as his. "As I said before, and as Officer Bonnefaçon will confirm, the project is a top-secret development. An extremely confidential venture between Albion and Laterre."

Alouette and the admiral both turned toward Marcellus. His heart was pounding so loudly in his chest, he was certain everyone in the flight bridge could hear it. Alouette met his gaze, communicating two simple words with those expressive brown eyes of hers.

Stay calm.

Marcellus shook out his still clenched fists and attempted to swallow. "Yes," he said in a raspy voice. "That's right. We were given strict orders not to mention it to anyone." He forced himself to look the admiral in the eye. "That's why the general issued us a special cloaking code, under which we were directed to land. But since you somehow managed to override that code, I am left with no choice but to divulge the purpose of our mission to you"—he gave a small, tight bow of his head—"Admiral Wellington."

Beads of sweat began to form on the back of Marcellus's neck as he watched the admiral for a reaction. One AirLink to Laterre, and they would be finished. Done. Not just imprisoned in an Albion prison, but worse. Much worse. Delivered back to Laterre for the *general's* punishment.

The admiral stood inhumanly still. The only visible movement was a slight twitch of his jaw.

He snapped his fingers at one of his guards, who promptly extended a wrist toward the admiral. A second later, something strapped to the guard's wrist glowed to life, and a hovering holographic image of a person materialized above it.

It appeared to be a woman, but Marcellus could only see the back of her head.

The Mad Queen?

"Lady Alexander, Your Grace," the admiral spoke, his tone suddenly docile and pleasant.

Not the Queen. An advisor perhaps?

"I have commandeered a foreign craft from the planet Laterre, aboard which an Officer Marcellus Bonnefaçon—grandson of General Bonnefaçon—and his . . ." He shot a skeptical look at Alouette. ". . . *entourage* claim to be here to—"

The admiral's voice was cut off as he listened to a response. He looked like he'd just eaten an insect. "Yes, Your Grace. I understand. Thank you. And Sols save the Queen."

The glowing image vanished, sucked back into the small device strapped to the guard's wrist. For a moment, the admiral didn't speak. Marcellus glanced uneasily at the other guard's assault lancer, still pressed into Alouette's chest.

Then, after a sweeping glance from Marcellus to Alouette to Cerise, and finally to Gabriel, Admiral Wellington cleared his throat. "Lady Alexander, her majesty's High Chancellor, has instructed me to escort you to the Queenstead spaceport. If it pleases you, one of my guards will pilot the ship the rest of the way to Albion, where awaiting transportation will take you to the Royal Ministry of Defence complex. Will that be satisfactory, Officer Bonnefaçon?"

Marcellus swallowed and shared a look of disbelief and uncertainty with Alouette.

He stood up a little straighter, trying to summon his grandfather's authoritative air and Alouette's calm confidence. "Yes, Admiral. That will be just fine. We are grateful for your hospitality."

CHAPTER 38

CHATINE

CHATINE WAITED UNTIL THE SKY WAS DARK AND THE camp was asleep. She slipped out of her bed, donned her Défecteur coat and mittens, and grabbed her crutches. On one of the shelves lining the walls of the treatment center, she located a small sac and filled it with supplies— bandages, ointment, more gauze, and a few vials of that magical goldenroot stuff. Everything she'd seen Brigitte use to treat her wounded leg.

The bag was unlike anything Chatine had ever seen before. It had a strange closing mechanism with two fuzzy fabric strips that magically sealed when she pushed them together. Also, the sac had two straps instead of one. What was Chatine supposed to do with two straps?

She deduced that one was for each arm, but when she looped her arms through, the bag sat oddly and uncomfortably against her chest and stomach, making her feel like one of those mothers in the Frets who attached their small children to the fronts of their bodies by fashioning old sheets and fabric scraps into slings. It made it even harder to maneuver around on the crutches, but eventually Chatine made her way through the door.

The air outside was freezing. Even more so now that night had fallen. It stung her cheeks and chapped her lips.

She followed the same route she had taken with Brigitte earlier, shuffling down the long, covered walkways, past the washroom and the grain silo before finally arriving at the storage chalet whose slitted windows glowed blue from the copious amounts of zyttrium inside. Chatine still couldn't wrap her head around the fact that the Défecteurs stole zyttrium from the Regime.

All this time, while the Ministère was busy manufacturing thousands of Skins each year, the Défecteurs had discovered how to use the zyttrium to hide themselves. To build stealth ships and invisible roofs.

She respected the con, for sure. There was always honor and respect among talented thieves, but she still felt angry at the sight of all of that stolen zyttrium. How many people had frozen and suffered and even died to wrench that precious metal out of the rock? People like her. And Henri. And Anaïs, who would never make it back to Laterre. Didn't it make these people—these *Défecteurs*—no better than the Regime?

Chatine glanced up at the building, her mind whirring to calculate how much just a single bloc of zyttrium could fetch from an illegal smuggler like the Capitaine. The dwindling deposits of it on Bastille and the Ministère's dependency on it would certainly make it worth a pretty larg. Enough to set Chatine up for a lifetime. Or two. Enough that she wouldn't have to ever steal again.

Her fingers itched. Her heart pounded. Her adrenaline spiked.

It was the same sensation she used to get in the Frets right before she lifted a First World relic from the neck of an unsuspecting Second Estater or pinched an apple from a passing cart.

The same sensation that used to fuel her, feed her, light the way through her darkest nights.

And yet, somehow, standing here right now, squinting through the narrow windows of the chalet, she didn't feel fueled. She didn't feel full. And she definitely didn't feel light, despite the iridescent blue glow that illuminated her face.

She only felt darkness.

And the blaze of her prisoner tattoo burning through the fabric of her coat. Five metallic bumps burned into her flesh like a brand. A constant reminder of the price she'd paid for her former life.

Gritting her teeth, she forced herself to turn away from the storage chalet and keep walking. With the heavy sac banging against her chest, she slowly made her way down the walkway, past the lodge, away from the protection of the chalets, and into the great unknown.

As she stared out at the dark, frozen terrain in front of her, she wondered if she was insane for doing this. For even considering it. She'd said so herself earlier: No one survives in the Terrain Perdu. But when she glanced back at the cluster of buildings behind her, she knew she couldn't stay here. Brigitte had been right: Some monsters you stay and confront. Some you turn away from.

Chatine knew what kind of monsters awaited her here if she stayed. If she lay around all day and did nothing while Henri was possibly still alive out there, lost and alone. They were not the kind of monsters she wanted to face. She'd spent the past twelve years believing he was dead when he wasn't. She wasn't going to make that same mistake again.

If he was alive, she would find him.

She'd found him once before. She could do it again. She would cross to the ends of the galaxy if that's what it took.

Balancing on her good leg, she planted her crutches on the ground, testing the feel of it. It was rugged and uneven. And frozen solid.

She swung herself forward and immediately felt the chill of the open air batter her face like one of her mother's slaps, but she kept going, holding Henri's face in her mind.

She was only a few mètres from the camp when her crutches hit a patch of icy ground and slid out from under her. She hit the ground hard. A bolt of pain shot up her left leg. She bit her lip to keep from crying out.

Feeling around in the darkness, she searched for her fallen crutch, but it was nowhere to be found. She let out a grunt of frustration and stretched farther, wishing she still had a Skin. The light would come in handy right about now.

She finally located the crutch, but when she tried to stand back up, the weight of the sac hanging off the front of her shoulders threw off her balance, and she went down again.

She wanted to scream. She wanted to punch something. No, she wanted to punch some*one*.

Suddenly, a light broke through the darkness, followed by the sound of booted footsteps crunching on the frozen terrain. Chatine squinted into the beam of a flashlight and rolled her eyes when she saw who was holding it.

Well, she *did* say she wanted someone to punch.

"What the fric do you think you're doing?" Etienne didn't sound concerned as he stalked toward her. He sounded annoyed and inconvenienced at being woken up in the middle of the night.

"What does it look like I'm doing?" she hissed back at him, digging the tip of her crutch into the ground and trying, once again, to stand up. "I'm getting out of here. And *you* are not going to stop me."

The crutch slipped and Chatine started to go down again. Etienne reached out to catch her, but Chatine managed to stabilize herself before he could get there.

"Well, this was a brilliant idea, wasn't it?" he asked.

Chatine snorted. "How did you find me anyway?"

"You're hobbling around a sleeping camp on metal poles. You're not exactly discreet."

Chatine bristled. She was used to being the one who followed, not the one *being* followed. These Sol-damn crutches had stolen her edge.

"I can't stay here," she said firmly. "I have to go find my brother."

A grimace passed over Etienne's face, and Chatine was immediately reminded of the story Brigitte had told her in the graveyard, as she'd bent over the small arrow-shaped pattern of stones.

"Etienne's father. He died in the last roundup."

Chatine felt a stab of sympathy for the young man standing in front of her, trying to block her path. As it turned out, she and Etienne had something in common. But the sympathy was stamped out a moment later when Etienne said, "And do you really think *this* is the best way to do that?"

Heat rose to Chatine's cheeks. He thought she was insane. Delusional for believing that Henri could still be alive. Could still be out there. She could hear the doubt in his voice, and it angered her.

Chatine stood up straighter—or as straight as she could while still leaning on her crutches. "Yes, as a matter of fact, I do."

Etienne looked like he wanted to say something but was trying to find the right way to phrase it. Chatine felt the heat spread to her chest. She already knew what he was going to say. He was going to tell her to just forget it. Let it go. The ship was gone. Henri was gone. Citizen Rousseau was gone. Everyone was gone. And there was no point risking death and frostbite to go looking for them.

But when he finally did speak, his words surprised her. "Did anyone ever tell you you're very restless?"

She was caught so off guard, it took her a moment to formulate a response. "I'm . . . I'm not *restless*. I'm opportunistic."

"Opportunistic, by its very nature, is restless."

"Whatever." Chatine tried to hobble past him. "Someone has to go looking for that ship."

She felt a hand fall upon her shoulder, pulling her to a halt. "Someone *is* looking for the ship." His voice was no longer laced with annoyance. It sounded gentle and bordering on pity. "Don't forget, one of our own is lost out there too. A great pilote. And a friend. We want to find them just as much as you do. We're not doing nothing. If they're out there to be found, we will find them."

If . . .

Chatine cringed at the word.

Sols, she hated that word.

Through her mittens, she felt for Marcellus's ring on her thumb, only to remember—yet again—that it was gone.

"Maybe you should just let our people do their job. I mean look at you! You're not exactly equipped to go on a rescue mission across the System Divine right now."

Chatine glanced down at her lumpy bag and dangling left leg and wobbly crutches. "But I can't just—"

Etienne bent down to look her in the eye. "Yes, you can."

"You don't even know what I was going to say."

He cracked a smile, his dark eyes sparkling in the beam of the flashlight. "Yes, I do."

Chatine let the defeat sink in. She loathed to admit that Etienne was right, but he was. She was in no condition to find anyone.

"And besides," Etienne added, "if you leave now, you won't get to meet the rest of the community. And everyone has been dying to meet you."

"Me?" Chatine thought of all those Défecteurs she'd seen in the lodge earlier and her gut twisted.

"Yes. Gridders are a bit of a novelty here. People are always fascinated by them. You're actually the third gridder to join us in the past month. And everyone *loves* Fabian and his wife, Gen. They arrived about two weeks before you. The people here can't get enough of them. They're like celebrities around the camp. I'm sure it'll be the same with you."

Chatine scoffed in disbelief. She'd spent so many years speculating about Défecteurs, she never even thought that they might be speculating about her.

"I hope they can deal with disappointment," she muttered. "My life is not all that interesting."

"Are you kidding? You were locked up on Bastille. *And* you escaped. You're already a hero in their eyes."

A hero who failed to save her own brother . . . twice.

"Well, then I *definitely* hope they can deal with disappointment."

"What were you on Bastille for anyway?" Etienne asked. "You never told me."

Chatine thought back to the long list of things she *should* have been sent to Bastille for over the years—theft, burglary, fraud, deceit, conning, pickpocketing, terrorization, unlawful manipulation of a Skin, assault of a Policier sergent, stealing from the dead, being born a Renard—and she was grateful that she didn't have to admit to any of those. She could just speak the truth.

"Treason," she said lightly, as though she were simply admitting to putting her shoes on the wrong feet.

Etienne barked out a laugh. "Treason?"

Chatine shrugged. "Yup."

"Really?"

"I was in possession of some very important intelligence, and I lied to General Bonnefaçon about it. That'll put you away for a long time."

Etienne's expression was so packed with astonishment, Chatine almost laughed.

"Makes your little stunt with the zyttrium look pretty tame, huh?" she asked.

Etienne shook his head. "Okay, traitor. C'mon. I'll help you back to the camp." The beam of his flashlight fell to the sac strapped around Chatine's chest and his expression suddenly shifted, his eyebrows knitting together. "What exactly is going on here?"

Chatine sighed. "I borrowed it, okay? I'm sorry."

Etienne continued to stare at the bag, the light from the flashlight illuminating the outline of his angular features, which were now twisted and taut, as though he were trying hard to stifle a laugh.

"What?" she demanded.

"You're supposed to wear it on your *back*." He reached forward and slowly began to untangle Chatine's arms from the straps, his body impossibly close to hers. She struggled to keep her balance on the crutches as he removed the bag from her shoulders and slipped his own arms through the straps before letting it fall against his back. "It's called a backpack. See?"

Okay, that makes much more sense.

What was it about this place—and him—that made her feel so stupide? As much as she hated life in the Frets, at least she knew how everything worked. She wasn't constantly making a fool of herself there. She knew how to wear a Sol-damn sac.

With a huff, she turned and began to hobble back to the camp. Etienne jogged to catch up to her. "Wait. Let me help you, at least."

She continued to swing efficiently on her crutches. "That's okay. I've got this."

But she clearly didn't have this, because a moment later, the crutch slipped out from under her again. This time, however, Etienne caught her, his hands landing on either one of her elbows.

"I have a better idea," he said once Chatine was stable. He slipped the backpack from his shoulders and spun it around, looping his arms through the straps and letting it settle over his chest, just as Chatine had worn it. Then, he bent down in front of her and pointed at his back.

"Hop on."

"Why would I do that?"

"So I can give you a lift."

For a moment Chatine just stared at the back of Etienne's puffy coat, confused by the gesture. "Why can't I just walk?"

"Um, maybe because we saw how well that worked a second ago? C'mon, jump on." He wiggled his hips slightly, making Chatine's mouth quirk into the tiniest of smiles.

She told herself it was only because she was injured. And freezing. And would probably get lost on her way back to the treatment center on her own. She told herself it meant nothing. And it certainly changed nothing. She swore to herself that it was a unique, one-time thing, as she handed Etienne her crutches and climbed onto his back.

CHAPTER 39

MARCELLUS

ALBION EMERGED LIKE A BLUE-AND-GREEN JEWEL IN the vast, dark blanket of space.

"There it is," Cerise said in a hushed and reverent voice. Reverent because of everything they'd gone through to get here. Hushed because of the Albion guard who had overridden the ship's autopilot and now sat at the flight console, forcing Marcellus, Gabriel, Alouette, and Cerise to communicate in furtive whispers and pointed gestures.

The guard's hands flew steadily and confidently across the controls, guiding the ship toward its final destination like a bird coasting on a stiff breeze.

Marcellus stared in awe through the window as the twinkling planet grew larger. Throughout his life, his grandfather had taken him on diplomatic missions to almost every planet in the System Divine. To the Matrone's home of Reichenstat. The System Alliance headquarters on Kaishi. The tropical beaches of Samsara. The newly liberated planet of Usonia. But never here. Albion had been the enemy of Laterre since the very beginning. Since the Human Conservation Commission first discovered the System Divine, and the wealthy families of the First World began to divvy up its planets. The only Laterrian he'd known to step foot on the planet was Commandeur Vernay, right before she was captured by the Mad Queen and executed.

"It's beautiful." Alouette's voice broke into his thoughts.

"Beautiful?" Marcellus repeated, turning his gaze back to the planet. No longer a small jewel in the sky, Albion now loomed large in the window of the voyageur. Its deep blue oceans, swirling clouds, and patchwork of emerald green continents—so strikingly different from Laterre's single landmass—were becoming clearer and more defined with each passing second.

But as hard as he tried, Marcellus could not see what Alouette saw. He could not see beauty. He could only see danger. Threat. And possible catastrophe. They were landing in the capital of an enemy planet, shielded only by a thinly veiled lie.

"What are we going to do about the source?" Cerise whispered, leaning in close to Marcellus. "We're supposed to meet them today at the coordinates they sent."

But Marcellus just shook his head. He didn't know what they were going to do about *any* of this.

"Arrival in Queenstead in three minutes," the guard announced from the console. "Please fasten your restraints."

"This better work," Gabriel muttered under his breath as he strapped himself into one of the flight seats.

The voyageur swooped down effortlessly through Albion's atmosphere and plummeted in a great descending arc until it was skimming like a bird just above the ocean's surface. Amid the choppy waves and eddying currents, islands began to appear, popping up like foreign ships on a detection scanner. Then, on the horizon, a much bigger land mass emerged. A craggy and high-cliffed coastline soon gave way to undulating hills and lush meadows, and finally, a huge city arose amid the greenery.

A grand wall snaked around Albion's capital, and as the voyageur cruised closer, Marcellus spied the four giant spires of the Queen's palace at the center of the city.

Gabriel is right. This better work. Or we're all dead.

The skies near the Queenstead spaceport were filled with aerocabs, Albion's version of cruiseurs, shuttling people back and forth across the land. The Albion guard expertly maneuvered the voyageur down, across the enormous spaceport complex, and into the gaping entrance of the terminal building.

Outside the window, Marcellus could see the terminal's vast curved roof above them, and all around was a myriad of idling ships. The voyageur came to a final halt at one of the gates, and the engines began to power down.

Marcellus tried to keep his hands from shaking as he unlatched his harness and adjusted the lapels on his jacket. He had changed back into his blinding-white officer's uniform, hoping to make the illusion more complete.

Together with Cerise, Gabriel, and Alouette, Marcellus descended the staircase to the primary hatch, where the loading ramp was already extended. As the four of them disembarked, they were immediately encircled by Albion guards, who wordlessly patted them down and searched their pockets for weapons.

"Well, this is certainly a warm welcome," Gabriel whispered, and Marcellus shot him a warning look.

When the security check was complete, one of the guards led them through the gigantic domed concourse, which was packed with passengers, port workers, and vendors selling last-minute food and goods for travel.

Finally, they emerged from the building and into the bright Sol-light. The first thing Marcellus noticed was the weather. It was as warm and as pleasant as the interior of Ledôme, the sky as bright and blue as the TéléSky, but everything just felt so much fresher. More authentic. He took in a deep breath, suddenly understanding how Thibault Paresse, the founding Patriarche of Laterre, could have started a five-hundred-year-long grudge against these people. They lived in a paradise. A paradise that Laterre had lost and Albion had won.

He pulled his gaze from the skies just as a black-domed aerocab pulled up in front of them. The door of the vehicle eased open like an insect's wing unfurling, and out stepped a woman in a purple knee-length jacket trimmed with white fur. Her monoglass gleamed in the late-afternoon light as her gaze swept over each one of them before finally landing on Marcellus. She flashed him a broad smile.

"Officer Bonnefaçon, welcome to Albion. I am Lady Alexander, High Chancellor to her majesty, Queen Matilda Bellingham, and your grandfather's primary liaison on Albion." She spoke in a silky, flawless accent that sounded deceptively soothing to Marcellus's ears. This must have been the person he had overheard his grandfather talking to in his study.

"Nice to meet you, your . . ." Marcellus struggled to remember the greeting the admiral had used on the ship. "Your Grace." He gestured toward Alouette, Gabriel, and Cerise. "These are my . . . um . . . associates."

Gabriel stepped forward and dipped into a low bow. "Your Grace."

Cerise grabbed him by the elbow and yanked him back, whispering hotly in his ear. "You only bow to the Queen, you idiot."

Lady Alexander smiled politely at Gabriel, but Marcellus could see the tug of annoyance at the corner of her lips. "My most humble apologies for the . . . how shall we put this? The *confusion* concerning your arrival. We were not expecting the general or any of his ambassadors. Up until this moment, all of our communications have been conducted remotely."

Even though her words sounded vaguely suspicious, her smile never faltered.

Marcellus cleared his throat. "Yes. I apologize for our surprise visit. My grandfather dispatched me fairly last-minute. We would have sent word of our arrival but . . . but . . ." He started to falter, the words feeling fat and clumsy on his lips.

"But we recently detected a breach in our normal communication channels," Cerise stepped in, offering Marcellus a reassuring nod. "We had to sever all outreach until the breach could be remedied."

Lady Alexander studied Cerise for a long moment, looking both thoughtful and apprehensive. Marcellus held his breath.

"I suppose that makes sense," she concluded after far too long a pause. "It has been a few days since I've heard from the general."

Marcellus swallowed hard. "Exactly. Apologies again for not keeping you better informed."

Lady Alexander nodded. "Not to worry. We are very pleased to welcome you to our planet." She gestured to the idling vehicle. "Shall we proceed to the laboratory?"

After sweeping over the dense and bustling parts of the capital, the aerocab glided onward, toward the less populated outskirts of Queenstead. Marcellus watched through the window as they passed rows and rows of what looked like fabriques and other industrial buildings.

Then they were flying out over the city walls and into the countryside beyond. Streams weaved and sparkled through meadows of grass. Forests and small villages dotted the landscape. To the left, the Sols were beginning to set behind a ridge of mountains that had loomed up nearby, and the sky was turning deep shades of violet, purple, and fiery gold.

Dangers aside, Marcellus had to admit that the sight *was* beautiful. Just as Alouette had said. Breathtaking, even. It reminded him of all the old stories he'd heard about the First World before it was engulfed by fires.

"Would you care for tea?" Lady Alexander asked. She pushed a button on her armrest, and from the floor of the aerocab, a titan tray glided upward, holding a set of porcelain cups and saucers with a matching teapot.

Marcellus exchanged confused glances with the others, and everyone hastily shook their heads.

"No, merci," said Marcellus.

With another push of the button, the tray disappeared beneath the floor again.

Finally, the aerocab banked to the right, and as they descended over a bluff, an enormous compound emerged in front of them. Albion's Royal Ministry of Defence.

Encircled in a glowing force field, the buildings inside the complex were arranged in a series of neat squares around equally neat lawns with pathways connecting them. Like all the other buildings on Albion, with their ornate gables and embellished windows, they looked like they'd been plucked from another time or transplanted from the First World.

The vehicle slowed to a stop at a security gate, where a squad of heavily armed Albion guards inspected the interior. Marcellus watched Lady Alexander's monoglass darken as her credentials were transmitted, and a moment later, a guard waved them through. Once inside the compound, Lady Alexander pulled a long, curving pipe from the inside pocket of her coat and placed it ceremoniously between her lips. After flicking a tiny switch on its side and taking a long drag on its tip, she puffed out a cloud of bluish-purple mist. Marcellus watched, transfixed. He'd seen delegates from Albion smoking these vapor pipes before, on his numerous trips to Kaishi when his grandfather would meet with the System Alliance. But now, up close, he could see that Lady Alexander's pipe was adorned with a small floral crest, carved into the titan plating.

"As you probably know," she said between puffs, "Albion's Royal Ministry of Defence has the most advanced laboratories in the System, dedicated to all manner of scientific inquiries." She gestured out the window as they passed a large, two-story building. "This facility houses our bioweapons department, while the building directly to your left is entirely devoted to new artillery development."

"Makes our Ministère tech labs look like First World relics," Cerise whispered to Marcellus.

"What was that?" Lady Alexander asked, her eyebrow arching clear above her monoglass.

"Nothing," Cerise muttered.

The vehicle glided to a halt in front of an imposing building with pointed-arch windows, a high vaulted roof, and ornate spires that stretched toward the sky. "And this," Lady Alexander announced with an air of importance, "is where our most classified and high-clearance research takes place. This is where we've housed the general's project."

Marcellus checked the time on the aerocab's clock. Their meeting with the source was scheduled to take place in less than two hours. How would they ever get out of this situation? Let alone sneak off to meet in secret with an Albion traitor?

"After you," Lady Alexander said cordially as the vehicle door swung open.

Marcellus climbed out and took an anxious look around. He was starting to severely doubt their decision to come here. Their cover could be blown at any moment.

"Officer Bonnefaçon," called another richly accented voice, and Marcellus turned to see a petite man in a trim white lab coat whisking toward them down a stone path. His wiry red hair—which appeared to have been, at one point in the day, confined with gel—now wisped in various directions around his head. As he moved toward them, he tried desperately to smooth down the rebellious strands. "We were so thrilled to hear of your visit. We are delighted to have you here."

Marcellus nodded to the man and forced a smile. "Merci. We are . . . *delighted* to be here, as well."

"I'm Dr. Cromwell," he said, his monoglass reflecting the blue sky and buildings around them. "I will be giving you and your associates a tour of our state-of-the-art lab. I think you and your grandfather will be very pleased to witness the progress that we have made."

Marcellus immediately noted the eagerness in the man's face. It was not too dissimilar from the way he'd been greeted by Lady Alexander when they'd stepped off the voyageur. It seemed this entire planet was bending over backward to please him. Or rather, to please the person they *thought* was working directly for the general.

Why were they so eager to make a good impression? What was the general promising them in return for this project?

Marcellus held back a shudder and forced himself to say, "Well, we can't wait to see it."

Dr. Cromwell beamed. "Right this way."

The scientist guided Marcellus and the others up the path to an unmarked entrance. With a hissing noise, the heavy arched doors eased open, revealing a wood-paneled hallway within.

"Welcome to the Filbright Wing," he said, ushering them through. "We don't generally like to boast, but we in the Filbright like to think that the work in our laboratories is at the cutting edge of Albion's developments."

Marcellus anxiously cleared his throat. "Wonderful."

"It's just through here," Dr. Cromwell said, leading them down the hallway and through another set of doors.

Inside was a room filled with consoles, monitoring equipment, and strange-looking contraptions with snaking tubes and thrumming pumps. They were met by two more scientists, who were introduced as Dr. Ward, an angular woman with sunken cheeks, and Dr. Collins, an older man with silver hair and a beard. The two scientists helped everyone into white lab coats.

"I was just telling the general during our last correspondence," Lady Alexander said as she buttoned the coat over her elegant purple jacket, "that the project is nearly ready."

Dr. Cromwell beamed again as he smoothed back another strand of escaped hair. "Oh yes. We're just completing our final round of tests." He turned to Marcellus. "Would you care for a demonstration?"

Marcellus looked to Alouette and Cerise who both nodded subtly. "Yes, yes. That's why we're here. To witness the . . . uh . . . product."

Dr. Cromwell beckoned them to follow him through another doorway into a room that contained nothing but an enormous cube in the center, constructed completely of transparent plastique.

"Is *that* the weapon?" Gabriel whispered, sounding slightly disappointed. Cerise immediately shushed him.

"Would anyone care for tea before we begin?" asked Dr. Cromwell.

Once again, they all shook their heads.

"Very well. Bring up the subjects, please!" Dr. Cromwell called out. *Subjects?*

There was silence for a few moments, followed by a faint humming sound coming from the cube. Marcellus's mind whirred with questions that he dared not ask. Then he watched in stunned silence as two trap-doors suddenly snapped open in the bare floor of the plastique cell. More humming noises and rumbling followed, before two circular platforms emerged from the gaps in the floor. On each of the platforms stood a man—barefoot, dirty, and disheveled, as though he'd spent the last few months locked in a cage. The rumbling stopped, and the two burly men faced each other in the center of the cube. They had shaved heads and wore nothing but flimsy green jumpsuits that strained over their big frames.

"What are they doing?" Alouette asked in a harsh whisper.

Marcellus glanced over at her. In her eyes, where, only a short while ago, he'd seen wonder and curiosity as they'd coasted toward Albion, he now saw a dark shadow descending.

She knew, just as he did, that something was about to happen.

Something very, *very* wrong.

"I don't know," he whispered back, and he could hear the tremor in his own voice.

"Remember, start very slowly," Dr. Cromwell said to Dr. Ward, who was prodding at a device in her hand that looked a lot like a TéléCom.

All three scientists and Lady Alexander had their gazes locked on the giant cube. Inside, the two men began pacing slowly around the plastique cell, eyeing each other with a mix of wariness and anticipation.

"What kind of a demonstration is this?" Cerise whispered.

But again, Marcellus couldn't answer. He couldn't even begin to imagine what they were about to witness.

"Increase to point five volts," Cromwell said in an eerily steady tone.

Marcellus's gaze snapped to the scientist for a moment before return-ing to the cube. The two men inside began to circle faster around each other. The taller one rotated his large shoulders. The other man blew out short, angry puffs of air. They were still glaring hard at each other.

"Up to one point five," Dr. Cromwell instructed. "And introduce the trigger."

Suddenly, the men stopped pacing and charged toward each other, their chests clashing like a pair of giant rocks. Marcellus felt Alouette flinch beside him, and his own stomach lurched.

What was going on? What were they—?

Thwaacckkkk!!

Marcellus leapt backward as something red and glittering splattered across the clear plastique wall in front of him. Blinking hard, he tried to process what had just happened. The shorter man was holding his face as a spurt of blood sprayed from his mouth like a fountain in the Palais gardens. The other man was a few mètres away shaking out his fist, crimson droplets falling down like rain from his knuckles.

Marcellus opened his mouth to say something—*anything*—to stop whatever in the name of the Sols was happening. But Dr. Cromwell spoke first, his voice cold and clinical. "Push it up to two point five, please."

Dr. Ward slid her finger across the surface of the device, and it was as if an invisible explosion detonated inside the huge plastique cube. The two men descended on each other like a pair of wild, untrammeled beasts. The shorter man led with a series of thudding, heaving punches to the other man's gut. But then his opponent managed to right himself and responded with a furious round of brutish kicks and wild punches to the stomach, chest, and face. More blood splattered the walls of the plastique cube, and feral growls shook the entire construction.

As Marcellus watched it all unfold, he felt like he was trapped inside a cell of his own. Alone. Isolated. And terrified. He wanted to scream, to make it stop, but his voice was lost and useless, locked behind a sheet of impenetrable plastique. Somewhere beside him, he heard Alouette let out a muffled gasp.

Marcellus glanced at Dr. Cromwell, Lady Alexander, and Dr. Ward. They were all focused on the cube, their faces relaxed and placid despite what was happening in front of them. But Marcellus suddenly realized that the other scientist, the gray-haired Dr. Collins, was not looking at the subjects. His head was upright and facing toward the plastique wall. But his eyes were trained downward, as though he couldn't bring himself to watch.

"Once General Bonnefaçon was able to supply us with the original blueprints of the implants," Dr. Cromwell was now saying, his calm, measured tone a disturbing contrast to the vicious snarls coming from the cube, "reversing the direction of the neuroelectricity to manipulate the subjects was fairly straightforward."

Implants?

The word tumbled violently around Marcellus's mind. What was he talking about? What implants?

"We've spent the majority of our time and resources developing the technology to not only control the power-supply field, but also to fine-tune its coordination, to assure accurate and precise results."

With a swift punch to the stomach, the smaller man went down, dropping to the ground like a sac of rocks. The other man took a menacing step toward him, glaring down at his opponent the entire time. He reared his foot back, ready to deliver a devastating blow.

"We are now pleased to report, after many tests, that we have finally perfected the algorithm and fully calibrated the voltage flow." Dr. Cromwell nodded to Dr. Ward. "Back down to zero, please."

Dr. Ward slid her finger across the screen of her device and, like a broadcast being paused in the middle of the playback, the tall man halted mid-kick. Then, a moment later, he lowered his foot and began to back away from his opponent.

Implants.

Neuroelectricity.

Power-supply field.

All of these words sat at the periphery of Marcellus's memory, just out of reach. He pressed a fingertip to his temple, as though trying to squeeze them all back into place.

"As you can see, with our newly designed operating system, we now have total control over the subjects." Dr. Cromwell turned back to his colleague. "Back up to two point five, please."

The reaction was almost instantaneous. The man on the ground leapt to his feet and hurled his body across the cube, attacking his opponent with a fresh, renewed enthusiasm. His eyes flashed with fury, his mouth twisted in an angry snarl, and his hands clawed at the air.

And that's when Marcellus noticed something he hadn't noticed before. In the tumult of the fight, the man's sleeve had ripped almost clean off, revealing . . .

Marcellus stepped up closer to the plastique, squinting under the bright lights of the lab.

Was he seeing that right?

No, he couldn't be. It was impossible.

But there it was. As clear as day. A small, rectangular screen embedded in the inside of the man's left arm.

An implant.

Marcellus's head throbbed as he struggled to make sense of what he was seeing. But it was Gabriel who got there first.

"He has a Skin," Gabriel breathed. His voice was smaller and thinner than Marcellus had ever heard it.

But he was right. Marcellus's gaze whipped to the other man, who was fighting back, arms swinging wildly, fist connecting everywhere. But possibly the most disturbing sight of all was his sleeve that had been just barely pushed up, revealing the short edge of another screen.

"Furthermore," Dr. Cromwell was now saying, "we have built in the ability to manipulate the subjects in any possible configuration. The application is completely customizable. You can group subjects manually or filter by similar characteristics such as age, gender, location, etc."

But Marcellus could barely hear him anymore. He was far too focused on the glowing screens embedded in the men's arms.

It's impossible, he thought again.

No one on Albion had a Skin.

They were a Laterrian technology. Developed over five hundred years ago to keep the Third Estate in line. Small, multifunctional implants powered by . . .

But just as the thoughts began to coalesce in his mind, just as he started to realize what all this might mean, Dr. Cromwell said, "And now, maximum voltage at five point zero."

Marcellus heard the command before he could process it. Before he could even begin to try to stop it.

"No," came Alouette's outraged whisper beside him. Barely audible.

Dr. Ward executed the order. Out of the corner of his eye, Marcellus saw Dr. Collins—the older scientist with the silver hair—visibly flinch. He turned back to the cube just in time to see the exposed Skins on the two subjects' arms flash a bright, iridescent red.

Then, anarchy.

Alouette shielded her eyes with her hand. But Marcellus couldn't bring himself to tear his gaze away. He was too transfixed. Too horrified. His mind too overloaded to do anything else but stare.

The two men attacked each other with more aggression, more ferocity than Marcellus had ever seen in a human being. They were tearing into each other's flesh with bare fingernails. They were delivering blows with the power of machines.

They weren't just fighting anymore.

They had an objective.

An endgame.

A gruesome finish line in sight.

And now it was only a matter of *who* would reach it first.

Neuroelectricity.

The information came streaming back to him now. He remembered. He remembered as though he were sitting in his Ministère officer training right now, hearing the words echoing through his audio patch.

"*. . . neuroelectricity is taken directly from the human brain, routed through a small power-supply field, and repurposed to fuel the circuitry of the implant, removing the need for any external power source.*"

The Skins ran on neuroelectricity.

But according to what Dr. Cromwell had just said and what Marcellus was now witnessing, that process could be reversed. It could be manipulated.

And these Albion scientists had done exactly that.

The Third Estate made up 95 percent of the Laterrian population. And the general was planning to use them as a weapon.

His weapon.

A deafening roar snapped Marcellus out of his trance. The shorter man had managed to break free from a choke hold like an animal suddenly unleashed from a cage. He grabbed his opponent by the shoulders, dragged him downward, and then proceeded to ram his face against the floor of the plastique cube. Over and over and over. Marcellus swore he could hear bones cracking, ligaments tearing, and of course the stomach-churning sound of spattering blood.

He heard Alouette's horrified chanting under her breath. "No, no, no, no."

Marcellus finally escaped the prison holding his lungs and body and voice hostage. He lunged toward the scientist holding the device. "Please, stop. Make it stop! Now!"

Dr. Ward and Dr. Collins both looked up, their expressions bemused. Dr. Ward turned to her boss, Dr. Cromwell, who raised a curious eyebrow. And Lady Alexander simply glanced at Marcellus with a cool unreadable look.

But before anyone could respond, the taller man in the cube managed to get under his opponent, hoist him on his back, and then lunge him violently into the air. His body flew up, as if it weighed nothing, and crashed into the wall of the cube. Right in front of Marcellus.

The plastique cracked. A thin, jagged, dark line that splintered not only the cube but Marcellus's vision as well.

Marcellus stood deathly still, frozen, paralyzed, as the man's body slid back down to the floor with the most horrific, shattering *thump*.

Then the room went silent.

Deafeningly, ferociously silent.

The other man stood in the plastique cell breathing raggedly, while his opponent was sprawled out on the floor.

Unmoving.

Lifeless.

Dead.

"So, what did you think?" Dr. Cromwell was the first to speak. His voice exhibited no sign of a reaction to what had just happened a mere mètre away. "General Bonnefaçon, I believe, will be very pleased, don't you agree?"

Somehow, Marcellus managed to drag his eyes away from the horrendous sight in front of him and focus his gaze on Dr. Cromwell. He was looking at Marcellus with a hopeful sparkle in his eyes and a small smile playing on his lips.

When Marcellus didn't respond, the scientist continued. "As I explained to the general, we still have a few more rounds of final tests, but we are working night and day to get this ready for him. And I'm certain we will be able to deliver the final product on schedule in one week."

The words bounced around in Marcellus's brain like a death sentence. And he supposed it was. The death sentence of a planet.

One week.

"Officer Bonnefaçon." Lady Alexander was suddenly in front of him, her eyes narrowing suspiciously. "Are you quite all right?"

"Y-y-yes," Marcellus stammered, his lips heavy and numb and useless. "Is there . . . um . . . somewhere my associates and I can go to discuss these . . . these results?"

Cromwell looked momentarily flummoxed as he pushed back a rogue strand of red hair. "Of course." He pointed toward a set of doors behind them. "There's a courtyard right through those—"

But Marcellus couldn't even wait for him to finish. Struggling to put one foot in front of the other and fighting for breath, he stumbled out of the lab. He could feel Alouette, Cerise, and Gabriel close behind him. He burst through the door to the outside. The Sols had set, but exterior lamps illuminated a small courtyard adorned with benches, a square lawn, planters of shrubs, and a fountain at the center.

"Marcellus?" he heard someone say. But he did not look back to confirm who had asked the question. He did not look back at all.

His stomach had turned to liquid, and his chest shuddered like a storm was about to hit. Holding up a hand, Marcellus ran to the shrubbery by the fountain and proceeded to be unceremoniously and horribly sick.

- PART 4 -
DÉFECTEURS

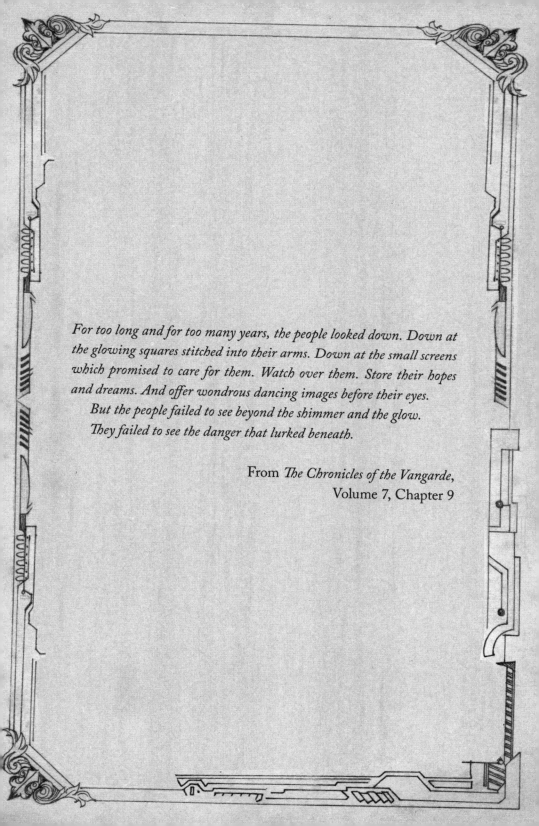

For too long and for too many years, the people looked down. Down at the glowing squares stitched into their arms. Down at the small screens which promised to care for them. Watch over them. Store their hopes and dreams. And offer wondrous dancing images before their eyes.

But the people failed to see beyond the shimmer and the glow.

They failed to see the danger that lurked beneath.

From *The Chronicles of the Vangarde*,
Volume 7, Chapter 9

CHAPTER 40

MARCELLUS

FOR A FULL MINUTE, THE PEACEFUL BUBBLING OF THE fountain in the center of the courtyard was the only sound Marcellus could hear. For a full minute, he could almost bring himself to believe that the last hour had never happened. That he hadn't just watched two men rip each other to pieces in a plastique prison. That he hadn't just emptied the contents of his stomach into a planter in the middle of a weapons development complex on the enemy planet of Albion.

But then, the minute was over, and the tranquil gurgling of the fountain was disrupted by Gabriel's frantic voice. "Can someone tell me what the fric just happened back there?"

Marcellus wiped his mouth and turned around to find Gabriel, Cerise, and Alouette all staring at him. Gabriel was looking a little queasy himself. His skin was clammy, and his eyes had gone glassy and dull.

Marcellus tried to speak. He tried to explain what they had just witnessed, but he couldn't put it into words. And the memory of that man lying lifeless and defeated on the ground, blood trickling from the wound on his head, brought another wave of nausea.

In the end, however, it was someone else who spoke.

A voice that seemed to come from the deep, dark corners of Marcellus's mind. A voice he had been dreading hearing since they'd landed. But a voice he knew would eventually return.

"Lady Alexander? This is certainly a surprise. I was not expecting to hear from you again so soon. Is there a problem with the delivery schedule?"

Marcellus froze as his grandfather's voice reverberated through his skull like a war drum. The general was back in his office. Talking to the very woman who stood just on the other side of that wall. Which meant only one thing.

She *knew*.

Lady Alexander had witnessed Marcellus's reaction to the demonstration, and now she knew.

"I'm sorry, can you repeat that?" The general sounded more bewildered than angry. "We must have a bad connection, because I'm certain I misunderstood you." He let out a low chuckle. "For a moment, I thought you said my *grandson* was on Albion."

"We have to get out of here!" Marcellus shouted.

Alouette was beside him in an instant, her eyes flooded with panic. "What's wrong?"

Marcellus's gaze darted anxiously around the courtyard. He could make out only one exit: the way they'd come in. "My grandfather knows we're here."

"What?!" Cerise bellowed. "How?"

"Lady Alexander just told him."

"You mean, she . . ." Alouette glanced anxiously between Marcellus and the door back to the labs.

"Yes," he answered her half-formed question as he eyed the three-mètre high brick wall surrounding the courtyard and scanned the surface for a good foothold. "We have to get over this wall. It's the only way out."

"That's impossible!" The general's voice in his ear was louder now, but Marcellus could hear the restraint. His grandfather was trying to keep his temper in check in the face of his shiny new ally.

"It's too high." Cerise's eyes tracked up to the top of the wall. "We can't scale it."

"Move aside, people," Gabriel said, pushing his way past Marcellus and Alouette. "Make way. Coming through." He interlaced his fingers together, extended his arms, and squatted down, creating a makeshift step. "Right this way." He nodded toward Cerise with a smug expression. "Ladies first."

For once, Cerise did not argue with him. Holding on to Gabriel's shoulders for balance, she tucked her foot into his hands.

"I'd just like to point out, for the record," Gabriel said with a grunt as he hoisted her up to the top of the wall, "that this was *my* idea, and I am helping the team with a very necessary *skill*."

Cerise grabbed onto the top of the wall. "Yes, yes, well done. You make an excellent step stool."

Gabriel gave Cerise a final push, which turned out to be just the *slightest* bit too hard. She was flung over the top of the wall and a moment later, they heard her land with an *"oomph"* on the other side.

"I did not appreciate that!" Cerise called back.

But Gabriel ignored her, already extending his hands out for Alouette. She disappeared over the top, landing with a much more innocuous sound.

"I most certainly did *not* sanction his visit!" the general thundered, and through Marcellus's audio patch, he could almost hear the walls of his grandfather's office trembling. "The stupide, worthless boy has hoodwinked you all. You must apprehend him immediately."

"Your turn, Officer." Gabriel proffered his makeshift step to Marcellus.

Marcellus glanced anxiously between Gabriel and the wall. "What about you?"

"Don't you worry about me. Criminal mastermind, remember? Climbing is second nature to me. Only surefire way to escape a droid. Now, hop on."

Pounding footsteps echoed from behind them. The door to the courtyard slammed open, and in the doorway stood Lady Alexander, the monoglass over her left eye glowing. "Don't worry, General," she said with a glare. "We have visual on him now. He will not get away."

"Go!" Gabriel screeched.

Marcellus stepped into his hands, and suddenly he was flying. Gabriel was stronger than he looked. Marcellus grabbed for the top of the wall to try to slow his descent, but he only managed to scrape up his palms and knees in the process. He crash-landed on the grassy lawn on the other side, rolling twice before coming to a stop in front of Alouette who helped him swiftly to his feet.

He could hear Lady Alexander's voice screaming from inside the courtyard. It was the most ruffled Marcellus had heard her since they'd arrived. "Security! Send all available guards to the Filbright Wing! We have a breach! I repeat a breach in the Hampstead courtyard."

A second later, Gabriel landed expertly in a crouch and beckoned to the rest of the group. "Follow me!"

They took off along the back side of the building. The skies above were now completely dark and lights from nearby windows cast long golden shadows on the pathways.

"I don't understand," the general was now saying in Marcellus's audio patch. "How did he even find out we were working together? He would have had to . . ." His grandfather's voice trailed off only to return a moment later in the form of a low, menacing growl. "I will get right back to you, Lady Alexander. In the meantime, find him."

Suddenly, sirens breached the night air, calling out across the complex. Above Marcellus's head, a parade of stark white search lights began to swoop over the darkened ground.

"Move!" Gabriel shouted as he darted across a grassy quad and down another shadowy, stone-flagged walkway with Marcellus, Cerise, and Alouette following close behind. Marcellus had no idea where they were running to. But he prayed Gabriel did.

Then, a moment later, Marcellus heard a fifth set of footsteps. Not behind them. Not pursuing them. But inside his head. The footsteps were coming from his audio patch, and they were accompanied by the sound of objects crashing to the ground.

His grandfather was searching for something.

Gabriel slowed at the edge of the next building, finding a narrow sliver of darkness between the glowing range of the search lights. He held up a hand and they all careened to a stop behind him. He crept forward and peered around the corner, scouting his route and waiting for a clear opening.

In his audio patch, Marcellus heard the scrape of a chair leg, the squeal of a drawer being yanked open, followed by the crash of something— perhaps a lamp—being overturned. They were the sounds of an office being ransacked. Scoured. Torn apart.

He knows I've been listening.

The general's footsteps soon quieted, and all Marcellus could hear was the sound of his own labored breathing as he pressed himself close to the wall.

He listened, waiting. He could almost see his grandfather now. Standing in the middle of his destroyed office, his skillful gaze scanning every centimètre, every corner. Trying to search out the source of the breach.

There was a tiny creak in Marcellus's ear. Followed by another. And another. Like a wild animal creeping up on its prey. Then Marcellus heard it. Soft and muted.

Clink.

Clink.

Clink.

The all-too-familiar sound of the Regiments board. The sound of pieces being lifted, checked, and replaced.

Clink.

Clink . . .

And then, a single word. "Sols."

Marcellus froze, listening to the shocked silence emanating across the galaxy, finding its way from his grandfather's study all the way here to Albion.

For a brief moment, the stars flickered, the planets wavered, and the universe felt out of sync. Because for a brief moment, General Bonnefaçon had been outsmarted by his stupide, worthless grandson.

Marcellus heard a rustle and a thud, and in a low, sinister voice, his grandfather whispered, "This is not over, Marcellus."

Then there was the distinct crunch of a boot striking the Palais's polished marble floor, destroying the auditeur, and silencing the sounds of his grandfather's office for good.

"This way!" Gabriel cried out.

Marcellus glanced up to see the group was on the move again, and as he ran to catch up with them, he suddenly understood that Gabriel was leading them back to the front of the Filbright Wing, where Marcellus could see Lady Alexander's aerocab was still docked, a row of lights on its underside blinking and glowing in the night.

They charged toward the vehicle. Cerise was the first to arrive. She pressed her hand to the panel on the side of the door, but nothing happened. "C'mon, c'mon," she urged, removing her hand and placing it down again. "Open, you Albion piece of junk!"

"Access denied," the vehicle responded in a pretentious accent that sounded eerily like Lady Alexander herself.

"It's locked." Cerise banged her palm against the door.

"Can't you hack it?" Gabriel asked breathlessly.

Cerise bent down and scrutinized the panel. "This is some special Albion technology. Maybe if I had fifteen minutes to bust it open and look around, I could figure it out."

Marcellus glanced up just as another aerocab came barreling around the corner, heading right toward them. The air rippled in its wake.

Guards.

"You have more like fifteen *seconds*," he informed her.

Cerise's head shot up, her eyes widening as her gaze landed on the incoming vehicle.

The aerocab lurched to a halt a few mètres away, and the door swung open. Marcellus sucked in a breath and turned, readying himself to run from the legion of guards that was about to pour out onto the roadway.

"Get in," said a deep, accented voice.

Confused, Marcellus spun back to the aerocab and peered at the single passenger sitting inside. Marcellus instantly recognized him from the lab. It was the older scientist. Dr. Collins. The one Marcellus had sworn he saw flinch during the demonstration. But what was he doing here?

Marcellus turned to Alouette, who was staring at the man with what appeared to be the same confusion.

"They won't get away, General. I assure you."

The voice startled Marcellus, and he glanced up to see that the doors to the Filbright Wing were splayed wide open and Lady Alexander was standing in the center, glaring hard at him from behind her shimmering monoglass. Then, not a second later, a troop of uniformed guards came streaming through the doors behind her, running straight toward them.

"GET IN," Dr. Collins bellowed from the awaiting vehicle.

Marcellus nodded once and the four of them dove inside.

The aerocab launched into the air, and Marcellus had to grab on to a seat to avoid being flung across the interior. An explosion of noise vibrated in his ears and shook the vehicle.

"Get down," Dr. Collins called out. "They're shooting."

Alouette, Cerise, and Gabriel all threw themselves onto the floor. But before Marcellus could duck, Dr. Collins thrust something into his hand. "We're almost to the security gate. When I cue you, throw this."

Marcellus looked down at a smooth metal cartridge in his hand.

"What is—?" he began to ask, but his words were cut off by the sharp blasts of more gunfire.

"Now!" said Dr. Collins, plunging his hand down on the console.

The window beside Marcellus slid open, and Marcellus hurled the small capsule out of the vehicle. It landed only mètres away from the security gate, and as soon as it hit the ground, a cloud of thick green smoke plumed into the air, swallowing up the squadron of guards who were shooting at them.

"Blinding gas," Dr. Collins explained as he sealed the window and revved the engine. The vehicle tore out of the complex.

Marcellus glanced back to see the smoke billowing behind them, obscuring the whole view of the tech labs. But even through the thick green fog, another round of gunfire rang out and Marcellus scrabbled down onto the floor. Something struck the side of the aerocab, leaving a large gaping hole in the metal that seemed to spread and blacken with each passing second, like it was alive.

Gabriel yelped. "What the fric kind of ammo are they firing?"

"Cluster bullets," Dr. Collins replied as he yanked on the contrôleur and pitched the aerocab into a steep upward climb. "A nasty Albion invention that you do not want to be on the receiving end of."

"No kidding," Gabriel muttered, still gaping, horrified, at the yawning puncture in the wall.

The aerocab juddered again but then evened out, and soon they were soaring across the sky, picking up speed. The sound of gunfire retreated into the distance, and Marcellus peeked out the window again to see the spires of the tech labs complex fading behind them.

"You're safe to get up now," Dr. Collins said without tearing his gaze from the front window.

Slowly, the four of them pushed themselves up from the floor and climbed onto the leather-covered benches. Marcellus shared an uneasy glance with Alouette, like they were deciding who would be the first to ask the question that was surely on all their minds.

But it was Cerise who blurted it out. "Why are you helping us?"

The aerocab lurched into a new gear, throwing everyone back against their seats.

"Why do you think?" the silver-haired scientist replied.

"I don't know," Cerise said impatiently. "That's why I'm asking!"

Dr. Collins glanced at Marcellus. "I assume all that gunfire means you're *not*, in fact, associated with General Bonnefaçon, as you claimed."

"He is my grandfather," Marcellus said with a grimace. "But no, I'm not associated with him. Not anymore, anyway."

"Then why are you here?" Dr. Collins asked.

"We're trying to stop him," said Marcellus.

Dr. Collins cocked a silver eyebrow and shot a look at Cerise. "As am I."

"What?" Cerise spat. "If you're trying to stop him, then why are you *working* with him?"

"Because he's the source," Alouette said softly, speaking for the first time since they'd scrambled into the aerocab.

Marcellus stared incredulously between Alouette and Dr. Collins. "*You're* the source?"

Dr. Collins darted a look back at Alouette. "What source?"

"You're the one who's been communicating with Denise," she said. It wasn't a question or an accusation. It was just a fact. And Marcellus was impressed that she'd been able to figure it out so quickly.

"How do you know Denise?" Dr. Collins asked.

"How do *you* know Denise?" Cerise fired back.

But Alouette answered first. "She . . . She sort of raised me. Or at least, she was one of the women who raised me."

"You're the Lark?" Dr. Collins asked in amazement.

Marcellus felt Alouette stiffen beside him. "Yes," she whispered.

"Did Denise send you here?" Dr. Collins steered the aerocab gently to the left.

"Not exactly," Alouette replied. "We intercepted your message for her. Denise taught me the code you've been using when I was little. That last transmission you received was from us. We pretended to be her so you would meet with us and hopefully tell us how to stop the general from using that awful"—she shuddered—"thing."

"Yeah, what exactly *was* that thing?" Gabriel asked.

"So, if you intercepted that transmission," Dr. Collins said, ignoring Gabriel's question. "Then where is Denise?"

Alouette stared down at her hands, her lips trembling. "She's . . ."

"My grandfather has her," Marcellus cut in, the familiar anger sharpening his tone. "He's taken her to a secret detention facility somewhere. We don't know where."

The aerocab fell very silent. Dr. Collins eased the contrôleur to the right and then down. The small craft ascended toward what looked like a very small town. Marcellus could make out a few neat rows of houses with gentle sloping roofs and square patches of grass behind them.

"Wait a minute," Cerise said, staring at the coordinates flashing across the console. "Isn't this the location where we were supposed to meet you?"

"It's a safe house," Dr. Collins said, "that the Ministry of Defence doesn't know about."

He silently steered the aerocab down a dark and quiet lane before pulling into a small docking shelter attached to one of the houses.

For a long moment, they all just sat there in the darkness. No one knew quite what to say or do next. Dr. Collins stared blankly through the front window, almost as though he were trying to summon the courage to move again.

Cerise was the first to speak. "So, are you going to tell us how you know Denise?"

At these words, the scientist seemed to break free from his trance. He jabbed at a button on the console, and the doors of the aerocab slid open. But just before stepping out, Dr. Collins glanced back at Cerise with a forlorn look, and said, "She's my daughter."

- CHAPTER 41 -
ALOUETTE

THE KETTLE ON THE STOVE LET OUT A LONG, HIGH-pitched whistle.

"Who would like tea?" Dr. Collins asked as he began pouring hot water into the teapot.

Alouette couldn't imagine stomaching anything right now. She just wanted answers. But she also didn't want to be rude, so she quietly raised her hand along with the others.

"You mecs really like your tea here, don't you?" Gabriel said.

Dr. Collins smiled as he took down five cups from a nearby shelf. "Yes. It must be an Albion thing. I suppose it comes from our ancestors on the First World. But mostly, I find tea helps me think." He carefully poured the tea and handed a cup to each of them. "And how about a bickie?"

Alouette shared a confused look with Gabriel.

Dr. Collins pushed a round silver container toward them. "You know, biscuits. Would you like a biscuit?" Then, after another series of blank looks, he said, "They're sweet."

Gabriel launched himself forward and grabbed for the container. "Thanks, mec. I'm starving."

After they'd each taken one—or in Gabriel's case, five—Alouette sipped at her tea and peered around the main room of this curious little house. It was as if she'd been transported back to the propagation room in the Refuge, where Sister Laurel used to produce all her herbal tinctures and medicinal syrups. Polished test tubes and cone-shaped beakers sat in neat rows on the shelves, and jars of powders and strange-colored liquids crowded every surface. A vast whiteboard held tangles of sketched drawings and diagrams, while a bank of cabinets hugged its way around the room. Even the ceilings were low like in the Refuge, and the blacked-out windows made Alouette feel like she was back underground.

"So, okay, apparently I'm the only one who's going to ask the million-larg question of the day," Gabriel said through a large mouthful of biscuit. "How did you end up building that . . . that . . . *thing* for General Bonnefaçon?"

Dr. Collins sipped his tea and leaned heavily on the kitchen counter, as though the answer itself was weighing him down. "I didn't know I was doing it. At least not at first. Dr. Cromwell and I are old colleagues, and he asked me to come and join him on what he called 'an exciting new research project.'" He cast an apologetic glance at Marcellus. "I promise, I had no idea what we were developing until it was too late. I thought we were expanding our research in the field of neuroelectricity. Dr. Cromwell said they desperately needed a neuroengineer, and I thought it was harmless. Then they started bringing in the test subjects and I heard the general's name mentioned a few times and I . . ." He grimaced. "I realized what the research was really for."

"What exactly *did* you develop?" Marcellus asked. He seemed to shudder at the memory of what they'd all just seen back in the labs.

Dr. Collins stared vacantly into his tea, a lifetime of regret playing out across his face. "The program is called TéléReversion. It's essentially a modified operating system for the Laterrian TéléSkins. The source code has been rewritten so that the neuroelectricity that powers the implanted interface can be manipulated and rerouted."

"I'm sorry," Gabriel said, looking mystified, "but *what*?"

Alouette placed a reassuring hand on his. "The Skins are powered by the naturally occurring electricity in the brain. Dr. Cromwell's team has managed to reverse that electricity so that instead of the brain powering the Skins, the Skins can now be used to manipulate the brain."

"Precisely," Dr. Collins said, tapping his finger against the edge of his teacup. "The TéléReversion program allows complete control over the mood and emotion of the subject at any given moment. For example, imagine the angriest, most destructive, most vengeful you've ever felt—"

"I'm getting there," Gabriel said through gritted teeth.

"Well, that's a reaction in your brain," Dr. Collins went on. "A neuro-response, we call it. Now multiply that feeling by a thousand, and essentially that's what the test subjects you witnessed earlier were experiencing. You see, there are particular areas of the brain—including the amygdala—that control your body's natural fight or flight responses. The new program directly stimulates these areas, prompting the test subjects to fight."

"But how do you control *who* they fight? Or what they attack?" Marcellus asked.

"That's where specific triggers come in. The program can send ideas or images to the brain to help direct the response. In the demonstration you witnessed, the subjects were triggered to attack each other. But the general will be able to transmit any trigger he wants, to any group of people, at any time."

"Holy fric." Gabriel pressed his fingertips into his temples.

"Holy fric is right," Dr. Collins agreed with a grave nod.

"A modification to the operating system," Cerise repeated, looking lost in thought. "But how do you modify every Third Estate Skin on the planet without anyone noticing?"

"That part was unnervingly easy," Dr. Collins said. "We wrote the source code to be inserted directly into a routine software update. They get sent out regularly from your Ministère, direct to the Skins. No one will even know what's happened until it's too late."

Cerise looked horrified. "When will the next update go out?"

"My guess is as soon as Dr. Cromwell delivers the final product to the general."

"One week," Alouette said numbly, remembering what Dr. Cromwell had told them back in the lab. "He said the program would be ready for delivery in one week."

Marcellus raked his hands through his thick hair. "And then what? Once the update goes out and all of the Third Estate are at the general's command, what is he planning to do with them?"

Dr. Collins sighed and shook his head. "I don't know. Whatever he wants, I suppose. But regardless of what he's planning, it can't be good."

"The scum of Laterre will soon be eliminated," Marcellus repeated his grandfather's horrible words. "The fat will be trimmed. The Regime will finally rid itself of the déchets and be brought to order."

"What?" Dr. Collins asked, his eyes widening with fear.

Marcellus blinked as though waking from a dream. "That's what my grandfather said. When he talked to Lady Alexander."

"What is a déchet?" Dr. Collins asked.

"It's what the pomps call us low-life Third Estaters," Gabriel muttered. "It means garbage."

"So he's planning to *eliminate* the entire Third Estate?" Dr. Collins asked.

"Probably not all of them," Marcellus said miserably. "He still needs some to serve as his own personal army."

"But he certainly doesn't need everyone," Gabriel said, his voice low and bitter. He let out a dark laugh. "I'm surprised he can even think of us as 'the fat,' when most of the Third Estate are starving."

"What are we going to do?" Marcellus asked, throwing up his hands in desperation.

"Hello? Isn't it obvious? We need to find the kill switch," Cerise said, which elicited a groan from both Marcellus and Gabriel.

"Cerise—" Marcellus started to object, but Cerise held up a hand to stop him and looked earnestly to Dr. Collins.

"You know more about the Skins than anyone I've met. There's a master switch, right? An emergency shutoff? A deactivation code? Something!"

Dr. Collins barked out a sharp laugh. "Wouldn't that be nice?"

"But it has to exist," Cerise insisted.

"It doesn't," Marcellus said irritably. "Just let it go."

"We received extensive intelligence on the TéléSkins at the start of this project," Dr. Collins said before taking another small sip of tea. "There was no mention of a kill switch. I would have remembered that."

"Why exactly are you telling us all of this?" Gabriel asked, his eyes suddenly brimming with suspicion as he glared at Dr. Collins. "Don't you hate Laterre like everyone else on this planet?"

Dr. Collins flashed Gabriel an empathetic look. "The Laterrian-Albion conflict that has been waging for centuries is not between us, my dear friend. It's between our leaders."

"So you're not loyal to the Mad Queen?" Gabriel asked with a snort.

Dr. Collins seemed to find amusement in the question. "That is a perfect example of how they pull us into their wars without our knowledge. Queen Matilda is no more 'mad' than you and me. In fact, she has a very brilliant and strategic mind. 'The Mad Queen' was a name coined by your Patriarche's father, Claude Paresse, to reinforce Laterre's hatred of Albion. We, here, have a similar phrase for your current leader: 'Lazy Lyon.'"

Gabriel snorted again. "Well, I'm not sure he didn't earn that one."

"What I'm getting at is that our leaders try to make us think that this five-hundred-year-long war has something to do with us, when it doesn't. It's a war about ego and titan, fought between despots who have nothing better to do than hold grudges. Sometimes I wonder if *they* even remember what they're fighting about."

Marcellus looked hopeful. "So do you know what the general is promising the Mad—Queen Matilda in return for this? What is Albion getting out of this alliance?"

Dr. Collins finished his tea and immediately poured himself a second cup. "I can't say for sure. But I can make a pretty good guess."

"What?" Marcellus asked.

"What's the one thing the Queen wants but doesn't have?"

Marcellus's body seemed to sag as the comprehension collapsed on him. "Usonia," he whispered, sending another chill through Alouette.

She remembered reading about Usonia in the Chronicles. How it started as one of the original self-governing planets of the System Divine, but then, years later, once titan was discovered under its surface, Albion moved swiftly. They invaded with their giant warships and ruthless guards. They slaughtered thousands of people, waging war on the small planet until it was fully under Albion's control. It wasn't until a few years ago that the planet finally fought back.

"The Patriarche helped Usonia win their war of independence," Marcellus went on, sounding dazed and full of agony, "and once General Bonnefaçon has control of the Regime, he's going to help the Queen get Usonia back."

"And he'll have the army to do it," Dr. Collins said grimly.

Marcellus jabbed his fingertips into his eyes and let out a hopeless groan.

"Unless," Dr. Collins went on with a raise of his eyebrow, "you can stop him."

Marcellus threw up his hands. "And how are we supposed to do that? You said so yourself, the program is already complete. Once the general sends out that update, he'll have the entire Third Estate at his beck and call. He'll be unstoppable."

Suddenly, Alouette remembered the coded message they intercepted from Dr. Collins. The one that sent them here in the first place.

Weapon nearly complete . . . I can stop it . . .

"You built something," Alouette blurted out. "To stop the TéléReversion program."

Dr. Collins smiled. "I can see now why my daughter spoke so highly of you."

Warmth spread over Alouette's body, allowing her, for just a second, to forget all the horrors in her mind—those two men fighting to the death, Denise and Jacqui being tortured in a cell somewhere, the surface of Bastille littered with the remains of Vangarde operatives—and just remember Denise as she was. As Alouette always wanted to remember her. Hunched over her workbench in the Refuge, peering curiously and intently at the inner workings of some Ministère gadget or device she'd disassembled.

"She taught me so much," Alouette whispered.

"And you're right," said Dr. Collins. "I *did* build something. Ever since I figured out that the general was the one behind this project, I've spent every free hour I've had here in this safe house, working on a way to stop him. I knew I couldn't keep Dr. Cromwell from delivering the program, or the general from sending it out to the Skins. The source code is too heavily guarded in the Filbright Wing. So I had to find another way."

Dr. Collins walked to a large cabinet with a line of glowing lights around its frame. As he opened its heavy, suction-sealed door, a cloud of icy steam billowed into the air. Donning a metallic glove, he reached inside and pulled out a tiny glass vial from one of the shelves. The faint white liquid inside bubbled and fizzed like it was alive.

Gabriel took a few cautious steps back. "What is it?"

"It's an inhibitor," said Dr. Collins. Then, upon seeing the blank expression on Gabriel's face, he clarified. "Think of it like a virus. Once inside the human body, it spreads and multiplies, making the carrier immune to neuroelectrical manipulation."

"A blocker," Alouette said, mesmerized.

"Precisely," said Dr. Collins. "The nanotechnology inside this vial essentially blocks the Skins from being able to transmit electricity back to the brain, effectively stopping the general's ability to trigger neuro-responses."

"That's genius!" Cerise said.

"Why, thank you." Dr. Collins smiled at the vial in his hand.

"Did Denise know about this?" Alouette asked.

Dr. Collins shook his head. "Not about the inhibitor, no. She knew about the TéléReversion program, and she knew I was working on something to neutralize it, but I didn't have a breakthrough until about a week ago."

"That's why you sent that last message to Denise," Alouette confirmed. "So she would come to Albion and bring the inhibitor back to Laterre."

"Yes," he replied. "My idea was for the Vangarde to distribute it into the water supply for the Third Estate. There are eleven water treatment centers on your planet: two in the city of Montfer; one in each of the towns of Delaine, Céleste, Adèle-sur-Mer, Lacrête, and Bûcheron; and four in Vallonay. If you can get one of these vials into each treatment center, the inhibitor will multiply and spread on its own, eventually infecting everyone with a Skin and rendering the TéléReversion program useless."

Marcellus stepped forward, looking grateful to have a plan. "We can do that. Are the vials ready now?"

"They will be by morning," Dr. Collins said.

"Um"—Cerise glanced impatiently between Marcellus and Dr. Collins—"are you all forgetting one very important thing? How are we supposed to get back to Laterre? Lady Alexander is still looking for us. I doubt she's just going to let us board our ship and fly off into the Sol-rise."

"Let me handle that," Dr. Collins said. "I've been monitoring my own security profile since we left the lab, and so far, they haven't revoked any of my clearances. Which means, I don't think they suspect me of helping you."

"So you can get us back into the spaceport?" Cerise confirmed.

"I will work on a plan," Dr. Collins assured her. "In the meantime, you all should rest. You've had quite the day. There are bedrooms and loos in the back. Make yourself at home."

"Loos?" Gabriel repeated.

"Sorry. Bathrooms."

Marcellus and Gabriel disappeared down a hall, presumably to seek out rest, while Cerise ventured into the kitchen for more tea. Dr. Collins sat down in front of one of his glowing screens and immediately seemed to fall into a trance. It reminded Alouette of the way Denise could so easily disappear into her devices. She tried to imagine what Denise might have been like as a child. As this man's daughter. There were so many questions she longed to ask Dr. Collins about the sister who had helped raise her.

Nibbling on her biscuit, she glanced around the room, and her gaze eventually landed on a familiar contraption perched on a nearby shelf. It was mounted on a wooden platform with a series of springs, cogs, and intertwined bolts holding up a hinged metal arm that, when in use, tapped down onto a small metal disk. Alouette stepped up closer to the shelf, her lips curving into a knowing smile. It was just like the device Denise had. The very one she had used to teach Alouette the First World code that had led them all here.

"That's how my daughter and I have been communicating."

Alouette looked up to find Dr. Collins watching her from his desk.

"I'm sorry, Dr. Collins," she said, quickly backing away from the shelf. "I didn't mean to bother you."

He smiled gently. "You're no bother. I'm just waiting for some processes to render. And please, call me Edward."

"Edward," she repeated quietly, liking the way the name sounded in his distinguished Albion accent. "I have to say"—Alouette nodded toward the contraption on the shelf—"sending signals through the old Human Conservation Commission space probe was a pretty brilliant idea."

Edward stood up and walked over until they were standing shoulder to shoulder, staring at the strange little device. "Thank you. That was all Vaness— Sorry, I forget she goes by Denise now. She found the probe when she was a little girl. She was always fascinated with space. Always listening to the skies. When she discovered that the probe was still transmitting through that old deep-space network from the First World, she figured out how to utilize it. She built this device so she could send me secret messages, using a First World code that she'd discovered. It was a game we used to play. Our own little secret." He caught Alouette's eye and tipped his teacup to her in a small salute.

Another rush of warmth shot through her. That was exactly what Denise had told Alouette when she'd taught her the code. *"Our own little secret."* Like she was passing down some ancient family wisdom. And now Alouette realized that she was.

A far-off look passed over Dr. Collins's face, as though there was more to the story than he was letting on. "She was always so much smarter than her old dad."

"Were you close?" Alouette asked.

Edward sighed. "We haven't been for a long time. This . . . This project is the thing that brought us back together. I haven't actually seen my daughter in thirty-five years."

"Thirty-five years?"

His eyes dimmed. "Yes. It's my fault, really. I became too obsessed with my work. And it drove her mother away. She was Laterrian. We met on Kaishi. At the headquarters of the System Alliance. I was representing Albion as a scientific diplomat, and she was there with her father, an ambassador for the former Patriarche."

"So she was Second Estate?" Alouette confirmed. The influx of new information was making her dizzy and thirsty for more. It had been so long since she'd studied, read, absorbed. She hadn't realized how much she'd missed it. Missed the rush she always felt when she learned something new. It was a rush she thought was only possible inside the Refuge library, under the careful watch and tutelage of the sisters. But here she was, on Albion, far away from everything she'd ever known, and she was experiencing that rush—that curiosity—all over again.

"Yes," Dr. Collins replied. "Josephine was Second Estate. She and I fell in love quickly. The way young people do. I convinced her to move to Albion. We had to sneak her in with fake credentials. Vanessa—or, as you know her, Denise—was born less than a year later, and I thought life couldn't get much better than it was. But then a few years passed, and I was called in on a special research project for the Ministry of Defence. I thought it would last a few months. It ended up lasting years and consuming all my time. I became reclusive and irritable and, in short, impossible to live with. Josephine left. She took our daughter back to Laterre. They moved into Ledôme, and eventually Vanessa signed herself up for the Cyborg Initiation Program, and I stopped hearing from her completely."

"Wait, she *chose* to become a cyborg?" someone asked, and Dr. Collins and Alouette both turned to see Cerise standing behind them. Her face was pulled into a look of utter disgust, as though the idea made her physically ill.

Edward nodded grimly. "I was furious when I found out. I knew they would only turn her into a heartless slave for the Ministère. They would take away everything that made her my daughter."

"But why would she choose to do that to herself?" Cerise asked, and Alouette couldn't help but feel like her reaction was just the slightest bit extreme. Of all the things they'd learned from this man today, Cerise seemed to be taking this one the hardest.

"Don't many people choose to become cyborgs?" Alouette asked.

Cerise snorted. "Maybe delusional ones."

"I have to agree," Dr. Collins said. "I don't understand why anyone would choose that life. With Vanessa, her mother died shortly before she signed up for the program, and I've always been convinced that she joined as a way to escape her grief."

"So then, how did you find out she'd started working with the Vangarde?" Alouette asked.

"I didn't until very recently. When she left the Ministère, several years later, and had her circuitries removed, she actually reached out to me. We were, by no means, reconciled at that point. She simply wanted me to know that she was no longer a cyborg, and that was that. She gave me no way to contact her. Then, when I started working on this project for the general, I knew I had to warn someone on Laterre. I found the old space probe signal that she used to send me secret messages when she was a little girl. I didn't know if she was still monitoring that signal or if she would even get my messages, but I had to try." He let out a sigh and stared longingly at the contraption on the shelf. His only remaining link to his daughter. "It's strange that, after all these years, General Bonnefaçon would be the one to bring us back together. And now he has her . . ." His voice suddenly cracked, and he glanced down at the floor, blinking back mist from his eyes. "My apologies."

Alouette's heart broke for the poor man. She reached out to put a hand on his shoulder but then remembered that Sister Denise didn't really like being touched. Perhaps her father was the same way. She let her hand drop, and instead, in the most earnest voice she could muster, she said, "Don't worry. We'll find her."

Of course, Alouette had no idea if her words were true. If they'd ever be able to find Jacqui and Denise. But she knew these were words she had to say aloud. For herself as much as for him.

- CHAPTER 42 -
CHATINE

"IT'S ACTUALLY BETTER IF YOU CHEW FIRST, *THEN* swallow." Etienne sat down next to Chatine in the half-empty lodge and began to scoop food from the brimming platters in the center of the table onto his plate.

Chatine looked up, her mouth crammed full of scrambled eggs. She swallowed and tried not to gag as the partially chewed food pushed its way down her throat. It had been two days since she'd tried to run away, and this morning, her appetite had magically returned. Just like that. She'd woken up with hunger pains deeper and more intense than anything she'd ever experienced in the Frets. Somehow Brigitte must have known, because when Chatine had asked if a tray could be brought into the treatment center for her, Brigitte had said with a curious sparkle in her eye, "How about you join us in the lodge for breakfast?" And that had been the end of it. Chatine often wondered if some of Brigitte's cyborg circuitry had been accidentally left in, because sometimes the woman seemed nothing short of a mind reader.

As soon as the food made its way down her throat, Chatine lunged for another bite.

Etienne laughed. "How are those wood chips?"

"Fantastique," Chatine managed to get out, after swallowing and before filling her mouth with a giant bite of what could only be described as crispy baked bread. It was crunchy and buttery and delicious.

"Glad to hear it." Etienne finished making up his plate and took a very normal-sized bite of eggs. They were the only two people at the table, but the room was filling up quickly.

"Wha dih yoo ga ah tha fah?" she tried to ask, but her words were garbled, and bread crumbs sprayed from her mouth as she spoke.

Etienne raised an eyebrow and made a show of brushing the crumbs from his face. "What was that? Apparently, I don't speak Hungry Gridder."

Chatine swallowed and wiped her mouth with her sleeve before repeating the question. "Where do you get all this food?"

"We grow it or make it ourselves. The eggs come from hens that we keep in our greenhouse. The bread is made from *real* wheat that we grow in our indoor fermes. No Ministère-engineered chou bread here. Every-one at the camp has tasks and assigned duties, but we all work together. We're completely self-sufficient. Well, except for the zyttrium. That we have to trade for. Hence why you're here."

Chatine took another bite of toast and tilted her head in confusion.

"The reason we met," he clarified. "You. Me. The roof of Bastille. My *daring* rescue mission? Any of this sounding familiar?"

Chatine swallowed. "Oh. Right." She was desperate to change the subject. It was bordering far too close to the danger zone. She'd built a fence around that zone in her mind and had made every attempt to steer clear of it. Despite what Brigitte had said, she couldn't face those monsters. They were too scary. Their eyes too dark. Their teeth too sharp. And if she couldn't be out there helping find Henri, she certainly wasn't going to sit around here and *think* about how she wasn't out there helping to find Henri.

"Well, anyway," Etienne went on, "the zyttrium allows us to live the way we want, but unfortunately a lot of it is required to keep our ships and roofs in good repair so we can stay hidden from the Regime. Which is why we have to trade for it."

"What do you trade?" Chatine asked before taking another bite of bread.

"Mostly our services. You know: rescue missions, stealth deliveries, medical procedures frowned upon by the Regime. Basically, anything people want to do in secret. Usonia was a decent customer for a while. All that drama with Albion. We helped them smuggle a lot of stuff in and out during the war."

Chatine nearly choked on her half-chewed mouthful of bread. "You've been to Usonia?"

Etienne beamed. "A few times. Nice place, but I wouldn't want to live there."

"Why not?"

"Too far from the Sols. Very cold. I'd get claustrophobic in those bubbles."

Defensiveness brewed in her gut. She'd spent the last ten years of her life trying to get to Usonia. "It's not like it's much warmer here, and what good are the Sols if you can't see them?"

Etienne tossed up his hands. "Well, well. Looks like I found another button. What's that one called? Oversensitive Defense Toggle?"

Chatine's fist clenched around her fork as a thousand rebuttals sprang to her mind at once. But instead, she glanced down at her plate and, noticing it was empty, reached for the serving spoon and began piling on more eggs.

Thankfully, Etienne changed the subject. "How's the leg?"

She shrugged. "Fine."

Etienne cocked another eyebrow. "Just fine?"

She sighed. "Actually, a lot better." It was still an understatement. When Brigitte had changed her bandages this morning, Chatine was shocked to see the wound was healing faster than she'd expected. She was even able to put weight on it and walk to the lodge without the use of her crutches. "Your maman is kind of magic."

Etienne smiled. "Yes, she is. She's very good at her job."

"Is that because she used to be a cyborg?"

Etienne shrugged. "Maybe. Maybe not. Some people just have a gift, you know? She understands things on a level that most people don't. It's hard to explain."

"I get it," Chatine said. Brigitte had a calmness about her. A quiet complexity that Chatine had never experienced before. It left Chatine feeling both at ease and desperately curious at the same time.

She scanned the lodge and spotted Brigitte sitting a few tables away. The woman caught Chatine's gaze, and as she smiled, the skin on the left side of her face crinkled around its maze of twisted scars.

"Why did she choose to take out her cyborg circuitry?" Chatine asked, keeping her voice low, even though they were still the only two at the table.

Etienne took a sip from his cup of hot chocolat. "She said it was because her soul finally caught up to what her mind was doing, and it broke her in half."

Chatine squinted at him. "What?"

Etienne sighed. "She doesn't talk about it much, but apparently when you're implanted with the cyborg circuitry, your mental capabilities are incredibly enhanced. But to protect the Regime from you turning your abilities against them, you're also programmed not to question authority or disobey orders. Which means your ability to navigate moral ambiguities becomes clouded." He chuckled. "*Her* words, obviously."

"You lost me," Chatine said.

Etienne leaned in closer to Chatine, his piercing dark eyes making it hard for her to swallow. "All I know is that right before she left, she was put on some special assignment that she won't talk about with anyone."

Chatine felt herself being pulled toward him. Partly because of those eyes, and partly because of her own curiosity. "What kind of assignment."

"I don't know. Like I said, she doesn't like to talk about it. But apparently, it was classified and very confidential. There was only one other cyborg working with her. A woman, I think. All Maman will say about the project is that it was bad. Disturbing. And when she realized its reper-cussions for the planet, she woke up from the 'cyborg sleep,' as she calls it. After that, she and this other woman removed each other's circuitries and left the Ministère."

"What happened to the other cyborg?"

Etienne shrugged. "She doesn't talk about her much either."

Chatine stole another glance at Brigitte before turning back to Etienne, prepared to ask another question. But just then, the door to the lodge burst open and a gaggle of children came barreling toward their table.

"No! I'm sitting next to him!" one of them shouted.

"No, I am!" another one said. "You sat next to him at dinner."

"I did not! That was Comète."

"You sat on the *other* side."

"Well, you'll have to beat me there!"

The mob continued to rush the table, elbowing one another to get ahead. Chatine felt the sudden inclination to run the other way. In the Frets, a gang of children charging at you meant only one thing: You were about to be jumped and robbed. They often worked in numbers to com-pensate for their size.

The group screeched to a halt in front of Chatine, their confused gazes darting between her and Etienne in the next chair, as though this seat-ing arrangement were some complicated puzzle they couldn't solve. Then their eyes swiveled toward the empty chair on the other side of Etienne, and four of them dove for it at once, pushing and shoving one another out of the way. Somehow, in the fray, the smallest of the bunch, a young girl with dark glittery eyes and a riot of curls, managed to squirm her way into the chair. She looked to be no older than four. A wide grin spread over her face, and her stubby legs swung gleefully.

"Astra! Get down!" one of the boys cried. "You can't sit there."

The little girl—Astra—stuck two fingers in her mouth and sucked on them contently. But she did not move.

The boy, who wore a giant hat with long, fuzzy ear flaps that nearly consumed his whole head, looked at Etienne for help. "Make her get down! I was supposed to sit there."

Astra removed her fingers from her mouth long enough to yell, "No!" before resuming her sucking.

This caused a chorus of shouts and complaints until Etienne raised his hands up and said, "Whoa, whoa. Everyone calm down. There's plenty of room at the table."

"Nuh-uh," said the boy in the hat. "Not with *her* there."

"Hey," Etienne said. "Perseus, that's not very nice. That's my new friend. Remember, the one I told you all about?"

Suddenly, every pair of eyes was on Chatine, any and all former disapproval instantly evaporating. Astra's fingers slipped from her mouth.

"You're a gridder?" Perseus asked. He was clearly the leader of this tiny gang.

"Uh," Chatine stammered, looking at all the mesmerized faces that surrounded her. "Yes. I guess, I am."

"*And* she was on Bastille," Etienne added.

"Can we see your tattoo?" Perseus asked, his eyes alight with mischief.

Chatine rolled up her sleeve to reveal the five clusters of metallic bumps burned into her flesh. "There it is. Prisoner 51562."

"Whoa," said one of the girls who reached out and ran her fingertips over the raised surface of the tattoo.

"Did you ever live in one of those crashed ships in Vallonay?" Perseus asked.

"They didn't crash," Etienne said, as though this had been a point of contention for a while. "They landed safely 505 years ago."

"Yes," Chatine agreed, "They're called the Frets. But they're so old and crumbling, sometimes it feels like they crashed. Half of the stairs aren't even there anymore."

"Soop," Perseus said, sliding into the chair next to Chatine.

"What's it like to have a Skin?" another girl asked.

Chatine spun to answer the question but was immediately bombarded by three more from different directions.

"Have you ever eaten chou bread?"

"Did you ever have to sell your blood?"

"Did you win the Ascension?"

Chatine snorted with laughter at that one. "No. Definitely not."

"What did I tell you?" Etienne leaned in to whisper. "Instant celebrity."

"Do you do magic tricks like Fabian?" one of the boys asked.

"Who?" said Chatine.

"One of the other gridders," Etienne reminded her. "Who arrived earlier this month."

"Fabian does magic tricks," Perseus explained. "He makes things disappear."

"Oh," Chatine said, turning back to the boy who'd originally asked the question. "No."

"Do you dance like Gen?" another asked.

"That's his wife," Etienne said. "She makes up funny dances."

"No."

"Can you brew a potion that makes people see stars?" another girl asked.

Chatine looked to Etienne. "What?"

"Weed wine," Etienne whispered with a wink. "Fabian told them it was a magic potion."

"Can you count to a million?"

"Can you pull a shiny button from my ear?"

Chatine was getting dizzy from all the questions being flung at her from every direction. Who were these mysterious Fabian and Gen? "No. I can't do any of those things."

"What *can* you do?" This was Astra, the youngest. She had climbed into Etienne's lap and was now staring at Chatine with her elbow propped on the table and her chin resting in her hand.

"I . . . uh . . . I can climb." She glanced down at her still-bandaged leg. "I mean, I *could* when I was . . ." but she trailed off as she realized that none of the children were even looking at her anymore. They'd all wandered off to find chairs at the table and were starting to help themselves to breakfast. All of them except Astra, who was still staring at Chatine from Etienne's lap. But in the place of her once fascinated expression, she now looked almost sorry for Chatine. She shrugged as if to say, *You can't do magic, what did you expect?*

"Told you they'd be disappointed," she whispered to Etienne.

Etienne chuckled. "Oh, this is normal. They have the attention spans of flies. You'll be a celebrity again in another few minutes." He lifted Astra and deposited her back into her chair. One of the other children had already filled her plate with food, and she began happily eating her breakfast.

Chatine warily eyed each of the tiny faces around the table, like she didn't quite trust them.

"You don't have a lot of experience with children, do you?" Etienne asked, and Chatine realized he'd been watching her.

"Um." She pressed a fingertip against a bread crumb on her plate and brought it to her mouth. "Not really, no. Third Estaters don't get to be children for very long. I mean, ever since I was five, I had to take care of—" An alarm bell went off in her head as she approached the danger zone. She quickly stepped back. "Anyway. Who are all these kids?"

Etienne looked surprised by the question, as though he thought the answer was obvious. "They're my siblings."

Shocked, Chatine quickly scanned the table, counting twelve in total. And some of them looked to be very similar in age. Her gaze flickered back to Brigitte a few tables away. "Wow. Your maman has been busy."

Etienne laughed. "They're not all biologically hers." Then, when Chatine gave him a confused look, he clarified, "I mean, she didn't give birth to all of them. When we lose members of our community, the children get assimilated into new families. But you'd never know the difference. We treat them just like our own. It helps everyone with the grieving process."

Chatine's eyes cut to Etienne. Was he referring to the roundups? She searched his face for a hint of that grimace she'd seen the other night. But his face remained neutral.

"Your maman said something about how the communities recently had to merge together," Chatine said, "because their numbers were so low. And how it's been a difficult adjustment."

Etienne nodded. "That's right." He gestured around at all the tables, which were now completely filled. "The problem was that our communities were all so different. We valued different things and had different skills. But it's all fine now, obviously. Everyone gets along."

Chatine glanced around the lodge. Chatter and laughter wafted through the room as easily as rain fell in the Marsh. The Défecteurs passed plates, banged their forks to make animated points, and leaned into one another to share stories and jokes. No one sat alone. No one lurked on the periphery, waiting to con or swindle or cheat the others out of a larg.

Her forefinger instinctively rubbed at her thumb, at the place where Marcellus's ring used to be. The memory of it was already growing fainter. She wondered if there would ever come a day when she stopped searching for it.

"What about your community? What were their skills?"

"We've always been shipbuilders. Maman says we descended from the people who built the original freightships that left the First World, but I don't know if that's really true."

Chatine gave a snort. "Yeah, I've been inside your ship. I don't think that's true."

Etienne scooped up a scrap of egg from his plate and flung it at Chatine's face. She ducked, and it landed on one of the ear flaps of Perseus's hat. He didn't seem to notice as he continued to heap food into his mouth.

"Anyway," Etienne went on, "now that we're one community, and have worked out the kinks, we've built the most advanced camp that any of us have ever lived in."

Chatine peered around at the other tables, taking a rough count. There were only about a hundred people in the room. Was that really all that was left of the Défecteurs?

"How many people used to be in your community?" she asked, her gaze still taking in all the unfamiliar faces. "Before the last roundup."

A rough scraping noise startled her and snapped her attention back to Etienne, but he was no longer in his seat. He had pushed his chair back and was now standing. "I should go. Marilyn still needs some more maintenance." Without another word, he left the table and carried his plate to the kitchen.

"He doesn't talk about the roundups."

Chatine looked over at Perseus in his big hat seated next to her. "Why not?"

He shrugged as he shoveled more food into his mouth. "He just doesn't."

She caught sight of Etienne walking toward the door of the lodge. There was something almost stiff and awkward about his steps.

"Have you ever asked him?" Chatine turned her attention back to Perseus. "Why he doesn't talk about it."

Perseus shook his head. "Nope. Maman said he'll talk about it when he's ready."

Chatine nodded, knowing from experience that that could quite possibly be never.

"Do you think Fabian will bring us back bonbons?" one of the girls asked to no one in particular.

"He said he would," replied Perseus. "And he never breaks a promise."

"What kind of bonbons do you think they'll be?" the girl asked. "Where do you think he'll get them?"

Perseus shrugged. "Who cares?"

Chatine glanced again around the room. The tables were starting to clear out as more people finished their breakfast. "And where *are* these famous gridders you keep talking about?"

"One of the pilotes took them to look for their lost children," said Perseus with a sad shake of his head.

"What happened to them?" Chatine asked.

"They got separated," one of the other children explained. "When the Policier came to their town and started to arrest people."

Perseus leaned in close to Chatine so that the other children couldn't hear and whispered, "Just between you and me, I don't think they're going to find them."

"Why not?" Chatine whispered back.

"Because when the Policier come, that's it. You're a goner."

Chatine felt a squeeze in her chest at this little boy's shrewd yet haunting observation. She glanced around the room once more. But this time, she found herself wondering how many people here had lost someone.

Just like Etienne.

Just like these other gridders.

Just like her.

"But they're coming back to the camp tomorrow," Astra said after plucking her fingers from her mouth. "They promised to be back for the cérémonie."

"What cérémonie?" Chatine asked.

"The linking cérémonie," said Perseus with an air of expertise that amused Chatine. "It's a huge deal. Everyone comes."

Chatine felt a sudden panic rush over her at the idea of any kind of social gathering with these people. "Well, I'll probably skip it."

Perseus stared at her as though she had just arrived from one of the farthest planets of the system. "No one *skips* a linking cérémonie," he said with a snort. "If you live here, you have to come."

- CHAPTER 43 -
ALOUETTE

"AND NOW THE SECOND SEQUENCE," ALOUETTE whispered into the darkness. *"Ghostly Stars."*

Wheeling her arms in front of her, she took three graceful steps forward. The dark skies of Albion seemed to echo her movements with their glowing moons and thousands of twinkling pinpricks of light.

"In this sequence we give thanks to the journey of our ancestors, who traveled far from their dying First World through endless space to establish a new life."

Sister Laurel's voice whispered in Alouette's memory as she moved through the sequence on the square patch of grass behind the small house. She knew she should probably stay inside, where Dr. Collins assured them it was safe. But after so many years living underground in a hidden-away Refuge, she yearned for these new sensations of being outside. The feeling of a breeze on her skin. The cool and dewy suck of grass under her bare feet. The curious sounds of a small sleeping town.

Alouette moved on to the next sequence, *Orbit of the Divine.* But with this movement, as her right arm arched up, she felt it. The thud and crack of her elbow meeting the officer's jaw. Her mind shifted back to Montfer and the Policier Precinct, remembering the electricity that had charged through her body. The ease with which her legs had kicked, her fists had flown, and her elbows had jabbed.

She picked up speed, moving faster now, through *The Darkest Night, The Gray Cloak,* and on to *Elevate the Meek.* Just as she had back in Montfer, she felt the strength of the moves. Their power. Their precision. Their secrets. Their—

The back door of the house opened with a soft creak, startling Alouette. She wobbled and nearly fell over. But a hand reached out to catch her. When she looked up, she saw Gabriel's big grin glinting in the darkness.

"Sorry," he muttered, looking sheepish for breaking her concentration. "Didn't mean to scare you."

"It's okay," Alouette said, catching her breath and finding her balance.

Gabriel let go of her waist and took a seat on the small flight of stone steps that led down to the tiny garden. "I couldn't stay in that house any longer. I was going out of my mind." He took a deep breath, but it did little to relax the taut muscles around his neck.

Alouette sat down next to him, wiping the beads of sweat from her brow. "Are you okay?"

"Sure, yeah, fantastique. The general wants to turn me into a weapon. So, you know, just another day in Third Estate paradise."

Alouette watched as his fingertips found their way under his sleeve and traced the bottom edge of his Skin, instantly reminding her of how much more real and terrifying this must be for him. Someone who actually was in danger of becoming one of the general's weapons.

She reached up to touch the scar on her wrist, where her own Skin used to be. She couldn't remember what it felt like to have one. Sister Denise had removed it when she and Hugo had first come to the Refuge. What must it feel like to have something implanted inside your body? Something watching over you, monitoring you, tracking you. Something that you can't escape from.

"Manacles of the mind," Sister Jacqui had always called them.

But they were physical manacles too, Alouette now realized. And they were about to become something even more than just chains.

Gabriel sighed and tipped his head back to look at the sky. "What a view, huh? Are those all moons?"

She let her gaze drift upward and linger on one of the glowing orbs hanging in the darkness. "Yes. Albion has more than fifteen moons, but only four are visible right now."

"Titanique," Gabriel whispered. "I could get used to this."

"Still thinking about moving here?" she asked.

"Huh?"

Alouette could feel Gabriel's eyes on her, but she kept her gaze locked on the sky. "Back in the voyageur, you said you wanted nothing to do with this mission and I couldn't help but notice that you are still here. You could have ditched us back at the defence complex and saved yourself. You could have slipped out the front door of Dr. Collins's house the moment we arrived. But you're"—she turned toward him, and their eyes met—"here."

Gabriel glanced away, looking caught out. "Yeah, well, you useless pomps clearly need my help."

Alouette cracked a smile. "Clearly."

"And if you all died trying to bring down the general, I'm just not sure I could live with that on my conscience."

"So you *do* have one of those?"

He flashed her a smirk. "Don't tell anyone."

"I wouldn't dream of it."

They fell silent and Gabriel returned his gaze to the sky. Alouette reached into her pocket and ran her fingertips over the metal tag of her devotion beads, thinking once again about that message Denise had sent her.

When the Lark flies home, the Regime will fall.

After everything they'd discovered today, Alouette was suddenly seeing Denise's words differently. With new meaning. New clarity.

Denise knew about the TéléReversion program. And she also knew that Alouette was the only other person on Laterre who could interpret Dr. Collins's code. That's why Denise had hacked Marcellus's TéléCom after being captured and sent Alouette that message

The certainty inside of Alouette was growing, filling her with light and purpose and determination. She now understood what Denise was trying to tell her. She could almost hear the sister's voice whispering in her ear.

Fly home, Little Lark. Go back to the Refuge. Join us. Help us. Fight this fight.

"Do you really think we can stop him?" Gabriel asked in a low whisper, breaking into her thoughts.

Alouette squeezed the tag of her devotion beads, trying to extract every last gramme of strength and conviction the sisters had ever bestowed on her. "Yes."

Gabriel turned to her with a doubtful expression.

"The general won't have the final TéléReversion program for another week," Alouette said. "That gives us just barely enough time to get back to Laterre and distribute Dr. Collins's inhibitor into the water supply before the Skins are updated."

"And then what?" Gabriel asked.

The question caught Alouette off guard. "What do you mean?"

"You don't honestly think the general will just give up after we interfere with his weapon, do you?"

Truthfully, Alouette hadn't thought that far ahead. What *would* happen if they succeeded? What would the general do next? She hadn't the faintest clue. She so longed to talk to the sisters. To ask them what they knew. What had they been planning for all these years? If she could go back now, if she could turn back time and stand in that Assemblée Room again, she knew without a shadow of a doubt that she wouldn't run away this time. She would stay. She would listen. She would ask the right questions, just like the sisters had taught her to do.

"We need your help, Little Lark."

She would say yes.

"What were you doing out here, anyway?" Gabriel asked.

Alouette shook herself from her reverie. "What?"

Gabriel made a strange looping gesture with his hands that Alouette soon realized was supposed to resemble a Tranquil Forme sequence.

"Oh," she said, feeling slightly embarrassed for having been seen. "I was just . . . practicing."

"For your next prize fight against Ministère officers?" Gabriel asked with another smirk.

Alouette couldn't help but laugh at that. "Sort of. I guess. It's actually called Tranquil Forme. It's supposed to be a sacred moving meditation. It keeps your mind focused and your body strong. But I've recently discovered it can also be used to fight."

"So *that's* your secret. Where did you learn that?"

Alouette felt a lump build in her throat. "From the women who raised me."

"The Vangarde?" he confirmed.

She nodded, feeling a flush of adrenaline at the name. It no longer brought her a sense of anger and betrayal. It now brought her strength. Courage. Determination. Perhaps exactly what the sisters had intended.

"So," Gabriel said, leaning back on his palms. "Let me see if I got all of this straight. You were raised by the Vangarde, one of which is this Denise person, except you didn't *know* you were being raised by the Vangarde. And when you found out, you bolted, because you were, understandably, a little pissed off. So you went looking for your mother at a blood bordel in Montfer, and now you're here, embroiled in this mess with us."

Alouette nodded, swallowing down the lump in her throat at the mention of the sisters. She still wasn't used to hearing other people talk about them. It was strange. They'd been her own secret for so many years. And now they were no one's secret. "That's about the gist of it," she whispered, trying to keep her voice from cracking.

"Is that why your biometrics are not in the Communiqué?" Gabriel asked, sounding like he'd just pieced this together. "Because the Vangarde were somehow able to erase them?"

Alouette thought back to the arrest warrant with her image on it. The one that had said, "Unknown Female." She shrugged. "I guess so. I guess they erased them at the same time they removed my Skin. When I first came to live with them after the Renards."

Gabriel let out a low whistle. "Wow. So you left some of the most despicable people on the planet to go live with the most famous rebel group on the planet. No one can accuse you of having a boring life."

"Is that what they accuse you of?"

"Me?" He snorted. "Are you kidding? No one would *dare* accuse me of being boring."

"Ah right," Alouette said, leaning back on her hands. "You're the criminal mastermind."

"And don't you forget it."

"I don't think you'd let me."

Gabriel grinned, and Alouette could suddenly feel his eyes on her again, studying her face in the near darkness. She turned. "What?"

"Nothing. I just . . ." Gabriel shook his head. "I'm glad you got out of that place. The Renards were horrible people. I can't imagine how you might have turned out if you'd stayed." He kicked at a loose rock with his toe. "Probably like me."

"You're not so bad."

"Well, that's true. But if there's any justice in the universe, those Renards are rotting on Bastille right now."

Alouette thought about the last time she'd seen the Renards. It was in the Forest Verdure when they'd kidnapped Hugo, the only real father she'd ever known, and were holding him ransom for Inspecteur Limier.

"What about their daughters?" Alouette asked, remembering the girl who had chased her into the forest on the moto. "Chatine? And Azelle?"

"What about them?"

"Do you know what happened to them?"

"No. Last I saw of any of the Renards was when they boarded the bateau to Vallonay. I assume those two girls turned out as wretched and miserable as their parents."

Alouette tilted her head back and stared up at the stars. "I hope not."

"You like to see the good in people, don't you?"

"Is that bad?"

"No. It's not bad, it's . . ." But when Gabriel couldn't seem to find the right word, he just said, "You clearly didn't grow up how I did. After you hang out with enough scum, you start to see it everywhere."

Alouette thought longingly about the dim hallways of the Refuge and the floors she used to clean every day.

"Maybe," she pondered, "there's always something good and clean underneath? Maybe some people just have more layers to scrub away?"

Gabriel threw his head back and laughed. "You can honestly still say that? After living with the Renards? Those people treated you like garbage. Turned you into their own personal slave. And *still* had the nerve to complain that your mother didn't pay them enough to take you in."

Alouette's gaze snapped toward him. "Were you there at the Jondrette when they took me in? Did you see my mother?"

"No," said Gabriel apologetically. "You were already living with them when my father started working there. But I just remember Monsieur and Madame Renard constantly griping about what a burden you were. And how the fifteen hundred largs your mother paid them to take you in wasn't enough."

Fifteen hundred largs?

Wasn't that the exact amount the madame had said she'd given Lisole before she left town? As an advance on her next blood extractions?

"Do you remember them saying anything else about her?" Alouette asked.

Gabriel shook his head. "Sorry. I wish I could be more help."

Once more, Alouette felt the hope drain from her. She was starting to wonder if she would ever find out the truth about Lisole Villette.

"But it sounds like these women who raised you were almost like mothers to you, right?"

Alouette could feel the grief rolling back toward her. But this time, it felt less like a catastrophic wave and more like a gentle swell lapping at the sides of a bateau. Maybe she had been right. Maybe she would never be still again. Maybe those swells would always be there, rocking her, guiding her, sometimes choppy, sometimes calm, but always reminding her that the ground beneath her feet will never be as solid as she wants it to be.

"Yes," Alouette said softly. "They were the only mother figures I had." She reached into her pocket once more and squeezed her fingers around the beads.

"And pretty feisty mothers, if you ask me," Gabriel said, nudging her with his shoulder. "I mean, *my* maman never taught me how to fight like that."

Alouette chuckled softly. "It's kind of funny. I was so mad at them for not telling me their secrets. Their truth. But it turns out, all along, they were actually giving me everything I needed to know. Wisdom, knowledge, history, philosophy, even the strength and focus and skills to fight." She paused, staring up at the dark sky. "I think," she went on softly, almost to herself. "I think they were preparing me for something."

"For what?" Gabriel asked.

She ran her fingers along the surface of the beads, remembering Principale Francine's words to her that last night in the Refuge.

"You are more useful than you realize."

Alouette sighed. "I'm not quite sure yet."

Another quiet lull fell between them before Gabriel said, "Well, you'll definitely have to teach me that Tranquil whatever stuff someday. Looks like it would be a useful skill for a criminal mastermind to have."

Alouette turned and raised an eyebrow. "How about now?"

"What? Here?" He glanced skeptically around the darkened garden. "Why not?"

He wiped the surprise from his face and leapt to his feet. "Okay. Sure. Yes. Let's . . . *fight*." He kicked off his boots and darted out onto the grass, looking so much like the little boy who lingered hazily in her memories.

Alouette pulled her hand from her pocket, drawing out her long string of devotion beads. The metal tag swung back and forth, its surface glinting in the light of four Albion moons. She caught it in her hand and stared down at the engraving that had once brought her so much pride and then so much heartache.

LITTLE LARK.

She thought about the secret Vangarde network the Ministère had found. A tiny, invisible thread, connecting these beads to all the others. Her only link to the sisters—their Refuge, their books, their wisdom and knowledge—now severed and dead.

"We were always going to tell you, Little Lark. We've just been waiting. . . . Waiting for you to be ready."

Alouette ran her fingertips over the engraving, feeling all the memories that were wrapped up in those ten little letters.

Sister Jacqui scribbling on her chalkboard.

Sister Laurel tending to her herbs.

Sister Denise tinkering at her work bench.

Sister Muriel darning the tunics.

Principale Francine meticulously arranging and maintaining the Chronicles.

The women who had raised her. The women who had protected the First World knowledge. The women who had tried to save the world.

Alouette lifted the beads above her head and carefully strung them around her neck. A shiver passed through her as the weight settled on her shoulders. It was familiar and yet brand new at the same time.

The Vangarde may have been gone, but *she* was still here.

"You coming?" Gabriel asked, and Alouette peered into the darkness to see him bouncing lightly on his toes. His fists were raised in front of his face like he was going to block a punch.

Alouette chuckled softly and joined him on the grass. "First rule," she said, her expression turning as hard and steely as Principale Francine's. "You master your mind, your breath, and the meditation first. *Then* you can use the sequences to fight."

She grabbed on to his wrists and eased his arms down to his sides. "Close your eyes and take a long breath in."

Gabriel shot her a wary look. "Is this a trick? Is this when you punch me in the face? Because I'm not sure I can take another punch in the face."

"I promise not to punch you in the face."

Gabriel scrutinized her for a long moment before finally closing his eyes and drawing in a breath.

"Now a long breath out," Alouette instructed. "Good. Do that again. And this time really focus. Feel the breath coming, deep and strong, into your lungs. Yes. Now feel the air leave. Every molecule evaporating out of you."

Gabriel peeked one eye open. "When do we start, you know, fighting?" He comically kicked the air.

Alouette shook her head and held a finger to her lips. Gabriel grunted and shut his eyes again.

"The first sequence is called *Sols Ascending*," Alouette said. "Open your eyes and follow me." She bent deeply at the knees and raised her arms slowly and gracefully into the air, her palms facing up. Gabriel's face was taut with concentration as he attempted to imitate her.

"Good. Try to relax," she told him. "Keep your muscles loose and your mind strong. Let's try the second sequence. It's called *Ghostly Stars*."

Alouette took three fluid steps forward, circling her arms in an alternating pattern in front of her. She could feel the reassuring clink of her devotion beads as she moved.

Behind her, there was a soft scuffle and then, "Sols!"

Turning back, she saw Gabriel tripping awkwardly over his own feet as his hands tangled around each other. She tried not to laugh as she walked toward him. "Here, let's get the arm sequence down first, then we'll work on the steps."

She spun him around and stood behind him. "Relax," she said, guiding his arms. "Keep your shoulders away from your ears. Keep your gaze straight ahead. Move the left hand up first like you're waving at a friend, and now follow with your right. The same easy—"

"What are you doing?"

Alouette jumped at the sound of the voice coming from the back door of the house. She and Gabriel both turned at once to see Marcellus standing there, watching them with an unreadable expression.

Alouette's hands fell from Gabriel's shoulders. "We were just . . . I was teaching Gabriel how to fight."

"Okay, that might be a tad inaccurate," Gabriel said, flustered. "Obviously I *know* how to fight. She was just showing me—"

"I think you should both come inside."

"What happened?" Alouette asked, her stomach twisting at the gravity she could now hear in Marcellus's tone.

"The Red Scar have sent another message to the Ministère."

CHAPTER 44

MARCELLUS

AT FIRST, THE TÉLÉCOM SHOWED NOTHING BUT darkness. A darkness that seemed to penetrate deep into Marcellus's bones. Cerise, Alouette, and Gabriel were gathered around him in Dr. Collins's kitchen, their gazes fixed on the screen. No one had breathed since he'd pressed play on the footage.

Then the darkness was speared by a glowing beam of light that flashed and bobbed, cutting through the void.

In his audio patch, Marcellus could hear muffled footsteps. The creak of a door opening. A scrape of metal. All the while the beam of what had to be a flashlight continued to sweep and bounce across the screen.

"Droids are cleared," a breathless voice crackled and wheezed, like it was being transmitted from elsewhere through some kind of communication device.

"Copy that," another voice responded. This one was crisp and clear. And even with just those two words, Marcellus recognized the voice and a chill whispered down his spine.

Maximilienne.

The footsteps grew louder, more hurried, as the flashlight beam dipped and juddered violently. They were on the move. Running.

Whoosh. Whoosh. Whoosh.

The high-pitched sound of rayonette pulses pierced Marcellus's ears. Light arched across the screen, white and blinding, and then there was the unmistakable thud of bodies falling. The flashlight beam fell to the ground, and Marcellus heard Alouette suck in a breath beside him. The crumpled forms of three Policier sergents filled the screen, each with a smoking black hole in the center of their forehead.

Not paralyzed, Marcellus realized instantly.

The Red Scar had gotten ahold of rayonettes. And they had set them to kill.

"This way," Maximilienne whispered, and once again, they were on the move.

A few seconds later, the footsteps were replaced by a barrage of furious clanging and something that sounded like drilling, followed by the squeal and bang of a door being thrown open. The beam of light whizzed around before landing on something silver and gleaming that was sitting in the center of a small, bare room.

Marcellus's stomach twisted painfully as the flashlight landed on two slim pillars of PermaSteel.

"What in the name of the Sols is that?" Cerise gasped.

But no one responded.

Marcellus turned to Alouette. The grim, haunted look on her face told him that she knew. She also recognized it. She, too, remembered the screams. The smell. Nadette's brilliant hair glinting under the blue light of the laser.

The TéléCom screen flooded with light, revealing the jutting, angular contraption that Marcellus had prayed he'd never have to see again.

Maximilienne stepped in front of the newly built exécuteur, addressing her comrades in red. "We will not allow the Regime to kill any more innocent people like my sister with this cruel device," she said, her fierce eyes blazing beneath her hood. "Regimes who misuse their weapons must lose those weapons."

Then the screen went black.

Marcellus dropped the TéléCom onto the counter like it had burned him.

"Wait a minute," Gabriel said. "That was the Blade wasn't it?"

Marcellus nodded and glanced toward Alouette. Her eyes were brimming with apprehension.

"What . . . What do you think the Red Scar are planning to do with that?" Cerise asked.

"Hopefully destroy it," Marcellus muttered with a shiver. "Just like the last one. No one should ever be put under that thing."

For a long time, no one spoke. Marcellus stared numbly at the blackened screen, trying to wrap his mind around this latest Red Scar threat. And it *was* a threat, right? Or was Maximilienne simply taunting the Ministère? Demonstrating what they were capable of?

Then, suddenly, the TéléCom was no longer dark. It lit up as a man's face flashed onto the screen. Marcellus leaned in closer, confusion and fear ebbing through him. The face was familiar but he couldn't, for the life of him, figure out why it was currently flashing on his TéléCom.

"Incoming AirLink request pending from Jolras Epernay," the device announced through Marcellus's audio patch.

"Who is that?" Gabriel asked, squinting at the screen.

"It's Maximilienne's brother," Marcellus replied numbly, his eyes still locked on the TéléCom. "He's another member of the Red Scar."

Alouette's eyes widened. "Why is he contacting you?"

Marcellus shook his head. "I have no idea. But I'm pretty sure he recognized me back at the Jondrette."

Cerise snatched the TéléCom out from under Marcellus and promptly dismissed the AirLink.

"What are you doing?" Marcellus asked.

"I'm sorry," Cerise replied sarcastically. "Did you want to answer an AirLink from a known terrorist?"

The screen flashed again as a second request came through.

"Incoming AirLink request pending from Jolras Epernay."

Cerise went to dismiss it again, but Marcellus stopped her with a look. "Can I please have *my* TéléCom back?"

Reluctantly, Cerise handed it back. "Don't accept that."

"Why not?" Gabriel asked. "What if it's important?"

Cerise huffed. "Trust me, whatever that man wants, it can't be good. Don't accept it."

"I think you should find out what this mec has to say," Gabriel argued.

"Incoming AirLink request pending from Jolras Epernay."

Marcellus stared down at the screen, into the young man's mysterious pale eyes. What could a member of the Red Scar possibly want with him?

His fingertip hovered indecisively above the screen. Part of him was terrified to accept the AirLink, while the other part was just plain curious. He could feel everyone's eyes watching him.

"It's ready," Dr. Collins said, slicing through the thick tension in the air.

Everyone turned to see the scientist standing in the doorway of the kitchen, holding a sleek silver canister. Marcellus felt a rush of relief.

The inhibitor.

He'd become so distracted by all this commotion from the Red Scar, he'd momentarily lost sight of the reason they'd risked their lives to come to this planet.

"Incoming AirLink request pending—"

Marcellus plunged his fingertip onto the screen of the TéléCom, dismissing the request and silencing the voice in his head.

The scientist delicately unscrewed the lid of the silver canister, and a gust of frosty steam hissed into the air. Inside, a round barrel held twelve glowing vials. "There is one dose for each of the water treatment centers on Laterre and one extra, just in case. The serum is designed to self-propagate. Which means once it's in the water supply, it will reproduce on its own."

Marcellus looked down at the canister and then back at the silver-haired man in front of him, a lump of gratitude forming in his throat. "Your work is going to save many lives. Your daughter would be proud."

Dr. Collins flashed him a kind smile. "Thank you. Or as I believe you say, *merci*." He carefully resealed the canister and handed it to Marcellus. "Try to keep it level, and make sure it doesn't undergo any jolts or serious vibrations. The inhibitor has to be stored in glass because it's less porous, which means the vials are very fragile."

Marcellus hooked his arms tightly around the canister, feeling the massive weight of such a small container. "We'll take care of it."

"Good," said Dr. Collins. "Now for the tricky part. I've managed to track down your ship. It's been impounded and moved to a military hangar at the Queenstead spaceport. My security clearances are all still in effect, so I can get you to that hangar, but I suggest we leave at once. Dawn will be arriving soon, and it will be much easier to sneak you in while it's still dark."

Marcellus couldn't see any reason to stay on this planet a second longer. "Then let's go."

Less than ten minutes later, they were all back inside the aerocab as it pushed out of the docking shelter and lifted easily into the air. In the darkness, the twinkling lights of the small house, then the street, and then the town receded behind them. They soared up and over a vast quilt of shadowy fields and rolling hills.

Everyone was silent. Marcellus hugged the canister with the inhibitor to his chest, as though he were afraid one dip of the aerocab might destroy this fragile hope he was holding on to.

One week.

The general would have his weapon in one week. It would take them five days to travel back to Laterre, which meant they'd have only two days to distribute the inhibitor into all eleven water treatment centers. And that was if nothing went wrong.

Sweat began to form beneath the collar of his uniform. He didn't like their odds or their timeframe. But failure was out of the question. He could not allow the general to take control of the Third Estate. He could not allow him to turn them all into weapons. People like Gabriel and Chatine.

Chatine.

The thought of her made his chest ache. The thought of her turning into one of those men in the plastique cage, fighting to the death, made his heart fill with rage. And he still didn't know where she was. He'd searched her location on his TéléCom a thousand times on the voyageur flight here, and each time, he'd received the same frustrating response.

"Location unknown."

Marcellus hugged the canister tighter to his chest and gazed out the window at one of Albion's many glowing moons. Wherever Chatine was, he would not allow her to be turned into a weapon. He would not let her down again.

Soon, Marcellus could see the Queenstead spaceport looming up ahead. Yesterday, the skies around the port had been dotted with aerocabs. But now, at this predawn hour, only the lights from the domed terminal building glittered in the darkness. The rest of the complex, which spread out for kilomètres around the terminal, was a shadowy puzzle of flat-roofed buildings, launching pads, and huge spacecraft hangars.

"Here we go," Dr. Collins said as the aerocab descended and they approached the security entrance to the spaceport's military wing, where Marcellus could see two guards stationed in front.

"Should we duck or something?" Gabriel asked.

"No," said Dr. Collins sharply as he maneuvered the aerocab to a stop in front of the entrance. "It will only draw suspicion. Act like you belong."

Marcellus sat up straighter, trying to wipe the pure and utter terror from his face. Dr. Collins opened the window, slipped his monoglass over his eye, and stared into a glowing control panel affixed to the side of the guard station.

Then, time slowed down.

The edges of Marcellus's vision fuzzed.

Albion seemed to complete a full orbit around Sol 1 before the panel finally glowed green and, in a lilting accent, the guard said, "Welcome, Dr. Collins. Please proceed."

Dr. Collins gave a tight, professional nod and proclaimed, "Sols save the Queen," before pushing up the throttle and gliding the aerocab swiftly toward the shimmering hangar in the distance.

"Oh my Sols," Cerise whispered once the window had resealed. "My heart is pounding so hard."

"I know!" said Gabriel. "The guard glanced at me for a second, and I swore I was going to throw up."

Cerise chuckled. "That probably would have given us away."

Marcellus exhaled loudly and glanced over at Alouette. But instead of seeing a mirror of his own relief reflected in her eyes, he saw only apprehension. "Are you okay?"

She bit her lip and darted a nervous look at Dr. Collins. "I don't know. I just . . ." She hesitated. "Did anyone else feel like that was, maybe, *too* easy?"

"There's no such thing as *too* easy when you're breaking into an enemy spaceport," Cerise said.

"She's right." Gabriel flashed Alouette a wide grin. "Relax. Don't overthink it. Dr. Collins said they didn't suspect him of helping us, and it's as simple as that. Right, mec?"

They all turned to the scientist for confirmation, and it was only then Marcellus noticed that Dr. Collins's body had gone rigid and his gaze was anxiously darting over the monitors on his console.

"Is something wrong?" Marcellus asked just as a massive high-powered tracking beam cut through the darkness in front of them. He glanced out the window, where he could make out four ominous crafts in the dark sky, glimmering like knife blades cutting through the air.

"What are those?" Gabriel asked, all evidence of his former easiness vanished.

"Aerodrones," replied Dr. Collins in a grim voice.

"What the fric is an—"

Dr. Collins jabbed at a switch on the console and the aerocab lurched forward, boosting them into top speed as they soared toward the massive metal hangar in the distance. Marcellus grabbed on to the edges of the seat for balance.

"What's going on?" Cerise asked.

"It was a trap," said Dr. Collins, peering back at the crafts retreating behind them. "My security clearances were evidently only active because they hoped I'd lead you right to them." He wrenched down on the contrôleur and maneuvered the vehicle into a sharp turn just as a shower of bullets sprayed across the back window, shattering it. Gabriel and Cerise screamed and ducked onto the floor.

"Bloody hell." Dr. Collins jabbed at another switch on the console. A second later, every light inside and outside the vehicle extinguished, plunging them into darkness. "Aerodrones are unmanned crafts," he explained. "They rely on light and movement to improve their aim."

"Oh my Sols, we're going to die!" Gabriel shouted.

Cerise groaned. "Don't make me punch you again."

"Don't worry," Dr. Collins assured them, pushing harder on the throttle. "I am going to get you to that—"

There was a sudden cracking sound, and the vehicle started to spin out of control, whipping around in circles and flinging Marcellus right off his seat.

Then someone screamed.

He couldn't be sure who it was. Cerise, Alouette, maybe Gabriel. But when Marcellus was finally able to right himself and look back at the driver's seat, he suddenly understood.

Dr. Collins was slumped over the console, his head shoved up against the contrôleur. Blood leaked in a sickening river from his right temple.

Before Marcellus could react, another round of cluster bullets exploded around them. The window beside him shattered. Marcellus glanced out through the broken plastique to see the glinting aerodrones circling overhead, like vultures waiting for something to die.

Adrenaline charging through his veins, Marcellus pushed the canister into Alouette's hands and then shoved Dr. Collins off the console. He maneuvered himself into the driver's seat and took a quick inventory of the controls. They weren't entirely like his moto, but they were close enough. He grabbed onto the contrôleur and yanked the vehicle out of its spin.

Through the splintered windshield, Marcellus saw another cluster bullet whiz by, barely missing the front of the aerocab. He jammed his hand against the throttle, and they exploded forward toward the hangar.

Shots rained down around them, one finding its way through the ceiling. Cerise and Alouette both screamed and jumped as the cluster bullet wedged itself into the seat cushion directly between them.

"Zigzag! Zigzag!" Gabriel shouted in his ear. "It's the best way to avoid getting shot."

Marcellus did as he was told, pulling the contrôleur left, then right, then left again. He was certain he going to be sick, but it was working. The aerodrones kept missing. Concrete burst up from the ground, creating a dust cloud of confusion, but most important, concealment.

"There's the ship!" Cerise exclaimed, leaning forward to point through the broken windshield.

Marcellus squinted. Cerise was right. Through the gaping mouth of the hangar, he could just make out their voyageur with its sleek wings and distinctive silvery shell.

So close . . .

He evened out the contrôleur and thrust the throttle as far forward as it would go, his gaze bouncing between the hangar and the rearview monitor.

"Wait," he said, staring at the dark, empty screen. "Where did the aerodrones go?"

Just then, one of the menacing crafts descended from the sky in front of them, blocking their path. Two others swooped in on either side while the fourth descended from above, until they were completely boxed in and Marcellus had no choice but to ease up on the throttle and allow the aerocab to drift to a stop and sink back down to the ground.

He glanced at Cerise, Alouette, and Gabriel, who all shared the same defeated expression. Their voyageur was so close. Marcellus could see it through the cracked window, less than twenty mètres away.

"Stop in the name of the Queen!" someone shouted, "Or we will fire."

They all turned to the left to see a squadron of Albion Royal Guards barreling out of a nearby building and sprinting toward them, assault lancers clutched in their fists.

"What do we do now?" Alouette asked Marcellus.

But it was Gabriel who answered. "I think we have to run for it."

"What?" Cerise gaped at him. "Are you insane? Those Albion fur-heads will be on us before we can even shout *Vive Laterre*."

"The voyageur is right there! We can make it." Gabriel scrounged around in one of the interior compartments before pulling out a small metallic cartridge, identical to the one Marcellus had thrown yesterday at the security gate of the Royal Ministry of Defence. "This will help."

Marcellus peered back at the incoming guards. Their uniforms were like an encroaching sea of red.

The Laterrian color of death.

"He's right," said Marcellus. "We have to run. On three."

Alouette and Cerise nodded, fear glistening in their eyes.

"One . . ." Marcellus positioned his hand on the door release. "Two . . ." He sucked in a breath. "Three!"

He slammed down on the console. The doors sprang open. Gabriel tossed the capsule in the direction of the incoming guards, and they ran. The blinding gas exploded in a plume of green smoke. Marcellus kept his head down as he surged toward the ship. He could see Alouette keeping pace beside him, Dr. Collins's canister of inhibitor clutched under her arm. The guards opened fire, shooting through the billowing fog of green. Cluster bullets showered around Marcellus like crooked rain. For a second, he thought he heard the sickening sound of one impaling into flesh, but he must have imagined it, because they were all still running.

Cerise had her TéléCom out of her pocket and was jabbing at the screen, her fingers fumbling as her legs pumped beneath her. The voyageur's loading ramp unfurled, and they charged through the hatch.

"Close it! Close it!" Marcellus ordered.

Bullets pinged off the ship's PermaSteel shell until finally, the side of the voyageur sealed around them, locking them inside.

"Prepare for launch!" Cerise shouted.

Marcellus pounded up the steps to the flight bridge. He barely had time to fasten his restraints before the engines rumbled and the ship swept out of the hangar and launched upward, away from the spaceport. Marcellus glanced at the other flight seats, breathing out a sigh of relief to see Alouette and Cerise were both strapped in, bracing themselves against the force of the takeoff.

It wasn't until they had broken through the thick atmosphere and were surrounded by the vast curtain of stars that Marcellus noticed the fourth seat was empty.

CHAPTER 45

CHATINE

EVEN FROM HALFWAY ACROSS THE CAMP, THE NOISE was thunderous. Chatine had no idea what the Défecteurs were doing out there—what this mysterious "linking cérémonie" was—but they certainly weren't being quiet or discreet about it. With all that banging and hammering and clanging, she was surprised every Ministère officer and Policier sergent on the planet hadn't been summoned to this very spot. After all the effort these people went through to shield themselves from the Regime, the ruckus they were making out there seemed decidedly counterproductive.

Chatine had been hiding out in the treatment center since dinner. If there was one thing she was certain about, it was that she wanted nothing to do with any Défecteur cérémonie of any kind. Just the word "cérémonie" made her hackles rise and all of her former prejudices about these people come bubbling back to the surface.

Then, somewhere far in the distance, in amongst the pounding and clanking, a melodic chorus of voices rose up, crooning in unison.

And now they're singing. Fantastique.

She was *definitely* not going out there.

The clanking and banging continued for what felt like hours. It would halt only long enough for a large group of people to shout something and cheer or break into another song. Chatine pulled a pillow over her head to try to block out the noise. Which is probably why she didn't hear the chalet door sliding open and the footsteps approaching.

When she felt a tiny *tap tap tap* against her arm, she screamed and sat up, wielding the pillow as a weapon. It was only when her eyes focused, the panic subsided, and she saw little four-year-old Astra standing in front of her—dressed in her reflective, hooded coat, with two fingers jammed in her mouth—that Chatine realized how ridiculous her reaction was. She lowered the pillow.

"Did I scare you?" Astra asked around her fingers. The notion seemed to delight her.

"No," Chatine said, but quickly changed her answer to the truth. "Maybe a little. What are you doing here?"

Astra removed her fingers from her mouth and dried them on the sleeve of her coat. "I'm supposed to come get you and bring you to the cérémonie."

Chatine shook her head. "Actually, I think I'm just going to stay here. I don't feel very good."

"He said you would say that, and he said to tell you that it's a lie."

"He?" Chatine cocked an eyebrow. "Let me guess, did Etienne send you to fetch me?"

Astra popped her fingers back into her mouth and nodded. Her face looked pretty adorable peeking out from her puffy, silver hood. Chatine had no doubt this was all part of Etienne's plan. Send the cutest one of the bunch, who was almost impossible to say no to.

"Uh-huh," Chatine said warily. "And what other excuses did he say I would give you?"

Astra tilted her head, as though trying to remember. She removed her fingers from her mouth again so she could count on them. "Your leg hurts. You have a headache. You ate too much bread at dinner. You have mensly cramps—no, *men-sta-rally* cramps." She huffed in frustration. *"Men-stu—"*

"Okay." Chatine stopped her. "I get it. Fine. I'll come. But only for a few minutes."

Astra beamed triumphantly before scampering to the door and standing on her tiptoes to pull down Chatine's coat from the nearby hook.

"Merci," Chatine said, sliding her arms into the sleeves.

She followed the little girl out of the chalet and in the direction of the noise, which was still going full force. Although Chatine could walk without her crutches, she was still slow moving. But with the girl's tiny stride, they turned out to be well matched. The light was dim in the sky, the Sols setting somewhere above the covered walkways, beyond the clouds. As they walked, she could hear Astra quietly slurping on her fingers, despite the cold outside.

"Why do you do that?" Chatine asked, glancing over at her.

"What?" Astra garbled.

"Suck on your fingers like that?"

Astra shrugged and pulled her hand down. "Because they taste good."

Chatine smiled. She couldn't think of a better answer.

As they passed through a cluster of chalets, the banging and clamoring seemed to reach a peak. Then they turned a corner, and Chatine froze when she saw the spectacle in front of her.

Every single Défecteur in the camp was here, and every single one of them was in motion. Working, chattering, hammering, digging, and most of them singing as they did it. They were gathered around a patch of muddied ground that had been dug into a neat square and bore a partially built metal frame. Men and women were carrying buckets of earth away from the site, while others shared the weight of long beams that were carried in and bolted into place. Some of the older children were hard at work too, digging and sifting over the ground, removing pebbles and stones from the site.

Chatine wasn't quite sure what she'd been expecting, but she knew it wasn't this. She stood frozen on the walkway, taking it all in. She was certain her mouth must have been hanging open, because she could feel a gust of cold air rush to the back of her throat.

"Don't just stand there like a sot, come on." Astra grabbed her hand and pulled her closer to the construction zone.

"What are they doing?" Chatine whispered, although she wasn't sure why. There was no way anyone else would be able to hear her over all this noise.

"They're building a new chalet!" Astra explained with great pride and enthusiasm. "For Saros and Castor."

"Who?" Chatine asked.

"Saros and Castor." Astra pointed to two men sitting on the sidelines of the construction zone. They were holding metal cups full of some steaming hot liquid and singing at the top of their lungs. Chatine watched, mesmerized, as one turned toward the other and they shared a long, passionate kiss.

"They're getting linked," Astra explained.

Chatine glanced between the half-finished chalet and the two men, trying to piece this all together in her mind. "So, the whole camp is building them a chalet?"

"Of course," Astra said, as though this were the most obvious conclusion to the chaos that ensued around them. "Whenever two people get linked, everyone helps build their chalet. Except Saros and Castor, obviously, since it's a gift for them. And us, little kids. We have to watch until we're old enough to help. But this time, I get to put on the connecteur at the end!"

"But *why*?" As soon as the question was out of her mouth, she realized how ignorant and stupid it sounded, yet it was the only question that seemed to come to her mind.

"So they have somewhere to live," Astra said. "Come over here. You can sit with me and watch."

Numbly, Chatine allowed Astra to guide her to a small area set up on the sidelines of the construction zone where the rest of the young children were gathered. But they weren't sitting in the chairs that had been set out. They were all on their feet singing and laughing and some even danced with each other. Chatine not only felt out of place in this festive energy, she felt like she'd crash-landed on the wrong planet.

Astra climbed into one of the chairs, and Chatine took the seat next to her. All Chatine could do was stare in wonderment at the new chalet rising up in front of her very eyes. Despite the chaotic noise, the whole operation looked surprisingly organized. And just like Astra had said, everyone seemed to have a job. Chatine had never witnessed anything so . . . She struggled to even think of the right word.

Collaborative.

Among the crew of hardworking men and women, Chatine spotted Etienne soldering a complicated corner joint onto the chalet's frame. He caught her eye, smirked, and then looked at Astra beside her and mouthed the words, "Good job." Astra giggled.

Chatine felt heat rise up inside of her. She didn't like being colluded against, and she definitely didn't like losing. She was about to get right back up and return to the treatment center—she'd come, she'd seen, she'd participated—but just then, a young woman came rushing up to her with a squirming baby in her hands and deposited the infant right into Chatine's lap.

"Oh, thank the Sols, you're here," the woman said hurriedly, "I have to work on the roof, and wiggly little Mercure here wiggled right out of his sling."

Chatine opened her mouth to protest, but the woman was already gone.

And now there was a baby on her lap.

A *baby.*

A baby that was heavy and drooling and definitely not hers. She hoisted it out in front of her like it was a batch of rotten eggs she didn't want to get too close to for fear of the smell.

The baby—Mercure—was dressed in a shimmering silver, one-piece outfit that seemed to be made of the same material as Chatine's coat. A single dark curl sprang out from underneath his puffy hood. Chatine stared at the infant, shocked and incredulous. He stared back, looking equally shocked and incredulous, his huge dark eyes open wide.

Then he began to cry.

No, not just cry. *Wail.* A piercing, shrieking, earsplitting wail. The sound—Chatine was certain—was louder than the construction noise. An impressive feat for something so tiny.

"What is happening?" Chatine asked to no one in particular. She still held the child at arm's length as it howled and squirmed in her hands.

"Make him stop crying," Astra replied, as though this were the easiest, simplest feat in the world and why hadn't Chatine thought of it?

"What?" Chatine shouted over the noise. "I don't know how to do that. This is not my baby!"

"So?"

"So?" Chatine repeated, frustrated. "Why would that woman just dump a baby on me that's not mine? And then expect me to shut it up?"

Astra gave Chatine a very strange look. As though Chatine were speaking with words too complex for her little four-year-old brain to comprehend. "Babies are everyone's," Astra finally said.

"No, they're not."

"Yes, they are."

Chatine huffed. "No, they're not!" she shouted, which only made the baby startle and then scream louder. Chatine didn't even realize that was possible. How many more levels did this thing have?

All the small children had stopped dancing and singing, and were now just standing there, staring at her.

"Why are you holding him like that?" one of the boys asked. It was Perseus.

"How am I supposed to hold him?" Chatine fired back.

"Not like *that*," Perseus replied unhelpfully. "Don't you know how to hold a baby?"

No, Chatine thought. She did not hold babies. She did not associate with babies. *Not anymore.*

Gruffly, she stood up, keeping the crying infant extended out in front of her as she scanned the construction site for the child's mother. She spotted her high up on the chalet frame, affixing a rafter for the flat roof. Chatine sighed and searched for another capable-looking adult or older child, but they were all occupied in the building of the chalet. With the frame now almost complete, people were busy bolting together sheets of metal to make the walls, and the older kids were laying down big interlocking tiles for the floors. In desperation, Chatine turned toward the couple seated off to the side, but they had gone back to kissing.

Chatine glared at Mercure. Her ears were starting to burn from his earsplitting wail. "Um, excuse me," she said to him, trying to keep the frustration from her voice. "Can you please be quiet now?"

The baby just continued to cry, his face now twisted and angry, tears streaming down his cheeks while his little chest puffed from the effort.

"Look," Chatine said reasonably. "You're obviously upset. I get that. So why not just stop crying and we can all stop being upset. Doesn't that sound like a good solution?"

More tears as Mercure began to wriggle and squirm.

"Yeah, I don't like this situation any more than you do," Chatine said, glancing around the construction zone. "I'm trying to find someone who can—"

Mercure gave an angry, tearful wrench and slipped right through Chatine's hands. The baby fell. Chatine gasped and lunged, her arms outstretched. Her injured leg made a disturbing *ripping* sound, but she barely heard or felt anything except the infant's tiny body landing in her arms, just centimètres before striking the ground.

Shaken and breathless, Chatine clutched the infant to her chest and held it tightly as she slowly maneuvered herself back down into the chair. "Sols," she whispered into the baby's ear. "That was very stupid of you. Don't do that again."

And that's when she smelled it.

It wasn't the scent of rotten eggs.

It wasn't the scent of rotten anything.

It was sweet and warm and soothing. Like freshly baked bread. Like the nine-year-old memory of Sol-light on her face.

"Like Henri," said a quiet voice in her head.

Chatine shut her eyes and welcomed the voice back with open arms.

It had felt like forever since Azelle had spoken to her and Chatine had feared that she'd left her back on Bastille.

Yes, Chatine whispered back into her mind. *Like Henri.*

And just like that, she was past the fence. She was inside the danger zone. She was living in it as though it were right now. As though it had never ended. As though it had never become a place of danger to begin with.

For a few blissful seconds, she was back inside a time when *he* was the safe place.

I miss him, Chatine told Azelle. *I miss our little brother.*

"I know," Azelle whispered.

A lump formed in Chatine's throat as she searched for the courage to say the words that had been clinging to the back corners of her brain ever since she'd received the alert about the explosif that had taken Azelle's life. Words that had seemed to grow stale and soggy, like chou bread left out too long in the rain. But words that she knew she still needed to say.

And I miss you, Azelle. Every day. More than I ever thought I would.

Azelle made no reply. But Chatine could swear she felt her sister smile.

She brought her face closer to the baby's cheek and breathed in his beautiful, fresh scent. Her arms instinctively tightened around him, and she began to sway back and forth. As though she had no control. Her body moved separately from her mind. The memory took over.

And soon, she was whispering into his ear. "There are three Sols in the sky. Yes, three! Sol 1 is the white one, Sol 2 is the red one, and Sol 3 is the blue one. Aren't we lucky to live under so many stars?"

Tears blurred her vision. Her heart heaved. But when she squeezed her eyes shut tighter, bracing herself against the pain, she felt only light and weightlessness. Like a voyageur breaking through the clouds.

She buried her face in the side of the baby's hood, keeping her lips close to his ear. "When we're big," she went on, "we can go up there." Her voice was cracking. But it seemed like every other part of her was coming back together. Fusing like broken bones. Melding like healed skin. "We can zoom off in a big space voyageur, and we can see all the stars really close. Would you like that? Would you like to see the stars?"

Her cheeks were wet with tears now. They were flowing like water from a busted pipe. Pooling at the bottom of her chin. She shuddered and pulled the baby's tiny body closer, drawing strength from his scent, determination from his warmth, and courage from his innocence.

And there she fell into a deep, peaceful trance. She didn't know how long it had lasted. She hadn't even realized the baby had stopped crying. When Chatine lifted her head, she saw his tiny eyelids were closed, his eyelashes clumped and wet with tears. His breathing was now soft and even. All of his former anger and resentment having faded into dreams.

Only then did Chatine notice that all the children had gone back to dancing. Even Astra had joined them. The workers continued. The chalet rose before her like a feat of impossible hope. And Chatine was all alone. With a sleeping baby in her arms and a dead monster lying at her feet.

- CHAPTER 46 -
ALOUETTE

"GABRIEL!" CERISE WAS ALREADY UNBUCKLING HER
restraints and jumping to her feet before Alouette had even finished
processing the empty seat next to them.

They left him behind?

No. They couldn't have. Her mind scrambled to piece together the
pandemonium of the last five minutes. She'd seen him on the tarmac
when they were running to the ship. She swore she had. He had been
right next to her. But had she actually seen him *board* the ship?

Her stomach seized.

It had been too chaotic. First the aerodrones, then Dr. Collins getting
shot, then the guards firing at them. It had been impossible to make sense
of anything. She'd been so focused on getting to the ship, getting *on* the
ship and getting as far away from that planet as possible, she hadn't even
noticed Gabriel was . . .

The breath hitched in her chest.

They left him behind.

She heard voices around the ship, calling his name. Searching for
him. "Gabriel?"

Hands trembling, Alouette fumbled with the buckle of her restraints until the latch popped open. She set Dr. Collins's canister down on the seat, and then she was running. Darting from room to room. The galley. The sleeping couchettes. The—

"Oh my Sols, Gabriel!" Cerise's voice howled from the cargo hold.

Alouette hammered down the steps, but her feet skidded to a halt as she took in the scene in front of her, her mind struggling to make sense of it.

Blood. So much blood. Rivers of blood. Leading to . . .

A body. Lying on its side. Curled in on itself, as though trying—and failing—to keep all that blood inside. Cerise was already on the ground, assessing the situation, her hands and clothes stained red.

"He's been shot!" she cried. "I didn't even know. He just kept running. But he . . ." her voice trailed off as shudders overtook her. Tears swallowed her words. Gabriel's body started to tremble.

A cacophony of voices clamored for attention in Alouette's head.

"Stay calm. Panic will only cloud your judgment—"

"Staunch the flow—"

"You are strong, Little Lark—"

"Apply pressure—"

"You are ready, Alouette—"

It was the sisters. They were all speaking to her at once. She clutched her temples in an attempt to drown them all out and focus only on what was important right now.

Sister Laurel. Her wellness lessons. Alouette had never learned how to deal with a situation like this. They didn't have cluster bullets on Laterre. But the principles of any open wound had to be the same, right? Yes, it was just like when she'd helped Marcellus in the Frets that day they'd met. She needed to stop the bleeding.

Snapping out of her trance, she lunged toward Gabriel and fell to her knees beside him. She ran her fingers up and down the length of his back. The skin was intact. Which meant the cluster bullet was still inside of him.

"We need to flip him over so I can see the wound." Alouette was surprised by the calmness of her own voice. Her heart was pounding wildly in her chest, but her thoughts were clear and focused.

Cerise scooted back, making room, and together the two managed to gently roll Gabriel onto his back. Cerise let out a gasp that echoed the horror flashing through Alouette's mind. In the center of Gabriel's stomach, just below his rib cage, was a jagged, open gash, roughly the size of Alouette's thumb.

Blood was still spilling out of it, soaking his clothes and the floor. Alouette pressed down, trying to cover it with her hands. But it wasn't enough pressure. She needed more weight. Rocking back into her heels, she rearranged herself so that she could press one knee into Gabriel's abdomen. He groaned in response, his eyelids fluttering.

"Are you sure you should be doing that?" Cerise looked on, aghast.

"Yes."

Just then, Marcellus barreled down the stairs and stopped when he saw the carnage. His eyes grew wide. "W-w-what happened?"

"He's been shot," Alouette said matter-of-factly. "He's losing a lot of blood. There's probably a med kit in the infirmerie. Can you go look?"

Marcellus nodded numbly and disappeared back up the steps.

Gabriel let out a soft moan, drifting in and out of consciousness. Cerise started to sob into her hands.

Marcellus returned less than two minutes later, carrying a small leather box which he handed to Alouette. "Bad news," he said breathlessly. "The scans in the flight bridge are showing three warships within range."

Cerise instantly stopped crying. "The Albion Royal Space Fleet?"

Marcellus nodded. "Lady Alexander must have alerted them. If we don't do something to conceal ourselves, we're going to be surrounded by micro-fighters before we're ever able to accelerate to supervoyage."

"Fric! Fric! Fric!" Cerise swore.

Keeping her knee pressed firmly on the wound, Alouette tore open the med kit and riffled around. The supplies were slim, but she found some gauze, which she immediately pushed onto Gabriel's wound.

"Can you do something?" Marcellus asked Cerise.

Cerise looked up at him, her tearstained face splotchy and hopeless. "What can I possibly do? They've already overridden my cloaking code. I don't know what else to—"

"What about the moons?" Alouette said, peering up from her position beside Gabriel. "What's the closest one to the ship?"

"What?" Cerise asked, confused, but then a second later, her eyes lit up with comprehension. "A moon is big enough to shield us from their scans!" She wiped her cheeks, looking relieved to have something else to do besides stand there and watch Gabriel bleed. "I'm on it!" she called, bounding back up the steps to the bridge.

Alouette pressed more gauze into Gabriel's stomach. He moaned and murmured something unintelligible.

"Shhh," Alouette told him. "Be still. Don't try to talk."

She brushed a strand of hair from his forehead. It was tangled and damp with sweat, but in that moment, he looked just like the young boy she remembered from the inn. Vague and disjointed visions of him flickered through her mind: Gabriel smiling at her from behind a bubbling pot of stew. Gabriel offering to carry one of her heavy pails from the boglands. Gabriel snatching a scrap of bread from the table while Madame Renard's back was turned.

"Is he going to be okay?" Marcellus asked in a shattered whisper.

But Alouette didn't respond right away. The hastily made dressing on Gabriel's wound was already soaking through. She pulled more gauze out of the med kit and pressed it down.

"Cluster bullets are very lethal," she said evenly. "Once inside the body, they disintegrate and shoot off tiny pieces of shrapnel in all directions, ripping holes in delicate organs, veins, and lungs." She fought to keep her voice from breaking. She fought to channel Sister Laurel, who would not cry nor break down in the face of an injury like this. Because she knew it would hinder her ability to do her job. She had to stay calm. In control. Even though she felt like she had a cluster bullet lodged inside of her, too.

"How do you know this?" Marcellus asked.

"From the Chronicles. There was an entire volume about Albion. It was never my favorite because I always thought, *When would I ever need to know this?*" Alouette let out a breath. "If only I knew."

"Can you help him?" Marcellus asked, his eyes glassy.

"He needs surgery," she said quietly. "If the shrapnel is not removed with the right equipment, it will eventually become infected and will poison Gabriel from the inside."

Marcellus stood there, speechless and terrified. In his eyes, Alouette saw the desperation. The pleading. *Please, fix this. Find a way to fix this.* "Where are we going to get this equipment? We can't take him to a med center. He's wanted by the Ministère."

Alouette darted her eyes back to Gabriel's face. It was wan and drawn, as if every gramme of blood had seeped away.

She inhaled a long breath. "The Refuge. I can take him there while you and Cerise get the inhibitor into the water treatment centers."

"But the Vangarde are . . ." Marcellus's voice trailed off, and his gaze dropped to the ground, as though he was afraid to continue, as though he felt the need to protect Alouette from any reminder of the truth. But Alouette no longer needed protecting.

"I know," she said quietly, gazing up at Marcellus. "The Vangarde are gone. The Refuge is empty." She took a deep breath, steeling herself. "Which means I will have to find what I need from Sister Laurel's journals and perform the procedure myself."

- CHAPTER 47 -
CHATINE

"UP YOU GO!" ETIENNE SAID, HOISTING ASTRA ONTO his shoulder. Astra's face beamed with pride as she clipped a small piece of looped metal between the ends of two long cables, connecting the newly built chalet with its closest neighbor.

Instantly, the building glowed to life as the power channeled from the rest of the camp into the new dwelling, illuminating it from the inside.

Linked, Chatine thought with a smile.

Everyone cheered. Chatine stared at the spectacle in awe, marveling at how fast the construction had been completed. A single afternoon and a whole community working together, and suddenly these two people had a house. A home. And it was a thousand times nicer than any Third Estate dwelling.

As Chatine watched the newly linked couple—Saros and Castor—walk into their chalet for the first time, hands clasped and faces beaming, she felt a strange stirring inside of her that she couldn't identify. It was warm and sweet. Like the hot chocolat the Défecteurs had been passing around in metal cups.

But it wasn't just *their* faces that thawed Chatine from the inside. It was the faces of everyone here. All the people who had helped create this structure. They were beaming almost as much as the couple they had gifted it to.

Chatine tried to remember the last time she'd ever built something with her own hands. She'd fixed a leaky roof in her family's old couchette once, but that didn't count. And her face certainly hadn't looked like *that* afterward. She hadn't glowed with pride the way everyone around her was doing right now. Would she have felt that if she'd ever shown up for her job at the textile fabrique? Would she have glowed with pride over a sheet of fabric she'd woven for the Matrone's curtains? Or a fancy tablecloth for some Second Estate manoir?

No. Definitely not.

The difference, Chatine immediately realized, was that these people had built this structure for them. Not for anyone else. They weren't assigned to do it. An alert didn't go off on a device implanted in their arms, telling them it was time to work. They worked because they wanted to. Because they enjoyed it. Because the result made them glow.

Saros and Castor emerged from their newly built chalet. The crowd cheered, and then the entire camp broke out in pandemonium.

Handmade instruments suddenly appeared. Music erupted. More hot chocolat was poured. And then a fire was built in a small pit in the center of the festivities. Chatine gazed into the flames, transfixed. Fire-making had been prohibited on Laterre ever since the first ancestors had arrived. It was a skill she thought time had forgotten. But clearly not here. Not among these people. She watched on as the fire grew bigger, until eventually the curling flames licked and batted at the cold air. The warmth and glow felt like a small Sol had fallen from the sky and landed right here, in the middle of the frozen Terrain Perdu.

Suddenly, everyone was on their feet. There was so much dancing. Men, women, children. Even little baby Mercure—who, up until a few minutes ago, had been asleep on Chatine's lap—woke up and joined in on the festivities. His mother placed him back in his sling, and Chatine smiled as the woman spun and shimmied her way through the crowd, causing the baby to laugh and shriek.

It's a fête, Chatine soon realized. But she'd certainly never seen anything like it before. Not that she'd witnessed a lot of fêtes in her life. Sure, there were the First Estate fêtes that the Paresse family held at the Grand Palais and broadcasted to the rest of Laterre—like the annual Ascension banquet and the elaborate birthday celebrations of the Matrone. But those always felt so formal and pretentious and decidedly *not* fun. Chatine would have rather poked her eyes out with an exploit pick than attend one of those. But this fête was different. These people—these strange Défecteurs who lived so far away from the rest of the planet, who hid from the Regime by stealing their own resources—they knew how to celebrate.

They all looked to be having so much fun, Chatine *actually*, for one sliver of a second, wished that she could join. That her stupide leg wasn't still healing from that stupide Ministère explosif. But then her gaze landed on Etienne, jumping up and down and waving his arms like an idiot, and the moment passed quickly. Chatine was perfectly content to just sit by the warm fire and watch.

The music came to a halt a few minutes later, and Saros and Castor stepped up onto one of the ladders, and announced, "Okay, everyone! It's time for the connecteur scramble!"

The crowd cheered and Etienne was suddenly in front of Chatine, his breathing ragged from all the dancing, his forehead damp with sweat despite the chill in the air. "Come on!" he urged, reaching out a hand to help her to her feet. "Get up!"

Warily, Chatine stared at his outstretched hand. "Why?"

"Didn't you hear? It's the connecteur scramble."

"Yeah, I don't know what that is."

Etienne rolled his eyes. "It's only the best part of a linking cérémonie!"

"Still don't know what it is."

Etienne leaned forward, clasped onto Chatine's elbow, and dragged her to her feet. She hobbled slightly as she tried to balance on her good leg.

"Just trust me," he said, guiding her around the roaring fire. "You don't want to miss this."

Etienne led her toward the ladder where the couple was still standing.

Clasped in their hands was a small piece of looped metal, just like the one Astra had used earlier to connect the new chalet with the rest of the camp. In front of the couple, a large crowd had gathered. People were playfully jabbing each other with elbows, jostling for space. They all wore eager, determined expressions.

"What exactly am I supposed to do?" Chatine asked Etienne.

"Easy," he explained, as he pushed his way through the crowd and positioned Chatine near the front. "Just catch the connecteur."

"And why would I want to do that?"

"Because it's what you do. And it's fun." He reached out and pulled off her mittens, then removed his own and stuffed them all into the pocket of his coat. "Plus, legend has it, whoever catches the connecteur at a linking cérémonie will . . ." He stopped, looking pensive.

Chatine narrowed her eyes. "Will what?"

"Will have good luck for the rest of the year."

"Yeah, right."

"It's true! It's ancient *Défecteur* legend." He winked at her and then lowered his voice, sounding eerily like a droid. "The Sols shall shine and good fortune shall be bestowed on whoever shall catch the mighty connecteur."

Chatine snorted. "In case you hadn't noticed"—she pointed at her left leg—"I'm not exactly in any condition to be running after flying scraps of metal right now."

Etienne scoffed. "Oh, please. Three days ago, you were about to cross the Terrain Perdu on that leg, so stop with the excuses."

"Is everyone ready?" someone shouted. Chatine looked up to see that Castor was now waving the connecteur above his head.

The crowd around Chatine whooped and hollered.

"Are you sure?" Saros egged them on.

More cheering as people continued to jockey for position. Chatine was shoved from all directions.

"Nope, definitely not doing this." Chatine tried to remove herself from the group, but Etienne reached for her bare hand, stopping her.

"Wait." His fingers wrapped around hers, and she was overcome with a sudden flash of warmth. She looked down. As though she had to see it with her own eyes. See his hand covering hers. Covering the spot where Marcellus's ring used to be. Like he *knew*.

When she looked up again, Etienne had moved closer. His piercing, dark eyes locked onto hers. "I'll make you a deal," he said quietly, earnestly. "If you catch that connecteur, I will give you . . ." He paused, as though trying to give her anticipation time to build.

It worked. Something passed through her knees. It felt a lot like wooziness.

". . . all of my toast at breakfast for the next two months," Etienne finished.

Laughter erupted from her. She couldn't help herself. It was jittering and anxious, but it still worked to chase away the strange sensation that had taken her over just a moment ago.

"How about this?" Chatine countered, allowing her lips to curve into an all-too-familiar smirk. If there was anything that could make her feel like herself again, it was negotiating. "If I catch the connecteur, you will give me . . ."

She mirrored his pause. He leaned forward, rapt and waiting.

". . . flying lessons," she finished. "On Marilyn."

Now it was Etienne who laughed. Loud and boisterous and explosive. "No. No way. Nuh-uh. Never gonna happen. Not even if the Darkest Night miraculously ended tonight and the Blue Dawn came tomorrow. Not in a million *trillion* Blue Dawns. Not even in a million trillion *White Nights.* NEVER."

"Fine," Chatine said smugly as she turned again to leave. But Etienne was still holding on to her hand. She was suddenly acutely aware of how close he was. Not just because of his breath warming her face, but because she could feel him there. His presence was somehow both quiet and loud. Both infinitely massive and impossibly small. As though he was nowhere and everywhere at the same time.

"On the count of three!" Castor called out, the connecteur poised above his head. "One . . ."

Chatine tried to pull her hand free. Etienne squeezed it tighter.

"Two . . . ," said Saros from the ladder, grabbing on to the other end of the connecteur.

Chatine looked over at Etienne, who was staring right back at her, a mischievous look playing in his eyes. Like he knew something she didn't.

"Three!"

The couple cocked back their hands simultaneously and tossed the connecteur up into the air. In one swift motion, Etienne pulled Chatine toward him. The small piece of metal arced over the assembled crowd and headed straight toward Chatine. Etienne's hands wrapped around her waist, and suddenly she was flying too. Her feet left the ground. She was as weightless as she was in space. There was no time to think. No time to negotiate. The connecteur was within reach. She could see it. She extended her right arm out, past all the other hands reaching around her. Her fingertips stretched, her body lengthened. But the connecteur was curving the wrong way. It was curving away from her. She wasn't going to catch it. It was going to just barely graze her fingertips. Then she heard a grunt as Etienne hinged forward, pushing her closer, his arms shaking beneath her.

"You got it! You got it!" he shouted.

And he was right.

The looped piece of metal hit her palm, and she closed her fist triumphantly around it. But just as soon as she'd snagged the victory, she felt herself falling. Etienne was stumbling beneath her. They were both going down.

She felt a pair of hands land on her left arm. Then another on her right shoulder. The crowd had surrounded them, stabilizing them both. Chatine felt her feet land safely on the ground and she turned to look at Etienne, who was breathless and beaming.

He nodded toward the connecteur, and she lifted it high above her head. Everyone cheered and applauded. Chatine couldn't help the smile that spread across her face.

"And we have a victor!" Saros shouted. "Thanks to the (questionably legal) help of Etienne, Chatine has captured the connecteur! Congratulations on your future linking."

WHAT?

Chatine's gaze shot up the ladder toward Saros, who winked knowingly at her. She turned and skewered Etienne with her eyes. "What is he talking about?"

Etienne opened his mouth to speak, but it was Astra who answered. She suddenly appeared next to Chatine with a huge grin on her face. "Whoever catches the connecteur is the next one to get linked!"

Chatine peered up at Etienne, her face still twisted with confusion. Etienne grinned sheepishly back at her. "Did I forget to mention that part?"

She raised the connecteur, ready to toss it at Etienne's head. Etienne held up his hands to defend himself. But Chatine was stopped by a commotion at the back of the fête. There were voices, followed by a few shrieks. Chatine froze, her pulse spiking as her thoughts immediately went to the worst possible scenario.

Policier.

Ministère.

Roundups.

She lowered the connecteur and turned to Etienne for an explanation, but he looked just as confused—and concerned—as she did.

Then she heard a squeal of joy from below, and Chatine glanced down to see Astra taking off in the direction of the commotion.

"Astra! Wait!" Chatine called out, but the little girl was already too far away to stop.

"It's Fabian and Gen!" Astra shouted with glee. "They're back!"

Chatine stood on tiptoes to try to see through the crowd that had begun to migrate in the direction of the commotion. Relief streamed through her when she saw that she was not surrounded by expressions of dread, but rather expressions of delight.

"C'mon," Etienne said, taking her hand once again. "You finally get to meet our other gridders." As he guided her through the crowd, Chatine could just make out two people crouched down, their bodies covered with children who were all scrambling to get close to them. Chatine couldn't even see their faces.

"Did you find your children?" a small voice called out.

"Why did you take so long?" said another.

"We have a new gridder!" a third voice informed them. This one, Chatine recognized as Astra, who had squirmed her way through the crowd and now had her arms wrapped around a slender man's neck. His face was still obscured by the throng of children. "Her name is Chatine!" Astra went on elatedly, "And she's from Vallonay too!"

"Chatine?" replied a voice with a curious ring. "Well, isn't that a lovely name. Don't you think that's a lovely name, my dear Gen?"

In that instant, at the sound of that voice, Chatine's entire body froze. She was as cold as the coldest, loneliest night in the Terrain Perdu. She was made of nothing but ice and bones and fear.

Then the other voice spoke. "A very lovely name, Fabian. She must be a very lovely girl."

"Oh, she is!" Astra replied giddily, oblivious to the frost in the air. The tense, pulsing energy that seemed to spread through the entire camp, rendering Chatine immobile. Speechless. Useless.

The crowd finally parted, and Chatine stared numbly at the two people who had managed to seduce this entire camp. The two people whose reputations among the Défecteurs had reached the status of legendary. The two people she prayed she'd never have to see again.

Their appearances were modified slightly. They'd changed their hair and clothes. She looked slimmer and he looked slightly heavier. And they were both considerably cleaner. But it was the eyes that gave them away. They still twinkled with that same wickedness—that same wretchedness—that Chatine had known her entire life.

These were the people Chatine had spent the past ten years trying to escape. The people who had beaten her and stolen from her and used her over and over again.

These were the people who had sold off her little brother to pay a debt.

These were her parents.

The connecteur slipped from her grasp and clattered to the ground.

CHAPTER 48

ALOUETTE

OUTSIDE THE PORTHOLE WINDOW, THE MOON OF Adalisa glowed, vast and bright and blue. Its giant craters were obscured by a constant cycle of lunar dust storms, making its surface look strangely distorted and out of focus. And right now, that's pretty much how everything felt to Alouette. The whole universe was out of alignment. Nothing felt right anymore. Everything felt off-kilter, off balance, like one stiff breeze could knock it all down. The Sols, the stars, every planet and every moon.

Cerise had maneuvered the voyageur into Adalisa's orbit, and they were now cowering behind the gigantic blue moon like the fugitives they were. She'd also sent out a series of microprobes as scouts, and the latest update reported that three more warships from the Albion Royal Space Fleet had joined the hunt. There were now half a dozen deadly crafts scouring the skies, searching for them. While back on Laterre, the general—who had undoubtedly learned of their escape by now—was certainly preparing his own ships to intercept them if they dared try to reenter Laterrian airspace.

In short, they were trapped.

And every minute that passed, every minute spent hiding behind this moon, brought Gabriel closer to death and the weapon closer to the general's hands.

Alouette tore her gaze from the window and focused on Gabriel. He'd been asleep for a few hours now. His chest was rising and falling so peacefully, if it weren't for the swatch of bandages on his stomach, it would be impossible to tell he was even injured. His face was calm, his expression serene.

Once Alouette had gotten the bleeding under control, they'd managed to move him here, to the infirmerie, where Alouette had found an assortment of rudimentary supplies. Nothing even close to what was required to perform any complex medical procedures. Apparently, whoever equipped this ship never anticipated its passengers getting shot by Albion guards. But Alouette had quickly managed to locate biosutures, bandages, and some médicaments which were, at least, helping Gabriel rest and keeping the infection at bay. But she knew they wouldn't heal him. Everything she'd done to help him was just a temporary solution. If they couldn't get him back to the Refuge . . .

No. She wouldn't even let her thoughts go there.

Frustrated and fidgety, Alouette stood up and walked over to the monitor on the wall. She activated the microcams in the infirmerie, so she could see and hear Gabriel in case he woke up. Then she slipped through the door of the small cabin and navigated her way up to the flight bridge. It was dark apart from the flickering lights of the flight console, the blue glow of Adalisa through the curved windows, and the hologram flight map that still hovered above its pedestal in the center of the room. Her eyes skimmed across the twelve planets of the System Divine before finally settling on the ice-white sphere of Reichenstat.

For the first time in weeks, Alouette was glad that Hugo Taureau, the only father she'd ever known, had left. She was relieved he wouldn't be on Laterre to witness everything that was about to happen.

She extended her hand toward the planet, until the tip of her index finger was submerged in the brilliant, bright light of the hologram.

I hope you're okay, she whispered into the silence of her mind.

"Sols!" shouted a far-off voice, followed by a loud *crash.*

Startled, Alouette snapped her gaze to the viewing lounge, just off the bridge. The room appeared to be empty. But a moment later, she heard a *bang,* and then another slew of curse words. Curious, she followed the noise until she reached the ship's small galley and pulled to a halt in the doorway.

Every cupboard and drawer had been opened. There were dishes, utensils, and boxes of food scattered everywhere. A metal tin lay on the floor, brown liquid splashed around it. And in the center of it all was Cerise, looking frenzied and agitated.

"What are you doing?" Alouette was almost too afraid to ask.

Cerise gave a sheepish little shrug. "Baking relaxes me."

Alouette's brow arched. The girl looked *anything* but relaxed.

"I just don't know what to do with myself!" Cerise threw up her hands. "We've been hiding behind this moon for hours and those warships are still out there. I've been racking my brain trying to figure out how to get around them so we can get the fric out of here, but I've got nothing. There's no way out of here. We're going to be stuck behind this blasted moon forever. Or at least until they find us or give up. But by then Gabriel will be dead and the general will have his weapon and he'll send the update to the Skins and all of this will have been for nothing." Cerise glanced around at the debris and sighed, her voice softening a little. "I didn't know what else to do, so I came in here. I thought I'd make a gâteau. You know, for Gabriel when he wakes up. He said he's never had gâteau before. But the ship doesn't have all the ingredients and everything's just . . . just . . ."

"A mess?" Alouette speculated.

Cerise collapsed against the counter. "Yes. Exactly."

Alouette had never seen Cerise look so daunted. So weighed down. She was usually the buoyant one of the group. But apparently, everyone had a limit, and Cerise had reached hers.

"It's a nice gesture," Alouette offered. "I'm sure Gabriel will love it."

Her heart ached at the unspoken implication of her words.

If he wakes up.

Cerise gritted her teeth. "Yeah, well, he's a total pain in my rump, and if I have to listen to him call me 'Sparkles' one more time I might throw myself out the escape hatch of the ship. But . . ." Her voice trailed off as her eyes misted. "But everyone deserves the chance to try gâteau."

Alouette cracked the tiniest of smiles. She'd never really taken the time to get to know Cerise. But as the slender, obsidian-haired girl stood there, with a hurricane of baking equipment scattered around her and tears pricking her eyes, Alouette couldn't help but feel an overwhelming sense of affection for her.

"Come on." Alouette walked over and nudged Cerise with her elbow. "I'll help you clean this up." She grabbed a sponge from the sink and began to wipe down the counter. For a long time, Cerise just watched her, like Alouette was performing some unfamiliar ritual from another planet.

"I actually find cleaning to be pretty calming." Alouette wrung out the sponge. "I used to scrub the floors in the Refuge. That was one of my chores."

"The Refuge," Cerise repeated. "That's where you lived? With the Vangarde, right?"

Alouette drew in a shaky breath. Her first instinct was to clam up, conceal the truth, keep the sisters' secrets. But when she looked into Cerise's eyes, she knew she could trust her. Over the past few days, she, Cerise, Gabriel, and Marcellus had become a group. A *team*. And for the first time since Alouette had left the Refuge, she'd felt like she was part of something again. Part of a family. She may not have known her real family—and she might never find the answers she was looking for about her mother—but she knew that the word "family" could be as wide and as all-encompassing as the universe itself. The sisters had taught her that.

"Yes," Alouette finally said. "I lived with them for twelve years. They pretty much raised me. I just didn't know who they really were until recently. I called them sisters."

"And that's how you know Dr. Collins's daughter?" Cerise confirmed. "Denise?"

Alouette nodded and ran her sponge across the countertop, feeling a deep ache pulse through her as she thought of Dr. Collins's head slumped against the contrôleur of the aerocab. And the promise she'd made to him mere hours before he'd died.

"Don't worry. We'll find her."

"She's one of the only sisters left," Alouette said. "I have to find out where the general is keeping them, but I don't even know where to start looking."

Cerise leaned forward on the counter. "Well, who else might know where the general's detention facility is?"

Alouette shrugged. "Marcellus said, besides the general, only Inspecteur Limier knows. I guess he was the general's primary interrogator. But according to Marcellus, Inspecteur Limier's condition is—"

"Unknown," Cerise said with a nod. "Yeah. The last I heard, he was going into surgery. Subdural hematoma. Blood clot in the brain. It didn't sound good. Apparently, his cyborg circuitry was pretty fried."

Alouette scrubbed harder against the countertop, trying to keep the guilt from creeping in. Was it possible that their only lead to Jacqui and Denise's whereabouts was lost because of *her* finger on the trigger?

"Do you . . ." Cerise started to ask something, but stopped herself, clearly wrestling with the right words. "Did Denise ever talk to you about . . ." She huffed and finally finished her sentence in a rush, as though afraid if she didn't say it quickly, the words would float away from her. "Did she ever say anything about her decision to become a cyborg?"

Alouette's hand abruptly stopped on the countertop. She certainly wasn't expecting Cerise to ask about *that.* "No. Hardly any of the sisters talked about their lives before the Refuge."

Cerise nodded, looking disappointed. "It's just . . . I can't stop thinking about what Dr. Collins said. How she joined the program so willingly. Why would she do that? What was she thinking?"

Alouette shook her head. "I don't know."

"Would you ever *choose* to be a cyborg?" Cerise pressed, and there was something about the look in her eyes that made Alouette certain this was not just an idle question. As though Cerise's life depended on Alouette's answer.

Her grip around the sponge tightened. "No. I don't think I would."

Something cold and chilling flashed over Cerise's face. For a moment, it looked like she'd fallen into some kind of trance. And when she spoke next, her words were flat and distant. "My operation was supposed to be yesterday."

Alouette blinked, certain she'd misheard her. "What operation?"

Still Cerise didn't look at her. She kept her gaze straight ahead. "My cyborg operation."

The sponge fell from Alouette's hand. "You mean, to *become* a cyborg?"

"Papa signed me up for the program a few years ago, as soon as he started to notice that I had a knack with devices and networks. Of course, *he* had conveniently chosen not to have the procedure done on himself, which never seemed fair. But he expects me to become a technicien, and maybe even a directeur of a lab one day."

"Will you still be able to hack?"

"Oh, I'll be able to. I'll be the best hacker in the world. I just . . . you know . . . won't want to." Cerise let out a bitter laugh. "How's that for irony?"

Alouette immediately understood. Cyborgs were programmed to be obedient. Wired for precision and loyalty. The operation would make Cerise even more talented than she already was, but it would steal away every thread of her rebellious spirit. Essentially the very thing that made Cerise . . . Cerise.

"That's what you meant when you said, 'superficial is the safest thing to be,'" Alouette realized.

"Yeah. I figured that if I could fool my father into thinking I *wasn't* as smart as he thought, maybe he'd change his mind about the surgery. But I'm pretty sure he sees right through me." She let out a heavy sigh. "What do you think prompted Denise to take out her circuitry?"

"I don't know," Alouette repeated.

Cerise shook her head, like she was trying to jolt herself awake. "Well, anyway, that's the other reason I left Ledôme to track down Marcellus. I wanted to tell the Vangarde about the message I found, but also . . . I was running away."

"From the operation?"

Cerise nodded. "I couldn't stand to think of myself as one of them. A cyborg programmed to serve the Regime I despise. I was foolish enough to think I could change the planet. I thought I was destined for better things. Bigger things."

"Maybe you are."

But Cerise only chuckled. "Maybe I'm not. Maybe I'm just stupid. Papa always said I was too idealistic for my own good." She glanced around the messy kitchen. "Maybe that's true. I just wanted to help. I fancied myself a *sympathizeur.*"

"You *are* a sympathizeur. And the world needs more of them."

Cerise scoffed. "Yeah, but what does that even mean? Nothing. Gabriel was right. My life *is* a joke. I don't really do much besides sit around in my fancy manoir, trying to track down some elusive kill switch that probably doesn't even exist. It probably is just a stupid conspiracy theory that I've wasted far too much of my life trying to prove right."

"No one has proven it *wrong,*" Alouette pointed out.

Cerise scoffed. "I don't know. Maybe the kill switch is just a metaphor for everything that's wrong with me. Maybe I just want so badly to believe that there's this mythical fantasy solution to the world's problems, and if I just look hard enough, I'll find it. Meanwhile, I've never done anything that might actually make a difference."

"Cerise!" Alouette said incredulously. "Look outside the window. You're on a voyageur, hiding behind an Albion moon. You traveled to an enemy planet, came face-to-face with the System Divine's most formidable soldiers, and you lived to tell about it. If that's not *doing* something, I don't know what it is."

For a moment, Cerise looked hopeful. Like she truly wanted to believe

Alouette. Like she wanted to be the same person who had boarded this voyageur only a week ago. Confident. Optimistic. Bubbly. But a moment later, her gaze went glassy, and Alouette could swear she saw the hope seep right out of her. Then, in a vacant, haunted tone, Cerise said, "And yet we're probably still all going to die out here."

Alouette felt the threat of Cerise's words sink into her. Like they were creating their own gravity, pulling her to the ground. Was she right? Would they never find a way home?

"Sometimes," Alouette began, feeling her confidence falter, "it's our intentions that mean more than the results." It was the kind of thing Sister Jacqui would say, and it made her long for her favorite sister more than ever.

"Maybe," Cerise replied glumly. "But my intentions are not going to save Gabriel's life. And I'm sorry to say, neither are yours."

Alouette was at a loss for words. She wanted so badly to comfort Cerise. To comfort *herself*. To tell them both it would all be okay. Gabriel would live. They would find a way to evade the Albion warships and they would get home in time to stop the general. But she couldn't say any of those things.

For the first time in her life, she felt words fail her.

Like the world was forgetting them all over again.

She glanced down at a smudge of egg yolk starting to harden on the counter. And suddenly, all she could focus on was that stain. She bent down, grabbed the fallen sponge from the floor, and attacked the stain with the strength and devotion of a soldier taking on an insurgent army. She scrubbed and scrubbed and scrubbed until her knuckles ached. Until she felt Cerise's gentle hand land on hers.

"Hey," Cerise whispered, carefully prying the sponge from Alouette's grip. "It's okay. You don't have to do that. I'll finish cleaning."

Alouette started to protest. "But I—"

"I know." Cerise's smile was warm and fleeting and unexpected. "But it's my mess. I should be the one to clean it up."

* * *

Alouette needed to walk. To pace. To move. She was used to being in confined spaces. The Refuge wasn't much bigger than this ship. But she'd never, in her entire life, felt more trapped than she did right now.

"Are you okay?" a voice asked. She looked up to see Marcellus sitting at one of the tables in the viewing lounge with Dr. Collins's canister positioned on the chair next to him, like he was afraid to let it out of his sight.

She tried for a deep breath. "I'm . . ." She still couldn't find the words.

But it turned out, she didn't need them. "I know." Marcellus exhaled. "Me too."

Alouette had never seen him look so drained. So defeated. The events of the last few days had left his face gaunt and his vibrant hazel eyes hollow and haunted.

"I'm going out of my mind," he said. "I hate just sitting here while Gabriel gets worse and my grandfather gets closer to his weapon. As soon as Dr. Cromwell delivers the TéléReversion program and the general updates the Skins, that will be it. He'll activate his Third Estate army, and he'll take control of the Regime. And meanwhile, we're just sitting here, waiting for the fric-ing Albion Royal Space Fleet to find us."

Alouette glanced at the glowing, cratered moon that loomed just outside the window and wondered if the pull of it wasn't driving them all a little mad.

With a sigh, Marcellus dragged a hand roughly through his already disheveled hair. "I've been trying to distract myself with this, but clearly it's not working." He gestured to the table and Alouette caught sight of a familiar red spine. The Vangarde's compendium of reports was open in front of him.

Her eyebrows shot up in surprise. "You can read that? Have you been practicing the Forgotten Word?"

Marcellus shrugged. "It's still difficult. But I had to communicate with the Vangarde, so, yeah, I've been practicing. I was surprised, actually, at how quickly it came back to me. Once I stopped fighting it. It's like, for seven years, I was pressing against a door, trying to keep everything locked inside. Then, once I let go, the memories just rushed out." He caught Alouette's gaze and flashed her a half smile. "But it was you who first reminded me how to open it."

Alouette felt for the metal tag dangling from her neck, remembering how earnestly he'd struggled to read its engraving back in the Forest Verdure, when they'd sat around a fire that Marcellus had built. When the world felt full of possibility. Not heartache.

"I'm still pretty rusty though," Marcellus said. "Certain words and letter combinations trip me up. Like, is this how you spell your mother's name? *L-I-S-O-L-E*?"

Alouette tilted her head toward the book and saw that Marcellus was reading the report about her mother getting fired from the Palais. She nodded. "Yes. That's—" But the words evaporated on her tongue when her gaze snagged on the date scrawled at the top of the page.

Month 7, Day 4, 488.

She could have sworn the reports about her mother were all written in Month 6. Around the same time that the Rebellion of 488 ended.

"Let me see that," Alouette said hastily, turning the book toward her. Her eyes skimmed over the dense handwriting, butterflies taking flight in her stomach as she quickly realized that this was *not* the same report. This was a different report which mentioned her mother's name. Written more than a month later. Alouette had been so convinced she'd read all there was to read about her mother. And then the voyageur had been overtaken by the Trafalgar warship, and the book had been pushed to the back corners of her mind. She hadn't looked at it since.

"What is it?" Marcellus asked.

"It's another report. About my mother."

"Read it aloud!" he urged.

Alouette nodded and bent her head over the page.

Month 7, Day 4, 488
Operative: Mabelle Dubois
Location: The Frets, Vallonay

I found Lisole today in one of the dingiest, darkest hallways of Fret 10. Her couchette was leaking and cold, littered with cockroaches and dirty puddles. The sparkle had gone from her eyes. Her beautiful dark curls had been shorn off.

Even some of her teeth were missing.

" I borrowed money from the wrong people," she said, covering her still swollen mouth with one hand and waving me inside with the other.

She insisted I sit in the one rickety chair in the room, while she leaned against the filthy, cracked window.

I couldn't conceal my sadness and concern as I peered around the couchette.

"They wouldn't give me a work assignment." She glanced down and smoothed her hand over her belly, now a gentle curve under her ragged dress. " Not like this, anyway."

In a rush of words, I said all I'd come to say. I told her who we were. Our mission. I told her about our safe hideaway, concealed from the rest of the planet.

" You can live there. You and your baby will be safe in our protection. Guided by our love. The sisters will take care of you both."

But she shook her head. She refused. She told me she didn't want to get tangled up in any more trouble.

Our name, soiled from the recent failed rebellion, clearly terrified her.

I tried to explain that we were innocent in that horrific bombing that killed those exploit workers one month ago. I tried to tell her that we were framed. We are not the terrorists the Ministère has painted us to be. I don't know whether or not she believed me.

" I just want to find a quiet life," she said. " A life away from everyone and everything. Just the two of us." She stroked her belly again.

I warned her the world wasn't safe for her or her child. I

told her she could never have the quiet life she wanted. Trouble would follow her wherever she went. That seemed to stir something inside of her. She gazed out the broken window, looking distant and haunted and hopeless. She must have realized that I was right. That we were her and her child's only chance. Because she gave the tiniest, most fragile of nods.

"Okay," she whispered. " I'll come."

I told her to take a day to settle her affairs. I promised to return tomorrow to take her to safety. But just in case anything should happen to me, I gave her instructions on how to signal us.

I know that she has made the right choice. For her own sake and the sake of the child. We can protect them. We must protect them.

An electricity thrummed through Alouette. "She was pregnant," she said quietly, her mind struggling to make all the pieces fit. "She must have been pregnant before she left the Palais."

Using her finger to mark her place in the book, Alouette hastily flipped back through the pages until she reached the first set of reports. Her gaze slid over the handwritten words, stopping only a little below the top of the page. She quietly reread the lines aloud. "I rushed into the hallway to find Lisole fighting with a handsome auburn-haired Palais guard. Her eyes were puffy and red. Her hair was a mess, and across her cheek, I saw an angry red mark. I knew, immediately, that she'd been struck."

"Do you think . . . ," Marcellus began, clearly coming to the same conclusion as Alouette.

Alouette thought about her mother's titan box, still tucked away in her couchette. About those intertwined locks of hair. One dark and curly, the other a luminous shade of auburn.

"Did she try to tell him?" Alouette wondered aloud as she turned back to her marked page. "Did she tell him about the baby, and he wanted nothing to do with it, so he had her arrested? Made up some story about her stealing from the Palais?" Perhaps that was what Mabelle had meant before, when she wrote that she feared Lisole had "gotten herself in too deep."

"Look," Marcellus said. He had flipped forward a few pages and was now pointing at a new report, dated the very next day. "Her name appears here too."

Month 7, Day 5, 488
Operative: Mabelle Dubois
Location: The Frets, Vallonay

Today, I knocked on the door of her couchette, but all I heard were cold, empty echoes and the skittering feet of vermin. I waited. I knocked again. I called her name. But still, there was only silence behind the door.

Finally, a neighbor peeked out from the next couchette and told me that Lisole had left yesterday.

"Good riddance," he snarled. "I didn't want some baby screaming and wailing all night."

I asked if he knew where she'd gone, but he shook his head and shoved the door closed in my face.

It was then I realized that she never intended to come with me. She only agreed so that I would leave her alone. Our name—and every falsehood that has been tangled up with it—has become our downfall.

Obviously, we must look for her. We must never stop searching. She is my friend. We were once as close as sisters. I care for her. And obviously, I care for the welfare of the child. The baby will be like a daughter to me. To all of us.

Wherever she has gone, we will attempt to bring her back to Vallonay. But I fear, deep in my heart, that we may never find someone who doesn't want to be found.

When Alouette glanced up from the page again, she had tears in her eyes. She now understood why Principale Francine had given her this specific book. It was the beginning of a story. The story of how Alouette had found her way to the Refuge twelve years ago.

"Mabelle," she whispered wistfully. "She was my mother's friend. She . . . saved me."

And suddenly, the rest of the story unfurled before her like a long-buried path emerging from the mist. "She invited my mother to live in the Refuge. She gave her instructions on how to signal the sisters. At first, my mother was too scared to come, convinced she would be better off on her own than hiding out with a group of rebels. But she must have eventually changed her mind and given those instructions to Hugo before she died. She must have come to realize that the Refuge *was* the safest place for me, despite it being the base for the Vangarde." Alouette's mouth quirked into a tiny smile as she touched the string of devotion beads around her neck. "And she was right."

Marcellus winced, his jawline taut against the memory of his former governess and the horrible way she'd died. "So I guess, in a way, Mabelle saved us both."

She glanced up at him, and when their eyes locked, Alouette felt something inexplicable pass between them. An understanding. A kinship. A connection that she knew would never be broken. No matter how many warships arrived to search for them. No matter what the future held.

"I . . . ," she began to say, but she didn't quite know how to finish. And it didn't seem to matter anyway, because a moment later, Alouette heard a soft groaning sound coming from the ship's internal speakers. Her gaze shot toward the nearest monitor on the wall. Gabriel was no longer sleeping soundly. He was now thrashing violently on the bed.

Alouette was on the move in an instant, sprinting to the infirmerie with Marcellus close behind her.

The sheets of Gabriel's bed were a tangled mess, and he was clearly in pain. His face and arms were covered in sweat.

"Are the médicaments wearing off?" Cerise asked, appearing in the doorway.

Alouette shook her head. "They should be good for another few hours." She reached over and felt his forehead. It was hot and clammy. Her mind whirred.

Infection? This fast?

"What's wrong with him?" Cerise's small, broken voice made her sound like a child.

Alouette sighed and looked up into Cerise's eyes. They were rimmed with fear. "It's the cluster bullet. All those tiny pieces of shrapnel create prime breeding grounds for infection."

"Can't you do something for him?" Marcellus asked.

"I can give him more médicaments, but it will only help for so long. He *needs* surgery."

Cerise's gaze bounced to the glowing blue moon outside the porthole window of the infirmerie and then back again, obviously coming to the same conclusion as Alouette.

They were running of time.

Gabriel thrashed again, his hand flying up and nearly smacking Cerise in the face. She let out a sad little laugh, "Well, I suppose I had that coming."

"Marcellus. Help me." Alouette held Gabriel's right arm down and Marcellus rushed forward to grab his other arm. But instead of pinning it to the bed, he was just standing there, staring at the inside of Gabriel's left wrist.

"What's wrong?" Alouette glanced over to see that Gabriel's Skin was alight. Marcellus pushed up the fabric of his sleeve, revealing the whole of the screen. And that's when Alouette saw it. That's when they *all* saw it.

Flashing in the center of Gabriel's Skin was a curious orange rectangle that seemed to be gradually filling with color.

"What is that?" Alouette asked, although she had a gut-wrenching feeling she already knew.

Cerise tapped on the screen to link the Skin with the ship's internal speakers. The implanted device connected just in time for them to hear the eerie robotic voice announce, "Operating system upgrade complete. Your Skin has been updated."

CHAPTER 49

MARCELLUS

"NO," MARCELLUS WHISPERED, STARING WIDE-EYED AT Gabriel's now darkened Skin. "No! It's too soon."

"Was that it?" Cerise asked, looking desperately from Marcellus to Gabriel's arm then back to Marcellus. "Was that *the* update?"

Marcellus nodded dazedly. "I think it was."

"But," Alouette protested, "but I thought we had more time. Dr. Cromwell said he would send the TéléReversion program in a week. Why would he send it early?"

Marcellus had been asking himself that very same question. But strangely, it was the memory of his grandfather's voice that supplied the answer.

"This is not over, Marcellus."

That was the last thing the general had said to him, before he'd smashed the auditeur under the heel of his boot.

"Because he knows I was there," Marcellus replied, feeling a shiver crackle down his spine. "He knows I saw the demonstration. He knows we escaped Albion and are trying to get back to Laterre. He can't risk me interfering with his plans. He must have demanded Dr. Cromwell send the program before the final tests were complete." He paused, exhaling a shaky breath. "I think we have to assume that the general now has his weapon, and that every Third Estater on the planet is an explosif waiting to detonate."

A tense, grim silence fell across the room. For a moment, no one spoke. No one even dared to breathe. Even Gabriel, who was still unconscious on the bed next to them, seemed to still as this weight descended upon them.

At once, Marcellus, Cerise, and Alouette turned toward the window. Toward the massive moon of Adalisa that was holding them hostage.

"Sols!" Marcellus shouted. He spun around and sent his fist flying into one of the infirmerie cabinets. The door busted open and medical supplies came spilling out. Alouette and Cerise just stared at him, astonished, as he shook out his now-aching hand, drops of blood sprinkling onto the pristine white floor. "We're trapped here! We'll never get back to Laterre. Those warships won't give up until we're found and captured. I thought we could stop him. I thought . . ." But his voice trailed off. Because it didn't matter what he thought anymore. Nothing mattered anymore.

He had lost.

His grandfather had won, and Marcellus, the general's sad excuse for a protégé, had lost.

Marcellus leaned against the examination table and buried his head in his hands, once again feeling the sharp sting of his grandfather's clever, strategic mind. Once again feeling like no matter what he did, how far he traveled, he was still three moves behind.

Always three moves behind.

He thought about the metal canister filled with vials of Dr. Collins's inhibitor. Their one hope of stopping the general. And they'd never even be able to use them. "It's over," he whispered.

"Maybe not," said a soft yet pensive voice, and Marcellus looked up to see Cerise had moved over to the monitor on the wall and was now tapping furiously on the screen. "I can't believe I didn't think about it before, but now it's so obvious."

"What's obvious?" Alouette asked warily.

"We still don't know exactly what the general is going to *do* with the weapon, right?" Cerise peered at them from the monitor. "But he must have some sort of plan. A strategy. If we can get back to Laterre and get the inhibitor into the water supply *before* he implements his plan, maybe we can still stop him from doing any permanent damage."

Marcellus wasn't following. Had Cerise completely forgotten about the Albion warships lying in wait on the other side of this moon? "Cerise, what are you talking about? Even if we can somehow get past the warships, it'll still take five days to get back to Laterre. We'll be too late. Not to mention the general will be waiting there for us with his own ships."

"Exactly." Cerise resumed drumming on the screen as though that settled everything.

Marcellus glanced at Alouette with a look that said, *She's not okay, is she?*

Alouette bit her lip and placed a gentle hand on Cerise's shoulder. "Cerise. We'll be detected as soon as we try to accelerate to supervoyage."

"Which is why we can't use supervoyage."

She gave the screen one last tap and stepped back. A moment later, the ship's autopilot voice slipped through the speakers. "Estimated arrival on Laterre in twenty-two minutes."

"Hypervoyage?" Alouette asked incredulously.

"We would instantly disappear from all scans," Cerise explained. "We'd be able to get past the Albion Royal Space Fleet *and* the general's fleet. We could enter Laterrian airspace completely undetected."

Marcellus stood up straighter, his body now coursing with newfound strength. Newfound hope. "Are you sure?"

Cerise jutted out her chin. "I'm sure."

"Have you two lost your minds?" Alouette said, suddenly stepping between Marcellus and Cerise. "You can't hypervoyage within the System. It's too dangerous. It's only meant for deep space travel."

"Has anyone ever tried it?" Marcellus asked.

Alouette reeled on him. "No! Because everyone knows there are too many manmade objects in orbit around the planets. Satellites and voyageurs and spacecraft carriers. It's just too many variables to account for. You're likely to crash. Or worse, hypervoyage right *inside* of something and explode instantly."

"Likely," Cerise pointed out. "But not guaranteed."

Alouette threw up her hands. "Do you really want to debate semantics right now?" Marcellus was certain he'd never seen her so unhinged before. So desperate. "You're talking about *bending* space. Trust me, that's not something you want to mess with. The results could be catastrophic. Not just for us, but for anything that happens to be in our path."

"I'm just saying," Cerise countered, "there's a chance that it could work."

Frustration flashed in Alouette's eyes. "Fine, you want to talk chances? If we jump to hypervoyage inside the System Divine, there's a ninety-five percent chance it will end in disaster."

"And if we stay here," Cerise said, "then it's *one-hundred* percent certain that Gabriel will die, and the planet will fall into the hands of a madman. Pick your disaster."

"I hate to admit it, but I have to agree with Sparkles here."

They all spun to see that Gabriel's eyes were open. His forehead glistened with sweat and his mouth was twisted in a pained grimace, but he was awake.

"Gabriel!" Cerise ran to him and threw her arms around him, completely unmindful of his condition. He winced at the sudden impact.

Cerise sat up, her expression instantly morphing to fury. "How could you do that? How could you just go and get yourself shot? You're such an idiot!"

Gabriel chuckled hoarsely. "Are you gonna punch me again?"

Cerise huffed and stood up from the bed. "Maybe. But not until you're better."

"That's very considerate of you."

"Marcellus," Alouette warned, almost as though she could see the wheels in his head spinning frantically. "We can't do this."

"It's our only chance," Cerise argued. She pointed at Gabriel. "It's *his* only chance. You said so yourself, our intentions mean more than the results. And right now, our intentions are the only thing we have left."

Cerise tapped again on the screen and the display shifted. Now, the monitor showed nine blinking dots glowing ominously in the darkness of space. "The microprobes are reporting three more warships than there were an hour ago," Cerise went on. "They're not giving up. They're only sending more."

Cerise turned back to Marcellus, an expectant look in her eyes. He darted his gaze to Alouette who was staring at him with the exact same look. He clawed his fingers through his hair and closed his eyes, his thoughts a jumbled, chaotic mess.

Was Alouette right? Had he lost his mind? Were they insane to try this?

But what other choice did they have? His grandfather had his hands on a weapon that would certainly destroy the planet. He had his very own Third Estate army at his command now. Not to mention, if they stayed here, the Albion Royal Space Fleet would inevitably find them and throw them in the Tower. If they even let them get off this ship alive.

How could they *not* try this?

The familiar fire started to burn inside his chest. The flames of desperation. Of fury. Of vengeance. Of knowing he would rather die than see his grandfather take control of Laterre.

This is what Julien Bonnefaçon would have done. Marcellus was certain of it. If his father were alive today, he would stop at nothing to see General Bonnefaçon defeated. He would stop at nothing to save his planet.

Marcellus glanced at the monitor on the wall and stared vacantly at those tiny green dots combing through space, like hunting dogs spurred on by the fresh scent of prey.

He flashed Alouette an apologetic look, then turned to Cerise. "Prepare for hypervoyage."

PART 5

TERRAIN PERDU

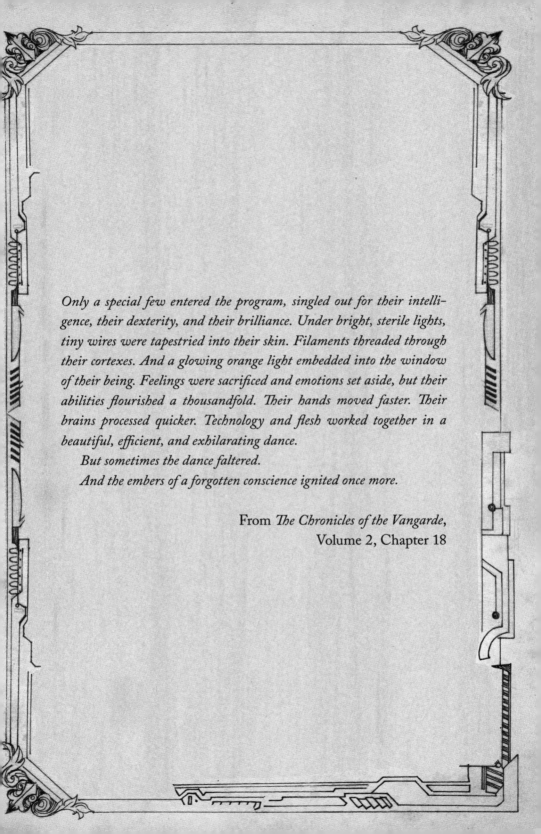

Only a special few entered the program, singled out for their intelligence, their dexterity, and their brilliance. Under bright, sterile lights, tiny wires were tapestried into their skin. Filaments threaded through their cortexes. And a glowing orange light embedded into the window of their being. Feelings were sacrificed and emotions set aside, but their abilities flourished a thousandfold. Their hands moved faster. Their brains processed quicker. Technology and flesh worked together in a beautiful, efficient, and exhilarating dance.

But sometimes the dance faltered.

And the embers of a forgotten conscience ignited once more.

From *The Chronicles of the Vangarde,*
Volume 2, Chapter 18

CHAPTER 50

CHATINE

ONCE AGAIN, CHATINE WAITED UNTIL EVERYONE WAS asleep. It took longer this time because of the fête. The Défecteurs didn't make their way back to their respective chalets until the early hours of the morning. Chatine could hear them outside, still dancing and singing and celebrating, while she lay on her bed in the treatment center, seething and raging and simmering, her breath a mess of gasps, her mind a tangle of bitter, dark thoughts.

Finally, however, the camp fell quiet and Chatine eased out of her bed, donned her coat, and slipped out into the darkness.

She limped down the grid of walkways, checking every corner, eyeing every door to make sure it remained closed. The last time she had snuck out in the middle of the night, Etienne had somehow found out and followed her. But she could not have him following her this time.

He was already suspicious enough. He'd seen Chatine's reaction when she'd come face-to-face with her parents. She'd probably looked like she'd seen a ghost. And she wished she had. All of Laterre would be better off if the Renards were dead. But they weren't dead, as she'd spent so long hoping. They were alive. They had somehow managed to escape the

Policier droids. And now they were here. The scums of Laterre. In this camp. With these innocent, unsuspecting, peaceful people.

Etienne had obviously sensed something was off. But when he'd tried to ask Chatine what was wrong, she'd dismissed him without an explanation. She'd simply muttered that her leg was bothering her before turning away and returning to the treatment center without another word.

Now, as she moved silently through the camp, she thought back through everything the Défecteurs had told her about their favorite new "gridders."

"Everyone loves *Fabian and his wife, Gen."*

"The people here can't get enough of them."

"One of the pilots took them to look for their lost children."

"Fabian does magic tricks. He makes things disappear."

Chatine grunted.

I bet he does.

It was a con. She was sure of it. That was the only reason her parents would infiltrate a Défecteur camp in the middle of the Terrain Perdu. The only reason they had gained these people's trust, invented new names and a ridiculous sob story about missing children.

As always, the Renards were plotting something.

Checking one last time to make sure she hadn't been followed, she eased open the door of the farthest chalet and slipped inside.

"There she is," came a gruff female voice. "Our darling daughter. Our *lost* child. We thought we'd never see you again."

Chatine squinted into the low light to find her parents sitting at a table in the corner, fabric scraps spread out around them. It took Chatine all of two seconds to realize they were sewing a collection of handmade sacs. Perfect for looting.

She clenched her teeth to keep from lashing out.

"Yes," her father added in a sugary tone that made the faint scar on Chatine's left palm twitch. "We heard you had a little run in with the Policier. Got yourself shipped off to Bastille. But I wasn't too worried. I knew you'd land on your feet. Just like you always do, my little kitty cat. After all, you have Renard blood running in your veins. And we all know the Renards always land on top. With all the squabbles and riots and silly rebellions on this planet, we're the ones who make it in the end."

"Stop," she spat. "Just stop. What are you doing here? What are you planning?"

Monsieur Renard tipped his head back and let out a long, deep belly laugh before sharing a knowing look with his wife. "Didn't I tell you, chérie? Didn't I predict she'd come here begging for a cut?"

"You're wrong," Chatine replied. "I don't want a cut. I don't want anything to do with you."

"Oh, but you *will* when you find out what we're after," Monsieur Renard said. "It's the con of the century, my dear. You'd be foolish not to want a cut." Chatine rolled her eyes. She'd been listening to her father claim he was planning the con of the century since she was a child. "And since you seem to have won these people over as well, we could probably use your help. How's ten percent?"

"No!" Chatine bellowed.

"Keep your voice down!" her father scolded her.

Chatine bristled but lowered her voice. "I don't want any of it. I want you to leave. Now."

Her mother chuckled. "Leave? Why would we leave when we're so close? We've already secured a buyer."

Comprehension struck Chatine in the chest. So that's what they were really doing this week while they were out "searching for their lost children."

"A buyer for what?" Chatine asked. "What are you selling these poor people out for?"

Her father let out a huff of frustration. "My sols, Chatine, you really can be dense sometimes, can't you? Sometimes I think you're even thicker than Azelle was."

Chatine flinched at the mention of her sister's name but fought to keep her expression neutral.

"Have you not noticed the stockpiles of a certain highly valuable metal these people have been hoarding?" her father asked.

Chatine clenched her fists. *The zyttrium.* Of course that's what her parents were after. It was the most valuable commodity in this camp. Bastille was running out of it. The Ministère needed it to keep the Third Estate Skinned and obedient. And the Défecteurs were rich in it. Her parents probably had no trouble at all finding someone who would pay top larg for it.

"You can't steal their zyttrium," she said.

Monsieur Renard snorted. "Why not? They stole it first."

"They need it to survive."

"So do we," Madame Renard said with a shrug.

"I won't let you go through with it."

Her father cackled and stood up from his chair. He began to stalk menacingly toward Chatine. She backed away until she was pressed up against the wall of the chalet. "And how on Laterre do you plan on stopping us? Are you going to chase after us in your condition?" He glanced down at her leg and let out a pitying cluck of his tongue. "Oh yes, I heard about your little injury." His hand reached toward her left knee. His fingers outstretched.

Chatine braced herself. The pain came a second later. A sharp, penetrating bolt as her father's grip squeezed around the fabric of her pants, twisting the flesh of her wound.

"You're not going to try to stop us," he breathed against her cheek, and Chatine flashed back to the thousands of other moments in her life when her father had threatened her. Hurt her. Breathed his rancid breath on her until she backed down.

Because she always backed down.

Because he was Monsieur Renard, leader of the Délabré gang. And she was just a lowly Fret rat, dependent on him for food and shelter and survival.

He squeezed her leg harder, and she felt a wave of dizziness rush through her. "You're going to keep your wretched little mouth shut and let us do what we came here to do. And if you help us out, we might even be nice and give you five percent."

"I thought it was ten," Chatine muttered through her clenched teeth.

Her father snorted. "Chatine, Chatine. Have I taught you nothing? First offers always come with an expiration. I suggest you take this second offer now before it, too, expires."

She grimaced through the pain, the anger building inside of her.

"Just think, Chatine," her father whispered silkily. "Five percent can set you up for good. Five percent can get you the life you always wanted."

The life she always wanted.

The words flittered jarringly through her mind, like they didn't quite fit together. The sentence was complete, but she couldn't make sense of it.

What was the life she always wanted? For a while, she thought it could be found on Usonia, far away from Laterre and its harsh laws and unjust Regime. But now? Somehow Usonia didn't seem far enough. Or maybe it was never the distance that she craved. Maybe it was something else.

Something that she'd stumbled upon without even knowing it.

With a sudden, fierce determination, Chatine lifted her hands and planted them on her father's chest. Grimacing through the pain, she shoved him as hard as she could. He stumbled back—more out of surprise than Chatine's actual strength—and fell onto the bed.

"What the—" he growled but Chatine cut him off.

"Shut up," she snapped. Her mother opened her mouth to speak but Chatine cut her with a glance. "Both of you. This is how it's going to work."

Her father's shock quickly gave way to a knowing smile. "Ah, there's the Chatine we know and love. A counteroffer. I'm listening."

Chatine took two purposeful steps toward him. "You're going to pack up your things and leave. Tonight. You're not going to speak to anyone. You're not going to take anything that doesn't belong to you. You're just going to leave and never come back."

Monsieur Renard leaned forward slightly, waiting for the rest. "And?"

"And nothing," Chatine fired back.

Monsieur Renard shared a look with his wife before they both broke into wild hoots of laughter. "Well, well, well," he said through his cackles. "Look at our little Fret rat all grown up and making demands she can't follow through on."

"I can follow through," Chatine swore.

"Oh yeah?" Madame Renard replied, amused. "You and what droid army?"

"I don't need an army." Chatine glared at her father. "You, of all people, must remember how quickly I can ruin your plans with nothing more than a scream. If you don't leave right now, I will scream. It will be the loudest thing you have ever heard. And then, when they all come running, I will tell them everything. I will tell them who you *really* are. I will tell them what you've done. All of it. Every con, every crime, and every severed toe. I will even tell them what you did to baby Henri."

Out of the corner of her eye, Chatine saw her mother flinch.

"Yes," she went on. "I know the truth. I know he wasn't really dead. I know you lied to me for twelve years, made me believe that that little girl Madeline killed him, when really you sold him off to pay for your own mistakes. You have robbed and cheated so many people, but nothing is more unforgivable then what you stole from me. You stole my life. And his life. And Azelle's life too. You stole my childhood. And my innocence. And my ability to believe in anything. And now, here, thanks to these people, I have managed to get a *sliver* of that back. And I will not let you take it away again. I will tell them exactly what you're planning, and then you can deal with *that* army."

For a split second, Monsieur Renard actually looked uncertain. But he quickly wiped the expression from his face and stood up. Again, he walked toward her. But this time, Chatine did not back away. She stood her ground. Even when her father pinned her with that dark, sinister stare that had haunted her for almost her entire life. "You wouldn't dare."

Chatine raised an eyebrow. "Try me."

"You like it here," Monsieur Renard stated as though this were a key piece of intel that Chatine had foolishly given away.

"So?"

"You like it here *too much*," he amended. "You've fallen in *love* with these ignorant dropouts."

Madame Renard chortled. Anger coursed through Chatine, but she fought to keep her hands and her breath steady.

"Didn't I ever tell you not to fall in love with your mark?" her father asked. "It's dangerous and . . . *messy*."

"That's where you're wrong," Chatine said confidently.

"You're not in love with them?"

"They're not my mark."

Madame Renard scoffed. "You expect us to believe that?"

"Believe whatever you want," Chatine spat at her, "but the truth remains, if you don't leave, I expose you."

"As I was saying," Monsieur Renard went on, undeterred, "you like it here. Too much. And if you expose us, we expose you. And then, it's adieu darling Défecteurs. Do you really think they'd let you stay after they find out you're a croc?"

Chatine snorted. "They know I'm a croc. They rescued me from Bastille. They've seen my tattoo."

"Sure, but do they know about your nefarious plot to steal zyttrium right out from under their noses?"

"What? I wasn't going to—"

"Who do you think they'll believe?" her mother chimed in, picking up right where her father left off in the coordinated dance they'd been performing all their lives. "You, a known convict with a criminal past? Or their *favorite* new friends? Fabian and Gen,"—she nodded at the scraps of fabric on the table—"who discovered these sacs hidden under your bed and became the heroes who exposed a con artist in their midst." She let out a scandalized gasp.

Monsieur Renard took another menacing step toward Chatine, his eyes narrowing wickedly. "Are you so sure they'll trust you over us? Are you willing to bet your life on it?"

Chatine's heart squeezed in her chest. She knew her parents were right. They were like celebrities in this place. Etienne had said so himself. Why would the Défecteurs believe her—someone they barely knew—over them?

Defeat started to clamp around her neck. Heavy and rusted like the chains on Bastille. When would she ever get out from under this shadow? When would she finally shed the burden of *their* name? Renard. As hard as she'd tried, she'd never been able to escape it.

Not when her family had run from Montfer and come to live in the Frets.

Not when Chatine had changed her identity and became a boy named Théo.

Not even on Bastille.

Everywhere she went, her past, her family, her blood followed her. And would continue to follow her. It had been branded on her as permanently as her prisoner tattoo.

When was she going to learn that she couldn't escape herself?

Now, she thought, standing up taller and sucking in a deep, courageous breath. *Right now.*

"Fine," she said, and her father seemed to sag ever so slightly in relief. That is, until she continued. "Expose me. Tell them who I am. Tell them whatever you want. I don't care. I'm prepared to leave. Just as long as you leave too. Because whatever you say, I will make sure that we all go down together."

Her father evidently wasn't expecting her to call their bluff, because for the first time in her life, Chatine saw fear flash in her father's eyes. True, genuine fear. He looked to Madame Renard, whose face was blank with shock. Clearly, they weren't willing to bet on the trust of the Défecteurs either.

Her parents shared one of their silent exchanges that Chatine had never been able to decipher, and then Monsieur Renard turned back to meet her unwavering gaze.

"I have a counteroffer."

Chatine smirked. "I'd expect no less."

"We'll go," he allowed, and Chatine tried to keep the triumph from her face. "*But* . . . we're not leaving empty-handed."

Her mother gave a resolute shake of her head and added, "We've worked too hard and put in too much effort to leave without anything to show for it."

Chatine narrowed her eyes. She didn't like where this was going, but she knew the rules of negotiation. You never got exactly what you came for, but if you were lucky, you walked away with more than you were willing to lose. "How much is it going to take to get you to leave quietly?"

Monsieur Renard sneered. For a moment, Chatine believed that he was actually enjoying this. And Chatine supposed she would be lying if she said she didn't get just the smallest drop of a thrill from it. She supposed all fathers and daughters had their thing. This was theirs.

"Ten blocs" Monsieur Renard announced. "That should give us enough to live on for a few years."

"Five," Chatine replied.

"*Seven*. And you have to steal it for us."

Chatine considered. Could she really remove seven blocs of zyttrium from the storage chalet without anyone noticing? She'd have to be strategic, move things around a little to cover her tracks. Her breath hitched, and she felt ill at the thought of the task that stood in front of her, but then she returned her gaze to what was *actually* standing in front of her—the most hideous, vile, despicable vermin on the face of the planet—and all her hesitation melted away.

She could do this. She could figure this out. She *had* to. One last time. One final job.

It *was* the con of the century. Because, for her, it was the con that would end all cons.

"Pack up your things," she said as she grabbed one of the handmade sacs from the table and turned toward the door. "I want you ready to go when I get back."

CHAPTER 51

ALOUETTE

THE HARNESS SLOWLY DESCENDED OVER ALOUETTE'S shoulders. There was a beeping noise as it snapped together and yanked her back into the seat. She could feel her blood running, fast and furious, through her veins. She didn't like how trapped and constricted she felt. It made her mind run back to that horrible bordel. The needle buried in her arm . . .

"Gabriel, how are you doing?" Cerise asked, and Alouette reminded herself that she wasn't the worst off in this situation. She glanced over at Gabriel, who was strapped into the seat next to her, the harness pushing down against his bandages.

He struggled to give Cerise a smile in return. "Titanique, Sparkles."

Alouette could hear the tremor in his voice. She couldn't even imagine how much pain he must have been in right now. Pain like she'd never experienced.

Despite his protests, they'd forced him to drink from the extra vial of the inhibitor that Dr. Collins had given them. So at the very least, Alouette knew Gabriel was safe from the general should he activate the

TéléReversion program. But it did little to reassure her. His injuries were bad and getting worse by the hour.

"So does anyone know what this is going to feel like?" Marcellus asked in an anxious tone. He was strapped into the seat on the other side of Alouette.

Cerise shook her head. "I've never hypervoyaged before."

"I've read accounts," Alouette offered. "I think you enter sort of a fugue state. At least at first. Until your body adjusts."

"What's a fugue state?" Cerise asked.

Thinking back to the sisters' Chronicles and the chapters devoted to space travel, Alouette tried to remember the descriptions that were recorded from the original settlers who had hypervoyaged from the First World to the System Divine. "I think you feel like you're sort of detached from your body. Disassociated from everything around you."

"Good," Gabriel said weakly. "If we crash and die, I don't want to feel it."

Alouette swallowed down what felt like razors in her throat. She knew Gabriel was trying to lighten the mood, like he always did. But there was also something morbidly accurate about his remark. She understood Marcellus's desperation to get back to Laterre quickly. She felt it too. But she knew the risks of hypervoyage. She'd read about them for years. And she couldn't shake the feeling that this was suicide. At first the autopilote hadn't even allowed them to activate the hypervoyage engines. Cerise had been forced to hack the safety override.

Now all Alouette could do was pray that she was wrong. That they would safely make it back to Laterre. That Alouette could get Gabriel to the Refuge, and that Marcellus and Cerise could get the inhibitor into the water supply before the general tore the planet apart.

"Where's Dr. Collins's canister?" Alouette asked, just now noticing that Marcellus didn't have it with him.

"I wrapped it in a thick blanket and secured it in a storage locker in the cargo hold," he told her. "I figured it would be safe from any turbulence there."

"Final checks complete," a calm robotic voice announced. "Commencing hypervoyage in fifteen . . . fourteen . . . thirteen . . ."

Alouette wished she could steal a smidgen of that calm and inject it straight into her veins.

There was a loud rumbling sound, followed by a cacophony of short, staccato beeps. Then the whole voyageur seemed to buck beneath them, like a giant animal scraping the ground, getting ready to pounce.

"Ten . . . nine . . . eight . . ."

Alouette opened her eyes and stared straight ahead of her, out of the bridge's front window. Stars hung everywhere in the vast sky, and somewhere among them was Laterre. And Vallonay. And the Frets. And the Refuge.

Home.

The word echoed in the far, deep corners of Alouette's mind. Ominous and impossible and hopeful all at the same time.

When the Lark flies home . . .

There was no more doubt behind Sister Denise's words now. No more bitterness festering inside her. There was only determination.

Yes, Sister Denise, she whispered into those far, deep corners of her mind. *I'm finally flying home.*

"Four . . . three . . . two . . ."

The ship was rumbling so hard now, Alouette's teeth were chattering and her spine began to ache. Her eyes darted to the left, to Marcellus's jump seat. He was looking at her, too, and when their gazes connected, it appeared that he was about to say something.

Au revoir?

Good luck?

I'll see you on the other side of space?

But he never got the chance.

"One."

The voyageur let out a boom and a roar. The world around Alouette shook violently. The stars outside the window blurred into a single infinite glow. Then, as if a switch had been flicked inside of her, every molecule of Alouette's body seemed to ignite and blast off. Backward, forward, downward, and outward, into the giant abyss of space.

Everything went dark.

Everything turned to nothing.

Alouette couldn't see anything or feel anything. And the only thing she could hear was a fast and rhythmic whooshing in her ears.

Ba-bummm. Ba-bummm. Ba-bummm.

At first, she wondered if this was what hypervoyage sounded like. If this was what bending space sounded like. It wasn't until the last shred of consciousness had deserted her body that she realized it was the sound of her own solitary and terrified heart.

- CHAPTER 52 -
MARCELLUS

BA-BUMMM. BA-BUMMM. BA-BUMMM.

Marcellus was surrounded by stars. So many stars. Bigger and brighter than he'd ever seen them. They made the ones that hung in the TéléSky of Ledôme feel insignificant and futile. Like sad little replicas that would never live up to their real inspirations.

"If you grow up to become general like me, you'll be able to visit the stars whenever you want. Would you like that, Marcellus?"

He could hear his grandfather's voice. But he knew it was not his grandfather of now. It was his grandfather of the past. The one who hung Bastille in the sky. The one who Marcellus yearned to be exactly like, but who always managed to make him feel like a fraud.

A sad little replica that would never live up to its real inspiration.

Ba-bummm. Ba-bummm. Ba-bummm.

"Yes, please, Grand-père. I would like that very much."

His grandfather laughed and ruffled Marcellus's hair. "Well, if you work hard every day, train diligently, and do exactly as I tell you, I have no doubt that one day you too will be the General of the Ministère. You too will command a planet."

Marcellus recognized the memory now. He was four years old, on his very first trip in a voyageur. His grandfather had taken him to Kaishi, where the general was scheduled to meet with the System Alliance as a delegate of Laterre.

He remembered the feeling of the supervoyage engines rumbling beneath him. The stars pulsating in the dark sky. His own wonderment as he took in everything. The whole universe laid out before his eyes.

But most of all, he remembered the want. That boiling determination to do exactly what his grandfather asked of him. To be the person his grandfather wanted him to be.

Had the general been plotting to take over the planet even then?

Which Regime had he been grooming Marcellus to govern?

The corrupt, divided one that currently resided over Laterre? Or this new, terrifying, "streamlined" version that his grandfather had been working so hard to instill?

Ba-bummm. Ba-bummm. Ba-bummm.

Slowly, Marcellus became aware of his own heartbeat, pulling him out of his memories, tugging at his consciousness. His mind scrambled to connect back with his senses. And then there it was. A tingling in his fingertips, in his palms, the soles of his feet, the tip of his scalp, the end of his nose. Every nerve felt like it was waking up, coming back online. His body, the seat under him, the floor below, began to reemerge through the nothingness to become real again.

Finally, light splintered in through his eyelids, unfurling in a mess of colors and glowing shards. He blinked once and then twice, and the fragments began to coalesce.

He saw, in front of him, not stars, but the whole world.

His world.

Great swirls and eddies of clouds enfolded themselves around the familiar, glowing planet. It spun on its axis like a great billowing ball of white and gray thread.

They'd made it. Laterre stood before them like an oasis in the sky, and they were alive.

The ship began to rumble beneath him. Gently at first, but rapidly building in intensity, until Marcellus's whole body was shuddering.

Is that normal?

He turned toward Alouette to gauge her reaction, but he couldn't even see her. The ship was shaking so badly now, his eyes could no longer focus on one object. Her face was jumbled and disfigured, like some of the First World paintings he'd seen hanging up in the Grand Palais—entire people reduced to nothing but colors and shapes.

She seemed to be shouting something, but he couldn't make it out.

"What's happening?" he tried to ask, but suddenly, something shot across his vision. A spark in the darkness. He turned back toward the window and just managed to catch the tail end of a large object hurtling through space. It almost looked like a comet.

No, Marcellus thought as a wave of panic crashed into him. *It looks like a . . .*

The voyageur pitched forward, sending Marcellus slamming into his restraints. Then a terrible sound crackled in his ears. It was blaring and violent and deafening.

A siren.

Definitely not normal.

And then a voice. Too calm to be human.

"Emergency. Primary engine critical. Emergency. Secondary reactor detached."

Detached?

Was that what he'd seen flying past the ship?

"Emergency. Primary engine critical. Emergency . . ." The recorded message proceeded to loop on and on, punctuated by the screech of the alarm.

"The ship!" Cerise shouted from somewhere beside him. "It's coming apart!"

Marcellus struggled to make sense of the words. But his head felt like it was splitting open. His brains would soon be splattered across this windshield.

Coming apart.

Another object flashed before him, and suddenly he understood. The ship was breaking.

"Oh my Sols! Look!" Cerise pointed to a monitor on the console that showed a view of the back of the ship. A great jagged gash had been torn across the voyageur's shell, and protruding between the two silver wings was a giant mess of fiery metal, twisted antennas, and shattered solar panels.

They'd hypervoyaged right into a satellite.

"Emergency. Tertiary reactor detached."

Marcellus finally found his voice. "We have to get to the escape pod before the hull breaches and sucks us all out into space!" He banged down on the mechanism controlling his restraints until his harness released with a low hiss. He leapt out of the seat and paused, waiting to see if he would stand or float. His feet stayed rooted to the ground, which meant the gravity simulator was still intact.

Alouette was already on the move, jumping out of her seat and rushing toward Gabriel. He was still unconscious. His head slumped against his chest.

"Help me get him out!" she cried, her fingers fiddling with the restraints.

As the ship continued to lurch back and forth, Marcellus staggered toward Gabriel's chair, his legs feeling wobbly beneath him, like he'd drunk too much champagne. Alouette managed to get the harness unlatched, and Gabriel tipped forward with a low moan. Marcellus dove to catch him before he slid clear out of the seat.

"What's happening, mec?" he garbled into Marcellus's shoulder. "Is the ship going to explode?"

"Yes!" Cerise shouted. "This time, the ship is *actually* going to explode."

Marcellus bent down and, with a grunt, managed to heave Gabriel over his left shoulder. He stood up, feeling the extra weight immediately.

Out the vast window, Laterre—blanketed in its thick swirl of gray and white clouds—was getting bigger and bigger, closer and closer by the second, and a fresh wave of panic slammed into Marcellus.

"Where is the escape pod?" Alouette asked.

"In the evacuation bay," Marcellus said. "Lowest deck."

"This way!" Cerise called out, leading them to the primary stairwell. Marcellus stumbled behind her, with Gabriel feeling like a sac of titan blocs on his shoulder. And the violent shuddering and screaming of the collapsing voyageur did not make it any easier. The alarms continued to carve permanent tunnels through Marcellus's ear drums.

"Emergency. Primary reactor detached."

"We get it!" Cerise shouted at the ceiling of the stairwell. "The ship is breaking!"

The voyageur jerked sideways in response, knocking Cerise off her feet. Her head smacked against the side wall, and she staggered to catch herself, pressing a hand to her right temple where there was now a bleeding gash.

"Are you all right?" Alouette called from behind Marcellus.

Cerise just let out a grunt in reply and surged forward down the last flight of steps. The evacuation bay was dim and low-ceilinged. Darker than even the cargo hold that they'd arrived in. At the end of the deck, Marcellus could see a large hexagonal hatch, locked with a single heavy lever.

The escape pod.

He allowed himself to breathe a sigh of relief. But it was a second too early, because just then the voyageur trembled violently. The extra weight of Gabriel on his shoulder caused him to lose his balance, and Marcellus was thrown forward. He reached out with his free hand to break his fall, and his palm slammed against the curved wall of the evacuation bay.

"Argh!" he cried, pulling back his hand. The metal was burning hot.

"It must be Laterre's atmosphere," Alouette called out. "We're too close."

Alouette's words were swallowed up by a terrible, ear-shattering sound that shook the whole voyageur. Then a bright, scalding, blinding light roared up in front of them.

Fire!

In an instant, the huge flames seemed to fill the deck, sucking in every molecule of oxygen and choking out great puffs of heat and terrible smoke. Marcellus could barely open his eyes. Every inch of his skin felt as if it were melting into the hull around him.

"Come on!" Cerise yelled, yanking down on the lever. The hatch of the escape pod screeched open. "Get in."

The fire licked and burned at Marcellus's back. He lunged forward and shoved Gabriel into the pod. Together with Cerise, they lowered him into one of the jump seats, and Cerise began to strap him in. Marcellus turned back for Alouette, only to find a wall of smoke where she once stood.

His stomach flipped as he struggled to see through the thick gray plumes. "Alouette?!" he screamed.

There was no reply.

He took a step forward, toward the wild, thundering blaze. The smoke burned and clawed at his throat. His eyes watered. But then, he saw it.

A flash of dark curls in the furious glow of the flames.

"Alouette!" he called again.

But she wasn't moving this way. She was moving back toward the stairs.

"What are you doing?"

Alouette shouted something back at him, but he couldn't hear it over the din of the fire and the screaming ship.

The voyageur gave another terrifying jolt as the sirens blared on and the fire lashed out at him like angry talons. "Alouette!" he called again. "You have to get into the—"

Just then, out of the smoke, Alouette came hurtling toward him, her hands clasped tightly around what looked like a piece of cloth. Was that her sac? Had she really risked her life for that?

Marcellus reached out a hand to her, but a moment later, a terrible roar detonated across the hull, and he watched in horror as Alouette was sucked backward, clean off her feet, pulled toward the spiraling and spewing flames.

"Alouette!" He charged forward.

The smoke was so thick now, he had to cover his mouth and nose with his sleeve. He could see nothing in front of him. He dropped to his knees and scoured the floor of the deck with outstretched hands. Until finally, his fingertips touched fabric. Then skin. Then hair. Heart pounding, he reached for her, pulling her fallen body to him. She let out a soft groan, and Marcellus nearly melted into the floor with relief.

Hooking his hands under Alouette's shoulders, Marcellus began to drag her backward, toward the hatch. Her body was still clutched protectively around that piece of cloth in her hands. By the time they both collapsed into the escape pod, Marcellus was coughing so badly, he could barely move.

Cerise pounded her fist against the panel on the wall. The door slid shut, and the pod began to rumble. Cerise helped Alouette up and into the jump seat. Marcellus struggled to follow, his muscles barely strong enough to fasten his restraints.

The engine let out a roar and then the pod released. In one swift jolt, they were hoisted out and away from the voyageur. The force of the blast pinned Marcellus to his seat, but just as the pod banked and they began their descent toward Laterre, he was able to turn his head long enough to steal a glance behind them. At the Galactique-class voyageur that had taken them to Albion and back. At the ship that was now exploding into a million shattering and burning pieces of light.

CHAPTER 53

CHATINE

OUTSIDE THE CHALET, THE AIR HAD NEVER TASTED SO fresh. So cleansing. So cold and delicious. Chatine gulped in huge lungfuls of it, thirsty for more and more and more. Still clutching the handmade sac, she collapsed forward and rested her hands on her knees, trying to calm herself. Her whole body was quivering. Her heart was thundering behind her rib cage. Her mind was on fire.

She couldn't believe what she'd just done.

She couldn't believe she'd gone to battle with her parents and actually won.

But she knew this victory wasn't just for herself. It was for Azelle, who had dreamed of a better life and had died working for it. And it was for Henri. For *Roche*, who had grown up parentless and abandoned and alone, wandering the streets, begging and conning for food, hiding under marketplace stalls and in the bases of statues.

This victory was for all of them.

The three lost Renard children, who had suffered simply for being Renards.

Chatine's breathing slowly returned to normal, and her head cleared as she reminded herself that this wasn't over yet. She still had to somehow break into the storage chalet and steal seven blocs of zyttrium.

Guilt streamed thick and heavy through her veins at the thought. She used to steal without remorse. It used to mean nothing to her. Just another part of her miserable day. But something had changed in her since she'd left Bastille. Since she'd seen that small raindrop-shaped birthmark on the back of Roche's shoulder. Since she'd woken up on Etienne's strange ship. Since she'd lost her Skin.

She flipped her arm over and rubbed at the healing incision. She would always have a scar. A reminder of the life she'd led. The chains she'd worn. But it was almost as though Brigitte had taken something else from her that day when she'd lifted the Ministère-manufactured implant from her body.

She'd taken away the ties to her past.

She'd freed Chatine from the person she used to be. The person her parents and the Regime had turned her into.

She couldn't steal from these people. She was suddenly certain of it. No matter the upside, she couldn't deceive them or con them or hurt them. She would just have to turn her parents in to the Défecteurs and deal with the consequences. Even if it meant she lost her place here too. Even if it meant she lost their trust.

On the horizon, a slither of clouds glowed pink and blue, a warning that the Sols would soon be rising. Brigitte's chalet, she knew, was on the other side of the camp, back near the treatment center. Chatine turned toward it and began walking. But she'd barely made it a few paces when she heard another set of footsteps.

She spun and blinked into the beam of a flashlight, her entire body tensing. She didn't need to see beyond that bright light to know who was behind it. The situation was too familiar. And his energy was too recognizable.

She swallowed.

There was no point in trying to play stupid or pretending she was just out on a late-night stroll through the camp. They were standing right next to her parents' chalet, and the walls weren't soundproof.

Chatine cleared her throat, but her voice still quavered. "How much did you hear?"

Etienne didn't reply as he took a step toward her and lowered the flashlight so that the beam landed right on her chest. Like a blade. Then, it traveled down to the sac still in her hand, and Chatine felt her blood turn to ice.

He knew. Of course he knew.

"Listen," she began. But Etienne held up a hand and didn't allow her to finish. Why should he? There was no use trying to explain now. He knew who she was, who her parents were. He'd heard her agree to their plan. He knew she was planning to steal zyttrium from the storage chalet.

"Come with me, please." His words were stark and cold, like they belonged to a stranger. Like he was *speaking* to a stranger. Not the girl he'd rescued from the roof of Bastille. Not the girl he'd smiled at from across the fête. Not the girl she so desperately wanted to become.

The girl she *had* become . . . if even for a splinter of a second.

Gripping the bag tightly in her hand, she kept her head down and followed behind him. He walked quietly, stiffly, the flashlight beam illuminating the walkway ahead of him. She didn't know where he was taking her, but she knew she wouldn't run. She would face up to her crime *and* her punishment.

It wasn't until they had made the final turn that Chatine recognized the path. Her gaze snapped up and she squinted at the shadowy shapes of the buildings around them, trying to confirm her suspicions.

The night's darkness was beginning to creep away, and, in the murky predawn gloom, she was now quite certain they were nearing the storage chalets. The buildings were taller and longer than the other structures, and their sides were punctured by slits instead of windows.

"What are we doing—" Chatine began to ask, but once again she was interrupted before she could finish as Etienne placed a single finger to his lips. She watched in astonishment and complete bewilderment as Etienne approached the door of the last chalet, pulled a small piece of metal from the pocket of his coat, turned it in the lock, and beckoned her inside.

All the breath seemed to leave her body at once as she gazed around the interior of the chalet. Chatine had seen zyttrium before. She'd spent seemingly endless hours mining it on Bastille. But never like this. And never so much of it. Shelves upon shelves bordered the entire space, and on every single one, small blocs of the processed metal were stacked in orderly piles. The whole place, even Etienne's clothes and hair, glowed blue. It was like she'd been transported into the hidden depths of a shimmering sea.

For a moment, Chatine wondered if this was some kind of trap. But then Etienne silently reached out and pried the handmade sac from her tight grip. Chatine's throat went dirt dry as she watched him count out seven gleaming blue blocs of zyttrium and place each one carefully and reverently into the bag.

Something stirred inside of her. Something so great and overwhelming and unfamiliar, she nearly sobbed. She reached out and braced herself against one of the shelves as the strange sensation trembled through her like a rolling explosion.

Once the Renards' sac was weighed down with the precious metal, Etienne turned to face her and finally answered her question, "I heard *all* of it."

He extended the bag toward her, and—with shaking, numb fingers—Chatine took it. It felt impossibly heavy in her hands. Heavier than seven blocs of zyttrium should feel.

Then Etienne offered her the tiniest, yet most monumental of smiles. "Flying lessons start after breakfast," he said before turning and leaving the chalet.

- CHAPTER 54 -
ALOUETTE

THE PARACHUTE DEPLOYED ABOVE THE ESCAPE POD, and suddenly they were drifting, buffeting across an endless gray-and-white sky.

"What were you thinking, going back in there?" Cerise bellowed at Alouette. "You could have gotten yourself killed! You could have gotten us *all* killed!"

"I had to . . . ," Alouette began weakly, but she couldn't find enough breath to speak. So instead, she carefully unfolded the blanket in her hands, like she was unswaddling a baby. And there, nestled in her arms, was the object she'd risked her life—all of their lives—to save.

Marcellus sucked in a sharp breath as his gaze fell upon the sleek silver canister. "The inhibitor," he whispered dazedly.

Alouette nodded and gave the barrel a sharp twist. The top hissed open with a puff of steam. Her vision cleared and then. . . every last ounce of hope leaked out of her.

Where there were once twelve intact, glowing vials, there was now a splatter of broken glass and congealed serum. All but *one* of Dr. Collins's doses of inhibitor had been destroyed.

Marcellus stared numbly down into the barrel, looking like he was staring into the barrel of a rayonette set to kill.

"No," he said, his voice shattering as quickly and violently as their voyageur had only moments ago. "No!" He banged his fist against the wall of the escape pod. "What are we going to do now? How are we going to stop him? We have nothing. No plan. No hope. No inhibitor."

"And it looks like no navigation, either," Cerise said somberly, poking at the flight controls. "The fire must have damaged the system."

"What does that mean?" Alouette asked, dread clawing at her voice.

"It means I have no way of controlling our landing. We're at the mercy of Laterre's gravity and winds now."

Marcellus leaned his head back against his jump seat and closed his eyes. Alouette could see his lips moving, like he was murmuring something under his breath. A prayer to the Sols, perhaps? Alouette turned toward Gabriel, who was passed out in the seat across from her. Unconscious. Near death.

She took deep, calming breaths, trying to tell herself that this, too, would be okay. This, too, they would survive. Just like they'd survived every catastrophe before this, against all odds.

They were still here. Injured and weary and bleeding, but still alive.

That had to count for something, right?

Outside the window of the pod, the nothingness and uncertainty of the Laterrian sky spread out around them. Thick gray clouds that seemed to go on forever, consuming everything. And for just a moment, Alouette wondered if they would ever touch the ground. If maybe they would just float in this misty limbo forever.

Suddenly, all she could think about was everything she'd left behind on that ship. Her mother's titan box, her screwdriver, the sisters' compendium of reports. They were all just things, Alouette knew that. Nowhere near as important as a human life. But she still felt the ache of their loss just the same.

That titan box was the only thing she'd had left of her mother. Her screwdriver had been a gift from Sister Denise. And Principale Francine had entrusted her with those reports—that small slice of Vangarde history. And now it was all nothing but space dust.

Something hammered against the sides of the pod, pulling Alouette's attention back to the window, which was now covered in tiny droplets of water. The soft gray blanket around them had turned dark and sinister as they'd continued their slow, undulating descent toward the ground. Then, moments later, light flooded the small pod and Alouette could suddenly see Laterre's great landmass stretching out below.

Squinting through the rain-splattered plastique, she could make out uneven terrain with patches of slick, foreboding ice and clusters of rocky outcrops. It wasn't until the ground drew closer that she realized where they were. And her heart nearly thudded to a stop. She recognized this unforgiving landscape. She'd read about it in the Chronicles.

It was a place no one survived.

Despite the parachute slowing their descent, their landing was hard. Rough. Jolting. The underbelly of the pod smacked down on the frozen tundra with a force so strong, it felt as though every bone and nerve in Alouette's body clashed and collided against one another. They slid along the slick surface of the ground before crashing into a jagged, jutting rock and finally skidding to a halt.

Alouette kept her gaze locked on the window, as though staring at their surroundings might possibly change them. Might possibly reverse time, change the direction of the winds, deliver them any place but here.

"This doesn't look good," croaked a voice, and everyone turned to see that Gabriel was awake, staring wide-eyed and slack-jawed at the barrenness outside the window.

"No," Marcellus agreed quietly, and when Alouette peered over at him, she saw that his face looked hopeless and defeated. "This is definitely not good."

Alouette's head fell back against the headrest in despair, just as the Terrain Perdu winds started to howl and pummel against the shell of their lonely, battered escape pod.

- CHAPTER 55 -
MARCELLUS

THE TINY SPARK CRACKLED IN THE WET MORNING AIR before immediately fizzling out. Marcellus cursed quietly under his breath and struck the small rock against the PermaSteel bolt again. His arms were tired, and he could barely feel his fingers anymore.

"Don't worry," he said to Gabriel through chattering teeth. "Just a few more seconds and I'll have this thing going and all of our troubles will be over."

It was a lie, of course.

Everything out of his mouth for the past three hours had been a lie.

"We'll be rescued."

"We'll find an AirLink signal."

"I can start a fire."

But it was better than the truth. Marcellus couldn't face the truth, let alone utter it aloud. The truth was unbearable. And morbid. And . . .

His fault.

This was all his fault.

Gabriel getting shot. The hypervoyage disaster. Their destroyed escape pod.

He pushed the thought from his mind and focused back on the small pile of twigs and spindly branches in front of him.

"Almost there," he said breathlessly to Gabriel. "We'll be warm soon."

Another lie. They might never be warm again.

But Marcellus kept telling himself that the lies didn't matter. Even if Gabriel was awake, he wouldn't be able to hear him anyway. The Terrain Perdu's winds howled and gnawed too loudly from every direction, and Gabriel was bundled too deeply inside layers of jackets, hoods, and emergency blankets that they'd managed to grab from the escape pod right before the floor—which had been pummeled during the crash-landing—collapsed out from under it. Then the rest of the pod had folded in on itself in a plume of shattering plastique and buckling PermaSteel.

Marcellus continued to bang the rock against the metal. He'd never started a fire without matches before. His matchbox had been in his sac on the voyageur, which was now nothing more than a pile of ash floating through space.

Alouette had told Marcellus she'd read in a book once that a spark could be created with nothing but a stone and a steel blade. The stone had been easy to find among the craggy outcrops, but, for the blade, they'd had to use a fragment of metal from the crumpled escape pod instead.

Another small spark ignited but, predictably, died before the kindling could catch. Everything in the Terrain Perdu was either frozen or wet or somewhere in between, making the fire nearly impossible to start. And the icy winds kept snatching away anything that even resembled a flame.

A low groan rumbled behind him, and Marcellus turned around to see Gabriel's eyes were half open. He looked like he was struggling to say something.

"Pi . . ." He winced at the effort. "Pi . . ."

"What's that?" Marcellus asked, leaning in closer.

"Pi . . . ," he murmured again.

As Marcellus watched the pain pull at Gabriel's face, more guilt bubbled up in his chest. He squeezed Gabriel's shoulder. "Hang in there, mec."

Gabriel's eyelids fluttered closed. Determined, Marcellus turned back to the paltry pile of frozen grass and sticks. His fingers were rigid from the cold, but he grabbed the stone and PermaSteel and struck them together with more ferociousness, more urgency than before.

Gabriel needed to get warm.

This fire *needed* to burn.

"Please," Marcellus muttered. "Please light."

Then, as if answering his prayer, a spark erupted. The twigs suddenly flickered to life. But no sooner had a beautiful orange flame danced before him, than a gust of wind swooped in and, like a cruel, icy joke, snuffed it out.

"For Sols-sake," Marcellus spat, and collapsed backward, tossing the pieces of stone and PermaSteel on the ground in front of him.

"Still no signal."

Marcellus looked up through the icy mist to see Cerise trudging toward him. Her cheeks glowed from the bitter cold, and he could see that every drop of blood had drained from her fingers, which were clutching her TéléCom.

"Nothing?" he shouted over the howling winds.

She dropped down next to him and blew into her hands. "No. Which means I know exactly where we are."

Marcellus pinned her with an eager stare. "You do?"

She let out a dark laugh. "Don't get your hopes up. It's not good. Due to the way the satellite orbits are set up, every three days there's a gap in coverage right over the center of the Terrain Perdu. Unfortunately, I have no idea where in the orbit cycle they are. So we could have signal in ten minutes . . . or three days."

Marcellus shivered. Both from the cold and from Cerise's words. He'd hoped that maybe they would be close enough to Montfer or the town of Lacrête to walk, but the center of the Terrain Perdu meant they were thousands of kilomètres from any city or civilization.

Cerise peered over at Gabriel wrapped in his myriad of blankets and clothing. "How's he doing?"

"He's hanging in," Marcellus said, somehow managing a smile again, despite their predicament.

Marcellus couldn't tell if the tears forming in Cerise's eyes were from the cold or from the sight of Gabriel's drawn, pained face.

"Unfortunately, this was all I could find," said another voice.

Marcellus looked up again to see that Alouette was back too. In her arms, she cradled a pile of brown grass and a few gnarled twigs, clearly picked from the sparse shrubs and bushes that managed to grow out in this wilderness. Alouette's frozen eyelashes shimmered in the afternoon light, and ice crystals clung to every tight coil of her hair.

"It was hard to find anything even close to dry," she said, setting down her armful of kindling next to Marcellus.

He sighed. "It doesn't really matter. I can't keep a flame lit. It would help if I had matches but . . ." He sighed, once again berating himself. "I don't."

Gabriel let out another moan, and Alouette immediately scrabbled toward him on her knees. She peeled back his blankets and started to check his wounds again. The narrow escape from the burning voyageur and then the boisterous crash-landing on the Terrain Perdu had not been kind to Gabriel. The bandages had been soaked with blood. Alouette had packed the wound with ice and used a spare blanket to make a new dressing, but it had been another temporary measure. And they all knew that.

"How is it?" Cerise asked.

Alouette was silent for a moment and then said, "Good. It looks good."

So, Marcellus wasn't the only one who had resorted to lying.

"Pi . . ." Gabriel whimpered, his eyelids struggling to open. "Pi . . ."

Cerise looked urgently from Gabriel to Alouette to Marcellus. "What is he saying?"

"I don't know," Marcellus said, shaking his head. "He's been mumbling that for a while."

Alouette reached over and felt Gabriel's forehead. "He's still a little feverish from the infection. But thankfully, I don't think it's gotten any worse. . . ."

Marcellus could have sworn he heard Alouette add the word "yet" under her breath. But like his momentary flame earlier, the word was stolen away by the brutal wind. He looked at Gabriel for a long time before snatching his abandoned pieces of stone and steel and banging them furiously together. But still, he could not achieve anything more than a useless spark. His jaw clenched with the effort. His freezing fingers struggled with the disobedient instruments.

Scrape . . . spark . . . nothing.

Scrape . . . spark . . . nothing.

Scrape . . . spark . . .

And then, fire.

But not blazing in front of him where it was supposed to be. This monstrous flame ignited *inside* of Marcellus. It was the same fire that had been burning inside him for weeks. Lit from the stinging heat of his grandfather's betrayal, the friction of this losing battle Marcellus had fought for his entire life, and the kindling of his hatred for the man who had raised him.

It all exploded inside of him, more colossal and destructive than ever, until his heart and body and mind were consumed by the roaring blaze, burning as wildly and violently as the flames that had once destroyed the First World.

"I did this!" he shouted, jumping to his feet. "I did this to Gabriel! To all of you."

"Marcellus," Alouette tried to argue, but he promptly cut her off.

"No. Gabriel is dying because of me. He was right. This *was* a suicide mission. Which means it should be *me* lying there with a cluster bullet wound in my stomach. Not him. And we're all going to freeze to death out here because of me. Because I can't defeat the almighty General Bonnefaçon. I've tried. Too many times now. And I always, *always* fail. He always wins and I always lose. We had the inhibitor. We had a sure-fire way to stop him. But we lost almost all of it because of my stupidity. And now the general has control of the Skins and the Third Estate and, soon, the planet. AND I CAN'T STOP HIM!"

Alouette and Cerise both stared up at him, startled.

"Marcellus—" Alouette tried again, but still, he would not allow her to finish.

"Stop! I never should have brought any of you into this. I never should have even let you onto that voyageur to Albion."

"Let us?" Cerise fired back. She was on her feet too, facing off against Marcellus, her cheeks puffed with sudden fury. "I'm sorry to break it to you, *Officer*, but you're not the Patriarche. I don't need your authorization. You didn't *let us* do anything. We volunteered. All of us. We volunteered knowing the dangers. And we didn't need you, your Sol-Almightiness, to give us permission."

This stopped Marcellus short. He was so taken aback by Cerise's outburst—by an anger that nearly matched his own—that he momentarily lost his train of thought.

"I'm sorry, Marcellus, but I'm tired of your pity parade," Cerise went on. "And your pathetic attempts at martyrdom. You're not the only one here who gets to feel guilty." Her voice cracked and her legs seemed to give out. She collapsed back down onto the ground, her gaze falling toward Gabriel. When she spoke next, her voice was quiet and full of regret. "I'm the one who suggested we go into hypervoyage. I'm the one who brought you that message from Dr. Collins in the first place. If you want to blame anyone, blame me."

"This is no one's fault," Alouette said, glancing between Marcellus and Cerise. "And I don't see how arguing over that will do anyone any good."

Flustered, Marcellus clenched and unclenched his fists. Alouette was right. It wouldn't do any good. They were running out of time.

With a growl, he turned and started off into the icy tundra.

"Marcellus!" Alouette shouted. "What are you doing?"

He could hear her footsteps chasing after him. "What does it look like I'm doing? I'm going to find help. I can't just stand here and watch Gabriel die. I can't just wait around here while the general destroys the planet. I have to do something, or I will implode."

"That's exactly why you *shouldn't* do anything." Alouette said.

Marcellus slowed to a halt. "What?"

He spun around and looked into her dark eyes—so strong and fierce and yet so tranquil at the same time.

"Marcellus," she said with a quiet urgency. "You don't even know what General Bonnefaçon is planning."

"All the more reason to get us out of here."

Alouette reached out and touched his arm. "Take a deep breath. Calm your mind. Let your thoughts settle before you—"

Marcellus threw up his hands. "Enough with your Sisterhood nonsense. I don't have time to listen to this. I have to go find help or we're all going to freeze to death!"

"I told you, we're in the middle of the Terrain Perdu!" Cerise shouted from beside Gabriel. "There's nothing out there for thousands of kilomètres."

"Then I guess I'll have to take my chances!" he shouted back. He turned and kept walking straight into the howling wind, which battered at his numb cheeks and ripped at his flimsy coat. It was so loud against his ears, he almost didn't hear it when Alouette spoke again.

"Is that what your grandfather would do?"

But he *did* hear it. He heard it and felt it everywhere. All the way down to his frozen toes. He spun back around, a new fury igniting inside of him. "Why would I care what my grandfather would do?" he said, his voice a deep, guttural growl.

Alouette's steady gaze never faltered. "Because you said so yourself: He always wins. He never loses. Why do you think that is?"

Marcellus's anger quickly gave way to bafflement. What on Laterre was she talking about?

"You may not agree with his motivations," Alouette went on, "but you can't argue with his success. Yes, he killed the Premier Enfant. He's caused chaos and destruction on this planet. He built a horrific weapon with Laterre's greatest enemy and is now poised to unleash it. Do you really think he accomplished all of that by 'taking his chances'?"

The words thrummed through Marcellus. Hitting him deep. Hitting him hard. He dug his fingernails into his palms and shut his eyes, trying to chase Alouette's voice from his mind. But it seemed to be clinging to the corners, gripping tightly like the fists of droids.

Then he could suddenly hear his grandfather's voice alongside it, harmonizing with Alouette's like a dark, haunting melody.

"Always so hasty to act, aren't you, Marcellus? Always rushing into things. You must learn to be more strategic. Plan your attack. Analyze your opponent. Play with your head, not your emotions."

The general didn't take chances. He didn't have to. He was always three moves ahead of everyone else.

Especially Marcellus.

Because Marcellus kept making the same mistakes time and time again. He kept starting over because he kept losing. He kept losing because he refused to play the game the way his grandfather did. The way his grandfather had *trained* him to play since he was a child.

What if Mabelle had been more right than she realized? What if this officer uniform he was still wearing was not a curse, but a gift? A key?

A key he had *yet* to use.

For eighteen years, he had trained under the general. For eighteen years, he had watched his grandfather maneuver and strategize. He'd sat in on countless briefings and meetings and broadcasts. He'd witnessed the general handle every problem under the Sols. He'd traveled across the System Divine and back—thousands of hours locked in a voyageur with Laterre's greatest military strategist.

For eighteen years, Marcellus had watched his mind work. He knew the general better than anyone.

What if the only way to defeat him was to be the one thing Marcellus swore he would never be?

Just like him.

"I . . . ," Marcellus began haltingly, but he didn't quite know how to finish. His mind was too tangled. His thoughts still a jumbled blur. He looked back at Alouette and drew in a long, slow breath.

Somewhere on the ground, Gabriel stirred. "Pi . . . ," he whimpered again.

Cerise turned to him. "Shhh . . . It's okay."

He twisted under his blankets. "Pi . . ." Once again, his voice seemed to give out on him.

Alouette ran back to Gabriel and pressed a hand across his forehead. "Are you okay? What are you trying to tell us?"

His eyelids heaved open and he looked straight at Cerise, holding her gaze for an impressively long time. He winced as he attempted to speak again. "My . . . my pocket."

Cerise pushed back the blanket and slipped her hand into Gabriel's coat pocket. "What is this?" she said as she pulled out a slim, curved object with titan plating that glittered in the Terrain Perdu's frozen light.

Marcellus stared, his gaze fixed on the small floral crest carved into the side. "Is that . . . ?"

"It's Lady Alexander's vapor pipe!" Cerise cried.

"Pi . . . ," Gabriel said again. "Pi . . . pe."

Cerise turned the titan device over in her cold fingers and gaped at it. "You stole this? From Lady Alexander? How did you do— *When* did you do that?"

She looked at Gabriel, but he only grinned lazily in return.

"We can use the heating element to light the fire," Alouette said. Cerise handed over the pipe, and Alouette pressed her fingertips against the seam to pop it open and began fiddling with the mechanism inside. She held the open pipe next to the kindling that Marcellus had layered beneath the twigs and branches. The wood caught fire. And a blast of light and warmth—beautiful, glowing warmth—sprang up, instantly shattering any lingering tension remaining in the air. Hurriedly, Marcellus fed the fire with more kindling, and Cerise protected the newborn flames from the ferocious winds with her coat.

Soon the small fire was roaring, its flames licking and twirling around one another.

Cerise looked back to Gabriel, who was smirking, despite his obvious pain. Her face lit up. Her dark eyes mirrored the flames. She moved closer to him and cradled his cheeks in her hands. "You, Gabriel, *are* a criminal mastermind."

Gabriel's smile widened and he tried, again, to speak. "Sparkles . . ."

But Cerise stopped him with a stern look. "No. Don't talk. Just shut up." Then, she carefully lowered herself down beside him and pulled his hand into hers.

Marcellus turned toward Alouette. She was smiling and staring into the orange blaze, her body seeming to melt from the beautiful heat and the even more beautiful relief.

But as Marcellus followed her gaze toward the roaring fire, he could not feel what she so obviously felt. He could not smile. Nor melt with relief. He felt only a looming dread of what was to come and what he would have to do.

Because he knew that fire—just like the one that had been burning inside of him, spurring him on, sending him across the System Divine and back—was a temporary solution. A fickle flame to ward off the inevitable and keep his fears at bay.

And all flames eventually have to burn out.

- CHAPTER 56 -
CHATINE

"NOW PULL BACK ON THE CONTRÔLEUR AND EASE into the turn. Nice and easy. Nice and easy. Not too steep. We're not dodging combatteur fire here. Now gently roll out of the turn and increase airspeed."

Gripping the contrôleur with both hands, Chatine carefully maneuvered the small ship, keeping her gaze on the beautiful white, untamed wilderness that spread out before her.

"Now trim the nose up just a bit," Etienne commanded.

Chatine reached for the dial to her left and rolled it forward. The ship started to dive.

"Nope!" Etienne shouted, gripping the edges of the jump seat. "Wrong way!"

Panicked, Chatine lunged for the dial and shoved it as far down as it would go. The ship immediately lurched into a sharp incline, until they were practically vertical and Chatine was staring up at Laterre's thick layer of gray clouds.

"Too much! Too much! Oh Sols, this was a mistake."

With her body thrust back in her seat, it was difficult for Chatine to reach the controls. She fought against the gravity pulling down on her arm until her shaky hand finally reached the dial.

The ship leveled off, and the horizon came back into view. But Chatine's stomach felt like it was still stuck in the incline.

"Okay," Etienne said, regathering his composure. "Okay. Everything's fine. No need to panic. You're doing great."

"Merci," Chatine replied bitterly. It was the first time Etienne had doled out even a hint of a compliment since they'd started this lesson.

"I was talking to Marilyn," Etienne said.

Chatine rolled her eyes. "Of course you were."

"Okay, now, have you checked your altitude monitor recently?"

She sighed. "Yes. Five seconds ago."

"Check it again."

Chatine pulled her gaze from the cockpit window and peered at the monitor just to the left of the contrôleur. "One point seven kilomètres," she announced.

"Too low. Way too low. Increase altitude immediately."

"But I like this view," Chatine complained. "I can't see anything from up there."

At this altitude she was just low enough to see through the patches of low-hanging clouds and make out the patterns and details of the craggy rocks, straggly bushes, and lakes of ice. She'd had no idea how truly fascinating the Terrain Perdu was.

"This isn't about the *view*," Etienne said sharply. "You can stare at the view all you want from the camp. This is about safety. What's the number one rule of flying?"

Chatine snickered. "No one flies Marilyn but you?"

Etienne shot her a sharp look. "Fine. What's the number two rule of flying."

"There is no number two rule," she parroted from their first flight together. "Rule number one is everything." Chatine struggled to keep a straight face, but Etienne was too much fun to tease. And the way his jaw muscles were tensing right now just made it all that more rewarding.

She reached over and poked his cheek. "Aha! Looks like you have some buttons of your own."

He swatted her hand away. "Let's just focus on *your* buttons." His face seemed to flush with embarrassment for a moment, and he quickly amended his statement. "I mean, the buttons in front of you. The *ship's* buttons."

Chatine chuckled, keeping her hands locked on the contrôleur.

Etienne cleared his throat and was all seriousness again. "The number *three* rule is to maintain altitude at all times. You can't always rely on stealth mode. It can fail. Which is why cloud coverage is our friend. It keeps us safe and hidden." He gave a curt nod of his head. "Or as we like to say, 'You fly high. You stay dry.'"

"Nothing on Laterre stays dry," Chatine pointed out.

Etienne huffed. "It means you stay hidden."

"Why don't you just say, 'You fly high. You stay hidden.'"

"Because it doesn't rhyme."

"Why does it have to rhyme?"

"Because—" Etienne stopped himself and took a breath. "Just stop talking and increase altitude."

Chatine shrugged and wrenched another dial. The ship shot up into the air in a heartbeat, causing Etienne to yelp.

"Too fast! *Way* too fast!"

Chatine tried to compensate with the contrôleur, plunging it downward. The ship started to dive back down toward the ground.

"Pull up! Pull up!" Etienne shouted.

"Are you talking to me or Marilyn this time?"

"YOU!"

Chatine eased up on the contrôleur, leveling off the ship at three kilomètres. She couldn't help the satisfied smile on her face. "*That* was a good button. I'll have to remember where that one was."

"That's it," Etienne said, unbuckling his restraint and standing up. "Get up. You're done. Flying lessons are over. This was a bad idea. You are not taking this seriously. You do not deserve to fly this ship."

"Okay, okay. Calm down." She surrendered her hands up and the ship started to pitch forward.

"Hands on the contrôleur!" Etienne barked.

Chatine dove for the contrôleur. "Sorry. Sit down. I'll stop fooling around."

Reluctantly, Etienne lowered back into his seat. The cockpit fell quiet, with only the soft purring sound of Marilyn's engine between them. Chatine glanced at Etienne out of the corner of her eye. He was as still as a statue, his gaze locked on her hands guiding his precious ship.

"Why did you agree to give me flying lessons, anyway?" Chatine asked.

Etienne's head snapped up, as though he were being awoken from a dream. "What?"

Chatine kept her eyes on the seemingly endless horizon. "You could have turned me in. Or kicked me out for being a thief. But instead, you told no one about me or my parents, you helped me steal zyttrium, and then you offered to teach me to fly."

"Are you still a thief?" he asked.

Chatine hesitated. Not because she didn't want to tell Etienne the truth, but because she *did* want to. She just needed a few seconds to come to terms with what the truth was now. "No."

"Well then, there you go."

Chatine glanced at him again. He was no longer looking at her or her hands, he was staring out the cockpit window. "You should know," he went on, "that we don't judge people by what they did in the past. We judge them by who they are now."

"Like your maman?" Chatine asked.

He peered at her. "What about her?"

"This classified project she was involved in, back when she was a cyborg. You said it was . . . bad?"

"Right. Yes, like that. She changed herself. More drastically than any of us, you could say. We have a lot of respect for people who can wake themselves up."

Chatine bit her lip, unsure if she should broach the subject she'd been desperately wanting to broach ever since Brigitte had shown her that graveyard. She took in a breath and tried to keep her voice light and casual, afraid that anything more might scare him away again. Thankfully, right now, he had nowhere to run to. "Was your papa a cyborg too?"

The reaction was instantaneous. Chatine didn't even need to take her eyes off the horizon to know it was there. She could sense it. Like a noxious gas filling up the cockpit, threatening to suffocate them both. And right away, Chatine knew she wasn't going to get an answer. The conversation would be over before it even began. He would make some critique about her altitude or speed and change the subject. He would—

"No."

The one-word response came swiftly and erratically, like he was afraid that if he didn't say it fast, he wouldn't say it at all.

"Was he born in a community? Like you?" Chatine could feel her hands shaking on the contrôleur, but thankfully the ship didn't shudder in response. Maybe, for once, Marilyn was on her side, helping her along.

"No," Etienne repeated, and just when Chatine thought it would end there again, he added, "He was Third Estate. From Vallonay. Like you. He used to love to tell me stories about living on the grid. The Frets, the Marsh, the Ascension, the droids—or 'bashers' as he used to call them. I never knew why."

"Because they bash their way through everything," Chatine explained bitterly. "And they can bash in your face without losing a drop of power." She swore she felt Etienne shudder at her description. "Have you ever seen one?"

He went silent again. Pensive. And then, "On the night of the roundup. There were hundreds. They were like monsters in the darkness. The things of nightmares."

"Is that what killed him?" she asked quietly. "Your father?"

"No." Etienne's voice was so cold and emotionless, it could have belonged to a basher itself. "The fires killed him."

"The fires?" Chatine repeated, but upon noticing Etienne flinch, she realized she had been too blunt, too fast. She softened her voice. "But I thought the Ministère didn't use fire."

"They don't," Etienne said. "We set them. To try to scare them off. It didn't work. Turns out droids aren't really scared of much."

Chatine kept her eyes trained on the sky, trying to give him privacy, and yet she yearned to turn and look at him. To see the pain on his face. Not because she could possibly fix it or erase it or even alleviate it. But because she understood it.

"How did he—" she began to ask, but Etienne cut her off. His response sharp and stinging, like a slap.

"Because of me."

Now she did turn to him. Just for an instant but an instant was all it took. His anguish was raw and fresh, as though it had happened not years ago but only yesterday. A wound that never closes but rather keeps opening wider and wider. Like a crack in the ground. The kind of crack that can suck in cities and mountains and oceans. The kind of crack Chatine knew all too well.

Etienne continued to stare out the window. "I went back. I shouldn't have gone back. We were safe. We were nearly away. But I went back. For a stupid toy. I thought I had left it in our chalet. The one that was burning to the ground. I let go of my father's hand and I ran. He, of course, ran after me and . . ."

He didn't finish. They both knew he didn't have to. Some endings didn't need words.

The silence returned in full force, consuming them in an instant. Chatine hadn't known what to say back in the graveyard when Brigitte had told her the beginning of this story, but somehow, she knew what to say now that Etienne had completed it.

"Merci."

Etienne's eyebrows pinched together. "For what?"

"For telling me."

His expression softened, looking almost embarrassed. "Well, you know . . . I did think I was going to die in this ship with you flying it, so I figured I better unburden myself before my trip to the Sols."

Chatine laughed politely. "Good thinking."

He breathed out a heavy sigh. "I miss him. Every day."

Chatine nodded, whispering the same words that Dead Azelle had whispered to her last night at the linking cérémonie. "I know."

"He was my mother's first patient."

"Really?"

"Yeah. She never got to work with patients when she was a cyborg, because she was assigned to medical research. But Papa arrived at our old camp shortly after she did. And since he was Third Estate, naturally he needed a Skin removal, so Maman did it. They used to tell this funny story about how he woke up in his goldenroot haze and fell instantly in love with her. And she told him, 'Wait until the herbs wear off, and then we'll talk.'" Out of the corner of her eye, Chatine noticed a ghost of a smile on his face. "I guess it wasn't just the goldenroot, because I was born less than a year later."

Chatine tried to match his fragile amusement. "Wow."

Etienne huffed out a laugh. "Yeah. I guess when you know, you know."

This time, when Chatine glanced at him, he was staring right at her, his gaze ready to capture hers.

"You know?" he whispered.

She turned away, unable to answer. Instead, she kept her gaze locked out the cockpit window and her hands wrapped tightly around the contrôleur.

Seconds passed. Possibly even minutes. Chatine didn't know. The sky out here seemed to consume time like a void.

"Why do you do that?" Etienne broke the silence, his voice no longer heavy and burdened, but light and inquisitive.

"Do what?"

"Touch your finger like that. I've seen you do it a few times. Like you're expecting something to be there."

Chatine peered down at the controls to see her forefinger was running

up and down the side of her thumb again, searching for Marcellus's
ring. She hadn't even realized she'd been doing it. "Oh," she said
clumsily. "I . . . just . . . I used to have a ring. I lost it somewhere when
I left Bastille. It's just . . . I guess I still touch the skin out of habit. It's
stupide."

"A ring?" Etienne asked, still staring at her finger.

Feeling self-conscious, Chatine repositioned her hands on the contrôleur so her naked thumb was concealed. "I wouldn't normally wear
one, it's just that this was . . ." she trailed off. For some reason, the thought
of telling Etienne about Marcellus felt wrong. Like the two existed in
separate galaxies, and should they ever be in the same one together, the
whole universe might explode. Or at the very least, the universe that lived
inside Chatine's mind.

". . . It belonged to someone I used to know," she finally finished. "And
I promised to keep it safe for them."

There was no response, and when Chatine glanced over at the jump
seat again, Etienne was no longer there. Keeping her hands firmly on the
contrôleur, she looked over her shoulder to find him rummaging around
in a cabinet in the rear of the cockpit. "What are you doing?" she asked.

"I didn't know what it was. I found it when I was cleaning out the ship
a few days ago. I should have guessed it belonged to you. The thought just
never crossed my mind."

Chatine held her breath as Etienne made his way back across the
cockpit. She wanted to close her eyes. Forever. She wanted to disappear
so she didn't have to see or feel or hear the implosion that she knew was
coming. But when Etienne appeared beside her, his hand outstretched,
she forced her eyes to stay open. She forced herself to look at the tiny,
silver ring.

Marcellus's ring.

Cupped protectively in Etienne's outstretched palm.

"Sorry," he murmured, clearly misinterpreting the conflict that was
playing out on her face. "I would have given it to you sooner. I forgot it
was even in here."

Slowly, hesitantly, Chatine reached out and prodded the ring with her fingertip. The touch of the metal burned her skin like ice and fire and snow and rain all combined into one.

"Here," Etienne said innocently. "Allow me."

And before Chatine could argue, her hand was clasped in his. The ring was pinched between his fingers. And she felt the metal slide onto her thumb, chafing against her skin like the edge of a dull knife.

Etienne released her hand, and it plummeted to her side like it was weighed down by stones.

"Watch the sky," he reminded her, nudging his chin toward the horizon.

Chatine blinked and refocused out the window, dragging her heavy, weighted hand back up to the contrôleur. As she stared into the icy abyss of the Terrain Perdu, she could feel tears pricking her eyes, but she couldn't, for the life of her, figure out where they were coming from. Was she crying for Etienne's lost father? Or her lost brother? Or sister? Was she crying for the ring? For the original bearer of it? Or was she crying for that look in Etienne's eyes when he'd slipped it on her finger?

So unassuming. So blissfully ignorant of everything. So prepared to not judge her for her past.

But this was a part of her past that he didn't know. That she wondered if she would ever be brave enough to tell him about.

"What on Laterre?" Etienne was suddenly leaning over the console, staring out the window. Chatine followed his gaze to the left, where she saw what had snagged his attention. Off in the distance—far below—in the vanishing light of the late afternoon, a small fire blazed. At least, that's what it appeared to be. Chatine had very little experience with fires. But before she could make sense of the strange spectacle, Etienne started yelling in her ear. "Increase altitude. Now!"

Chatine's hands dove for the controls, ready to blast them upward. But she stopped herself when she noticed something on the ground a short distance from the fire. A small, glimmering, oval-shaped craft with a giant blue cloth spread out around it that was snapping and billowing in the harsh Terrain Perdu winds.

"What is that?" Chatine asked, squinting through the window.

"Whatever it is, it's not our concern," Etienne replied hurriedly. "Increase altitude right now and turn this ship around."

But Chatine ignored him, pushing the ship closer to the ground so she could get a better look. "I think it might be a crash site."

Etienne let out an angry puff of air. "Even more reason to get out of here. Anyone flying over the Terrain Perdu is Ministère or at the very least Second Estate, and we're staying away from both of those. Now get up and hand over the controls. You're done."

"No!" Chatine fired back. "They might need help."

"Then they can call for a gridder to come help them. Now get up before I physically remove you from that seat."

Chatine held tight to the controls, continuing her steady descent toward the ground. "The code says if we can help without getting killed, then we help."

"And if we go down there, we'll probably *be* killed."

"You don't know that," Chatine pointed out.

"And you don't know it's safe. When in doubt, don't help."

Chatine shot him a glance. "Is that the community's code, or yours?"

That shut him up. If only for a moment. "We don't get involved! That's a rule!"

"Well, then, good thing you Défecteurs are really good at breaking rules," Chatine snapped, and guided the ship swiftly and steadily toward the ground.

CHAPTER 57

MARCELLUS

AT FIRST, MARCELLUS SAW NOTHING EXCEPT ENDLESS gray clouds. But the sound was getting louder. It rattled the air around them. It shook the ground beneath their feet. It plunged his heart into a frenzied panic.

Combatteurs.

They had found him. His grandfather had tracked the ship, tracked the escape pod, and now he was going to end it all in a rain of fiery, scorching explosifs from the sky.

And they were an easy target. Sitting in wide-open terrain with their blue parachute flapping in the wind like a homing beacon.

Marcellus turned to Alouette and then to Cerise. The fear in both their eyes told him they'd heard it too. They all looked to the sky with puzzled and terrified expressions. But still, there was nothing. Where was that sound coming from? No matter how hard he tried, he couldn't pinpoint its origins. But there was one thing for certain: It was getting closer.

"What is it?" Alouette asked.

Marcellus shook his head. "I don't know."

"Should we move?" Cerise asked, her eyes darting anxiously to Gabriel. Marcellus knew what she was thinking. How would they possibly move him without injuring him more?

"Where would we go?" Marcellus asked. "If it's a craft, it'll move faster than we could ever travel by foot. And if it's already spotted us, then there's no hope."

"But if it's a craft," Alouette said, craning her neck, "why can't we see it? Is it concealed by the clouds?"

"I don't know," Marcellus said again, this time with a shudder.

A second later, the air around them started to whip and thrash, battering against Marcellus's ears until he couldn't decipher the sound from the mysterious rumble of what he knew to be engines. Their chute flapped violently, locked in place only by the tethers that were still secured to the abandoned pod.

It's landing, Marcellus thought, desperately scanning the horizon.

And then he saw it. The faintest shadow on the ground. Something blocking the afternoon light from the three Sols hidden behind the clouds.

"How is it . . . ," Alouette began to ask, but her question drifted into the wind when suddenly, as if carved right into the air, a door emerged and hissed open.

Cerise gasped. Alouette sucked in a sharp breath. Gabriel let out another groan. And Marcellus could only stare. Speechlessly. Incredulously. Breathlessly.

A figure stepped out of the invisible ship, dressed in strange clothing flecked with white and gray that was almost camouflage against the backdrop of the Terrain Perdu.

Without warning, Marcellus's heart swelled to the size of a Sol. His skin prickled. His legs felt like they might surrender beneath him and bring him thudding helplessly to the ground.

And strangely, his eyes were the last to recognize her.

He let out a breath so shocked and sudden, he wondered for a moment if it might be his last.

Then, somehow, through the battering wind and the roaring engine and the kilomètres and kilomètres of lost land that surrounded them, Marcellus managed to find his voice.

"Chatine?"

- CHAPTER 58 -
CHATINE

MARCELLUS.

Sitting across from her in a cruiseur, his hazel eyes twinkling, his lips quirked into a small smile.

Marcellus.

Crouched down in front of her chair in the interrogation room, gazing up at her, pleading with her to help him.

Marcellus.

Kissing her on the rooftop of the garment fabrique. Deeply. Intensely. Endlessly.

And finally, *Marcellus.*

Turning away from her. Calling her a traitor. Walking out of her life forever.

That was what she had always believed. Those were the thoughts and visions and memories that had cycled through her mind during all those lonely days and nights on Bastille.

But now . . .

Marcellus.

Standing in front of her in the middle of the Terrain Perdu, surrounded by a dying fire and the crashed wreckage of an escape pod. Staring at her like she was a ghost. A phantom. A vision.

Just as she was staring at him.

Because he *was* a ghost to her. He had been just as dead to her as little baby Henri. He had been just as impossible to bring back as her brother. And yet somehow, at some point, they had both come back to her.

Chatine rubbed her finger against the silver ring that encircled her thumb. The one that she swore had saved her from Bastille. And the one that she was now certain had guided her right here. Right now. To this very spot. Like a tiny Sol, lighting a path through the darkness.

Marcellus was the first to speak, shattering the silence that seemed to have encapsulated them like a dome. "Chatine?"

But as desperately as Chatine wanted to reply, wanted to tell him all the things she'd ever dreamt of telling him while she'd lain awake at night, locked in that dingy tower on the moon—how she was sorry, how she didn't mean to betray him, how she was selfish and stupid and blind—when she opened her mouth, nothing came out.

Marcellus also seemed to be struggling. "How did you . . . ? I thought you were . . . ? What happened . . . ?" He huffed, frustrated with his own babbling, before finally sputtering out, "Who is that?"

Chatine turned around to see Etienne standing behind her, his eyes dark and narrowed, his mouth pressed into a tight line. She nearly startled at the sight of him. As though she didn't even recognize him. As though she'd been transported a month into the past, before she had ever been sent to Bastille, before she had ever been rescued by a strange and alluring pilote, before she had been welcomed into his home. It seemed to be the only way this situation made sense. It's as if she were somehow living two different timelines at the same moment. Existing in two different worlds at once.

How long had he been standing there?

Chatine glanced back and forth between Etienne and Marcellus before finally managing to utter her first syllable. "Uh . . ." It wasn't much, but it still felt like progress. She tried again. "He's . . . um . . . well . . ."

"She's been living with me," Etienne said, stepping up to stand next to Chatine.

Chatine felt her entire face explode with heat, and suddenly the words not only came to her, they wouldn't *stop* coming to her. "Well, yes, technically, that's true because he rescued me from Bastille because I was injured trying to escape and he brought me back to his camp where his mother helped heal my leg because she used to be a médecin and also she removed my Skin because they don't like Skins there because they sort of do their own thing but I've been living there because I didn't have anywhere else to go and you know, because of the injury thing but now that I'm better I'm really not sure what I'm going to do because—"

"A médecin?" someone asked, mercifully cutting Chatine off before she talked herself dizzy.

Chatine glanced over Marcellus's shoulder, noticing, for the first time, that he wasn't alone out here in the middle of this frozen wilderness.

"Did you say that you know a médecin?" the same voice asked, and Chatine could now see it belonged to a girl. A girl with dark curls as wild as the Terrain Perdu and eyes as dark as the Darkest Night. A girl who instinctively made every fiber of Chatine's body tremble with envy and guilt and anger and remorse.

It was her.

It was Madeline.

The girl who had lived with Chatine's family for three years. Who had been wrongfully blamed for Henri's death. Who had captured Marcellus's attention in the Frets. Who he'd called *Alouette*.

Chatine now glanced back and forth between Marcellus and Madeline, standing only a mètre apart, both dirty and disheveled and shivering from the cold, clearly having landed here *together*.

"Is this médecin nearby?" Madeline continued. "Can she help us? Our friend is in really bad condition." She gestured back toward the dying fire, where Chatine could see a man bundled in a layer of blankets, his eyes half closed, his face covered in a sheening layer of sweat despite the freezing temperatures out here.

"What happened to him?" Etienne was suddenly on the move, striding purposefully toward the man. He knelt down to examine him.

"He was shot," said a girl who Chatine didn't recognize. But from the style of her clothes—despite their ragged and dirty appearance—Chatine guessed she had to be Second Estate.

"Shot?" Etienne asked, confused. "By a paralyzeur?"

"No," Marcellus said, speaking for the first time since he'd bombarded Chatine with questions. "It was a cluster bullet."

Chatine scowled. *What the fric is a cluster bullet?*

Etienne scoffed and jokingly asked. "A cluster bullet? What, was he on Albion?"

"Yes," Marcellus said, and the graveness in his tone hardened Etienne's expression.

Chatine spun to face Marcellus. "What were you doing on—"

"There's no time," Etienne cut her off. "His infection is bad. We need to get him back to the camp immediately."

"Is he going to be okay?" the Second Estate girl asked, her voice barely a whimper.

"I don't know," Etienne said bluntly. "My maman is a healer. She'll be able to tell us more. Help me lift him."

Marcellus, who had been watching Etienne with a strange mix of confusion and distrust, suddenly sprang into action. With the help of Madeline, they lifted the injured man and carried him swiftly yet carefully toward the idling ship.

"Chatine, open the cargo hold," Etienne called out.

Chatine darted into the cockpit and quickly found the controls for the hatch. The loading ramp clanked and clattered open, and she jumped back out to see Etienne, Marcellus, and Madeline carrying the man into the hold. Once he was safely aboard, Etienne grabbed Chatine by the elbow and pulled her out of earshot of the others.

"Do you know these people?" he asked. His eyes flickered toward the loading ramp and seemed to land directly on Marcellus. "Can we trust them?"

Chatine followed his gaze, once again marveling at the events that had brought them here. Brought all of them together. Chatine, Etienne, Marcellus, Madeline. Her present and past—both near and far—all colliding like reckless stars. The Sols were either trying to send her some kind of cryptic message, or they just had a really whacked sense of humor.

Either way, she knew what her answer had to be.

"Yes," she said decisively, knowing that single word would seal her fate in ways she couldn't even begin to imagine.

- CHAPTER 59 -
MARCELLUS

"WHAT'S TAKING SO LONG? WHY ISN'T HE OUT YET?"

Cerise hadn't stopped pacing the length of the small Med Center since they'd arrived. She was like a cat prowling the gardens behind the Grand Palais kitchens, waiting for scraps of food. Every time she reached one end of the room and turned, the thermal blanket wrapped around her slender frame would snap and crackle.

"He's going to be fine," Alouette said for what had to be the tenth time, and yet it was as though Cerise could hear nothing but the fears playing out in her own head.

"He should be out by now. How long does it take to remove a cluster bullet?"

"A long time," Alouette replied. "You saw the wound. It was bad. And cluster bullets are designed to spread and do as much damage as possible."

Once again, Marcellus was amazed by her seemingly endless well of patience. With Cerise. With him back in the Terrain Perdu when he foolishly thought he could walk to find help. With everyone. She just seemed to have a natural gift for calming people and talking sense when everything else felt senseless.

Cerise made another sharp turn and continued pacing, her gaze never leaving the door that Gabriel had been carried through earlier. They'd been told it led to some kind of operating room, but Cerise hadn't looked convinced. And to be honest, Marcellus hadn't been all that convinced either.

After boarding the strange ship with Chatine and being forced to don blindfolds, they'd arrived at a camp in the middle of the Terrain Perdu with odd-shaped buildings that were nearly invisible from the air. Just like the ship had been when it had landed near their crash site.

Défecteurs, Marcellus had soon surmised, but he was still struggling to wrap his mind around it. He'd always heard rumors that some of them had survived his grandfather's roundups, but he was never quite sure. He'd had a hard time believing that they could exist *anywhere* without the Ministère knowing. And yet here they were.

Marcellus took a sip of hot chocolat from the cup clutched between his slowly thawing fingers. He pulled his thermal blanket tighter over his shoulders and glanced around the peculiar little Med Center. The shelves were stacked with supplies, and there was a row of neatly made-up cots, like the one he and Alouette were currently sitting on. He was in complete awe of all of it. This camp. This hiding place of the Défecteurs. He'd only ever known about one other Défecteur camp, buried deep in the Forest Verdure. But that one had been abandoned.

That one had been *his* hiding place.

Cerise completed another lap of the room. "What kind of Med Center is this, anyway? It doesn't look like a real Med Center, and that woman who took Gabriel in there didn't look like a real médecin." She was whispering even though the three of them were the only ones in the room.

After they'd arrived and Gabriel had disappeared behind the operating room door with a woman who had quickly introduced herself as Brigitte, Chatine had run off somewhere with that tall, chisel-jawed pilote. Etienne, she'd called him. Marcellus wasn't exactly sure why, but he didn't have a good feeling about him.

That was another thing Marcellus hadn't yet been able to wrap his mind around. Chatine Renard had escaped from Bastille? And was now living with Défecteurs who had removed her Skin? That was why his constant searches for her had always come back with "Location unknown?"

"Cerise," Alouette said gently, "why don't you sit down and have some hot chocolat? It'll help calm you down."

But Cerise ignored her and continued pacing.

Marcellus finished off his drink but kept the cup gripped in his hands. Now that he was getting warm, he was also starting to feel antsy being cooped up in here. He still had no idea what was happening on the rest of Laterre. They'd been unable to get a signal in the Terrain Perdu, and the Défecteurs had confiscated their two TéléComs the moment they'd arrived at the camp, despite Cerise's insistence that neither of them were trackable. Apparently, they didn't approve of Ministère devices around here. Not that Marcellus could blame them. But he was anxious to find out what the general was doing. Had he already started his war? Had he already taken command of his Third Estate army?

What was he planning next?

That was the question that was killing Marcellus. He had half a mind to start pacing right alongside Cerise.

"How do we even know that woman knows what she's doing?" Cerise jerked her thumb toward the operating room door. "She might do more harm to him than good in there."

Marcellus heard something that sounded like a growl, and his gaze snapped toward the other end of the room where, in the doorway, Etienne now stood with Chatine.

"That *woman* is my maman," Etienne said in a low, threatening voice. "And she knows exactly what she's doing."

Cerise looked momentarily stunned by Etienne's presence and slightly alarmed by his tone, but then she flicked her long dark hair defiantly over her shoulder and pulled her spine straight. "I have no doubt she *thinks* she knows what she's doing. But I'm just saying, she might not have the experience to—"

"Did you see the scars on her face?" Etienne said, moving farther into the room. Marcellus couldn't help but notice that his fists were clenching and unclenching at his sides like pistons. Apparently, *he* didn't have a good feeling about *them*, either.

"That's where her circuitry used to be," he went on, shooting a pointed look at Cerise. "From when she was a *cyborg*." Etienne positioned himself in the corner and crossed his arms over his chest. "So, like I said, she knows exactly what she's doing."

Cerise's mouth fell open. "Another one? She . . ." But the words faded on her lips, as her mind seemed to fritz and whirl.

Marcellus's mind was whirling too as he remembered the scars that he'd briefly glimpsed on Brigitte's face. Now that he thought about it, they looked almost identical to the scars that he'd seen on Denise's face.

He cut his gaze to Alouette, who was chewing on her bottom lip, lost in what he assumed to be the exact same thoughts.

"I brought you some more hot chocolat."

Marcellus glanced up to see Chatine standing in front of him, a silver flask in her hand. She unscrewed the top and filled his cup with more of the steaming liquid before walking tentatively over to Alouette.

"It's Alouette now, right?" she asked in a voice Marcellus had never heard before. It was quiet and gentle. "Your name?"

Alouette nodded. "My father changed it from Madeline after we left the inn."

Marcellus watched in confusion as something powerful and strangely tender passed between the two girls. Some kind of unspoken conversation that he could not even begin to understand.

"You two know each other," he said dazedly as he suddenly remembered something Chatine had told him back at the Vallonay Policier Precinct before she was sent to Bastille. His brow furrowed, trying to recall the details. "You used to live together?"

Chatine nodded. "She stayed with my family at the Jondrette."

Marcellus's gaze snapped to Alouette as he thought back to that rundown inn that was now nothing more than a pile of ashes. "You *lived* there?"

Alouette nodded. "When I was very young. Before Hugo brought me to the sisters."

"We . . . ," Chatine began before turning to Alouette with wide, apologetic eyes. "We treated her very badly."

A hint of a smile broke onto Alouette's face. A silent gesture of forgiveness. Chatine filled Alouette's cup with hot chocolat, and Alouette focused back on Cerise, who was still pacing the room. Chatine sat down next to Marcellus on the cot. Marcellus could feel Etienne's dark eyes watching them from the other side of the room.

"So," Marcellus said uneasily to Chatine, clutching his cup, "are you going to tell me what happened, or do I have to guess?"

Chatine flashed him a playful smirk. "Whatever do you mean, Officer?"

Marcellus rolled his eyes. "You're living with Défecteurs? I didn't think they'd exactly be your style."

"Actually," Chatine said in a low, conspiratorial tone, "it turns out they really don't like being called that."

Marcellus snorted and then, upon realizing that Chatine was not joking, schooled his expression. "Oh. So, what *do* they like to be called?"

Chatine flicked her eyes toward Etienne, who was still glowering at them from the corner, looking not too unlike those guards who had boarded their voyageur on Albion. "They're really not label people."

Marcellus gaped at her. With the short hair, that strange white-and-gray clothing, and this new relaxed air about her, he barely recognized the girl. Then again, he'd spent most of their time together thinking she was someone else. He wondered if he'd ever truly known the real Chatine Renard at all.

"Why are you looking at me like that?" Chatine asked, nervously raking a hand through her cropped hair. "You don't like it."

Marcellus cleared his throat. "No, I do," he rushed to say. "A *lot*. I just . . ."

Chatine cracked a smile, and Marcellus felt his cheeks flood with heat. He dropped his gaze down to his hands and muttered, "I'm just having a hard time getting my head around all of this. You living here. With them."

"They're nothing like I thought they'd be. They're good people. They saved me. And they're going to save your friend in there. Who, by the way, doesn't exactly look like *your* style either. Since when do you hang out with shaggy-haired Third Estaters?"

"Well," Marcellus said, a grin pulling on his lips. "I did know this boy once named Théo. He had pretty shaggy hair too. I just never saw it because—"

"Right, right," Chatine interrupted. "I stand corrected." She ran her fingers over her scalp again, as though trying to remember what it felt like before all the hair was shaved off.

Marcellus's smile instantly faded, and his stomach clenched. "Was it bad? Up there on Bastille?"

"No," she deadpanned. "It was paradise. All the chou bread you can eat and hours of stimulating conversation down in the zyttrium exploits."

Marcellus knew she was making a joke, but he still felt chastised. Of course it was bad up there. It was horrible. The worst conditions a human being could endure. He took a breath, steeling himself to ask the question that had been secretly plaguing him ever since he'd first watched Chatine's arrest report. "Was it my fault?"

Chatine's head snapped toward him. "What?"

"Your arrest. Was it my fault? Did you get sent to Bastille because of me?"

"Why would you think that?"

"Because Marcellus is always trying to take credit for other people's misfortunes," Cerise muttered. She turned toward the operating room door. "Argh! Would it kill someone to give us an update or something! He could be lying dead in there for all we know!"

Alouette shared a knowing look with Marcellus before jumping to her feet and guiding Cerise back to the cot with her. Cerise sat down on the thin mattress, and Alouette handed her a mug of hot chocolat. "Sit here. Drink this. Don't move." Alouette sat down beside her and linked her arm with Cerise's. The gesture, Marcellus was certain, was meant to be both comforting and restraining.

"It wasn't your fault," Chatine whispered.

"I just . . ." Marcellus floundered for words. "You never would have been sent there if it weren't for me. The general never would have hired you to spy on me and you never—"

"I never would have gotten out of there if it weren't for you. You *saved* me. Your message from the droid—if it weren't for that, I might have died in that tower."

"Why *were* you on Bastille?" Marcellus turned back to her to see the lightness had vanished from her eyes. "Your arrest alert just said treason."

"I lied to the general," she explained without meeting his gaze. "I discovered where the Vangarde base was, and I told him I would lead him to it. But I lied. I led him somewhere else, and he had me sent straight to Bastille."

At this admission, Alouette glanced over at Chatine. "You found the Refuge?"

"Refuge?" Chatine repeated curiously.

"That's what the Vangarde call their base," Marcellus explained.

"Yes. I found it."

"And you protected it?" Alouette asked.

"I protected the Frets. I protected my people. And I guess, yes, I protected the Vangarde, too."

Chatine turned to meet Marcellus's gaze, her intense gray eyes the color of Laterre's sky. And at that moment, something flowed through Marcellus. Something unnerving yet comforting, irritating yet familiar. He'd been so wrong about her. So many times. This girl who'd spied on him. Who'd deceived him. This girl who'd joked with him. Challenged him.

Kissed him.

This last memory made Marcellus's frozen toes feel warmer than they'd felt in a lifetime. He hastily pulled his gaze away from hers only to have it land on Etienne. The Défecteur was glaring at Marcellus as though he had microcams affixed to the inside of Marcellus's brain, monitoring all of his thoughts and emotions. As though he, too, were watching Marcellus and Chatine kiss on that rooftop in an endless loop.

Marcellus cleared his throat and instead turned his eyes to Alouette, but looking at her only made his heart clench with some other emotion he couldn't quite identify. He dropped his gaze to the floor, which right now felt like the only safe place in the room.

"How did you escape?" Alouette asked Chatine.

"I . . . ," Chatine began with difficulty. "I escaped when the Vangarde was breaking out Citizen Rousseau." She looked like she was about to cry. She opened her mouth to say more, but no sound came out. Instead, it was Etienne who spoke.

He took a step out of his corner and unlocked his arms from across his broad chest. "There were two ships on the mission, but we lost contact with the other one shortly after it took off."

Comprehension suddenly crashed into Marcellus. *These* people had helped the Vangarde break out Citizen Rousseau? That strange ship he'd seen on the roof belonged to them?

Etienne looked to Chatine, who was staring numbly at the ground, and the hardness of his gaze softened. "Her little brother was on the other ship."

"Roche," Chatine whispered, her voice cracking. "It was Roche. He was my lost baby brother, and I didn't even know until it was too late. Back then, we called him—"

"Henri," Alouette said with sudden realization. "I remember now. At the inn. Late at night, I would wake up to the sound of his cries. You would go to him. You would sing to him."

As Marcellus watched the rivulets of tears make their way down Chatine's cheeks, he felt like the whole planet was imploding around him. His insides caved in on themselves. The walls of the chalet came crumbling down. Not only had his grandfather killed Citizen Rousseau and Mabelle and Alouette's beloved sisters in that attack. He'd also killed Roche. That clever boy Marcellus had interrogated in the Precinct. Chatine's little brother.

General Bonnefaçon had destroyed all their lives. He was an enemy to everyone in this room. To Chatine, who'd suffered on Bastille. To Alouette, who'd lost the only family she'd ever known. To Gabriel, who was fighting for his life in that operating room right now. To Cerise, who'd left behind her comfortable life in Ledôme only to be stuck here, staring at a door and praying to the Sols that Gabriel would make it out. Even to these Défecteurs, who had been banished to the frozen tundra of the Terrain Perdu in an attempt to escape the Ministère's wrath. They were all victims of his grandfather's vicious game. They'd all been made miserable because of him.

And for all they knew, he could be destroying even more lives right this minute.

The thought made the room spin. Marcellus gripped tightly to the edge of his cot and tried to take deep breaths. He didn't know how much longer he could stay locked up here. He didn't know how much more waiting he could take.

"Your friend is stable."

The voice came from behind Cerise, startling everyone. Marcellus looked up to see Brigitte, the former cyborg médecin, standing in the doorway of the operating room dressed in her medical scrubs, her scarred face covered by a surgical mask that stopped just below her eyes.

Cerise's gaze seemed to track right to the splatters of blood on the front of Brigitte's shirt. "Oh my Sols! He's alive? He's going to be okay?"

Brigitte grabbed Cerise's hands in hers and squeezed them tightly. "He's going to be okay. I was able to get all the fragments of the cluster bullet out. And I went ahead and removed his TéléSkin while he was under. He's going to make it. He's a fighter."

Cerise collapsed in relief onto the nearest cot. "Oh, thank the Sols."

"Pretty nasty things, those cluster bullets," said Brigitte. "Do you want to tell me how he got shot?"

Cerise looked to Alouette, who looked to Marcellus, who looked to the floor again. "We were pursued by the Royal Guard." He swallowed. "On Albion."

He expected Brigitte to react with shock. It wasn't every day you met a Laterrian who had been to Albion. But she simply nodded for him to continue.

Marcellus anxiously cleared his throat. "My grandfather, as you might know, is General Bonnefaçon." Once again, the Défecteur's expression remained neutral, even in the face of her enemy. "But I swear I don't work for him anymore. You don't have to worry about me—"

"If I was worried," Brigitte interrupted calmly, "you wouldn't be here."

"Right." Marcellus felt a flicker of relief, followed quickly by confusion. "Wait, *why* aren't you worried?"

Brigitte cracked a small smile. "Let's just say we have some of the same friends."

Marcellus wasn't quite sure what to do with that, so he simply stored it away to be questioned later. "Well, anyway, we went to Albion to track down a source who had been working with the general to build a weapon."

Chatine stiffened. "What kind of weapon?"

Marcellus looked to Cerise, who looked to Alouette, who held Chatine's gaze with unwavering strength. "It's an update. For the Third Estate Skins. It gives the general the ability to control people. To make them violent."

"We believe he wants to turn the Third Estate into his own personal army," Marcellus added.

"What?" Chatine said in a breathless whisper.

"Our source on Albion designed an inhibitor that would prevent the general from being able to control people through the Skins," Marcellus explained. "But unfortunately, the majority of it was destroyed."

"What exactly does he plan to do with this weapon?" Chatine asked.

"We don't know yet," said Marcellus. "All we know is that he wants control of the Regime, and he's going to use the Third Estate to get it."

Chatine glanced down at her left wrist, and Marcellus could make out a faint red scar where her Skin used to be.

It was only then that Marcellus realized the médecin still hadn't reacted to what he'd just told them. And when he peered back up at Brigitte, he noticed she was not looking at him. She was looking back into the operating room, a pensive, almost troubled expression on her face.

"What is it?" Marcellus asked, alarmed.

It felt like forever before Brigitte spoke. Her gaze was still trained on the operating room door, her mind clearly working. "Something happened when I was operating on your friend."

"What?" Cerise asked.

"Right before I removed his Skin," Brigitte said haltingly, like she was trying to organize her thoughts and speak at the same time, "something appeared on the screen. I believe it was one of your Universal Alerts."

Marcellus's stomach rolled. His grandfather. The weapon. It was already starting. "What was it?" he asked desperately, leaping to his feet. "What did the general say?"

When Brigitte finally turned back to Marcellus, there was something in her eyes that told him it was even worse than he imagined. "No, not the general. It was the Patriarche."

- CHAPTER 60 -
MARCELLUS

"FELLOW LATERRIANS. OUR PLANET HAS RECENTLY experienced several disturbing setbacks."

The stout, jowly face of Lyon Paresse filled the screen of the strange Défecteur device. Just like their ships, it was unlike anything Marcellus had ever seen. It was the same shape as a TéléCom, but it looked ancient. Like an old First World relic, with its maze of wires, hard black casing, and winking lights.

Everyone in the Med Center was gathered around the screen, listening to the Patriarche's voice seep out of the device's small, tinny speakers.

"A few weeks ago, we said good-bye to our beloved daughter and Premier Enfant, Marie Paresse. At barely three years old, she was taken from us by a brutal, depraved group of terrorists. Thankfully, we were able to apprehend Marie's murderer, Nadette Epernay, and bring her to justice."

Marcellus cringed as the view on the screen changed from the Patriarche's bereft face to the archived footage of Marie's governess being marched to her death. Two hulking droids led her across the stage at the center of the Marsh, toward the terrible exécuteur with its glowing blue laser fuzzing and sparking ominously in the wet air. The girl was young. Beautiful. And so innocent. Framed for a crime she didn't commit. Just another pawn in the general's terrifying game of power and corruption.

Marcellus knew exactly why they were replaying this footage for the entire planet to see. It was a reminder. A threat. That any of them could be next.

The footage continued and Marcellus watched, once again, as the head of Nadette Epernay was severed from her body in one blinding, remorseless slice of blue light. Beside him, Chatine winced and averted her eyes.

As the dreadful smell of burning flesh flooded Marcellus's memory, the Patriarche's voice resumed over the ghastly images.

"Because of this fateful event and the turmoil that followed, we were forced to cancel the annual Ascension until balance and order could be restored to our planet."

The archived footage ended, and the Patriarche returned to the screen. But even though it was Lyon Paresse's face being broadcast to all of Laterre, Marcellus knew these weren't his words. He recognized his grandfather's precise language and diplomatic phrasing. And judging from the Patriarche's stilted tone, Marcellus had no doubt that these carefully considered words were being broadcast into an audio patch for him to parrot.

"And now, I am pleased to announce," the Patriarche continued with a taut, forced smile, "as I'm sure you will all be pleased to hear, that not only has the annual Ascension ceremony been rescheduled, it will begin promptly in five minutes."

Alouette glanced up from the device long enough to share a wary look with Marcellus. She was clearly as suspicious and distrusting of this turn of events as he was. After all, it had been less than a week since the Patriarche had shot down the idea of a rescheduled Ascension. Which meant whatever was happening here, whatever the general had convinced the Patriarche to agree to, it wasn't a coincidence.

It wasn't the general "taking his chances," as Alouette had said.

"This, however, will be a very different kind of Ascension," the Patriarche went on, drawing Marcellus's focus back to the screen. "Unlike any we have experienced on Laterre before. I realize that despite the recent"—the Patriarche paused, looking displeased by the general's choice of words—"…*setbacks*, there are still many of you—the majority of you, in fact—who have chosen *not* to rebel. Who have not participated in the chaos and turmoil that has invaded our planet. There are many of you who have continued to perform your honest work for an honest chance and who have continued to show loyalty to me, my family, and our beloved and beautiful Regime. And I would like to personally demonstrate my deepest appreciation and gratitude to you."

The Patriarche took a long, rehearsed pause. Marcellus felt like his lungs were trapped in a vise.

"Which is why," Lyon Paresse continued, "for this special Ascension ceremony, we will be choosing not *one* person to Ascend to the Second Estate, but *fifty*."

"Fifty!?" Cerise spat, her gaze snapping up from the device. "That's unheard of."

Marcellus nodded, his gut twisting more with every passing second. "Yes, it is."

"That's right, my fellow Laterrians," the Patriarche said, his forced smile widening to the point where he looked like a broken toy. "In just a few minutes, fifty lucky members of the Third Estate will be chosen to Ascend. And of course, like every winner before them, all fifty Ascendants and their families will receive brand-new manoirs in Ledôme and will be invited to attend the Ascension banquet at the Grand Palais tomorrow night. There, my wife, Matrone Veronik Paresse, and I will personally welcome you all to your new life."

The Patriarche's lips pulled back again to reveal his perfectly white teeth in an expression that was undoubtedly supposed to appear pleasing but ended up only looking disquieting. As though some part of him knew there was something very sinister about this turn of events.

"Fifty winners?" Chatine repeated, dumbfounded.

"And their families," Cerise added.

"That has to be close to two *hundred* people," Alouette said.

Marcellus closed his eyes, feeling the planet wobble beneath his feet like a rumbling foreshadow of what was to come. "It's the Peasant's Revolt," he whispered as a chilling tingle shot down his spine.

Cerise turned to him. "You mean from the Regiments game?"

Marcellus nodded. "Surround and capture the Monarch. He's going to use the Third Estate to kill the Patriarche."

"What?" Chatine asked.

Marcellus's breath was coming fast and furious now. "It's the perfect plan. Ledôme is nearly impenetrable. Its perimeter is guarded by droids at all times. Normally, the Third Estate aren't allowed inside, and the Patriarche never leaves it. Apart from a few strongly vetted servants and Palais staff, the Patriarche never comes close to the Third Estate."

"Except during Ascension banquets," Cerise whispered, the pieces evidently clicking into place in her mind as well.

"Exactly," Marcellus said. "That's how he plans to take control of the Regime. By sending in the Third Estate to murder the Patriarche and put an end to the Paresse family for good. He just had to find a way to get enough of them inside." Marcellus released a shudder of a breath, once again in awe of his grandfather's brilliant mind.

He glanced back at the screen of the strange Défecteur device. The Ascension ceremony had already begun. Faces spun across the screen, randomly stopping at winner after winner after winner.

The general's unwitting army mobilizing before his very eyes.

This was how the Regime would end. This was how the general would pull off his master plan. His Peasant's Revolt. By convincing the Monarch to *invite* the Peasants into his home so that they could destroy him. This was no longer the fool's move that Marcellus had always believed it to be. Now it was the move that would secure General Bonnefaçon his long-awaited and hard-fought victory.

"The Regime will finally rid itself of the déchets and be brought to order."

Marcellus had interpreted his grandfather's words all wrong. The "déchets" he was referring to were not the Third Estate. They were the *First* Estate. Those were the people the general thought of as "garbage."

Fat to be trimmed. Scum to be eliminated. And he was going to use the Third Estate to do it.

"I don't understand." Chatine started to pace. "If all he has to do to take control of the Regime is kill the Patriarche, why doesn't he just do it himself? Smother him with a pillow in his sleep? Mess with his hunting gun so it blows up in his face? Poison him like he did with the Premier Enfant? I can think of several easier ways to kill someone than going through all this trouble."

It was a valid question. One that Marcellus didn't immediately have an answer to. But he was grateful that someone else in the room did.

"Because," Alouette said, her voice soft and pensive, "the System Alliance will never support his claim to the Regime if it looks like a military coup."

"She's right," Marcellus said, a shiver of comprehension passing through him. "The System Alliance is funded and run by the twelve heads of state of the System Divine. If they get wind of a possible plot to overthrow one of them, there will be resistance and most likely war."

"But," Alouette went on, "if he mimics what happened on Usonia and makes it look like a *revolution*, like this is the people's doing—"

"—and *he's* the hero who steps in to restore order . . ." Marcellus added.

"Then the Alliance has no choice but to support him and back his claim to the Regime," Alouette finished with a nod.

"But first he needs to make it *look* like a people's revolution," said Marcellus gravely. "Once the Patriarche is gone, nothing will stand in his way."

A tense, grim silence fell across the little Med Center. For a moment, no one spoke. No one even dared to breathe as this heavy, noxious cloud descended upon them. Upon their home planet.

Laterre had known clouds.

It had known storms.

But never one like this.

Marcellus now understood it all. The real reason the general had to kill the Premier Enfant, the last remaining Paresse heir, was not to start a riot. That was just a convenient side effect. It was so that he could finally inherit the keys to the Regime. The Regime he believed he deserved all along.

Check mate.

No. It couldn't be. This could not be the end. There had to be another way.

Marcellus could suddenly hear his grandfather's voice in his mind. As clear as if they were still sitting in front of that Regiment's board, a carnage of fallen pieces scattered across the table.

"Sooner or later, Marcellus, you're going to have to start playing the game like someone who actually wants to win."

"We have to do something." Cerise was back on her feet, pacing again. "We have to stop him."

"How?" Chatine asked.

Cerise threw up her hands. "I don't know! But if there's a kill switch out there, then now is the time to find it."

"What's a kill switch?" Chatine glanced curiously at Cerise.

Marcellus groaned and was about to respond that they were wasting their time talking about fantasy solutions instead of trying to find a *real* solution, but Cerise spoke first. "Many people believe," she shot a look at Marcellus, "that the Skins were originally designed with a switch that can disable them."

"All of them?" Chatine sounded dubious. "At once?"

"It's not unheard of," Cerise said defensively. "Any good hacker or technicien knows that you should always build a kill switch into any large-scale system in case something goes wrong and you need to shut it down. If we can find this switch, we can disable the Skins. All of them. And stop the general from using the Third Estate as a weapon."

Chatine snapped her gaze to Marcellus, a hopeful twinkle in her eye. "Have you heard of this?"

Marcellus sighed. "It's just a conspiracy theory! Wishful thinking. There is no kill switch. It doesn't exist."

"Actually, it does."

Everyone turned to see who had spoken, and Marcellus's gaze landed on Brigitte. It was only now that Marcellus realized the two Défecteurs in the room—Etienne and his mother—hadn't uttered a single word since the Universal Alert had begun. Etienne still bore a displeased expression, and the médecin was just standing there, watching them all with relaxed interest.

"She's right," Brigitte went on. "There is a kill switch. It was built when the original engineers designed the TéléSkins. As a precaution."

Marcellus scoffed. Of all the people to believe in ridiculous Laterrian conspiracies, a former cyborg living in a Défecteur camp would be the last person Marcellus would suspect.

"Do you know where it is?" Cerise asked eagerly.

Brigitte gave a single, tight nod.

Cerise's eyes widened. "You have to tell us! You heard the Patriarche! You know what the general is planning. We have to stop him. You have to help us."

A shadow of regret seemed to pass over the woman's scarred features. "It's no use. Even if I told you where it was, there's no way you could ever get access to it."

"Oh, I'll get access," Cerise said confidently.

Brigitte shook her head and let out a sigh. "No, you won't."

"How do you know?" Cerise sounded mildly offended. "I happen to be an expert hacker."

"Because the kill switch is guarded by a very special technology. A unique DNA lock. To be opened only by someone who possesses a direct ancestral link to the Paresse line. It's completely unhackable."

Marcellus could feel the room turn very cold. Colder, dare he say, than even the Terrain Perdu outside. "What are you talking about?"

Brigitte turned to him. "I'm talking about a vault so secure that only the Patriarche or his descendants can ever get inside."

Marcellus squeezed his temples. This couldn't be real. This woman was delusional. Insane. If there was a kill switch for the Skins, wouldn't he have been told about it?

"Maman?" a voice broke into Marcellus's thoughts. It was Etienne. He was staring incredulously at Brigitte, speaking for the first time in what felt like hours. "How do you know all of this? How do you know about this DNA lock?"

Brigitte flashed a weak smile that caused her scars—the ghosts of her vanquished circuitries—to glint and stretch. "Because, chéri, I invented it."

- CHAPTER 61 -
CHATINE

CHATINE WAS AWARE OF THE MUFFLED VOICES AROUND her, but for a full minute, all she could hear was the sound of her own heavy, uneven breaths. And the hazy echoes of her disbelief hanging in the air.

A switch that disables the Skins?

An Ascension banquet for fifty winners?

A weapon that will give the general command of the entire Third Estate?

She glanced down again at the inside of her left arm, at the long, rectangular scar where her Skin used to be. Where this weapon *would* have been if Brigitte hadn't removed it. And now she understood why the Défecteurs didn't trust any of the Ministère technology, especially not the Skins.

"I knew it! I knew it was real!" a screeching voice yanked Chatine out of her reverie and back into the treatment center. She turned to see who had spoken. It was the girl Marcellus had introduced earlier as Cerise.

"I don't understand." Marcellus was holding his head in his hands like he was afraid his brain might explode. "There's a kill switch for the Skins hidden behind a DNA-locked vault?"

"Yes," said Brigitte, and Chatine swung her gaze back to Etienne's mother. "It's called the Forteresse. It was the last project I worked on before I left the Ministère."

"That was the special assignment you refuse to talk about?" Etienne sounded stunned and almost disgusted. "You built a lock that protects the Skins?"

Brigitte lowered her eyes. "I'm not proud of it. That's why I left. And I vowed to spend the rest of my life removing as many of those evil devices as I could."

"So, this Forteresse," Cerise said, sounding somewhat hopeful. "If you built it, then you must know how to break into it. A backdoor? A loophole? If we can access it, we can shut down the Skins before the general can—"

Brigitte shook her head. "There is no backdoor. There is no loophole."

Cerise frowned. "But every good hacker puts in a backdoor."

"Not cyborgs," Brigitte said solemnly. "It goes against their programming. By the time we realized what we'd done, it was too late. The Forteresse—and the kill switch for the Skins—was locked to anyone who wasn't a Paresse descendant. Even us."

"Us?" Cerise repeated. "You were working with someone?"

Brigitte nodded. "There were two of us on the project. We left together. Her name was—"

"Vanessa," Alouette said quietly, and Chatine could swear she saw the girl shiver.

Brigitte's eyebrows shot up. "How did you know?"

"She goes by Denise now." Alouette kneaded her hands in her lap. "She . . . She was one of the women who raised me."

"You were raised by the Sisterhood?" Brigitte asked.

"How do you know about the Sisterhood?" Marcellus shot back.

"I told you." Brigitte flashed him a smile. "We have some of the same friends."

"Yes. They raised me." Alouette nodded, but in her eyes, Chatine saw a hint of grief.

"Vanessa—or Denise as you call her—was a dear friend," Brigitte explained. "We were placed on the Forteresse assignment together because of our mutual expertise in the field of genetics. Patriarche Claude wanted to safeguard the Skins and his family's sovereignty over the Third Estate. The Rebellion of 488 was still three years away, but unrest was already rumbling. The kill switch was originally located in a bunker inside the Grand Palais, but Claude didn't think that was safe enough. He worried about the Palais being stormed and the bunker raided. He wanted to make sure that, even in the face of a rebellion, no one could shut down the Skins. Because he knew, as I'm sure you do, that the Skins are the only way to keep the Third Estate controlled."

Chatine scoffed, feeling a familiar hatred for the First Estate roll through her. *Arrogant pomps.*

"So," Brigitte went on, "Vanessa and I built the Forteresse to protect the kill switch. And Patriarche Claude had a special tower erected to house it."

"The Paresse Tower?" Cerise asked in astonishment.

Brigitte nodded. "It was a clever decision on Claude's part: to hide the kill switch in plain sight but protect it by the most advanced lock on the planet. Most people think the tower is just decorative. A symbol of the Regime. But there's a small chamber at the top that only a few people know about."

"Who?" Cerise insisted. "Who else knows about it?"

Brigitte let out an unsteady breath. Chatine could tell that recounting this story was making her anxious, dredging up old regrets. "The current Patriarche, of course. General Bonnefaçon, who was there when the project was initiated. Vanessa—or Denise. Me. And now the people in this room."

"The general knows," Cerise repeated numbly, casting a glance at Marcellus, but he appeared to be lost in thought.

"How does a lock like that even work?" Alouette asked.

Brigitte wrung her hands together. "Well, as a cyborg, Vanessa had been a frontrunner in the field of gene editing—the process of modifying targeted strands of the human genome. It would have been easy to build a lock that opens to anyone with Paresse DNA, but the Patriarche didn't want that. Most members of the First Estate have at least some Paresse DNA, and he didn't want a disgruntled cousin or uncle shutting off the Skins. He wanted this lock to *only* open for his direct descendants. He also wanted to make sure that someone couldn't just snatch a strand of hair from his head and use it to unlock the Forteresse and gain access to the kill switch. So Vanessa figured out a way to edit the Patriarche's genetic code and create a modified gene. We called it the Sovereign gene."

Brigitte seemed to shudder at the name. "This modified gene can only be found in certain cells of the brain, and the modification is only triggered once a Paresse heir has come of age. If she'd lived, little Marie Paresse would have eventually had the ability to open the Forteresse." Brigitte paused, as though taking a moment of silence to mourn the lost child. "Once the creation of the Sovereign gene was complete, the DNA of Claude's young son, Lyon, was also edited. And I started work on the lock itself. I was able to develop a technology that can not only read the modified Sovereign gene in the brain and confirm its validity, but also eliminate any chance of sabotage. The lock on the Forteresse, for example, can't be accessed if more than one person is present, eliminating the chance of the Patriarche being coerced into opening it. The person accessing the lock must also be alive and not under duress." She sighed and looked to Cerise with apologetic eyes. "In other words, we did our job too well."

"So it's hopeless, then." Cerise collapsed back down onto the cot, a darkness seeming to descend over her. "The kill switch exists, but we can't get to it. And now we just have to sit idly by and watch the general take control of the planet."

"We don't need the kill switch," Marcellus said quietly. He was leaning against the wall with his arms crossed over his chest. It was the first time he'd spoken in several minutes.

Cerise peered at him. "What do you mean?"

Marcellus stood up straighter, as though waking from a dream. "Think about it," he said, his gaze fierce and determined. "For the very first time in . . .well, *forever*, we're not three moves behind him."

"What?" Chatine asked.

"Don't you see?" Marcellus's face was flushed with adrenaline. "We know exactly what the general is going to do next. We know he plans to use the Ascension banquet to bring two hundred Third Estaters into Ledôme to kill the Patriarche. And now that we know his strategy, we can stop him. We can *defeat* him."

Chatine and Cerise exchanged a wary look. But Alouette somehow seemed to be following what Marcellus was saying. She was gazing up at him, her own eyes alight with something that looked like pride.

"How?" Chatine asked, still trying to keep up.

"My grandfather always says that the only way to win is to analyze your opponent and plan your attack accordingly."

"But couldn't we just, I don't know, *warn* the Patriarche?" Chatine asked. "If he knew what the general was planning, he'd probably cancel the banquet and have the general arrested."

"It won't work," said Marcellus. "We'd never be able to get close enough to the Patriarche in time to warn him, and the general has installed guardian controls on the Patriarche's TéléCom, making it impossible to send him an AirLink without the general knowing about it. Which means we have to stop him another way."

Marcellus turned to Chatine, his eyes as grave and unwavering as his voice. And in that moment, she suddenly understood. This tall, determined man standing before her was not the same Marcellus Bonnefaçon she'd met less than a month ago in the Vallonay Med Center morgue. That shiny-haired, goofy-smiled, inept young officer was gone. And in his place, Chatine saw what she knew his grandfather had always hoped to see.

His protégé.

A little sliver of General Bonnefaçon.

Chatine felt a shiver ripple through her. "So," she began warily, "does that mean you have a plan?"

PART 6

THE PATRIARCHE

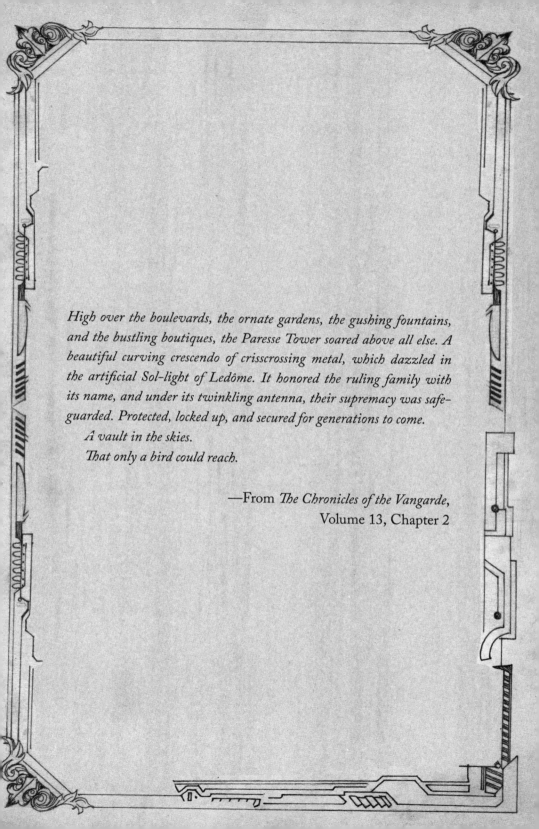

High over the boulevards, the ornate gardens, the gushing fountains, and the bustling boutiques, the Paresse Tower soared above all else. A beautiful curving crescendo of crisscrossing metal, which dazzled in the artificial Sol-light of Ledôme. It honored the ruling family with its name, and under its twinkling antenna, their supremacy was safe-guarded. Protected, locked up, and secured for generations to come.

A vault in the skies.

That only a bird could reach.

—From *The Chronicles of the Vangarde*,
Volume 13, Chapter 2

- CHAPTER 62 -
CHATINE

A SHARP WIND WHIPPED OFF THE ICY LAND, CAUSING Chatine to yank the hood of her puffy coat tighter under her chin. The Sols had risen just a few minutes ago, lighting up the blanket of clouds above and the frigid ground below. Idling nearby was Etienne's ship, which had delivered them all the way out here, far from the camp and its hidden location. Out in the distance, somewhere beyond all this frozen nothingness, was Vallonay. Beckoning them. Waiting for them. And behind, past kilomètres of craggy rocks and sweeping bluffs, was the community that had welcomed Chatine with open arms. She didn't dare look over her shoulder. If she looked back, toward the memory of their chalets, and walkways, and the warm glowing lights of the lodge, she might lose her nerve. She might never leave.

Two worlds. One in front of her. One behind her. Both somehow hers and somehow not.

"He's nearly here," Cerise said. Chatine looked over to see the Second Estate girl jabbing at a TéléCom with gloved fingers. Beside her stood Marcellus and Alouette, both bundled in thick, glimmering jackets. And nearby, huddled by themselves next to the ship, were Etienne and Brigitte.

"Do you really think this plan is going to work?"

Chatine recognized Alouette's voice, but it took a moment for her to realize she was talking to *her*. She glanced over to see Alouette shivering slightly in the coat she'd borrowed from Brigitte. Her hands were wrapped around a silver canister, which Chatine had been told held the last remaining vial of this miraculous inhibitor that was supposed to somehow neutralize the general's weapon.

Chatine took a deep breath, pondering the question. *Do I really think this plan is going to work?* She stole a glance over at Marcellus. There was an intense flicker in his hazel eyes as he stared out at the frozen wilderness, pensive yet determined, brave yet terrified.

"I think . . . ," she began haltingly, "I think it *has* to work."

"There he is!" Cerise called out as a sudden gust of frigid morning wind kicked up and the purr of an engine pulled Chatine out of her thoughts. She looked up to see a cargo transporteur emerging from the frozen mist. The vehicle looked like a giant insect with its sleek black sides shimmering in the early light. It slowed to an idling hover in front of them, and then the massive loading door hissed open in a plume of warm steam and glowing light.

"Didn't I just put you on a voyageur?" said a voice from inside.

Blinking against the brightness, Chatine could just make out a slender-framed man with neatly parted hair who had swiveled around in his seat to grin broadly at Cerise.

"Grantaire!" Cerise said, looking relieved. "You are seriously the hero of the hour."

"The hero of the *week*," he corrected. "This is the second time I've bailed you out, Chevalier."

"I know, I know. I owe *you* one now. But listen, we really need a ride back to Vallonay."

He let out a deep belly laugh and rubbed his hands over the vehicle's contrôleur. "Of course you do." He peered out at their desolate surroundings. "So, are you going to tell me what you're doing out here freezing in the middle of the Terrain Perdu?"

Cerise glanced at Marcellus, and Chatine immediately recognized the distrust in his eyes.

"Um, probably not. No," Cerise said. "But I will regale you with all the details of how I once hacked Papa's TéléCom to play his AirLink messages backward."

Grantaire snorted. "Then, you'd owe me *two* favors."

The smile suddenly slid from Cerise's face. "Look, you know I wouldn't ask if it weren't important."

Grantaire's gaze drifted from Cerise to Marcellus to Alouette to Chatine before finally settling back on Cerise. Then he exhaled a heavy sigh. "It's a good thing I have no life. Get in already. You're letting all the cold air in."

Cerise clambered into the transporteur and beckoned for the rest of them to follow. Alouette climbed aboard next, while Marcellus turned toward Brigitte and reached out his hands for her to take.

"Merci," he said. "For saving him. For keeping him safe here. And for helping us."

Brigitte nodded. "You're welcome. Good luck."

Marcellus released her hands with a squeeze and boarded the transporteur. As Chatine watched him disappear inside the hovering vehicle, she felt a hotness under her collar. A burning in her cheeks. Her gaze snapped to the left to see that Etienne was watching her. Glaring at her. Those huge dark eyes of his boring into her like a médecin's laser.

She opened her mouth to say something but was cut off by Cerise, who suddenly came tumbling back out of the transporteur.

"Brigitte! Wait." She ran back to Etienne's mother and fidgeted awkwardly with her hands. "Watch out for Gabriel, okay?"

"Of course. I will take good care of him."

Cerise cracked a smile. "No, I mean, *you* watch out. He's a criminal mastermind, you know. A good one. And he can be extremely disagreeable."

Brigitte chuckled. "Merci for the warning."

As Cerise watched Brigitte turn and head back to Etienne's ship, tears began to pool in her eyes. She seemed frozen to the ground until Alouette re-emerged from the transporteur and guided Cerise back inside.

And then, Chatine was alone with Etienne.

But with the distance between them, she may as well have been out here all by herself. He was standing a few mètres from her, but he felt oceans away. From the moment she'd defied him and landed his ship in the Terrain Perdu, he'd been acting so strange. So different. His playful, jesting nature was gone, consumed by a darkness that had settled around his whole body, dimming his eyes.

Etienne was the first to speak, and his words felt like daggers through her heart. "You don't want to get involved in this, Chatine. This is exactly the kind of trouble you should stay away from."

Chatine dropped her gaze to the ground, feeling hot tears of frustration prick her eyes. "I have to do this. Did you not hear what Marcellus said?"

"I heard everything he said," Etienne muttered and then under his breath added, "and didn't say."

Chatine wasn't quite sure what he meant by that, but she brushed past it. "The general is going to turn the Third Estate into an army. An army only he can control. Do you know how many are going to be killed if we don't try to stop him?"

"You?" he fired back. "Why do *you* need to do anything about this? This doesn't concern you. We don't get involved in matters of the Regime, remember?"

"That's right," Chatine snapped. "Because you only look out for your own, right? You only protect your *own* people. Well, these *are* my people. You can take away my Skin and hide me out here in the middle of nowhere, but I am still Third Estate. I am still one of them. And I will not let the general use them as a weapon."

Etienne huffed. "The code says—"

"Fric the code!" Chatine shouted. "It's not my code, it's yours. I lived by a code of my own for years. A code that said I only help myself. And it brought me nothing but grief. I'm done with codes. And if you keep insisting on living by yours, eventually you're going to become one of the general's weapons too."

The line of Etienne's jaw pulsed. Chatine knew he was trying to think of what to say next, but it didn't matter. Her mind was made up.

This place—this community of kind, caring, hard-working people—had somehow managed to extinguish her anger and soothe the pain she'd carried around all of her life. But this was a new kind of anger. This was a new kind of pain.

This was a pain that would not just be felt by her.

It would be felt by the whole planet.

And General Bonnefaçon was not the kind of monster you walked away from.

"Au revoir, Etienne." She spun toward the transporteur but stopped when Etienne's hand wrapped around her wrist.

"Wait." His voice was urgent. Hurried. With a heavy breath, he reached into his pocket and pulled out a small, crudely made device, roughly the size of a Skin. "Take this," he said, shoving it into her hand. "You might need it."

Chatine removed her gloves and turned the device around in her hand. She had started to get used to the community's strange, unfamiliar gadgets. But she'd certainly never seen this one before. "What is it?"

"That is how we took out the power on Bastille."

Chatine's mind flickered back to that night she'd awoken to pure darkness in the Trésor tower. Everything around her had gone out: the microcams, the doors, the locks on the vents.

"You did that with this?" she said incredulously, waving the slender contraption.

"Don't be fooled by appearances. The Ministère wants you to believe that power has to come in a flashy package. But it's that very shortsightedness that has allowed us to outsmart them for all these years." He nodded toward the device. "It's called an impulsion. It will take out everything connected to the nearest power grid. Lights, locks, monitors. But it won't work on anything self-powering, like Skins or TéléComs or droids."

As Chatine stared down at the handmade contraption, a sudden sadness began to settle over her. "I guess there's no way to convince you to come with us?"

Of course, she already knew the answer. But hearing it spoken aloud felt like she was being hit by explosif shrapnel on the roof of Bastille all over again.

"I don't get involved." His voice was suddenly so cold, so fitting for this barren landscape around them.

"Not even . . ." She bit her lip to keep the courage from rushing right out of her. "Not even for me?"

For just a split second, the darkness faded, the walls came down, the old Etienne was visible through the lingering shadows, and Chatine felt her heavy heart lift.

"I—" he began tentatively.

"Chatine? Are you coming?" Marcellus's head suddenly appeared in the loading door of the transporteur, staring down at Chatine with those flecked hazel eyes.

She nodded, her throat dirt dry. "One minute."

Marcellus disappeared back inside the vehicle, and without even thinking, Chatine's fingertips went straight to the ring. Like it was a Sol and she was a lonely, barren planet with no orbit. Like it was titan and she was a croc on the prowl for something to steal.

Etienne's gaze dragged downward until his eyes were locked on the silver band around her thumb. Then he looked up at the open door of the transporteur, and Chatine could clock the second that he figured it out.

When she focused back on his face, the old Etienne was gone again, consumed by the darkness, as though he'd never been there at all.

"I don't think you need me to get involved for you," he said before turning and walking back toward the ship, the glowing morning skies reflecting off his coat.

"Etienne!" Chatine shouted into the void of the Terrain Perdu. But her voice felt just as lost as the land that surrounded her.

"Good luck, Chatine," he called over his shoulder. And with that, the new Etienne was gone too.

Chatine watched him go just long enough for her anger to build, to rise up, to fuel her, to push her into that transporteur, and to not look back.

- CHAPTER 63 -
MARCELLUS

THE VAST TÉLÉSKY OF LEDÔME ARCED ABOVE THE transporteur, glowing and blue and dazzling with the three Sols hanging in the center in all their sparkle and grandeur. Marcellus had been gone less than two weeks, but the whole thing seemed so much brighter and more vivid than he remembered. Now, having seen real blue sky and the real Sols setting over the Albion horizon, the charade of all this was more obvious to him than ever. Almost like *these* artificial Sols, hanging in their artificial sky, were trying too hard.

"I never thought I'd find myself back here," Marcellus muttered under his breath as he gazed out the window.

Chatine barked out a laugh. "Me neither."

The guards hadn't even checked the cargo hold of the transporteur when Grantaire stopped at Ledôme's west gate, scanned his biometrics in, and explained that he was making a special delivery for his mother, the Policier inspecteur of Montfer. They'd simply waved him through. Now Marcellus, Chatine, Cerise, and Alouette were seated in the front compartment of the vehicle, watching the bright and colorful sights pass by through the windows.

With every turn and tiny jolt of the transporteur, Marcellus felt like his heart might thump right out of his chest. Their plan had been cycling through his mind on a never-ending loop since they'd left the Terrain Perdu. On some level, it seemed so easy. Simple. As though nothing could possibly go wrong. And yet, at the same time, it also felt close to impossible. As though they were fools for even trying.

But fools or not, Marcellus knew they *had* to try.

"So," Grantaire said, nudging Marcellus with his elbow as the transporteur turned off the main avenue and into a quiet neighborhood. "I can't help but notice that we're here. We made it. I got you safely into Ledôme."

Confused, Marcellus glanced uneasily at Grantaire, unsure what he was getting at. "Yes. Merci. We really appreciate it."

Grantaire held up his hands. "Okay, I get it. I get it. Officer Bonnefaçon still doesn't trust me."

"W-w-what?" Marcellus stammered, taken back. "That's not true."

"It is true," Grantaire deadpanned, and upon seeing Marcellus's baffled expression added, "You can't be the son of a celebrated Policier inspecteur without picking up *some* of her skills. But I don't need cyborg circuitry to sense when someone doesn't like me."

Marcellus faltered, searching for an excuse, but nothing came.

"Hey, it's okay," Grantaire said. "I have to earn your trust. I respect that. I'll work on it." Grantaire winked at him. "I like a challenge."

Marcellus fell quiet and returned his gaze to the window. Outside, nestled behind towering oak and chestnut trees, the manoirs of the Second Estate looked like over-frosted gâteaus. Gaudy painted reliefs covered their walls and pediments. Ornate golden tiles decorated the roofs, and tall, striped columns guarded the front doors.

The transporteur pitched to the left and glided into a long circular driveway before coming to a stop beside a gushing fountain. This manoir was just as grand and opulent as the rest, with a myriad of windows that dazzled in the artificial Sol-light.

Cerise gave Grantaire a hug before hopping out of the vehicle and calling back, "You're the best!"

Grantaire waved and called back, "If only my maman felt that way!"

"I owe you one!" Cerise said before blowing him a kiss.

Alouette and Chatine both thanked Grantaire and stepped out onto the driveway, so that Marcellus was the only one left.

"Look," he began, feeling awkward. "It's not that . . . I just . . ."

Grantaire smirked at him, like he was enjoying this.

Marcellus wrung his hands together and huffed out a breath. "Just get out of Ledôme, okay?"

The smirk evaporated instantly from Grantaire's face. "What? Why? What's going on?" His eyes narrowed. "Does this have something to do with the Ascension banquet? Fifty winners is—"

"Just go. Turn around and get back to Montfer."

Then, before Grantaire could ask him any more questions, Marcellus climbed out of the transporteur and hurried up the driveway.

"Well, here we are," Cerise said, gazing up at the manor. "Home sweet home."

Marcellus couldn't help but remark on the sadness in her voice. It was as though this was the last place Cerise ever thought she'd end up. Marcellus felt the same way. When he'd left Ledôme and the Grand Palais behind, he'd been certain he would never come back.

And yet, here they were. About to infiltrate an Ascension banquet.

But first, they needed supplies.

"You *live* here?" Chatine said, doing very little to hide her disbelief and what sounded like a hint of disgust.

"Unfortunately," Cerise muttered.

She guided them all through the front doors and into a large foyer. Polished marble floors stretched out under their feet, and above their heads, a vast chandelier bloomed with a thousand tiny crystals. They passed gilt-framed paintings, opulent handcrafted sculptures, and a sprawling, intricately woven rug that led to the base of a sweeping staircase.

In her arms, Alouette held tightly to Dr. Collins's canister like it was a lifeline. And it was. It was crucial to their plan. Tonight, that one remaining vial of inhibitor would mean the difference between life and death for a lot of people.

"Are you sure your parents aren't going to come home?" Chatine asked, still gawking at the interior of the house as though the walls were crafted out of pure titan.

Cerise snorted at this. "Come home? Right. Now *that* would be a surprise."

"Your parents don't come home?" Chatine clarified. "Ever?"

"Well, not like *ever*. I mean, Maman does need a place to unpack and repack her suitcase. But mostly never. Papa practically lives at the Ministère headquarters, and Maman prefers Samsara this time of year."

"You mean," Alouette began cautiously, peering into a vast salon with floor-to-ceiling windows that looked out over a sparkling blue-water pool and sprawling green lawns, "you live here alone?"

"Pretty much." Cerise beckoned for them to follow her up to the second floor, and as Marcellus climbed the steps and glanced back over the railing at the magnificent marble foyer below, he suddenly noted the emptiness of it. The coldness of it. Their feet on the stairs echoed across the great manoir like there was nothing around for kilomètres to stop the sound.

They reached a large set of double doors at the end of the hallway, which Cerise opened with a flourish. Stepping inside, she threw out her arms. "And this is my room," she announced.

The bed chamber was large and filled with light from its ribbon of high-arched windows. A vast canopy bed covered with a mountain of colorful silk pillows stood like a regal centerpiece in the middle of the room. Paintings lined every wall, and a deep-pile rug sprawled across the polished floors.

"It's . . . nice," Chatine muttered. She looked extremely uncomfortable inside the room. Her hands were tucked into the pockets of her gray-and-white Défecteur pants and her elbows were pinned to her sides, like she was afraid of knocking into things.

"But the piece de résistance is in *here*." Cerise led them through a door, and their jaws all immediately dropped open at the sight in front of them. Technically, the room could be described as a closet. But it was unlike any closet Marcellus had ever seen before. There were racks and racks of shoes of all shapes, styles, and colors. Pristine leather handbags were displayed behind illuminated plastique panels. Every centimètre of hanging space was filled to the brim with blouses, skirts, and dresses in every shade and fabric Marcellus could imagine. And, on the far back wall, were floor-to-ceiling shelves stocked with more gadgets than he'd ever seen outside of the Cyborg and Technology Labs.

"Holy fric," said Chatine. Her eyes were as wide as moons. She turned to Cerise with what could only be described as admiration. "You're like a Second Estate croc."

Cerise grinned. "Merci." She spun around and plucked a gadget from one of the bins on the back shelf before placing it atop a chest of drawers in the center of the room. A moment later, the device glowed to life, and a large-scale hologram map of Ledôme fanned out across the closet.

"Okay," Marcellus said, stepping forward to take command of the map. He zoomed in on the Grand Palais. "The Ascension banquet starts in two hours. Here. On the Imperial Lawn." He pinched his fingers, directing the hologram to a large swatch of bright green grass that stretched out behind the Palais. "Chatine and I are going in as guests. We will enter here, at the main security checkpoint in the administration wing." He zoomed in farther to reveal a courtyard at the far end of the Imperial Lawn, opposite the Palais's main building.

"That's where your biometrics will be scanned," Cerise added, "and cross-referenced with the guest list."

"Are you sure you can pull this off?" Marcellus's heart raced at just the idea of getting anywhere near a Ministère scan.

Cerise flashed him an annoyed look. "Haven't we been over this? Expert hacker, right here."

"Wouldn't it be easier if we just scaled a wall or something?" Chatine asked, looking anxiously at the map.

Cerise huffed. "Trust me. I got this."

"All right," Marcellus said, trying to capture air in his rapidly constricting lungs. He turned to Chatine. "If anything goes wrong and you need to escape, use one of the loopholes in the security shield around the Palais." He reached back toward the hologram and zoomed out until the perimeter fence was in view. "Mabelle engineered them years ago, and as far as I know, all four are still intact. She marked their locations by bending the fleur-de-lis ornament at a slight angle." He pointed to three spots around the perimeter of the fence before dragging his finger to a fourth point near one of the numerous gardens. "This one is closest to the banquet, so it's our best escape route."

"Why aren't we just using those to sneak into the banquet?" Chatine asked.

"Too risky." Marcellus shook his head. "There are always extra guards on patrol during Ascension banquets. We're far better off entering as guests."

Chatine nodded, but still didn't look convinced.

"Which means you're going to have to blend in with the other guests." Cerise turned to riffle through the rows of hangers behind her. "Marcellus, you can borrow one of Papa's tuxedos, and for Chatine . . ." She paused and plucked a hanger from the rack. A plume of pale green fabric seemed to spill out into the closet like a gushing fountain. It was long and billowy with a never-ending train of silk and ruffles. "This color will be wonderful with your complexion."

Marcellus had never seen a more horrified expression than the one that had just descended over Chatine's face.

Chatine barked out a dark laugh. "You're joking, right?"

Cerise looked down at the dress, confused. "I don't joke about ball gowns."

"I'm not wearing that." Chatine was eyeing the explosion of a dress like it was made of jagged shards of glass, not what appeared to be layers of fine Samsarian silk.

"But you have to. It's the Ascension banquet. Everyone will be dressed up. Even the Third Estaters." She opened a drawer and pulled out a pair of long silk gloves. "And these will cover the scar from your Skin."

Chatine crossed her arms over her chest. "I haven't worn a dress since I was eight years old, and I'm certainly not going to start again now."

"Well, what did you expect to do? Waltz into the gardens wearing *that*?"

Chatine glanced down at her Défecteur clothes and a shadow of doubt flickered over her face. "I . . . ," she began, but her voice trailed off.

"This is the Grand Palais. You have to blend in. And if you don't blend in, you *die*!"

Everyone startled at Cerise's drastic change of tone. Her mood seemed to have gone from confident to morbid in an instant. Clearly, the stress of this endeavor was taking its toll on all of them.

"Or maybe *you* want to break into the Ministère headquarters and hack the guest list and *I'll* go to the banquet." Cerise went on, her voice still strained.

Chatine's arms fell back to her sides, and without another word, she reached out and took the dress from Cerise.

"Merci," Cerise said tightly. "Oh, and one more thing." She disappeared around a corner of the closet and returned a moment later holding what looked like a clump of human hair.

"A wig?" Chatine asked in disbelief.

"As much as I love this look." Cerise gestured to Chatine's short crop of newly grown hair. "Very razor chic. I do worry it *might* make you look like you just escaped from Bastille."

"I did just escape from Bastille."

"Right." Cerise extended out the wig.

As Chatine took it and ran her fingers through the long, dark brown locks, a disturbed, almost haunted expression passed over her face. "This looks a lot like the hair I sold two years ago."

Cerise flashed a hurried smile. "Good, then it'll look natural. And you." She reeled on Marcellus and squinted at his face like he was out of focus. "Hmm. The stubble definitely helps. And we'll get you a hat. But it won't be enough." She rummaged around in another drawer before pulling out a pair of dark Sol-glasses and handing them over.

Marcellus slid the glasses over his eyes and watched the closet tint a reddish gold. It made him think of Albion sunsets and death. He slid the glasses off before refocusing on the hologram.

"Alouette and Cerise, you will be here." He maneuvered the map away from the Palais and pushed in on the dark structure that sat like a giant festering wound amidst the vibrant colors of the rest of Ledôme. The two black towers of the Ministère headquarters soared out of the hologram like a pair of ominous sentinels, and the rows and rows of windows, black and glassy, shone like a battalion of unblinking eyes.

"The service entrance in the back is your best option," Marcellus continued, fighting off a shudder at the sight of that building. "Most of the employees who use that entrance leave at 19.00. You can sneak in through the door as someone is leaving."

"Right." Cerise opened a drawer, pulled out two bundles of fabric, and handed one to Alouette. "This will be our cover."

Alouette unfurled the material to find a simple black pair of pants and a short-sleeved blue shirt with a crisp black collar, simple black buttons, and two deep pockets sewn at the waist.

"Cleaner's uniform," explained Cerise. Then, upon Alouette's questioning look, she added, "Let's just say this is not the first time I've had to sneak into the Ministère."

"Have you figured out how to get into the server room yet?" Marcellus asked Cerise.

"I can disable the security feeds, because they're on an accessible network, but I can't hack a biometric lock. At least not without raising a lot of alarms." She turned expectantly to Alouette, as though they'd already come to a decision.

"I'm going to disable the lock on the server room door," Alouette said.

Chatine and Marcellus both stared at her with wide, unblinking eyes. "You can do that?" Marcellus asked.

Alouette nodded. "Sister Denise taught me how to disassemble my first Ministère lock when I was eight. Now I know why."

Once all the disguises had been distributed, Cerise directed them to private bathrooms to shower and change clothes. The steaming hot water raining down on Marcellus, washing away the dirt and ash and lingering chill of the Terrain Perdu, felt so good. For a moment, he nearly forgot what they had all gathered here to do. But then, as he reached to shut off the faucet, Marcellus's gaze snagged on a window set high in the bathroom wall where, slicing through the darkening TéléSky outside, he could make out a soaring, glinting antenna.

Even from way out here, among the manoirs of Ledôme, the Paresse Tower was visible. Marcellus still couldn't believe what Brigitte had told them. A kill switch for the Skins? Hidden right in front of him—in front of *everyone*—this whole time? Looking up at it now, Marcellus felt like the tower was taunting him. Reminding him of everything that was at stake tonight.

He stood naked and shivering, running through the plan in his mind, thinking about everything that could possibly go wrong. There were no real Sols to pray to inside Ledôme, and he wasn't about to trust the fake ones. Which meant he had no choice but to rely on himself and the people he now called his friends.

Hastily, he grabbed for a towel and dried himself off before pulling on his borrowed tuxedo. It wasn't as scratchy and stiff as his officer uniform, but the touch of the fabric still made him cringe.

He was just knotting the tie when his TéléCom lit up on the bathroom counter.

"Incoming AirLink request pending from Jolras Epernay," a voice said in his audio patch.

Marcellus froze as his gaze traveled down to the screen and the now all-too-familiar face of Maximilienne's brother. He was AirLinking Marcellus again? What could that Red Scar monster possibly want with him?

There was a rap at the door and Cerise called out, "Almost ready?"

Marcellus blinked down at the screen again, where Jolras's face was still waiting.

"Yes!" he shouted back through the door as he hastily swiped at the screen, declining the request. Tonight, he only had the time and energy to think about *one* threat to Laterre. And that was his grandfather.

When he emerged from the bathroom, he found Cerise was the only one waiting for him.

"Where is everyone else?" he asked.

"Still getting ready," she said, and Marcellus noticed a dark shadow descend over her face. "I thought we could do this last part alone."

Marcellus nodded grimly and followed behind her as they walked in silence down the long hallway of the second floor. With each step, Marcellus felt his breath grow shallower and his heart grow heavier. He thought back to that early morning when he'd darted around the abandoned copper exploit, looking for Mabelle and feeling like a traitor. At that moment, he'd wanted nothing more than to join the Vangarde, avenge his father's wrongful incarceration and death, and stop General Bonnefaçon from destroying a planet.

Little did he know, those fateful steps that morning would lead to these ones.

Would lead him here.

Cerise entered a large wood-paneled study and stopped in front of a framed painting of a peaceful First World landscape. She pushed the frame aside to reveal a thick PermaSteel vault embedded into the wall.

"Last chance to back out," Cerise said. "Are you sure about this?"

Marcellus nodded, feeling the significance of such a simple gesture crash down around him. "The general must be stopped. It's the only way."

Cerise sighed and pressed her palm to the glowing panel beside the door. The vault clicked open, and Marcellus sucked in a sharp breath when his eyes fell upon dozens of silver rayonettes hanging from a wooden rack in neat, shimmering rows.

"Papa's been stealing weapons from the Ministère ever since the last rebellion," Cerise explained, and for a moment her eyes went glassy. "The truth is, I don't think he's one hundred percent convinced we won't see another one."

Marcellus reached inside the vault and delicately plucked a rayonette from the rack. Every nerve in his body caught fire as his fingers closed around the glittering handle. He'd held weapons almost his entire life. His grandfather had placed his first rayonette in his hands when he was only eight years old. But he'd never felt its true weight and power and responsibility until right now.

In his mind, he could still hear his grandfather's words from that day ten years ago.

"Hold it steady, Marcellus. In the face of your enemy, a wavering hand can cost you your life."

"Don't hesitate. As soon as you have your best shot, you take it. Never give your opponent the chance to shoot first."

"See this switch? This activates the lethal mode. Only use it in the most dire of circumstances."

Marcellus rolled his thumb back and forth over the toggle. He couldn't think of more dire circumstances than the ones they now faced. And when the time came, he would not hesitate. His hands would not waver. He would not give his grandfather the chance to shoot first.

The thought brought him a rush of terror, then sickness, and then finally, a rush of conviction.

Marcellus had waited a long time for this moment. Longer than he'd even realized. He had suffered, lost, grieved, raged, fought, froze, and traveled across the stars and back for this one chance to stop the general. A chance to make things right.

With a *snap* that reverberated throughout the room, Marcellus flicked the switch on the rayonette and tucked it into the waistband of his pants. "Your father is wrong," he said gravely to Cerise. "Laterre won't see another rebellion."

Cerise blinked up at him with questioning eyes.

"Because no matter what happens tonight," Marcellus said, "there's going to be a revolution."

- CHAPTER 64 -
ALOUETTE

THE MINISTÈRE HEADQUARTERS WAS A COLD AND
sterile place that made Alouette grateful she and Cerise had come here
at night. The hallways were mostly empty, with the exception of a few
patrolling guards who paid no attention to them in their uniforms and
pushing their cleaning carts. Alouette couldn't imagine what this place
must feel like during the day, when the labs were bustling with activity
and cyborgs roamed the halls.

They'd slipped in through the service entrance as the employees of
the day shift were leaving. And now, as Alouette darted behind Cerise
down another long, silent corridor, she swore she could hear her erratic
heartbeat echoing off the spotless white walls. She'd never been more
nervous in all her life. Not when she'd first snuck out of the Refuge.
Not when she and Hugo had been kidnapped by the Renards. Not
when the voyageur started to break apart. Not even when the escape
pod had stranded them in the Terrain Perdu and she was certain they
were all going to die.

There was just something about this place. This building, with its
bare, austere hallways; swift, soundless elevators; and echoing, polished

floors. They seemed to suck the courage right out of her. Like leeches on her skin.

Cerise pulled to a stop in front of an unmarked door and glanced over both shoulders before pulling out her TéléCom and unfolding it. Alouette looked at the screen to see a grid of squares, each one showing a different view of the Ministère headquarters. She immediately recognized the bottom right feed as the hallway they were now standing in, and the two figures dressed in black and blue uniforms as them.

"I can buy you about forty-five seconds. Sixty at the most," Cerise said, tapping furiously at the screen. A dizzying array of panels and blueprints flashed by so quickly, Alouette could barely keep up. "Will that be enough to disable the lock?"

Alouette drew in an unsteady breath. She'd never done this with a clock ticking over her. But she knew there was only one answer to give at this point. Either she did it or the entire plan failed. "Yes."

Cerise prodded at the TéléCom once more. "Okay. Ready? Go."

The bottom right square of the grid went dark, and Alouette sprang into motion. Bending down, she studied the locking mechanism secured to the wall next to the door. She pulled up the hem of her shirt to reveal the small selection of tools she'd collected from Cerise's closet, tucked into a makeshift toolbelt. She reached for the screwdriver first and carefully removed each of the screws on the lock's outer casing. The plastique panel popped off and her gaze roved quickly over the complicated nest of circuitry inside, while her hands switched out her screwdriver for the small power cell she'd removed from a light fixture in Cerise's manoir. She'd spent nearly an hour finding one with the perfect voltage and another fifteen minutes attaching a short extension wire to the output.

"Twenty seconds left," Cerise said beside her.

Alouette carefully maneuvered the power cell into the lock's circuitry, but her fingers were trembling so badly, the tiny cylinder slipped from her hand and clattered to the floor. Crouching down to retrieve it, she reminded herself to breathe, calm down. Her nerves would only cause her to make mistakes. As she tried again, gently guiding the power cell into the lock, she pictured Sister Denise, sitting at her workbench, disassembling Ministère gadgets and soldering circuit boards, always with a delicate but assured hand. She was a woman of very few words. But every time Alouette had watched her break open a device and explore the mechanisms inside, it was like watching poetry in motion. A skilled musician with their favorite instrument.

"Every device has an inherent flaw in its design," Sister Denise had once told her. *"If you search long enough, eventually you'll find it."*

Sister Denise's words in her mind filled Alouette with strength and resolve and, more important, steadiness. She slipped the power cell farther into the lock, until she felt an almost infinitesimal spark as the extension wire connected with the circuitboard.

"After analyzing Ministère locks for years, I discovered that if you introduce just the right voltage of power to the circuitboard, it momentarily overloads the system and disables the device."

A soft hissing sound followed, and the door swept open.

Cerise wasted no time. She grabbed Alouette by the elbow and shuffled her through the door before sealing it shut behind them. Rows upon rows of glowing machines lined the room, each one taller than Alouette and blinking with tiny blue lights. At the center of the pristine white ceiling, amid a complicated grid of vents and fans, a cooling unit hummed.

"Cerise, what's the status?" Marcellus's voice suddenly slipped into Alouette's ear, startling her. She wasn't used to wearing an audio patch, but Cerise insisted she be able to talk to everyone, so she'd equipped them all with audio patches and TéléComs and set up a multi-channel AirLink that allowed them to communicate.

"We just got into server room 12," Cerise replied. "I just need to find the right router." She was already moving through the aisles, her gaze flicking expertly over the shelves before pulling to a decisive halt. Crouching down, she opened her bag and pulled out a small flat contraption, which she promptly affixed to the front of a glowing panel. Cerise's small device illuminated, its tiny screen flashing erratically. She began tapping on the device, pausing only long enough to hand Alouette her

TéléCom. "Take this. Keep an eye on the cams. Warn me if anyone is coming."

Alouette lowered herself to the ground next to Cerise and kept her eyes locked on the grid of security feeds. She diligently flicked her finger across the screen, revealing more and more chilling views of the Ministère headquarters. Each one sent a shiver of fear through her.

The Ministère had always been an enemy to Alouette. A danger to her way of life and to the precious books she'd sworn to protect. But now, as she stared at the countless rooms and labs and offices, she suddenly saw it—and the threat it posed—with new eyes. Now that she knew the sisters had been more than just guardians of the Forgotten Word, that they had been crusaders trying to fix a broken planet, she understood what this building had really represented to them. And what it now represented to her.

It was a stronghold of the Regime. A symbol of corruption. It was where cruel weapons were developed, imperious cyborgs were created, and soldiers of injustice were trained.

"Nearly there," Cerise said, her gaze swiveling between her contraption and the machine it was attached to. "Once the network bridge is online, I'll be able to intercept the data being sent from the banquet's security checkpoint."

Alouette quickly swiped back to the view of the hallway outside the server room, passing over numerous grids and security feeds. But her finger slowed to a halt as something in one of the feeds caught her eye and her breath. Her chest squeezed as she struggled to make sense of what she was seeing. She tapped twice on the feed, prompting it to fill the entire screen.

And suddenly it was as though she were back in the Terrain Perdu, every centimètre of her body frozen in the icy air. Marcellus's words to her on the voyageur floated above her head like tiny flecks of snow.

"My grandfather has a detention facility hidden somewhere. . . ."

"There are only two people on the planet who know where it is. . . ."

"What's wrong?" Cerise asked. "Is someone coming?"

Alouette's mind was racing too fast to respond. But as soon as Cerise leaned over and saw the image that filled the TéléCom screen, she seemed to understand. She inhaled a sharp breath. "He must have made it through the surgery," she said quietly. Pensively.

"Do you think . . . ?" Alouette couldn't even whisper all the words. They felt too dangerous. Too laced with hazardous hope.

But Cerise plucked the question right out of Alouette's mind. "That his memories have been restored?"

Alouette nodded, her throat constricting. Going dry. Turning to hot, desert sand.

"I think," Cerise began, locking onto Alouette's eyes with a fierceness and determination that made Alouette shiver, ". . . that there's only one way to find out."

All at once, Alouette understood. Cerise's eyes were speaking so much louder than her words. Alouette thought briefly of her promise to Dr. Collins before he died. Her promise to find Jacqui and Denise. To find his daughter.

And she knew what Cerise was thinking. Because it was what they were *both* thinking.

This might be our only chance.

"Cerise," Marcellus's voice shattered the silence of the server room, causing Cerise's and Alouette's gazes to break apart. "Chatine and I are almost to the banquet. Is everything in place?"

Cerise blinked, as though shaking herself from a trance, and focused back on the panel in front of her. She tapped once on the screen and nodded approvingly. "Yes. The network bridge is online. Are you and Chatine ready?"

There was a long pause, in which Alouette's heart instantly ratcheted up three notches. Finally, Marcellus replied, "Yes. We're ready."

Cerise took a deep breath and turned to Alouette as her lips formed a single, silent syllable. The most terrifying and hopeful syllable Alouette had ever known. *Go.*

- CHAPTER 65 -
CHATINE

CHATINE COULD BARELY BREATHE. PARTLY BECAUSE OF
her frazzled nerves, but mostly because of the dress. It was impossibly
tight and clung to her body in the most awkward of places. The fabric fell all the way to the floor, some of it even dragging behind her.
Cerise had called it a train. In the Frets, it would have been called a
"mud trap."

And she didn't even want to get started on the shoes.

"Chatine and I are almost to the banquet. Is everything in place?"
Marcellus whispered into his audio patch beside her. They were striding
across a large courtyard, flanked on either side by the Palais's adminis-
trative buildings. Finely dressed banquet guests swarmed around them.
Even though he was walking right next to her, Chatine had to keep
glancing at Marcellus out of the corner of her eye to make sure it was
really him. With his sleek tuxedo, black hat, Sol-glasses, and the dark
stubble shadowing his chin, he was barely recognizable. Both of them
were. As much as Chatine hated to admit it, Cerise had done an excellent
job disguising them.

"Yes, the network bridge is online," Cerise replied in Chatine's ear, causing her to wince. She still hadn't gotten used to hearing voices in her head again. "Are you and Chatine ready?"

Marcellus glanced over at her, his eyebrows raised in a silent question. It was such a simple question. And yet, the answer made Chatine feel faint. Back in the Défecteur camp, when Marcellus had first laid out this plan, it had all felt so easy. So straightforward. But the distance had clearly softened her perspective. Her anger at discovering what the general was planning had placed a hazy filter on the reality of the situation.

A reality that hadn't fully hit her until they'd passed through the gates of the Grand Palais. Until the memory of the last time she'd been here stabbed her like a knife. Now the responsibility, the gravity of what they had come here to do was finally sinking in. And it dragged on her body even more so than this ridiculous dress.

She gave Marcellus a small, hesitant nod.

"Yes," he replied to Cerise through his audio patch. "We're ready."

They continued to follow the throng of banquet guests toward the entrance. Chatine tried to take deep breaths to settle her nerves. She'd performed a thousand cons in her life, but never one of this magnitude. And never in shoes this tall.

"You're doing great," Marcellus whispered to her. "You totally blend in."

"I feel like a pastry," she whispered back.

"A very elegant pastry," he amended, and Chatine was grateful for the humor. It immediately put her at ease. "Of course, I do miss the Fret rat look."

Chatine shrugged. "What can I say? Black is my color."

The entrance to the Ascension banquet was a long archway made of tiny flowers and fluttering leaves. Chatine and Marcellus joined the queue of guests waiting to pass through the security checkpoint. Up ahead, five officers in bright white uniforms stood guard, the glistening rayonettes strapped to their belts making Chatine's heart flutter.

"Are you sure this is going to work?" she whispered hotly into her audio patch. If *any* one of those officers recognized her or Marcellus, this would all be over before it even began.

"Calm down," Cerise replied smoothly. "Everything is set up. It's going to work."

Chatine didn't like the fact that their entire mission was dependent on this Second Estate girl she barely knew who *claimed* to be a hacker. But Marcellus and Alouette seemed to trust her, and so Chatine had had no choice but to go along with it. If it had been up to her, they'd be climbing walls in dark camouflage. Not walking right into the lion's den dressed like brightly colored pieces of meat.

"Skins, please," said a deep voice.

They had reached the front of the line, and Chatine looked up to see two officers brandishing TéléComs toward them.

"Second Estate," Marcellus clarified in a voice that sounded nothing like his own.

"Biometrics, then," the guard said.

Chatine's heart started to pound as she dropped her gaze, figuring the less eye contact the better. Marcellus gave her an encouraging nod before confidently placing his palm against one of the outstretched screens. Like it was nothing. Like those screens couldn't reveal the truth about both of them in the blink of an eye.

Convict.

Traitor.

Escaped from Bastille.

Wanted by the Regime.

Chatine swallowed hard, removed her right glove, and extended her hand. She nearly recoiled at the touch of the TéléCom. Was it just her imagination or was it burning hot? As the screen glowed orange under her fingers and the scan initiated, Chatine's mind flashed back to every other time she'd been scanned. Tracked. Logged. Marked. She'd stood under the watchful eye of cyborgs, succumbed to the degrading searches of officers, suffered the invasive inspections of droids who would just as soon bash in her head as let her go.

Her entire life was a seemingly endless collage of Ministère surveillance.

And now, for the first time, she was offering it up willingly.

"Okay, I've got you," Cerise whispered in her ear. "Your biometrics are coming in. I'm routing them through the network bridge now and transmitting your fake profiles."

Chatine tried to release the breath that was caught in her chest, but her lungs seemed to be holding it captive. All she could think about was what would happen if Cerise's hack failed. If this scan revealed the truth. Her *real* profile.

A shrill beeping sound cut through the air. Panicked, Chatine glanced back down at the screens of the TéléComs to see they had both turned red. She shared a fleeting look with Marcellus, silently asking which direction they should start running in.

"That's strange," one of the officers said, frowning at something evidently being reported into his ear. "Your biometrics aren't seeming to register with the—" The beeping sound came to an abrupt halt and the angry red screens turned instantly back to orange. "Ah, here we are." The officer looked up and flashed Chatine and Marcellus a smile. "Welcome, Monsieur and Madame Pontmercy. Sorry about that. Must have been a glitch."

"Quite all right," Chatine murmured, trying her best to return the smile. But it was difficult to do with her heart in her throat.

As they shuffled forward, through the archway, Chatine struggled to catch her breath. "What the fric?" she whispered once they were far enough away from the officers.

"Sorry!" came Cerise's far-too-chipper reply. "I mixed up the profiles and nearly sent Marcellus's to your scan and yours to Marcellus's. Anyway, I had to abort in the middle. It wasn't pretty. But the good news is, you're in."

"Barely," Chatine muttered.

They approached a set of stone stairs that led from the courtyard down to the Imperial Lawn below. For a moment, as Chatine took in the breathtaking view, all remnants of her former anxiety seemed to vanish.

The Sols had set in the TéléSky above, but the Palais gardens glowed with a thousand tiny, twinkling lights that were hung in the trees and ornate shrubbery. Every flower imaginable glimmered in the magical half-light, and a series of illuminated fountains chugged water high into the air in a coordinated dance. And, at the far end of the Imperial Lawn, up a majestic sweeping staircase, stood the Grand Palais itself. The ocean-blue walls of the vast building looked almost purple in this light, and every one of its hundreds of windows reflected back the twinkling glow from the gardens.

A poke at her arm jolted her from her thoughts, and she looked down to see Marcellus was nudging her with his elbow. She nudged him back, assuming it was some kind of attempt to reassure her. But Marcellus just laughed.

"I'm offering you my arm," he explained.

She stared at him, dumbfounded. "What would I want with your arm?"

He grabbed her gloved hand and looped it around the crook of his elbow. "It's proper etiquette for a wife to take the arm of her husband." His eyes twinkled as he added, "*Madame* Pontmercy."

Chatine fought back a snort. "Proper etiquette?" She lowered her voice to a whisper and jutted her chin at the pocket of his tuxedo jacket, where she'd seen him hide his rayonette. "I think we're far beyond that now."

His expression darkened, as though he were just now remembering what the weapon was for. "Fine. Then it's to help you down the stairs."

Chatine rolled her eyes and removed her hand. "I've scaled walls in the Frets. I don't need help walking down stairs."

But as she descended the first step, the ridiculously tall shoes Cerise had made her wear wobbled beneath her and she began to fall. Marcellus reached out to catch her just in time and, with an infuriating smirk, returned her hand to his arm. "And now we understand the etiquette."

Chatine grumbled in response, but this time kept her grip locked on his elbow as she carefully maneuvered down the steps and into the heart of the festivities. How was she *ever* supposed to successfully do anything covert in this ridiculous getup? She was used to blending into shadows. The only thing she would blend into in this dress was the gâteau.

"Don't worry," Marcellus whispered as they waded into the crowd. "If you fall again, just blame the wine."

Even though the Patriarche and the general wouldn't be making their grand entrance for at least another thirty minutes, the banquet was already in full swing. Music wafted through the warm night breeze, and hundreds of Third Estaters—invited in from the gray, damp world outside—were now dancing, chattering, and milling excitedly around vast tables laden with food and wine. Chatine spotted silver dishes bearing whole roasted chickens, platters of sizzling fish, towers of brightly colored fruit, and vast boards of every kind of cheese imaginable. And on the center table stood a line of embellished gâteaus, green and frosted, with dozens of cream-filled layers.

A true First Estate fête.

Chatine's mind involuntarily fluttered back to the last fête she had attended. The linking cérémonie at the camp. Sols, how much she would rather have been there than here. The memory of Etienne's face as he turned away from her in the Terrain Perdu had been like a permanent knife burrowed in her side ever since she'd left.

Marcellus guided her off to the side, where a row of delicately trimmed hedges flanked the perimeter of the lawn. From here, they could observe the rest of the fête without being easily spotted.

"Can you see the champagne fountain yet?" Cerise's voice slipped back into her ear.

"I'm looking." Marcellus craned his neck to peer above the sea of coiffed hairdos, wide-brimmed hats, and feathered hairpieces. "Okay, it looks like they're just bringing it out now."

Chatine followed his gaze and tilted forward on the tips of her shoes, momentarily grateful for the extra height. She spotted two waiters guiding a large cart across the lawn. On it, a glorious fountain glimmered with bubbling golden liquid that cascaded over its numerous tiers. The surrounding crowd stopped to gawk and admire the spectacle while some Third Estaters captured footage on their Skins.

"Got it," Chatine said. "Will anyone be guarding it?"

Marcellus shook his head. "I highly doubt it. I don't think my grandfather has any suspicion that we're about to bring down his entire plan with champagne."

Chatine nodded and surreptitiously ran her hand under the bottom edge of the dress's suffocating corset, feeling for the two objects she'd stuffed in there before leaving the manoir.

The first was the strange contraption Etienne had given her back at the camp. He'd called it an impulsion. She still wasn't sure what she would need it for, or if it would even work, but she figured it didn't hurt to have it with her. The second object was the vial of inhibitor. Alouette had warned her to keep it secure, and Chatine could think of no better place. *Nothing* was moving around in this dress.

As the waiters positioned the fountain amongst the other banquet tables, Chatine angled her body toward the hedge and reached down the front of her dress to pull out the vial. For a moment, she studied the small container, wondering how these few drops of liquid could possibly protect all these people from the general's weapon. But Alouette had assured her it would be enough, spouting something about self-propagation.

"All good?" Marcellus asked.

Chatine nodded as she tucked the vial into her palm, making it disappear like she'd done so many times with precious relics lifted from unsuspecting marks.

"Remember," Marcellus said, "you need to get the inhibitor into the fountain before they start filling glasses for the toast. It's the only way to be sure that everyone here drinks it and the weapon is neutralized before the general has a chance to activate it from his TéléCom."

"But what about everyone else?" Chatine asked, a potential flaw in the plan just now occurring to her. "All the Third Estaters not at this banquet. If he tries to activate the weapon, won't they all—"

Marcellus shook his head. "No. The scientists on Albion told us that the program is configurable to any size group. This is a targeted attack. The general has only one goal today. He has no reason to activate anyone else."

Chatine released a breath. *It's just another con,* she told herself. *Like the countless you've done before. A sleight of hand. A quick tip of the wrist and it's over.*

She peered up at the vast TéléSky above their heads, where countless stars shimmered and winked like tiny, precious gems around a white moon.

And suddenly, just like that, she was back there. *Up* there. The last time she'd looked at a great dusting of stars like this, she'd been on Bastille. A chain tugging at her neck, choking her breaths. Her fingertips raw and shredded from a long shift in the exploit. And every part of her cold. So very cold.

Chatine's knees went weak. Like they were made of nothing stronger than flimsy twigs. She could feel her confidence drifting away on Ledôme's artificial breeze.

"Sols, I can't do this," she said under her breath.

Marcellus positioned himself in front of her, his face only centimètres away. He slid the Sol-glasses off, and suddenly all she could see were the endless flecks of green and brown in his eyes. "Yes, you can. You can do this, Chatine."

"I—I can't . . . ," she stammered, shaking her head. "I can't go back there. If anyone recognizes me—"

"No one is going to recognize you," Marcellus assured her. "You are the master of disguise, remember?" A small smile quirked on his lips. "You fooled me into thinking you were a boy for a whole week. You can fool anyone here."

Chatine glanced around, focusing on the hundreds of Third Estaters crammed into the garden. All of them were dressed in sharp tuxedoes and plush gowns which glittered under the lamps that dangled over the lawn like rows of miniature Sols.

Yet, despite their elegance, their excitement, their awe at the food and the music and the opulence of the Palais, Chatine could see in their faces and their awkward stances that they felt just as out of place as she did. For beneath the gauzy sleeves of the ball gowns and the crisp white tuxedo shirts, their Skins still glowed bright, just waiting to turn them from unassuming Ascension winners to vicious killers. At the touch of a button.

The thought made Chatine's gut twist and her resolve strengthen. And suddenly she remembered why she was here.

For them. And for him. For Henri.

"Welcome, Ascension Winners!" The music lulled to a halt and the crowd hushed as an eager voice slipped into the air through the powerful speakers that were hidden among shrubs and flowerbeds.

"I am Georges Bissette, and I will be your master of cérémonies for the night. First and foremost, I would like to personally welcome you to the Grand Palais and, of course, congratulate you on your triumphant Ascension to the Second Estate!"

Cheers broke out across the Imperial Lawn. Chatine glanced toward the stage constructed in the center, where she could now see a man in a bright blue tailcoat who was addressing the crowd.

"You'll be very pleased to hear," Georges went on, "that the Patriarche and Matrone will be arriving shortly to officially kick off the festivities."

Marcellus looked to Chatine, warmth and reassurance flickering in his eyes. "It's time."

She nodded, took another steeling breath, and squeezed the vial in her hand before slowly turning around.

"Good luck," Marcellus whispered behind her.

"Wait." She spun back, grabbed Marcellus by the sleeve, and guided him farther into the cluster of hedges, until they had entirely disappeared from the banquet and were surrounded by a cocoon of twinkling, glowing green. The tiny lights threading through the bushes seemed to make every leaf glimmer and dance.

"I . . ." She hastily searched for the right words. "Before we go through with this, there's something I have to do."

Marcellus stared back at her, those intense hazel eyes of his deep and boundless. She'd spent so many nights lying awake on Bastille thinking about those eyes, wondering if she'd ever see them again. Now here they were.

And she could not wait a second longer.

She pulled the long silk glove from her left hand and slowly slid the ring from her thumb.

For a moment, Marcellus just stared down at it, something indecipherable playing out on his face. Chatine couldn't tell if it was anger, relief, surprise, or something else entirely. Something she couldn't even begin to comprehend.

He tried to speak, but the words came out choppy and stammering. "You . . . How . . ."

"I stole it from you. In the cruiseur on the way back from Montfer."

"Montfer?" Marcellus spat, his mind clearly doing the mental calculations, counting back how long ago that had been. How much had happened since then.

An execution.

A riot.

An imprisonment.

An escape.

Countless deaths.

And now a banquet that could change the course of a planet.

Yet here it was. Safe and sound.

"I'm convinced it protected me," Chatine said quietly. "On Bastille."

Marcellus's gaze snapped up to look at her. To collide with her. To crash into her and pull them both back to the roof of that fabrique. When she'd let down her hair and scrubbed the dirt from her face and shown him who she really was.

When she'd kissed him and he'd called her a traitor.

"But it doesn't belong to me," she whispered, as she took hold of Marcellus's wrist, pried his fingers open, and dropped the silver band into his palm. "It never did."

Then, without another word, she darted out from the hedges and faded into the crowd.

- CHAPTER 66 -
ALOUETTE

ALOUETTE MOVED SWIFTLY DOWN THE HALLWAYS OF the Ministère's Cyborg and Technology labs. With every corner she turned and every stark, echoing hallway she crossed, her heart pounded harder.

"Turn left. Then another left. Do you see the door to your right? That's the infirmerie."

She was grateful for the audio patch behind her ear and Cerise's steady voice to guide her. She could never have made it here on her own. Alouette approached the door to the infirmerie and reached for the screwdriver on her toolbelt.

"Wait!" Cerise called out, causing Alouette to recoil. "There's a médicin coming out of there right now!"

Panicked, Alouette spun around, trying to figure out how to blend in in the middle of this bleak white hallway. Unfortunately, she'd left her cleaning cart back inside the server room. She grabbed for a cloth tucked into her tool belt and made a show of wiping down a nearby window.

"Stay calm," Cerise warned. "Remember, cyborgs can sense elevated body temperatures and heart rates."

Alouette took a deep breath. Behind her, she heard the infirmerie door open and footsteps echo on the polished floor. She glanced over her shoulder to see a woman in green scrubs retreating down the hallway. Alouette turned and darted through the open door just before it sealed shut.

Leaning against the wall, she took a moment to try to steady herself. The sound of heavy, labored breathing punctured the air. Alouette was certain it had to be coming from her, but when she finally turned around and her gaze fell upon the real source of the sound, something fierce and hot and panicked bubbled up in her chest.

Even though she knew what she had come here to do, even though she'd been mentally preparing herself from the moment she'd left the server room, she still hadn't prepared herself for *this*. Nothing could have prepared her for this.

In the center of the room, a large machine puffed and wheezed. Lights flashed along its underside, and a tangle of tubes and wires snaked in and out of a long, cylindrical dome on top. And laying under the curved and clear plastique, still and silent as the dead, was Inspecteur Limier.

Except he wasn't dead.

Not quite.

His eyes were closed. His skin was waxy and his head bandaged. Oxygen pumped into his lungs, moving his chest up and down. And the circuitry implanted into the left side of his face hummed and blinked. Just as it had done the night he'd tried to kill her. Just as it had done the moment before Alouette had fired that rayonette into the wet air of the Forest Verdure and watched the pulse bury itself into his temple before exploding in a shower of sparks.

"Okay, I've deactivated the security feed to that room." Cerise jolted her out of her memories. "But it's only a matter of time before someone notices the outage, so be quick."

Steeling herself, Alouette scurried across the room toward a small console connected to the side of the plastique dome. "Search internal memory chip," she whispered shakily. "Filter for files logged with detention facility and interrogation."

The control panel emitted a soft beep as results started to populate the screen.

"It's working," she reported back to Cerise. "Lots of files are coming up."

"Good. Let's hope one of them is intact."

Alouette stared down at Inspecteur Limier as the program rooted around in his damaged brain. She knew that by the time Sister Jacqui and Sister Denise had been transferred to the general's facility, Inspecteur Limier had already been incapacitated. But Marcellus had been certain Limier knew where the facility was located.

Please, she thought desperately. *Please tell us where they are.*

As the screen continued to fill with search results, the circuitry implanted in the side of the inspecteur's face gave a sharp, rapid flash and suddenly, a memory started to push its way to the surface of Alouette's mind. As if that program were rooting around in her own brain as well. She suddenly recalled something Limier had said to her back in the Forest Verdure, minutes before he had tried to kill her and Alouette had turned him into this.

"If it isn't little Madeline. Alive and well. I thought you were dead. Pity. It would have made all of this so much tidier."

The words sent a shiver down Alouette's spine. At the time, she hadn't thought much of them. They were just the nonsensical babblings of a man possessed. But that was before she'd been to the blood bordel in Montfer. That was before she'd spoken to the madame. Before she'd learned that she was, indeed, supposed to be dead.

The Communiqué had confirmed it.

Madeline Villette had died in 490.

But how did Inspecteur Limier know that? Or more important, why did he even care? Madeline Villette had just been some random baby, born to a Third Estate servant, living in Montfer. While Limier had been a cyborg inspecteur working halfway across the planet.

But then, Alouette recalled the clue that had sent her on this desperate quest to begin with.

"You are a criminal," Inspecteur Limier had said to Hugo. *"And she is the daughter of a worthless blood whore. The Regime has no use for either of you."*

Something was tickling at the edges of Alouette's consciousness. Something that made her legs feel wobbly and her scalp tingle.

Inspecteur Limier had clearly known her mother. He knew that she'd sold her blood. He knew that she'd had a daughter. And that she'd named her Madeline.

A daughter he thought was dead.

The control panel let out a soft ding, alerting Alouette that the search was complete. She peered back at the screen, reminding herself to stay focused. Any minute now, another médecin could walk through that door.

"What do you see?" Cerise prompted.

Alouette squinted at the panel. "There are a lot of files. Are these really all logged with detention facility and interrogation?"

"He *was* the inspecteur of the Vallonay Policier Precinct. So probably yes."

Alouette's stomach turned as she braved another glance at the incapacitated inspecteur. How many people had been tortured by this man?

She tapped on the first file. A moment later, one of the monitors on the wall of the room blinked to life. Grainy blackness filled the screen, followed by a loud screeching noise. She winced and scrubbed forward in the footage, only to find more static. She tried a different file, but it was the same. File after file of nothing but darkness or the indecipherable jumble of shapes.

"They're all corrupted," she whispered to Cerise, feeling the hope squeeze out of her.

"Keep looking."

Alouette tapped the next file on the screen. Then the next. Until she was quickly nearing the end of the search results. She let out a small whimper of frustration. *She* was the reason all of these files were corrupt. *She* was the one who put that pulse in the inspecteur's head. Jacqui and Denise were the only two sisters left in the world. If she couldn't find them—if she couldn't fulfill her promise to Dr. Collins—would it be her fault?

She clicked on the next file but froze when she heard something behind her. It was the unmistakable sound of heavy breathing.

Someone else was in the room with her.

Alouette spun around, pulse racing, fingertips tingling. But there was no one there. The room was empty apart from . . .

She turned back toward the bed of the unconscious inspecteur and watched as he took in a long, noisy breath. This one, however, wasn't assisted by the tubes that tunneled down his throat. This was a lengthy, deliberate inhale through his nose. Almost as though he was trying to capture every scent in the room.

Alouette staggered back. "Cerise," she whispered urgently. "I think he's waking up."

"What?"

The inspecteur inhaled again, his nostrils flaring.

"You should get out of there," Cerise said.

Alouette turned toward the door, preparing to run, but a slight movement caught her eye. She snapped her gaze back to the monitor on the wall just in time to see a face flicker into view. The image strained against the static, like it was fighting to be seen. Sounds came, distorted and echoing, and then the face appeared again. This time closer. Clearer. It was a man. His haunted, terrified eyes were bulging, and his haggard cheeks were streaked with tears. Alouette could just make out some kind of metal wire pinching at his neck before the soundtrack screeched and the footage warped again, replaced with a sequence of flickering images—a fist punching through the air, a pool of blood, wrists bound by chains.

Alouette squirmed at the sight but still forced herself to step closer to the monitor, to the jagged splintered footage, trying to make out any detail that might reveal where it was captured. But everything was so jumbled and hazy.

"What are you doing?" Cerise screeched.

Ignoring her, Alouette hurried back to the control panel. She darted a look at the inspecteur. His eyes were still closed, but his circuitry was flickering with more intensity now. More alertness.

"Requesting coordinates," she whispered to the panel.

There was a hesitant pause before the reply came. "No coordinates found."

Alouette bit her lip, trying to organize her thoughts. There had to be a way to figure out where this memory was captured. She stared down at the inspecteur, who was still breathing deeply, his eyelids fluttering as though he was dreaming about this very same memory. Walking back through it in his own mind.

And an idea came to her.

Hastily, Alouette jabbed at the control panel. "Requesting time stamp."

There was another pause, but this time, the console reported back, "Month 8, Day 19, Year 504. 11.29."

"Find all memories dated one hour before."

The program went to work again, and soon a new file started to play. Black static filled the screen, and Alouette's heart sank again as she assumed it was another corrupted file. But then, a moment later, she realized, the static was *moving*. Rushing past. Because it was not static at all. But rather, a vast and dark ocean.

The Secana Sea! Alouette realized with a jolt of adrenaline.

Limier was flying over the Secana Sea. The soundtrack whooshed and roared as the vehicle—a cruiseur, perhaps?—drew closer to something in the distance. It almost looked like an island.

There was an island somewhere on Laterre? But Alouette had always been taught the planet consisted of a single landmass. She lunged for the control panel again and reversed the footage on high speed, mesmerized as Limier's memory tracked all the way back to Vallonay. Over the docklands. Into the Frets. And back to a cruiseur station just outside the Policier Precinct.

Jabbing her hand down, Alouette stopped the footage and scrubbed it forward a few seconds. On the monitor, in juddering, splintered pieces, Alouette watched the inspecteur board the cruiser and, in his gruff, monotonous tone, articulate a long string of coordinates.

Her breath shuddered in her chest.

He was giving the cruiser a destination.

A location.

Hastily, she pulled out the TéléCom Cerise had loaned her and recited the coordinates into the screen. Sure enough, a single orange dot appeared off the northwest coast of Laterre's great landmass. An island. A *secret* island. Where her beloved sisters awaited.

Relief flooded through Alouette. It was beautiful and intoxicating and distracting. So distracting, she didn't even see the hand reaching out from the bed beside her until it wrapped around her wrist. She screamed and scrambled backward, shaking herself from Limier's grasp. When she looked back at the inspecteur, she saw that his eyes were open—one a dark brown, the other a vibrant cybernetic orange. And they were both looking at her.

Alouette rushed back toward the door and scurried into the hallway. She tried to keep her pace slow, natural, all the while glancing over her shoulder for the inspecteur. "Cerise," she whispered breathlessly into her audio patch as she turned the corner and exited the door to the cyborg labs. "I've got it. I've got the coordinates. I know where they are."

There was no response. And it was only then that Alouette realized she'd hadn't heard anything from Cerise in a while. Her footsteps slowed.

"Cerise?" she asked quietly.

Still nothing.

Alouette's hackles rose. Something was wrong.

She quickened her pace, trying desperately to remember the path she'd taken from server room 12, but the hallways were long and daunting, and they all looked the same. She had no idea if she was getting closer or farther away.

"Alouette?"

The voice was like a song in her ears. "Cerise! Are you okay? What happened? I can't find my way back. I—"

"Don't come back."

Alouette skidded to a halt. "What?"

"Don't come back here." Cerise's voice was harsh and cold. It sent a chill through Alouette. "Get out of the Ministère. Now. And whatever you do, don't try to rescue me."

"I—I don't understand. What happened?"

"Just promise me you won't try to rescue me."

"Cerise," Alouette tried, something hot clawing at her throat.

"Promise me," she repeated. Her tone was unlike Alouette had ever heard it. Desperation mixed with something akin to anger.

"Okay," she finally said in a broken whisper. "I promise. But will you please just tell me—"

"Vive La Vangarde," Cerise said quietly. And then there was nothing but silence.

"Cerise?" Alouette whispered into her audio patch, but the line had gone dead.

Terrified and winded, she glanced around the empty hallway, as though she expected the answer to this impossible situation to appear through the nearest door. *Leave the Ministère? Without Cerise?*

No, she couldn't do that. She couldn't just—

Heavy footsteps reverberated through the empty hallway. It sounded like an invading army. Alouette readied herself to run until she heard a deep, angry voice bellow, "She's in server room 12. I want guards stationed all down this hallway. She is not getting away."

Quietly, Alouette followed the sound of the voice, tiptoeing toward the nearest corner. When she poked her head around the edge, she saw a man in a black tuxedo standing outside the same closed door that she had broken into earlier. The man was flanked by two guards in Ministère uniforms and a female cyborg in a white lab coat.

Alouette's gut twisted, and she had to clamp her mouth shut to keep from crying out. She had to do something. Cause a diversion. Distract them. Lead them away from that door. She could not let Cerise go down for this. But before she could even begin to formulate a plan, the door to the server room swept open and Alouette heard Cerise's bright and chipper voice call out, "Papa! Bonsoir! How have you been? You look well. That tux is simply divine on you. How is the banquet going?"

Papa?

Alouette squinted down the hallway at the girl who had just appeared through the door with a wide grin on her face. And suddenly Alouette understood. This man in the tuxedo who was glaring at Cerise with a deep scowl cut into his face—this was the infamous Directeur Chevalier.

"I've missed you so, so much, Papa!" Cerise said, leaning in to pull the directeur into an embrace.

He grabbed her by the arms and brusquely pushed her back before snapping his fingers at the cyborg and pointing toward the server room. "Rolland, find out what she's been up to in there."

Alouette felt her legs go wobbly as she watched the woman in the lab coat stride into the room. But Cerise didn't look concerned. She gave a playful little snort. "Up to? Papa I wasn't up to anything. I got lost looking for *you*. I thought you might be in this—" she glanced back into the server room and crumpled her forehead in confusion—"room with all the flashy lights."

"Save it, Cerise," the directeur snapped. "I'm not falling for it. Not this time. You've been gone over a week. Vanished without a trace. Your maman has been out of her mind with worry on Samsara. I had people searching all over Ledôme for you. Fortunately, a neighbor saw you coming home earlier today with some friends and AirLinked me to let me know. Where have you been?"

For just a split second, Cerise seemed to falter, as though she wasn't sure how to respond to that. But when she spoke again, her voice was as breezy as ever. "Oh, you wouldn't believe it, Papa. I was kidnapped by this violent rebel group and then I got caught up in this wild space adventure where Albion warships were chasing us and the aerodrones were firing at us. Oh, and then we crash-landed in the Terrain Perdu and

I thought we were going to die." She let out an exaggerated sigh. "It was exhausting. I would have AirLinked, but I'm pretty sure we were being tracked by the Mad Queen so—"

"Stop." Directeur Chevalier pressed his fingertips into his temples. "Just stop. No more lies, Cerise. No more stories. You are not getting out of this. I know the games you've been trying to play with me. And they won't work."

"But Papa, I swear I'm not—"

"No," the directeur interrupted again. "You can't keep running away from your future, Cerise. I've rescheduled your operation for tomorrow morning. And until then, you'll be under constant surveillance. It's done."

Operation.

Alouette's heart clutched in her chest. Her throat burned. She could not let this happen to Cerise. She could not let them take her and turn her into a cyborg. She readied herself to burst down this hallway. To fight. To cry. To scream. Until she remembered her promise to Cerise only moments ago.

"Get out of the Ministère. Now. And whatever you do, don't try to rescue me."

Cerise must have seen her father coming on the security feeds. She knew what was about to happen. She knew she was about to get caught. Why hadn't she run? Why hadn't she saved herself?

The cyborg reappeared through the doorway of the server room with Cerise's network bridge in her hand. "I located this. Without further analysis, I can't be precisely sure what she was using it for. She covered her tracks pretty well. Any traces of network tampering seem to have been erased."

Then, like a series of stars colliding into one another, it all became suddenly clear to Alouette.

Cerise hadn't saved herself because she'd chosen to save them. Instead of running, she'd tried to erase the evidence. Even though she knew that if she got caught, it would end like this. Her brain would be cut open. Cybernetics would be implanted behind her skull. Fiberoptics would be laced through her neurons. A web of flashing circuitry would be artfully embedded into her skin. And one of her twinkling dark eyes would glow an eerie, probing orange.

And still, she chose to save them.

"Take her to the surgical ward and lock her in a room." Directeur Chevalier motioned toward the two guards, who grabbed Cerise by either arm and began to lead her down the hallway. Cerise struggled in their clutches, bucking and twisting, but they were too strong.

"Papa!" she shouted down the hallway. "Please, just listen to me! I swear I can explain everything!"

Alouette kneaded her hands together in quiet desperation. Could she really just stand there and let them take her? Could she really keep her promise to Cerise?

"Directeur, I might have found something."

Alouette's head snapped up to see the cyborg handing the network bridge over to Cerise's father. The directeur scrutinized something on the screen, his expression morphing from confusion to comprehension to alarm. "Marcellus Bonnefaçon?"

The cyborg nodded. "It appears his biometrics were scanned by a guard at the security checkpoint of the Ascension banquet. Cerise passed the signal through this bridge and sent back a fake profile in response. But in her haste to cover her tracks, she evidently forgot to erase the log, and when I ran the biometric markers through the Communiqué, I got this."

The directeur hastily shoved the device back at the cyborg and pulled out his TéléCom. "Urgent AirLink request for General Bonnefaçon." There was a heart-stopping pause, during which Alouette was certain she was going to faint, before the directeur spoke again. "General. I'm afraid I have bad news. Your grandson is at the Ascension banquet."

- CHAPTER 67 -
ALOUETTE

ALOUETTE'S LUNGS BURNED FROM RUNNING, AND her heart was thudding like a drum in her chest. The twin towers of the Ministère were now just an eerie glow in the night sky behind her.

"Marcellus!" she shouted hoarsely into her audio patch for what felt like the hundredth time. "Marcellus, are you there?" Still no response. Cerise had evidently cut the connection when she'd seen her father coming down the hallway. But it didn't stop Alouette from trying to make contact. Again and again and again.

She *had* to warn Marcellus. The general knew he was there. Their entire plan—not to mention the lives of everyone at that banquet—was in jeopardy.

She could see the darkened outline of the Grand Palais in the distance. As she ran breathlessly toward it, she tried to recall the details Marcellus had given earlier about the loopholes in the security shields. There were four, she remembered. One that was closest to the gardens. That was her best option.

As soon as she reached the Palais fence, she pulled out her borrowed TéléCom and used the light to illuminate the little fleur-de-lis ornaments on the top of each post. She walked briskly along the perimeter until she located the one that was bent at an angle, and then she scrabbled over the fence.

She hit the ground hard but was up in an instant before she was running again. The north end of the Palais was in sight. It was vast and incredibly well lit. Just ahead, she could make out a small staircase leading up to the side of the Grand Terrace. From there, she'd be able to see out over the entire banquet. She bounded toward it, her muscles crying out, her breathing ragged.

Almost there.

She pounded up the steps and charged onto the terrace just as a pair of Palais doors swung open. Alouette skidded to a halt and searched for a place to hide, but there was nothing. And there was no time.

"This fête better not last all night," said a deep, booming voice. "I have better things to do, you know?"

"It should only take a few minutes, Monsieur," said another voice.

When Alouette's gaze fell upon the two men exiting through the Palais door, her whole body went completely and utterly numb. The first man—an advisor in a dark green robe—she didn't recognize. But the other? Just the sight of him made her gut twist and her knees go weak. His thick and immaculately coiffed auburn hair glinted in the terrace lights. Of course she recognized him. There wasn't a soul on Laterre who wouldn't.

It was Patriarche Lyon Paresse, the leader of Laterre.

And he was staring right at her.

She wanted to run. She wanted to flee. But for some reason, she couldn't move. There was something about the way he was looking at her—slack-jawed and spellbound, like he'd just come face-to-face with a ghost—that made Alouette feel like her feet were bolted to the ground.

And then he spoke, uttering the only two syllables in the universe that could cause Alouette's heart to stop beating and the world to come crashing to a halt.

"Lisole?"

It was barely a whisper from the Patriarche's lips. A murmur of shock and surprise and . . .

Recognition, Alouette suddenly realized.

Except it wasn't *her* he recognized. He was staring at Alouette with the exact same bewilderment and disbelief as Madame Blanchard had done back in Montfer. His watery gray eyes were wide and unblinking, entranced by the sight of her.

No.

By the sight of who he *thought* she was.

"Monsieur Patriarche," the advisor said, casting an uneasy glance at Alouette and her cleaner's uniform. "I think we should proceed to the banquet. The Matrone is waiting for you." He tried to usher the Patriarche away, across the terrace, but Lyon resisted, pushing his way back to Alouette.

"Lisole!" he said again. This time, it wasn't a question. It was an answer. A sigh of relief. "I thought you were . . . They told me you were . . ." His voice trailed off. And that's when Alouette saw something on his face that confounded her to the very core of her being.

Affection.

Confused and overwhelmed, Alouette started to back away, but something on the advisor's green robe caught her attention, freezing her in place again. Her gaze fell to his front pocket, where an intricate emblem was stitched into the fabric.

And suddenly, every sound for thousands of kilomètres seemed to fade from existence, and all she could hear was an intense drone in her ears.

She felt herself leaning closer, like she was being pulled into the gravity of that small image.

Two lions standing on their hind legs, mouths open mid-roar, paws in the air.

They were the exact same lions as the ones that had been engraved into the lid of her mother's titan box. The box had been destroyed on the voyageur, but Alouette had stared at its surface for so many hours, she'd studied its intricate carvings and designs for so long, she could have reconstructed it from memory.

And yet, for some reason, she hadn't pieced it together.

This was the Paresse family crest.

She'd seen drawings of the majestic insignia countless times in the Chronicles. But she hadn't associated it with the engraving on her mother's box until now. Maybe it was because the two things seemed so unrelated. Her mother and the Paresse family were as far apart as Usonia and Sol 1.

What had her mother been doing with a titan box adorned with the Paresse family crest?

"Monsieur Patriarche," came another voice. This one was low and clipped, and even though Alouette had never heard it before, it chilled her to the bone. "Is something wrong? We are waiting for you on the other side of the terrace. We must proceed to the banquet now."

At first, all Alouette saw was the white jacket coming toward her, with its row of dazzling titan buttons. Then she saw the tall frame, the wide shoulders, the thick hair, the hazel eyes—almost identical to Marcellus's—and every molecule inside of her clattered and collided like an exploding sol.

"But look, General!" the Patriarche blustered, his words garbled and his eyes glassy with confusion. Like someone just waking from a dream. "It's her! It's Lisole. H-h-how is this possible? You told me she was dead."

The general's cruel, piercing gaze settled on Alouette, and something in the clench of his jaw and the slight widening of his eyes told her he knew *exactly* who she was. "I agree, the resemblance is uncanny," he said evenly. "Why don't you join your wife and proceed to the banquet, and I will sort this out."

Run.

The word flittered through Alouette's mind, and she knew instantly that it was her only option. But evidently, so did the general, because before she could take a single step, his large hand wrapped around her arm, and he began to drag her back toward the side staircase.

She struggled against his grasp, trying to wrench herself free, but he was too strong. He gave her a rough yank and whispered angrily into her

BETWEEN BURNING WORLDS   603

ear, "I know why you're here. I know what you're after. But I have not worked this hard and for this long to have everything stolen from me by the daughter of a worthless blood whore."

He snapped his fingers at two officers in white uniforms who were patrolling nearby and beckoned them over. Alouette swallowed hard, feeling like her heart might beat right out of her chest.

"Officers," he said in an impervious tone. "This servant was caught trying to steal from the Patriarche. Take her into custody and I will handle the situation after the banquet is over. Do *not* let her get away."

CHAPTER 68

MARCELLUS

"PLEASE WELCOME YOUR ILLUSTRIOUS HOSTS FOR this evening, Patriarche Lyon Paresse and his beautiful wife, Matrone Veronik Paresse!"

The entrance was a grand one. The Patriarche was dressed in a forest-green jacket with a plush silk cravat tied around his neck. The Matrone was wearing a billowing dress that was almost as wide as she was tall, and her dark curls were wound up into a towering structure that was held together by a dazzling tiara encrusted with a rainbow of multicolored gems. They were flanked by advisors in deep green robes and handmaids who swarmed like fluttering butterflies in lacy, brightly colored gowns. As the entourage slowly descended the curving stone steps from the Palais's vast terrace, a chorus of trumpets and cheers erupted from the Imperial Lawn below.

Marcellus watched the procession from his hiding spot in the hedges, his heart whirring into a tempest. He had attended Ascension banquets all his life, but he'd never seen anything quite like this. The sheer number of people packed into this garden was staggering. Normally, when one winner was chosen, the guest list consisted of the lucky

Ascendant, their immediate family, and a host of important Second Estate members. But predictably, with *fifty* winners, the Third Estate far outnumbered the Second Estate. Which was exactly how his grandfather had intended it.

"Don't they look fantastique, everyone?" Georges Bissette exclaimed from the stage in the center of the lawn. But no one was looking at the well-coiffed man in the bright blue tailcoat anymore. All the Third Estate eyes were trained on the Patriarche. On the great leader of Laterre. The very person they had unknowingly been brought here to kill.

Marcellus darted his gaze to the champagne fountain, where a flock of waiters dressed in velvet, high-collared jackets was already beginning to arrange crystal flutes to fill for the toast. His eyes tracked outward until he spotted a flash of color. A green gem glittering amongst a sea of shimmering silks. Chatine was almost to the fountain, her long dress billowing behind her like smoke.

"Absolutely radiant!" said Georges Bissett as the trumpets gave way to a rousing anthem played by a string quartet and the Patriarche and Matrone continued their long procession down the stairs. Marcellus couldn't help but remark that the Patriarche looked somewhat unsettled, as though something was troubling him.

Across the Imperial Lawn, the crowd's cheers had lulled to a swarm of awed whispers.

"They look so different in person."

"She's much thinner than I imagined."

"Well, she did just lose her precious bébé. I'm sure she hasn't eaten in weeks."

Marcellus kept his gaze locked on Chatine, still weaving through the crowd. She was now only a few mètres from the fountain. *Nearly there,* he told himself, trying to calm his frazzled nerves.

So far, everything had gone according to plan. Cerise and Alouette had broken into the Ministère server room. Chatine and Marcellus had infiltrated the banquet. Marcellus was in prime position with a perfect view of the terrace steps, which his grandfather would be descending at any moment. Now all they had to do was get that inhibitor into the champagne before the official toast.

"The Matrone's ceremonial tiara is made of one hundred percent titan and is encrusted with over two thousand First World jewels," Georges Bissett explained, causing the crowd to gasp and sigh.

The Patriarche and Matrone had almost reached the bottom of the steps. Marcellus scanned their parade of advisors and escorts. There was still no sign of his grandfather.

He turned back to Chatine and the fountain, but something flickered in the periphery of his vision, snagging his attention. It was a figure dressed in a dark uniform prowling through the crowd, only a few mètres behind Chatine. As Marcellus focused on the complex network of circuitry implanted in the man's face, dread immediately began to ripple through him.

Inspecteur Chacal.

What was he doing here? Had he spotted Chatine? Had he recognized her?

"And tonight, the Patriarche is wearing a stunning satin cravat imported straight from Samsara," Georges announced as the Patriarche and Matrone reached the base of the stone steps and waved cordially out into the crowd.

"Chatine," Marcellus whispered urgently into his audio patch. "We might be in trouble. Chacal is right behind you."

He watched Chatine continue to move toward the fountain. She didn't even so much as flinch at his words.

"Chatine?" he said again. "Can you hear me?"

Nothing.

"Cerise? Alouette? Is anyone there?"

The silence brought Marcellus's galloping heart to a lurching stop. He hastily pulled out his TéléCom and checked the connection. It was dead.

Fear prickled his skin and blurred the corners of his vision. Why had the AirLink been severed? But he didn't have time to dwell on the answer. If Chatine couldn't get the inhibitor into the champagne and neutralize the weapon, the rest of the plan would fail.

Marcellus edged out from his hiding place and darted toward the fountain, concealing himself behind one of the many elaborate ice sculptures punctuating the garden. Chatine was steps away from the champagne now. But Chacal was strangely nowhere to be found. Marcellus scanned the lawn, craning his neck to see over the crowd, but it was as if the inspecteur had suddenly vanished.

A loud *crash* rang out from the direction of the fountain. Marcellus snapped his gaze back, certain he would see Chacal tackling Chatine. But instead, he saw that Chatine had fallen into one of the waiters, knocking over a tray of empty champagne flutes.

"Oh! Excusez-moi, monsieur. I must have tripped on this beautiful dress," she said, but there was something off about her voice. Something wasn't right.

"I'm so sorry," Chatine went on. Her words were almost garbled, like she was struggling to get them out of her mouth. She swayed again on her feet, looking like she might pass out.

"Are you okay, mademoiselle?" the waiter asked, reaching out to steady her.

"I . . . ," she said woozily, her eyes rolling back into her head. "I . . . think I had too much . . . wine."

Then she dropped. The waiter dove to catch her and she slumped forward into his arms. Marcellus darted out from the cover of the statue, but stopped a split second later when he noticed a flicker of movement behind the waiter's back. Chatine's left hand was tilting toward the bubbling spring of champagne. It happened so fast, if Marcellus hadn't known what he was looking for, he would have surely missed it.

"Are you all right?" the waiter asked, helping Chatine back onto her feet.

She let out a dramatic sigh. "Yes, quite all right. Merci." And as she staggered away from the fountain, she surreptitiously slipped the now-empty vial back down the front of her dress.

It was done. Dr. Collins's serum was now spreading and multiplying in the gurgling fountain, helped along by the churn and whir of the pumps.

Tucking himself back into the protection of the hedges, Marcellus exhaled in a rush of relief as he watched the waiters begin to fill champagne flutes from the fountain and arrange them on trays.

"And it appears our final guest of honor has arrived!" Georges Bissette's voice slipped back into the air. "Here comes the distinguished and celebrated head of our glorious Ministère. The man who keeps us all safe. Who keeps the planet safe. General Bonnefaçon!"

The guests cheered and clapped wildly. Marcellus's head snapped up, and suddenly, there he was. The general stood at the top of the stone steps, looking immaculate and impossibly composed. His cool steady gaze surveilled the oversized crowd with what looked like approval.

Marcellus's stomach clenched at the sight of him. It was the first time he'd seen his grandfather since that fateful night he'd sped off from the Palais on his moto, convinced he'd never return.

And yet here he was.

And there the general was.

Two opponents finally coming face-to-face on this lush, exquisite battlefield.

The general descended the stone staircase and took his place next to the Patriarche. Instantly, that familiar rage began to pulse inside of Marcellus. He gripped his fingers around the cool handle of the rayonette tucked into his waistband, his fingers itching, his heart racing. He longed to charge out from his hiding place, push his way through the crowd, take aim, and pull the trigger right this very second. But, as he glanced around again at the hundreds of Third Estaters packed into this garden, he knew that decision would be rash, impulsive, and more importantly, disastrous if he missed.

This whole situation—this banquet, these guests—was like an explosif on the verge of going off. One wrong move and the general could pull out his TéléCom and detonate. Marcellus had to wait for the TéléReversion program to be deactivatied. Wait for the inhibitor to be consumed and render the general helpless and vulnerable.

Marcellus could not play the game the way he'd been playing it for his entire life. As much as it tormented him and made his whole body break out into a cold sweat, he had to be patient. He had to fight the urge to take his first shot. So that he could take his *best* shot.

"And now for the moment I'm sure you've all been waiting for," Georges Bissette crooned loudly from the stage. "The champagne toast!"

Waiters moved through the crowd with trays, handing out glasses filled to the top with sparkling, golden champagne. Marcellus's grip around his rayonette tightened. His pulse vibrated in his ear drums. He kept his eyes locked on the general.

"To lead us in a congratulatory toast and officially welcome you to your new life in Ledôme, please welcome to the stage, the honorable, the distinguished, the unrivaled Patriarche Lyon Paresse!"

Marcellus startled and his hand momentarily slipped from his rayonette. *What?*

The Patriarche was going to give the toast? He never spoke at Ascension banquets. It was always the master of cérémonies who did all the talking. The Patriarche and Matrone just descended the steps, waved at the crowd, took a ceremonial sip of champagne, and left. That had always been the way of things.

The cheers in the Grand Palais gardens built to a frenzy as a troop of officers in pristine white uniforms parted the crowd, clearing a walkway from the stone steps to the stage. The Patriarche smiled and waved as he made his way across the lawn.

Marcellus didn't like this. It felt slippery and suspicious. Like a trap.

No, like another one of his grandfather's strategic plays.

His gaze darted back to the general, who was watching the proceedings with cool, relaxed interest, his hands clasped casually behind his back. Marcellus tracked the Patriarche's path to the stage, perfectly positioned right in the center of the crowd. The Patriarche ascended the steps and turned in a slow circle, waving at the hundreds of people packed into this garden.

He was completely surrounded.

Nowhere to run.

A trapped Monarch.

"Welcome! Welcome!" the Patriarche boomed out, his voice as artificial and bright as the stars twinkling above their heads. "Laterre and its glorious Regime is the envy of the System Divine. Through honest work for an honest chance, the good people of our planet can rise up and Ascend to a better life. A life led in this beautiful Ledôme."

Cheers and shouts went off like fireworks around him. Marcellus startled at the sound, his nerves now frayed beyond recognition. He darted another glance at his grandfather, who was reaching into his pocket to withdraw his TéléCom.

"Today, *you* are those people," the Patriarche continued, his face beaming. "You have worked hard, with honesty and integrity. You have won the Ascension, and now you will live out the rest of your days under this beautiful and magical TéléSky!"

Someone handed the Patriarche a flute of champagne, and he raised it high in the air, as though he were toasting the stars. "So, now please raise your glass!"

In front of Marcellus, hundreds of hands raised into the air. Hundreds of glasses filled with sparkling golden liquid launched toward the sky. Heart racing, Marcellus reached for his rayonette again, his fingers gripping the handle.

Come on, he silently urged the crowd. *Drink. Just drink it!*

"Tonight, we drink to your health, your happiness, and your prosperity. Tonight, we drink to your *Ascension!*" The Patriarche slowly lowered his glass to his lips. The crowd did the same. "Congratul—"

"Arrête!"

The Patriarche jolted to a halt, as someone suddenly charged up the steps of the stage. But it was not a banquet guest, as Marcellus feared. It was Pascal Chaumont, the Patriarche's advisor. His dark green robes billowed behind him as he hurried toward Lyon Paresse and knocked the champagne flute from his hands. The glass crashed to the floor of the stage and shattered on impact. "Don't drink!" he shouted into the crowd. "Don't drink it!"

Murmurs of confusion percolated across the Imperial Lawn. Marcellus's eyes darted every which way until he found Chatine again. She was staring back at him with an expression that mirrored his own: part puzzlement and part dread.

Chaumont struggled to catch his breath. "I've just been informed that we have reason to believe the champagne tonight has been poisoned."

All the color seemed to drain from the Patriarche's face in an instant. Someone screamed. And Marcellus felt his limbs go numb as, all around him, he heard a cacophony of glass shattering.

When he peered back toward the stone steps on the far side of the lawn, General Bonnefaçon's eyes were already staring back at him. Watching. Waiting. As though he'd known exactly where to look this whole time.

As their gazes locked, the general's eyebrow cocked ever so slightly, and his lips curled into a ghost of a smile. As if to say, *Nice try, Marcellus.*

Marcellus faded farther back into the hedges, his throat burning with the bitter taste of defeat.

How did the general know? Had he witnessed Chatine pouring the inhibitor into the champagne? Or had someone *else* seen it? Someone who had been flitting around the crowd like a phantom?

And just as the memory of his face slipped into Marcellus's mind, he felt the cold barrel of a rayonette press against his left temple and an even colder voice say, "Welcome back, Officer Bonnefaçon."

- CHAPTER 69 -
MARCELLUS

OUT OF THE CORNER OF HIS EYE, MARCELLUS SAW THE
flicker of circuitry. The glimmer of a glowing orange eye. And the
unsettling sneer of an inspecteur who had waited a long time for this
moment to come.

"If it were up to me, I'd pull the trigger right now," Chacal said in a low
snarl, pressing the rayonette harder against the side of Marcellus's head.
"You have made me look like a fool one too many times, Bonnefaçon,
and I would like nothing more than to see a smoking black hole in your
déchet-loving head."

Marcellus sucked in a breath, his gaze darting around for Chatine.
But his view was obscured by the hedges. He could no longer find her in
the crowd.

"But unfortunately," Chacal went on, "the general requests the plea-
sure of putting a pulse through your skull *himself.*"

"Chacal," Marcellus began desperately, "I don't think you understand. You don't know what he has planned. You have to listen to me. My
grandfather—"

"Shut up!" Chacal hissed in his ear. "You don't outrank me anymore.

You have *no* rank anymore. You are nothing but a useless traitor. Just like your father. And I am about to become a hero, delivering the general's most wanted fugitive right into his hands."

Marcellus saw it only moments before it happened. Chatine moved in a blur, her hands fumbling to attach some kind of small device to a nearby garden light. *What is she doing?*

Then, a strange zapping sound exploded in Marcellus's ears. Like an electrical current shorting out. The entire banquet was suddenly swallowed in darkness as every light in the garden winked out in perfect unison.

The diversion worked. Marcellus felt the barrel fall away from his temple in a moment of surprise. He didn't hesitate. He jabbed his hand into the air, knocking the rayonette out of Chacal's hand.

"Sols!" Chacal swore, and Marcellus could hear the inspecteur rooting around on the ground, searching through the darkness for his fallen weapon.

Marcellus charged out of the hedges, moving in the direction of the stone steps, where he'd last seen his grandfather. He withdrew his own rayonette from the waistband of his pants and blinked rapidly, trying to adjust his vision, but still, he saw nothing. Nothing but a pristine, unblemished, and uninterrupted blanket of black that the stars in the TéléSky were too weak to penetrate.

Screams were erupting all around Marcellus. He was shoved violently from every direction as the crowd grew more restless and panicked in the darkness. He fought to keep his balance, but eventually the tide became too strong, and he felt himself getting swept up in its current.

Elbows jabbed at him and feet trampled on his toes. There was a splash behind him as someone fell into one of the fountains and began to flounder and cry out. Marcellus jostled through the commotion, trying to get closer to the steps.

Finally, he stopped and pulled his TéléCom out of his pocket, using the faint glow from the screen to light his way. He directed the light up ahead, toward the curving stone staircase, but he didn't see the general.

All around Marcellus, more lights came on as Skins were illuminated and TéléComs were unfolded.

Urgently, he swept his gaze around the garden, through the panicked turmoil. He could see officers and advisors stumbling and rushing toward the stage in the center of the Imperial Lawn, attempting to form a tight, protective circle around the Patriarche. Marcellus continued scanning the garden in a slow circle, casting the light from his device in front of him, until he was staring back at the stone steps.

But his grandfather was still nowhere to be found.

"Fric!" Marcellus swore aloud. He started to push his way to the stairs. He would search this whole Sol-damn Palais if he had to, but he would *find* General Bonnefaçon.

Another body slammed into him, knocking his TéléCom to the ground. Marcellus was plunged back into darkness. He dropped to his knees and raked his fingertips across the grass, which was wet and sticky from the spilt champagne. Shards of broken glass bit and snagged at his skin, but finally he grabbed hold of the Télécom, the device slick in his bloodied fingers.

He sprang to his feet and staggered the rest of the way toward the stairs, dodging banquet guests and panicked advisors and assistants trying to restore some semblance of order.

He was halfway up the steps when he heard the silence descend behind him. Eerie and sudden like the flick of a switch. It was as though Chatine had not only zapped the power from the garden lights, but from the crowd as well.

Marcellus's feet dragged to a halt, and when he turned around, every droplet of blood in his body pooled, in one great showering gush, down to his toes.

In the darkness, it almost looked like fireflies. Innocent sparks of light twinkling amongst the hedges and the flowerbeds. Two hundred Skins flickering at once, flashing a deep, crimson shade of red.

CHAPTER 70

ALOUETTE

ALOUETTE SQUINTED THROUGH THE DARKNESS AT the two officers lying by her feet. Unconscious but not dead. She peered at her hands, raw and thrumming from the energy still pulsing through them.

They hadn't even had a chance to fight back. As soon as the general had disappeared down the terrace steps, the familiar sensation had bloomed inside of her like the brilliant rays of a Sol. Warm and strong and deadly. Her muscles had tightened and coiled. Her body had tingled with anticipation. And her pulse had slowed to a steady, even hum.

Within minutes, they were both on the ground.

Every time Alouette performed Tranquil Forme as a weapon, she felt as though she were separate from her body. Detached from her own mind and thoughts and emotions. Yet, at the same time, she felt as if her body and her mind were strangely part of everything too. The skies above, the ground beneath her, and even the guards she was fighting. They all seemed connected. But now, as she finally returned to herself and settled once more into her skin, her thoughts came rushing back as well. Everything that had happened in the past few minutes slammed into her like a tidal wave.

Lisole.

The Patriarche had called her by her mother's name. He'd thought that *she* was Lisole. He had *known* her mother.

Her heart started to pound again.

Something was happening to her. Something she couldn't quite explain. She suddenly felt like she was back on that voyageur, space bending impossibly around her, warping her thoughts, detaching her mind. She sank to the ground, leaning back against the pedestal of a nearby statue.

Black tendrils clawed at the corners of her vision. Her senses all tangled together until she could taste her fear and see her breath and hear the darkness rushing toward her.

The planet spun. Round and round and round.

Lisole.

Fired from the Palais.

Forced to sell her blood.

A fake funeral.

The Renards.

A giant crushing hole gaped inside Alouette's chest. It was a hole that had been growing for weeks.

Ever since she'd discovered that Hugo Taureau was not her real father.

Ever since she'd aimed that rayonette at Inspecteur Limier's head.

Ever since that message—*When the Lark flies home, the Regime will fall*—had appeared on Marcellus's TéléCom.

Ever since she'd walked into the Assemblée room to find that the sisters had been lying to her for twelve years.

Ever since the Patriarche—the most powerful man on the planet—called her by her *mother's* name.

Wider and wider and wider the hole grew. Until it felt like it would drown her. Consume her. Become her. Until she no longer bore any semblance to the girl she thought she was. Where was that person now? Where was Alouette Taureau? Lost in the abyss? Swallowed by a truth that seemed to keep expanding and stretching and changing?

Every. Minute. Changing.

Who am I?

She'd been chasing the answer to that question for so long, she'd forgotten what it felt like to be content. To be satisfied with ignorance. And now that she was certain she was brushing up against the real answer—the *complete* answer—she wasn't sure she wanted to know anymore.

Because suddenly the truth felt like a blazing hot atmosphere, ready to burn her alive upon entry. Ready to scald away any hopes of ever being satisfied with that blissful ignorance again.

She thought back to that small titan box whose ashes were now drifting and dancing through space. The one thing her mother had protected, guarded, defended. For all those years. Like a baby bird too young to fly.

Like a secret too dangerous to reveal.

Alouette shut her eyes and tried to remember the feel of the intricate design carved into the lid. Two lions facing off, claws outstretched, teeth bared.

The same symbol etched into that man's green robe.

The Paresse family crest.

She squeezed her eyes tighter and forced her mind to go back to that ship. To that couchette. To that moment lost in time when she'd held the titan box in her hands and pried open the lid to find two strands of hair tucked inside. One dark and curly, like her own, the other a glimmering shade of auburn. The same shade she'd seen only moments ago. As the Patriarche had stood in front of her and called her Lisole.

She didn't want to accept it. She didn't know if she could ever survive the aftermath. But she knew now that she didn't have a choice. You can't unstrike a match. Or repack an explosion. You can't unbreak a lock. Or stuff the contents back inside.

And you can't unknow the truth.

Who am I?

I am the daughter of the Patriarche.

Who am I?

I am a Paresse.

Who am I?

I am the Lark who has finally flown home.

For minutes—maybe hours, maybe lightyears—Alouette sat perfectly still. As though this terrace floor that propped her up was made of nothing more stable than withered First World paper, and a single twitch might cause it all to come crashing down. As though every breath she took from here on out held a different meaning. As though the next move she made might decide the fate of a planet.

When the Lark flies home, the Regime will fall.

Sister Denise knew. She knew who Alouette was. That was what she'd been trying to tell her through the message on Marcellus's TéléCom.

"Home" wasn't the Refuge, as Alouette had believed all this time. Home was here. Ledôme. The Grand Palais.

Alouette was a Paresse. The Paresse heir. The *only* heir.

A petrified scream punctuated the darkness of the terrace, and Alouette leapt to her feet. More screams followed, and then Alouette heard the unmistakable sound of bodies colliding. Hundreds of them. She ran toward the stone staircase that led down to the gardens and froze. The Imperial Lawn was a blanket of blackness, pierced only by the flicker of glowing Skins. And in the dim light, Alouette saw her worst nightmare come to life.

Fists punching and hands clawing and mouths open in bellowing roars.

It was like Dr. Cromwell's lab on Albion multiplied by a hundred. No, by *two* hundred. Two hundred guests turned into weapons.

The general had activated the TéléReversion program.

Breath shuddering in her chest, Alouette charged down the first few steps toward the lawn, readying herself to fight again. But a second later, something in the distance caught her eye, pulling her to a halt.

Far off, in the darkness of Ledôme, a lone star twinkled.

Alouette stood paralyzed and speechless, her thoughts blurring in and out of focus. It couldn't be a star. It was too low in the sky. But somehow, it seemed to be calling out to her. Like a beacon. A monument of hope.

Twinkling just for her.

The Paresse Tower.

Suddenly, like a Sol exploding, sending shards of light to the far reaches of the galaxy, a thousand voices from a thousand moments in time rushed into her mind at once.

"... *we need your help, Little Lark* ..."

"*It's called the Forteresse* ..."

"... *you should always build a kill switch into any large-scale system* ..."

"*He wanted this lock to only open for his direct descendants* ..."

"*It makes sense to hide it, right?*"

"*We called it the Sovereign gene.*"

"*You are more useful than you realize, Alouette* ..."

"... *it only activates after a Paresse heir has come of age.*"

Alouette sucked in a breath, steadying herself on the handrail of the staircase as all the voices slowly morphed into one. One voice. One sentence. One destiny.

"*We've just been waiting. . . . Waiting for you to be ready.*"

Those were Principale Francine's words to her that night she left the Refuge. That night she turned her back on the Sisterhood. On the Vangarde. On her planet.

When the Lark flies home, the Regime will fall.

Alouette now understood everything.

"Home" was both the Palais *and* the Refuge.

Denise knew, just as all the sisters knew, that Alouette was important to the fate of Laterre. To the war that was coming. To the revolution. But not *only* as the Paresse heir.

Because the truth was, Alouette was not just Paresse.

She was also a sister.

She was also Vangarde.

She was also the Little Lark.

And she would see the fall of this Regime.

- CHAPTER 71 -
MARCELLUS

MARCELLUS COULD HEAR THE CARNAGE ON THE IMPE-
rial Lawn in front of him. Bodies slamming together. Great guttural
roars scraping the air. And the screams. The heart-wrenching, piercing
screams that he knew would haunt his dreams forever. But it wasn't
until the lights came back on and illuminated the Palais gardens that
he could see the devastation with his very eyes.

And he almost wished the lights would go back out again.

In his few short years of training as an officer and then a commandeur, Marcellus had seen little violence. A few Fret fights over scraps of
food, one or two disputes between workers in the fabriques and exploits,
and of course the recent riots. But those incidents paled in comparison to
the brutality that was playing out in front of him now.

In the blink of an eye, two hundred Third Estaters had been transformed from happy, docile banquet guests into enraged, wild-eyed fighters. They used every weapon they could find—overturned tables, shards
of broken champagne flutes, titan food platters, even their own fists. They
fought and yelled and destroyed, but this was so much more than just a
riot. This felt like a war. A war in the Patriarche's own backyard.

Most of the Third Estaters stormed the stage where the Patriarche still cowered behind a circular wall of officers and advisors who struggled to fight off the attackers. Others, who couldn't reach the stage, turned on one another or on the unsuspecting and unarmed Second Estate guests who were unable to flee.

The officers and guards tried to fight back, firing a barrage of rayonette pulses at anyone they could find, but it seemed they didn't quite know what to do with this turn of events. They weren't used to fighting without the help of the droids. They were overwhelmed and outnumbered.

"No, stop! I beg you! I have children at home! Please!" The cry came from somewhere below him, and Marcellus looked down at the lawn to see a man in a blue tuxedo looming over a defenseless Second Estate woman, a shard of stone from a busted fountain in his hand. Marcellus toggled his rayonette back to paralyze mode and took aim. A pulse rippled through the air, finding its way into the man's leg. He cried out in pain and slumped over the woman, who hastily pushed him away before fleeing from the gardens.

Marcellus desperately scanned the crowd for Chatine, praying she'd had the foresight to run as soon as those Skins had flickered red. He thought of Alouette and Cerise and hoped that they were still in the Ministère, far away from this anarchy.

There was a horrified scream followed by a thump, and Marcellus glanced down to see Georges Bissette, the Ascension banquet host, lying at the foot of the steps, his head cracked open on the stone as a woman in a dark silk gown stood over him with a glint of untrammeled fury in her eyes.

"Oh my Sols!" someone shrieked next to Marcellus. "She just . . . He just . . . What is happening?"

He glanced up to see one of the Matrone's handmaids—a young woman named Margaux—staring wide-eyed at the body. Her eyes rolled back in her head, and then she went down. Marcellus dove to catch her before she hit the ground. "Get the Matrone inside!" he shouted to no one in particular. Most of her handmaids were crying hysterically, but one of them took control of the situation and began to usher the Matrone and the rest of the women up the steps to the Palais terrace. An advisor in a dark green robe appeared beside Marcellus, scooped Margaux into his arms, and followed after the others.

Marcellus continued to fire paralyzeur pulses into the crowd, trying to incapacitate as many Third Estaters as he could.

"Ma chéri!" the Matrone called. She had stopped halfway up the steps and was now staring into the gardens with a look of utter terror on her face.

Marcellus's gaze darted back toward the stage in the center of the lawn, where the Patriarche's guards diligently fought off attacker after attacker, each one charging with more determination, more ferocity, than the last.

"We have to get the Patriarche back inside the Palais!" someone called from the stage. Marcellus squinted into the mayhem to see Chaumont shouting at a female officer who was currently trying to ward off a man wielding half of a broken chair.

She nodded and gestured toward one of her colleagues. "Call in all guards stationed around Ledôme. Tell them to abandon their posts and get to the Palais now. And gather any nearby sergents and officers you can find. We need to clear a path for the Patriarche." She shoved the Third Estater back with the heel of her boot and then fired a paralyzing pulse into each of his legs. The man crumpled with a whimper.

"What in the name of the Sols is going on!" the Patriarche bellowed to Chaumont. "Why are they rioting? They *won*!"

"I don't know, Monsieur," Chaumont replied breathlessly before turning to the female officer. "He can't stay here."

"I know," she replied, glancing out into the fray. Marcellus followed her gaze to see her requested reinforcements were on their way. She shouted out orders to the officers around her, and they began to reposition. Some ventured down the stage steps to clear a path, others stayed huddled around the Patriarche. "We go on my command! Ready . . ."

But just then, another undulating flicker of red permeated the crowd. Marcellus's stomach clenched violently as he gazed out at two hundred Skins flashing the deadly crimson color.

Within an instant, the rioter's anger seemed to escalate. Tables were overturned, people were shoved into hedges and flowerbeds, and a group of twelve men started to storm the Patriarche's stage, fire and fury in their eyes.

He's increasing the voltage.

The horrific sounds around Marcellus continued to intensify as the new, elevated voltage took hold, pushing the Third Estaters into a higher, more deadly gear. For a moment, he stood paralyzed on the steps, just watching it all unfold, unable to move.

But then a small, frantic voice yanked him from his trance.

"Maman? *Maman!*"

Marcellus peered out to see a little girl in a violet billowing dress standing on the edge of the lawn—her dark, coiled hair whipping across her round, tear-stained cheeks—as she looked desperately around for her mother.

Nearby, a man in a shimmering silver suit was shoving through the chaos of bodies, searching for the next place to direct his rage. His shoulders were hunched, his fists clenched. Marcellus watched the man's eyes zero in, horrifically and unequivocally, on the little girl, and his paralysis shattered in an instant.

Bounding down the stone steps two at a time, he launched himself across the grass, snatching up the girl in one hand while the other fired his rayonette. The pulse was sloppy and badly aimed. It grazed the man's elbow, but he didn't stop. In fact, the pain only seemed to fuel his rage. He lunged at Marcellus and the girl. Marcellus aimed his weapon again, but another body slammed into him and knocked it right out of his hand. The man in the silver suit attacked. Marcellus threw a punch into his jaw. It felt like every bone in his fingers crunched on impact, but it wasn't enough. The man only staggered slightly before descending again.

Marcellus hunched his body over the little girl, trying to protect her from the strike that was surely coming but somehow never did. When Marcellus unfurled himself a moment later, he saw a female sergent in a dark uniform landing a graceful, arcing kick to the man's chest that sent him soaring backward and crashing into one of the green and pink frosted gâteaus. He didn't get back up.

Marcellus stared dazedly at the woman who had delivered the blow. She was now inserting herself back into the brawl, fighting off attackers with a relaxed ease that gnawed at the edges of Marcellus's memory. There was something strange, yet familiar about the way she moved. Like she wasn't fighting, but . . . dancing?

"Allie!" A woman in a burgundy gown bustled up to Marcellus, sobbing with relief as she reached for the little girl still in Marcellus's arms, "Oh, Allie. Thank the Sols."

"Get her inside the Palais!" Marcellus yelled over the roar.

The mother nodded, teary eyed, and swooped the little girl from Marcellus's arms before bounding up the steps. Marcellus snatched up his fallen rayonette from the grass and followed after her.

Peering back at the stage, he saw more officers and sergents arriving to protect the Patriarche. They were trying to form a human wall from the stage to the steps, to give the Patriarche a clear passageway to flee. But it seemed that with every new officer that arrived, another was dragged backward into the fray.

Then, a dark-haired man in a torn tuxedo slipped through the barrier of guards and climbed onto the stage. Marcellus saw a flash of metal and was instantly certain this was the end. The man had somehow gotten hold of a rayonette, and he was now moving toward the Patriarche, the weapon outstretched.

A pulse was fired.

"No!" someone shouted. It was Chaumont. He stepped in front of the Patriarche and a second later wilted to the ground, dark smoke drifting up from the wound in his chest. Two of the other officers tackled the assailant, wrestling the weapon from his grasp and using it to put an end to the threat.

A sickening sensation of defeat started to settle over Marcellus. The

Patriarche's chances of getting out of here alive, he now realized, were slim at best. Soon, the general would have exactly what he wanted. He had all but won. He had activated the weapon. He was controlling them all.

Controlling them.

The thought burst into Marcellus's mind, and his gaze shot back toward the gardens. Third Estaters in dresses and tuxedos were still punching and bludgeoning and clobbering anyone they could find. But, of course, none of them were in control of their own fury. All of them were being manipulated.

Which meant the general had to be close. He had to be watching.

Marcellus scanned the Imperial Lawn, searching for the source of this anarchy. At the base of the steps, two Third Estaters pummeled an officer in a white uniform, dragging him to the ground.

And that's when Marcellus lifted his eyes skyward. That's when he realized his grandfather would not be down *here*, putting his own life in danger. He would be somewhere safe. Somewhere high up, where he could manipulate his soldiers. Move his little peasant pieces across the board. Observe his victory unharmed.

Then, almost as if his grandfather had shouted out to him, Marcellus's gaze instinctively tracked up to the second floor of the Grand Palais.

And there he was.

General Bonnefaçon stood on a balcony, half hidden behind the door. Marcellus instantly recognized the location as his own rooms, the very place where he'd been arrested a little more than a week ago. The general's body was rigid, his face stoic, his eyes scanning the massacre with a mild curiosity. And clutched in his hands was his TéléCom.

A calm suddenly spread over Marcellus. Deep and profound. The deafening sounds around him faded away, as though they were nothing more than quiet ripples, traveling outward on a pond. Every distraction in his mind stilled. Every thought solidified. Until he felt more focused, more determined, than he ever had.

"Always so hasty to act, aren't you, Marcellus? Always rushing into things."

Not this time. This time, he was playing to win. And there was only one move left to make.

Spinning around, he climbed the stone steps to the terrace and slipped quietly through the door. Compared to the Imperial Lawn outside, the Palais was quiet. Eerily so. Like it was keeping vigil, holding its breath for the outcome of this night.

Marcellus silently crept up the servants' staircase and down the long corridor of the south wing. The door to his old rooms was left slightly ajar, just as it had been the last time he was here. Before he'd stormed in to discover that General Bonnefaçon was framing Marcellus for his own crime.

Never underestimate the element of surprise. His grandfather had taught him that. His grandfather had taught him everything.

With steady hands, he flicked his thumb over the toggle switch on his rayonette, hoisted it in the air, and stepped into the room.

Check mate.

CHAPTER 72

ALOUETTE

GARGANTUAN AND COMPLETELY DWARFING, THE structure soared above Alouette. The latticed metalwork glinted and glistened under the inky star-filled TéléSky, and its four massive feet hulked around her like the claws of a strange, gleaming giant.

"The Paresse Tower," she murmured under her breath, as she looked up and up and up, tracing its great bowing ascent into the air. Standing here, under this massive, intimidating edifice, Alouette felt so infinitesimal, so insignificant, so small.

Yet, she knew she was not small. And she was certainly not insignificant.

For somewhere up there, so high it almost touched the artificial Sols, was a vault that only she could open. A stronghold of corruption that only she could bring down.

A Forteresse.

The guard station at the base of the tower was empty, the officers clearly having been called to the commotion at the Palais. Alouette stepped into the tiny elevator and crouched down to examine the control panel affixed to the side of the cage. It was a complex mechanism, undoubtedly with layers of security. Yet, a knowing smile crept over her lips as she reached for her toolbelt, now truly understanding why Denise had taught her so much about the inner workings of Ministère technology.

The elevator moved swiftly, like a bird swooping toward the sky. There were no plastique windows or solid walls inside the car, just a frame of intricate curling metalwork that allowed the artificial Ledôme breeze to whip through and tug at Alouette's curls as she ascended. She gazed down at the ground receding below. The whole of Ledôme stretched out beneath her. The boulevards with their twinkling streetlamps spreading out likes rays from a glimmering star. The parks, the gardens, the ponds shimmering in the moonlight. And not far off, the Grand Palais. From way up here, the great building seemed so peaceful and serene. Untouched by the horror and carnage that was unfolding right at this very moment.

The memory of it brought her another wave of resolve.

Finally, the elevator began to slow. Alouette looked up again as a single bird swooped and darted through the light from the dazzling beacon at the top of the tower. For a moment, as the car whined to a stop, all Alouette could see and feel and think about was that bird. What was it doing out here so late at night? Why was it up here so high?

She watched it flutter and dip as it played obliviously in the rippling air currents.

And then, it was gone. Swooping gracefully upward and disappearing into the dark night sky.

The elevator clanked into place, and its metal door rumbled open to reveal a small, octagonal room with gleaming marble floor tiles and decorative mirrors on each wall. Inside, a miniature chandelier hung from the ceiling and a heavy titan-embossed door stood like a sentry before her.

She slowly stepped off the elevator and into the chamber. It was like stepping into a tiny version of the Grand Palais. Or how she'd always imagined the Grand Palais to look.

Her heart gave a heavy thump as the door behind her clanged shut, sealing her inside.

There were no windows in here. Just her own terrified face reflected back at her an infinite number of times.

Uncertainly, she glanced around. Was she supposed to do something? Or say something? Her thoughts were cut off by a sudden whirring noise. Alouette yelped in shock just as the sound crescendoed to a high-pitched squeal. A blinding flash seared at her eyes, and all the mirrors in the room morphed into a series of glowing panels. Some of them glimmered with waterfalls of white dots, while others flashed with rows of pulsating red and blue lines. A dizzying sequence of synchronized lights roved and darted across Alouette's face, then her neck, her chest, her stomach, her hips, her legs, and finally her feet.

Fear instantly began to rise up inside of her. Like an unwanted and engulfing wave. It ramped up her pulse and gnawed at her gut until she felt like she might faint.

And then, a siren blared.

Loud and boisterous and most definitely *wrong*.

Alouette's breath quickened as panic overtook her. On one of the panels, the glowing red and blue lines flickered harder and faster like an ominous warning sign.

Doubt started to creep in. Had this been a mistake? Was this fragile hope she held in her heart nothing more than the whims and fantasies of a motherless girl desperate to give her life and past meaning?

Alouette turned around and lunged toward the elevator door. She ran her fingertips around the surface, searching for a handle or control panel, but there was nothing. She banged mercilessly, but it didn't open.

The sirens continued to blare, and the strips of red and blue lights pulsated harder, peaking at the top of the panel. It was as if the whole room was screaming at her to get out. Telling her how wrong she'd been to come here in the first place.

Alouette's knees buckled, and she sank down to the marble floor. She held her hands over her ears, trying to block out the sirens, but it only made the sound of her own pounding heart louder.

BumBumBumBumBumBum.

It sounded like an engine running on full throttle, moving faster and faster with no hope of slowing down. And all around her, her fear was mirrored in those pulsing blue and red lights.

BumBumBumBumBumBum.

They seemed to move in perfect synchronicity with her heart. Almost as though they were . . .

She gasped and stared in wonderment at the ring of glowing panels.

. . . monitoring her.

Then, in a moment of sudden realization, Brigitte's words came rushing back.

"The person accessing the lock must also be alive and not under duress."

Alouette shut her eyes and tried to reach out to her favorite sister, far across the Secana Sea, imprisoned on that little, unknown island. Alouette had to believe that she was still alive and that if she just listened hard enough, Jacqui would speak to her.

"Fear is like a wave. It comes and then it goes away. Just try to breathe."

Alouette knew the voice was only a memory. An echo of a long-ago time. But, like always, the simple, unadorned words were just what she needed to hear.

She drew in a long, deep breath through her nose and exhaled through her mouth. Then again. And again. As she breathed deeply, she allowed her mind to drift back to the only place she could think to go.

The low-lit hallways and rugged walls. The smell of her father's bread baking in the oven. The sound of Sister Muriel's beads rattling through her fingers as she ate. The warm glow of the lights in Sister Laurel's propagation room. Sister Jacqui's kind smile. Principale Francine's stern, but always steady gaze.

A safe place. A refuge.

Her heart began to slow.

Her fear evaporated.

She opened her eyes and peered upward. The red and blue lines had calmed to a low, even flutter on the panel above. And the small chamber had fallen silent.

Slowly and calmly, Alouette got back to her feet.

"Initial phase complete," a pleasant voice rang out across the room, and Alouette let out a long, shuddering breath. "Commencing phase two."

Suddenly, something protruded from the ceiling and clamped around Alouette's neck and head, holding her in place. She yelped and her heart immediately started to race again.

The red and blue lights on the panel pulsated angrily in response.

Deep breaths, she reminded herself. *Relax.*

The clamp tightened around her head and a high-pitched whine reverberated into her ears.

"You are the bird," she whispered soothingly. "A Little Lark drifting in the warm currents."

And then she felt it. Quick and sharp and painful, puncturing the top of her head. She fought back a shriek as something burrowed into her skull. She longed to scream, to lunge with her hands and stop whatever was happening. But then, the panel in front of her flickered and changed. A strange honeycomb grid of light began to form and spread and connect. Like puzzle pieces coming together from all sides, creating a complex web of intersecting shapes that then proceeded to shrink and morph into something bigger. Something even more beautiful and elegant and twisting, like two entwined, dancing snakes. Alouette recognized the imagery from her studies. The panel was mapping out an intricate network of molecules.

The double helix of her very being.

"A modified gene that can only be found in certain cells of the brain," she whispered aloud, remembering Brigitte's words.

This horrifying device was analyzing her brain from the inside. A moment later, she felt the needle retract. The squealing sound abated— both inside the room and in her mind—and the clamps finally released her.

Alouette reached up and touched the sore spot on the top of her scalp. When she pulled her fingers away, they were dotted with blood.

Her blood.

Paresse blood.

From a direct descendant of the Patriarche.

Alouette knew this to be true even before the voice in the small chamber announced, "Match confirmed," and the heavy PermaSteel door in front of her eased open.

- CHAPTER 73 -
MARCELLUS

GENERAL BONNEFAÇON TURNED AROUND.

Marcellus took a step closer.

General Bonnefaçon's gaze flicked to the weapon clutched in Marcellus's hand.

Marcellus aimed.

General Bonnefaçon laughed.

It was a cruel, mirthless laugh that sent shivers down Marcellus's spine and caused his finger to hesitate, ever so slightly, against the trigger.

"Put down the TéléCom," Marcellus commanded, surprised to hear the steadiness in his voice. The noticeable lack of a tremor. "It's over, Grand-père."

The general peered back at the carnage on the Imperial Lawn below. "It's not over, Marcellus. It's not even close to being over."

"Put it down now."

The general's grip around the device tightened.

"Put it down, or I'll shoot."

This made the general laugh again. "No, you won't. You don't have what it takes to shoot me. You never did. You were never a fighter,

Marcellus. You were never the great strategist I tried so desperately to raise you to be."

"I'm here, aren't I?" Marcellus countered.

That seemed to amuse the general. He tilted his head, considering. "That is true. But unfortunately, you've already lost."

Marcellus felt his temper flare at the words. He gritted his teeth. "No, I haven't. *You* have."

His grandfather clucked his tongue. "Don't you see, Marcellus? You are all alone. There's no one to help you now. You have no allies left. Your friends are gone. Your little hacker is back in the directeur's custody. Your beloved Fret rat is somewhere down there probably getting torn limb from limb. And I already caught your blood whore."

Marcellus flinched at the words. Blood whore? Was he talking about Alouette? Had she and Cerise really both been caught?

"She thought she was so clever," the general spat, his knuckles turning white around the edges of the TéléCom. "Little Madeline Villette. She thought she could swoop in here and take everything I've worked so hard to achieve."

Marcellus's brow furrowed. What was he talking about? Was he trying to distract Marcellus? Confuse him into lowering his weapon? It wouldn't work. Marcellus held his rayonette strong and steady, the barrel pointed directly at his grandfather's chest.

"But the blood whore gave herself away when she walked into that bordel last week," the general went on. "I never believed for a second that she was really dead. Did her mother actually think that I would buy her desperate, pathetic story and give up? Just like that? I have spent the past sixteen years setting traps for that girl. Monitoring blood at the bordels, the med centers, the Policier Precincts. I have searched to the ends of this system for her. But up until a week ago, it was as though the wretched girl had simply disappeared. I knew she was still out there, though. And I knew that one day she would make a mistake. She would reveal herself. As usual, I was right."

Marcellus still had no idea what his grandfather was talking about.

He'd been trying to track down Alouette for sixteen years? Why? Marcellus told himself to remain calm. Stay focused. His grandfather was just toying with him, attempting to break his concentration. But he would not break. He would pull this trigger, and he would put an end to it all.

Do it.

Do it now!

From the balcony, Marcellus could still hear the mayhem on the Imperial Lawn below. Bodies being torn apart. People screaming. Officers shouting commands to try to restore order. And yet, somehow, his finger was frozen. Paralyzed.

Why couldn't he do it?

"I told you," General Bonnefaçon sneered, mocking Marcellus's hesitation. "Your heart is too soft. It's always been a flaw of yours that I despised. Don't think I haven't noticed that you've never brought down a single bird on all those hunting trips. Not because you can't shoot. But because you can't kill. It's not in your nature, Marcellus." He let out a low chuckle. "It's a shame really. You got your father's cowardice and your mother's tender heart. A terrible combination."

Every molecule inside of Marcellus caught fire at once. "My father was a hero!" he roared. "He had the courage to stand up to you and this entire Regime. He joined the Vangarde because he wanted to make the planet a better place. And so did I." A heavy lump formed in his throat, softening his voice. "I still do. Which is why you won't get away with this. I know everything. I know you framed my father for the copper exploit. I know you killed the Premier Enfant. I know you're trying to kill the Patriarche so you can take control of the planet. And I won't let you get away with it."

Suddenly, there was a blur of movement as the general launched himself toward Marcellus. Marcellus pulled the trigger, but it was too late. He didn't have the aim. He didn't have the steadiness. His grandfather barreled into him like a voyageur breaking atmosphere. He heard something crack that he was pretty sure was a rib. The rayonette slipped from his grasp. He fell to the ground, the impact knocking the breath and the fight right out of him.

No! he thought desperately. He would not let this happen again. He would not lie down on another cold marble floor and let himself be beaten. He was not that boy anymore.

He was the son of Julien Bonnefaçon.

He was raised by Mabelle Dubois.

He had the blood of rebels in his veins and the words of revolution-aries in his head.

The kick came, swift and powerful and merciless. Marcellus rolled, dodging his grandfather's boot just before it made contact with his side. He scrabbled up to his knees and reached for the rayonette, but another kick landed on his hand and he cried out in pain. The general bent down to grab the weapon. Marcellus let out a roar and dove toward him, clobbering him with his entire aching, sore body. The rayonette skittered across the room, disappearing under a chaise on the balcony.

The two men clashed like First World warriors, throwing punches wherever they would land, grabbing clothes and limbs and flesh, fighting for position. Out of the corner of his eye, Marcellus saw a glint of something shiny on the floor. A screen. It was his grandfather's TéléCom, obviously having been dropped in the scuffle. And the TéléReversion program was still running. Still controlling all those people outside. Compelling them to fight. To kill.

Something exploded in Marcellus's chest. A mixture of hope and desperation and fire. He jumped to his feet and darted forward, his fingers grasping desperately for the device, but he was halted by a splinter of pain that suddenly shot down his spine as his grandfather's fist slammed into his back. The TéléCom slipped from his hand. The room spun. Marcellus swayed dizzily and felt himself starting to go down again. Another fist came flying at his face. Marcellus staggered backward from the blow, blood spurting from his nose.

When his vision finally cleared, his stomach clenched at the sight of the general reaching toward the holster on his belt, pulling out his own rayonette, and taking aim at Marcellus's head.

"Fortunately for me, you and I don't have the same problem. I *can* pull the trigger."

The general's finger squeezed. Marcellus shut his eyes. He didn't want the last thing he ever saw in this life to be his grandfather. Instead, he thought of his father. He thought of Alouette. And Cerise. And Gabriel. And of course, Chatine.

He hoped they were safe.

Even though he knew they were not.

No one was safe anymore.

And he *was* all alone.

A hush fell over the room. Over the entire Palais. Marcellus was certain the silence was proof that it had already happened. That he was already dead. But a moment later, his eyelids fluttered open and he saw that the general was no longer standing in front of him with his rayonette raised. He was standing on the balcony, staring out at the Imperial Lawn. In his hands, he held his TéléCom again, and he was jabbing mercilessly at the screen.

And that's when Marcellus realized what the silence really was.

The fighting had stopped.

The Imperial Lawn had fallen deathly quiet. Like someone had pushed pause on a broadcast.

Marcellus rushed out to the balcony to see the miracle for himself, and just as he suspected, the banquet guests were all just standing there, motionless in their ripped and bloodied dresses and tuxedos. They were wearied soldiers who had just woken from a deadly trance and were now staring in bewilderment at the aftermath of a battle they never chose to fight.

The silence was broken by a commotion and people yelling. Marcellus's gaze snapped toward the stage in the center of the lawn to see a flutter of activity and the flash of the Patriarche's recognizable auburn hair as his guards ushered him across the grass, up the stone steps, and into the safety of the Palais.

"Sols!" the general swore, prodding relentlessly at his TéléCom. On the screen, Marcellus could see the TéléReversion program was still running. But no one was fighting.

What happened?

He stared out at the carnage on the Imperial Lawn. Bodies were strewn everywhere. Some still stirring. Some not moving at all. So much blood. So much death. And for what? The general had failed. The Patriarche still lived.

One man in a ripped blue tuxedo was standing dazedly over a fallen officer. But he wasn't looking down at his victim. He was looking at his Skin, which Marcellus suddenly noticed was completely black.

Marcellus cast his eyes farther across the lawn and saw more Third Estaters doing the same. Peering down at a darkened void implanted in their arms. One woman tapped hastily on the screen, another tried to speak into her Skin, but nothing happened.

It was as though they were no longer Skins at all.

They were just empty shackles, connected to nothing.

With a roar of frustration, the general's head snapped up from his TéléCom and focused on something in the distance. Something far away from the Palais gardens. Confused, Marcellus tried to follow his gaze, but before he could make sense of what he was looking at, his grandfather spun around and stalked toward the door to the hallway. It was as though Marcellus was suddenly invisible. Their previous altercation forgotten. The general was on a new mission now. One that apparently only *he* understood.

But Marcellus had not forgotten.

Ducking down, he reached under the chaise for his fallen rayonette and hoisted it into the air, taking aim at his grandfather once more.

"Arrête," he said in a low, ominous tone.

The general turned around and, upon seeing the weapon back in Marcellus's hand, let out a deep groan, as though Marcellus had turned from a minor threat to a major inconvenience.

"Haven't we been through this already?" his grandfather snapped.

"I can't let you walk out that door, General."

"And, as we've established, you can't kill me. So, it appears we are at an impasse."

"I don't have to kill you to stop you."

His grandfather snorted out a laugh, like this was the most ridiculous, childish thing Marcellus had ever said in his life.

And maybe it was. Maybe Marcellus was still a child. A child with a tender heart he'd inherited from his mother. A child who had never even been able to shoot down a bird. Maybe he would always be that child. And maybe that was exactly what the planet needed right now.

More tender hearts and less death.

More wisdom and less violence.

More people like his father and less people like his grandfather.

It was no longer just the blood of a three-year-old child and her innocent governess on the general's hands. It was now the blood of all those people down there.

"I came here tonight to end you," Marcellus went on, gaining certainty and clarity with every word. "I was convinced that was what my father would have wanted. What he would have done himself. But I was wrong. Julien Bonnefaçon joined the Vangarde to *stop* the violence. He never would have wanted this. He would have found another way. He would have made sure that you answered for your crimes. Every single one of them. Just as I will."

For a flicker of an instant, Marcellus swore he saw something unfamiliar in his grandfather's expression. Something akin to fear. Not the kind that comes when you face your own mortality, but the kind that comes when you face your own conscience.

"I don't have time for this, Marcellus," his grandfather snapped before turning and continuing toward the door.

With a calm, steady composure, Marcellus flicked the switch on the rayonette once more, toggling it back to paralyze mode. To non-lethal mode.

To the *other* way.

The one that didn't avenge his father, but rather exonerated him.

Marcellus took aim at his grandfather's left leg and squeezed the trigger. But just then, the whoosh of a rayonette pulse came from somewhere behind him, followed by the sound of flesh tearing. Marcellus cried out as the sting of a thousand lasers ripped through his shoulder.

He staggered back, dizzy from the pain. A dark veil curtained his vision. He squinted through it to see his grandfather rushing toward the door and fleeing into the hallway. Marcellus tried to take aim again, but he could barely raise his arm. The pain was excruciating. The rayonette clattered to the ground. Marcellus buckled over on the balcony and stifled another cry. When he glanced down at his right shoulder, he saw the fabric of his tuxedo jacket was charred and smoldering, the exposed skin underneath nothing more than an oozing blackened wound from what had to be the graze of a lethal pulse.

But who had fired it?

Struggling to stay upright, Marcellus spun around on the balcony and glanced over the railing, at the terrace. To where Inspecteur Chacal was raising his weapon again and aiming it straight at Marcellus's head.

Marcellus barely had time to register the danger before a plume of green silk seemed to emerge from nowhere. It charged into the inspecteur with the force of a droid. The rayonette flew from his hand and clattered down the stairs. Chacal crashed onto his back with his assailant landing on top of him.

Marcellus's heart stopped.

It was Chatine. The green dress was ragged and torn. Her face was streaked with blood. But she was unharmed. At least, for now.

She tried to scramble away from the fallen inspecteur. But he grabbed her by the ankle and yanked her back with a growl. She clawed at the ground, but it was no use. The inspecteur's hold was too tight. And he was too angry.

"You filthy, good-for-nothing déchet!" he roared. His orange eye gleamed with fury as he withdrew the metal baton from his belt and raised it above her head.

Chatine twisted under his grasp, just managing to dodge the blow as she flipped onto her back.

Panicked, Marcellus hoisted up his rayonette, but his right arm screamed in pain. He switched to his other hand and fired but the pulse exploded against the base of a flower planter a few mètres away, nowhere even near his target.

Chatine scrabbled backward across the terrace. Chacal launched himself toward her, abandoning his baton and instead reaching for her neck with his bare hands. Marcellus watched in horror as he began to squeeze.

Chatine's eyes bulged. Her strangled voice tried to cry out. Her feet kicked and her hands grappled on the ground for something to use as a weapon. But there was nothing.

The inspecteur squeezed harder. A vicious, spiteful determination lighting up *both* of his eyes.

Marcellus took off at a run, charging out the door of his rooms, through the corridor, and down the imperial staircase. His ribcage throbbed in pain, like someone was stabbing him repeatedly in the side. He spilled out onto the terrace and crashed to a halt when he saw Chatine was no longer on her back. And the inspecteur was no longer strangling her. He was standing upright, grasping at something impaled in his neck. Blood oozed from the wound. His throat made a strange gurgling sound. He staggered backward, looking surprised and infuriated, the circuitry across his face flickering violently.

Marcellus's gaze pivoted from Chacal to Chatine. She was still on the ground, panting furiously, her wide, petrified eyes locked on the inspecteur. The hem of her dress was pushed slightly up, revealing one bare foot.

And that's when Marcellus recognized the weapon protruding from the inspecteur's neck.

It was the sharp stiletto heel of a shoe.

The inspecteur continued to stagger backward as he tried desperately to dislodge the object. And then it was as if the whole world slowed to a juddering, lumbering crawl. Marcellus could only watch, numbed by the searing pain in his shoulder and the fear clutching at his chest, as the inspecteur's right boot snagged beneath him. Suddenly, he was falling, tumbling like a planet spun off its orbit, down the sweeping stone stairs to the Imperial Lawn below.

With each step, his cybernetic eye flashed and flickered.

Until his body hit the giant flagstone at the bottom of the staircase, and the cruel orange light winked out.

- CHAPTER 74 -
CHATINE

CHATINE RENARD HAD KNOWN DEATH ALL HER LIFE.
When you were born into the Third Estate, it surrounded you wherever
you went. It hid in the shadows of the Frets. It lurked in the darkness of
Bastille exploits. It waited for you to fall asleep every night so it could
plague your dreams. For Chatine, death had always been a permanent
fixture. A crack in the ground that you were forever straddling.

But nothing could have prepared her for this.

She sat on the top step of the curving stone staircase next to Marcellus,
wordlessly taking in the world below. And that was exactly what the Imperial Lawn looked like now. Another world.

Amid broken tables, destroyed gâteaus, and a sea of broken glass,
bodies lay twisted and wide-eyed and eerily still. Blood was everywhere. On the once-pristine tablecloths. On the shredded remains
of silk gowns. On the discarded shoes. Even on the row of glowing
lamps strung overhead. A few survivors knelt over the mangled bodies,
weeping silently. Others wandered the lawn in an astounded, horrified
daze, like sleepwalkers locked in a bad dream. The only sounds were the

fountains, still gushing and bubbling obliviously up into the night air, and the mournful hoot of a lone owl off in the trees.

Chatine wasn't sure how long they'd been sitting there before the sound of sirens punctured the silence. Officers and sergents and even droids started to file into the gardens. Chatine was quite certain that, under normal circumstances, droids weren't even allowed in Ledôme. But these were clearly not normal circumstances.

"We have to get out of here," she whispered to Marcellus. It was the first time either of them had spoken since they'd watched Inspecteur Chacal plummet to his death from this very step.

Marcellus nodded but didn't speak. Chatine was sure he was in some kind of trance. Death had a tendency to do that. She stood up and offered her hands to help him to his feet. But he didn't move. Nor did he look at her.

"Alouette," he said numbly, his eyes glazed and unblinking. "And Cerise. They . . . My grandfather said . . . We have to find them."

"We will," Chatine assured him, glancing over her shoulder at the uniformed men and women filling the gardens. They were already starting to take survivors into custody. "But first we need to get away from the Palais."

She offered her hands again, and this time he took them, wincing in pain as she pulled him to his feet. Chatine glanced down and, for the first time, noticed the gruesome gash on his right shoulder. It was blackened and charred like overcooked meat.

That can't be good.

Scurrying across the terrace, they found their way down a back set of stairs and into another garden dotted with ornate ponds and marble statues. "How do we get out of here?" Chatine asked.

Marcellus pointed up ahead at the glimmering fence that marked the edge of the Palais grounds. "The loophole is just up there." He seemed to struggle with his speech, as though each word required effort to pronounce.

Chatine nodded and took a step toward the fence but glanced back just in time to see Marcellus teetering on his feet. His eyes rolled back into his head and he started to go down. "Marcellus!" Chatine dove to catch him, but he was too heavy. She felt her knees buckling under his weight. A second later, another figure emerged, darting out from a nearby hedge. It was a woman in a dark Policier uniform. A sergent.

Chatine's hopes plummeted. Marcellus would be recognized for sure. He had lost his hat and Sol-glasses somewhere in the battle, and the dirt and blood on his face did little to disguise him.

The woman rushed over to Chatine and helped lower Marcellus onto the ground. "What happened to him?" she asked, speaking in hushed, urgent tones.

Chatine tried to respond, but nothing came out. She stared at the woman in confusion as she gently slapped Marcellus's cheeks, trying to rouse him. Why wasn't she arresting him?

Marcellus's eyes dragged open and his gaze settled on the sergent's face. But instead of reacting in fear, as Chatine had, his face twisted in what looked like recognition. "You're that woman I saw fighting . . . ," he started to say, but his words were garbled and eventually died completely.

"It's okay," she said, reaching down the front of her uniform and pulling out a long string of what looked like metal beads. On the end hung a small rectangular tag, which she showed to Marcellus as though it was supposed to mean something to him. "I'm on your side. My name is Sister Laurel. I'm going to help you."

"Sister?" Marcellus's forehead crumpled weakly. "But the general said . . . We thought you were all . . ."

"Shh," Laurel whispered. "Don't try to speak. Just relax."

With delicate fingers, she peeled back what was left of Marcellus's tuxedo jacket and shirt. He winced sharply at her touch and looked like he might lose consciousness again. "Was this from a lethal pulse?" she asked Chatine.

"I-I don't know," Chatine finally managed to stammer out. "What if it was?"

"Then it needs to be tended to immediately." Laurel reached into the pocket of her sergent's uniform and pulled out a small vial. She uncorked it and ran it under Marcellus's nose. Chatine had no idea what was in that vial, but Marcellus jerked violently awake at the smell of it. Like he'd been doused with ice cold water. Laurel helped him back to his feet before turning to Chatine. "That should help a little with the pain and keep him conscious, but you need to take him back to the Refuge. There are motos parked just outside the fence, near the entrance to the hunting grounds."

The Refuge. The word clattered noisily around Chatine's mind. Wasn't that what Alouette had called the Vangarde's secret base? Chatine looked at the woman in the uniform again, suddenly seeing her with new eyes.

She was one of them.

"No," Marcellus said, shaking his head. He seemed clearer now. More lucid. "I can't go back. I have to find Alouette."

"*You* have to get medical attention," Laurel said sternly. "Let me worry about Alouette. I have a team of operatives here. And we know where she is."

"Where—" Marcellus started to ask but was cut off by a noise behind them. The rustle of footsteps on grass.

Laurel gave Chatine a pointed look. "Go. Now."

Chatine guided the moto through the darkened Vallonay landscape. Marcellus clung to her waist as she steered toward the cluster of rusting, crooked edifices in the distance.

Another place she never thought she'd return to.

The Frets were exactly as Chatine had remembered them. Two weeks on Bastille and nearly another two in the Terrain Perdu, and nothing had changed. The Marsh still smelled like rotting seaweed. The ground around the shuttered market stalls was still littered with the scraps of mangy vegetables. And the clang and whir of patrolling droids was still deafening. But for some reason, Chatine felt immune to it all. She observed the stacks of trash and dank, grimy passageways with a distant curiosity. Almost as though she were a visitor from another planet. A foreign dignitary sent on a diplomatic mission to chronicle the state of the system.

As she and Marcellus weaved through the marketplace in the direction of Fret 7, she no longer felt the coldness in her bones, the hunger in her belly, or the suffering in her heart. The misery that had followed her around this planet for the past eighteen years was somehow nowhere to be found. Vanished in the stiff, biting winds of the Terrain Perdu.

"Are you sure you remember where it is?" Marcellus asked her for what had to be the fifth time since they'd left the Grand Palais.

"Yes," Chatine said. "I went to Bastille protecting this place. Trust me, I remember where it is."

They entered the long, dark hallway of Fret 7, a place Chatine had once called home. In a former lifetime. With one arm dangling limp at his side and the other clutching his ribcage, Marcellus followed closely behind her, his gaze darting anxiously at each closed couchette door that they passed.

She didn't blame him for being nervous. In their blood-stained formal attire, they didn't exactly blend in around here.

The mechanical room was damp and dingy, with rusting machines, a tangle of knotted pipes and cobwebs, and a giant greasy puddle in the center of the floor. Marcellus glanced around in awe, his gaze halting at a broken pipe that was dangling from one of the PermaSteel walls. He stared at it like he was staring straight into his past. Into *his* other lifetime. "I can't believe the base has been right here," he whispered dazedly, "this whole time."

"The best crocs hide in plain sight."

He looked at her, and for a moment, their gazes locked, a thousand silent words streaming between them, their two former lifetimes crashing back together. The old Marcellus and the old Chatine saying their adieus.

Chatine offered him a small smile before hurrying behind a large, decrepit piece of machinery and kneeling down. She wedged her fingernails under the rusting metal and slid the grate to the side, uncovering a dark cylindrical shaft cut into the floor. In the dim light of the mechanical room, they could see a single ladder leading down, eventually swallowed by the darkness below.

Marcellus looked up at Chatine with a slightly petrified expression and quirked an eyebrow. "Ladies first?"

She snorted. "Then, by all means, after you."

With a smirk, Marcellus maneuvered himself onto the ladder, cringing in pain as he grabbed the first rung. Once he'd reached the bottom and called back up to her, Chatine took a deep breath and crept toward the edge. She had climbed up countless walls in these Frets, but never had she climbed down beneath them. As she replaced the grate above her head and descended the ladder, she tried to chase away the barrage of disturbing memories that flooded her mind. Memories of being trapped in those dark exploits, under the surface of Bastille. Whatever happened next, wherever her new path may lead, she was determined to *never* set foot on that moon again.

She felt Marcellus's hand at her back, indicating she'd reached the bottom. She hopped off the ladder and found herself in a dim, hollowed-out space with a large PermaSteel door cut into the wall.

She looked to Marcellus. "What do we do now?"

He shrugged. "I suppose we could just knock."

"Knock?" Chatine said with a roll of her eyes. "We're standing at the door of the most famous rebel group on the planet, and you want to *knock*?"

He scoffed. "Well, do you have a better idea? Do you want to try to ram the door open with your—"

Suddenly, a deep, ominous click echoed off the bedrock walls, sending a shiver through Chatine. She turned to Marcellus again, unsure what to do. Then, out of the corner of her eye, Chatine saw the flicker of movement. Her gaze snapped back to the door, and she leapt out of the way just as the large, solid bloc of PermaSteel began to swing toward them.

- CHAPTER 75 -
ALOUETTE

THE ELEVATOR WHISKED DOWN, LIKE A PLUMMETING rock. Alouette gripped hold of the ornate metalwork as the breeze battered at her hair. Below, the lights of Ledôme's boulevards, parks, and manoirs grew larger and brighter as she descended, and in the distance, the windows and floodlit lawns of the Grand Palais glowed into view.

Looking over it all, Alouette felt strangely numb and completely alive, all at the same time. It was as if she'd gone up this tower as one person, and now she was returning to the ground as another. Something had shifted inside her, and everything was now reforming, reshaping, evolving. Who she was. Where she came from. What she was capable of.

She was still Alouette Taureau, the girl who'd been saved and loved by a convict named Jean LeGrand. She was still the Little Lark, too, the girl who'd been raised, nurtured, and trained by the Sisterhood. But she'd flown beyond those names now. There was something new brewing inside her. Beginning to emerge.

These half-formed and dream-like thoughts cycled through Alouette's mind as the elevator finally touched down and its door clanged open. She stepped out, and for a second, gazed up at the vast TéléSky. The stars blinked and sparkled in the blackness.

She thought of the world beyond Ledôme, where shimmering starlight like this was never seen. Where the clouds blanketed everything, offering only rain and dampness and never-ending gray. Where people lived in the rusting remains of old freightships. Where the stomachs of children growled and girls sold their blood for a few extra largs.

The discrepancy, the inequality, and the injustice of this twisted and wrenched deep inside Alouette. But the feeling was quickly replaced by another. This one was stronger. More profound. Rooted into the very core of who she was.

It was the feeling of resolve.

She reached down, into the collar of her uniform, and pulled out her devotion beads. Her last remaining link to the sisters who'd raised her. The women who'd trained her. The rebels who'd made her who she was.

The sudden sound of footsteps on gravel cut off her thoughts. Before Alouette could turn to see who was approaching, someone grabbed her arms and pinned them behind her back.

Instantly her body electrified. She could feel every nerve and sinew inside her switching on. Her mind went calm like a lake and her breath stilled to almost nothing.

Elevate the Meek, she thought, as she prepared to move into a twisting lunge.

But the blow to her head came a moment later, spiraling her vision into darkness. She felt the ground come rushing toward her. She felt her chin knock against the stone. And just before the stars twinkled out completely, she heard a gruff voice say, "Madeline Villette. Somehow I just can't seem to get rid of you."

CHAPTER 76

MARCELLUS

THE WOMAN WHO STOOD BEFORE THEM IN THE SMALL vestibule was wiry, gray-haired, and wearing a long plain tunic. With flinty eyes, she peered at Marcellus and Chatine over a pair of half-moon glasses. Marcellus guessed, from Alouette's descriptions and stories about the sisters, that this must be Francine, the Principale of the Refuge.

"He needs help," Chatine blurted out. "We were told we could—"

"Yes," Francine said, ushering them inside. "This way. We'll get you to the infirmerie. Sister Laurel will be back soon."

They followed the woman down a long, dimly lit corridor. The bedrock walls were unadorned, and the floors were plain but immaculately polished. Through a few of the open doors, Marcellus could see bedrooms containing little more than a neatly made bed and a small nightstand.

Everything was so simple and neat.

So silent and calm.

A refuge from the boisterous, unraveling planet above.

He still couldn't wrap his head around the fact that anyone was here. He'd been so certain the Vangarde were dead. And yet, here he was, being led through their secret base by one of their leaders. And that woman at the banquet had said she'd brought operatives with her.

"Sister Laurel," Marcellus repeated the name, remembering the way the woman had fought with the same familiar grace and relaxed ease as he'd observed Alouette do in Inspecteur Limier's memory file. "Why was she at the banquet? Did you know what the general was planning?"

Francine slowed her pace slightly and shook her head. "No. When the Ascension was rescheduled, and it was announced that fifty winners would be chosen, we were understandably suspicious of something. So we sent Sister Laurel and a team of operatives to investigate. We never expected . . ." She cleared her throat, sounding grieved. "It is awful what has transpired tonight."

"That was the weapon the general has been working on." The words exploded out of Marcellus. It felt like he'd been waiting years to say them. Ever since Mabelle had first recruited him in that leaky, dilapidated cabin at the copper exploit, pleading with him to find out more about the weapon. "That's what Denise was trying to stop. It's a program that reverses the neuroelectricity to the Skins so the general can force the Third Estate to fight for him. And what's worse, he still has it. He could activate the program again at any time and command his Third Estate army."

"No, he can't."

The words came so unexpectedly, so swiftly, Marcellus was almost certain he misunderstood. He squinted at the gray-haired woman in front him. "What?"

"The Skins have been turned off," she said simply.

Turned off?

Baffled, Marcellus thought back to the balcony, when he'd stood beside his grandfather and watched the survivors stare down at the darkened screens in their arms.

Did the Vangarde discover a way to get around the Forteresse?

"Still, tonight was a travesty," Principale Francine said, bowing her head solemnly. "And unfortunately, we were too late to stop it."

"I tried to tell you," Marcellus insisted. "I swear I tried to make contact, but I couldn't get through. After Bastille, I thought . . . *We* thought you were all . . ."

"Dead?" Francine guessed.

Chatine's gaze darted curiously toward the woman.

Marcellus nodded, trying to catch his breath. "Yes."

Francine stopped in front of a closed wooden door and turned around to face Marcellus. In that moment, her eyes looked kind and her face looked earnest. "Merci for everything you've done for the Vangarde. You have been a loyal and faithful servant. Just like your father. Mabelle was right to insist we recruit you. Given the circumstances, however, we were forced to employ a few very extreme tactics. And, unfortunately, we had to keep many of our operatives in the dark about it. I'm terribly sorry about that. But you must understand it was for the benefit and safety of everyone involved."

Marcellus's brow furrowed. *Extreme tactics?* "You mean you weren't communicating on purpose? You were *pretending* to be dead?"

She flashed him a knowing look. "It wouldn't be the first time."

His thoughts drifted painfully back to that night in the warden's office. When they'd all gathered around a bank of monitors and watched Citizen Rousseau's finger unexpectedly twitch on the screen.

They've been playing dead.

"The general has been trying to track us down for years," Francine explained. "We had to make sure he stopped looking for us. Which is why we chose to go completely silent. We couldn't take the risk of any of our correspondence being intercepted. And that, unfortunately, included cutting off our own internal network among the Sisterhood."

"The beads," Marcellus said suddenly.

Francine nodded. "Yes. Traditionally our devotion beads are linked together so that we can stay connected to each other. But knowing that two of our operatives were in custody, and that their belongings would surely be confiscated and analyzed, we decided to use that to our advantage. Severing the connection was a difficult choice to make, however, because it meant we were no longer able to track Alouette. But we had to trust that our teachings had prepared her for the world and that she would be able to take care of herself. And we simply couldn't risk the Ministère hunting us down. Especially after Bastille. We needed General Bonnefaçon and the Patriarche to believe that we didn't succeed up there. And that they had won."

Something dark and heavy lifted instantly from Marcellus's chest. "You mean, you *did* succeed?"

For the first time, a small smile broke through the woman's hardened facade. And she looked almost proud. "Yes."

Marcellus tried to pull his thoughts into focus, but they were spinning too quickly. Round and round until all he could see was the roof of the Trésor tower and that strange little ship vanishing from the sky in a gust of smoke and fire.

There was a small yelp beside him, and Chatine's mouth fell open in shock. "Citizen Rousseau is *alive*?"

At that, Francine turned around and opened the door in front of them. Inside, a woman lay stretched out on a narrow bed with a wooden frame. She was so still, only a slight movement of the sheet indicated that she was breathing. Her silver hair had been gently brushed and plaited into a long braid, which now lay across the crisp white pillow. The crevices and lines in her skin looked less deep, less angry, less battered here, under the soft glow of the infirmerie lights. But the hollows under her cheek bones were just as sunken and shadowed and beaten as Marcellus had remembered from years of staring at her on a security feed.

Citizen Rousseau.

The woman who had led a rebellion and failed.

The woman who Marcellus's father had died for.

The woman who had inspired hope in a people who had lost theirs centuries ago.

Could she do it again?

Looking at her frail, brittle body now, it felt unlikely.

"Bastille was not kind to her," Francine said. "And the tincture we gave her to slow her heart so she would be transferred to the morgue nearly killed her. We almost lost her on the journey home. Laurel had to induce a coma to keep her stable until she recovered. But our dear sister has finally returned to us. And soon, when her vitals are stronger, we will be able to wake her and finish what we started."

"You mean the ship made it back?" Chatine asked, her voice was quiet, almost wary, as though she were afraid the answer might destroy her.

"Yes," Francine said. "The stealth mode helped complete the illusion of the Ministère's victory. However, our pilote was injured by an explosif shortly before we took off. She managed to get us back safely to Laterre, and we did everything we could for her here. But we lost her the very next day."

Marcellus pressed his fingertips into his temples trying to make sense of everything. That ship he'd seen on Bastille hadn't been blown out of the sky. It had taken off. It had made it back here.

With Citizen Rousseau inside.

But Marcellus could hardly process his own reaction to this news, because he was too busy trying to interpret Chatine's. Tears were swimming in her eyes, and a sob of what could only be described as life-altering relief seemed to shudder through her.

Chatine wiped at her wet cheeks. "If the ship made it back, then that means—"

"Did you know the First World had only one Sol?"

Marcellus, Chatine, and Francine all turned at once to see a boy standing in the hallway with a half-eaten apple in one hand and an open book in the other.

When the boy's gaze landed on Chatine, his lips curved into a wide grin. "Hey, you're here! Isn't this place soop? They have much better food than on Bastille, and they're teaching me to read the Forgotten Word!"

"Henri!" In a heartbeat, Chatine was running at supervoyage speed. She crashed into the boy and wrapped her arms so tightly around him, Marcellus honestly couldn't tell if she meant to embrace him or suffocate him.

The boy seemed slightly confused by her reaction. He patted her awkwardly on the shoulder. "Um, it's nice to see you, too." Then, after a moment, and another noisy bite of apple, his eyebrows shot up. "Wait a minute. Who's Henri?"

Chatine laughed and squeezed him tighter. For a long time, they just stood like that. The boy eating his apple and Chatine clutching his skinny body to hers, like she might never let go. But the sound of a heavy metal door clanging shut a moment later broke all of them from their trances.

Marcellus peered down the low-lit hallway to see Sister Laurel moving steadily toward them. She was still dressed in her bloodied and ripped sergent's uniform.

He looked to her with hope brimming in his eyes. "Did you find her? Did you find Alouette?"

She shot a brief, indecipherable glance at Francine before replying, "Not yet. But my operatives are still looking. We will—"

Marcellus didn't even allow her to finish. He was already on the move, already charging down the Refuge hallway, back toward that heavy PermaSteel door. He could feel Sister Laurel's temporary médicaments wearing off and the pain and nausea creeping back in, but he didn't care. He couldn't just sit down here and wait while she was still out there.

"Marcellus!" Footsteps pounded after him, but he didn't stop. Couldn't stop. Something sharp and throbbing stabbed at his side. He doubled over as a groan clawed its way up his throat.

Suddenly, Sister Laurel was in front of him. Her kind, dark eyes staring intensely into his. "You need help. Your ribs might be broken. You still have a lethal paralyzeur pulse in your shoulder. You need medical attention. You cannot go out there."

"But . . ." He tried to speak. Every syllable, every breath was an agonizing effort that drained him. "Alouette."

"I know you're worried about her," Sister Laurel said. "So are we. But take a breath and really think this through. Do you really think you're in any condition to go searching for her right now?"

Marcellus turned from her, his eyes falling on the small vestibule at the end of the hallway. The door that stood between him and the outside world.

"We *will* find her," Sister Laurel promised, her voice stern and heart-breakingly earnest. "Let my operatives do their job. And let me treat you."

Marcellus could feel his irrational resolve slipping. He pulled his gaze from the door and focused back on Laurel. There were two of her and she was swaying.

"I can't abandon her," he said, his voice cracking like a child's.

"You're not," Laurel said. And maybe it was the tone of her voice or the honesty in her eyes or the promise of her help, but for some outlandish, indescribable reason, in that moment, he believed her.

He took a deep breath and allowed his head to fall into a nod. He allowed himself to be guided back to the infirmerie. And, as he lay down on an empty cot next to the unconscious form of Laterre's most infamous rebel leader, he allowed himself to believe that any minute now, Alouette would come walking through that Refuge door.

CHAPTER 77

CHATINE

EVERYTHING ABOUT HIM WAS FAMILIAR. HIS CHIN. HIS eyelashes. His cheeks. The way his lips moved ever so slightly while he dreamed. As she watched him sleep, curled up in a tiny ball under the blankets just like he used to do when he was a baby, Chatine felt foolish for not seeing it before. For not recognizing him the moment she first laid eyes on him.

The resemblance seemed too obvious to miss now.

But she, of all people, knew how the heart could play evil tricks on the mind. And that the eyes could be as devious and deceitful as a pair of crocs.

None of that mattered now, though. All that mattered was that he was here. And she was here. And they were together. The two lost Renard children finally reunited. And she would never lose him again.

The door to the small bedroom creaked open, and Chatine looked up to see Marcellus standing in the doorway. She straightened up in the chair next to the bed, where she'd been sitting for the past few hours, and beckoned him inside. "How are you?" she asked.

With a wince, he lowered himself onto the edge of the bed. "Apparently, I'm going to live."

Chatine chuckled softly. "That's good. I'd be pretty bummed if you didn't."

Marcellus nodded toward Henri, still fast asleep. "How is he?"

Chatine allowed her eyes to drift back toward her brother. Her *brother*. It felt so good to finally hold that word in her mind again and not be plagued with guilt and fear and crushing sadness. "He's fine. More than fine, actually. Talked my ear off for twenty minutes about his bravery during what he's calling the Great Bastille Escape of 505." She snorted and adjusted the blankets under his chin, a delicate smile playing on her lips. "I used to watch him sleep when he was a baby. He slept the exact same way. I just can't believe they brought him back to me."

"The Vangarde?" Marcellus asked.

She shook her head. "The Sols."

Chatine could feel Marcellus's eyes on her, warm and inquisitive. "Yes, they can certainly be mysterious like that."

With a contented sigh, Chatine finally pulled her gaze from Henri and glanced around the room. It was modest and bare, with uneven walls, a nightstand next to the bed, and a small closet cut into the bedrock and covered with a simple black curtain.

"I think this is Alouette's room," Chatine said quietly. She wasn't sure if she should mention her name. The sisters still hadn't given any indication that she'd been located, and Chatine was starting to worry that something had gone very wrong.

A flicker of uneasiness flashed in Marcellus's eyes, but he quickly concealed it. "How do you know?"

"Because I found this." Chatine reached under her chair and pulled out an old, faded doll with long, silky hair and a tattered yellow dress. She stood it up on her lap and stared into its glassy gray eyes, feeling the same haunting sensation she'd felt when she'd first discovered it laying on the bed. It was like looking into a mirror that warped time, and the reflection staring back at her was some younger, forgotten version of herself.

She swallowed and ran her fingers through the doll's dark nylon curls. "For the longest time this doll represented everything I wanted to be and never could. Funny how it's been right here, so close this whole time, and I never knew."

"I don't understand," Marcellus said, his brow furrowed. "Have you seen it before?"

"Not only have I seen it, I took a souvenir." She pivoted the doll on her lap so Marcellus could see the empty sleeve hanging loose from the dress. Chatine pushed it back to reveal a small hole just below the shoulder.

Something strange and chilling passed over Marcellus's face as he stared at the spot where the doll's little arm used to be. Then, as though moving in slow motion, he reached into his pocket and, with an unsteady breath, withdrew his hand and extended it toward Chatine.

She let out a tiny, uncontrolled gasp when she saw what was nestled in his palm. Like a long-lost remnant washed up at sea. A fragment of misplaced time.

"How?" she murmured, barely a whisper. "How do you have this?"

"I found it in your couchette."

Chatine's thoughts spun dizzily through her mind. *He went to my couchette? He looked through my room? And of all the things he would have found there, this is what he took?*

He let out a short laugh and shook his head. "When I think about all the times that I could have lost it, or forgotten it, or accidentally left it aboard the voyageur to be shattered into a million pieces, it almost seems impossible that I still have it."

"B-b-but . . . ," she stammered, still confused. "Why did you keep it?"

Silent and still, Marcellus stared down at the lonely little doll arm still resting in his palm. "I guess . . . ," he began, the answer seeming to come to him in a rush of certainty. He lifted his eyes to meet hers. "For the same reason you kept my mother's ring."

Warmth instantly flooded the small room, cocooning Chatine the way she imagined these Refuge walls were designed to do. She didn't speak as she delicately picked up the little piece of plastique from Marcellus's hand and guided it into the empty slot just below the doll's left shoulder. It made a quiet clicking sound as it slipped into place. And Chatine could swear she heard it echo for kilomètres. For years into the past. Back to when she was torn apart just like this doll, forced to face the world with a missing limb and a hole that seemed impossible to fill.

Until, one day, someone miraculously showed up and proved her wrong.

For a long time, she just sat there, staring into the doll's tiny gray eyes, sharing silent stories and promises. She might even have stayed like that all night. They both might have. If it weren't for Marcellus's TéléCom.

He startled as something evidently pinged in his ear, prompting him to remove the device from his pocket and glance down at the screen. The blood drained instantly from his face.

"What is it?" Chatine asked, peering over his shoulder. She recognized the alert as an AirLink request, but the face flashing on the screen—a man with intense pale eyes, curly hair, and a high, pronounced brow—was unfamiliar to her.

Marcellus hastily reached to dismiss the request but Chatine placed a hand on his, stopping him. "Wait. Who is that?"

"He's . . ." He breathed out an uneasy sigh as his gaze flickered anxiously to her. "His name is Jolras Epernay. And he's part of the group responsible for your sister's death."

Chatine felt a sudden stab at the reminder of Azelle and the horrible way she died, but she swallowed and forced herself to ask, "Why is he AirLinking you?"

Marcellus shook his head. "I don't know. He's been doing it for days now. But I refuse to answer."

He glanced down at the screen, where the face of this man—this *Jolras*—still flashed persistently.

"Maybe you should answer," Chatine said quietly.

Marcellus flinched, clearly not expecting to hear that. "Why? This group is incredibly dangerous. They call themselves the Red Scar. Their leader is a mad woman who is unpredictable and disturbingly violent."

"Isn't that exactly why you *should* answer?"

Marcellus seemed to consider Chatine's logic. After everything that had transpired tonight, it just might have been the only logic that made sense anymore.

He bit his lip and stared down at the TéléCom. The light from the flashing screen reflected ominously in his hazel eyes. Then, after sucking in a breath, Marcellus swiped on the screen and accepted the request.

CHAPTER 78

MARCELLUS

THE OLD FREIGHTSHIP WAS DARK AND EMPTY AT FIRST. But as they wove onward, through the hallway of Fret 7, Marcellus began to hear noises. Heavy footsteps rattling across the metal floors above. Distant shouts echoing and vibrating down the old rusting pipes that snaked along the walls. Even though it was the middle of the night and well past curfew, the whole Fret felt as if it were coming alive.

"This way," Chatine said, leading him deftly through the corridors toward the exit.

The alleyway between the Frets was teeming with people. All of them on the move. All of them heading determinedly in the direction of the Marsh. Marcellus's gaze flitted around, astounded, as they joined the moving crowd.

"What's going on?" Chatine asked, fear glimmering in her cat-like gray eyes.

Marcellus shook his head. "I don't know."

The AirLink conversation had been brief. Too brief to make sense of.

"Meet me in the Marsh. Near the west entrance. She's gone too far."

And then it had been over. The pale-eyed man had vanished, leaving Marcellus and Chatine in a stunned silence. At first Marcellus had believed it was a trap. But there was something about the urgency in his voice and the fear in his eyes. It was real.

A Third Estate man in a ragged hood shoved Marcellus from behind. "Better hurry up, or you'll miss it," he growled before disappearing into the river of streaming people.

Marcellus and Chatine shared an anxious glance before picking up their pace. Jostled and breathless, they finally reached the Marsh and both came to a skidding, astonished halt. The marketplace, even though it was the dead of night, was jammed. Marcellus had never seen so many people crammed into this space, even on the busiest of market days. The shuttered stalls had been shoved aside, some even pushed over, and the thrumming, vibrating, boisterous crowd were all moving in the same direction. Toward the center of the Marsh.

Toward the towering statue of Thibault Paresse, the Patriarche who had founded this planet.

"What is this?" Marcellus asked as a shiver traveled down his spine.

"It's her," came a voice behind them.

Marcellus and Chatine spun to find themselves face-to-face with the man from the TéléCom screen. The man who had stood idly by as a hothouse was demolished and three innocent superviseurs were killed in the blast. The man who had held Cerise down while his sister tried to brand her with a laser. The man who had played a vital part in the death of Azelle Renard.

The brother of both an innocent victim and a guilty terrorist.

Jolras Epernay.

Marcellus felt his blood grow hot at the sight of him standing there, trying to remain still amidst the jostling crowd that pushed past them from every direction.

"It's Max," he said, and Marcellus could hear that same urgency and fear in his voice.

"Who?" Marcellus asked.

"My sister," Jolras said. "Maximilienne. She's . . . She's out of control. I've been trying to warn you for days."

"Why me?"

"Because I saw the arrest warrant," Jolras said. "I know you're with the Vangarde. And we need their help if we want to stop her."

"I am not your ally," Marcellus spat. "I don't want anything to do with the Red Scar."

"Neither do I," Jolras said. It came like a slap. Fast and unexpected with the sting of surprise.

"What?" Marcellus snapped.

Jolras glanced around at the thick sea of bodies and huffed out an impatient sigh. As though he wasn't sure how much time they had for explanations. "At first, yes, I was excited about the idea. I was angry about what the Ministère did to Nadette, and it felt good to be doing something to retaliate. But Max, she . . ." His voice trailed off and he tugged brutally at the end of one of his curls. "Her anger goes beyond reason. Beyond limits. She's turned into someone I don't even recognize. Something has to be done. She's . . ." And then he repeated the same chilling words he'd said on the TéléCom. "She's gone too far."

Marcellus narrowed his eyes. "What do you mean?" he asked.

But it was the crowd who answered. A raucous, deafening cheer exploded all around them, and they were suddenly shoved forward. Marcellus tried to peer up ahead, in the direction everyone was moving. At first, through the gloom, he could see nothing but bodies and the shadows of the giant Frets looming over the Marsh. But as the tide jostled the three of them deeper into the marketplace, toward the looming statue up ahead, Marcellus caught sight of something he'd wished and prayed he would never see again.

It was the blue glow he spotted first.

And then, as he moved closer still, he saw the perfectly straight line of light sending sparks and blinding azure flashes into the misty air.

His body went cold. Colder than it had been crammed into a crate full of ice packs in the cargo hold of a voyageur. Colder than it had been trapped in the frozen tundra of the Terrain Perdu.

This was a cold that gripped not only his limbs. But his mind and his heart and his hope.

Chatine let out a gasp, her eyes locked on the sight in front of her. "Is that the—?"

But she never got a chance to finish the question, because just then, they were shoved again from behind and pushed forward.

Closer and closer.

Until Marcellus could see it all.

The flat bed of metal.

The two jutting PermaSteel columns.

The blue laser sparking furiously between them.

"The Blade," someone whispered behind them, answering Chatine's unfinished question and sending a shudder through Marcellus's frozen body.

The Red Scar hadn't stolen it to destroy it. They'd stolen it to use it.

Chatine glanced around, her eyes wide with horror and panic. "Where are the droids?" she whispered, and Marcellus suddenly realized she was right. That was what was missing here. The three-mètre-high monsters that had become a permanent fixture in the Frets were nowhere to be found in this madness.

"They were called to deal with several disturbances strategically spread out among the city and the outskirts," Jolras whispered back. "An explosion in the fabriques, another two in the exploits, a ransack of the power plant in Lacrête, and a handful of riots in the fermes. Timed diversions. All premeditated. All in preparation for this."

Marcellus shivered at the implication. Thousands of Third Estaters crammed into the Marsh after curfew, with no means of policing them.

Then, as if echoing his very fears, the crowd around them roared, and Marcellus found himself being shoved again from all sides. He reached out and grabbed on to Chatine's hand. But when he turned to look for Jolras, he was nowhere to be found, swallowed by this thrumming, vibrating sea of people who were now cheering and shouting, raising their fists into the air.

But, despite the deafening noise, there was one voice he could hear above them all.

"It is time to end the tyranny. It is time to end our hunger and our misery."

Marcellus knew the voice instantly. There was no mistaking it.

Up ahead, on a makeshift stage positioned right below Thibault Paresse's feet, he spotted her.

Maximilienne.

She stood beside the gleaming, purring exécuteur, her shaved head glowing in the blue light of the laser. Her red hood was pushed back to reveal the whole of her face and her fist was punched fiercely into the night air.

"It is time to end the injustice, the servitude, the hours we spend toiling for the upper estates so they can live in luxury in their precious Ledôme."

The crowd around Marcellus shouted in response. He could feel the coiled tension, the awakened excitement, and the hunger for something more than food, radiating off them.

"It is time for them to see that *we* are the power. *We* are the true beating heart of this planet. We, the Third Estate, are everything. And now that our Skins have been turned off and our life-long shackles removed, we can finally take control of what is rightfully ours."

Another resounding, deafening roar erupted around them.

It was almost more terrifying than watching the general's weapon. Because these Third Estaters were being fueled by their *own* minds. Their own desire to fight.

"It is time to destroy that which destroys us and destroys our children. It is time to look into the eyes of our enemy for the last and final time." With that, Maximilienne raised a single hand into the air, like she was calling forth the skies.

Behind her, Marcellus could see a group of her comarades in red hoods shuffling forward, dragging something with them. His stomach knew what it was before his eyes could even make sense of it.

Grasped between two of the hooded men, shivering and cowed and dressed in nothing but a battered cloth, was . . .

"It is time to remove that which oppresses us."

As she said these words, the figures in the red hoods shoved forward their captive.

The bare-footed man.

The quavering man.

The Patriarche.

Suddenly, the roaring and shouting stopped. The whole Marsh fell silent. The man they'd only ever seen on their Skins was now in front of them, as clear as if the Sols had risen and were shining down onto the stage. But gone were the Patriarche's fine clothes and polished shoes. Gone was his powdered, smooth skin and perfectly coiffed hair. Now he looked like one of them. A Third Estater. Battered and damp and beaten, shivering from the cold air—and the fear.

"Our beloved, fearless leader was caught trying to flee from our planet," Maximilienne explained with a biting sharpness in her tone. "We captured him on his way to the Vallonay spaceport. He was trying to abandon us in our time of need. Just like he and his wretched family have abandoned us for centuries."

Marcellus felt his knees weaken, and as though sensing his waning strength, Chatine tightened her grasp around his hand.

"It's time to put an end to our Darkest Night and welcome in our new dawn," Maximilienne bellowed.

The figures in red grabbed the Patriarche again and pushed him fiercely down onto the metal block of the exécuteur. His whole body shone blue from the strip of blinding light above him. His auburn hair flopped to the side like a discarded mop, and his terrified eyes flashed like two shining pebbles. His mouth opened and closed, as if he wanted to say something, to shout something. But nothing came out.

The crowd whooped and jeered at the sight.

"Are they really going to do this?" Chatine asked, her voice trembling and barely audible above the din.

Marcellus could do nothing but numbly shake his head.

He did not know the answer to that question. Nor the answer to every question that seemed to line up behind it.

Marcellus glanced up at the statue that towered above them all. The founding Patriarche loomed over this spectacle like a disappointed father, reprimanding his children. And then Marcellus looked back at the current Patriarche, shivering and whimpering as his head was pressed down against the block.

A once-mighty man reduced to nothing.

Marcellus had always known Lyon Paresse to be a fool. A greedy, selfish leader. But he didn't deserve this. No one deserved this.

Marcellus tried to push his way closer to the stage, but it was impossible. The people were unyielding. Unmoving. Like a battalion of impenetrable droids.

Then a crackling sound reverberated through the crowd. Marcellus snapped his gaze back to the stage to see the laser beginning to move.

Beginning to descend.

Beginning to slice its way through the swirling, wet air.

The crowd fell silent again. The hum and sizzle of the laser was more deafening than any shout or roar of a riled up Third Estater. The blue light sparked and flashed, consuming every molecule of mist in its path.

And then it happened.

The laser cut through the Patriarche's neck in one clean and crackling slice.

There was no blood, no scream, no sound. Except the thud of the Patriarche's head as it dropped onto the metal slats of the stage.

Then, like a dream, like a nightmare unfurling, came the smell.

The familiar, terrible smell of burning flesh.

The smell of a planet about to ignite.

ACKNOWLEDGMENTS

They say sequels are the hardest books to write. We wish we could say this one was an exception. This book was quite the exciting voyager ride, with some wobbly liftoffs, rocky asteroid belts, and interplanetary flight turbulence, but thanks to the help of some truly amazing people, we arrived safely.

Merci, as always, to our *fantastique* editor, Nicole Ellul, whose commitment to and belief in this series has never faltered. You are truly a superstar and we couldn't do this without you! Thanks to our 'soop agent, Jim McCarthy, and the whole team at Simon & Schuster, including (but certainly not limited to), Mara Anastas, Liesa Abrams, Chriscynethia Floyd, Mary Nubla, Christine Foye, Ruqayyah Daud, Julie Jarema, Emily Hutton, Michael Rosamilia, Heather Palisi, Nicole Overton, Elizabeth Mims, Lauren Carr, Nicole Russo, Caitlin Sweeny, Alissa Nigro, Annika Voss, and Anna Jarzab. And a special shout out to Clare McGlade, our amazing copyeditor, who we have now renamed "Sister Clare." You're a genius and truly deserve your own set of Devotion Beads!

Huge thank you to the wonderful and inspiring Marissa Meyer, Stephanie Garber, Beth Revis, Jessica Khoury, Danielle Paige, and Brendan Reichs for supporting this series! We are so honored to have your names on our book! And thank you to Caitlin O'Brient Bauer and the "Sky Pod"—Stephanie, Brittany Michelle L, Dayle, Michelle B, Christy, Becca, and Mariana—for everything you did to launch this series so epically into space!

We were fortunate to have access to some pretty amazing minds when creating this world and particularly when writing this book. First off, thank you to our incredible teen beta readers, Nini Kauffman-O'Hehir and Fae Leonard-Mann (who read this book at impressive hypervoyage speeds!) and to our star-studded team of experts (we claim full responsibility for any errors or fictional liberties that we took!) Marguerite Syverston, once again, you kept our stars aligned, our orbits orbiting, and our hurtling asteroids at a safe distance. Steven Williams, thank you for the crash course in genetics, DNA editing, and something called CRISPR. (Which we initially thought was a snack . . . good thing we had you!) Author Jussi Valtonen, thanks for keeping all the brains in check (both ours and our characters') with your neuroscience expertise! *Merci beaucoup,* Caroline Roland-Levy for being our *"rock française!"* and for never getting tired of our late-night frantic texts asking questions like, "What do French pilots call the thing that steers the plane?" Thank you also to author and Chess Grandmaster Jennifer Shahade, Electrical Engineer Bill Herz, and Cybersecurity expert Patterson Cake.

Wow, Billelis! You did it again with another truly stunning book cover that we still cannot stop staring at! And Francesca Baerald, you put the "divine" in System Divine. Your maps bring this world to life and we thank you for every beautifully drawn wave, mountain, and craggy coastline!

We are infinitely grateful to all the indie booksellers of the world who supported this book, displayed it on your beautiful shelves, and placed it in the hands of readers. You make author dreams come true every single day. Special thanks to A Great Good Place for Books, Blue Willow Bookshop, Books Inc., Books of Wonder, Left Bank Books, Main Street Books, Mysterious Galaxy Bookstore, Oblong Books & Music, Once Upon a Time, Powell's, Red Balloon Bookshop, Rediscovered Books, RJ Julia Booksellers, Square Books, Tattered Cover, Third Place Books, University Bookstore, and Vintage Books.

And last but never least, thank you to all our amazing readers. We love that you love Chatine, Marcellus, and Alouette as much as we do and we can't wait for you to find out what's in store for them next! *Vive* Laterre and *vive* all of you!

—Joanne and Jessica

So many thanks, as always, to all my friends who have supported my books and who helped pick up the slack when I had to shut myself away, writing and editing. In particular, huge thank yous to Donna Lewis, Pamela Mann, Lesley Sawhill, and Ron Aja. And Jess! My cowriter, *capitaine,* and (most of all) friend. You inspire me every day!

Thank you to my family, especially my mum, Kate Matthews who is always one of my first readers and Jana and Alan Lewis who are the most loving and supportive in-laws I could imagine. And, of course, Benny Rendell and Brad Lewis. Thank you for your endless support and patience during all the hours I was pulled into deep space by this book, and for how rich, fun, and infinitely interesting you make my life back on Earth!

—Joanne

Thank you to my J-Team: Jess, Jo, and Jenn for your pep talks, late-night texts, funny gifs, final-hour brainstorm calls, and all-around awesomeness. If speed dial was still a thing, you three would have the top spots.

I would never be able to do what I do without my tremendously supportive (and often-times quirky) family behind me. Thank you to Michael and Laura Brody for listening, reading, offering advice, and entertaining the dogs when this book kept me locked away for days. Thank you to my fabulous sister Terra Brody, my equally fabulous brother-in-law, Pier, and my Texas family, Vicki, George, and Jen. And as always, thank you to Charlie, my heart and Sol, my rock, and my *cocapitaine.* You've read more drafts than I can count, have seen *Les Misérables* more times than I'm sure you want to count, and have listened to me go round and round in plot circles more times than I thought possible. And yet, you're still here. *Merci.*

—Jessica